Catherine Wells

Stones of Destiny

CATHERINE WELLS

Stones of Destiny

Cover Design, Text and Illustrations copyright © 2007 Catherine Wells
Original Cover Design by DA Design

First edition published in Great Britain in 2007 by Four O' Clock Press

ISBN13 978-1-90614-619-1

The right of Catherine Wells to be identified as the Author of the Work has been asserted by her in accordance with the Copyright, Designs and Patent Act 1988

A Four O' Clock Press title from Discovered Authors

All rights reserved.
No part of this publication may be reproduced, stored in a retrieval system, or transmitted, in any form or by any means without the prior written permission of the Author

Printed in the UK by BookForce

Available from Discovered Authors Online –
All major online retailers and available to order through all UK bookshops

Or contact:

Books
Discovered Authors
50 Albemarle Street, London
W1S 4BD

+(44) 207 529 37 29

books@discoveredauthors.co.uk

BookForce UK's policy is to use papers that are natural, renewable and recyclable products and made from wood grown in sustainable forests where ever possible

BookForce UK Ltd.
50 Albemarle Street
London W1S 4BD
www.bookforce.co.uk
www.discoveredauthors.co.uk

BOOK ONE

Prologue

The summer sun was well up in the sky, but a damp wind blew across the lowlands, causing the stranger to draw her cloak tighter. Or perhaps it was not the breeze that chilled her. "Are you Fionna?" she asked.

The old woman nodded. "I am called that." She studied the stranger with hard, clear eyes, wondering if this could be the king's woman her stones whispered of. Surely not; this was a peasant, tall and large-boned, her blond hair gone mostly to gray. Perhaps once she had been beautiful—before children and hard work and wars had taken their toll—but there was nothing of a queen's manner about her.

"My name is Kelda," the woman said, and a foreign lilt in her speech said the Scots' Gaelic was not her native tongue. "I was told you might help me."

Fionna's suppressed a sigh. People always came to her when the need was desperate. The older she got, the more she resented it; often as not, there was little she could do to help them. Their trust wore at her. Now here was a foreigner, a Norsewoman by her speech, asking for help. Why waste time on this one?

But the whispers still echoed in Fionna's mind, quiet sussurations of the stones only she could hear. The king's woman, the king's woman—but not the queen. And if not the queen, then who?

"Come," Fionna said, beckoning the stranger to follow.

There was rain in the air now, unwelcome with crops curing toward harvest, but not surprising. Far to the west, a royal cortege trundled its inexorable way toward the Isle of Iona, and the days had been damp and cold as if the land itself mourned the passing of its husbandman. Fionna picked her way through the grass and heather, around the little hillocks that dotted this lonely stretch of land and made a maze of it. Finally she stopped in front of one grassy mound and pulled back a hide to reveal an entrance. The mound was in fact a stone hut, sodded over decades before and blending now into the natural contours of the earth. She motioned her visitor inside.

A tiny fire sizzled in a slight recess along the wall, keeping the chill at bay. Kelda settled on the floor beside it, still holding her cloak close around her, clutching something beneath it. Fionna could not tell what it was, but she felt the power in it.

A pot of water heated at the edge of the fire. Fionna added herbs to brew a drink for her guest, something warming, something to clear the cobwebs from old memories. As it steeped, she drew her basket of stones onto her lap. The pebbles were worn smooth with time and use, and each bore a single symbol. Fionna selected four, placing them in a circle on the hard-packed ground: Birth, Puberty, Marriage, Death. This was the Cycle of Life, the arena for all that was. To the left she placed the Moon, to the right, the Sun. Then she poured a cup of her brew, handed it to Kelda and asked, "What of Macbeatha?"

Kelda sipped at the drink before answering. "Macbeatha is dead," she said dully, but the grief which had gone from her voice still rang in her blood and echoed off the stone walls of the tiny chamber.

"That is not what I meant." Fionna took two more stones, rolled them between her palms, then gazed at them. "The stones have spoken to me many times over the years of this king, this Macbeatha mac Findlaech of the House of Loarn, but still I do not understand. Why do they speak of this king, and not the one who was before, or the one who will surely follow?" Her eyes narrowed. "You knew him. Tell me: what is the sense of it all? Why Macbeatha?"

Kelda sighed, a great emptying sigh as the sorrow of now escaped her with a sibilant hiss. Drawing a deep breath, she let then fill her. One more sip of the brew and the trace of a saucy smile touched her lips, her eye turned inward, and she began to speak.

Chapter One

I never understood how Macbeatha's mind worked—but then, it was never his mind I was much interested in. I left that for his wife, the Lady Gruoch. I'm sure the pleasure she got of his mind was not half what I got of the rest of him. And as for the others—as for Duncan and Thorfinn and Alba, this kingdom of the Scots—I think they had more of him, too, than she. It must be said we all got what we wanted—Macbeatha most of all. And in the end, we all paid the price.

But when I first saw Macbeatha, there was no thought of price in my head at all! I was fourteen, serving in the hall of my lord Thorfinn, mormaer of Caithness and Sutherland—or jarl of the Orkneys, depending on whether you were Scot or Norse. Thorfinn was whichever it suited him to be at the moment. It didn't matter to me. Scot or Norse, he was the most important thing in my world. He represented power and protection and the brightest hope an impudent slave girl could imagine: to be a royal concubine and bear sons so remarkable that, of course, Thorfinn would adopt them as legitimate heirs. Perhaps they would go a-viking with him, and bring back shiploads of silver ... Such were the dreams that danced in my foolish, naïve head the day Macbeatha walked up from the shore into the *huseby* yard surrounded by Thorfinn and his warriors.

At first I took him for some brigand my lord had apprehended and brought back for sport. He had a wild look to him: dressed in a coarse, sleeveless tunic that bloused over a rope belt, his bare feet covered with sand, and his braided hair sticking out in odd directions. I had never seen a savage before, though I knew they dwelled in the highlands to the south and west, and there in the safety of the *huseby,* I was curious. Coming closer, I saw his clothes were dirty, his hair bleached by the sun, and his face wind-burned; and though he wore bands of gold on his neck and arms, I thought they were stolen, for he looked like nothing so much as a churl caught raiding my lord's nets or stealing a sheep.

Then Thorfinn slapped him on the back, roaring with good spirits, and this savage smiled the most dazzling smile. By that I knew the stranger was not to be our evening's entertainment, for no one smiles so when he is at Thorfinn's mercy. Realizing this was a guest, I was about to run and tell my mother when the clouds parted and a shaft of sunlight struck his hair, touching it with fire.

I gasped aloud. I had never seen hair of reddish gold on a living man before and, child that I was, I thought it must be the aspect of Thor resting on him. Oh, he was beautiful! The savageness of his dress dropped away and I saw instead that he was tall and golden and pulsing with life— In an instant I knew that, god or man, I must have his attention, must have that smile turn on me.

So I raced for the hall, shouting a warning to the kitchen that Jarl Thorfinn had returned from sailing. Then I grabbed up two tankards and dunked them into an ale cask, scorning the bung for taking too long. A moment later I was dashing back outside with the dripping tankards in my hands, sloshing the yeasty brew on my clothes as I ran.

Thorfinn looked up when he saw me coming and called out merrily, "Ho-ho! A Valkyrie, Macbeatha, come to greet us and make stout-hearted warriors welcome! Just what a thirsty man needs, eh?" The Valkyries are ladies—Christians would call them angels, I think—who greet dead warriors when they arrive at Odin's hall, Valhalla. I was modest enough yet to blush at the compliment, and at my lord's approval, but not so modest I didn't feel smug satisfaction as I handed him one tankard, and turned to give the other to his guest.

My previous master had tried—unsuccessfully—to teach me not to look into the face of my betters. Tell me, though, who could resist stealing a closer look at that red-gold hair? Even had I not been impudent—which I most decidedly was—I think I would have glanced upward as I handed this man his ale. What a shock, then, that my gaze never got beyond his eyes.

There was always a fire in the eyes of Macbeatha, even when he smiled. They were vivid green, like a cat's eyes; they told me he had a single purpose in life, and woe to the creature who got in his way. I guessed he must be twenty or twenty-two, to have such an unshakable opinion of himself and his destiny, and so he was—though at fifty, he had lost not one speck of that certainty. Only by then, he knew the cost of it all ...

As I stood there, gazing up into his wild face and wondering at the strangeness of him, he in turn looked down at me—or rather, down the front of my dress where my shawl had fallen open, and I saw I distracted him momentarily from his single-minded ambition. It ever pleased me to distract men. Odin gave to my lord and his warriors strong arms to bend others to their will; he gave to me a fair face and large breasts to do the same.

When Macbeatha raised his glance to my face, his lips were twisted in a wry smile of approval. "A Valkyrie, indeed," he agreed, and the soft burr in his voice gave him away.

"You're a Scot," I blurted.

A sly look came over his face and he asked, "Are you sure? I might be a *petta*-warrior, you know." Then there came into his exotic eyes such a devilish gleam that I gasped, wondering if the blood of such frightful beings might indeed run in his veins.

But Thorfinn slapped him on the back again. "Come inside and dry yourself by the hearth!" he invited. I decided this stranger with the captivating eyes had been teasing me. The *petta*-folk are a tale the Norse tell their children to frighten them, and this man was simply trying to frighten me. I did not know then that his grandmother was, indeed, of the old Pictish race.

As they pushed past me and on toward the hall, Thorfinn called for water so he and Macbeatha could wash the sea spray from their faces and mustaches. I ran to do his bidding. I had known two masters before Thorfinn, and even had I not desired to be his concubine, I would have run for him out of gratitude for the life I knew in his hall.

Like most Norse halls, it was long and narrow with a trench-like hearth running its length; but unlike the earth-and-stone longhouse where I grew up, it was made of stout timbers and dressed stone. At one end, partitions running between the roof braces created small sleeping chambers for my lord and other people of rank. He had no wife then, but his mother had her own room, as did Thorkel Fosterer when he stayed with us.

An entryway had been built on the front of the house; here Thorfinn and his guest paused to wash before they retired with their tankards to one of the long benches standing along the walls. Nearly a dozen men had accompanied Macbeatha, and as they seated themselves across from my lord's *hird*—his warband—they cast nervous glances at their hosts. And well they might: in the four years I had been at Thorfinn's hall, we had battled the Scots more than once. It made Macbeatha all the more fascinating and mysterious to me. Why should my lord greet an enemy in such a friendly fashion?

I brought ale to the men of the *hird* then, leaving poor Nisse to wait upon the Scots, but I kept my ears tuned to the conversation between my lord and his guest. "How are things at my grandfather's court?" Thorfinn asked.

"It has been more than a year since I was there," Macbeatha told him in passable, if accented, Norn. Thorfinn's grandfather was Malcolm mac Kenneth, King of Scots. It was from him Thorfinn got his black hair and harsh features—the gods know, only a Scot could ever be that ugly. Still, Thorfinn was the height of my desire, until that day.

Macbeatha drank deeply of his ale and wiped the foam from his bright red mustaches with the back of his hand. "I've been in Strathclyde this winter, visiting your cousin Duncan."

Thorfinn's face grew sour. "And how is Duncan?" he asked, his mouth puckering as he spoke the name.

"Still an ass," Macbeatha assured him. "Only now he's a royal ass!" Then the two of them roared with laughter and called for more ale, which I was quick to supply. I had no idea what the joke was—should a Norse slave girl know who the king of Cumbria and Strathclyde is?--but I grinned anyway and made sure to stoop over strategically as I filled their tankards from my pitcher. Both men's eyes wandered to the wares I displayed, and I sauntered away, insufferably pleased with myself.

I look back now and think how my poor mother despaired over my behavior! She knew, of course, that it is no great accomplishment to tempt men with female flesh. Having spent most of her life as a serving woman and bed wench, she knew it is usually easier to attract a man's attention than to avoid it. But that afternoon

I strolled back to the ale cask thinking I would be in the bed of one or the other that night, while Nisse and Haldana sulked in the kitchen.

Little did I know that in three days time, I would wish I had never laid eyes upon the Scottish prince.

Chapter Two

My service as a bed wench had begun just that spring, and I had as yet only been called to my lord's bed once. It's not likely I'd have been there even that one time—for he found my brazen flirtation more amusing than anything else—had not Ivarr Thorkelsson taken a fancy to me.

I call him Ivarr Thorkelsson because everyone knew he was Thorkel's son, though Thorkel never acknowledged him. Born of a servant in the Fosterer's house at Sandwick, he proved to be a sturdy boy and a pugnacious scrapper. After Thorkel came to Caithness to foster Thorfinn, Ivarr came to live there, too, and the two boys grew up together. Side by side they learned the warrior's arts, though Thorfinn was older and always the stronger.

But Ivarr was fifteen that winter and had been promised he could go out with the *hird* when they sailed to war in the spring. It was a sore point with him to have been left behind the previous year, for Thorfinn was only fourteen when *he* first went to battle. Ivarr was bitterly jealous of his father's fosterling who, it seemed to him, had everything without having earned it, while Ivarr did not even have his father's name.

"Who made him Jarl of Caithness, anyway?" Ivarr said to me once. "That old bag of wind who calls himself King of Scots? Pah! He had no right to give Caithness and Sutherland to anyone—they were Jarl Sigurd's, not his! If it hadn't been for Thorkel Fosterer, Sigurd's *Norse* sons would have taken this land from Thorfinn and fed him to the cod."

When I told my mother this tale, she scoffed at Ivarr: what a foolish boy, to think Thorfinn did not control his own jarldom, and more foolish still to say so! At nineteen, Thorfinn already held half his father's realm, and he was twice the warrior Ivarr would ever be. Ivarr had grown up bitter because Thorkel never publicly acknowledged him, though he acted as a father toward him. Ivarr resented the love Thorkel bore toward high-born Thorfinn, seeing himself as poorer for all that Thorfinn was rich.

Thorfinn must have understood this, for he tolerated a degree of disrespect from Ivarr that he would never have tolerated from anyone else. Yet they quarreled often, being more like brothers than lord and man. I suppose that is why, when I flaunted my blossoming womanhood in front of Thorfinn, it was Ivarr whose attention I drew.

Please understand, I was not averse to this attention. Ivarr was the image of his father: handsome, fair-haired and even-featured. And although he was not technically a foster brother to my lord, being so obviously Thorkel's son made him a person of some importance in the household. Thorfinn still thought of me as the brazen child he'd bought for a single silver mark, I reasoned, but if I teased Ivarr so he asked Thorfinn for permission to lie with me, perhaps that would open Thorfinn's eyes.

Now, I understand that in most Norse halls, it is not necessary to have a man's permission to lie with his slave girls, even when the master of the hall is Christian. But most Norse halls are not run by the Lady Plantula, daughter of the High King of Alba. According to the older servants, when Plantula came to Sigurd as a bride, she was horrified at the casual way in which men fornicated with the slave girls in her husband's hall—and in her very presence. So was her priest. Neither, however, could tell Sigurd what to do in his own hall. Although he had been baptized a Christian, his practice of Christian ways was patchy at best.

But when Sigurd was killed at Clontarf, she resolved to make a few changes. Thorkel Amundsson wanted very much to foster five-year-old Thorfinn in the Norse way, serving as his regent, so Plantula struck a bargain with him. She would accept Thorkel as fosterer, provided she could make some changes in the way the hall was run. One of those changes was to forbid fornication with Thorfinn's slave girls in the hall. Thorkel protested. Men would call the young jarl inhospitable. They would refuse to fight for such a stingy jarl. Furthermore, he could hardly be held accountable for the actions of the slaves, if they chose to make merry with the men of the *hird*.

Eventually, they reached a compromise. Plantula allowed that a man might do as he pleased with his *own* slaves—outside her presence—but the women who served her and her son were not to be molested. Any complaint by a bondwoman would find a receptive ear with her. But how they chose to deport themselves in private, she would not inquire.

I am told this arrangement worked quite well until Thorfinn approached manhood and decided he, too, could do as he pleased with his slave girls—including offering their services to his guests and loyal men. A warrior need only ask his permission. By that point, the Lady Plantula could do precious little about it, so she settled for making sure Thorfinn went to confession, and retiring to her room early in the evening.

Until that winter, though, if someone asked Thorfinn for me, he would scowl and say, "She's too young. Choose another." So I teased Ivarr, hoping since he himself was young, Thorfinn's answer to him might be different.

My mother, dear woman, saw a disaster in the making as her virgin daughter flirted with a hasty and inexperienced boy, and she intervened with Thorkel Fosterer on my behalf. Though she served in Thorfinn's hall, Mother was actually Thorkel's bondwoman, and a favorite of his for her gentle manner and quiet beauty. Therefore, it was the Fosterer who asked permission to lie with me first, and he gave me a gentler introduction to the ways of men and women than I would ever have had at the hands of his fifteen-year-old son.

Still, my first experience was a rude surprise, to say the least. Thorkel was a patient teacher, though, and I a determined student. Once initiated, I was sure I could please Thorfinn better than any other woman in his hall. Still, it was Ivarr who grabbed at me as I served at the long tables, who pulled me into his lap and worked his hand beneath the hem of my short gown to find bare flesh. I did not complain, for my blood ran hot even at that early age. But the night he pulled me over to his corner of the hall and made to spread his blanket over the two of us, Thorfinn's voice rang out.

"Ivarr. That is not your slave."

Ivarr stopped short, his face twisted in anger and embarrassment at having been called out for bad manners in front of the *hird*. But instead of apologizing, he cried, "Well, *you* don't use her—what do you care if I do?"

"Because I have not bedded her yet," said Thorfinn, "doesn't make it less my right, nor more yours."

Even then, if Ivarr had only said, "Your pardon, lord. I did not mean to intrude on your privilege; but if you have no plans for her company tonight, do you mind if I keep her here?"—if only he'd said something like that, I believe Thorfinn would have accepted his apology and the two of us might have passed an enjoyable night together. But Ivarr was more stubborn than wise. He came to his feet with his fists clenched at his sides. "Are you never satisfied?" he hissed. "Must you take everything away from me?"

At that, Thorfinn rose from his place in the high seat and came to tower over Ivarr, for he was almost a full head taller than the boy. His eyes burned like black coals in his craggy face, though his voice was soft. "How can I take away from you what is already mine, and was never yours for a moment?"

Full of myself as I was, even I knew it was not about me. It was about Thorfinn's authority in his own hall; and it was about the love of a man they both knew as father.

Ivarr grabbed my arm and jerked me back to my feet. "Take her, then!" he snapped.

And Thorfinn did. But it was the only time, and I suspect he refrained because he didn't really want to make more trouble with Ivarr. Soon after, the weather broke and Thorfinn set sail with his *hird* to visit his holdings in the Orkneys, while his freemen and bondsmen went about the work of delivering calves and lambs, shearing sheep, working manure into the soil, planting barley, and all the other tasks of a thriving *huseby.*

A huseby is a royal farm, but one that controls and protects the surrounding district. Thorfinn's holdings stretched along the fertile northern coast and back up into the rugged highlands and required many people to tend them; but in addition, he had jurisdiction over the adjoining lands of many freemen and *bønders*: they looked to his *hird* for protection, and in return supplied him with food and other goods. He always kept a very large hird. Having become jarl at the tender age of five, only Thorkel Fosterer and a very large hird had kept him in power.

Now, though, the Fosterer had mostly withdrawn from control, letting Thorfinn rule on his own. Just a week before Macbeatha arrived, my lord had returned from his lands in the Orkneys accompanied, not only by his own ships, but by a dozen others as men joined his *hird* for the summer, drawn by his growing reputation as a fierce warrior and successful raider. Thorkel and Ivarr had not come, though; they tarried at the Fosterer's estate at Sandwick, where he kept his wife and younger children.

So with Ivarr out of the way, I had great hopes of drawing Thorfinn's eye. But all my posturing was for nothing. Though I lingered near where the men practiced with their swords and spears, and cast seductive glances from under long lashes as I served at table, I rarely got more than a smile or a wink from my lord. I began to look forward to Ivarr's return when *someone*, at least, would notice my eagerness to please.

Macbeatha's arrival changed all that. He was the most exciting man, and I soon found myself sitting on his lap, stroking that long, red mustache of his while he and Thorfinn talked of politics. They spoke Norn mostly, at Macbeatha's request. "It's the only chance I get to practice," he explained.

"Your accent is terrible," Thorfinn reproved. "Kelda speaks better Norn than you."

"I speak perfect Norn!" I objected with a pout.

Both men laughed, and I got a little squeeze from Macbeatha. "And what are you doing, listening to the conversation of your betters?" he demanded playfully.

"I can listen to what I please, as long as I don't repeat it," I told him. "My mother says a slave who keeps her ears open and her mouth shut is a valuable commodity."

They laughed again, and I was glad I amused them, for I wanted to stay right where I was for a while.

"And what have you learned by listening to us this afternoon?" Macbeatha asked, his green eyes glittering.

"That you came from Cumbria by boat across a large dale, because you were afraid to sail through the Western Isles for fear you'd run into my lord and his *hird* and have to fight him. Only I don't understand how you can take a boat through a large valley."

Chuckling, he settled me more comfortably on his lap. "The Great Glen has rivers and long, deep lakes for most its length. We sailed our boat up an inlet as far as we could, then pulled it out of the water and slid it on—" Here he consulted Thorfinn for a word he did not know. "On rollers, on logs, to a lake. Then we sailed again, then crossed a small piece of land, then sailed, and so on, until we reached the Firth of Moray."

"Ah." I nodded wisely. "And there you stopped with your kinsmen." His hand was sliding in a most intriguing way along my bare arm, under my shawl. "Is Jarl Hundi really your kinsman?" I had heard tales of the Dog Earl who made war against Thorfinn's father Sigurd, claiming Caithness was his.

Macbeatha laughed. "Yes, but don't hold it against me, will you? He's been dead a long time."

"Would the same were true of his sons," Thorfinn muttered into his tankard.

"Well, I can't choose my relatives, cousin," said Macbeatha, "or I would never have chosen someone as ugly as you."

My jaw must have dropped to my knees. "You are my lord's kinsman?"

"Of course, didn't you know?" he asked in all sincerity. "Our mothers are sisters."

I looked carefully from him to Thorfinn and back, but Thorfinn's face was concealed in his tankard as he drank deeply, and there was no guile to be found in Macbeatha's countenance—that in itself made me suspicious. "Truly?" I asked uncertainly. "I've never heard you spoken of as a kinsman."

"Thorfinn!" Macbeatha cuffed my lord playfully. "You don't speak of me in your hall? Your kinsman, who saved your life on three occasions?"

Thorfinn nearly choked on his ale.

For as long as I knew him, I could never tell when Macbeatha was lying. I have seen him swear most sincerely to outrageous falsehood, and give the truth with such a sly look, his listener instantly discredits it. "I don't believe you," I decided.

That brought a wounded look to his face. "Which, that I am Thorfinn's cousin, or that I saved his life three times?"

"You spoke of *his* cousin Duncan," I said slowly as I reasoned it out, "not *your* cousin Duncan. And he said *my* grandfather, not *our* grandfather. So I don't think you're his cousin. And as for saving his life—" It occurred to me, thankfully, to be a bit politic as I called the man a liar. "I'm sure my lord Thorfinn hasn't needed saving, except perhaps once, as a small child."

Macbeatha roared with laughter. "By God, but she's clever, too, Thorfinn!"

For his part, Thorfinn stretched his long frame out on the bench where they were sitting. "It was only twice," he grumbled, setting his tankard on the floor and folding his hands comfortably across his chest. They had both drunk quite a lot by this time, and Thorfinn was clearly sleepy. "And I wouldn't call it saving my life, exactly. More like saving me a beating." Then fire kindled in his dark eyes as he said to me, "But he is my kinsman."

"As you say, lord," I responded quickly, not wanting to offend him.

"He's my kinsman because sometimes you *can* choose your relatives." Thorfinn extended an arm toward Macbeatha. "And I chose this one long ago."

Macbeatha reached over to clasp Thorfinn's arm, and I saw there a bond between them that went beyond words. "More kinsman than the sons of Maelbrighde will ever be," he vowed in fierce tones. Then he added lightly, "And it was three times. You forget the spring you and your mother came to Inverness, and I saved you from the clutches of the evil *petta* woman."

At that Thorfinn burst into laughter and rolled off the bench onto the floor. "What was I, nine years old? I don't know who was more terrified, me or the old witch!"

I smiled, too, although I had no idea what they were talking about. But I liked being cuddled, and I liked Macbeatha's smile, and his red mustaches intrigued me. There inside, his hair lost its red hue, but the mustaches fairly glowed their fiery color. "Will you stay long, lord?" I asked, reaching out a tentative finger to stroke the length of one.

"Perhaps. As long as the food is good and the company pleasant." Here he slipped a hand through the drooping neckline of my gown and found a breast to fondle. "Long enough to make sure your lord sails his warband west, and not south."

Thorfinn snorted and picked himself up off the floor. "I never look south for trouble," he grumbled. "But if your cousin Maelcolm comes begging for a fight, he'll get one." He plopped himself back down on the bench, rattling it considerably. "I'm for the Hebrides this summer, and maybe some raiding along the Irish coast. I've promised Ivarr his pleasure with a few Irish girls if he does well in battle."

"Tell him to bring one back for me," Macbeatha said, brushing strands of hair away from my neck and dropping light kisses on it. It made me shiver deliciously.

"Your mustaches tickle," I informed him.

Then, of course, he made a point of tickling me with them, till I squirmed and squealed. Thorfinn looked over at us with mild scorn. "You're spoiling her with all this attention, you know."

"I intend to do worse with her before the night is out." Macbeatha leaned back against the wall and left off tickling me in favor of slowly bunching up the skirt of my gown, intent on finding a way underneath it. "With your kind permission."

Thorfinn shrugged. "What's mine is yours. It might be amusing to have one or two red-haired brats running around here."

Red-haired children! The thought excited me nearly as much as Macbeatha's touch. I thought I should like nothing better than to give birth to a red-haired child of his. Of course, the child would be a slave, and there was no chance Thorfinn would adopt a child so obviously not his own. But perhaps he would take the boy into battle, where he could win his freedom by his courageous fighting— I stroked the long red mustaches and dreamed ...

Just then a boy ran in shouting. "Jarl Thorfinn! A ship approaches, and it looks to be Thorkel!"

Chapter Three

With a glad cry, Thorfinn heaved himself to his feet. "Come, kinsman," he bade Macbeatha, "put the girl down and let's go meet Thorkel."

With an abrupt motion I was swept from my warm perch, deposited on the bench and forgotten—forgotten!--as the two men headed out the door.

I was quick after them, but my mother called to me from the dairy where she had been helping with the evening milking. "Kelda! Take your brother to see the ship land."

Normally I didn't mind taking little Hakon with me anywhere— I just adored him! He was three winters old, bright-eyed and flaxen-haired and curious about everything. And I knew very well what my mother had in mind: Hakon was Thorkel's child, and she wanted to remind the Fosterer what a strong, fine boy Hakon was. If he were charmed by that roguish smile and willful temper and the hero worship in those clear blue eyes, perhaps-- Though she never spoke of it, I knew how badly my mother wanted Thorkel to adopt Hakon.

So I turned aside to scoop up my baby brother and carry him along. "Oof! You're getting so heavy!" I gasped as I hoisted him into my arms.

"I can walk!" Hakon protested, squirming to get down.

I didn't want to fall behind the crowd, though, waiting for a dawdling child. "Can you walk on your hands?" I teased, turning him upside-down and holding him by his ankles. He squealed with delight, a noise that brought favorable glances in his direction. Everyone smiles to see a little boy behaving like a little boy.

But it was awkward, trying to carry a squirming three-year-old at arm's length, and I quickly gave it up. "Climb on my shoulders," I commanded as I turned him upright again. "Can you see the ship racing for the shore? Guess who is on that ship."

"Thorkel!" he shouted, clapping his hands in delight as I hoisted him to my shoulders. Then he clamped his arms around my forehead and commanded, "Run, Kelda, run!" So we ran toward the shore, his eyes fixed on the brightly striped sail of Thorkel's ship, mine fixed on the golden-red hair of Macbeatha.

Thorkel's longboat had sixteen pairs of oars, but they were tied up on racks over the heads of the crew as she ran before a stiff breeze. Slender as an arrow, she knifed through the waves like a fish, her keel soaring proudly at bow and stern. Her distinctive figurehead, a snarling beast that looked part wolf and part boar, had already been taken down. Such figures are to frighten the protective spirits of ones enemies, so they are taken down when coming to a friendly port.

Just beyond the breakers, men cast out the anchors and she lay to among the other longboats. Two smaller vessels were already rowing out to meet her, but Thorfinn and Macbeatha grabbed yet another and plunged into the icy waters with it, wet up to their thighs before they clambered into the craft and began to pull on the oars. The two of them rowed strongly, muscular arms and backs accustomed to hard work.

Hakon and I waited impatiently, peering to see which boat would ferry Thorkel. Before long we saw him standing in the prow of his fosterling's boat, shouting over the sound of the waves with great good humor, exhorting Thorfinn and Macbeatha to put their backs into it. As soon as the boat scraped on the sand, all those aboard jumped out and dragged the heavy wooden vessel past the tide line as if it were a toy.

Then there was hand clapping and back slapping as greetings, delayed during the transport, were exchanged. "Thor's hammer, but it's good to see you boy!" Thorkel roared at Macbeatha. "I was afraid we'd have to come to Burghead to see you again, and then you'd be launching spears at us."

Ivarr stood close by his father's elbow. Macbeatha turned to him and asked, "Is this Ivarr? Thorkel, you breed sons like trees!

Look at those shoulders!" Ivarr puffed up his chest a little but did not smile. "I hear you will go to war against the Irish this summer."

Ivarr shrugged, his blue eyes cold. "I will fight Irish, or Scots—it makes no difference to me," he said bluntly. "As long as their guts are spread for the eagles and the ravens, I will rejoice."

Now, that is the way all Norsemen speak of their glory and ferocity in battle. But for Ivarr to include the Scots, when he knew this one was a friend, bordered on bad manners. If Macbeatha was offended, though, he gave no sign.

"Thorkel, Thorkel!" shouted the child on my shoulders, impatient to be noticed.

"Well, look at this!" Thorkel laughed, plucking up the boy and tossing him in the air. "Hakon, you get bigger every time I turn around!"

Hakon shrieked with delight at the playful treatment. "Again!" he commanded, so Thorkel tossed him in the air again, catching him in large, strong hands. It made me beam to see them enjoy each other.

Then without a word, Thorkel passed Hakon back to me and turned away, dropping a heavy arm across Macbeatha's shoulders. "Tell me, boy, what news from Alba? Is the High King still in good health?"

"Hale as ever, last I heard," Macbeatha replied. "Still keeping the Northumbrians at bay, and the Bernicians under his thumb."

Trudging along close behind them, I heard the change in Thorkel's voice as he asked. "Do you come from Inverness?"

"I stopped there for a few days," Macbeatha answered in the same covered tone. "I go back when I leave here. It's not good for a prince to be too long from his own country, once he comes of age."

"And the king of Moray—"

"Mormaer," Macbeatha corrected gently. "My cousin is the mormaer of Moray, steward of the High King."

"Mormaer, then," Thorkel said with distaste. "Does he still look toward Caithness?"

Macbeatha gave a humorless chuckle. "The sons of Maelbrighde will always look toward Caithness, and whinny and blow and stamp their feet like a stallion in the presence of mares. But Maelcolm, at least, is no fool. He seeks to win the affection of the tribes along Dornach Firth before he tries to strike deeper into your territory."

"And will you fight beside him when he does?"

At the pointed question, Macbeatha broke into a grin. "Only if I believe we can win!" Then, "We'll speak of politics later, when the wind doesn't carry our words. In the meantime, I've brought gifts—one in particular I know you like. Owen!" he called to one of his men, and gave some instruction that sent the man hurrying off to their beached boat. "After supper tonight," he promised his companions, "we'll drink of the water of life!"

I would have liked to hear more, but just then someone grabbed me from behind and I nearly lost my grip on Hakon. "Ivarr!" I gasped when I saw who it was. "You nearly made me drop the baby!"

Ivarr scowled. "Oh, put the brat down. Let him walk."

I did, but I was still unhappy at being distracted when I wanted so to hear Macbeatha's every word. "That brat," I told Ivarr crossly, "is your half-brother."

It was the wrong thing to say. His scowl darkened and he sneered, "He's a thrall, the son of a thrall, and he can be bought and sold like any cow." His own mother, you see, was a freewoman. "And you, Kelda—" He grabbed my arm roughly and put his lips next to my ear. "You're a thrall, too. Don't forget that."

"Which makes it my duty to serve my *lord's* pleasure," I retorted, not liking the idea that my little brother might be sold, and unwilling to *think* I might ever have to leave Thorfinn's hall.

Ivarr's face twisted with bitterness at my galling reminder, and he shoved me roughly aside, sending me sprawling in the dirt. Then he walked on after the rest of the men without a backward glance. Cheeks burning, I sat up and brushed the dirt from my skinned palms. There and then I planned how I would hurt Ivarr—and feed my own growing desire at the same time.

There was no chance that night. Some eighty or ninety warriors were staying at Thorfinn's hall, and just feeding them was a chore that took hours. The lady Plantula herself served Thorfinn in his high seat, and Macbeatha in the lower high seat across the hearth. It irked me because *I* wanted to serve Macbeatha. Then, much to my chagrin, as soon as the boards were cleared, Thorfinn sent all the women out of the hall. All! Lady Plantula retired to her room with her maid while the rest of us filed out. Pouting like the child I was, I stomped across the yard to the kitchen with the others.

"It would do you no good to flaunt your charms in the hall tonight," my mother chided. "They will drink themselves stupid, and though they may desire what you offer, they will be unable to take advantage of it."

What pearls of wisdom my mother tried to bestow upon me! And how different my life would have been had I taken her warnings to heart. But I was young, and I stamped my foot and thrust out my lower lip and said, "I don't see why I can't at least serve him ale. What harm in that?"

"Because when men drink themselves stupid, they often drink themselves ugly as well. When they are ugly and stupid, and their own flesh denies them the satisfaction of their desires, they sometimes take it out on the woman who inflames them. Thorfinn sent us away because he doesn't want us hurt. Be glad he is so considerate."

She was right. The next day a good many hirdmen staggered around ashen-faced and bleary-eyed, wincing at the shrill shrieking of children and the ringing of the carpenter's hammer.

It was the Christian Sabbath, and the withered old Scot priest who attended Lady Plantula said mass in the yard. All were allowed to attend, slave and freeman, warrior and maid, for my lord had insisted his entire household be baptized. Normally I avoided services, but that morning as the wooden altar was set up, I eagerly joined those clustering in the yard, hoping to glimpse the object of my ardor.

When he came outside, I saw he had put on clean clothes: a tunic, or *léine,* as the Scots call it, bloused up over his belt and a colorful *brat,* a rectangular cloak, slung over his left shoulder. Standing in the front ranks of worshippers beside Thorfinn and Lady Plantula, he showed no signs of hangover, but bowed his golden head piously during the prayers, listened attentively to the readings, and received the Holy Sacrament with reverence. I thought him very devout; but as he returned from the altar and caught my gaze, he *winked* at me.

After mass he and Thorfinn went off hunting, and I did not see them again until evening. With that morning's headache still fresh in mind, the men drank more moderately, and we women were allowed to stay after the meal. Arnor the *skald* gave us a great story about Thorfinn's father Sigurd Hlodversson, whom we call Sigurd the Stout. Then he told another about Thorfinn himself, and how at fourteen he had led his hird against his half-brother Einar to get his just share of Sigurd's inheritance.

As I moved up and down the benches with pitchers of ale, I noticed Ivarr watching me. Another time, I would have sauntered casually in his direction and lingered overlong in filling his drinking horn; but that night I avoided him, remembering the soreness of my palms and the scuffs of dirt on my clothes. I crossed instead to the other side of the hall where the Scots sat and served them with great courtesy. To my mind they were strange, ugly men, mostly small and dark and hairy, but they were Macbeatha's men, so I went out of my way to smile and show them hospitality. I also went out of my way to pass before Macbeatha as many times as possible.

He gave no sign that he noticed. The men were telling riddles now, and Macbeatha would turn aside to translate the game into Scots for his men so they could guess, too. Then he proposed a liar's contest, and it was great fun. Men told stories about talking wolves and birds that flew backwards and fish that swallowed longboats whole. Halfdan told a randy tale of a *fian* wife who, dissatisfied with her husband's performance, replaced his organ with that of a bull. The teller went into great detail about the *fian* wife's resulting pleasure, and the serving girls began to blush. "Imagine her surprise, though," he concluded, "when her first child was born with four hoofed feet and a ring through its nose."

The men roared with laughter and called Halfdan's tale the best lie so far. "Do we have another contender?" asked Thorfinn. "Or shall we name Halfdan the winner?"

"I believe Macbeatha will contend," said Thorkel slyly, his eyes challenging the younger man across the fire.

"Lord knows Scots are the greatest liars in the world," Thorfinn agreed. "Macbeatha, can you do Halfdan one better?"

Macbeatha looked surprised, surveyed the men on both sides of the long hearth, then leaned forward in his chair toward the smug Halfdan. "That was a lie?" he asked with unparalleled sincerity. "Why, I believed you!"

The hall erupted in laughter that shook the roof beams. Tears rolled down Thorfinn's cheeks, he laughed so hard, and even Halfdan had to admit Macbeatha's lie was greater. "Kelda!" Thorfinn called to me. "Pour more ale for the winner."

I had been squatting on the ground at Macbeatha's feet, waiting for such an opportunity. But as I reached forward with my pitcher, he seized me around the waist. "Forget the ale," he said, "I'll take this." Pulling me roughly into his lap, he teased, "Come to my chamber, I'll show you what the *fian* wife gave me." Before I could respond, he covered my mouth with his in a kiss that kindle fire all the way to my toes.

They told me later how Ivarr leapt up with a murderous fury in his eyes.

Then just as abruptly as he had grabbed me, Macbeatha set me back on my feet and, with a gentle slap on my behind, sent me on my way. I staggered a bit, giddy and weak with the rush of longing through my veins, but he seemed to feel nothing. "Thorkel," he called out. "We have not yet partaken of the water of life I promised you. Owen, where is that cask? Bring it out, we must drink to our host and his good Fosterer."

The cask was brought, and Macbeatha served out a small measure for Thorfinn and Thorkel and himself. *"Uisge beatha,"* he pronounced as he poured. "The water of life. Liquid fire that warms the soul but steals the breath. Halfdan, will you drink with us?" It was his way of recognizing the second-best liar in the hall.

"That I will," said Halfdan, sending his drinking horn around.

"Who is the bravest man in the hall, save those now served?" Macbeatha asked. "Who will drink of the water of life with us?"

The Scots all held their horns out eagerly—they did not need to be asked twice. But the Norsemen were slower. "I will taste," said first one hirdman, and then another.

Suddenly Ivarr came to his feet, eyes blazing with hatred. "I will drink," he snarled. "There is nothing a Scot takes into his gullet that will give a Norseman pause."

I was confused. Why this look of loathing on Ivarr's face? Silly as it seems now, I had no idea then what caused him to bear such ill will toward my golden Macbeatha.

But Macbeatha was not confused. For as long as I knew him, I only saw him confused once, and that over a woman. "This is a drink for men," he goaded, "not for boys."

"I am a man!" Ivarr shouted. "I will drink anything you drink, be it water or blood."

Macbeatha chuckled low in his throat. "Then pass me your horn, man, and I will measure your life into it."

The horn was passed, and the look in Macbeatha's eye as he sent it back put a chill in my blood. In that moment I was sorry for Ivarr, though I did not know why.

"Drink it slowly," Thorkel cautioned from his seat on Thorfinn's right. "It burns."

But Macbeatha tossed his measure back in a single gulp, then smiled and lifted merciless green eyes to Ivarr. When Ivarr tried to do the same, he choked and coughed and gasped for breath like a fish flopping on the sand. The men around the hearth laughed at him, Norse and Scot alike, excepting Thorkel and Thorfinn. The former looked sad, the latter, grim.

"Come," whispered Haldana, tugging at my sleeve. She was only seventeen, but wise enough to know a man's shame is compounded if a woman should witness it. She drew me out of the hall into the cool night where stars glittered above the restless sea. Standing in the shadow of the hall, she put her hands to the small of her back, emphasizing the bulge in her stomach where Thorfinn's child grew. "You like this Macbeatha, don't you?" she asked.

"Does he not bear the aspect of Thor?" I answered rapturously.

"He does dazzle," she admitted. "But listen to me: he will go back whence he came, and Ivarr will stay. Think on it, Kelda. Don't trade a night or two of fascination for a life of scorn."

I knew what she meant. But I was young, and I wanted what I wanted. When we were sure Ivarr had recovered from his spasm, we went back inside.

Chapter Four

For the rest of the evening, Macbeatha ignored me. I was quite hurt—I *knew* he wanted me. Had he not already asked Thorfinn for permission? Yet his eyes never strayed to where I sat, nor did he try to touch me when I refilled his tankard. Moreover, no one else would touch me, either. The other bondwomen were grabbed and stroked and teased all night long, while the most I got was a leering look and a crude remark.

I understand that women who are born free find such attention offensive, but born in slavery as I was, it was what I expected, and an affirmation that I was pleasing. I wanted men to play with me and surrender to the fire of lust I kindled in them. I was quite put out that Macbeatha wouldn't oblige.

"Better watch out," Nisse goaded, "or Thorfinn will give you to those Scot savages. They probably have lice."

"He wouldn't let such men take liberties with his property," I retorted, hoping that was true. "Maybe he's decided he wants me for himself tonight, and that's why Macbeatha ignores me."

"The Scot ignores you," Haldana said wearily, "because Ivarr looked ready to kill over the one kiss. Your Macbeatha doesn't want trouble in his cousin's hall, it would be bad manners. No slave girl is worth that."

I protested, of course, but as I thought about it, I knew she was right. Still it rankled—why should Ivarr control my destiny when he didn't own me? So when Thorfinn commanded the fires to be banked for the night, I slipped unseen into the guest chamber prepared for Macbeatha.

It was a dark and windowless room, but someone had put coals in the brazier and lit a rush lamp which cast quiet, flickering shadows around. A soft feather-stuffed mattress lay on the sleeping platform, with several thick wool blankets and a stack of furs spread on it. It was as fine as the bed in Thorfinn's room, and I thought for a moment of snuggling down in it to wait. But a small sea chest sat against a wall, and I was consumed with curiosity. What manner of things did a Scot carry when he traveled? Kneeling in front of it, I reached out to lift the lid and peek inside.

The next thing I knew, my arms were pinned and a rough hand held a thin, cold blade flat against my neck. I was too terrified to breathe, let alone scream.

Then, "You!" Macbeatha said in disgust.

His tone hurt more than his grip. "Pardon, lord," I whimpered. "I only—" Words failed me. I only what? I had no business opening his sea chest, and no convenient lie came to my frozen mind. Besides, I doubted any lie would fool him. "Pardon," I repeated, knowing there was nothing else I could say.

His grip relaxed just a little, but he did not let go. "Did you come here to rob me?" he demanded harshly.

"No, lord! I came to wait for you. Only I saw the chest, and I was curious ..." I wanted to smile at him to demonstrate the innocence of my intent, but he had my back pinned tight to his chest and the blade still at my throat. I dared not move.

"Curious if I carried silver?" His mouth was so close to my ear, I could feel his warm breath.

"Just curious what a barbarian prince carries in his sea chest," I squeaked. "Please, lord—I came to give to you, not take."

Finally I heard a chuckle low in his throat, and I suspected he had been teasing me the whole time. But by Thor's hammer, it was always so hard to tell with him! "You think you have something I might want, do you?" he asked with mirth in his voice.

"You said as much, earlier. To Thorfinn."

Still he did not release me, but held me helpless in a grip as unyielding as stone. "So I did. But you're far too trusting, Kelda. Never believe what a man promises when he has his hand inside your dress." Slowly he began to stroke the sharp edge of his knife across my neck as though shaving it. "Never turn your back to a door when you are alone, either." My heart pounded and I hardly dared to breathe lest the soft caress of that blade turn deadly.

"And never—" He held it poised at the curve of my throat where a pulse beat frantically. "—*never* enter a warrior's room without permission. I could cut your throat, pay Thorfinn a single mark for his loss, and be quit of the deed."

The truth of it stung; but I wasn't about to let him know. "Even so, lord," I agreed. "But I can give you little pleasure dead. Alive, I can sweeten more nights than this one."

I tell you now with the wisdom of years that Macbeatha loved power. It was the sweetest elixir he knew: to be in control of the lives of others, to command their loyalty, or their fear—or both. Stroking his knife across my throat, he savored the power he had over me—to take my life or yield it back to me. But I tell you as well, it was never his nature to exercise power unjustly, nor to break those who gave themselves into his hand.

The low chuckle sounded in his throat again. "By God, you are clever," he whispered, and the twinkle I could not see in his eye, I heard in his voice. The knife disappeared and he released me at last, sitting down on the floor beside me. "Do you want to see what's in the chest?" he asked.

"As you please, lord," I said carefully, although I had quite lost interest in it.

He laughed again and reached for the latch. "Someone has trained you well."

"Someone has tried. It comes back to me when there's a knife at my throat."

Then he grinned broadly, lifted the lid of his sea chest, and rifled through its contents for me. There was nothing too remarkable: a linen tunic, finely embroidered; a whetstone, iron and flint; several bone fishhooks folded in a scrap of leather; an oilskin cloak; and a leather wallet with a folded sheet of vellum inside. My hand went to the tunic, examining the delicate stitches in it. "She sews very neatly," I said.

"Who sews?" he asked with a teasing look.

"I thought you might tell me. A mother? A sister? A wife?"

"A wife," he admitted. "But not mine!"

I closed up the sea chest for him. "I would ask whose wife, but if her husband doesn't know, it's hardly right that I should."

He laughed and reached out to pluck the bone pick from the wooden brooch holding my coarse woolen shawl together. "You're very cunning, little bondmaid," he said with that soft burr like music in his voice and the lamplight glinting on his golden hair. "I find you amusing, even with your clothes on." He laid my shawl carefully aside and turned deft fingers to the brooches fastening the straps of my gown. "I can't wait to see how much fun you are with them off."

Perhaps it was because the look of him was so exotic to my eyes; perhaps it was because my body had finally begun to understand this sort of thing; or perhaps it was the playfulness with which Macbeatha took me. Whatever the reason, that night was the first time I truly felt pleasure in a man's bed. Thorkel had been gentle with me, but I got no pleasure of him. Even with Thorfinn, whom I greatly desired, there was the warm satisfaction of accomplishment, but nothing like pleasure. Nothing like *this*. I felt like the *fian*-wife in Halfdan's story, panting and straining until my need burst forth, and I was consumed in ecstasy.

Then to settle into his arms feeling safe and protected-- I had intended to slip away afterward, to go back to the kitchen and gloat to Nisse. But I fell asleep there and hardly stirred until the dawn, when birds began to twitter and Macbeatha jerked awake with a soft, guttural utterance that could only have been a Scottish curse.

"Lord?" I asked softly, feeling his arms grow rigid.

With a groan, he went limp again.

Belatedly, I remembered what Haldana had said about not causing trouble in Thorfinn's hall. "You meant for me to be gone by morning, didn't you?" I guessed.

He flopped over on his back and stared up at the roof beams of the still-dark room. "It would have been convenient."

"I can go now," I offered, struggling free of the warm covers and swinging my feet onto the rushes covering the chilly stone floor.

But he caught me around the waist and tugged me back into the bed. "No point in that," he said, wrapping arms and legs around me. "Someone will see you steal away and the word will travel." He nuzzled his face against my neck. "I will have to bear the consequences—I may as well have full enjoyment of the deed."

So it was full daylight before I scurried out of his room and off to the kitchen to help prepare the morning's meal. I know not what was said to him when he joined the other men outside—probably just the usual bawdy banter that men exchange after such escapades. By the time they came back into the hall for their meal, conversation had turned to other topics, such as who was the strongest rower, who could throw a knife with the greatest precision, and whether the long-legged youth from Birsay could run faster than Macbeatha's bandy-legged steersman.

The only way to decide these vital questions, of course, was to have a series of contests and competitions. It was all in good fun, and there was a great deal of wagering, all the while giving warriors who had been idle over the winter a chance to test their skills before going into battle. Freemen left their fields to watch, visitors arrived from neighboring farms, and even we slaves were allowed to slip away from our duties to watch a race or a wrestling match. A holiday atmosphere fill everyone—except Ivarr.

He had been unusually surly at table that morning, and when I passed by him with a kettle of porridge, he tripped me up and sent me sprawling, the hot porridge scalding my arms. "Clumsy," he sneered. "That is a waste of good food."

"It is you who wasted it," I retorted, "tripping me like that."

"I never touched you!" he shouted. "You're just clumsy, and trying to blame me for your stupidity."

I bit back the hasty reply that came to mind and forced myself to be more cunning. "Indeed, lord, I am clumsy this morning," I agreed. "Perhaps it is because I slept so little last night, and my legs still quiver under me."

His face went purple. But there was nothing he could say to that. As I picked up the kettle and wiped its brim with rushes from the floor, I glanced across the fire to see how Macbeatha liked my wit. He was not looking at me, but he had his head down and a hand in front of his mouth. Hiding a smile? Perhaps. Thorfinn's look, however, was easy to read. He glared down at Ivarr from his high seat.

I took care to keep away from Ivarr for the rest of the meal. Such a display of ill temper was strongly reminiscent of my previous master, and I had learned young and learned well that the best course of action with such a man is to stay out of his way.

When the boards had been cleared, the men filed outside to organize their competitions. Thorfinn and Macbeatha stood just inside the door debating how they would contend with each other. Thorfinn challenged his friend to a wrestling match, but Macbeatha conceded with a laugh. Thorfinn was not only taller, he was heavier into the bargain, and it would have been a very brief match. My lord received much the same response to a rowing contest—Macbeatha had been fostered at the Scottish court in Scone, far from the pounding of the sea. Rowing had been only a small part of his training.

Nor would Thorfinn face Macbeatha at spear throwing. "You'll conjure up one of those unholy Pictish spells," he accused, "and make the wind blow just as I make my cast."

"Swords, then?" asked Macbeatha. "I promise to do nothing unholy there, just my strong right arm against yours."

Ivarr was passing by on his way out. "A Scot's promise is worth spit," he sneered.

I was cleaning the floor where the porridge had spilled and looked up to see the spark that flashed in Macbeatha's eye. But it was Thorfinn who replied. "My mother is a Scot," he reminded the boy.

Ivarr struggled a moment to extricate himself. "Nobly born and nobly bred," he revised rather belatedly. "Too bad it's not true of other Scots." Then with a look of pure hatred for Macbeatha, he stalked out of the hall.

"Your fosterer's son has poor manners," Macbeatha said darkly.

"But a strong arm and a stout heart. I think he will prove himself worthy this summer."

"If he can control himself. Arm and heart are nothing without good judgment. I wonder if he has that?"

Thorfinn shrugged. "He'll learn."

"If he lives long enough." Macbeatha stretched himself and adjusted the heavy gold armbands he wore. "I've half a mind to teach him a lesson before I leave."

Furrows appeared on Thorfinn's brow. "Though he is not truly my foster brother," he cautioned Macbeatha, "I think of him as kin."

At that a broad smile overtook Macbeatha's countenance. "Don't worry. I'll be as gentle as you would."

Thorfinn pulled a face. "That's no comfort. At times, I'm tempted to kill him!"

Macbeatha laughed. "I promise not to do that. If, that is, my promise is worth more than spit."

Thorfinn laughed, too, and clapped his friend on the shoulder. "As long as you don't have your hand in my money pouch," he quipped. "Come, I'll put half a mark against that gold armband of yours that my man takes the footrace." And off they went, Macbeatha protesting that half a mark was hardly fair for a family heirloom.

It didn't matter: the Scot won the footrace, which surprised us all—who would have thought such speed could lurk in such a compact body? But out of six wrestling matches, five were won by Norsemen. In knife-throwing, an Orkneyman named Turolf took first place, though Macbeatha ran him a close second, and Thorfinn lost money because he had bet heavily on Macbeatha to win. Neither prince competed in archery—Thorfinn disliked it, and the Scots disdain archery as unfair and unmanly. Instead, they bet on the spear-throwing contest, which was taken by a local boy with barely a dusting of fuzz on his upper lip.

"Where are you from, boy?" Macbeatha asked as he paid Thorfinn his wager.

"Sutherland," the gangly youth replied. "Along the Oykel River."

"Ha," said Macbeatha. "Probably more Scot than Norse."

"It doesn't matter," Thorfinn told him. "The Oykel is mine, that makes him my man."

"Yours for now. Once, the Oykel belonged to my kin."

"If they think to take it again, they'll find me ready."

"And what if it's me who comes to take it?" Macbeatha asked easily, tucking his purse away inside the blousy fold of his tunic.

"You'll find me ready."

"Perhaps we should test our swords today, then," Macbeatha suggested with a smile. "What do you say? Caithness against Moray, with Sutherland as the prize."

Thorfinn gave a barking laugh. "That's too rich a purse for honesty—you'll cheat."

"Without hesitation, cousin. All right, let's have a smaller prize for our contest, then." Word was spreading rapidly that Jarl Thorfinn and the Scottish nobleman would play at swords, and a crowd began to collect around them. "Nothing you can't afford to lose. Say that knife with the silver handle you showed me."

Thorfinn sent someone to fetch their weapons. "You have nothing of equal value to wager against my knife, though. Not after my spearman took yours."

Then Ivarr stepped up. "What need of prizes? Thorfinn, take his right hand as a trophy."

The Scots bristled, and Macbeatha turned cold green eyes on the boy. "Even with one hand, I could slit you from navel to chin and go happily to my bed." A wolfish grin twisted his face. "Provided Kelda was there to sweeten it."

There was a spattering of laughter, and Ivarr flushed a bright pink.

"Leave off," Thorfinn commanded. "This is not a fight for blood. We'll draw a circle in the dirt: whoever forces the other out first is the winner." A man had arrived with two swords and two round shields. "There, Macbeatha, those are yours, are they not?"

Macbeatha took his sword, drawing it from its wooden scabbard. "Yes, this is mine," he acknowledged as he inspected its edge. "Though I could do as well with another. After all—" He cast a wicked grin in Ivarr's direction. "As any woman will tell you, it's not the weapon, but how one wields it. Isn't that so, Kelda?"

I didn't bother to answer; I knew he wasn't speaking to me.

"Halfdan!" Thorfinn barked, taking up his weapons. "Make us a circle the size of two ox hides."

Chapter Five

Since this was only a friendly contest, both men wore leather jerkins with extra strips of leather sewn on for protection. They also had their shields, for those are as much a part of any combat as swords and axes. Thorfinn's was painted bright red and edged with black, made of thin boards covered with leather and bound together by an iron bar across the back. A hole was cut in the center of the boards so a man could grasp the bar, and his knuckles were protected by an iron boss fitted over the hole. That was the only metal on the shield; metal adds too much weight, and a warrior depends on quickness and agility to keep the shield between himself and his enemy.

Macbeatha's shield was of similar construction, but there was a design painted on it: two circles linked by inward curving lines. It looked like two cart wheels with a slackened rope wrapped around them. The whole emblem was cut through by a zigzagged bar, like a stick broken in two places. I had seen that image the night before: it was etched in blue woad just below Macbeatha's collarbone.

Thorkel Fostcred acted as judge for the fight, though he was clearly unhappy with the contest. Had the crowd not drawn in, watching eagerly and wagering with abandon, I believe he would have tried to stop it. "No strikes to the head or legs," he ordered.

"We have yet to settle on a prize," Macbeatha called out as he drew near the circle Halfdan had scratched in the hardpacked dirt of the yard. "Though beating you in front of your men will be prize enough. Still, let us have some small trifle to be awarded to the winner." His mustaches gleamed bright red in the daylight, and the westering sun glinted like fire on his braided hair as he flexed his powerful arms and swung his sword to get the feel of it.

"I would have your brass shaving knife," Thorfinn decided, "to use on my own throat each morning."

"Just be careful whose hands you put it in," Macbeatha laughed, for it is Norse custom that a man's wife or bondwoman should shave him. "And from you I would have the use of your slave girl for another night."

Thorfinn balked in the act of stepping up to the circle. "That you could have for hospitality," he protested, frowning. "I will not fight over that. She already thinks too much of herself."

"Let us say, rather, that you give her into my hand for one day. To wait upon me and only me from the setting of this sun to the setting of the next. To do whatever I bid, for me to do with as I please." He grinned wickedly. "Of course, I may ruin her, for she will surely never find satisfaction in your bed again."

"Ha!" cried Thorfinn, taking his place. "It is well you left your bed wench behind in Cumbria, or I could have demanded her in return. Then she would fall at my feet and beg to stay with me, for to go back to you would be like following a bull with a goose."

"A fate she already knows," Macbeatha rejoined, "for I left her with your goose of a cousin, Duncan!" With that, he stepped into the ring and the match began.

They circled warily at first, baiting each other with words and false lunges. Then Thorfinn attacked, hacking wickedly against Macbeatha's shield, and my heart rose in my throat. One slip, and either of them could be maimed or killed.

But there was no murder on their minds. Macbeatha countered with a roar that ended in laughter as he pulled his stroke and only tapped Thorfinn's shield. They knew what they were doing, it seemed. I began to breathe again.

Round and round the circle they went, feeling each other out, exchanging good-natured insults, each looking for a way to throw the other off balance enough to force him out of the ring. It was more about strategy than strength—but that was always Macbeatha's finest weapon. He gave ground under Thorfinn's onslaught, and gave ground, and gave ground, and then stepped to the side to let Thorfinn propel himself nearly out of bounds. Thorfinn was no fool, however; he caught himself and twirled just in time to deflect a flat-side blow from Macbeatha's sword.

"If I meet you in battle," Macbeatha told him, "it won't be the flat of my sword."

"If you meet me in battle, stepping out of a circle won't save you."

Then they both laughed and began to circle each other again. Thorkel, I noticed, was not laughing. Neither was Ivarr.

Once again they clashed, and Macbeatha was nearly forced out, but he twisted away and hammered fiercely on Thorfinn's shield until Thorfinn fell back. Now it was Thorfinn who gave ground, but not for long—he had the reach of Macbeatha, and raw strength. Still, Macbeatha was older and more experienced. In the end he lured Thorfinn to the circle's edge and caught a glancing blow on his shield just so that Thorfinn's foot slipped and went over the line.

"Hold!" cried Thorkel quickly. "The line is crossed. Macbeatha is the winner."

There was a great roar from the Scots, and grudging admiration from the Norsemen, with bets won and lost and everyone agreeing it had been great sport to watch two princes compete. Both men were puffing and blowing, sweat dripping from brows and chins, soaking their shirts beneath the leather armor. The scent of them was pungent in my nostrils as I rushed forward with tankards of ale I had kept at the ready.

Thorfinn drank greedily of his, Macbeatha only sparingly. "At sundown, Kelda," he said loudly, "begins the happiest day of your life. You are to serve only me at supper, and sit at my feet, and keep my tankard full. And if you are good, perhaps I shall hold you upon my lap. Then when the fire burns low—" He gave a most lecherous grin. "—I shall kindle another fire in you, to make you pant and sweat as I do now." Bending at the waist, he rested his hands on his knees. "Only let me catch my wind, for the fighting has stolen it. By sundown I shall be recovered, though, and we shall rival the owls with our hooting all the night." Men laughed, while the gentlewomen blushed and pretend they didn't wish to be in my place.

"Unless, of course," he added, "someone here manages to take my prize from me."

In that frozen instant I knew what would happen, knew it had never been my company he sought. He had laid a trap, and I was only the bait.

Ivarr stepped forward. "I will take her from you."

"No!" Thorkel said firmly, stepping between them.

Macbeatha's chest still labored with his breathing, but his eyes were cold with victory. "I have just fought fiercely with your lord," he said. "But give me a moment—"

"Now," Ivarr insisted, a nasty curl to his lips. "In battle, a man must turn from one opponent to the next." Drawing his sword, he picked up the shield Thorfinn had dropped. "Face me now, or admit cowardice and surrender the prize to me."

"This is not a battle!" Thorkel hissed.

"The boy is right," Macbeatha replied, handing me the tankard he had only sipped from. "In battle there is no respite for the weary warrior, and no matching of age and strength—only the enemy God or the devil throws at you." Then he took the shield in his right hand and picked up his sword with his left. "And you never know what manner of evil that will be."

At first I did not realize he had done, but Ivarr saw right away, and a shadow passed across his sunburned face. He gazed uneasily at his sword in his opponent's left hand. But he stuffed his fear under a carpet of arrogance and sneered, "Two-handed, are you? All Norsemen are two-handed."

Macbeatha chuckled without humor as his eyes narrowed and he began to circle his opponent. "Come, boy," he taunted, not breathing nearly so hard as he had been a moment before. "When was the last time you faced an opponent who attacked from the left?" Gone was the bantering tone he had used on Thorfinn. "It requires an entirely different defense. Oh, but you know that, don't you? All Norsemen are two-handed, you say. Come, boy—come, show me. Show me how you meet a left-handed warrior."

Suddenly he struck, a lightning swift blow that clove Ivarr's shield in two. "Toss him another!" Macbeatha commanded, and someone did. Then he attacked again. Ivarr staggered back, nearly out of bounds, and Macbeatha laughed at him. Furious, Ivarr launched himself at his enemy, sword flailing, but Macbeatha caught the blows on his shield or on the flat of his own blade, making sparks fly as the two swords clashed.

I watched in dismay, for it was a poor contest. Ivarr had strength and speed, Thorfinn had been right about that, but he lacked experience—especially any experience in defending himself against a left-handed attacker. Nor were his broad shoulders and heavily muscles arms any match for Macbeatha's experience and cunning. Time and again Macbeatha caught him with the flat of his sword; had he used its edge, poor Ivarr would have died a dozen times. With each stroke Macbeatha pulled, each blow he turned, Ivarr's humiliation grew until Thorkel Fosterer turned to the jarl and said softly, "Stop this."

"Macbeatha," Thorfinn called out over the clanging of swords. "Enough."

But Ivarr would not stop his assault. If it was obvious to all that Macbeatha was turning his blows, it was equally obvious Ivarr was not. He struck full force with the lethal edge of his sword. Finally Macbeatha's shield went to pieces under the onslaught, but Ivarr would not stop to let him get another—foul manners for a contest such at this. "Ivarr!" Thorfinn called more loudly. "Enough!"

"Yield!" Ivarr snarled at Macbeatha.

But Macbeatha would never yield. In the years I knew him, he might avoid a fight, or retreat from a slaughter, but he would never yield. Casting the bits of his broken shield aside, he took his sword in both hands and launched himself at Ivarr. In a matter of moments he had destroyed the boy's shield, driven him back over the line, and struck a blow that sent him sprawling backward in the dust. Then Macbeatha stopped, one foot on Ivarr's chest and the edge of his sword at Ivarr's neck. "You are a strong warrior," he panted. "But you need a cool head to go with that fiery arm. Take a lesson from this, young Ivarr—it may save your life in battle. Never let your weakness show: you wear your lust for that girl like a target for men to strike. And never grasp at the thing you hunger for until you have sniffed around for a trap. And for the love of Christ, if you can learn about your enemy before you fight him, do it. You had only to ask Thorkel or Thorfinn—they would have told you my left hand is stronger than my right."

Finally he stood back and extended a hand to the fallen boy. "Now, come drink with me, and sit beside me in the hall, and Kelda shall wait on us both for supper."

But Ivarr rejected the proffered hand, clambering to his feet without aid. "I will sit in hell first," he snarled, and walked stiffly away.

I saw Ivarr only once more that day: he and Thorfinn were in a heated discussion near the shore, where tents had been pitched to house the overflow of men. Thorfinn stormed back to where

Macbeatha polished his weapons in the shade. "Stubborn boy!" he blurted. "Not only does he refuse to make peace with you, he says he won't come into the hall while there are Scots here."

"'Filthy Scot bastards,'" Macbeatha corrected. "If I read his lips correctly."

"Damn him! I am a Scot, too! It was Malcolm of Alba who first gave me warriors to hold Caithness, and if Olaf hadn't put my back against the wall ..."

Macbeatha snorted. "You're about as much Scot as I am Pict. Norse is how you live, Norse is what you are. Although Grandfather may never forgive you for acknowledging the Norse king as your overlord."

"Does he know?" Thorfinn asked worriedly.

Macbeatha shrugged his shoulders. "Word trickles in. He has heard the story, but he calls it a lie. Publicly. I'm not so sure what actually goes on in that agile brain of his."

"Hrmph." Thorfinn sagged up against the wall of the house, casting dark eyes on me. I was lurking nearby, working with a spindle and waiting for Macbeatha to crook his finger. "Are you hearing all this, Kelda?"

"Only as much as you want me to," I replied, rather deftly, I thought.

Thorfinn swore, but Macbeatha reached out a hand to calm him. "Let her be, it's not her fault," he said gently. "She didn't ask to be the object of Ivarr's attention, nor mine. But if it will ease the situation any, I'll send her to the kitchen tonight."

Tears sprang to my eyes—I did not want to be sent away! Thankfully, Thorfinn said, "No, you can't send her away now. You can't give way in the face of Ivarr's bad temper. She is my slave, and it is not for him to decide who I can and cannot give her to! Keep her in the hall, keep her plainly with you, and let no man doubt: what I have bestowed on you, no other can take away."

And so at last I got what I wanted. I served my Thor-like Scot at supper, and he kept me at his feet, or on his lap, the rest of the evening. I was petted and fondled, albeit with rather casual indifference, and I imagined each man in the hall envied Macbeatha as he led me off to his chamber for the night. There we did not, actually, rival the owls, for he was tired from the day's competitions, and sleepy with food and drink. But he kept me late in his chamber the next morning, so when we ventured out at last, the dozen or so men still lounging in the hall hooted and crowed and bandied ribald comments with Macbeatha. He sauntered casually through their midst saying, "I think I must get myself a bondmaid, Thorfinn, though the priests frown on slavery—of Christians, anyway. A nice pagan wench would suit me well, though. Are there any pagans left in Norway, cousin?"

"Not while Olaf is king," Thorfinn replied. "Should he fall, no doubt plenty will go back to the old ways. But if you are worried about what the priests think, stay here with us. Old Father Macmuir will only grant a man one wife, but he doesn't squawk about slaves, as long as they're baptized."

"You are a gracious host," Macbeatha replied as they strolled outside, away from the other men, "but my future is in Alba. It's south to Moray for me on tomorrow's tide."

"So soon? It's been two years since I saw you, and you stay only two or three days?"

"To stay longer would anger my blood cousins unnecessarily. Our friendship goes hard on them, just as my father's loyalty to your grandfather did. Besides, I have made an enemy here, and I did not intend to do that."

"Ivarr?" Thorfinn shrugged. "He'll get over it. By the time we subdue the Western Isles—and their women—he'll have forgotten all about Kelda."

"No doubt," laughed Macbeatha. "Perhaps next time I'll bring him one of my wenches as a peace offering. I know one or two who would make him dizzy."

Thorfinn's brow furrowed. "Well, for now, best leave that kind offer unspoken."

Macbeatha found his men and gave them instructions to prepare to sail on the morrow. They all looked relieved and hurried off toward where their boat was beached. I trailed along behind him, pouting a little because he had not looked at me since we came out of his chamber. "Does my lord have any tasks for me?" I asked plaintively.

"No, Kelda," he answered wearily. "I don't require your services any more today. Go back to the kitchen, or wherever it is you usually go."

How disappointed I was to be so dismissed! Particularly when my golden warrior would leave the next morning. But a slave's life is filled with disappointments. I was always one to make the best of a poor situation, and this was no different. If Macbeatha didn't want me around, perhaps I could wheedle a boon from him. "If it please you, lord," I said, "my mother is working in her own field today. May I go and help her?"

He gave a dismissive wave of his hand. "Yes. Go."

So off I trotted, planning what I would do once he had sailed back to Alba. Now that he had taken such a fancy to me and extolled the pleasures of my company, maybe Thorfinn would take a keener interest in me. And after Ivarr's insolence, maybe he would no longer defer to the younger man's jealousy, but take me again to his bed.

It never occurred to me to wonder what Ivarr thought of all this.

Chapter Six

Thorkel's lands lay hard by Thorfinn's, and he had given my mother a small plot there on which to grow whatever she pleased. One day a week, and one hour every evening, she was allowed to tend it; and whatever she grew, Thorkel would buy from her. She had already saved more than a mark. When she had two, he had promised she could buy her freedom, and Hakon's.

After that she would continue to work for him, but she would be paid a small wage. With Thorfinn's approval, she could take a husband from among the freemen who worked his property, and together they would have their own plot of land. Her service was still required, and she could not leave Caithness without Thorkel's permission, but she would be free. She could return at last to the pride she had known as a child growing up in the timberlands north of Bergen in Norway.

My mother had not been born a slave, you see, but the daughter of a Norse merchant. She was captured by Vikings—the word only means *pirates*, you know, and they preyed on Norse shipping as well as that of foreigners. In fact, she was snatched from the bridal ship that carried her to her promised husband, a wealthy merchant in Kaupang. Her dowry went for plunder, and her maidenhead to the first Viking who entered her tent. Not that it mattered which—half a dozen others followed. But instead of being sold on the slave market afterward, the Viking captain decided to keep her for himself. So she came to be his thrall on a small island in the far northwest of the Orkneys.

It was important to my mother to regain her freedom, therefore important to me that she do so. I did not like field work, but when the Lady Plantula would allow it, I went out to help Mother. So having been dismissed by Macbeatha, and obtaining his permission, I went to her field.

I brought food along, for I hadn't eaten yet, and I doubted Mother had either. She was most grateful. We ate there among the new barley sprouts and went right back to work. I strengthened the low stone wall bordering her plot, to keep cattle and sheep out of the grain. She hoed diligently at the thistles trying to overtake her patch of ground.

After a time she announced, "I'm having another baby. In the fall."

I stopped my work and looked over at her. "That's good, isn't it?" I loved babies and couldn't wait to have one of my own.

She only shrugged. "Thorkel was pleased. He said if it's a boy, he'll give me a lamb next spring, and all the wool from it will be mine."

That seemed generous to me, but I said nothing. I knew what seemed generous to my mother was that she didn't have to fear for the child's life. It had not been so long ago, nor had I been so young, that I could not appreciate what she had endured at the hands of our last master.

I was only six when the Viking captain, who I suppose was my father, died, and so I remember little of him except that he gave me sweets and called me Dumpling. But I do remember his funeral. People came from all the surrounding islands to honor him, and they pitched their colorful tents around the house. His longboat was dragged up onto the shore and propped up between four posts with a great pile of wood and brush heaped around it. All manner of goods were loaded aboard for the journey to the Otherworld: food and clothing, brass utensils and wooden figurines, tables and chairs and a huge horsecart. And yes, the horses to draw the cart. They were killed with swords, cut up into pieces, and cast into the boat.

As soon as the old master had died, his sons and his friends came around to the slave girls and asked, "Which of you will go with your master to the Otherworld?" We kept the old ways there, and a man took with him into death everything he would need for his comfort. Sometimes a man's wife accompanied him, but the old master's was already dead. Besides, a good wife was valuable whereas a slave girl was cheap. So they came to my mother and the others and asked who would go.

I remember looking up at her to see if she would agree, for I was frightened she might go away from me. As I searched her face, I saw only a look of stone; but her fingers dug into my arms where she held me, and she would not meet the eyes of the men who asked the question.

Finally, "I will go," said one of the others, and relief wash over me. They took her away immediately to get her ready.

Mother said it was just like a wedding. They dressed up the girl and for three days ahead of time, she ate and drank and sang and was merry. On the day of the funeral, she went to the tents of all the old master's friends, where they each took her as the groomsmen take the bride on her wedding night. They gave of their potency to add to the master's vitality in his new life. After that, men lifted her on their hands to peek over a wooden frame, as though she were looking over the barrier of death into the Otherworld. "I see my mother!" she called as she peered over that frame; and the next time she was lifted, "I see my father!"

At last they boosted her over the gunwale onto the deck of the longboat, where the old master's body had been laid out under his orange and yellow tent, its sides rolled up so all could see. My mother lifted me onto her shoulder, and I saw him stretched on a couch covered with fine blankets and rugs brought back from his viking expeditions. There was a fat old woman there, too, an "angel of death" who had been hired to oversee the ceremony. She gave the slave girl a potion, and the girl sang a song of farewell to her friends. Then the fat old Valkyrie, the angel, sent her inside the tent.

After what had been done to the horses and other animals, I had some idea what was coming, but still it surprised me. Four men held the girl's arms and legs, while outside the boat others shouted and banged on their shields with sticks or swords. If she screamed, no one heard. The Valkyrie wrapped a strap of leather around her neck and handed the ends to two other men. When they snapped the thong taut, the Valkyrie took a broad knife and jabbed it in between the victim's ribs two or three times—not deeply, maybe an inch—and dark liquid stained her fine gown. I could see her struggling, in spite of the potion and the men holding her down; but her struggles grew weaker and weaker, until finally they ceased altogether.

When they were sure she was dead, the six men released her, and the fat angel arranged her body. Then everyone climbed out of the boat and it was set on fire. I wondered why so much wood was used, for trees are scarce on the isles; but as the inferno raged, one of the older slaves grinned and pointed to the plume of smoke rising high into the heavens. "See how quickly it will carry the master to Valhalla!" he said.

Valhalla—the Hall of the Slain, Odin's residence in the Otherworld. I remember thinking how lucky that girl was, going to Valhalla with the old master. There is no Otherworld for slaves, you see. It is only for warriors and their women.

Much of what happened over the next few years I did not understand at the time, but from the whispering of the other servants and my own wisdom of near fifty years, I can piece it together now. Hrafn, eldest son of the old master, took control of the farm, but he had a cruel nature. He argued bitterly with his two younger brothers, who took their share of the inheritance and left.

After that he became unbearable. He beat the slaves, and even his wife, and he never went himself to work in the fields or fish in the sea as the old master had done. Instead he sat by the fire drinking ale while his bondsmen and freedmen did all the work. In the spring he would join his friends and go a-viking—for he had no ship of his own, as his father had—and in the fall, when the harvest was in, he would do the same. Those were periods of great relief for everyone in the household.

Everyone except my mother. Hrafn's wife hated her, and gave her all the worst jobs to do, and hit her if she didn't do them fast enough or well enough—and sometimes even if she did. For some reason, you see, Hrafn had become obsessed with my mother. He would come to her in the middle of the day when she was working and force himself on her, or he might stop in the midst of a meal to do the same. Then at night he would take her away from me again, and if I whimpered, he slapped me across the face.

That first winter she gave birth to a boy, the last issue of the old master. But when the steward came to tell the master he had another slave, Hrafn growled, "Go and cast it into the sea."

The steward stood stupefied. "But—sir," he stammered, "it is a boy, a strong and healthy one. He will give you many years of good labor—"

"He will eat my food and drink my ale for twelve years before he's good for anything! Take him away and cast him into the sea, or I shall do it myself and cast your own son after him!"

The steward shrank away and did as he was told.

My mother screamed. She shrieked and wept until the master hit her in the face with his fist and knocked out two of her teeth. Perhaps that's why she never smiled again.

In those years I learned to be small as a mouse when the master was at home. In the summer while he was away, I grew rambunctious and impudent, for I was a favorite of all the other slaves, and they spoiled me. But during the winter, as he drank by the fire, I melted into the shadows and said not a word.

Two more children did my mother labor to deliver; two more were cast into the sea. With the first of these, I was old enough to understand the horror of it; with the second I was old enough to fear for my own life. The master seemed to enjoy hurting others, just to prove he had the power to do it. He killed my siblings, his own babes, because it gave him pleasure to cause my mother such suffering. How much pleasure, I wondered, would it give him to kill me, as well?

It was only by the grace of Freya—or perhaps the Christian Mary—that Thorkel Fosterer and his young lord, Thorfinn, decided to take shelter on our island from an autumn squall.

Talk of the young jarl was everywhere that fall. Not yet fifteen winters, he had been to King Olaf's court in Norway, where he was favorably received and granted custody of lands belonging to a deceased half-brother. Then, when another half-brother, Einar Wry-mouth, challenged him for lands, Thorfinn led his hird out personally to meet the contender. No doubt all this was orchestrated by Thorkel Fosterer, but he gave all credit and respect to Thorfinn, and so the whole of the Orkneys was a-buzz was with tales of him.

And to think the two of them landed there, on our island! They had been sailing up and down the coast, introducing the new jarl to his people. While stopping with a noble family across the water on the main island, the two of them decided to go out together in a rowing boat—that's when the squall came up. Finding our island close by, they beached their small craft and came pounding on the door of the longhouse.

It was late in the season, and the master was back from his autumn viking, but he had been drinking since early morning, and it was now mid-afternoon. The mistress woke her husband from his ale-sodden sleep by the hearth, and he roused himself enough to greet his noble guests. Then he went back to snoring and gargling, leaving the rest of us to wait on the rain-soaked visitors.

The mistress was quick to see to their needs—but I was quicker. Here was my golden opportunity! She called for blankets, but I fetched dry clothes from the master's trunk. "Here, I know he would want you to wear these while yours dry. See the fine stitching on this one? My mother made that." I dropped myself down in front of Thorfinn, whose long legs were stretched out toward the hearth. "Allow me, lord," I chirped, and began to tug off his soggy boots.

When I had done the same for Thorkel, I stuffed their wet boots with straw to draw out the moisture. Then I laid out their wet clothes by the hearth, inspecting them as I did. "There's a tear in your sleeve, Jarl Thorfinn," I announced. "My mother can fix that for you—she's very clever with a needle. See how smooth and even the threads of that blanket are? My mother spun the wool herself. And wove it. Is it not beautiful? She has a wondrous eye for color."

Throughout the evening, there was nothing to be done for our guests that I did not anticipate and labor to accomplish. All the while, I chattered on about my mother's virtues. "Here is some bread and cheese while you wait for supper. My mother made the cheese. That is she, lord, sitting quiet in the corner with her needle-work. Doesn't she have a fair face? Here, let me fill your horn. We've heard all about your courage, lord, and what a fine warrior you are. My mother tells me the stories every night."

On and on I went, and the light of amusement twinkled in Thorfinn's eye. "It sounds like your master is a lucky man," he would say, "to have such a perfect bondmaid as your mother. Wouldn't you say so, Thorkel?" And Thorkel would agree my mother must be the most amazing bondmaid in the isles.

The mistress tried to hush me once. "Kelda, leave off. Your chattering annoys the jarl."

"On the contrary," Thorfinn said, "it is nice to be so eagerly welcomed. Not all in this part of the Orkneys have been so glad to see me."

Taking a cue from that, I went on at great length about the tales we had heard of his valor—most of which I made up on the spot. Thorkel Fosterer was hard pressed to keep from laughing at some of them; and when I said we had heard how Thorfinn single-handedly rowed a longboat—a ship which holds forty or fifty men—across the ocean from Bergen to the Shetlands, he finally threw back his head and roared. So did Thorfinn. "If she were not a girl," he said, "I would take her back as apprentice to our skald. By God, but she's clever!"

I beamed up at him and refilled his drinking horn.

Finally, as the boards were set to form our tables, the master awoke. He seemed surprised to find guests in his house; his wife had to explain again who they were and how they had come to be there. "They have graciously accepted to stay the night," she finished.

Hrafn growled and coughed and hawked and spat into the fire, and then he stomped over to take his place in the high seat.

The mistress was mortified. "Sir, give place to the jarl," she hissed.

Bleary-eyed, the master swung his shaggy head around to glare at young Thorfinn, who though tall and broad of shoulder was still a bit gangly, with a face marked by the blemishes of youth. "To this boy?" he demanded. "Not in my house."

Thorfinn's shoulder muscles bunched, and rage blazed in his dark eyes.

"Sir," the mistress urged again, "he is the jarl. Sigurd's son. Give place."

But the master settled his bulk into the high seat and sneered, "Not for long, he won't be. Einar Wry-mouth will see to that."

Thorfinn leaped to his feet with Thorkel only a beat behind. The Fosterer caught his lord's shoulder with a strong hand and whispered something in his ear that made Thorfinn consider a moment. But then the jarl marched up to Hrafn, mounting the platform of the high seat so he could bend down and stare the older man in the face. "Einar barked like a seal," he told the master coldly, "but his army fled before me. He will not be back. I and I alone am jarl here; and you will give me due respect, as well as pay me lawful *skatt*, or I will return in the spring with my longboats, and your fine house will be a memory."

The master gave a sharp laugh, but a deadly silence had fallen in the house, and he stopped short. Warily he cast his eyes first to one side of the long room and then to the other and saw no warrior in the place except Thorkel, who was Thorfinn's man. In a sickening rush, he realized not a slave or a freedman who sat at his hearth was likely to raise a hand in his defense. He had no friends in his own house.

"King Olaf has recognized Thorfinn as jarl," the mistress said softly. "Who are we to do otherwise?"

Finally Hrafn stirred in his chair. "Who, indeed," he echoed, and got down from the high seat. "Please, lord," he said tightly, gesturing to the spot he had just vacated. "You honor us with your presence."

His moment of good judgment did not last, however. He was surly and rude the rest of the evening, and it was probably that more than anything I did which led to our eventual deliverance. But it came about like this. As the fires were banked and we all found our places on straw ticks along the walls—the master having fallen asleep earlier—I crept to where Thorfinn was spreading out the fine blanket I'd brought him. He looked up with a twinkle in his eye. "Now, don't offer to warm my covers," he teased, "you're too young for that. Or did you have in mind to offer your mother, that paragon of every womanly virtue?"

"Please, lord," I whispered earnestly, "take us back with you. You are a great jarl; you need many slaves. Buy us both, you will not regret it. My mother is clever and fair, and I will work very hard, and you've seen how I can make you laugh. Please, lord ...?"

What a sight I must have been! Ten years old, all arms and legs and matted hair, in a dirty white slave's dress with goose grease smudged on my cheek. Thorfinn reached out and wiped the grease away with his thumb, and there was a look of sadness in his dark eyes. "A slave's lot is given him by God, little one," he whispered back. "You must accept it and bear your cross humbly."

"Which god is that?" I asked. "Odin? Thor? Only tell me what a cross is, and I will bear it."

Well, of course I knew what a cross was, and that Thorfinn worshipped the Christian god—everyone knew that! But I reasoned that if he thought my soul was imperiled, he'd be more apt to rescue my mother and me.

It worked. A stricken look came to his face. Then he patted my cheek and bade me sleep; but when I had gone, he turned to whisper conspiratorially with his fosterer.

The next morning the Fosterer challenged Hrafn to a friendly game of knucklebones. The master was quick to bring out his set of bones with their painted marks, for he loved to gamble. Soon they had a board set up between them and were rattling and tossing the cube-shaped bones with alacrity. They wagered small things first, and my master won quite a lot, but then his luck turned. By the time they finished, he owed Thorkel the equivalent of two silver marks.

"Time for us to go," young Thorfinn announced. "Come, Thorkel, let us say good-bye to our host and be on our way."

"No, wait!" the master cried, panic-stricken. "Things are out of balance, you can't leave now. Give me a chance to win back what I've lost."

But Thorkel brushed him off. "No, no, the jarl is right; we have overstayed already. Only give me my two marks for now, and we will play again when I return to collect *skatt*."

"I haven't any silver just now," the master whined, and I remembered the steward telling Thorkel that. "I've just laid in my supplies for winter. Come back in the spring—"

Now Thorkel's face grew dark. "The winter is a long time to trust a man for two marks. What if you die before spring? No, no, I will take it in goods, then. What do you think, Jarl Thorfinn? Can we fit a couple of slaves into our rowing boat?" He looked around the room as though making a choice. "I'll take that one," he said, pointing to my mother.

"No, not that one!" shrieked the master, who coveted my mother over all the rest. "Take one of the other girls. Take Hulda or Iduna or—"

"That one," Thorkel repeated firmly.

"But—but—" sniveled the master.

"And her child."

Now the master realized he had been tricked, and his eyes grew flinty. "No!" he growled, drawing himself up to his full height, which would have been impressive had he run to muscle instead of blubber. "The mother is worth two marks by herself. Take her for the debt, but the child you cannot have. And do not expect to find hospitality in my house again!"

"How much for the child?" young Thorfinn asked.

The master's eyebrows flew up—it hadn't occurred to him anyone would pay money to keep a mother and child together.

"Two marks covers them both," Thorkel said firmly. "No slave is worth more than one."

"This one is," the master insisted. "She's well-trained, and obedient—no backtalk from that one. And she bears healthy babes. Two marks is the price of her."

Thorfinn had fished a coin from the pouch at his belt. "And one," he replied, "is the price of the child. Here." He tossed the coin at Hrafn's feet. "You are paid in full, and generously at that. And you will grant me hospitality whenever I desire it, or you will wake one night to find your house in flames and yourself roasting in it like the honking goose you are." Then he turned and stalked out the door.

I snatched up my mother's hand and pulled her out after him.

Chapter Seven

So we came to Thorfinn's hall in Caithness, and a life of comfort that encouraged me to careless impudence. Thorfinn was ever amused by my quick wit, and I used it to curry favor in the household. When the roundness of my cheeks began to surface in other parts of my body, I learned how to use that to please others, too. It is no wonder I harbored such hopes of becoming Thorfinn's concubine—he was my savior.

I thought much of this as I worked in my mother's field that day, laying plans to insinuate myself into his bed the moment Macbeatha was gone. Such daydreams raised a heat in me that rivaled the midday sun, so I grew less and less inclined to keep pace with my mother. Finally I told her I must go see if Macbeatha needed anything of me before his day of service was up, and she, accustomed to such excuses, bade me go.

As I trotted across the fields toward home, danger was far from my mind. Here in the heart of Thorfinn's realm, no outlaw would dare accost one of his thralls! Stopping by the stream, I cast no wary glances before bending down to splash water on my sweaty face and neck.

Rough hands seized me from behind and threw me to the ground, knocking my head against it. Stunned, I gasped and blinked and tried to make out the face of my attacker.

It was Ivarr. He straddled me and pinned my wrists with his hands, an ugly look on his face. Then he locked one of my arms against his side with his knee and drew his knife, bringing it dangerously close to my eye. "What do you say now, Kelda?" he sneered. "Where's your clever tongue? Say one word, and I'll cut it out!"

I said nothing, trembling and watching the point of the knife.

"I'll bet you wish now you hadn't thrown yourself at that barbarian!" he gloated, his eyes glinting like a wolf about to bring down its prey. "You were supposed to be mine, you know. Thorfinn promised me. At the end of summer, if I proved myself in battle, he was going to let me buy you from him."

My breath stopped. Thorfinn, sell me? To Ivarr? Oh, no, he couldn't!

"But I don't want you any more. Not after that dirty Scot had you. You're not fit to be my bondmaid now." The tip of his knife made a small circle in the air above my eye. "And when I'm through with you, no one else will want you, either."

Panic surged through me. What was he going to do? Wasn't there anyone nearby to stop him? A whimper escaped me.

That only made him smile viciously. "How do you think your filthy Scot will like you with only one eye, Kelda? Or one ear missing? Or better yet—what if I cut off your nose? Yes, that's what I'll do. Nothing but a raw, ugly scar in the middle of your face."

"Oh, please, Ivarr!" I cried out, hysterical at the thought of pain and disfigurement. "Please, no! What do you want of me? Please, I will do anything you ask. I'll lie with you whenever you want. I won't tell Thorfinn. Please, Ivarr, please—"

His lips still curled in that grotesque grin. "We'll see how well Thorfinn likes you after that. He'll probably give you to his herdsmen for their amusement. They'll put a sack over your head so they won't have to look at you while they hump you." He set his blade to the side of my nose, and I screamed.

"Ivarr!"

Ivarr jerked back around, keeping the knife pressed to my flesh. His father stood behind him, glaring down at us.

"Ivarr, let the girl go," Thorkel commanded.

"I'm going to cut her nose off!" he shouted. "That will teach her!"

"She's not your slave!" his father snapped. "Let her go."

"She made a fool of me!" Ivarr howled.

"You have made that of yourself. Now, let her go, or when the hird sails in two weeks, you will not be with us."

Fear replaced the madness in Ivarr's eyes. "No! You promised I could go this year! Thorfinn said I could!"

"Then let the girl go," his father repeated, "or we'll leave you at home like the child you show yourself to be!"

For an agonizing moment Ivarr sat poised, struggling to find a way to have both things he wanted. In the end, it couldn't be done. He released me with a curse and got to his feet. Then he kicked me in the ribs, hard, and walked away.

"Get up, girl," Thorkel said softly. "Go to your mother; and for the love of God, stay out of the hall tonight."

I needed no encouragement on either count. Scrambling to my feet, I staggered back along the path I had come, sobbing and clutching my bruised ribs.

I spent a very bad night. My side hurt, there was a lump on the back of my head where it had hit the ground, and I wept in terror every time I thought about what had almost happened to me. Mother slept beside me in the kitchen, with Hakon between us, as though she would protect us both from any evil. But she couldn't, and I knew she couldn't. And for the first time since I'd come to Thorfinn's hall, I knew that he couldn't, either. All Ivarr had to do was catch me alone, or just slip up to me in the night, and mutilate me. He could even cut my throat, and the only consequence he would bear was paying Thorfinn one silver mark for the loss of his property. How was I ever to feel safe again?

I slept little, for Ivarr haunted my dreams. What was I to do? Nothing. Any doing would be done by Thorfinn, and what would that be? He was not likely to punish Ivarr. Threaten him, yes, but not punish him. Even if he did, that would only serve to make Ivarr angrier with me. How had I come to this place, I asked myself. What had I done that was so wrong? I resolved that if I ever got out of this situation, I would turn my charms on no one but Thorfinn, my lawful master. No flirting with the hirdmen, no fawning on guests. And I would *never* go anywhere alone again.

Finally dawn came, and others began to stir. Cook and his helpers started making the bread, and great kettles of porridge were set on the fire. While it cooked, I went with my mother to work in the dairy.

Churning is a mindless task and I usually hated it, but that morning there was a certain comfort in it. It felt good to do battle with something. The frustration of my helplessness, my anger at

Ivarr, all went into plying the handle of the churn. As the cream inside resisted my push and sucked back against my pull, I felt as if I were the churn, being thrust down and then tugged up, pushed and pulled through the thick, heedless morass of this world, with no end in sight. I almost didn't notice when the Lady Plantula came in.

"Kelda," she said, "my son would speak with you in the hall."

Tears sprang to my mother's eyes, and a terrible foreboding came over me. Numb with fear, I walked slowly to the hall. Inside, Thorfinn waited with Macbeatha close at hand. When he saw me, my lord's face grew grim. "What a problem you have set me," he said. I stood with head bowed and tried very hard not to tremble. "I had hoped Ivarr's preoccupation with you would fade when he went to battle, but now he has made threats he will feel honor-bound to carry out. I cannot let him harm you—I would lose face if I couldn't protect my own property in my own hall. Nor can I punish him severely—he is a freeman and Thorkel's get, and you are but a slave. I had hoped to solve all this by giving you to him when we return from the Hebrides, but he has vowed he won't have you. I must find another solution."

My stomach twisted and turned, and I sank slowly to my knees.

"I am sorry for the choice I must make, Kelda, for you have always amused me."

I dared not breathe.

"I'm giving you into the hand of Macbeatha."

Breath rushed back into my lungs, and I felt giddy with relief.

"She is yours now, my friend," he told Macbeatha. "Do with her as you will."

My head came up as Macbeatha walked to where I knelt. His face was solemn, and in his hands was a thin strip of leather somewhat longer than his arm from elbow to fingertips. My eyes went to it as he wrapped and unwrapped its ends around his hands in an idle gesture. I remembered the slave girl who was killed at the old master's funeral: it was a leather strap they had used to throttle her.

He must have seen the anguish on my face as I stared at that leather thong. "Kelda," he said softly. "Do you trust me?"

Slowly I forced my eyes to meet his, searching the swirling depths of those cat-green orbs for something I could trust.

"Bare your neck," he instructed.

There was nothing in his face to tell me his intent, no reason at all for me to believe in him—yet I did. In that moment I found something solid at the core of Macbeatha, something as unshakable as the earth itself. He asked me to trust him. That I would do. If it was the end of my life, then I would go as a warrior goes, without fear or hesitation. I tugged the shawl away from my neck and lifted my hair up out of the way.

Leaning over me, he brought the strap around my throat. I felt it caress my skin, felt the pressure of it being drawn snug against my neck. Forcing myself to breathe deeply, I closed my eyes and waited.

Deftly, gently, his fingers tied a strong knot in the strap, and then the leather lay slack against my throat. "In Alba," he said, "we mark our slaves so, with leather collars. When we reach my home there, I will put my mark on a piece of lead and fix it on your collar, so all men will know you belong to me." Then he stepped back. "Now, go bid your mother farewell. We sail with the tide."

Chapter Eight

In Fionna's hut

Fionna handed Kelda a bowl of thin porridge and watched as her guest stirred a spoon listlessly through it. She wondered if the Norsewoman was too exhausted to eat. "For a little strength," she encouraged, gesturing to the bowl. "To tell me your tale."

As though it were a task that needed doing, like tending the fire or lacing a boot, Kelda put the spoon in her mouth.

While she ate, Fionna considered what Kelda's tale bespoke. There were pieces of the story she had overlooked—the Norse jarl, for one. It had not occurred to Fionna he had anything to do with this, but he had been Macbeatha's friend in their younger days. And as they both grew in power? What had happened then?

Patiently the old one sorted through her stones. Here, the double circle slashed with the rod, the sign of Macbeatha's house—or more accurately, his grandmother's house. Like Fionna, his grandmother had been of the old Pictish race, long subdued and mostly forgotten. But Macbeatha had borne the ancient clan mark both on his shield and on his body; and when the stones whispered their elusive messages, they gave to Macbeatha, King of Scots, that same sign.

By what sign would they call the Norse jarl? Fionna strewed the stones across the floor in one pattern after another until they chose: two wolves with their heads twined. Ah—the fierce warrior who was both Scot and Norse. Fionna put his stone in her palm *along with Macbeatha's. Then she chose three others at random from her basket. Cupping them in her hands, she shook them once, twice, thrice, and cast them across the Cycle of Life.*

The stones thumped against the hard-packed earth, two of them clicking loudly as they landed side by side in the North: the twin circles and the twin wolves. That made sense: both were warriors from the north. Near them landed the Rod, the emblem of power—for kings, of course. Or those who strove to be kings. Yet the circles and the wolves were side by side, equal. That spoke of an alliance between them.

A black stone with a red jag rested between Birth and Puberty: the Fallen Foe. Who was that? And what was the meaning of his stone landing there? Childhood? Spring? A new beginning? Fionna frowned.

Another stone lay far above the Fallen Foe, on a line that passed through Macbeatha's stone. This one had landed upside down; Fionna turned it over carefully. Scone: the city of the Scot high kings since the days of mac Alpin, and of Picti kings before him. Was the Fallen Foe a king?

With a sigh, she turned her eyes to the last two stones. A plain blue pebble of Blessing lay in Summer—that was hardly in dispute. The summer of Macbeatha's life had been filled with blessings. But the last stone—salt water? "Was he a sailor, the high king?"

"He knew his way around a ship," Kelda replied, putting the bowl of porridge aside. "And he kept a navy, though he preferred to avoid battles at sea. The Norse are better at them than the Scots, and he would not put himself at a disadvantage. But we came to Inverness by ship the first time, and to Scone at the last ..." Her voice trailed off with the pain of some memory.

Fionna poured Kelda another cup of the brew mulling at the fire. "Tell me about the first time," she said, drawing the Norse woman's mind back to the tale. "Tell me about coming to Inverness."

Kelda fingered the cup in her hands, blowing idly on its contents as her thoughts drifted backward once more.

* * *

I hated Gillecomgain the moment I met him. He swaggered down to the riverbank to meet our boat like a cock strutting on a wall, convinced the sun rises at his command. The two cousins were built the same—tall and lean and hard-muscled—but Gillecomgain was dark and swarthy, with a jagged scar on the left side of his face that ran from his lip to the corner of his eye. It gave the impression he was constantly sneering—and perhaps he was. I don't think I ever heard him speak in a tone that concealed his contempt for everyone around him.

As soon as I splashed ashore, Gillecomgain came up and walked around me, looking me up and down as one might look over a heifer one considered buying—or roasting. I had been born a slave, and lived in thralldom for fourteen years, but that was the first time I felt like goods in a market stall. When Macbeatha hoisted his sea chest to his shoulder and bade me follow him up the hill toward town, I did so quickly, terrified to be left alone in this foreign place with barbarians like Gillecomgain.

The trip from Thorfinn's stronghold had not been pleasant for me, as you might guess. When I parted from my mother, knowing I would likely never see her again, I had found myself on a boat filled with strangers who barked at me in words I did not understand, then shoved me roughly when I did not do as they had commanded. Plainly, they did not like having me aboard. Scots believe women on ships are bad luck.

Macbeatha barked at me, too, but at least he did it in Norn. Most of the time. Yet it was clear he was not happy with the situation, either. He sent me to sit in the bow of the ship and told me to stay put and keep out of the way. Once we turned into the Moray Firth, he came to join me where I sat alternately watching the shore and glancing back at him forlornly. I tried to smile as he flopped down on a stack of otter hides—a gift from Thorfinn—but as soon as I twitched the corners of my mouth, my tears began to flow. A sigh of exasperation rattled up from his throat, and I felt I just couldn't bear another rebuke. "Oh, please don't be angry with me, lord!" I sobbed.

But instead of chiding me for my foolish tears, Macbeatha gathered me in his arms and held me close against his chest. "I'm not angry with you," he sighed in my ear. "If anything, I'm angry with myself for not having foreseen Ivarr's deed. I thought to instruct him on underestimating his adversary, but I erred as badly as he did, and now it is you who must pay the price."

I only clung to him and sobbed even harder.

"Yes, go ahead and cry, Kelda," he soothed. "Cry for all you have lost: your mother, your country, your comfortable life. Weep until there are no tears left in you, for once we reach Moray, you must never weep again. There you must be strong, and hard, and show no weakness, for they will have no mercy on a foreigner. There you must take your bitter sorrow and turn it into a hard rock to plant your feet upon and make your stand. If you stand tall and strong, they will turn away from you, for it is easier to find a weaker person to assail."

The tone in his voice suggested he spoke from experience. "Is that what you have done?" I asked, looking up at him through my tears.

He smiled ruefully then and told me of his two cousins, Maelcolm and Gillecomgain, the sons of Maelbrighde (whom we Norse called Jarl Hundi, the Hound Earl). Both were older than he, though his father was the elder of theirs, for Findlaech's first wife had been childless. When Macbeatha was a boy, Jarl Hundi and another man, Maelsnechti, convinced Findlaech to try wresting Caithness back from Jarl Sigurd, for the family of Jarl Hundi's wife had once been rulers there. The three of them took a small fleet up the Moray Firth and issued a challenge to Sigurd.

In a great battle off Duncansby Head, the Scots were beaten back. Maelsnechti was killed outright, and Jarl Hundi was gravely wounded. Only the arrival—conveniently late—of High King Malcolm mac Kenneth and a sizeable land army had saved them. It was a great humiliation, watching the southern Scots ride in the day after the battle, then having King Malcolm go to treat with Sigurd like a father coming in to settle a squabble between two small boys. Shortly afterward, Jarl Hundi died of his wounds, leaving to his two sons the quest for Caithness. When Findlaech would not pursue the matter, his nephews were much aggrieved. Their father had died trying to take the province; they felt it was Findlaech's duty to wage war until he succeeded.

There were two reasons he did not. One, the tribes of Moray were unwilling to support such a costly war—they were happy with a truce. Two, when Malcolm mac Kenneth had come to the aid of the Moraymen at Duncansby, he resolved the conflict by giving his youngest daughter to Jarl Sigurd as wife in a marriage alliance. For Findlaech to attack Sigurd would earn him the wrath of the High King and a war on two fronts.

But Jarl Hundi's sons wanted Caithness, wanted their father avenged, and wanted nothing to do with Malcolm and his kingdom of Alba. They considered Moray a separate nation and were furious that Findlaech styled himself "mormaer" or "high steward" to Malcolm, rather than a king in his own right. It was only a matter of time until they challenged him. So when he was stricken with grief on the passing of his wife, Macbeatha's mother, they marshaled their forces and presented themselves before the fortress at Inverness, ready to do battle.

Findlaech had only his personal guard and one other company with him, twenty men in all. Outnumbered, he rode forth alone to do single combat with one of his nephews. Gillecomgain, younger of the two, met him on the field; he was eighteen then, young and agile and absolutely fearless. Findlaech was old and tired and had buried his heart with his wife. He cut that gash in Gillecomgain's left cheek, but when he stepped back to ask if his nephew would surrender, the young man responded with an upward sweep of his sword that caught Findlaech in the ribs and killed him. Macbeatha was fifteen at the time, away in fosterage.

"Why did you not become mormaer after your father?" I asked in genuine puzzlement.

He gave me a wry smile. "Our customs are different than yours. Among the Scots, a man must be eighteen before he can contend for such an office—I was too young. Furthermore, no Scot rules simply because his father ruled before him. We demand that a man prove himself before we pledge him our support. He must be *rigdomnae,* the stuff of kings, not only by birth, but by character. And then, the leaders of the tribes must choose to have him. My cousin Maelcolm was my father's *tanist,* his second, named by my father himself to succeed, and he had the support to do so."

He reached out a finger to stroke my cheek. "I will yet rule in Moray, Kelda, that I promise you. I have made a rock of my bitterness, and from it I will bring down the sons of Maelbrighde. But I am not ready to challenge them just now. I was fostered at Scone, you see, which will serve me well later on, but it kept me out of Moray for ten years. Many chieftains still do not know me or have reason to trust me. I will need more time to change that."

Then he smiled. "But you will keep that a secret, won't you, my pet?" he asked. "Keep your ears open and your mouth shut, as your mother taught you. For now, my cousins must believe I am loyal, serving them as a good kinsman should—and so I do. But my feet are planted on that hard rock, and I will not be moved from it. See that yours are as well."

Once I had met Gillecomgain, I could hardly wait for Macbeatha to challenge him. But that would be years ahead, and as we hiked up the path from the shore that first day, I was more concerned with my immediate future. "Do you have a wife, lord?" I asked.

At that, he laughed. "No, not yet. The kind of connections I need to make through marriage, I cannot make until I have better established my reputation."

"Who keeps your house?" I pressed. Clearly, whoever that was would be in charge of me.

"I have a sister, Brenna. She runs the household, with assistance from our chief steward, my kinsman Donn. Brenna is the real reason I visited Thorfinn this spring."

"Oh?"

"I had hoped to betroth her to him, ending forever the quarrel over Caithness and Sutherland. But Thorfinn was not interested in the match. If he hopes to gain the rest of the Orkneys—and he does—he cannot afford a Scottish wife. He needs the daughter of a Norseman, preferably a powerful one with royal connections. I don't blame him for that."

I gave no more thought to Brenna, then, for we had entered the town. Inverness is a sprawling, meandering thing that crawls up from the river into the hills, a hodge-podge of wattle and daub huts clustered below an ancient stone fortress. Children and pigs wandered the streets, which were mere patches of bare ground accidentally left between the houses and shops. The town had long been a trading center, lying as it does where a river connects the sea to Loch Ness, a long and deep lake that slices a route through the Highlands. A livestock market and a bartering ground, Inverness bustled with all the squalid life such places attract. To a girl raised on farms, even a large farm like Thorfinn's, such a collection of buildings and people crowding in on one another was an amazement.

Macbeatha's lands were actually across the firth in Ross, but he had a house in Inverness, far from the shore on a road to Forres. It was larger and finer than any of the houses we passed, made of split timbers well chinked with straw and mud. Even the thatched roof seemed thicker and more luxurious than any I had seen before.

There was a second floor for sleeping, so it looked strangely tall to me, though it was not so long as the houses I had known. Shutters stood open to the spring air.

The people at work in the yard looked foreign and therefore frightening. My steps slowed unconsciously and I lifted a hand to the amulet hung around my neck, hoping Macbeatha's sister had his sunny disposition.

His hand on my shoulder stopped me in the path. Carefully he took the wooden amulet from my fingers and examined it. "It is a cross," I said quickly, for the design was a clever one, with a hole drilled in the short piece above the crossbar, letting it hang suspended from its thong like a Christian cross.

But he was not fooled. Turning it upside down, he swung it back and forth by the longer end of the upright. "It is Thor's hammer," he said. "Luckily, most people here wouldn't know Thor's hammer if it struck them in the head. Go on, wear it, but inside your gown, lest someone be wise enough to guess. And remember to cross yourself on occasion, and go to mass so there won't be any talk. Have you been baptized?"

"When Thorfinn bought me," I assured him, tucking the amulet into my bosom. "I am a Christian now."

He snorted. "Provided I don't hold your faith to a candle. Come along, now, there's my sister waiting."

Brenna stood like a queen amidst a flock of clamoring geese. Small of stature and of bone, she had a regal bearing that made one forget how tiny she was. Her hair was a rich, brown-black tangle flowing around her shoulders, her dark eyes large in a fair face. Her shift of soft, fine wool was a colorful weave of deep blues and greens, belted at her tiny waist with a bronze chain. Gold lay at her throat, sparkled on her fingers, and dangled from her ears. No one could doubt her family's royal standing.

But to my surprise, she greeted her brother in cold tones. Though I did not speak Gaelic then, I later learned the match he had proposed to Thorfinn did not please her—she despised her Norse cousin. So Macbeatha teased and baited her a bit before admitting Thorfinn had declined. Finally he promised to take her to the High King's court that winter, to seek an alliance for her among the princes of Alba.

Upon hearing this, her haughtiness vanished, her eyes lit, and I thought she might fling her arms around his neck like a child, though she managed to restrain herself. I breathed a sigh of relief to see her happy face.

And then she saw me.

I didn't have to know her language—her tone conveyed her contempt. Macbeatha did not rise to her anger, though, responding sweetly as if it meant nothing—and to him, it probably did not. Eventually she stalked into the house, her back stiff as a broom. "I don't think she likes me," I ventured, tears brimming in my eyes.

"She doesn't know you," he said simply. "And I neglect her badly, so she resents anyone else whose company I keep. But don't worry, she's not an unkind person. Besides, I intend to have her married in a year's time."

I wonder if he knew how long that year would be for me.

Chapter Nine

As soon as Brenna had gone, others of the household came up to greet Macbeatha with smiles and hand clasps and light in their eyes. There was Donn, the steward, a tall and stately gentleman with one eye missing; a lumbering wrangler called Engus; his wife Aithne, the cook; and there was Siusan.

Siusan was the eldest of Engus and Aithne's three children, a young woman of perhaps seventeen or eighteen. She was tall and large boned, with a handsome face and a thick, brown braid that fell just to her nicely rounded posterior. As she came forward to greet Macbeatha, her manner was deferential, as befit a *doer cheile*, a client of lowly status, but the smoldering way their eyes met told me that behind closed doors, they were on much more familiar terms. And the look she turned on me was one of pure hatred.

Now, I had never expected to be the only one catering to Macbeatha's carnal appetites. After all, Thorfinn had taken his pleasure with any of a half dozen serving girls, and even when I'd hoped to be his concubine, it never occurred to me to wish he would give up the others. Getting children on slave girls was one way to increase his wealth. Scots, however, have a different viewpoint. For centuries, their priests have taught them that servants—even slaves—are fellow Christians, and female servants are not to be used for their lords' pleasure. Not that men didn't keep mistresses, nor did they suffered much penalty for seducing a maid here and there, but it was done with a wink and a nod, not in flagrant defiance of the Christian commandments. Furthermore, it was a sin that needed confessing before a man died, or he might go to that dark side of the Otherworld the Christians call Hell.

But that a girl so purloined should resent other girls sinning with her man was beyond my comprehension.

Macbeatha pretended not to notice the look Siusan gave me, though it could not have escaped his sharp eye. Instead he took her in one hand and me in the other and introduced us in our two languages. Siusan was Brenna's maid, he explained, and did spinning and sewing, as well as helping her mother with the cooking. And I, he told Siusan, was a gift from his cousin the mormaer of Caithness, and would likewise help in the house. Then he bade Siusan take me inside and show me where to put my miserable little bundle of belongings, which consisted of a comb and a pair of winter boots wrapped in my cloak. He himself went off with Donn to discuss how his holdings in Ross fared.

They fared better than I, I can assure you of that. The first time Siusan bumped into me, I thought it was an accident. We were standing near the fire pit in the center of the house, and when her shoulder caught me, I stumbled against one of the stones, nearly losing my balance. Siusan exclaimed something that sounded like an apology and caught my arm to steady me, but her eyes, when I looked into them, had a wicked gleam.

Later on we went out into the yard, and when her shoulder slammed into mine again, and I into the door jamb, I knew it was intentional. I wanted to tell her to stop, that I knew what she was doing. Not knowing her language, I could only look daggers at her.

But the third time, when she shoved me against the big wooden cistern so I nearly went in headfirst, I turned around swinging.

Her mother Aithne managed to pull us apart, though not before Siusan had clawed vicious stripes down my cheek, and I had yanked out a tuft of her hair. Aithne smacked her daughter hard across the face and sent her sobbing into the house. Then, to be impartial, she smacked me with equal force and made it clear that I was to sit by the door of the house and not move until Macbeatha came back.

I was happy to do just that. Nisse, Haldana and I had had our little spats, our rivalries back and forth, but no one had struck me since I came to Thorfinn's hall. Tears welled in my eyes and I thought how desperately I wanted to be back there---

Except I didn't. Not with Ivarr there. I resolved that no matter how Siusan pushed or slapped me, I would push and slap right back. She was no bigger than me, and no stronger; I didn't have to be afraid of her the way I was of Ivarr. It was as Macbeatha said: if I stood up to her, if I made it cost her every time she struck me, she would soon find someone weaker to pick on. Or so I hoped.

When Macbeatha came back, Aithne met him with an explanation. As he examined the marks on my face, I could see he was angry, but all he said was, "Come inside."

Next he found Siusan where she sat spinning with Brenna. She was quick to show him her wounded scalp, with a flood of words which, I have no doubt, laid the blame entirely upon me. Again, he said only two words, and she followed him to where I lingered in the light from the open door. With her in one hand and me in the other, he spoke first in Gaelic and then in Norn: "Any time I find a mark on either one of you, I won't ask who put it there—I will simply put the same mark on the other one. So each of you had better see that nothing happens to the other. And if you are caught fighting again, I will bind you together, ankle and wrist, and so you will stay until it pleases me to release you."

Then he informed the others in the household that they were all to teach me their language, and he expected me to be conversant in it by the end of harvest. Finally, to Siusan he said, "If Kelda cannot speak four sentences in a row without stumbling by then, you will have a stroke of my hand for every word she misses."

She blanched, whimpering an objection—she must have realized how easily I could pretend I didn't know, just to get her in trouble. It certainly crossed *my* mind. He replied with a sly look, probably pointing out the advantage of making friends rather than enemies.

By the time supper had been served and cleared, I had learned a dozen words; and at the end of the evening, as everyone began to settle down for the night, Macbeatha invited me to his sleeping chamber in the loft to learn a few more.

The scratches on my cheek had crusted over, but a foot that ached every time I stepped on it still reminded me of Siusan's attack. "Lord, I would follow you anywhere," I sighed in Norn, "and learn the name of every pleasure you desire. But perhaps it would be wiser if you took Siusan to your bed tonight."

He blinked, then gave a little chuckle and kissed my injured cheek. "Perhaps it would," he agreed. "If it can be done discreetly. All right, rest you by the fire tonight—I will have Siusan get you a warm blanket of your own." He spoke briefly to Siusan, then climbed the steep, ladder-like stairs to the loft.

Why it must be done discreetly, I did not then understand, so I was surprised when, after bringing me a thick wolf hide for a blanket, she did not follow Macbeatha upstairs. Instead, she stretched out her bed on the rush-strewn floor beside her younger brothers and closed her eyes. Only when the house was quiet and the boys were asleep, did she rise from her place and climb silently up the stairs.

The lesson of discretion I failed to learn from Siusan that night was to cost me dearly in the years to come.

Three nights later Gillecomgain came to the house to speak with Macbeatha. I had learned by then that Gaillecomgain was his brother's *tanist,* named by Maelcolm to take his place should he fall in battle. It was the place my lord coveted, but the two of them sat by the fire polishing their weapons and drinking ale and laughing as though they were the best of comrades. I was pleased I could pick out a word here and there, but I could not begin to make sense of what they said.

The next morning Macbeatha told me he and his cousin were going out with a warband to Moray's lands along the Great Glen, where the Scots of Atholl were wont to raid the herds of Moray—and vice versa. They would not be back until the harvest.

It rained all day.

Chapter Ten

In Fionna's hut

Kelda watched Fionna's hands move deftly over her stones, moving, shifting, rearranging. "What are they?" she asked with passing curiosity.

"Stones."

"But what do they mean?"

Fionna shrugged. "Many things."

The patterns on the floor swam in and out of focus for Kelda, their colors bleeding together like a length of breachan, the Scottish multi-colored cloth. "Are they from the gods?"

A sigh escaped the old woman. "They must be. Who else would take such delight in confusing me?"

"Mmm." Kelda's eyelids fluttered a bit. "The old gods are like that," she agreed dreamily. "I have to say, although Macbeatha told me many wonderful stories about the Christian god, I never warmed to him. The stories were good enough—full of love and forgiveness—but seeing the kind of people who claim to worship him, I can't say I've found much of love or forgiveness in them. So many are hard and flinty and full of hatred for anything different." She sighed. "Hatred, and jealousy."

Fionna grunted. "But not Macbeatha," she guessed.

"Oh, no." A smile spread again on Kelda's face as she drifted back into remembering. "No, not Macbeatha..."

* * *

He had Engus fix the lead stamp on my collar before he left that spring, marking me his slave with that curious double circle. Then he smiled his dazzling smile at me, chucked me under the chin, and promised to bring me a pretty bauble when he returned. I asked for a crow fattened on the blood of his enemies. He laughed loudly at that, called me his little Valkyrie, and told me to be waiting with a drinking horn when he came home, just as the Valkyries wait for valorous warriors at Odin's hall. Then I started to cry, and he kissed me and held me and reminded me that I must be tough as old leather while he was gone.

It was advice I had to employ almost immediately. No sooner had he ridden out of the yard with his guardsmen, sun glinting red on his golden hair, than Siusan took care to step heavily on my toes. I didn't wait for an apology; I kicked her as hard as I could in the calf muscle. She gasped and turned to me with a hand drawn back to slap me, but I only smiled wickedly and pointed to my cheek, daring her to make a mark there. She thought better of it, knowing Macbeatha had instructed Donn to act in his place should we quarrel. Letting her hand fall, she turned and limped away.

So it went for the first week: she would pinch my waist, and I would throw an elbow into her ribs. She would trip me and I would shove her into the mud and rub her face in it. Oh, I got a few bruises from Donn for my trouble, because I was quite brazen in my retribution, but they were worth it. Siusan quickly learned that whatever she gave out, she might get back the same from Donn, but she'd get worse from me.

The Lady Brenna, of course, took Siusan's part in everything, and once even undertook to beat me herself. However, I was bigger than she, so I simply took the stick away from her and broke it into little bits. Oh, she was furious! She came at me with both hands scratching, but she was such a little thing, I just picked her up off the ground and carried her out to Donn, who was mending a harness under a tree near the stables. There followed a dreadful argument—dreadful for Brenna, at least, who shouted and waved her arms and stamped her feet. Donn only answered in calm and patient tones, his agile fingers never pausing in their work. Eventually Brenna stormed off.

It was easy to see who was truly in charge of Macbeatha's household, and why. Kneeling in the damp dirt at Donn's feet, I turned mournful eyes up to his single bright blue one. "I—" I began, then slumped because I had no idea what Scots word I wanted. "I am ..." Not knowing how else to convey it, I folded my hands in front of me and put on my most repentant look.

"Sorry," he guessed. "You are sorry."

"I sorry I much trouble," I said. "Good girl."

A smile twitched at his lips, and there was a twinkle in that single blue orb reminiscent of his younger kinsman. "Yes, good girl," he repeated, patting my hair as he would that of a child. "Brenna is a good girl, too, only—temper." He made a comic motion of screaming and waving his hands alongside his face. "Understand? Temper."

"Temper." I thought I did. Then, "Macbeatha, no temper," I told him.

Donn laughed roundly, his lean and lined face falling into even more wrinkles. "Oh, yes, Macbeatha has a temper. Only—" He pantomimed catching something in his fist, something that wriggled and squirmed as he tried to hold it. Then he placed his other hand on top of the fist and gradually subdued it. "Control," he told me. "Macbeatha controls his temper. Very much."

I thought of Macbeatha's duel with Ivarr, and I knew what Donn meant. It sent a small chill through me.

Having found physical abuse too costly, Siusan turned to a more clever tactic for tormenting me. Aithne and Donn, and even Engus, were conscientious about teaching me the Scots language—and the children were best of all—but from Siusan and Brenna I learned only such phrases as "stupid girl" and "clumsy creature"—until one day, Siusan seemed to have a change of heart. We were sitting out in the morning sun, sewing new clothes for Brenna to wear at court that winter—she had traded sharply in the marketplace and come home with, not only fine linen for a gown, but enough actual silk to make one. Even the Lady Plantula, Thorfinn's mother, never had an entire gown made of silk.

"Did you know silk is made by caterpillars?" Brenna asked her maid rather importantly.

Siusan looked a bit skeptical. "Caterpillars?" she questioned.

The word was new and unfamiliar to me, so I echoed it. "Caterpillars?"

Brenna, pleased to be the possessor of so much refined knowledge, proceeded to use her index finger to demonstrate a caterpillar's inching motion. "Caterpillar," she repeated, and then made a fluttering motion with her hands to indicate a butterfly.

"Ah!" My face lit up as I understood what she meant. "Caterpillar," I said, mimicking her finger motion, "and—what?" I made the fluttering motion with my hands and lifted inquiring eyes to her.

"Cowpie," Siusan supplied promptly.

If Brenna made any sound or gesture to betray her maid, I never saw it. "Cowpie," I echoed, pleased to learn a new word.

Next Siusan pointed to the roses growing wild along the rail fence that surrounded the vegetable garden, keeping the horses and cattle from eating the plants. "Maggots," she told me.

I was so excited that she had at last decided to be civil, I dropped my work and ran to the fence, plucking a pink blossom and bringing it back to her. "Maggot," I said proudly as I presented it to her.

The smile on her face was smug but charming. "Thank you, Kelda," she said. "I like to spit maggots in my hair. Spit, see?" And she plaited the flower into her long brown braid.

"Spit many maggots for you," I offered, and collecting numerous blossoms, I plaited them into a wreath and set it on her head.

She and Brenna smiled and laughed with such delight, I was thrilled. At last, it seemed, I had made friends of them. "Spit maggots for you, too," I told Brenna, and plaited another wreath for her. Then, giddy with joy at this accomplishment, I began to dance around the yard.

"Vomiting," Siusan told me, getting up to dance a step or two herself. "You vomit in the summer with many maggots spit in your hair."

Aithne heard the three of us laughing and came out from inside the house to investigate. Her round face split into a grin as she saw us dancing with flowers in our hair. Our fighting and bickering had been a sore trial for her. "Look, look!" I cried, scampering to the fence for more roses. "We are happy! I spit maggots for your hair, too, Aithne!"

The cook's jaw dropped and she stared at me.

"Maggots, see?" I repeated, holding out a handful of blossoms, unable to understand why she looked at me that way. "It is all right, yes, to spit maggots for the hair?"

Now Aithne's lips sealed in a straight line and she glared at her daughter, who had the decency to hang her head just a little. With an exasperated sigh, the older woman stalked into the house. A moment later she returned with a bowl full of oatmeal that had gone bad. "Maggots," she said firmly, pointing at the fat gray worms squirming in the spoiled food. "These are maggots, Kelda. Those—" She pointed at my wreaths. "—are roses."

My cheeks burned as I realized the trick that had been played on me.

But the lesson was not over. "Spit," Aithne said, and then demonstrated that action. "You would spit maggots, certainly, if you bit into them, but you do not spit roses. You pick them, you weave them or plait them or twine them, but you do not spit them."

I looked down at the flowers in my hands and imagined them full of ugly, wriggling maggots—and suddenly I began to laugh. "Maggots in the hair!" I shouted, tossing the roses up in the air as the hilarity of the notion struck me. My knees grew week with mirth and I sank into the grass laughing. "Look, look!" I pantomimed spitting into my hand, then weaving the unseen creatures into a wreath which I perched on my head. "I spit maggots for the hair!" I rocked back and forth, giggling.

Siusan's face grew bright red, and a moment later the laughter burst forth from her, too. She bent over her sewing and tears dripped down onto the fine cloth as she laughed. Even Brenna giggled a little. Jumping up, I danced over to Brenna and snatched the wreath from her hair. "Ooo, ooo, maggots!" I cried, tossing the flowers away in mock revulsion. Then I began to dance around the fallen wreath.

Suddenly I stopped. "What is called?" I asked Aithne suspiciously. "This, what is called?" and I danced a few steps more.

"Dancing," she told me.

I wagged a finger at Siusan. "When Macbeatha home comes, I say, 'I be happy and vomiting for see you,' and what say he?" I asked sternly.

Brenna covered her mouth with a hand to stop up her giggles, and Siusan cringed momentarily—but then she burst out laughing once more, setting down her sewing and clutching her sides, which had begun to ache from so much merriment. "Please come vomiting with me, Macbeatha," she mocked, and went off in peals of laughter that made her topple right off the bench and onto the ground.

Aithne only shook her head and went back into the house.

"What is vomiting?" I asked Siusan when we had both caught our breath a little. She pantomimed throwing up her breakfast, complete with descriptive noises, and then we were off again, rolling on the ground with laughter.

I can't say we became fast friends after that, for Siusan continued to play tricks on me whenever she could. But if she got too mean or spiteful, I had only to say something like, "Excuse me while I go spit maggots in my hair," and she would start laughing again, and the bad moment would pass.

She still tried to teach me the wrong words for things, so I had to check everything I learned from her with someone more trustworthy; but she was very good at correcting me on the order of my words. I think it made her feel superior to correct me. And as I learned more and more Scot words, we began to have actual conversations.

Finally I was able to ask her what I had wanted to ask from the day I met her.

There were some pieces of my vocabulary missing yet, so I fished for those first. It was "jealousy" I was after, so as we skimmed cream from buckets of milk in the dairy that day, I asked, "If you have something and I want it, what is that called?"

"Covetousness," Siusan replied primly. "That is a sin."

As far as I knew, jealousy wasn't actually a sin—it was senseless and harmful, but it wasn't a sin. So I tried again. "What if I have something you want borrow—not have, only borrow—"

"You don't have anything I want," she snipped.

I gave an exasperated sigh. "I have basket of flowers, many flowers," I persisted, then added—"heather and maggots." Siusan stifled a guffaw. "I have many, many flowers, and you want only three or four, but I say no—"

"Selfish," Siusan pronounced. "You are selfish if you will not share your flowers with me."

"Selfish." It was the other side of what I was looking for, but it had the right ring to it. I had heard the word before, and I thought it was genuine, not another of her pranks. *"You* are selfish, Siusan," I told her seriously.

Her eyebrows flew up. "I, selfish?"

"I take nothing from you, but you will not—share." That was the word she had used, I was sure. "Macbeatha is much man, for two girls, why not share?"

That was when I learned the words "godless heathen" and "stinking whore."

This occurred just after the Midsummer festival, and it was a full week before Siusan would even speak to me again. It made me angry, especially when I finally understood what the word "whore" meant, and in what low esteem such women were held. As a slave, I was only serving the desires of my lawful master; Siusan was not his slave, only his servant. If fulfilling my obligations made me a whore, what did her actions make her? I endeavored, with my limited command of Scots, to ask her. Unfortunately, I did so in front of Brenna.

To this day I do not understand why Brenna should have concerned herself with who shared her brother's bed. His pleasure was his business, and none of hers. But she was clearly furious to learn he had been taking advantage of her maid. I hadn't realized it was a secret, so it shocked me when Brenna began first to shout at Siusan, and then to beat her with a stick that lay at hand. Aithne came running, surprised to see the other two in combat, rather than me. But when Brenna told her why she was hitting Siusan, Aithne slapped her own daughter and propelled her from the house, then burst into tears.

I was distraught to see what my inadvertent revelation had wrought. I ran out after Siusan and found her in the stable, sobbing bitterly on a mound of hay. When I tried to apologize, she only screamed at me, calling me names and groping around for a stone or other handy object to throw at me. Finding nothing better, she threw fistfuls of hay. Weeping, I knelt down beside her and tried to calm her, but she struck at me with her hands and told me I'd ruined everything, that now they'd watch her and she would never be able to go to Macbeatha again.

Not knowing what else to do, I ran to find Donn, the one reliably rational presence in the household. Through my tears I explained as best I could what had happened. He sighed and limped—for he had a bad leg as well as a missing eye—to the stable to find Siusan.

"You hate me!" Siusan shrieked. "You all hate me, I know you do."

"I cannot speak for the others," Donn said gently and sensibly, "but I certainly do not hate you. You are far too young and pretty to hate."

That stemmed the hysteria to a gurgling sob. "My father will beat me," she whimpered.

"Your father? I doubt that. He has taken as many gifts from Macbeatha's hand as you have in recompense."

Siusan's jaw dropped and outrage flashed through her brown eyes. Donn only shrugged. "It would be disrespectful to do otherwise, for either of them. And they have great respect for each other."

"My mother hit me," Siusan whined. "And when I come out of here, she'll beat me soundly."

"That may be," Donn agreed, "for she is a virtuous woman; but her anger will pass. Like many things in life, you must live through this, and come out the other side."

"And she'll make my father marry me to the first stupid boy who asks!"

"He cannot do so without Macbeatha's permission," Donn pointed out. "And do you think Macbeatha would see you miserable?"

Siusan sniffled and wiped her nose on her sleeve. "No," she admitted.

"Now," said Donn with decision. "It is Brenna we must placate, for no doubt her sensibilities are more offended than even your mother's."

Here I tugged at his sleeve. "I will say I lie," I volunteered. "I will say I lie to get Siusan trouble. Lady can beat me for lying, it is all right."

They both turned to look at me in amazement. Tell me, why were they surprised that I wanted to undo the harm I had clearly done?

"I doubt she will believe you," Donn ventured. "Brenna is quick to believe evil of everyone but herself."

"You would let her beat you to spare me?" Siusan asked incredulously.

I shrugged, not looking forward to the prospect at all. "Macbeatha said no make marks on me, how bad can be?" I scoffed with all the bravado I could muster.

"Perhaps we can try to mend this," Donn said. "Both of you come with me."

Chapter Eleven

When he had gathered Brenna, Siusan's parents, and we two girls in the house, he sat in a chair before us, like a father before his children, and began. "This is how the matter has come to me. Kelda—implied—that Siusan has not kept herself pure, and her statement has caused much anguish in this household. We cannot have such disharmony. Kelda knows she was wrong to say this, and she wishes to apologize. Don't you, Kelda?"

"I am sorry," I offered contritely, hanging my head. "I say lie to hurt Siusan."

"Lying slut!" Brenna hissed, but Aithne only looked troubled, and Engus rubbed his face uncomfortably.

Donn scowled at the outburst, then continued. "Kelda didn't know how much trouble it would cause to say such a thing. She does not know our ways."

"Heathen—" Brenna began, but Donn cut her off with a warning gesture.

"Clearly there has been a wrong done here, and it must be punished. I understand Siusan has already been beaten," he observed dryly, "so it is only fair that Kelda receive likewise; and since Siusan is the one who suffered, she is the one who should administer the beating."

Siusan, who had been silent with her head bowed, looked up in surprise.

"Will everyone agree this is a fair and just settlement of this matter?"

Brenna looked as if she would like to add further invectives, but she held her tongue.

"And when it is done, there is to be no more said of this, and it shall be as if this incident never happened."

Engus nodded enthusiastically, quite relieved. His wife eyed him suspiciously, but she, too, nodded her head. "I shall be happy to assist you, Siusan," Brenna offered, "if you need it."

"No," Siusan croaked hoarsely. "I can beat her well enough myself."

"Then I shall take the girls out to the stable and see the thing done," Donn decreed. Siusan and I turned to leave with him.

"No," Brenna said firmly.

Donn gave her a withering look.

"Siusan's humiliation was before her family and me. I demand that Kelda's should be so as well."

Donn raised his eyes to the two of us. "It is fair," I said quickly. Crossing to the hearth, I picked up a stick of green willow that had been used as a poker and took it to Siusan. "No marks," I reminded her under my breath.

"Just scream," she whispered back.

Oh, I felt the blows, but they were as light as they could be in front of witnesses. And I winced and shrieked enough to satisfy Brenna's greedy lust for punishment. Then Donn said, "Enough," but Brenna snatched the switch from Siusan's hand and smacked it across my neck.

"That's for lying to me," she snarled.

Donn leaped to his feet, eyes blazing, and for a moment I thought he would use the switch on his kinswoman; but he only took it away and cast it into the fire, where it smoked and popped. "You had better hope that heals before your brother gets home," he warned the young lady, "or he'll put one just like it on you." Then to the rest of us he said, "This matter is ended, and it will not be spoken of again. Not even to Macbeatha."

That night, after the others were asleep, Siusan slipped over to where I had my bed stretched by the fire. "Does it hurt much?" she asked.

"Just here," I replied, pointing to the welt on my neck.

For a moment she was silent, staring down at her hands. "You know, you didn't have to do that. Brenna will be watching me after this, and if she catches me, the beating will have been for nothing.

Except now," she added, "Macbeatha probably won't want me anymore, so then I won't get caught, will I?" Tears glittered in her eyes.

I raised myself up on one elbow and looked at her curiously. "Why he will not want you?" I asked. "You are plump and pretty and agreeable—except to me," I added with an arched eyebrow. "Of course, he will still want you. And if Brenna makes trouble for this, I help you again. Not take beating again," I hastened, "but I make up stories so she not know."

Siusan looked at me with something like horror and amazement mixed in her eyes. Then, "You are very different than we are," she whispered, shaking her head, and slipped back to her own bed.

The harvest was already underway when Maelcolm, the mormaer, came back from campaign with his warband, driving herds and flocks before him and bearing sacks of goods, not from plunder, but from *conveth,* the hospitality rent due him as ruler of Moray. He had been to the mouth of the River Ythan in the east, and all along the northern coast, but there had been no Viking invasions that year. To keep his army from getting too restless, he had harassed the Norse settlers around Elgin and Banff, but they were mere skirmishes.

His kinsman Bothan came back two days later, having crossed to the west side of Moray Firth that summer and "protected" the Scots living along the border of Sutherland. This had brought him into conflict with some of Thorfinn's men—not his hirdmen, mind you, just some *bønders* who claimed allegiance to the jarl and liked to break up their summer by fighting with any Scots who were game for a good tussle. Bothan had suffered several casualties, including two dead and three others who were so maimed they would not take up arms again. However, they had given as good as they got, and came away with some Norse swords and some odds and ends of silver for their trouble. They, too, had collected cattle and sheep for *conveth,* and these they turned over to Maelcolm with great pride.

The summer rains—coming daily for weeks on end—grew infrequent with the approach of autumn. Long days of sunshine dried out the grain, and men began to look at the oats and barley and say, "Tomorrow, or the day after ..." I fretted that Macbeatha was not home yet, and Brenna fretted, too, fearing some harm had befallen him and his reckless cousin Gillecomgain. But Donn only smiled serenely and said, "He has a weather eye, does that one. He'll be here before the first frost."

And so he was. Dhui, Engus's youngest son and our reliable harbinger, came racing into the yard late of an afternoon shouting, "Macbeatha comes! He comes with horses and boats and a Viking ship!" It was only a fishing boat, of course, but Scots in Moray did not build ships in that design, so to Dhui it was a Viking ship.

We all jumped up and Brenna was ready to run for the loch, but she caught herself and began to give orders instead. "Kill three fat geese and set them to roasting, the men will be hungry. And run to the market for fresh fish—we'll stuff them with sausage and bread and bake them as well. Bake all the bread the ovens would hold, bring up another barrel of ale, and don't salt any of the butter from the dairy today—sweet butter will be wanted for the feast." We scampered about like a flock of eider startled by a seal. Men were called in from their chores in the pastures and the pens, women darted around the house and the dairy, faces were scrubbed, clothes were brushed, and the entire household stood by to meet the returning warriors when at last they rode their horses into the yard.

Brenna fairly glowed as her brother swung down from his horse to greet her. His hair gleamed red in the westering sun, and his face and arms were darkened with sun, or grime, or both. Seizing her by the waist, he lifted her high in the air and swung her around like a child, which made her laugh aloud in delight. Then she hugged him, heedless of the stains it put on her light woolen gown, and bade him welcome home.

Donn was next to greet him, and then older servants and retainers crowded around, all wanting to share in this joyous homecoming. I saw Siusan slip in to take Macbeatha's helmet and shield from his horse before it was led away. Seeing her, he reached over to pat her bottom playfully; then, as though reminded, he turned and began to look around. "Where is my Valkyrie?" he called out. "Where is Kelda?"

The crowd seemed to part before him as they all joined in his search. Brenna had tried to send me off to the market for some last-minute trifle, but I had ignored her, for his parting words to me were not forgotten. Now I advanced toward him, a brimming horn in one hand and a pitcher of ale in the other, with no need to elbow a path. "I am here, lord," I told him proudly in Scots, holding out the horn.

He took it from my hand, but before he drank he looked me up and down with satisfaction. "You seem to have prospered," he observed, green eyes alight. Then, "What is that in your hair?"

It was a circlet of grasses I had woven and perched on my head. "It is a ... wreath," I said, hesitating just slightly. On her way into the house, Siusan stopped short and turned back to stare. "There are no ... flowers," I went on, hesitating again for effect. It was not lost on Siusan—she stood frozen in place, a look of dread in her eyes. "In the spring, when there are flowers, I—" The air hung heavy around me as I drew out the pause. "I plait flowers for my hair," I finished. "Roses, lots of roses, and I go dancing. That was four sentences, yes?"

"Yes!" Macbeatha cried in delight, and I could almost hear the great intake of air as Siusan began to breathe again. "Yes, four very nice sentences, Kelda. Siusan! You have done well. You have all done very well." Then he lifted his horn in toast to us all, and downed the ale in a single draught.

There was much merrymaking that night, and I grinned broadly as I moved among the crowd with my pitcher, refilling horns and tankards everywhere. There were some bad moments early on, for not all the men had come back; their families came expecting a feast and went away keening. But for the rest, there was much joy and laughter and singing. It felt good to serve in a hall again, even a Scot hall. The men smiled at me, and patted and grabbed in a friendly fashion. When there was a moment's peace, I settled myself at Macbeatha's feet, and he smiled down at me. As long as he was home, I knew everything would be all right.

Then the mormaer arrived, flanked by his brother Gillecomgain. I had seen Maelcolm only once before, when he returned with his warband. Like Macbeatha, he was a tall man, though more heavily built, with bowed legs and hairy arms that looked as if they could snap a tree trunk in two. His hair was a coppery red, much darker than my lord's, but his full beard was the same bright shade as his kinsman's mustaches. Advancing on Macbeatha, he opened his arms in a sincere but restrained gesture. "Well done, cousin," he said matter-of-factly.

Macbeatha rose and embraced Maelcolm. "I believe we did Moray some credit," he replied in the same subdued fashion. My lord always had the trick of adapting his style to that of the people around him. Maelcolm was a taciturn and understated man, so Macbeatha addressed him in similar tones.

When Maelcolm had greeted Brenna, my lord offered him the place of honor, and Gillecomgain the seat next to it. "Good people, raise your horns," Macbeatha proclaimed to the crowd. "Let us salute the leader of our Great Tribe, who sent us forth, and also his brother, who led us into battle with unfailing courage."

So we drank to the mormaer, whom everyone called *righ* or king in his presence; and to Gillecomgain, whose stupidity we had been deploring before he walked in; and to Macbeatha, who had engineered a raid on a fortified hall; and to Alistair, who—oh, I can't remember why we drank to him, but I'm sure we did. Then we drank to the men who had fallen in battle, and to Moray and the ancestral House of Loarn, and to courage, and to valor, and soon we were all very drunk.

Then the stories began, greatly embellished tales of the expedition down the Great Glen and each battle along the way. Gillecomgain grew quite ebullient, painting himself the hero in true Scottish fashion. Macbeatha, however, let others tell of his cunning and prowess, which they were quick enough to do. The men were tired from their travels, however, and soon began to nod in the corners and along the walls.

Finally Maelcolm called for a bed, and we brought out the blankets and straw ticks we had stuffed earlier to accommodate our guests. Brenna said the hearth blessing as she covered the fire for the evening; but Gillecomgain called for more ale, making no move toward the bed prepared for him.

Macbeatha rose and stretched broadly. "Well, cousin," he said with a yawn, "I bid you good night."

"What? To bed so soon?" Gillecomgain prodded. "Dawn is yet far off for men such as we."

"Aye, so it is," my lord agreed, picking me up and tossing me over his shoulder. "There is bed, and then there is sleep. It's bed for me." Then, to the sound of Gillecomgain's coarse guffaws, he carried me toward the ladder that led upstairs, leaving his cousin to his own devices.

It had been such a joyous evening, I was surprised that when we reached the loft, Macbeatha fell abruptly silent. It was as if all his joy and warmth had been left behind at the hearth. In the pale light filtering through the smoke hole, his face was hard and dark with anger. But why? Was it something I had done? Something that happened in the hall? As we approached his chamber at the end of the loft, I feared what demon would emerge when he closed the door behind us.

Chapter Twelve

From the tales told in the hall earlier that evening, I knew some of what had transpired during the campaign, but nothing that might cause this reaction in my lord. It was not until much later I got the ugly parts of it from Weylin, one of the warriors in Macbeatha's guard. Piecing it together, it went like this.

There were 21 of them who set out from Inverness that season: Alistair mac Laughlin had nine men with him, and Macbeatha his nine, and Gillecomgain rode at their head. They traveled down the Great Glen toward the lands of Atholl, for there is no love between the Great Tribe of Moray and the Great Tribe of Atholl, and each likes to prey upon the other's cattle. It is a chance for young warriors to make their reputations, and if all goes well, to bring home some prizes. It is like Norse men going a-viking, except along the Great Glen, neither tribe has much worth stealing.

Below Loch Ness, the lands of Atholl lie on the east side of the Glen and the lands of Moray on the west, and it was here most of the fighting took place. Gillecomgain's warband got away with 26 cows in a raid near Lochaber, then had to battle the Athollmen who came to steal them back. A rich tribe south of Inverlochy was relieved of a hundred head of stock, and the local Moraymen helped prevent Atholl from chasing back up the Glen after them. But Gillecomgain was incensed when Athollmen crossed into Moray's lands and set fire to a village and mill.

"We'll make them pay!" he raged. "A hundred head of cattle? We'll take five hundred! And what we can't take with us, we'll kill! There'll be keening this winter in Atholl, by God!"

It was mid-July, and rain poured down outside the inn where they had taken shelter. Macbeatha sat languidly by the fire, whittling a charm from a piece of kindling. Without looking up, he said, "I hear there's much wealth in Dunglas."

"Dunglas!" Gillecomgain looked blankly at his kinsman. Dunglas sat on a sea loch well down the Glen. "We can't drive cattle back from Dunglas, it's too far."

My lord shrugged negligently. "We'll be lucky if we can drive this hundred head back up the Glen. Myself, I'd trade them for wool and cheese, which we can take by ship. But the chieftain who keeps the fortress at Dunglas married an Irish Dane, and his father-in-law brings him all kinds of rich gifts from his travels: tapestries, pearls, plundered silver, swords ..."

Around the room, men moistened their lips and leaned a little closer.

"How many men at the fortress?" Gillecomgain asked warily. It was one thing to raid the countryside, where only one or two dozen men could be mustered on a moment's notice. It was quite another to attack a fortress, where surely there were guardsmen nearby, and a sizeable village that could provide men and arms for a defense.

Macbeatha cast a glance over his shoulder at their host, a tribesman whose duty it was to run this inn for travelers. "What would you think, Cyric? Fifty?"

"Without warning, perhaps only thirty-five," the portly gentleman estimated. "If you issue a challenge, Liosliath might raise a hundred."

"And how many can we raise?" Gillecomgain asked.

"There's fifty hereabouts would go with you," Cyric assured him. "Maybe another dozen or two you could pick up along the way."

Gillecomgain considered that. "It could be an even fight then," he said, his eyes glittering. "Even in numbers, that is. Everyone knows one Morayman is worth two Atholl swine!" There was a ripple of approving laughter from the men in the room.

"And we can carry our rewards back up the Great Glen on boats," Macbeatha suggested. "Leave the cattle here for those who lost all in the fire. No doubt we can pick up more along the way."

And so it was planned. *Laochraidh,* those tribesmen whose right it is to bear arms, came in from the straths and the glens, lured by the promise of glory and plunder. Over a hundred in number now, they celebrated Midsummer in high spirits, cavorting around a bonfire and bragging to the women present how their swords would be reddened and their purses filled, and promising lavish gifts to the lady who would sweeten the sending with her favor. Then, with the bulk of summer behind them, they set out in a light drizzle to ravish Dunglas.

Unfortunately, Gillecomgain chose to ride through hostile country below Inverlochy. They were caught crossing a loch and lost half a dozen men to Atholl spearmen on the shore. Macbeatha urged his cousin to take to the river and come at Dunglas from the southeast, but Gillecomgain wouldn't hear of it. "Bring them on!" he shouted, shaking his fist at the Athollmen they knew must be watching them from behind rocks and trees on the steep upward reaches of the narrow glen. "Gillecomgain of Moray is afraid to fight no man!"

And so they were ambushed again crossing a swift stream.

Now the two cousins sat in their tent arguing for hours. Some of the locals drifted away, deciding they'd rather go home with a whole skin than follow a madman for treasure. The warband was down to fifty, and a quarter of those were untried boys. "We cannot challenge them with fifty!" Macbeatha could be heard to shout.

"We are seventy-five if we are one!" Gillecomgain roared back. "I will take seventy-five men of Moray against *two* hundred Athollmen. *Three* hundred. We'll burn them in their fortress."

Suddenly it got very quiet. Some minutes later the two combatants came out of the tent grinning like conspirators. "I have a plan," Gillecomgain announced, and everyone knew full well whose plan it was.

First they pounced on the nearest settlement and stole every head of livestock they could find: thirteen cows, three goats, six sheep, and five pigs. They made a great show of roasting one sheep and two half-grown pigs and feasting on them; then they packed their gear and retreated up the Great Glen with their wounded and their plunder.

Under cover of the first darkness, however, Gillecomgain, Macbeatha, and the sound men of their warband stole away and back down the river toward the coast. They kept to the friendly shore, traveling only at night, and taking ship in two coracles just where the water turned from fresh to salt. Then, when they were near the mouth of the sealoch they sought, the small band crossed over into hostile territory and crept their way afoot through forest and fen to the island fortress of Dunglas.

The fortress was actually a *crannog,* a house built on an artificial island near the south shore of the loch. Pilings had been driven into the lake bottom, a platform of wood and stones laid upon them, and finally the house with its surrounding stone wall constructed on top of that. The house itself was timber, covered with sheets of lead, which probably gave the fortress its name of *Dunglas,* gray rock. A narrow stone causeway connected Dunglas to the mainland, where a cluster of wattle and daub huts housed the chieftain's close kin, his more distant tribesmen, and a few clients who helped work the land. Guessing ten warriors in the fortress and two dozen more in the village, the innkeeper's estimate of thirty-five was deemed fairly accurate.

But there were less than half that many Moraymen by then, and they would have no lead walls to hide behind. An attack by water would be suicidal, for the defenders could pick them off as they scaled the stone wall; and the narrow causeway leading to the fortress lay under water most of the time, as the sealoch's level rose and fell slightly with the tides. There was a small lip of land just before the gate, a staging area for goods brought out by boat or raft. Above it rose a tower from which one man with a crossbow could keep the area quite clean of invaders.

The three leaders stood in a thicket across the narrow loch and gazed at the daunting fortress. "We could give the alarm and send them all scurrying into the fortress, then make off with their cattle and sheep," Alistair suggested half-heartedly.

"I want what's inside that fortress," Gillecomgain growled.

"I have an idea," said Macbeatha. "Owen, Weylin, you're with me. The rest of you men, build a raft, a sturdy one, twice the length of a man in both directions. And keep it and yourselves out of sight." Then off he strode, seeming not to notice he had given orders as though he were in charge; and the men jumped to obey, as though it were true.

"What are we doing?" Weylin asked as they slipped away through the marshes.

"Stealing a boat."

Weylin wasn't sure why they should steal a boat when they'd left three perfectly good coracles not far away, but he knew enough not to question Macbeatha. They bypassed two or three others at small holdings along the north shore, working their way toward the sea until they came upon a fisherman's hut with a fine, trim craft tied up outside. "It looks like a Viking boat," Owen remarked, noting the high prow and stern, the perfect shiplapping of the staves, the thinness of the hull. "Only smaller."

"Exactly," Macbeatha agreed. "It's just what we need."

There were dogs at the cottage; they had to slip into the loch and swim quietly around to come at the boat from the stern. Macbeatha cut the line and they eased the small craft away from the shore, letting it drift out toward the sea while they clung to the gunwale on the far side. Only when they were safely away did they haul themselves, cold and shivering, into the boat and take up the oars to row her back toward Dunglas.

By the time they had hidden the boat in some rushes and hiked back to their camp, the raft was completed. Macbeatha surveyed the sturdy platform of logs with satisfaction. "Good. That should hold a fair amount of wealth, wouldn't you say? Now, which of you speaks any of the Viking tongue?"

The men looked dumbly from one to the other. Finally, "I can say, 'Your sister sleeps with horses,'" one man ventured. "And 'shit-eating coward.'"

"Aye, I can curse a bit," offered another.

"Good! Each of you will teach your insults and curses to three other men, whoever has the quickest ear and the nimblest tongue. If Liosliath has a Danish wife, he should recognize a few curses. Now Alistair, this is what you'll say—it means, 'Is the master at home? We bring gifts from Swein.' That's Liosliath's father-in-law."

They spent the day resting and constructing the few additional items they would need, making jokes to bolster each other's courage. Just as the long summer twilight began to settle over the land, Macbeatha and Alistair took the boat, with two men concealed under an oilskin in the stern and two more under a blanket in the stem, and rowed out from their hiding place, making for the fortress as though they came from the sea. Owen, Weylin and the others poled the raft eastward through the marshes until they could cross the loch, hidden from watchful eyes by the deepening shadows, using crude paddles to propel themselves toward the southern shore while the outgoing tide carried them slowly back toward Dunglas.

As the raft approached the fortress, those aboard slid into the water and clung to the sides of their craft, guiding it quietly toward the back side of the crannog. They were just another shadow among the many flickering across the loch. The twilight was still and deep, with stars beginning to wink into being overhead, and they could hear the voices of their comrades as the boat approached Dunglas from the west. "Halloooo!" called Macbeatha in a voice comically accented to sound like a Norseman speaking Gaelic. "Liosliath! We come to Liosliath from Swein! You know Swein!"

From the water they saw him standing boldly amidships with a broad and rather stupid smile on his face, his hair pulled back at the nape of his neck to look like a Norseman. Alistair added his speech about gifts, and Macbeatha echoed, "Ja! Gifts! Here, you see?" He prodded the oilskin in the stern where two of his men hid. "Silk! You know silk? For the lady, from her father!"

Sounds drifted over the fortress wall as people scurried about inside, and torches were brought to the open gate. A woman appeared, her gold jewelry sparkling in the flickering light. She and Macbeatha conversed briefly in Norn, then she nodded to the guards, who reached out to take the line Macbeatha tossed them and hook it around a mooring post. As they did, the raft drifted up against the back side of the crannog. As quietly as they could, men dragged themselves from the water back onto the raft to wait, using the paddles to keep the craft in place against the pull of the tide. Though they could still hear voices, they couldn't make out any words, and they could not see the gate from this vantage. Then came Macbeatha's voice, clear as a bell on the night air: "Lady, can you swim?"

There followed a loud splash, and chaos erupted. Angry shouts filled the air as men burst from hiding aboard the boat; then came the ringing of swords and the cries of wounded warriors. But a moment more, and three ladders of vines dropped over the fortress wall. Owen, Weylin and the others climbed up and across, dropping into the courtyard of the fortress with sword and shield at the ready. They pushed the defenders back toward the gate, catching them between Macbeatha's party and their own. The battle was fierce, but in the end, all the defenders lay dead on the blood-slick flagstones before the house.

Lights danced on the shore now, torches coming toward the water as men hurried to find out what all the commotion was. The soggy Danish mistress of Dunglas had clambered onto the submerged causeway and was slogging her way toward land. "Shall I kill her?" asked Alistair, who had mounted the tower with a crossbow and was waiting for the first villager to try charging across toward them.

"No," Macbeatha barked curtly. "We are only *pretending* to be Vikings. All of you, say nothing in Gaelic. Those who can, give out Viking curses, loud enough for those on shore to hear. Into the house, now—let's see what's worth taking away!"

They burst into the house with a will, overturning furniture and tossing it into the fire, rolling gold and silver dishes into carpets and tapestries. A dozen servants cringed at one end of the hall, and upstairs, three children and their nurse huddled quaking in a loft bedroom. It was here things began to go awry, for Gillecomgain judged one of the girls old enough to be raped, and so he did; but he had to kill the old nurse in the process. Macbeatha was not pleased. War is for men, he says, and women and children ought to be left out of it—unless, of course, one comes at you with a weapon, and then you do what you must. But Gillecomgain did what suited him, and the girl suited him, and the old woman was in the way.

It left a sour taste in more than one mouth, though, and men were anxious to be on their way. They were hauling the bundled valuables over the wall to where the raft was tied when the angry Athollmen launched several wicker coracles from the shore. Macbeatha and several others climbed back into the boat, cursing freely in Norn, and headed down the loch toward the sea, drawing the Athollmen after them while the raft slipped quietly across the water toward the northern shore with their plunder. Macbeatha had grabbed a torch from the ruined house, and Alistair sent one flaming crossbow bolt after another toward their pursuers. One pierced the lead coracle, and the pitch-coated wicker exploded in flames. After that, the other boats fell off, giving up the chase.

Gillecomgain was so pleased with the Viking ruse, he insisted on using it two or three more times as they worked their way back toward Inverlochy. They were just little hit-and-run raids, stopping to slaughter a few sheep and steal some kegs of ale, taking the one or two silver brooches or gold armbands that could be had, and moving on. Macbeatha was cross at these interruptions—he wanted to run northward with what they had, not to alarm the countryside to their passage—but Gillecomgain thrust out his jaw stubbornly and said it was payback for the village burned near Inverlochy. He was the *tanist,* after all, and it was hard to argue with a man who might be mormaer in due time.

But the last of these raids set Macbeatha to seething.

From a distance, the cluster of huts looked like just another village on the Atholl side of the river, with some pigs rooting around and some goats grazing on a rocky slope nearby. It wasn't until they landed that they saw a cross mounted on the lodgepole of one of the huts.

Gillecomgain was in rare form. With his hair pulled back like a Viking's, he roared the single curse he had mastered and swung his sword at a fleeing villager, cutting the man almost in half. Macbeatha was appalled—the man was tonsured, a priest or a monk. He hadn't even been armed. When a woman ran from her hut, dragging two small children by the hand, Macbeatha seized his cousin by the neck of his tunic and hauled him back to stay his hand. "Let her go!" he screamed over the din of shouting. "We are here for treasure, not murder!"

Gillecomgain snarled at his kinsman, but he left off chasing the fleeing villagers and began poking through the wattle huts. It was soon apparent there was nothing in this village worth taking, except a single sword whose aging owner had tried valiantly to purchase time for his family to escape. Gillecomgain was furious at the lack of spoils. "Burn the place!" he commanded. So they set two or three huts on fire; then Macbeatha summoned his men and they started back toward their boats.

"Burn it *all!"* Gillecomgain raged, grabbing a brand from one of the fires and tearing through the village touching roof after thatched roof with his makeshift torch.

Macbeatha met him face to face in front of the wattle hut with the cross mounted over the door. "It's a church," he hissed at his cousin.

Gillecomgain giggled maniacally. "So? Vikings burn churches!"

"But Christians do not!" Macbeatha grated through clenched teeth. "Turn back *now."*

Gillecomgain only sneered his peculiar, twisted sneer, with the scar on his face warping his countenance out of all proportion. "God doesn't dwell in an *Atholl* church," he cackled, and tossed the brand onto the roof.

Macbeatha's arm snapped out to stop him, but it wasn't quick enough. The fire caught in the thatch, and in a moment the entire structure was ablaze. Still the two men stood face to face, their eyes filled with hate, until finally Macbeatha lifted his gaze to watch as flames engulfed the cross. Then he turned back to Gillecomgain. "May all the fires of hell consume you as they have this church," he said quietly, and walked away.

They reached Inverness without further incident, but plainly these matters still preyed on my lord's mind as he left the victory feast and brought me to his chamber. There he closed the door without a word, then opened the shutters and let the cold night air rush in. Shivering, I sat quickly on the bed and drew the blankets around me, watching his face in the moonlight. His jaw worked, his eyes glittered like the stars outside, and he drank in the blackness and the cold of the night as if it could cleanse him of some cloying evil.

Finally he closed the shutters and came to me, speaking no word but making manifold demands with his mouth and his hands. That night there was none of the playfulness or pleasure I had so enjoyed with him before. That night there was only a driving force inside him that needed to consume everything in its path, and I was merely fuel to feed that fire. I felt frightened, yet exhilarated, as a sacrifice must feel as it is offered up to some god. Wordlessly I clutched him to me, surrendering without complaint all that he was greedy to take.

He spent himself quickly and collapsed exhausted at my side. Lying there, confused and a little frightened to find this turmoil inside him, I began to stroke his arms and his chest, hoping to soothe him to sleep. I had no idea then what was wrong, whether it was something that happened while he was away or just his persistent hatred of his cousins. But instead of comforting, my touch roused him again. Surprised, I nurtured this spark while he lay, for some time, quiescent beneath my hands. When at last he reached for me, it was without haste. There was still no joy in him, but the savageness was gone from his needing, and there was more warmth in his desire. This time he carried me with him, and as we fell back sweating upon the pillows, I knew whatever demon had possessed him was beaten back.

For a time we were silent, and I was drifting toward sleep when finally he spoke. "We burned a church," he said softly. It was all he ever said of the matter, and at first I did not understand the significance of it. A church was only a building, after all, like a house or a stable or a shop. Men burn many buildings when they go raiding. Why should it matter if he burned a church?

Then I thought about the places where we Norse worshipped, those who kept the old ways. It was, I realized, like burning a sacred grove where men and animals hung silent from the trees, offerings to the gods. Suddenly the horror of it came through to me and I flinched. "Ah, my sweet one!" I gasped, reaching out to gather him in my arms.

Trembling like a child, he clung to me, his face buried in my neck. I held him and soothed him until at last he slept.

The next day we left Inverness for Ross, where the harvest was in progress. Harvest has always been a joyous time for me. There is much labor, to be sure, and men fret and watch the skies in fear that a storm will come and make their labor all for naught. But throughout the years I knew Macbeatha, I never once saw a harvest that was less than bountiful.

In all the decisions of when to harvest and how much to slaughter, Macbeatha was the authority, and his sound judgments led men to trust him. But he never failed to seek counsel of his steward and kinsman, Donn. It was done in private, so if they should disagree, it was only between them; but it was clear to me Macbeatha regarded Donn as he would a fosterer or a father. This applied not only to matters of husbandry, but to politics as well. I stumbled across them one day, deep in conversation, when I went to hang strings of mushrooms and onions in the drying shed.

"Pardon, lord," I said immediately, surprised to find them in that remote place, and I turned to go.

"It's all right, Kelda," Macbeatha said with an indifferent wave of his hand. "Go on with your chores." And he went back to telling Donn who would be arriving at Maelcolm's fortress in Inverness for the Hallowmass feast.

I hung my strings of vegetables very slowly, concentrating on deciphering what they said without seeming to do so. The names confused me—so many *Mael's* and *Gille's*, and everyone a *mac,* or son, of so-and-so. But I gathered that Macbeatha sought corroboration on whose daughter to charm, and whose wife not to, and together they considered whether to seek a wife for Donn's grandson, to form a marriage alliance for the house.

"Do you understand all this, Kelda?" Donn asked as I lingered over the last string, retying a knot I knew was perfectly secure.

"Understand what, lord?" I asked blithely as I picked up my empty basket and prepared to leave.

Macbeatha chuckled. "I'll wager you could put coals under her feet and she wouldn't let on they were hot unless she was supposed to know it."

"You could beat her with a stick, I'm sure of that," Donn agreed dryly.

"Come, Kelda," Macbeatha invited, drawing me under one arm, "I want to know how your study of our language progresses. Tell me what you understood of our conversation."

So I repeated back all I had gleaned. Here and there I gave them a chuckle because I had misconstrued something, or mispronounced a word, but on the whole I must have gotten most of it right, for Donn winked at his young lord and said, "You would do better to take *her* to court with you, and leave Brenna somewhere along the way."

Macbeatha gave a hearty laugh. "I had thought some of taking her with me, just for amusement," he admitted. "And to boast of my Viking bondmaid."

I laughed and objected. "I'm not a *viking*. Can you see me with sword or spear, fighting on a longboat?"

"We say *viking* for all Norsemen," he told me. "Even their wenches. It will make you more exotic at court to call you a Viking, and everyone will envy me."

Do you know, I believed him? Perhaps at that time he believed it himself.

At any rate, I was thrilled to learn I would go with him to the High King's court in Scone. The prospect of a winter without him was dull indeed. But then I wondered if perhaps he intended for me to wait upon Brenna, and to leave Siusan behind. Oh, how she would hate me for that! And how furious Brenna would be.

But he had other plans for my service. "Kelda," he said the next morning as his old servant Murdock took up a shaving knife to pare the red stubble from my lord's chin. "Do you know how to shave a man, as your mother shaves her lord Thorkel?"

My eyes grew wide and my jaw dropped. "N-no, lord," I stammered, trying to imagine holding a knife to his or any other royal throat.

"Learn."

So I studied the art of shaving. First I watched Murdock. Then I practiced with a knife by shaving the hair from my arms—that was simple enough, for arms are long and smooth. Next I tried shaving around my ankles and knees, for they were lumpy and bumpy and more difficult. When I could do that without a nick or a scratch, I convinced Engus's older son to let me practice on him. He was fifteen, with hardly enough beard to bother, but it was a face, and that was what counted.

Finally, on the morning of the Hallowmass feast, I told Macbeatha that on the morrow I would be ready to shave him.

"Tomorrow?" he echoed, cocking a reddish eyebrow as he took his chair by the fire where Murdock waited with water and knife. "Why not start today?"

"Because if I slip and nick you, you will have a mark on your face at the feast."

His green eyes sparkled as he smiled at me. "You will not nick me," he said confidently. "I know you, Kelda—your feet are planted on a hard rock, are they not? Come." He clasped my wrist with one strong hand and drew me toward his chair. "Murdock, give her the knife. Let's see what she can do."

"Oh, please, lord!" I protested, trying to pull away from him, though it was impossible. "Let me start tomorrow. I am so nervy now to start."

"Nervous," he corrected, for my Gaelic failed me when I was upset. "You are nervous; but you must do this anyway. Do you understand me?" His eyes caught mine and there was no laughter in them now, only a fire of purpose. "Strength means doing what needs to be done, even when you are nervous or afraid."

So I shaved him. I shaved him that day, and every other day we were together, from then until now. I shaved him the day he took the white rod of Moray; I shaved him the day he was inaugurated as High King. I shaved and washed him clean before they laid him upon his bier, for I could not send him to Heaven or Valhalla or wherever he goes with dust on his forehead and stubble on his chin. And in all those years, the only time I ever nicked him was on his wedding day.

Chapter Thirteen

We went a-horseback to Scone, and even Siusan and I were given ponies to ride. Brenna, of course, was an excellent rider, being a noblewoman and much practiced in the art. She had a special saddle which allowed her to ride with both legs to one side, which showed off her fine clothes to best advantage. We servant girls were another story. Siusan simply pulled her shift up through her belt, blousing it like a man's tunic, and rode astride. I copied her.

Since we were traveling with a lady, it was necessary to have a large company of warriors in attendance. I'm sure it was not necessary to have quite the number we took, but Macbeatha intended to make a grand impression as he trotted the length of Moray with his beautiful sister and their retinue. In addition to his nine guardsmen, Macbeatha enlisted three other companies of ten men each. This, of course, necessitated a large baggage train and several servants to act as porters and wranglers. We were well over fifty in number when, with banners flying and a song on the lips of the warriors, we rode out of Inverness and between the fallow fields, northeast toward Elgin.

Macbeatha carefully plotted his route to arrive each evening at the home of some tribal leader who, in the tradition of the Scots, offered hospitality to these two members of Moray's royal family and their entourage. At supper, Macbeatha was sure to charm the wives and daughters of his host, while Brenna slew every highborn man in the hall with her elegant manners, her dainty form, her handsome face, and her razor wit. Macbeatha must have received at least one query about a marriage for her at every place we stopped.

Word preceded us to a fortress at the mouth of the Ythan River, north of Aberdeen, where Fergus mac Mhuire was chieftain. Fergus rode out to meet us with a company of warriors, greeting my lord and his sister as if they were his own children. He insisted we stay the week so he might give a feast in their honor. This was done in high style with musicians and entertainers, races and competitions, feasting and drinking for an entire day. One might have thought it was the High King himself who graced this event, rather than cousins of the Mormaer of Moray.

Of course, to the people of Moray, the mormaer *was* the king. Oh, they might drink the health of the High King in Scone, but they'd spit afterwards. They answered to Fergus mac Mhuire first, to Maelcolm of Moray second, and to Malcolm of Alba only if it pleased them. Close kin of the mormaer had greater honor among them than any relative of the High King ever would.

But beyond that, Fergus had been a fosterling of Macbeatha's father Findlaech some twenty years before, and he cherished my lord and his sister as close kin. He told us repeatedly how he had wept when he heard of the Lady Doada's passing, and that he was not surprised Findlaech had fallen in combat soon afterward. "Never did a man bear such love for a woman as Findlaech bore for the sweet Lady Doada," he vowed the night we arrived, as he and Macbeatha sat drinking in the hall.

Macbeatha gave a bitter twist of a smile. "My cousin Gillecomgain said something similar, so I'm told."

"Oh?" Fergus's face darkened as he caught an undercurrent of animosity.

"As my father lay mortally wounded," Macbeatha explained, "he told his guard, 'I would rather walk forever in death with my Doada than live another moment on this earth without her.' And Gillecomgain, who had slain him, said, 'No man should love a woman that much.'"

Fire flashed in Fergus's eyes. "A man who does not understand such devotion," he growled, "can hardly understand other passions. Like loyalty. And honor." Then his eyes narrowed as he studied his young guest carefully. "He who has no understanding of the passions of men," he said slowly, "ought never to be king of Moray."

"And so he is not," Macbeatha replied benignly. "He is only the *tanist,* and the tanist does not always become king. He needs the approval of men like yourself."

A smile spread across Fergus's face. "And we may choose someone else," he agreed, pulling a pitcher of ale closer to them and filling Macbeatha's horn. "Come, my foster brother, let us drink to men who are truly *rigdomnae*—the stuff of kings." Then he and Macbeatha drank and clasped hands, two men who have come to an agreement.

It was the day after the feast that Raghallach came down out of the hills.

He rode at the head of a hundred warriors, all mounted and decked in the glittering gold armbands and neck chains of noble families. A messenger came ahead to assure Fergus of their peaceful intent—although who would be foolish enough to attack that stronghold with only a hundred men, I don't know. Certainly not Raghallach, for he was no one's fool.

Siusan and I watched from behind the doorposts of a stable as Raghallach and his men clattered into the yard, horses puffing and blowing in the frosty air. The Highland chieftain wore a great cloak of otter pelts and a pair of *rivelin,* those boots made from the untanned hide of a cow's hind legs, worn with the hairy side out and the dew claws coming on either side of the heel. He was a great hulk of a man with a black curling beard shot through with silver white, and his graying hair twisted into a single braid at the side of his head.

Fergus met him with caution, for they were not the best of neighbors. I have never understood the Scots' penchant for thievery back and forth between their tribes, and Macbeatha could never explain it to me, except that it was expected. Raghallach came down out of the hills and stole Fergus's cattle, and Fergus rode up into the hills to steal them back, plus a few more. It was a point of honor to try to gain the advantage of the other fellow, and be a dozen or so head up on him, which was silly—you knew he was only going to come and steal them back, plus a few horses and sheep into the bargain. Several men were wounded or even killed each year, some babies died of starvation, and neither tribe got much richer. Why didn't they take ship, as the Norse did, and sail to some other coast to do their raiding, where the inhabitants couldn't come back after them?

Nevertheless, Fergus and Raghallach were old adversaries in this game of larceny, and it was highly unusual for one to ride into the stronghold of the other. "Welcome," Fergus greeted soberly as his rival's tribesmen glared belligerently around the oval enclosure of the fortress. "To what do I owe the honor of your visit?"

Raghallach dismounted and stood before Fergus, arms akimbo, his great cloak flung aside to show the glittering gold chains on a chest as broad as a bull's. "I understand there is a princess of the House of Moray here," he said bluntly. "I have come to see if she is as fair as the reports which come to me claim."

Siusan and I gasped and stared at each other. Was this man truly a suitor for Brenna's hand?

Siusan scurried off to bear the news to her mistress, but I headed for the hall to see what I could learn. Raghallach looked to be three times Brenna's age, and while that was not unusual—particularly in political marriages—it was not exactly the match a girl of sixteen dreamed about. I smiled to myself, thinking how furious she was going to be.

But I learned nothing that evening. With all the extra mouths to feed, we servants were very busy indeed. I assumed the task of serving ale, my favorite job, for it kept me amongst the men and near my lord. Yet nothing of importance transpired that evening, except that Brenna was the object of many long looks and no few compliments from Raghallach. But even after she and the other ladies retired for the evening, the conversation was one of harvests and Viking raids and the summer's campaigns. Brenna's name was not mentioned.

The next morning, however, when everyone had struggled awake and was setting about the day's activities, Raghallach clapped a huge paw on Macbeatha's shoulder and said, "Come take a walk with me, mac Findlaech. This is fine, warm weather you have here on the coast, and I would be outside these walls for a time."

Macbeatha nodded and shifted his cloak up over his shoulders, for only a Highlander would have thought the day warm.

It was late afternoon before we learned what had transpired. Macbeatha came to Brenna where she sat sewing in a cozy chamber with its own fire, in the company of several of Fergus's kinswomen. At a word and a smile from him they left, along with their maids; but Siusan and I sat fast where we were. He frowned at us momentarily, then shrugged. No doubt he anticipated one would have to be deaf not to hear the conversation which ensued.

"I have found a husband for you, sister," he began.

Brenna looked up sharply. "What, not that great oaf who rode down from the hills last night!"

"That great oaf is a very powerful man," Macbeatha said pointedly. "He controls the highlands from the Don to the Spey, and he can muster a goodly number of foot, as well as his cavalry. We need him."

"You need him!" she spat.

"And is this not your quarrel as well?" he asked in dangerous tones. "Or do you wish me to forgive our dear cousins for conspiring against our father, and forego my right to challenge them?"

"I hate Gillecomgain as much as you!" she hissed back. "Not only for what he did, but because he is a godless, black-hearted piece of filth who makes my skin crawl. But think what you ask of me, Macbeatha! You condemn me to a life of poverty and deprivation in those hills. Isolated, with no markets for two days' travel, and outlaws and knaves hiding in caves and hollow hills!"

"Nonsense," he replied mildly, with a lift of his eyebrows. "An outlaw couldn't support himself in that country: there's nothing to eat and no one worth robbing."

"You see what I mean!" she snapped. "You would take me to court in Scone, and then banish me forever to the desolate fastness of Raghallach's hills?"

A stick of pine snapped in the fire and ejected a glowing ember into the room. Macbeatha nudged it gently with the toe of his boot, scooting it back across the stone flooring into the hearth. "Actually, I would not take you to Scone at all."

Brenna's jaw dropped. "What?!"

"The trip to Scone was a lure. I've arranged to meet the new tanist of the Isles in Cirech, where he's visiting his sister. I meant to traipse you across the breadth of Moray, charming every chieftain and his kinsmen along our journey, then marry you to Bowen when we reached Inverbervie."

"Bowen?" Brenna repeated dumbly, for she had met her brother's friend and foster brother. "You would marry me to *Bowen?* That clumsy rail of a stick man with buck teeth and a nose an eagle could perch on—you would marry me to *that?"*

"If he'd have you," Macbeatha replied innocently. "After all, he's apt to be king of the Isles after his uncle. Atholl has offered him a marriage alliance already—Duncan's niece, I think—but he promised to wait till I brought you—"

"I will *never* marry Bowen!" Brenna raged. "I don't care if he stood to be High King! And I won't marry Raghallach, either—that aging, battle-scarred hulk! And I *will* go to Scone for Christmas!" She stamped her little slippered foot on the unforgiving stone.

Macbeatha only laughed. "Well, you're right about two things, my little princess," he agreed. "You won't marry Bowen, and you won't marry Raghallach. As to Scone for Christmas, that will depend on your new husband."

Her tirade fell off and she stared at her brother in utter confusion. "But if not Raghallach ..."

"Raghallach already has a wife who, by all accounts, is too ornery to die and too well-connected to divorce. You are to marry their son."

"Son?"

"He's off on a timbering expedition, doesn't know a thing about it yet. It seems you'll be as much a surprise to him as he is to you."

She continued to sit slack-jawed, at a loss for words, for several moments. Finally she stirred. "If he is off timbering," she ventured, "we could go on to Scone and return in the spring—"

"You go back with Raghallach," Macbeatha said firmly. "If you don't want a priest till spring, or even Misdummer, that's fine. I'll come to your wedding if you wait till Midsummer. But you go with him tomorrow. I've sent word to Donn as to your dowry, and he will see it is delivered when the weather permits. In the meantime, take all that wonderful baggage you packed, and Siusan. And Gilda, too, if you like. A princess of Moray should come with at least two maids."

Now Brenna's eyes narrowed and took on a wicked glint. "Give me Kelda," she said.

"Oh, no!" Macbeatha laughed. "She's far too entertaining to part with just now. Besides, you'd abuse her for no purpose. Kelda goes with me."

"You'd take your Viking whore to see Scone, and not me!" she shrieked.

His green eyes flashed, but his tone was still light. "Perhaps I'll take Siusan, too, and leave you only Gilda."

"You are a beast without parallel!"

"I love you, too," he replied easily, turning for the door. "Kelda, come pack my things. We leave in the morning, as well."

As I rose to follow him from the room, Brenna jumped to her feet. "Macbeatha!" she called in a most pitiful, pleading tone.

We both turned back, and I could see the tears she fought not to shed. But she lifted her little chin high. "Does he have a name, this son?" she asked tightly.

Even in defeat, she was proud. Oddly enough, in defeat, this pride was most becoming. I have known Brenna many years, and she is not a gracious winner—her eyes grow small and nasty, and her voice squeaks. But defeat brings out in her a nobility that makes people want to fall down and worship.

While Macbeatha might have been inured to her anger, he was not insensible to her fear. "Dufflach," he answered softly. "His name is Dufflach."

"And does he favor his father in appearance, or perhaps he is only *half* as broad as a ox?" she asked with an imperious toss of her head that could not disguise the tremor in her voice.

He shrugged. "You'll know soon enough."

I met Dufflach one summer, and as it turned out, Brenna had worried for nothing. He was handsome and well-formed, with good manners and eloquent speech, and witty into the bargain. Had he come himself to woo her, I think she might have fallen smitten at his feet. But at that moment she knew nothing of him except his name; and I, a Norse serving girl, pitied the princess of Moray who was, in this matter, as much a slave as I.

Sorry as I felt for her, though, it was Siusan I pitied most. By the next morning, Brenna had composed herself, reconciled to her fate, and she even managed to say a polite farewell to her brother. Then she mounted her horse looking regal and haughty, a princess through and through. But poor Siusan! As she took the reins of her sturdy pony, her eyes were red from weeping, and she looked timid as a mouse. She had left Inverness on a great adventure, thinking to follow her pampered mistress to the stronghold of the High King; now, instead, she was sent off to the Highlands in winter, parted forever from her father and mother and brothers with no chance for a final good-bye.

Her eyes, when they met mine, grew dark and angry, and I knew she wished I might be condemned to serve in her place while she went on to Scone with her lord. But that was not the tapestry the Fates had woven. I could only tell her I was sorry to part from her and hoped to see her again in the spring—and it was mostly true. She had been my nemesis, but also my teacher and my lodestone; I felt a little lost at the prospect of continuing the journey without Siusan.

I was truly sorry to learn she took a fever the following winter and died.

Chapter Fourteen

We stayed in Cirech two weeks, and I liked Bowen. He was as gangly and big-nosed as Brenna had painted him, but he had such a merry spirit, one easily forgave his appearance. With high-born ladies he was uncomfortable, and I don't believe he was the least bit disappointed to learn Macbeatha had given his sharp-tongued sister to someone else for wife. A match between them would have been harder on him than on her. In the company of men or of servants, though, he laughed and talked and made bawdy jokes. He could mimic animals and people with amazing accuracy, which was fine entertainment after a meal, and also a great asset in hunting and, they tell me, in warfare.

Best of all, he kept a bed wench named Myrna who was a warm-hearted soul, and part Norse herself. She made me feel more comfortable than I had since I left Thorfinn's hall. We passed many pleasant evenings seated at the hearth with Myrna on Bowen's lap and me on Macbeatha's, laughing and cuddling and drinking ale. It was a warm respite before the coldness of Scone.

Scone itself is not very impressive for a royal city. There is a great tower that looms up above the trees, but other than that, you can hardly see any of it until you get quite close. Its daub and wattle huts and timber houses are set far back from the banks of the River Tay, which tend to be marshy and unfit to build upon. But there is a river crossing just there, the first one beyond the reach of tidal flooding, and the fortress at Scone was no doubt built to guard it. Fife lay just to the south, beyond the town of Perth, while Scone itself belongs to Atholl; no doubt in former times the tribes of Fife were as prone to raiding Atholl as Moray still is, and one imagines there were many battles between them at the ford by Scone.

Near the tower, and enclosed by the fortress walls, lies the *bruigheann,* the royal residence of the High King. It is a great stone building, three stories high, although the bottom story is short, windowless, and used only for storing goods. A wooden staircase leads from the ground to the second floor, constructed so that anyone coming up it has his sword arm against the wall, while anyone coming down has his free. The great hall is on this second level, where all the windows are tall and narrow; a spear or an arrow can pass out, but an attacker would be hard pressed to get one in.

Also within the walls of the fortress are a number of other large houses, homes of the close kin and loyal clients of the High King. There are stables and storehouses, as well, and barracks and pens. Trees have been cleared for a goodly distance from the fortress wall, so no enemy can approach undetected. In this open space between the stronghold and the woods are pasture lands, and as we approached that winter day, a good many fine red cattle could be seen cropping at the dry, yellow grass.

We had to pass through most of the town before we reached the fortress gate. Macbeatha rode at the head of his nine guardsmen, the only warriors still with us. All the others had been sent back after Brenna's departure, which was just as well. Being few in number, Macbeatha and his guard could ride into Scone in full battle regalia without being viewed as a threat. Each wore a padded leather jerkin under a multi-colored cloak trimmed with fur, and each carried a lance. It was a fine, cold day, and the metal trappings of their bridles and saddles glinted with the same brightness as the sparkling river water. Owen carried Macbeatha's banner, that double circle in blue on a field of red.

As I rode behind on the long track toward the royal residence, I couldn't help feeling proud of my lord and his splendid warriors. Even my pony felt the excitement in the air; he picked up his head and pranced on his broad hooves, aware of every eye turned in our direction. When we neared the gate, Macbeatha undid the pin that fastened his cloak at his right shoulder, letting it fall away to reveal the golden hilt of his sword, his golden armband, and all his other finery.

Shouts of welcome rang out, and grooms came running to take our horses. Macbeatha dismounted with flair, throwing one leg over his horse's head and sliding deftly to the ground. A man of about fifty, who I imagined must be the High King, strode out of the hall and down the wooden stairs to greet Macbeatha with a warm embrace. But my lord called him Donall and asked, "How is my grandfather?"

Then another man appeared in the door of the hall, a tall, broad-shouldered man in rich woolen clothes, with a hawkish face that was instantly familiar—I had seen that stamp on my lord Thorfinn's visage. His gray hair had grown thin, for he was well past seventy even then, and his pointed beard was a snowy white. But there was an iron spark in his blue eyes that betrayed no weakness. "Macbeatha!" he called out strongly. "I began to despair that we should see you at all this winter."

"And could I stay away two years in a row?" my lord asked, taking the stairs two at a bound to embrace the High King. "Who would keep my wits sharp, if I did not hone them against your own?"

Then they laughed, and Malcolm mac Kenneth, High King of Scots, clapped an arm around my lord's shoulders and ushered him into the house.

Whether he was actually Malcolm's grandson or not, Macbeatha was treated as such in Scone. We carried his trunks to a chamber on the third floor, a place reserved for the family of the High King. The room was hung with rich tapestries, and the rushes on the floor were laid over with a thick carpet. Beeswax candles burned in a sconce—an unbelievable luxury to me!--and as we set the trunks down, a servant came in with fresh coals for the brazier, to take the chill off the room.

Malcolm's wife was long dead, his daughters grown and gone, so his household was run by an arrogant woman named Shayla. Shayla had accompanied Malcolm's late wife across the sea from Ireland and was, I believe, some sort of kinswoman to the dead queen. It was she who showed us the room, then chased all the porters back down into the yard to look after their own pack animals. She tried to chase me out, too.

"You, girl, leave that," she ordered imperiously. "The kitchen is across the way, near the wall. Go make yourself useful to the cook."

I turned and looked at her blankly. *"Ja?"* I asked innocently.

"I said go make yourself useful!" she repeated. "Macbeatha may bring his wenches with him if he likes, but they'll do more than warm his bed. Now, off to the kitchen with you."

But I only blinked and smiled sheepishly. "Macbeatha," I said, pointing at the trunks.

"Blessed Mary, help me," Shayla sighed, and tried to explain herself with gestures. "Leave the trunks," she said slowly, closing the lid of one and laying her arms across it. "I can't stay and watch you, and I won't leave a heathen alone in the family's chambers. You—" She took me by the arm and tugged me toward the door. "—go downstairs—"

But I was not so small that she could tug me anywhere I did not wish to go. "Macbeatha," I repeated firmly, and showed her the leather collar I wore with my lord's stamp on it. "Macbeatha," I said once again, pointing to the trunks.

"Macbeatha—downstairs," she pronounced loudly, as though raising her voice would help me to understand her better. She pointed toward the hall below. "You go downstairs to Macbeatha, all right? Unpack later, when someone can keep an eye on you."

I pretended to finally understand. "Macbeatha," I parroted, pointing in the same direction; then, just to show that I was cleverer than she, I used my fingers to pantomime walking. "Kelda ... Macbeatha."

"Yes, yes, Kelda go to Macbeatha," she said in exasperation, taking up my finger-walking gesture. "Please."

"Please!" I echoed in a parody of stupid delight. Then off I bounced, leaving Shayla to pick up her skirts and waddle after me, afraid I might wander somewhere I shouldn't if left unsupervised.

Though the hall was crowded with men and women milling about, my lord spotted me the moment I entered and beckoned to me. "You do have an eye for the wenches," the High King observed as I drew near. "This one's a gift from Thorfinn, you say?"

"A genuine Norse beauty," Macbeatha replied. "Look at that shining hair!"

Shayla came panting up behind. "Hrmph," she sniffed. "Probably rinses it in sheep urine. Filthy Viking wretch."

King Malcolm's eye grew dark. "Shayla."

"You know they are, lord," she persisted, undaunted by the king's expression. "And stupid into the bargain. This one can't speak a word, except his name." She nodded disapprovingly toward Macbeatha.

Not a flicker of surprise passed my lord's face. Still, I jumped in quickly. "Would you like some ale, lord?" I asked in Norn. "This ill-mannered woman has been so busy making sure I didn't steal anything upstairs, it appears she has forgotten to offer you refreshment. But I see a cask and some drinking horns in the corner; perhaps the High King would allow me to serve you both."

During this King Malcolm suddenly stifled a laugh, and Macbeatha's lips twitched in sympathy. "With your permission, sir?" Macbeatha asked the king.

"What? What did she say?" Shayla asked, flushed with ire.

"She wants to serve us ale," Malcolm informed his matron. "And she thinks you have bad manners for not offering to do so yourself."

Shayla turned beet red, and I skipped quickly away to get the ale.

"It's all good and well for you to bring your wench with you," Shayla scolded Macbeatha, "but you ought to teach her respect. At the very least, you ought to teach her to speak properly, not prattle on in that foreign nonsense."

He shrugged indifferently. "She does everything I tell her to," he replied. "And since she is *my* slave, I don't see why anyone else should mind."

I flounced my way back, letting my backside sway fetchingly as I approached my lord and his liege, and noting the way the aging king's eyes took in the display. Then I smiled my most charming smile as I filled two drinking horns from the pitcher I carried.

"Thank you, Kelda," Malcolm said in rudimentary Norn. "You are a good girl, and very pretty."

By his speech, I discerned that he understood more Norn than he spoke. But I blushed and bobbed my head, then asked, "May I serve my lord's guardsmen, or will your woman do that?" I shot a derisive glance over my shoulder at Shayla.

Again Malcolm stifled a laugh. "Serve the men, girl," he said.

"What? What did she say?" Shayla demanded, eyes flashing.

"She wants to serve ale to my men," Macbeatha translated.

"Good. Let her be useful for something," Shayla grumbled, turning for the door.

"Oh, she's useful for a great many things," Macbeatha assured her blithely.

Shayla spared him a dark glare, then lumbered away. "When she has finished, send her to the kitchen," she called over her shoulder. "It will be time for supper soon, and she can help serve." Then she tugged a heavy wooden door open and was gone.

When I had served my lord's warriors, I returned to squat by Macbeatha's feet, and he patted my head affectionately. "She has that Norse insolence," he told the king, "but she really is devoted to me."

"And does she speak no Gaelic at all?" Malcolm asked, holding out his drinking horn for me to refill. I believe he was more interested in the gap I allowed in the neckline of my shift, than in having his cup refilled.

Macbeatha shrugged. "A few words." He named some which would never be used in the presence of ladies, but were a source of great pleasure to the two of us. All the warriors within hearing laughed, including the High King. "There isn't much else she needs to know," my lord concluded.

They went on then to discuss other things, and I sat there looking happy and complacent, refilling their horns when it was required, until Macbeatha told me, in Norn, "Go help with the serving." Then he leaned forward and whispered in my ear, "See what you can learn by speaking no Gaelic."

Dinner was always a grand affair at the High King's court. Besides the warriors and the noble guests who seemed always to be present, there were the requisite pipers—nine of them, blowing odd harmonies on their wooden whistles—and drummers and other musicians and entertainers. I was not allowed to serve at the head table, though—Shayla had that honor—nor would she let me serve the ale afterwards, but had two other young girls doing that. All I could do was sit with the other servants in a corner of the hall far from the warriors, making a supper of the leftovers from the feast.

Macbeatha handled my absence with no apparent inconvenience, pinching whichever girl came to fill his cup and letting his eyes wander over the rest of them. It put me in a bad mood, and I was pouting when at last he sent me upstairs to ready his chamber. Shayla followed me, and would not leave until Macbeatha arrived.

"Why this storm on your brow?" he asked with a chuckle when she had gone.

"I hate that stupid woman!" I snapped. "She thinks I'm a thief, or a murderess, or something. She wouldn't let me draw a pitcher to serve you ale—did she think I was going to drink it myself?"

"Shayla sees it as her sworn duty to find fault with all servants," he replied. "And most freemen. Tell me, what prompted you to pretend you don't speak our language?"

"She tried to shoo me off to the kitchen, and I didn't want to go. I just knew she would try bossing me the whole time we're here, so I pretended I didn't understand her."

"What a clever girl you are!" he laughed, and kissed me on the mouth. "Now tell me, what have you learned tonight by being stupid?"

"That you are the first of many guests expected for the Christmas feasting," I told him. "And that the king still talks of wenches, but does little with them. And that some high-born person named Cronin is coming, who behaves as if he were High King instead of Malcolm."

"Crinan," Macbeatha corrected. "Crinan, Abbot of Dunkeld, the king's son-in-law. Yes, that's an apt description."

"Except he defers to the king in the king's presence," I added. "Is he Duncan's father?"

"Yes," my lord confirmed, pleased that I was beginning to piece things together. "What else was said about Crinan?"

"That he'd be a better king than Duncan." I cocked my head. "Why is Duncan to become king after Malcolm?"

At that, Macbeatha frowned and began to draw off his outer clothes. "It's all part of Malcolm's scheme," he explained, tossing his cloak to me to fold. "Malcolm had no sons, you see; but for conquering the world, he found daughters much more useful. He married his eldest, Bethoc, to Crinan of Atholl, the most powerful man in the southern regions of Alba. Then he married the youngest, Plantula, to Sigurd of Orkney, binding him in a marriage alliance. But to gain the high kingship, he needed my father, and he was one daughter short. So when his kinsman died and left a young daughter, Malcolm took the girl in and raised her as his own. That was my mother, Doada."

"Then you are not truly a grandson to the king!"

A sly smile slid across his face. "Am I not? Rumor has it that Malcolm was more than passing fond of his kinsman's wife, and there was a reason beyond friendship that prompted him to take my mother in."

Blast the man! He would always hold that Malcolm was his grandfather, but I *still* don't believe it. I don't think he did, either, but it served his purpose to pretend he did.

"Anyway, he offered my father Doada in exchange for his support, and my father accepted for two reasons: One, his first wife was childless, and he was ready to divorce her and seek another who could bear him children. Second, if he married a princess of the royal house, he himself would have a claim to the high kingship."

I digested this carefully. "But she wasn't really a princess," I pointed out.

His smile turned sardonic. "A fact Malcolm neglected to tell my father."

"Oh! Your father must have been furious when he found out!" I exclaimed. "And yet, everyone says how much he loved your mother. How did that come to be?"

He dropped onto the bed and stuck his long legs out for me to remove his boots. "Because my mother, knowing he had been deceived, stole away from her women and sought out my father before the wedding. She revealed Malcolm's deception to him and gave him the opportunity to renege on the marriage contract."

"But he didn't."

"It would have meant war between Moray and Alba. And besides, he was quite taken with Mother's honesty, and her courage. So he went through with the marriage—and it's a good thing for him that he did."

"Because he came to love your mother so much?" I asked, my heart touched by this romantic story.

"No, because he got *me!* And the world would be a much poorer place, had I not been born!" Then he tumbled me onto the bed with him and commenced to prove just how much poorer *my* world would be, at any rate, if Findlaech had declined to marry Doada.

In the quiet aftermath, as we drifted toward sleep, I lay with my head pillowed on his chest and asked, "Do you hate the High King for tricking your father?"

"No!" Macbeatha laughed, making my head bounce on his chest, and I heard his voice one way with my open ear and another with the one pressed to his flesh. "I rather like my grandfather, actually. He's devilishly clever, and he's always been very good to me. But," he added, stroking my hair, "I don't trust him for a minute. He will use anyone or anything to get what he wants; and unfortunately, what he wants is not necessarily what I want."

"And that is?"

"Well, he does want me to be Mormaer in Moray, and there we are agreed," he conceded. "But he wants Duncan to be king after him, and Thorfinn and me to be Duncan's vassals; and there we are very much opposed."

"But he doesn't know that," I guessed.

"And never will. So keep it in your pretty little head, and go on pretending you don't speak our language, and we shall see how best to thwart my cunning grandfather and his arrogant offspring."

And so I became Macbeatha's special ears in the residence of the High King. It proved useful on more than one occasion. Most especially, there was a time when it saved the life of a woman and her child; and without them, who knows if he would ever have become High King? But I get ahead of myself. Before all that, there was Duncan.

Chapter Fifteen

My duties were light that winter: some sewing, some serving, and a lot of listening. My supposed ignorance of Gaelic allowed me to ignore those tasks I disliked, and volunteer to do only what pleased me. Shayla persisted in her rudeness to me, so I developed what I thought of as my "stupid cow" look—because that's what she called me when I stared at her so uncomprehendingly.

It was lonely, though, having no one to talk to, for only King Malcolm, Macbeatha, and a few other warriors spoke any Norn at all, and they spent little time speaking to serving girls. So sometimes, when I felt restless and when I had nothing very important to do, I would go out to the tower and climb up to its top. From there I could look out over the trees and see up and down the Strathmore, which is what they call the broad valley of the River Tay. It refreshed my spirits to be able to see the land as a raven sees it.

The tower was not roofed, but it had a walkway just below the top where watchmen could pace. There were always two on duty, one looking north and one looking south, but I stayed out of their way and they paid me no attention. Sometimes Macbeatha would join me up there—he liked to sit on the tower's rim with his feet dangling over the edge, a habit that made me shiver. One fine, crisp morning, as the hall filled with guests arriving for the Christmas feasting, he was perched there as we discussed—in Norn, of course—the Lady Airgiod's penchant for pickled onions, and the resultant sour odor. Then abruptly, his back stiffened and his hands snapped out to catch the wall on either side.

My heart thudding, I clutched at him instinctively, fearful lest he lose his balance on that precarious height. "What?" I demanded.

"It's him," he hissed, eyes riveted on the south road. "Duncan."

Following his gaze, I saw an entourage approaching the ford, red and gold banners flying in the breeze. With twenty mounted warriors, a company of foot, two horsecarts and several servants, the king of Strathclyde and Cumbria was making his stately way toward Scone. Then, even as I watched, the hard, flinty look in my lord's eye melted away and he chuckled. "I might have known he'd find me in this tower! Well, my sweet, you've met a high king—time for you to meet a low one." He swung one leg to the inside of the tower, straddling the wall, the better to watch the royal embassy approach.

"Why do you dislike him so much?" I asked.

"Dislike him? What makes you think I dislike him?"

"Oh, come, lord!" I poked him in the chest with a mittened finger. "You're always calling him names and making jokes at his expense. In Thorfinn's hall, you called him a royal ass. Why is that?"

"I call him a royal ass," Macbeatha explained patiently, "because that's what he *is*. Only you mustn't repeat that. As far as everyone else here is concerned, he is my beloved kinsman and foster brother, and all that passed between us as boys has been forgotten."

"And what was that?"

"Well, let's see." He paused to consider, which made me think he was about to tell some outlandish lie. Or some outlandish truth. "We were fostered together here in Scone, and I had plenty of run-ins with him them. But my first recollection of Duncan is from the winter when I was five and he was nine, and my mother had brought me to Scone while she visited her sisters, the king's daughters. Thorfinn was just a year old, and quite the darling of all the ladies—although why, I don't know, because he was as ugly a baby as I've ever seen. But since *I* was no longer the darling, and feeling a little put out about it, I went off exploring on my own."

The cavalcade was splashing through the water now, for the Tay never freezes so close to the sea. Macbeatha's eyes never left the progress of those red and gold banners, or the warrior riding proudly on a jet black horse. "As I approached this tower, I could see Duncan and another boy standing at the top, throwing stones at the hounds and pigs in the yard below. Now, I hadn't much sympathy for the pigs, but that's no way to treat a good hound. So I shouted up at them to stop."

"I take it they didn't."

"No, they challenged me to come up and make them. Well, my grandmother Gia had taught me a prince must never refuse a challenge, or his people will not respect him. So up the stairs I marched to tell these southern boys that a good warrior never mistreats his hounds." The cavalcade had cleared the ford now and was making its way toward the village along a wide track well trodden by the High King's guests.

"What happened?" I prompted, having a clear vision of a five-year-old, red-haired dynamo marching up the tower stairs to confront two belligerent boys twice his age.

"I never made it to the top—the two of them waylaid me inside, just under the watchmen's perch where they couldn't be seen. Then they picked me up, each one took an ankle, and they dangled me out over the central shaft of the tower and threatened to drop me."

I gasped involuntarily, for I knew how long that unrestricted drop was. "What did you do?"

"Do?" Macbeatha laughed. "Why, I told them very calmly that if they intended to drop me, they'd better have a very good story to tell my grandfather the High King. And if they didn't intend to drop me, they might as well put me back on my feet before I used magic to change myself into a bat."

"A *bat?*" I cried.

"Well, I was hanging upside down at the time—it was the first thing that came to mind. And I was counting on them having heard my grandmother was a *petta* woman, and believing I had some magical spells at my command."

"But weren't you *terrified?*" I demanded incredulously.

Again he laughed. "Of course, I was! But there was something inside me that knew what Duncan wanted, more than to hurt me, was to scare me." He turned briefly to look me full in the face. "And I wasn't going to give him the satisfaction."

There in the cold green fire of his eyes, I saw that this, at least, was true. Whatever enemies he faced, Macbeatha would never give them the satisfaction of dictating his response.

"Well, it must have worked," I observed, "since you are here today with your skull intact."

He shrugged, his eyes going back to Duncan's train as it snaked its way now among the outlying huts of Scone. "They didn't drop me, no. They did carry me down the stairs and rub my face in a manure pile, then throw me into a horse trough. But I suffered no permanent damage, although my mother fretted for days that I would begin to wheeze from the dousing. I got even with them, though."

"Oh?" I was curious what a boy of five could do to get even with two nine-year-old bullies.

"I muttered some nonsensical incantations and told them I'd cast a spell so the whites of their eyes would turn green. They spent the next two weeks peering at each other's eyes to make sure they weren't changing color."

I laughed, until I remembered how convincing Macbeatha could be when he chose. "Did they really think your grandmother was a *petta* woman?" I asked.

"Well, she was," he said simply.

My eyes must have grown as wide as an owl's.

Glancing up, he laughed at my expression. "I don't mean she was a sorceress," he explained. "Just that she was *Picti*. One of the Old Race that lived in Moray before we Scots came. Half of Moray has Pictish blood in them, you know—they just aren't likely to admit it. No one wants to be associated with the powerless, and the Picti lost their power generations ago."

It took me several moments to digest this information. I was raised to be terrified of the *petta* woman who would put a spell on me if I was caught outside after dark, or wandered off into the hills alone. Now to learn that my lord's grandmother was this thing I'd been taught to fear-- "Well, that explains it," I said finally.

"Explains what?" He was still watching the red and gold banners make their way through the village.

"How you have such power over women. Clearly you put a spell on them so they cannot resist you."

He tugged me into his arms then. "Well, the Lady Morag seems to be resisting just fine," he complained playfully. The lady in question was the young wife of an aging nobleman from Fortriu, and my lord had taken a fancy to her—probably because she was in the radiant bloom of her first pregnancy. Nothing attracted him more than a woman in her fourth or fifth month, when the sickness has abated and that glow takes hold, and the full rush of her maternity is almost tangible.

"Oh, that can be fixed," I promised, for although the lady was formal and distant to his face, I had seen the lingering looks that followed him when his back was turned. We laid plans together, then, for how and where he might seduce her. I never minded his dalliances, for it pleased me to see him well pleased. And when the lady was conquered—or not, if he deemed it too dangerous politically—I was always there to snuggle against him and play games and keep him satisfied, as he kept me.

But this day, not even such talk could keep him long distracted from the approaching retinue. When they had wound their way through the zigzag streets and neared the gate to the fortress, he started down from the tower, and I followed him. As we stood in the yard waiting, he said to me in a low voice, "Quick, Kelda, run up to my room and fetch my sword and shield."

I balked, the hair on my neck rising in apprehension. But, "Go, quickly," he urged. "It will be all right, don't worry." So I ran into the hall to do as he bade, then brought his arms back to where he waited in the yard. He had only tied his swordbelt in place when the vanguard entered through the gate. My lord sauntered up to meet them with his rich blue and green cloak, fastened at the right shoulder, thrown back to leave his sword clearly visible. "Who goes there?" he demanded in a rough voice.

The guardsmen were quite undaunted. "Duncan mac Crinan, king of Strathclyde and Cumbria, and tanist to Malcolm mac Kenneth, King of Scots."

"Duncan!" barked Macbeatha. "Duncan dares show his face here? Duncan mac Crinan, come down from your horse and face me! There is the matter of a woman I would discuss with you."

At that point Duncan pushed his way past his men, horse dancing at the tone of malice in Macbeatha's voice. I saw that he was a tall man, well-made, with muddy brown hair and his grandfather's fierce blue eyes. A thick gold torc gleamed at his throat, and the gilt on his horse's trappings was profuse. It was not hard to believe he was a king. "Macbeatha!" he shouted. "What in God's name are you talking about?"

"As if you didn't know," my lord persisted in low and challenging tones. "Come down from that horse and face me like a man!"

A look of puzzlement crossed Duncan's face—it was clear he had no idea what his foster kinsman was talking about. But he swung his leg over his horse's head and slid to the ground, tossing the reins to a groom. "A woman, you say? What woman is that?"

Macbeatha's answer was to draw his sword. "Blackguard!" he thundered. "Knave!"

Duncan fell back a step, and a shadow of fear ran through his eyes. "Macbeatha! What—"

"Draw your sword!"

Not knowing what else to do, but clearly not understanding the quarrel, Duncan unhooked the small, colorful shield from his saddle and drew his sword. His guardsmen shifted uncomfortably in their saddles; servants stopped their work in the yard to stare; men drifted out from the hall to stand along the wooden stairs. With a feral cry, Macbeatha raised his sword and struck at the Cumbrian king.

Duncan caught the blow on his shield, but gave ground before its fury. "Macbeatha, have you gone mad?" he demanded.

"Women always drive me mad!" Again my lord struck; again Duncan gave ground.

"Will you at least tell me what woman we're talking about?" Duncan pleaded.

"Why, my brother's wife, of course!" Macbeatha declared. "Did you think her honor would go unavenged?" He struck again.

"Your broth—Do you mean your cousin's wife?" the poor, bewildered Duncan asked as he pushed his horse aside to give himself more room to retreat.

"What? Have you besmirched her, too?" Macbeatha demanded. "If you have, your life is twice forfeit!"

"Christ, no! I don't even know your cousin's wife!" Duncan protested. "I don't—" Suddenly he backed off two paces and dropped the point of his sword. "Macbeatha, you don't *have* a brother," he accused.

At that my lord dissolved into laughter. "Oh, the look on your face, man!" he snickered. "But never, never drop your point like that. I could have killed you twice over if I wanted."

"Damn you, Macbeatha, I never know when you're joking," Duncan grumbled. "What a madman you are! You're lucky I didn't take your head off."

It didn't look to me as though there had been any danger of that.

"You are too serious, cousin!" my lord laughed. "Come, put up your sword and embrace me!"

Duncan made to do so but stopped suddenly. "Damn you, Moray, you know it's not right to put up our swords until there's blood on them!" he swore. "There are some things not to be joked with!"

But Macbeatha shrugged. "Blood is cheap," he said easily, and without thought or flinching he cut the heel of his own palm along the edge of his sword. "There. Now there's blood on mine." He wiped his weapon clean with a handful of dried grass and sheathed it.

Duncan only stood looking stupidly at his blade, then glanced uncomfortably at his own palm.

"Oh, here!" Macbeatha exclaimed deprecatingly, as though he spoke to a child. He smeared blood from his hand along the flat of Duncan's sword. "Remember this, it's the only time you can say you've had my blood on your sword. Now, put it up and embrace me as a kinsman should!"

With a dark look and muttered curses, Duncan cleaned his sword and sheathed it, but then he did open his arms and embrace Macbeatha, albeit somewhat grudgingly.

"Are you still enjoying the wench I left you?" Macbeatha asked as the two of them started for the hall, arms draped across each other's shoulders.

"For as long as I can," Duncan grumbled. "I'm to be married next year, you know."

"What have marriage and wenches to do with each other?" Macbeatha beckoned to me. "Here, let me show you my new wench. Isn't she marvelous? Young and ripe, and best of all, playful. Aren't you, Kelda?" As I drew near he caught me to him and nuzzled my neck. "But you can't have this one, I own her right and proper. A gift from your true cousin."

"What, that Norse troll?" Duncan sneered, pulling away from Macbeatha.

"Oho, you should see the troll now! Taller than either of us, shoulders like an ox, and he swings a sword with enough force to hew a tree at one stroke!"

Duncan told Macbeatha what he was full of, and the two of them passed into the hall with me trailing closely behind. I intended to clean and bind that cut on my lord's hand lest it become poisoned.

Duncan spent the next several hours bragging about his exploits in Cumbria, riding roughshod over the natives. Unlike Atholl and Fortriu and Moray, which are Great Tribes of Alba, Strathclyde and Cumbria had been a separate kingdom—or was it two kingdoms? I was never quite sure. At any rate, the Scots had conquered the Brythons there long before and put an overlord in charge of the kingdom, with a large warband to enforce his rule. So unlike the mormaers of the seven Great Tribes, the king of Strathclyde and Cumbria was appointed by the High King, not elected by his peers. For generations, it had been the habit of Scottish high kings to appoint their tanists, the men they wished to succeed them, to this vassal kingship. It was a sort of training ground for high kings. So when, in his eighteenth year, Duncan mac Crinan was named king of Strathclyde and Cumbria, he became the heir to his grandfather's kingdom, as well.

Now I must say, Duncan was a much pleasanter person than Gillecomgain. He didn't sneer at anyone, and no look of his ever made my flesh crawl. He was short-tempered and easily offended, but that is often true of powerful men. They are accustomed to having their way, and to being treated with respect, so they quickly grow irritated if they are not instantly obeyed. My lord himself could be like that from time to time once he came into office, though he rarely indulged in displays of temper.

But there was something just—well, oafish about Duncan. He had no sense of humor—or at least, a very poor one. What there was consisted of deriding other people. He was not a bad-looking man—his features were just sharp enough to make him appear formidable, without being severe—but he had no idea how to charm ladies. This, of course, did not stop him from trying. To put a capstone on it, he never knew when he had transgressed good manners with them.

Furthermore, for one who had been educated at the royal court in Scone, he wasn't quite as accomplished as the other nobles I've met. Every high-born Scot plays an instrument of some sort—

Macbeatha played the *feadan*, a wooden pipe, and his fingers were quite nimble at it. Duncan tried to play the *fhidheall*, but either he could not tune the strings properly, or he didn't place his fingers in quite the right places, so his notes sounded a bit sour. He did, however, have a fine, deep voice that everyone loved to hear. During the long winter evenings, as people gathered in the hall to tell tales and sing songs of glory and battle, Duncan would saw at his *fhidheall* for one or two songs, then just hold it the rest of the evening—much to everyone's relief—while he sang lustily.

He spoke only a phrase or two of Norn, which was unfortunate because his prospective bride was a Northumbrian Dane, and the language they speak is very close to mine. He claimed to speak Latin, but I never heard a word of it—not that I would have known if he spoke it well or badly. Macbeatha spoke Latin, though, as well as Norn and Scots, and he acquired Anglish and Greek in later years. It was not hard for him to make Duncan look pale, and he took every opportunity to do so.

This did not please the High King. He came to Macbeatha's chamber the night of Duncan's arrival, where I was re-dressing the cut on his hand before bed. After inquiring pleasantly if he might come in, and greeting me briefly in Norn, he strolled over to the tapestry covering the window and inspected its warp. Then, "It was poor form, drawing your sword on Duncan today," he informed Macbeatha in Gaelic.

My lord sat on the bed as I rubbed grease into his cut and laid a piece of wool over it. "It was a jest," he said mildly. "You know I can't resist having fun with Duncan. No harm intended."

"You mean having fun at his expense," Malcolm corrected. "And what you intended was to show yourself a superior swordsman."

My lord shrugged and did not try to lie his way out of it. "He shouldn't have given ground like that."

"You placed him at a disadvantage," Malcolm admonished, turning toward us. "He could not understand why his cousin and friend should be attacking him. He did the right thing, giving ground until he understood what was going on. You are the one who looked bad, Macbeatha, not he. A warrior doesn't draw his sword as a jest."

My lord said nothing, but I could see the color rising in his cheeks.

"He is your foster brother, and one day he will be your High King. It is your duty to show him to best advantage, not worst. No one gains by divisiveness. Our strength lies in uniting against the Angles, the Danes, the Norse. That is why I have worked so hard to bind my kingdom together. This quarrel between Moray and Atholl must stop."

"Tell Duncan," said Macbeatha softly.

Malcolm's brow furrowed and his eyes narrowed. "I am telling you," he said sharply, "because you understand it better than he. That makes it your responsibility. Oh, yes," he went on with a dismissive wave of his hand, "I know you're cleverer and more astute, you don't need to prove that to me. But that is precisely why I need you in Moray, why Duncan needs you there. I know your cousin styles himself king and is quick to point out that it was not he who pledged me support at my inauguration. Alba is still two nations, north and south. But it cannot go on so, or we shall all perish; and you are the one who can stop it."

He took a step closer to Macbeatha and glared down at him. "This is a marriage I propose in which you are the bride and Moray is the dowry. The bride cannot make her husband look bad without causing harm to the family; you cannot show up Duncan before the court without causing harm to Alba. Do you understand me?"

I had finished bandaging my lord's hand, but I was afraid to move, so I folded and refolded the extra scraps of wool and wiped grease from my hands onto my leather boots. Macbeatha lifted cool green eyes to the king. "Moray is not mine to give," he said quietly.

Now a chuckle rumbled up from the king's chest and a smile tugged at the corner of his lips. "Oh, it will be, lad," he assured his former fosterling. "One day it will be. I have never doubted it." Then with the look of a father well pleased, the King of Scots turned from his man and left the room.

The silence hung heavily for a long moment. Finally, "Oh, there shall be a marriage, all right," Macbeatha whispered softly. "But it is I who shall be the husband, and all of Alba shall be my bride."

Chapter Sixteen

He was not much fun that night, nor the next morning; but all trace of ill humor vanished when he left his chamber and went out among his fellow Scots. To see him at table with Duncan, one would have thought they were bosom companions, not contenders for the same prize. Had I not witnessed the king's rebuke on the previous night, I would never have known Macbeatha suffered from anything other than infectious high spirits. Yet suffer he did, and I felt every pang in my own heart.

After breakfast he and his men rode out to hunt, for a dusting of snow had fallen up in the Sidlaw Hills overnight, and they were sure to find fresh tracks. Having noticed a tear in the sleeve of his favorite tunic, the one with gold threads in the embroidery, I fetched the garment and my sewing basket, then wandered in search of a room where some ladies and their maids might be sewing.

Instead, I stumbled across a well-lit chamber where the High King sat at a table with vellum and quill, scratching away. He looked up as my shadow passed the door, and smiled with interest. "Good morning, Kelda," he greeted in Norn.

I stopped and smiled my most charming smile, bowing low enough to display that which he desired to see. He sighed a little and went back to his vellum; I turned to continue down the corridor.

Then, on an impulse, I turned back. "Is there anything my lord needs?" I asked. "Ale, or another lamp, or perhaps a baked apple?" I had noticed he didn't take much food in the hall, and almost no meat, but he had a fondness for apples baked with cinnamon.

He started to decline—I could see the refusal on his lips and in his eyes—but then he changed his mind. "Perhaps you could, ah ..." His eyes wandered briefly about the room. "Stir the fire," he suggested, for this room had its own fireplace, vented through a chimney against the wall.

Grinning happily, I put my sewing down on a stool near the hearth, pushed my shawl back out of the way, and knelt by the fire. I could feel his eyes on me as I leaned over to poke at the embers with a stick. Taking my time, I broke up the remnants of a pine log and placed another from the wood basket on its coals. It was dry and well seasoned; in no time the flames were licking around its girth like hungry little kittens searching for a nipple to suck.

When I had stalled as long as I could, I turned back to the king just in time to see Duncan appear in the doorway. "Good morning, Grandfather," he greeted in that smooth, rich voice of his. Then he saw me. "What's this, Macbeatha's wench?"

Malcolm grunted. "Luscious, isn't she?" he asked in Gaelic.

I turned and bowed to Duncan, endeavoring to prove the king's point.

"What are you doing with her?" Duncan asked stupidly. At least, *I* thought it was stupid.

The king sighed again. "The only thing an old man like me can do: watching."

Duncan snorted. "I can think of a thing or two *I'd* like to do with her."

"I'm sure you can. But you'd better keep such thoughts in your head. You can ill afford to offend your cousin."

"He's not my cousin," Duncan protested. "And he gave me his last wench."

Malcolm shrugged. "If a man offers you his horse, you can take it. But it doesn't do to ask for it when you have a stable full of your own. And you must call him cousin, as he calls you, anywhere except before a judge. Under the law he is not your cousin, but in courtesy, he is. Remember that."

Duncan's response was a rude noise.

I had picked up my sewing again, but I was reluctant to leave. "Is there anything else my lord needs?" I inquired politely. "Macbeatha is gone hunting, and I would be happy to serve you. Oh!" I exclaimed, catching up a lap blanket he had laid aside when his grandson came in. "This begins to unravel, may I not mend it for you?"

"Yes, thank you," the king agreed. I brought a stool near to where he sat, plopped myself down upon it, and began to mend the fraying blanket.

"What did she say?" Duncan wanted to know.

"She just wants to be useful," the king explained. "I think she gets quite lonely, not speaking our language."

"Let her learn it." Duncan dropped himself into a chair across from his grandfather. "He spoils her, you know. Spoils all his women. They lose their respect for you if you spoil them."

"A silken cord may look gentle, but it is surprisingly strong. Macbeatha is no fool, make no mistake of that."

I looked up with a smile at the mention of my lord's name. "Yes, you heard that, didn't you?" Malcolm cooed in Gaelic. "We're talking about your master. Smile at her, Duncan."

Duncan flashed me a smile, then turned back to his grandfather. I returned to my sewing.

"He's soft, though," Duncan insisted, careful not to use a name.

Malcolm shifted his gaze from me to Duncan and shook his head. "If you believe that, then *you're* the fool."

Duncan's face darkened. "He rode with me, last winter—we made some raids along the Mercian border before the snow set in. I've seen him fight: there are better swords, and stronger arms."

The king's eyes narrowed. "Yours?"

Duncan thrust out his chin. "I could take him."

"Not if you drop your point, like you did yesterday."

Duncan threw his hands in the air, springing from his chair and stalking toward the fire in disgust. "He surprised me. I didn't know what he was on about. Then when he started talking about his brother's wife, I knew he was joking. Either that, or mad."

"Let me tell you something," the High King advised. "Moray will always surprise you. And Moray *is* mad, will always be mad. They're a different breed, up there in the north. Pictish blood mixed in. Findlaech fought with me against Kenneth mac Dubh, turned the tide for me with his support—I would not be High King today without him. But I never trusted him. There was a madness in those dark eyes of his, an accusation that it ought to have been *him* taking the rod of office. The son is like that. Mark my words, and keep Macbeatha close to you—but never let him slip behind your back."

A blank look came over Duncan's face. "He's of the House of Loarn," he said stupidly. "So was his father. There have been no high kings of that House for a dozen generations. A man can't be High King unless he's within four degrees of kinship to another high king."

A sinister smile twisted Malcolm's lips. "Then pray, be sure you do not give your sister or niece in marriage to Macbeatha," he warned. "For then he will have what I was careful not to give his father—and you, my lad, will have a war on your hands."

Duncan remained unconvinced. "The Great Tribes will never accept a Morayman as High King," he scoffed. "It's as you say—they're all crazy, and everyone knows it. But if you think Macbeatha is a threat ..." He grinned wickedly. "Why not remove him?"

At that Malcolm scowled. "You need him. You'll never hold Moray without him."

"So I don't hold Moray," Duncan sneered. "Who needs it?"

"You need it!" Malcolm barked as he jumped up from his chair and slapped his hand on the table. "You need Moray, and you need Caithness, or you'll have the Norwegian king camped on your northern border! You need Lothian because it's rich, and it keeps the Northumbrian earls humbled in the east! And you need Strathclyde to keep the Norse in Dublin from marching across your southern border to fight the Danes in York! Alba is first among the nations of these isles, because I have kept her together and kept her strong, and you will do the same—"

Just then he broke off in a fit of coughing. I sprang to my feet, snatched up a pitcher and cup from a nearby table, and brought him a measure of whatever was in the pitcher. It did not smell like ale.

"Are you all right, Grandfather?" Duncan asked worriedly.

"Yes, yes," Malcolm sputtered between sips of the liquid. "Dry throat, that's all. This does the trick." Then he turned to me. "Thank you, Kelda, you may go now."

He had spoken in Gaelic. I gave him my stupid cow look.

Did something sparkle in his eye? I was never sure. "Go, please," he repeated in Norn.

So I gathered up my sewing, albeit reluctantly, and started for the door. Just before I left, Malcolm said softly to Duncan, "It's a good thing Macbeatha doesn't know there's a granddaughter of

Kenneth mac Dubh in fosterage near Pitlochry. He'd probably swim the Firth of Tay to arrange a marriage into that family."

I had much to tell my lord when he returned from hunting that afternoon. But I said nothing about the woman in Pitlochry.

Chapter Seventeen

After that I was very careful around the High King. I continued to show him more courtesy than I would another, and more flesh, for what harm was there in giving him a moment's pleasure? But I never went out of my way to be near him in my lord's absence, lest he think I was eavesdropping; and more than once he tried to trip me up by telling a tale or asking a question in Gaelic, to see if I would respond. Fortunately, my stupid cow look did not fail me, and I survived the winter in my ruse.

With Duncan, I had no need to be cautious. There was no guile in him, and no artifice. He said what he thought, and did as he said, and cared little for the consequences. Every servant in the hall knew he dreaded being saddled with a Northumbrian wife, that he thought his cousin Thorfinn was a traitor to the Scots, and that he dared the king of Dublin to try marching an army across Cumbria. Harassing Mercians along his southern border was not satisfying to Duncan; he wanted a good *war,* with some real plunder, and a host of enemies on whom to test his sword.

The men often practiced with their arms during the short winter days, if weather permitted. They hacked and hewed at posts, threw their spears at stacks of straw, and taught each other tricks with knives. Sometimes they would try each other at swords, and the surgeon stitched one or two wounds on account of it, but mostly they preened and boasted and rode their horses full tilt at wooden targets. Duncan excelled in these games, for he was both strong and quick, and because of it the men thought he must be as great a warrior as he boasted to be. I was never sure if Macbeatha *could* not beat him, or *would* not, after the High King's admonition.

On days when the weather was poor, they sat in the hall and polished their weapons, or mended their tack, or played at board games like *brandub* or my lord's favorite, chess. Macbeatha let Duncan win at these games, or so his men said. To me, the odd wooden playing pieces leapfrogged here and there in random patterns—I knew nothing of their strategy. Such bouts always ended with Duncan in high spirits, and Macbeatha poorer by a quarter penny or two of Anglish silver.

"You gamble too much," I scolded him once, after he had lost what looked like seven or eight silver mites.

Macbeatha only laughed. "That's not gambling. That's buying goodwill with bits of metal. A bargain."

Still, I was glad when Twelfth Night arrived, for it meant Duncan and his retinue would take their leave the following day. This dicey game of protocol my lord played with him made me nervous. But as they pondered over the chess board that day, a guest arrived with information that would change Macbeatha's life.

"Brother Maelgirc!" my lord shouted in glee when he saw the man, rushing to throw arms around him with more genuine affection than I had seen since he parted from Thorfinn. "Now, here's a Twelfth Night treat. How are you? What brings you here?"

Maelgirc was a short but burly monk, who looked almost fierce in spite of his ear-to-ear tonsure. He caught my lord in a grip that practically lifted him off the ground—no easy task. "When I heard two of my former pupils were at court, I decided it was worth the trip. How are you, lad?"

Macbeatha responded in what I suppose was Latin, and they chattered back and forth in that for a moment. Then the visitor turned to Duncan, who had casually swapped two of Macbeatha's playing pieces when the latter got up from his seat to greet the monk. "And Duncan! You've filled out a bit since your grandfather made you king of Cumbria. How long has it been? Ten years now?"

"Even so," Duncan replied, coming to greet the cleric with considerably less enthusiasm than Macbeatha. "But you know, it still seems odd to come in from the hunt here and not find you waiting with a lesson board, spewing Latin grammar at me."

Brother Maelgirc laughed heartily.

I don't care much for churchmen, I never have—they make me uncomfortable. I kept my distance, for I had learned what a dim view of slavery and of bed wenches they held—particularly monks. A priest might have a wife or a mistress—there was Duncan's father Crinan, for instance, who was the Abbot of Dunkeld, as well as the king's son-in-law—but monks are generally celibate. This makes them intolerant of women in general, and bed wenches in particular. So I was understandably apprehensive after supper when Brother Maelgirc called me over. "Are you a Christian, girl?" he demanded with a scowl on his face.

I answered with my stupid cow look.

"Christian," he repeated, holding up the cross he wore around his neck. "You—Christian?" He jabbed a broad, stubby finger at me.

In response I drew the amulet from my breast and showed it in its cross position.

"Thorfinn had her baptized," my lord assured him.

"How does she go to confession, if she speaks no Gaelic?" the monk persisted.

Macbeatha's jaw fell. "Well ... she ... I ..."

"There is a priest at Abernethy who is fluent in the Viking tongue," Maelgirc declared. "I advise you to take her to him, Macbeatha. If you're going to keep that slave collar on her, you take responsibility for the well-being of her soul, as well as her body."

Macbeatha bowed his head meekly and agreed.

I should have known he would never be so meek unless it served a purpose. Of course, it was all a ruse. The monk had set up a meeting for my lord at Abernethy, one he did not want the High King to know about. My need for a priest was only an excuse for Macbeatha to ride there without arousing suspicion.

All this he explained to me that night, for he was more excited than I had ever seen him. "She's there, and Maelgirc has convinced her to speak to me!" he exclaimed in covered tones, eyes bright with victory.

"Who?" I asked, wondering which woman he intended to seduce now, and how he managed to have a churchman helping him.

"A very great lady," he replied. "One I need to cultivate. One who can give me the *Lia Fail.*"

"A stone?" I asked in confusion. "What kind of stone is it?"

He laughed and hugged me, more from his excitement than his amusement at my mistake. "The *Lia Fáil,* the Stone of Destiny," he explained. "Upon this stone have the high kings of Alba been invested since the days of Saint Colm. It is the stone Kenneth mac Alpin took from my ancestors of the House of Loarn; it is the stone I intend to take back." His green eyes burned with the fire of passions most men never imagine.

"And how can she give it to you?" I wondered.

"She is Boite, the daughter of Kenneth mac Dubh, who was High King before Malcolm."

I was still having trouble sorting all this out. "Is she King Malcolm's aunt, then?"

"No!" he laughed. "No, she is of a different house entirely—but a royal house. There are two lines of mac Alpin, you see, and they are supposed to alternate in the high kingship: the king from one selects his tanist from the other, and vice versa. But when Malcolm fought Kenneth mac Dubh, all the princes of that house died in battle with him. It opened the door for Malcolm to choose a tanist from his own house."

"Duncan," I deduced. "Is this Boite unmarried?" I was beginning to see where his hopes lay, for among the Scots, a man who marries into royalty can then become king.

"Boite's husband lost an arm in battle. It makes him ineligible to be High King," Macbeatha explained. "But he was quite able to father children."

The hair began to prickle on the back of my neck. "So there is a granddaughter of Kenneth mac Dubh." Perhaps it hadn't been a lie Malcolm had fed me, when he said such a person was near Pitlochry.

"A granddaughter, and a grandson, both hidden away in fosterage somewhere. Boite doesn't trust my grandfather, can you imagine that? She's afraid some strange accident might befall her children." My lord giggled foolishly. "And I don't think she's come of age yet—the granddaughter, I mean—but I am a patient man. Only I did not think Boite would speak with me, since my father sided with Malcolm against hers."

Then he hugged me again, unable to contain his joy at this opportunity which had fallen in his lap. "But Maelgirc has arranged it—I was always his favorite pupil, whereas he despaired of Duncan.

He would a thousand times rather see me as High King than that bully. And if I can only speak to Boite, I am sure I can convince her, as well."

I truly did not understand the intricacies of the situation, but Macbeatha was so happy at the prospect of this interview, I couldn't help being caught up in his excitement. It also made him exceedingly amorous, which was enough for me. We celebrated far into the long winter night, nestled on the finest of feather beds, our laughter muffled by thick woolen covers; and how many slave girls have ever known such luxury?

Unfortunately, the promised interview did not go quite as Macbeatha had planned.

Boite was waiting in the sacristy of the little church at Abernethy in Fife, where Macbeatha and Owen had taken me according to the subterfuge arranged by Maelgirc. The priest there conducted my lord and me inside, while Owen watched at the door. The lady stood with her face to the wall, where a beautiful cross was carved into the stone. She was as tall as me, with graying brown hair caught back in a ribbon, and her cloak was black. More than that I could not tell.

The priest left discreetly, and I lingered near the door to the chapel. Macbeatha unpinned his cloak, leaving it draped over his left shoulder only, the better to display his fine clothes and impressive physique. Then, adopting a humble manner, he began, "Lady, I am honored."

From Boite came a voice strong but weary. "Sir, you are ambitious," she said bluntly. "Let us be plain with one another."

His countenance fell and his humble attitude dropped away like a silk cloth from a lady's shoulders. But Boite turned around slowly, and by the time she faced him, all trace of surprise and disappointment was gone from her mien. He held his face in a neutral expression, though his eyes were soft as he met her gaze expectantly.

For her part, the lady seemed to take him in at a glance. "Hrrm," she grunted, unimpressed. "So you are Moray."

"I am Macbeatha mac Findlaech, of the House of Moray," he elaborated, with just a hint of pride.

"Mac Findlaech, yes," she mused darkly. "Now, there was another one who thought to rise above himself through marriage."

At that, my lord bristled a bit, and the accustomed fire came into his eyes. "The House of Moray is the royal family of the House of Loarn," he informed her. "Many a high king of Dalriada was born of it. Our place is high enough, we do not need to rise from it."

Boite grunted again and turned to pace the length of the small room. I could see now she was an angular woman with cheeks and neck beginning to grow slack with age. She bore herself with great dignity, moving with a deliberate step. Stopping near to me, she turned her dark eyes upon me. I bowed quickly. "Who is this?" she demanded.

"My serving girl," Macbeatha replied. "She speaks no Gaelic; your words will not travel beyond these walls."

The look she turned on him was hard and cold. "Do you imagine I will say something here that I do not wish widely known? No, no, Moray," she said with a mirthless chuckle, "I am giving away no secrets here. If there is a need for confidence, it is yours, not mine." Then she waited, holding him in a mocking gaze.

"The matter I wish to discuss, the High King would not approve," Macbeatha told her carefully.

Again that cold laugh. "So you don't think your grandfather wants you within reach of the *Lia Faíl,* do you? I don't blame him. If I were High King, I wouldn't want such a bright and ambitious man anywhere near my seat of power."

A wry smile cracked Macbeatha's face. "I see Maelgirc has given a good accounting of me," he observed.

The mocking look disappeared, and Boite turned away again. "Brother Maelgirc has done a great service to my family," she replied. "Because he asked it, I have agreed to speak with you. So here I am, young Moray. Speak."

Again her forthright manner stole the moment from Macbeatha. He shifted his stance, raised his chin, and took it back. "As you have already guessed, I seek a marriage alliance with your House. Quite specifically, I wish to marry your daughter, when she comes of age."

"And not a moment too soon," said Boite dryly, "since that will be at the Festival of Bride. Well, one can see easily why such an alliance would be to your advantage, Moray. But what of me? How would it benefit the House of mac Dubh?"

"Protection for your children. You fear what may befall them at Malcolm's hand. I will take your daughter deep into Moray. Alban kings have died upon our doorstep, but not one has ever taken from Moray what Moray did not willingly release. And when your son completes his fosterage, I will welcome him into my hall and my warband. I will see that he gets the experience a warrior needs so that one day, together, we shall bring down the House of Malcolm."

For a long moment they held each other's eyes, two strong wills testing one another. Finally, "And are you king in Moray?" Boite asked sarcastically.

"Not yet."

"Tanist, perhaps?"

He did not flinch, though the barb pricked him, I know. "My cousin Gillecomgain is a warrior known more for his courage than for his cunning," he responded. "It is likely he will die gloriously—but rather young."

"And should I not fear the same fate for you?"

"I am more cunning than my cousin. Lady, let us speak plainly once more. If I take your daughter to wife, I will do whatever is necessary to protect her, and to assure that your progeny take their rightful place as rulers in Alba."

"Ah, but there is not a prince in the kingdom who will not swear the same thing to me," Boite said stubbornly. "And despite your brave words, you are Malcolm's fosterling, and his man, even if there be no blood of his in your veins. That, Moray, is a stain not easily removed."

With that, the lady turned on her heel and stalked from the room.

He brooded for days. Not when anyone else was watching, mind you, but alone with me, his eye was dark and his mind churned visibly. What thoughts they were, I cannot tell you, for he never confided them to me. I only coaxed him to seek another expression for his passions, that he might know the comfort of a loving heart and a good night's sleep.

As winter began to fade, he sought passage on a ship to take us home, but the weather was not promising. He and Owen argued whether they should go by land, perhaps up the Strathmore, or cross the hills through Atholl and go up the Great Glen. "Let's wait and see what word Dougal brings from the harbor today," Macbeatha said at last. "If the shipmaster is not willing to set out by week's end—"

As if summoned by his name, Dougal, youngest of Macbeatha's guardsmen, burst into the hall. He was pale and breathless, as though he had ridden back upriver from the seaport at breakneck speed. "Lord!" he cried. Every face in the hall turned toward him, but he did not notice as he strode to where Macbeatha stood. "A ship just came from Aberdeen, with a message from Fergus mac Mhuire. Your cousin Maelcolm is dead."

The color drained from Macbeatha's face. "Dead?"

"His horse stumbled on the ice and threw him—broke his neck."

For a long moment there was stunned silence throughout the hall. Then everyone sprang into motion. "Owen!" Macbeatha barked. "Saddle my horse, and yours. We leave now. Weylin! Get the rest of my retinue packed and follow as soon as you can—no later than Saturday. Kelda, go to the kitchen and get us some travel rations."

"In Norn, lord," I prompted him softly, and he barked the command again in the language I was known to understand. I scurried off to do his bidding.

When I returned, he and Owen were in the yard, already mounted on their horses, and King Malcolm was with them. "You'll need more men if you're going to challenge Gillecomgain," the High King was saying. "I have a company of foot here that does nothing more useful than see my meat doesn't grow rancid. Let me send them after you—"

"Don't bother," Macbeatha said sharply, catching up the bag of bread, cheese, and dried fish I handed him. "With all due respect, a company of Athollmen will do me more harm than good. No one in the north will elect a prince who's backed by southern troops. No, if I'm going to take Moray, I must do it on my own. Fergus will back me, and Raghallach, and a dozen others. If I can get just one or two more of the powerful ones to pledge themselves to me, it can be done." Then he called down to Weylin, "Take care as you come, but come quickly. I will need every friend I have in these next weeks."

"God speed you, Macbeatha," Malcolm said fervently. "We shall pray for your success."

My lord nodded in acknowledgment, then kicked his horse into motion and thundered out of the yard.

Chapter Eighteen

How many times have I heard the story? Even Owen loved to tell it, and he is a man of few words. The two of them pounded north along roads wet with melting snow, trading horses as they wore out the sturdy beasts who bore them. They followed the Glen Esk, reaching Aboyne in only two days, and stopped at the monastery there for a few hours' sleep. Then it was off before the late winter sun had risen, crossing the River Dee near Creag Faire. There they met some of Raghallach's men, who guided them through the Grampian Mountains by ways known only to the Highlanders. A night's rest in a hut on the Spey, another hard day of riding, and they arrived at last in darkness at Macbeatha's house in Inverness.

No soul stirred at their coming, for spirits and faeries go about after dark, and it wouldn't do to open the door and let one in. But at Macbeatha's hail, a quick and alert voice responded, "Who goes there?"

"Macbeatha and Owen, half dead and starving, and two horses in worse condition," Macbeatha shouted back.

Before he finished speaking the door was flung open and people poured into the yard. They had been expecting him. Grooms led the tired horses away, and Donn ushered them to the fire where Aithne was dishing up trenchers of savory venison stew. Dhui came running with large tankards full of cool ale. "God, I have dreamed of this since we took horse this morning," Macbeatha groaned as he threw himself into his chair and reached for the steaming platter

Aithne offered him. Then, before the first mouthful was swallowed, "Donn, tell us how things stand."

The old steward drew up his chair and filled them in. A week past, the mormaer and his brother had been out hunting with a party of men. They were chasing down a stag when Maelcolm's horse lost its footing on icy ground and pitched the ruler against a tree. His neck had snapped, killing him instantly. Donn had sent three riders immediately, each by a different route, but the ship from Fergus had been faster. "He was bidden come for the election of a new mormaer," Macbeatha explained. "He tarries on his way, to give me what time he can."

"Ah." Donn's brow furrowed. "Gillecomgain prowls the fortress, nervous as a cat, waiting for the chieftains to assemble. He knows you are the only one who can reasonably contest him, and he does not relish your challenge. He has made gifts to every abbey in Moray, asking the monks to pray for his dead brother, but he's really trying to buy the Church's support."

"Who do we have?"

Donn ticked off the names, counting up to eight on his fingers, and ending with, "Bridei mac Fergus will support us in a vote, but not a fight. The same is true of Uchtan the White."

"Cowards," muttered Owen.

"Cautious," said Donn. "They had a bad winter, with many dead. They need their men to plant the crops. If Maelcolm had had the good grace to die after planting, we'd have stood a better chance."

"Do you think it will come to a fight?" Macbeatha asked his elder kinsman.

Donn rubbed at his scarred eyesocket. "If you do not challenge Gillecomgain to fight, your claim will not be taken seriously by many of the chieftains. They don't know you. You have no major battles to your credit. It will take a fight to prove to them that you are the better man."

Macbeatha chewed his food thoughtfully, green eyes whirling as they looked inward. Then, "He can muster more men than I, can't he?"

"At this moment, yes."

"Then I will have to challenge him to single combat."

Silence hung like smoke around the fire. At last Donn said, "He is fearsome."

An uncomfortable feeling crept over the room as Macbeatha and Donn gazed at each other. "Ah," Macbeatha said softly. Then, "Does he expect me to fight?"

"He fears it."

"That was not the question." Macbeatha still held his kinsman's eye in a steady gaze. "Does Gillecomgain—do the chieftains—*expect* me to fight."

"If you do not fight," Donn told him, "it will be said you are afraid."

Finally Macbeatha's gaze shifted to the fire. "Ah."

Those who knew him, of course, knew if Macbeatha chose not to fight, it would not be for lack of courage. It would be because he had thought things through carefully and decided not fighting was a better choice. But as Donn had pointed out, far too many in Moray did not know him.

"There is another possibility," Donn said carefully.

My lord looked at him, and they seemed to read each other's thoughts. "The tanistry," Macbeatha said softly.

"You are only twenty-three, Macbeatha. Time is your friend, and Gillecomgain's enemy. He is rash; he is hasty; he will make mistakes. Your chance will come 'round again."

Macbeatha poked at his food, staring gloomily at the contents of his trencher. "He'll want to wage war on Thorfinn," he said unhappily.

Old Donn cocked an eyebrow. "He'll want to wage war on everyone. It will be your job to direct him."

"His desire for Caithness is too deep. He won't listen to me there."

"Then you may have to make difficult choices."

Setting aside the half-eaten stew, Macbeatha rose and paced to the wall and back. "I cannot refuse to go to war, or I will lose all credibility with the tribes."

"I know you will go to war," Donn agreed. "It's just a matter of where, and against whom."

Again the two of them looked at each other.

"The tanist becomes the most dangerous man in the Great Tribe," Donn continued. "It is not uncommon for a king to send his tanist to another district, to police and protect it, off where he cannot raise a challenge to a beleaguered king. You have many friends in the east, do you not?"

"After my last journey there, I certainly do. And there is always danger of Vikings raiding along the eastern seaboard."

"So you see," Donn concluded, "the tanistry could be good for you. A chance to fight Vikings as head of your own warband, a chance to establish your reputation as a leader of warriors. It is always better to be voted in unanimously, than to force the vote by eliminating your rivals. With a few more campaigns under your belt, and some firm ties with the Great Tribes of Cirech and Ce, you will be in a much better position to hold Moray."

"And the more firmly I hold Moray, the stronger my position in Alba as a whole."

"Exactly."

Macbeatha paced to the wall and back again, then flung himself into his chair. There he sat, hands clasped, staring into the fire for several moments. "But how do I get the tanistry, and keep the good opinion of those who would have me fight for the mormaership?"

To that question, even Donn had no answer.

"Let us see who will come to my banner," my lord said finally. "Let us give every appearance of preparing to challenge Gillecomgain, but deny vociferously that I intend to do so. When men come and ask, we will say these preparations are just for the coming season, not to fight Gillecomgain. But we make our preparations open. Say one thing with our words, another with our deeds. Let everyone, including Gillecomgain, see just how strong Macbeatha mac Findlaech is. And then, I shall go to my cousin and see what terms I can dictate."

It was a glorious time, with the air freshening toward spring and a growing number of warriors camping around Macbeatha's hall in Inverness. By the time I arrived from the south, he hosted no less than a dozen chieftains in his house, with others quartered on his kinsmen in and around Inverness. It was a rousing sight, that many swaggering heads of tribes in their holiday best, with gold, silver and bronze flashing in the sun, wearing colorful cloaks over long tunics, rustling like the willow branches by the stream. Men polished their swords and honed their axes, and Owen grumbled it was a waste not to make war on Gillecomgain with this fine host.

But no one spoke openly of war. We waited patiently for the Abbot of Deer, who had to journey slowly by horsecart because of an affliction of his foot. Once he arrived, the meetings would begin at which the leaders of Moray would discuss Gillecomgain's claim to the mormaership, his ability to rule, and the possible fate of Moray under his leadership.

Yet on the lips of every craftsman and herdsman and shopkeeper was the question: will Macbeatha challenge his cousin? Will the ruddy warrior challenge the dark?

Macbeatha walked the streets of Inverness with a smile on his face, greeting high and low alike, flirting with the women and laughing heartily with the men. He called at the fortress to offer his sympathy to Maelcolm's wife and her two children. He attended mass, and made a donation for a special requiem for the fallen mormaer. And any time he was asked—and he was asked often—whether he would challenge Gillecomgain, he would smile and say, "Now is not the time to speak of that. Let us grieve for our dead while we may, and worry about the living in their due time."

Days passed, with Gillecomgain growing more and more nervous as the numbers around Macbeatha swelled. Finally, when the Abbot of Deer's entourage was spotted coming up the road from Forres, Macbeatha called his staunchest supporters to him and set out for the fortress. They took their time, parading through the streets of Inverness on horseback. Fergus mac Mhuire rode at Macbeatha's right hand and Owen at his left, bearing Macbeatha's standard. Other chieftains and guardsmen followed. I had hurried ahead on foot and was already in the courtyard when they arrived and dismounted. In the commotion of servants and dogs and children, I slipped inside.

When my lord entered the timber hall through its mighty stone façade, he found Gillecomgain waiting for them with thirty or forty armed men at his back. "Greetings, cousin," Macbeatha saluted him pleasantly.

Gillecomgain touched the hilt of his sword, as though assuring himself it was still there. "And to you, cousin."

"How is your sister-in-law?" It was a solicitous inquiry after the widow.

A twitch plucked at Gillecomgain's lip. "She has gone to her mother's house in Urquhart, with her children." He did not say, "For protection," but that was the reason. She was afraid Macbeatha might destroy the progeny of the former ruler. That was uncharitable of her: Macbeatha would visit no harm on widows and children, for to do so was dishonorable. Whatever tricks he employed to get what he wanted, he was a man of honor.

"What a pity she is gone," my lord lamented, "for the children should be here to see their uncle invested as mormaer."

Surprise jolted Gillecomgain. His eyes widened and his mouth parted, and for a moment he could not speak. Then his eyes narrowed again in suspicion. "What do you mean to say, Macbeatha?"

"Why, only that these good men with me have come to pledge you their support. Surely the vote cannot go against you now."

Distrust made the scarred side of his face squint more than the other. "You would throw your support to me? Why? To what purpose?"

Macbeatha smiled broadly. "Come, come, cousin. Surely you can see that, divided, we bring only bloodshed and ruin to Moray. But *united*— Ah, cousin, how powerful we shall be!"

"United?" Gillecomgain looked quizzical first; then fear ran through his eyes as he comprehended. "You would be my tanist."

My lord gave a courteous nod. "Our House should stand as one, as it did when your father was tanist to mine." He gestured toward the chieftains flanking him. "These good men have urged it."

For a moment Gillecomgain looked like a cornered fox; then his eyes narrowed again as he considered it. Behind him, his own men shifted uncomfortably. At last he smiled. "The two of us, leading Moray into battle," he said, savoring the thought. "A stronger Moray than has been seen since our two fathers fought side by side against the Viking chief."

It seemed an odd thing to recall, since Sigurd had defeated the brothers, and Macbeatha allowed no time for anyone to dwell on it. "No one will dare threaten Moray, when we two are of one mind," he assured his cousin, advancing to meet him.

"We will make Moray whole again," Gillecomgain agreed, reaching out to clasp his cousin's arm in token of their solidarity. "It will be as it was in a bygone age, when the other Great Tribes trembled before Moray's power." A maniacal gleam spread from his eyes to the whole of his twisted face. "We shall take back what was once ours," he vowed in a ringing voice. "We will be kings once more!"

Suddenly light filled the room as a cloud scuttled away from the sun and golden rays flooded the hall. "Let the nations beware!" Macbeatha declared, his voice swelling as the light glinted off his reddish hair. "This day marks the beginning of a new age in Moray.

The grandsons of Ruadhri will raise the House of Loarn to new glory!"

Every tribesman in the hall roared his approbation, and those who had shields on their backs unslung them and pounded on them with their sword hilts. The great and joyous clamor echoed off the walls like waves breaking against a cliff.

The moment was so stirring, I almost believed it myself.

Macbeatha won great favor among the tribes for joining forces with Gillecomgain, and those who had mistrusted him before gained new respect for Findlaech's son. It was true he had been fostered in the south, but he was a Morayman in his heart. With Gillecomgain's boldness and Macbeatha's good sense, they felt, Moray could not only protect itself, but even grow rich at the cost of her enemies and her neighbors.

After that, little time was lost in approving Gillecomgain's claim. His investiture as Mormaer was set for the day before the Festival of Bride, or the Feast of St. Brigid, as the priests called it. This year, the celebration on the first day of February would symbolize a new beginning for Moray, as well as a new cycle of planting and harvest, birth and death. Everyone was in high spirits, full of hope for a bright future.

Then Crinan of Atholl rode into Inverness.

Chapter Nineteen

Crinan, you may recall, was the Mormaer of Atholl and Malcolm's son-in-law. But he was also the abbot of Dunkeld, and he came to Inverness in his abbot's robes, rather than warrior's garb, accompanied only by monks from his abbey in Dunkeld. That should have been a relief, as it signalled his peaceful intentions; however, why he should come at all was a mystery to us. The ancient feud between Moray and Atholl made it suspicious, and the fact that he came the day before Gillecomgain was to be inaugurated made the hair on everyone's neck rise.

There was a community of monks at Inverness who celebrated the various holy offices at the town's cathedral, and to them did their Dunkeld brethren go for hospitality. But Crinan presented himself at the fortress, and asked hospitality of Gillecomgain there. It was fitting, to be sure, for one mormaer to expect hospitality of another; it was also a compact of peaceful intentions, for guest and host were bound by ancient custom not to raise arms against one another.

Still, no one could understand why Crinan had come.

Macbeatha called on him as soon as he heard, taking Owen with him. That was Owen's idea, not Macbeatha's. "If you're to be in a room with both Gillecomgain and Atholl, you'll not go without a man to guard your back," he growled. Macbeatha rolled his eyes and threw up his hands, but he allowed Owen to come.

As soon as they had gone out of the yard, I went after them, for with Brenna gone, who would gainsay me? As an excuse, I asked Aithne if I might take a wheel of cheese to the fortress, to add to their feast, and she said yes. So I went first to the kitchen with

Macbeatha's gift, and from there it was no problem to slip into the hall. I wanted to see this man who had the whole town on edge.

Crinan was a fearsome looking man for a churchman. His frontal tonsure only emphasized the squareness of his head, and the lack of a beard left his hard jaw in plain view. What hair he had was thick, dark and curling, though heavily salted with white. Piercing blue eyes glared out from a strong face with regular features, heavy eyebrows, and the lines of fifty-some years. But beyond his appearance, it was the way he moved that made Crinan look so fearsome. Even in his plain brown churchman's *tunica*, Crinan walked like a warrior.

Macbeatha crossed the hall and greeted the older man warmly, as was his habit with those he distrusted. "I had hoped to see you at Christmas," he said. "I would not have guessed we would meet here in Inverness!"

"I imagine not," Crinan replied with a smile that was none too warm. "God makes a mockery of human plans, doesn't he? Come, sit by the fire with your cousin and me." He drew Macbeatha to the hearth where Gillecomgain sat glowering openly. "I have not been to Inverness since you were a babe, and much has changed. This hall was your father's then, and your mother its most gracious mistress." The abbot looked around him with a hint of distaste. "Much has changed, indeed."

Gillecomgain put on a fair feast for such short notice, though it was clear he'd have preferred a different guest. Still, the ritual formalities were observed, with Crinan offering a gift of bread, and the meal progressed. Drinking horns were lifted to the dead mormaer, to the newly elected one, to the prospective tanist, and to the honored guest. Then Crinan offered an accolade to the High King, and Gillecomgain balked; but at a subtle prodding from Macbeatha, he drank. That done, Crinan lifted his horn once more. "To my nephew Thorfinn mac Sigurd," he proposed, "our neighbor and fellow mormaer in Caithness."

Gillecomgain slammed his horn down and turned blazing eyes on Crinan. Macbeatha put a hand on his cousin's shoulder and said smoothly, "Let us drink rather to *all* duly elected mormaers," he suggested, "and have done with it, or we shall not finish these courtesies before I have to excuse myself to answer a call of nature."

Crinan chuckled, though I think it was less at the jest than at Macbeatha's adroit handling of the situation. "To all mormaers, then," he agreed, leaving out the reference to election, since Thorfinn had been appointed by his grandfather, and not elected at all.

He did not let the subject drop, though. Later in the evening he asked Macbeatha about his visit to Thorfinn the previous spring, and how my old master fared. Macbeatha answered pleasantly, but very carefully, and Gillecomgain grew more and more surly. Crinan pretended not to notice, and kept right on. "They say he swore allegiance to Olaf of Norway," he said conversationally. "Is that true?"

Macbeatha laughed. "Thorfinn's allegiance is to Thorfinn," he replied. "He'll placate Olaf until he's gotten all the Orkneys, and probably the Shetlands, too. Then I'd like to see Olaf control him."

"If he grows that strong," Crinan remarked, "I'd like to see *someone* control him."

At that point Gillecomgain pushed to his feet. *"If* he grows so strong!" he snarled. "There are those who would pull the wolf's teeth while he's still a pup. Then what difference does it make who his master is?" With that, he stalked away from the table.

"Your cousin seems a bit testy," Crinan observed casually. "Perhaps it's the thought of all that responsibility he'll be taking on tomorrow."

"More likely something has soured his stomach," Macbeatha replied. "It only takes a particle of something noxious to burn one's insides. Isn't that true?"

Crinan regarded him suspiciously, not sure if he had been insulted. "No doubt he'll feel better in the morning," he said after a moment.

"As for myself, I fancy the atmosphere has grown somewhat foul in here. I could do with a breath of fresh air. Perhaps you would join me?" He smiled at Crinan, but his eyes glittered coldly.

Crinan's glittered right back. "I would be delighted."

Seeing them make for the door, I slipped out just ahead of them and busied myself at a water barrel by the wall. As the two of them passed, Macbeatha saw me and scowled, but he did not bid me leave. So I took my time doing nothing and listened carefully.

They stopped near the wide opening that served as gate in the fortress wall. Timbers were stacked nearby, for Gillecomgain had been ready to stop it up if Crinan came with warriors, rather than monks. The abbot fixed my lord with a cold eye. "I rather expected to find *you* taking up the rod of office tomorrow," he said. "Or at least fighting for it!"

My lord's voice was as frosty as the night air. "I choose not to weaken Moray with internal conflict just now."

"Your grandfather will be disappointed that you surrendered without a fight."

"I surrendered nothing!" he snapped. "The tanistry suits me fine for the present. But you—what are you up to, goading Gillecomgain about Caithness? What do you think will be accomplished by a war between him and Thorfinn?"

"War?" Crinan protested with mock sincerity. "Why, I want no war between them. Thorfinn is my nephew, and lawful ruler in Caithness, I don't want him unseated. And I may not like Gillecomgain, but he serves as a useful buffer between Atholl and the Vikings. I don't want to see either defeat the other."

"No, but you'd like to see them both weaker, wouldn't you?" Macbeatha retorted. "Less trouble for you, if Gillecomgain takes his army north instead of south. Less chance of raiding in your western lands if Thorfinn is busy fighting off an attack from Moray!"

Crinan's chuckle was cold in the darkness. "I am a shepherd, Macbeatha. A good shepherd looks after his flock."

"He does not send the wolves of war on his neighbor's flock!"

At that Crinan drew back. "Gillecomgain is the wolf," he said harshly. "It is his nature to destroy. The only question is, who will be his prey?" Again came the cold chuckle. "Like you, Macbeatha, I do what I can to direct him." Then Crinan turned and strode back toward the hall.

The investiture proceeded smoothly, with mass and communion and the reading of psalms as everyone walked in procession to a hill outside the city. They put much store in hills, the Scots do. Once there, the leading chieftains gathered round Gillecomgain as the Bishop of Inverness handed him the rod of office, and the people raised an acclamation. Then a yearling bull was killed—for the feast, everyone said, but its blood was spilt upon the ground very like a sacrifice. Gillecomgain ate of the raw liver—for good luck, they told me, and not to consume the fertility of the bull for himself and for Moray. That was pagan thinking and, as Aithne took pains to remind me, they were all Christians.

Crinan stood on the sidelines throughout, smiling to himself, even as the *seanchaidh* recited the generations of Gillecomgain's family back to the kings of Dalriada and beyond, to Gaidheal Glas, son of Scota, daughter of the Pharaoh Chenthres. Then, as the old bard retired, the Abbot of Dunkeld stepped forward. "Gillecomgain mac Maelbrighde, Mormaer of Moray," he intoned—and it was the first time that day anyone had used the term *mormaer,* or high steward, rather than king— "I bring to you the blessings of your high king, Malcolm mac Kenneth, and his urgent desire that, as his faithful steward, you be strong and just and live in peace with your neighbors. Let me take to him your assurance that you will strive to do as he asks, and pray God's help to strengthen you in that resolve."

Jaws dropped. Apparently it was unheard of for high kings to meddle in the investiture of their mormaers, and certainly not to extract a promise like that! Macbeatha was clearly furious; but it was Gillecomgain, of course, who erupted.

"You go back to Malcolm stinking mac Kenneth," he swore, "and tell him Moray will live and fight as it has always done, to keep what belongs to us and take back what has been stolen!" Then he pushed Crinan roughly aside and stormed off the hill, followed by most of the chieftains and his entire guard.

I was standing near Macbeatha and Owen among the stunned onlookers who lingered on the hill, staring at the abbot and whispering to each other about what this meant. Clouds were scudding up in the southwest, and it looked as though a late winter storm might darken our festivities—not that Crinan hadn't done that already. "Did he come all the way from Atholl just to antagonize us?" Owen asked, as Crinan sauntered back toward the town like a warrior who had just taken the head of a rival.

"I believe he did," Macbeatha replied tightly. Then, as I watched, my lord's jaw relaxed, his eyes took on a keener light, and a small smile touched one corner of his mouth. "Do you know what I think?" he said with a hint of amusement in his voice. "I think Gillecomgain will want to make the traditional *crech righ,* the raid of a new king upon his neighbors to demonstrate his courage and the wealth he will bring his followers."

"Aye," Owen agreed, tugging at his black beard. "Do you think he'll try for Duncansby again? God knows they're rich enough. I know you don't want to fight Thorfinn, but—"

"I was thinking I might suggest an alternate target," my lord interrupted. "Someplace that won't be expecting him—because Thorfinn will, I assure you. Someplace rich in cattle and goods; someplace that thinks itself fat and secure."

Owen's brows bunched together over his nose. "Where is that?" he asked suspiciously.

Macbeatha looked smugly after the retreating abbot. "Dunkeld," he said softly. "I say we attack Dunkeld."

Gillecomgain was captivated by the plan. Thorfinn could wait—he had waited this long, hadn't he? What did it matter if they struck him this spring or next fall? Or even next year? But Dunkeld— The new ruler of Moray chuckled and rubbed his hands together in anticipation of the look on Crinan's face when he found himself under attack in his own town!

They had to wait for the snow to clear from the Pass of Drumochter, for that was Macbeatha's plan—to cut through the Highlands, down Glen Garry to pick up the River Tay and follow it until they reached Dunkeld. They would hide up in the hills, sending only a few men in to scout the defenses. The attack would come at dusk, with one group sacking the town and another driving the cattle from the nearby meadows. Night would cover their retreat into the Highlands. Then, as soon as they crossed the pass, they would scatter to the four winds, each chieftain returning to his own home with a share of the cattle and other plunder, leaving Crinan no single location at which to strike back to recover his lost wealth.

Surprise was essential to success, so Macbeatha had his cousin send small parties into Sutherland, as though they were reconnoitering prior to a raid. He also sent ships up the Moray Firth, prowling along its western shore, to hint at a possible sea battle. Word had gone out that those who hungered for gain and glory should come to Gillecomgain's banner, but only when the pass was cleared of snow was the true plan revealed. Then off they went to pay Crinan a call.

Dunkeld sits in valley of the River Tay, which in that season was green and lush. Dykes held the burgeoning Tay within its banks, but no one was foolish enough to try crossing it at the ford just southwest of the town. In the fields along the river, new barley and oat sprouts pushed their way up from the reddish soil to stretch slender blades before the sun. Meadows shimmered with the pale colors of wild flowers, and young calves kicked up their heels.

According to Owen, the Moraymen watched the town most of the day, spotting the largest houses, seeing which roads got the most use, noting how the stone-walled abbey, the abbey church, and other defensible places were in the south part of the town. Macbeatha suggested they sweep in from three sides—north, east and west—and try to herd its citizens toward these sanctuaries, leaving the houses and shops to be looted by the raiders. Then, as Crinan organized his defenders into a force, the attackers would scatter with their booty. Gillecomgain approved; orders were passed to all the men hiding in the hills, and they began to creep toward the town.

In the fading light, they got quite close before the alarm went up. Then with a whoop and a cry, Gillecomgain led his horsemen to the attack from the north, while Macbeatha led those from the east, and men on foot rushed up from the dikeworks along the river. Townspeople fled before them, trying to reach the abbey or some other haven, leaving their household goods behind.

The attackers had worked their way to the center of town when they saw a red glow brightening in the night at the south end of town. Someone had put a torch to the abbey. Cursing violently, Macbeatha urged his horse toward the flames, ignoring the flow of Moraymen who were beginning to leave the city with their plunder.

He found Gillecomgain and some fifty men just out of range of the spearmen on the abbey walls. The thatched roofs of a stable and several other outbuildings were ablaze, and from within the compound came the shouts of people calling for buckets of water. Forcing his way through the press to his cousin, Macbeatha seized him roughly by the tunic and almost unseated him. "Are you mad?" he demanded.

Battle lust was written on Gillecomgain's face. "He's in there!" he snarled back. "Crinan is in there!"

"So are the women and children," Macbeatha retorted. "This was not part of the plan!"

"I'm *making* it part of the plan!" Gillecomgain roared back, loosing himself from Macbeatha's grip. "The houses!" he shouted to men nearby. "Fire the houses! Burn the whole town!" Warriors rushed to do his bidding.

Rage blazed on Macbeatha's countenance to rival the flames consuming the abbey's buildings. "You'll trap our own men!" he hissed. "Rescind the order! Give our foot time to get out."

Then, as Owen tells it, Gillecomgain's eyes widened in horror as he realized his error; but I wonder if perhaps, in that moment, he realized just how dangerous was this cousin of his. At any rate, he hesitated only a moment before he commanded his men to stop. "We'll hold them inside the abbey until our foot have retreated," he said. "Then we'll fire the town as we withdraw."

At that moment the gates of the abbey opened and a contingent of Athollmen burst forth to engage their assailants. Gillecomgain led the charge against them, and soon they were beaten back within the walls. From up above, the defenders rained down stones and spears upon the Moraymen, but they had no archers, which was a lucky thing. "Enough," Macbeatha told his cousin when the Athollmen were back behind their protective wall. "Time to go." This time Gillecomgain did not hesitate, and they were off, retreating into the hills and to Moray.

For the rest of the summer, Atholl kept trying to return the favor, but without much success. Word had circulated that the plan had been Macbeatha's, and so as the raid was sung in halls across the land, my lord's fame began to grow. That was what he wanted, what he needed, and he accepted the accolades; but it went hard on him to have his name linked with the burning of Dunkeld. There was no honor in setting fire to the town, and he took care to whisper about that Gillecomgain had thrown the first torch.

For one man, it made no difference. Crinan had stood in the upstairs window of his abbey house and seen, by the light of his burning town, the faces of those in the street below. He knew who had been there, and he would never forget.

Chapter Twenty

In Fionna's hut

Fionna stood at the entrance to her mound home, holding back the hide door and peering out into the lingering daylight. Someone else was coming, though she did not know who or why; but it was unlikely he could find this place unless she wished it. Slowly she turned from the opening, letting the hide fall back into place. Kelda had finished the oat porridge, and she looked less haggard now. "So Crinan saw Macbeatha at the burning of Dunkeld," Fionna said. "The old High King could not have been pleased."

"No, he was not," Kelda agreed. "A raid of cattle and some looting was one thing. Burning the town, and the abbey—" She shook her head.

"What did he do?" Fionna asked. "How did he make amends?"

Kelda's brow furrowed a little. "I was never quite sure ..."

* * *

Perhaps King Malcolm eventually forgave him—or appeared to—because Macbeatha quickly separated himself from his incautious cousin. At the very least, that made it convenient for Malcolm, and even Duncan, to overlook my lord's pivotal role in the affair. But that first winter, he didn't dare show his face in Scone, nor in Cumbria, and though he wished to speak again with the Lady Boite in Fife, now that he was tanist, with Crinan's wrath so high—and the High King's, too—he knew better than to venture south. So we stayed in Inverness, where he began a sly campaign to divorce himself from Gillecomgain.

He plotted it with Raghallach, when he went to the Highlands at Midsummer for his sister's wedding. As summer paled and the fall butchering began, they sent a minor chieftain to whisper in Gillecomgain's ear: How clever Macbeatha was, and how ambitious. "A good man to have at your side, but not at your back." He reminded the new mormaer how, in the tales of the old gods, the warm sun Lugh was overcome by his tanist, the cold sun, bringing winter to the land. And how Macbeatha took for his symbol the double sun, embracing both cold and warm aspects.

Others warned Gillecomgain, as well, for it is an old story, that of the tanist impatient for his turn to rule who brings arms against his own kin. Hadn't Macbeatha's cousins done it to their uncle, Findlaech? Hadn't a hundred others, over the centuries?

In the weeks just after his inauguration, Gillecomgain had required my lord's presence almost every day. But after the whispers began, Macbeatha was called less and less to the fortress. The shortening days served to recall the legend of Lugh's fall to his tanist, and over the winter, we heard from Gillecomgain only thrice. In the spring, everyone was occupied with planting and lambing, but finally, as Black Friday gave way to Easter and thoughts turned to the summer's campaigning, Gillecomgain called Macbeatha to him.

My lord came home with a smug look on his face. "I am to take a warband east," he said, "and patrol, in case the Danes come up the coast."

"Oh!" I cried, jumping up. "May I come with you?" I hated the thought of being separated from him for another summer.

"Of course, you may!" he laughed, picking me up and planting a kiss on my forehead. "We shall be quartered with the various chieftains when we are not fighting, so you will be safe enough, and no trouble."

"I am never any trouble," I pouted, and he laughed again and put me down.

"You are the opposite of trouble," he agreed. "I only meant when there are hardships and hard riding, I won't worry for your comfort or your needs because you will be with others who can take care of you. My mind will rest easy if I know that."

I was glad his mind rested easy, for mine was troubled that spring. There was a matter of which I hadn't spoken to anyone—I was afraid to, as though speaking of it would make it so. But I carried it in my heart and worried that because of it, Macbeatha would one day turn away from me to some other wench for his comforts. I was sixteen winters old, you see, and I had warmed my lord's bed for two years, but there was as yet no trace of a child in my womb.

I was terribly afraid I was barren.

Following the camp was not nearly as much fun as I had hoped. Macbeatha spent most of his time with his men, and I had only the other servants for company. I did see more of him than if I had stayed in Inverness, but not a great deal. My chief delight lay in greeting him each time he came back from an outing with a smile on my face and a horn of ale in my hand. Then he would call me his Valkyrie, and my world would be as bright as the sunshine that fell golden across the land.

There were no pirate attacks that year, but there was a band of thieves near Mortlach that troubled the clerics there, as well as the farmers. Macbeatha and his warband rode after them and had great fun rooting them out of the hills. He came back with several heads tied to his saddle and not a mark on him, except a bruise on one shin that he apparently had acquired in a tussle of a different nature.

I have never understood the Scottish fascination with taking heads. What gruesome trophies they are, with their lips stretched back and their eyes rolled up and flies clustering about the mouth and nose and severed neck. Yet Macbeatha was quite pleased with his string of three, and not at all happy when he tried to hand them to me and I refused to take them. "What's wrong with you now?" he demanded.

"They're *ugly*," I protested, drawing back in horror. Ugly! They were revolting.

"They're the heads of my enemies," he said, as though that explained everything. "Here, take them and clean them up for me."

"Do *what?*"

He was growing quite irritated. "Clean them up," he repeated. "Wash the blood off them. I'm going to hang them on my tent."

I stared at him, hoping he was joking. Now, I can understand hanging the heads of outlaws outside a village or a farm, as a warning to others what fate awaits those who would make mischief there. But what point is there in hanging them on the pole of your tent in camp? Who's going to see them but your friends, and the people you're protecting?

But he wasn't joking. "You want me to—to t-touch them?" I stammered.

"Of course!" He proffered the heads again. "I kill them, you clean them. That's the way it works."

I took another step backwards. "Are you going to eat them?" I asked in a whisper.

He laughed heartily. "No, you silly goose! I told you, I'm going to hang them on my tent. Look, I've got three, no one else got more than one. Now, take them and clean them up for me."

Gingerly I reached out for the knot of leather that tied the hair of the three heads together. "It's just like handling a boar's head, or a calf's," he assured me, but I did not find it so. How my skin crawled as I washed those three heads and combed out their beards. And just as I thought I was finished with the most vile task I had ever performed in my life, Owen showed up with another head. Owen was now captain of my lord's guardsmen. "This one thought to cast his spear at Macbeatha's back," he said as he shoved it at me. "I took his arm off for him."

"Did you bring me that, too?" I asked testily.

His brow furrowed. "Why would I do that?"

"Nevermind," I sighed, and I took the noxious thing from him.

For a few moments he stood there and watched me as I soaked the thing's beard with my wet rag to soften the dried blood in it. Finally I asked, "Is there something else?"

"No." Owen shifted his weight from one foot to the other. "I told him you wouldn't do it," he said. "I was wrong." Then he turned and lumbered off.

Tears sprang to my eyes as I watched him go. I had never had such high praise from Owen before.

As Midsummer drew near, we received word that Gillecomgain had managed to cross the Oykel before he ran headlong into Thorfinn and his *hird*. There had been a few skirmishes along the way, in which the Scots had overwhelmed their assailants, but the battle against Thorfinn himself had gone rather badly. To Gillecomgain's surprise, the people of the countryside took up arms with the Norsemen, and he found himself outnumbered. Even the Scots among the locals refused to provide supplies willingly or to aid Gillecomgain's army in any way. They had already paid *skatt* to Thorfinn, so they didn't intend to pay *conveth* to Moray, as well. After one fierce battle, the angry mormaer had to withdraw, burning a few farms and driving off some livestock as he went.

Now he was back at Inverness, and he wanted to talk to Macbeatha.

Macbeatha left his brother-in-law Dufflach in charge of the warband and rode back to Inverness with his guard. We had only been at Forres, which is an easy ride from Inverness, so he let me come along. Bored with waiting in camp while he hunted scoundrels, I was glad of the opportunity.

We reached Inverness just at suppertime and went straight to the fortress, where Gillecomgain's steward urged us to stay and eat. There we learned Gillecomgain had been wounded in Caithness, taking a bad sword cut on his leg. It had grown infected, but with the application of poultices and some herbal concoction a local woman supplied, he was now recovering well, although his leg was stiff and he limped badly. "I will be well enough by Midsummer, though," he insisted.

When the men had eaten their fill, and I had settled myself at my lord's feet to eat my own bread and butter, Gillecomgain addressed his cousin. "I need you to do something for me."

"What is that?" Macbeatha asked, handing me a piece of roast duck he had saved for me.

"I've arranged for a bride," Gillecomgain said, growing a little crimson at the edges of his black beard. "I was to bring her here for Midsummer so we could be wed, but the doctors say I should not make the journey and risk opening this wound."

This was the first we had heard of a bride, and I knew Macbeatha must be as surprised as I was. The only clue he gave, however, was a brief pause before he replied. "That is unfortunate for you," he said carefully. "Will you postpone the wedding?"

"I was hoping you would fetch her for me."

The pause was longer this time. What was Macbeatha thinking, I wonder? All I know is that he said, "I would be honored, cousin. Where is she?"

Gillecomgain grimaced. "In Fife. Fostered with an abbot at Loch Leven. I know it's a long way, but-- You know the territory around there better than I do, anyway. And by the time you get back with her, my leg will be better, and she won't think she's getting a cripple ..." His voice trailed off.

Macbeatha gave a long, low chuckle. "Why, cousin," he teased, "I believe you're afraid of this girl."

"Bah!" Gillecomgain scoffed, but it was clear that he was. "I've nothing to say to gentlewomen, that's all. I've nothing to say to other women, either, but with them it doesn't matter. You've spent time at court, you know how to charm them— Just bring her back. I don't want her weeping and hysterical when she arrives."

No, I thought, save that for when she looks at you.

"Fife," Macbeatha mused. "That's a long reach for you. How did all this come about?"

But Gillecomgain only shrugged. "Her kin approached me last winter. It took till Beltaine to reach an agreement. She's young, healthy, good family—I wasn't crazy about having a southern bride, but I suppose it's all right. Your mother was from the south, and she was always ..." He looked a bit wistful as he spoke of the Lady Doada. "I liked her. She was ... gentle."

Macbeatha drained off his horn and rose, stretching luxuriously. "Well, if you want the lady back here by Midsummer, I had better see about getting a ship tomorrow. I'm proud of you, cousin," he added, slapping Gillecomgain on the back good-naturedly. "I was afraid it would take you years to get around to finding a wife. You need one, you know. Every king needs one. So I'll be happy to go and fetch her back for you." Then he asked, "Who is she, by the way?"

"Her name is Gruoch," Gillecomgain said. "Her mother is Boite, daughter of old King Kenneth mac Dubh."

The moon and stars stopped in their courses. I took one look at my lord's face and began to cough loudly, bringing everyone's attention to me. Macbeatha bent quickly to raise me up and pat my back, but what he was really doing was composing his features before he could turn back to the assemblage. "Sorry," I apologized loudly, still coughing. "I swallowed wrong."

"Too tired to swallow straight, are you?" Macbeatha said in a bantering tone that sounded only a little forced. "Time for me to go, anyway, since I have a journey to arrange." As he turned once more to the mormaer, his smile was back in place. "I will leave as soon as I can hire a ship. I'll have her here well before Midsummer." Then he bade his guardsmen stay and enjoy the mormaer's hospitality, and I followed him out of the hall.

As soon as we were out of sight of the fortress, Macbeatha began to curse. He cursed thoroughly in Scots, then went on at length in Norn, and finally turned to something I did not recognize. Anglish, perhaps? When he had worn out cursing, he jumped down from his horse, drew his sword, and attacked a nearby tree. He hacked at it with a fury until the poor thing cracked through—for it was a small tree—and fell with a great splintering groan beside the road. For a moment he stood panting; then he returned and vaulted onto his horse. We walked the rest of the way home in silence.

The household was asleep when we arrived, but young Dhui let us in. From the gallery above, Donn peered down. "Everything all right?" he asked quietly.

"Not quite everything," my lord growled.

We went up the ladder to the loft, but while I went off to Macbeatha's chamber to prepare his bed, he disappeared into Donn's room. I was sound asleep before he came in. The next morning, he woke with a groan and flung back the covers, forcing himself into a sitting position. It was a sure sign he dreaded the day's events. Rising up on one elbow, I began to rub his back. "Did Donn have no words of advice for you?"

Macbeatha snorted. "Yes. He said if Gillecomgain's first child is a girl, in another fifteen years I can marry her. Fifteen years! I'm not about to wait that long."

"Is there no other?" I asked helplessly. "Duncan has a married sister, doesn't he? Is there a daughter—"

"Two boys, and one of them sickly. Not that anyone in his family would give me a wife, anyway. No, it has to be from the other royal family, the line of Kenneth mac Dubh. There is one daughter of a cousin, a hawk-faced old widow, and there is this granddaughter. I really didn't want to court the old crone—she has stayed a widow for nearly twenty years, undoubtedly for a reason. But now I'll have to." With a sigh he fell back into the bed and wrapped his arms around me. "But not today." I purred and held him close. "Oh, Kelda," he sighed. "I really wanted someone young and lively."

"Well, Gillecomgain is stupid enough to send you after his bride: Why can't you just carry her off and marry her yourself?"

He drew back and looked at me, startled. "That would be dishonorable! I could never show my face in Moray again if I did that!"

To this day, the Scots' sense of honor seems totally capricious to me. Why was it all right for him to seduce a married woman, but not to wed another's betrothed? "Too bad," I said with mock sorrow. "I guess you'll have to settle for stealing her heart, and making a cuckold of your cousin before he's even wed."

It took a moment, but then the corners of his mouth started to twitch, and finally he buried his face in my hair and laughed. "I like the way you think," he chuckled. "Oh, I dare not actually sully her, at least not before the wedding; but I can at least toy with her affections. It will be some small compensation for the evil her mother has done me, and the fact that I will have to go court the old widow."

His kisses grew warm then, and I knew I had taken some of the misery out of his day. "Do you think, lord," I ventured as he began to lose himself in the pleasures I offered, "that I might come along and watch you seduce the young lady?"

At that moment, I think he would have promised me anything.

Chapter Twenty-One

It took us five days to reach Loch Leven, and the last part of the journey was on horseback. Not only was there an abbey at Loch Leven, but a community of—what do they call them? Nuns. Women monks. When Macbeatha told me they were Christian women who lived apart from the world, I thought they were like the old priestesses who dedicated themselves to Freya or Odin or some other god or goddess, and offered themselves as vessels for men who wished to reach that deity. My lord choked on his ale when I suggested that, and he hastily assured me that they were *not* like such priestesses at all. These women live as virgins their whole lives, like the Holy Mother. It still seems strange to me. Virginity may be well and good for the Holy Mother, but I cannot imagine anything so sad as a life without the ecstasy I found in Macbeatha's arms.

He made it clear, though, that we would share no such delights while we tarried at Loch Leven. We must ask hospitality of the abbot of St. Serf's, who was Gruoch's fosterer, and he did not wish to be so flagrant with his sin as to exhibit it to the household of an abbot. I made a face at him. "And as I travel with four men," I mocked, "where do you imagine they will think I spent the last four nights?"

Our party was approaching the village on the shores of the lake, where the abbot and his wife had a house, and Macbeatha was growing grumpier by the minute. "We'll tell them you're Owen's wench," he said.

Now it was Owen, riding at Macbeatha's flank, who threw him a dark look. "And will you explain to my wife," he asked, "why the Lady Gruoch thinks Kelda is my wench?"

"You can tell them she's my wench," offered Weylin, who rode behind. "But only if I can have her for the night!"

Now, Weylin was a handsome fellow in those days, and good natured into the bargain, and I wouldn't have minded a bit if my lord had passed me off to him for a night or two. But Macbeatha never seemed inclined to act on such suggestions. Not that he took offense at them—he didn't. He just seemed to think they required no response.

So he ignored Weylin, as though his words were chaff the wind blew away. Instead he declared, "Why should I have to tell them anything? Kelda is my servant who has come to wait upon the lady for her journey, and they need no more explanation than that. Let them think what they will."

But I was not to come to his bed in the abbot's house.

We paused long enough to break out Macbeatha's standard, which Weylin carried ahead, leaving old Gramus and me in the rear with our pack horses and the sleek, sturdy mare Gillecomgain had sent for his lady. Gillecomgain had tried to press his standard on Macbeatha, but the latter had refused deftly, saying the people of Fife wouldn't know one from the other, and Gillecomgain ought to have his in case Thorfinn tried to pay a visit. However, my lord did cajole a large purse of gold and silver from the mormaer, so his bride could make the journey in the greatest comfort—and so, incidentally, could Macbeatha.

Finally we reached our destination, a large timber house in the center of the village. All the townsfolk came out of their huts to stare as we dismounted, their eyes round at the sight of a strange standard flapping in the breeze and armed warriors calling on the gentle abbot and his wife. "Moray," we heard them whisper, and "prince of the House of Loarn."

The abbot himself leaned out a window and peered at us, shading his eyes against the sun. "Good day to you, Reverend Abbot," Macbeatha called. "I am Macbeatha mac Findlaech, cousin to Gillecomgain mac Maelbrighde, the mormaer of Moray. My cousin begs your pardon that he cannot attend upon the Lady Gruoch in person, but he has suffered a minor injury and his doctors advise against traveling until it is healed." He patted the wallet tucked into the folds of his cloak. "I have here a letter from him."

A moment later the portly abbot shuffled out of the house with his stout wife trailing two steps behind. "Mac Findlaech, you say?"

Charm shimmered around Macbeatha like a halo. "Yes, Macbeatha mac Findlaech. I am Gillecomgain's cousin, and his tanist. He fought the Vikings not many weeks ago and, though his enemies fell before him like straw, he did suffer a wound upon his leg which prevents him riding just yet. He would not hear of postponing the happy day of his marriage to the Lady Gruoch, however, and so he asked me to bring her to him." Macbeatha smiled that dazzling smile of his. "Is the lady at home?"

The abbot seemed to have trouble taking this in. "No—no, she is not," he mumbled. "A letter? You say you have a letter?"

Immediately Macbeatha produced the letter and handed it over. The abbot squinted first at the seal, then at Macbeatha, then at the writing on the outside, then at Macbeatha again. Finally he broke the seal and squinted at the markings there, his lips moving silently as he poured over the contents. Then he squinted one more time at Macbeatha, peered around my lord's shoulder to squint at the rest of us, and announced, "We were expecting Gillecomgain."

Patiently my lord explained again the reason for the substitution. "But I have pledged my life to bring her safely to her promised husband," he concluded. "You have my word of honor before God that that is what I shall do."

This last seemed to penetrate the abbot's perplexity, for he called to a serving girl to go fetch the Lady Gruoch and her foster sister Ailean from the convent, where they had gone to pray with the sisters. "Please," he invited us, "come inside."

It was clear the abbot was quite nearsighted, and from the way he asked the same questions over and over, I thought perhaps he was hard of hearing as well. Macbeatha's temper was as sweet and smooth as heavy cream while he explained about the gifts Gillecomgain had sent, the horse chosen from the finest animals he owned, the ship we had hired, the ports where we would stop, how many days it would take us—

"Then you can tarry with us a day, can you not?" asked the abbot when he had calculated—very quickly, mind you—how many days before Midsummer we should arrive.

"Gillecomgain is most anxious," Macbeatha prefaced, "but if the Lady Gruoch desires a day of preparation for her journey, he would be the last to gainsay her. And I, of course, am both his servant, and hers."

And, I thought, that gives him an extra day to insinuate himself into the lady's favor.

"Mac Findlaech," the abbot mused. "You were fostered by the High King, were you not?"

There was that slight hesitation before my lord answered. "I was a hostage there, yes," he replied. "Along with princes from several places."

"But your father was Malcolm's man."

"Like the other mormaers, he came into the house of Malcolm."

The abbot was not looking at Macbeatha—no doubt he could have seen little of my lord's expression—but he had his head cocked to one side and was listening intently. "And you, Mael—Maelbeatha, was it?"

"Macbeatha," my lord corrected in an even tone.

"Yes, yes, Macbeatha," the abbot demurred, rising from his chair to take two cups of mead his wife had filled from a cask in one corner. "Both names are quite common in Moray, I think. But you, Macbeatha," he continued as he brought one cup to my lord, "you yourself were a suitor for my little Gruoch's hand, were you not?"

Now it became clear the abbot was not the dull-witted fool he had first seemed. All his questions, all his hesitations, had not been from stupidity, but from caution. He had expected the winner of the contest, and here came the loser in his place. The abbot watched his guest's face closely from his new vantage point not an arm's length away.

"I see you are in the Lady Boite's confidence," Macbeatha replied wryly. Then he lifted his chin so his questioner could see his countenance clearly. "Yes, I brought my suit for the young lady's hand to her mother; but it seems that honorable woman has decided on another. And I will respect her decision." He sipped at the mead. "I regret it," he admitted with a twinkle in his eye, "but I respect it."

For a long moment the abbot held his gaze; then the cleric nodded and returned to his chair. "I have heard a thing or two of you here and there, Macbeatha mac Findlaech," he said as he eased himself back down. "But nothing that casts doubt upon your honor."

"I am pleased to hear it," Macbeatha told him coolly, "for I would be obliged to kill any man who said otherwise."

That made the abbot chuckle. "Pray keep your sword in its sheath, my young warrior. No one here is foolish enough to question the honor of one of Donall's protégés." Donall was the swordmaster at the High King's court, and he had a well-earned reputation for training warriors.

Just then a shout was raised outside, and the mistress of the house leaned out a window to see what it was. "Oh, she's here!" that lady cried. "She's come with Ailean, and now you shall meet her: our angel, our sunlit meadow, our little Gruoch!" With that, the abbot's wife bustled out the front door to meet the two girls and their maid. Macbeatha rose to his feet with an eagerness on his face, a light in his eyes, for here was his quarry: she whose body had escaped his hand, but whose heart he would possess to spite Gillecomgain, the Lady Boite, and all others who sought to confound his plans.

At first we could not see her, for the abbot's wife ushered her in with one plump arm draped around the girl's shoulders, and her shawl concealed most of Gruoch's slender form. But then our hostess turned and presented the prospective bride. "Gruoch, heart, here is the man what's come to fetch you to your husband."

Gruoch had, to her credit, the fairest complexion I have ever seen: pale and smooth, the color high in her cheeks from walking back from the convent. Beyond that, I could not see much to fuss over. Her nose was straight and small, her eyes some color between blue and gray, her hair—where it was not covered by a scarf—so dark a brown as to seem almost black. Though slender, she was not tiny the way Brenna was. Her height was somewhat less than mine, her bosom certainly not of my proportions, and her hips almost bony by comparison. Oh, perhaps I am being unkind. No, I *know* I am being unkind. She was attractive enough, she was just not the sort Macbeatha usually fancied.

One would never know it from the look on his face, though. He bowed to the young woman—younger than *me,* mind you, and he called *me* a child still—and he said in his most sonorous voice, "Ah, lady, your kinsmen represented you as gentle and good, but they failed to mention your beauty causes the moon to blush for envy."

Gruoch's mouth slacked open slightly as she stared at my golden-haired warrior, my Thor, with his dazzling green eyes and his bewitching smile—and then she laughed. It was a short, harsh laugh. "And why should Moray care if I am beautiful, or even gentle?" she demanded. "It is my family that interests Gillecomgain, and nothing more."

"Gruoch!" the abbot's wife chided.

Macbeatha blinked, regrouped, and tried again. "If that were true, lady," he said with a wry smile, "then he should be a bigger fool than I take him for."

"And do you take your mormaer for a fool?" she rejoined quickly.

"Only that he did not come himself on this errand. And had he seen the glamour you cast with your violet eyes, he would not have allowed a mere mortal like myself within reach of your spell."

She made a disgusted noise and rolled her eyes. "They're not violet, they're blue," she said flatly. "And you're about as subtle as the serpent in the Garden of Eden."

"Gruoch!" the abbot chided now, frowning.

"Well, he is," Gruoch defended. "Does he think I'm so stupid as to believe his flattery? Maybe the giddy-headed women in Moray find such talk exciting, but I do not." With that she turned on her heel and stalked toward the back of the house.

"Gruoch! Where are you going?" the abbot demanded.

"To pack," she called without turning. "I assume we leave in the morning."

"No, lady, we do not." My lord didn't exactly shout, but his voice rang, loud enough and sharp enough that Gruoch stopped short and turned slowly around to glare at him. He glared right back with a look that has chilled the blood of many a warrior. It phased Gruoch not at all. "The good abbot has requested we tarry with him a day," he continued in a voice not so loud, but every bit as forceful. "I imagine he means to ascertain that I am indeed my cousin's emissary, and not some brigand come to spirit you off into the evil clutches of the High King. So we shall tarry and make him any reassurance he requires, whether to break bread or to swear upon a stone or to make a vow to the Holy Mother herself. And *then*, lady—*then* we shall leave."

"Then you needn't have called me from my prayers," she responded archly. "And I shall go now to my room to complete them."

I sighed and shook my head slightly. He had met the mother—he might have guessed the daughter would have the same tongue.

Chapter Twenty-Two

That evening Macbeatha presented the various gifts Gillecomgain had sent: golden earrings, a silver mirror and comb, fragrant water of roses, and a necklace set with some sort of green stones. Ailean was quite enchanted with them all, and with Macbeatha, too. All night long her eyes kept sliding to his, and when he winked at her she would blush furiously and turn away. She was a plain-faced girl with dull yellow hair and a washed-out complexion, obviously accustomed to running Gruoch a poor second, and yet there was no resentment in her. She squealed with delight at each object Macbeatha produced.

Gruoch received the tokens politely enough, though she lacked Ailean's enthusiasm. When the last had been presented, she said, "My bridegroom is most generous. I will thank him when I meet him, and wear his gifts with pride."

My lord had spoken little to her during supper, chatting amiably with the abbot and his wife instead, and flirting quietly with Ailean. Now, taking heart at Gruoch's apparently softened mood, he told her, "Gillecomgain has sent a horse, as well: a fine mare, which he hopes will make your journey to the port a pleasant one."

"I am not much experienced with horses," she said rather stiffly, "but I shall rely upon the judgment of my future husband and trust the animal is worthy."

"Then perhaps, lady," Macbeatha suggested with a hint of coldness, "you will also rely upon his judgment in the matter of an escort, and trust that I, too, am worthy."

"I never said otherwise. Only I do not care to be treated like a child or a simpleton, and you would be better off saving your charm for ladies who draw their nourishment from it. I do not."

"And from what *do* you draw your nourishment?" he asked frankly.

"From God," she replied immediately. "And from Holy Scripture. And from other books—Cicero and Adomnan and other scholars—and from poetry. But I'm sure such things hold no interest for a warrior like yourself. No doubt you draw your nourishment from blood and *uisge beatha* and girls like that one in the corner."

I know I should have kept quiet, but I couldn't help it. The attack was so unwarranted. "My lord reads books," I defended. "Lots of them. And his sword—"

"Kelda," he said sharply, and I subsided. Then to Gruoch he gave a cold smile—almost a sneer—and said, "Cicero! I have read his works, but I prefer those of Caesar. Have you read him, lady? His recounting of battles stirs me."

She leaned over to adjust her slipper—and showed not one morsel of flesh, for she was covered to the neck, although it was mid-summer. "And my husband-to-be—does he also enjoy reading Caesar?" she asked.

Macbeatha gave a small contemptuous snort. "He might—if he could read Latin."

"Ah, yes." She smiled artfully. "He had not the benefit of your fine education, I understand—being schooled, as you were, at the knee of Malcolm mac Kenneth."

"No, he was never held hostage for his father's good behavior, as I was. There was no need, as his father was dead and no threat to the High King."

"That is what I shall enjoy most about Moray, I think," sighed Gruoch with all the sincerity of a monk in a whorehouse. "That it is so far removed from such conflicts, and that my groom has no traffic at all with the High King."

Macbeatha opened his mouth to speak, then thought better of it. "As you say, lady," he conceded. "That is one of Gillecomgain's many fine qualities."

Personally, I couldn't think of *any* fine qualities to attribute to Gillecomgain.

"You will probably appreciate as well," my lord went on, "the courage and tenacity of your groom in battle." He then proceeded to relate the burning of Dunkeld, much to the horror of the abbot and his family. But Macbeatha told the tale with relish, watching Gruoch grow pale at the story of heads lopped off, and children trampled, and old women run through—things I had not heard before, and I doubt most of them actually happened. Yet he painted them in gruesome and gory detail, attributing some to Gillecomgain and others to himself, until Gruoch's lips grew quite thin and colorless, and her jaw clenched so tight I thought her cheeks would pop with the strain.

Finally the abbot interrupted, calling attention to the late hour and suggesting such fair flowers as Ailean and Gruoch needed to retire. "You and your warriors may sleep here, in the hall," he told Macbeatha, "and your girl ... ah ..." He paused awkwardly.

"She shall attend me, of course," Gruoch interceded deftly. "If she is to be my attendant for the journey, then she and Maisie should get acquainted. Let her join us in our chamber above." So reluctantly I followed Ailean and the Lady Gruoch up the narrow stairs to their sleeping chamber, leaving my lord and his men below.

Maisie was a sweet thing, a little simple, and several years older than Gruoch and Ailean. If allowed, she would have waited on me as well as the other two; in spite of my slave collar, I had some trouble convincing her I was not a guest. Gruoch was kind to both of us, though she held herself distant as befit her station. I was prepared to dislike her, because she had such disdain for my lord; but she was too gracious and thoughtful with her servants for me to summon up any hatred. She reminded me in many ways of the Lady Plantula, Thorfinn's mother—I don't know why. And when I thought about her being married to Gillecomgain, all I could feel for her was pity.

Ailean cooed and trilled and carried on about Macbeatha and the gifts, and quizzed me for more details about my lord. How old was he? Did he have a wife? Was he rich? Was he really the fierce warrior he claimed to be? Taking a cue from my lord's story earlier that evening, I told her about the heads he had brought back from battle. Ailean blanched and squealed, "Ooohh! And you *touched* them?"

"Of course," I replied airily. "I washed them and combed the beards so they would look fine hanging from my lord's tent post."

Ailean squealed again, and I threw a wicked glance back at Gruoch to see how she had received all this.

But although her face was set in grim lines as she packed away her new jewelry, she managed to keep her voice even and unperturbed. "Don't be such a silly," she told her foster sister. "Warriors always take heads, to show how powerful they are, and what the fate of their enemies will be. When my grandfather was High King, he had the heads of a hundred of his enemies hung outside his hall; and those of three very powerful kings he kept in a casket, and brought them out to show visitors."

Ailean shivered and dove under the covers of her bed. "Oh, how brave you are, Gruoch, to go off to such a distant place and live among such ferocious people!" she exclaimed, yet there was a distinct note of envy in her voice.

Gruoch knelt by her bed to pray, but before she began, I heard her say quietly, "I wasn't given a choice."

The long and lingering twilight had finally faded almost to blackness when I heard Gruoch rise softly from her bed. Ailean and Maisie had chattered incessantly until Gruoch snapped at them to be quiet or she would brain them both with her new mirror; then they were asleep almost instantly. But the lady herself had tossed and turned fitfully in her bed.

Being spoiled by sleeping in fine beds with my lord, I found a straw tick on the floor quite uncomfortable, so I, too, was awake when finally Gruoch rose and crept to the window. The shutters had been closed to darken the room for sleeping, but she cracked one open and sat on the sill, gazing out into the night. Her pale linen shift glowed in the quiet light of moon and stars, and I thought, "Poor thing! She was given no more choice in this than Macbeatha gave Brenna. And to be stuck with Gillecomgain, that pig! If she dislikes Macbeatha, wait till she meets him!"

Then she did the most astonishing thing: taking a shawl from a peg near her bed, she wrapped it around her, slipped out the window, and vanished. Seeing it, I rose from my own bed and hurried to discover how a maiden could disappear out a second-story window.

There was an oak tree near to the house, and one of its forks grew up right by the window. Gruoch had climbed out onto it and was crawling deftly toward the trunk. I suspected she had often slipped out this way, for there was no hesitation as she clutched the limb and swung down, nor any searching about as her foot found purchase on the stub of an old branch. She crouched there momentarily, then dropped with a soft thud upon the dirt below, wrapped the shawl close around her, and started for the stable.

I waited only long enough to see where she was going. Then I hurried from the room, closing the door quietly behind me, and crept down to the hall below.

Macbeatha rose up on one elbow as I approached—he had not been asleep, either. "Kelda!" he whispered angrily when I knelt beside him. "I told you—"

"She's gone out the window," I said.

There was a moment's pause. "Gruoch?" he asked in surprise.

"I wouldn't bother to tell you if it were Ailean," I snipped. "Of course, Gruoch. She climbed down an oak tree and headed for the stable."

"Is she running away?"

"Not without shoes and cloak, surely. I don't know what she intends to do, but I thought ... you might like to find out?"

He grinned in the dimness, then kissed me quickly. "Come along. If she is frightened and calls out, I want another woman there to keep things respectable."

So we slipped from the house and stole across the yard to the stable. The door was ajar; Macbeatha hid himself in the shadow of the building while he peered around it at the inside. "She's looking at the mare," he reported. "You go in first, tell her you were concerned for her and followed. She'll feel more comfortable if she knows she is not alone. I want to startle her, but I don't want to frighten her so she screams."

"She doesn't strike me as a screamer," I sniffed, but I went through the opening while he waited outside.

"Lady?" I called softly, seeing the glow of her pale garment perched on the edge of a stall. "Are you all right?"

Her head snapped around. "Yes," she said after an instant. "Yes, I'm fine, I just couldn't sleep. I get restless sometimes. Go on back to bed."

But I had instructions to the contrary. "She's a fine horse," I ventured, coming further into the stable. "Very well-behaved—not like that stupid pony I ride. My lord picked her himself, from all Gillecomgain's horses—"

"You mean Gillecomgain picked her," Gruoch interrupted.

"No, lady, it was Macbeatha's idea. He—"

Her eyes bored into me in the darkness. "You are mistaken," she said firmly. "Think again. Your master clearly said the mare was a gift from Gillecomgain." She climbed down from the stall and came toward me. "Of course that means my bridegroom himself was thoughtful for my welfare, and so he directed your master to go and choose this horse." Now she stood right before me, her eyes hard and commanding, though her voice was gentle. "Isn't that right?"

I dropped my gaze. "Yes, lady," I answered politely. "Of course, you must be right."

Then, as though the moon had slipped behind a cloud, the light spilling through the doorway disappeared as a soft and sonorous voice came to us like moonbeams on a loch:

"By night on my bed I sought him whom my soul loveth:
I sought him, but I found him not.
I will rise now, and go about the city in the streets,
And in the broad ways I will seek him whom my soul loveth:
I sought him, but I found him not."

At the first sound of his voice, Gruoch jerked around to see Macbeatha framed in the doorway, a shadow against the lesser night outside. Then she stood riveted, her breathing shallow, as his words floated like a falcon on the sighing wind.

"The watchmen that go about the city found me:
To whom I said, Saw ye him whom my soul loveth?"

Macbeatha stepped inside, and the light crept back into the stable behind him.

"It was but a little that I passed from them,
But I found him whom my soul loveth:
I held him, and would not let him go,
Until I had brought him into my mother's house,
And into the chamber of her that conceived me."

Now Gruoch mustered a voice, accusing, "You are a brazen one, mac Findlaech."

"You said you draw nourishment from Holy Scripture," he reminded her in a slightly mocking tone. "And from poetry. I give you both." Then, wickedly, "I thought you might be hungry."

"When I am hungry, you will never know it," she promised.

He laughed and began to close the distance between them as he continued:

"I charge you, O ye daughters of Jerusalem,
By the roes, and by the hinds of the field,
That ye stir not up, nor awake my love,
Till he please."

"Song of Solomon," Gruoch identified the passage. "The sisters say it speaks of Christ, the divine bridegroom."

Still he advanced.

"Who is this that cometh out of the wilderness
    like pillars of smoke,
Perfumed with myrrh and frankincense,
With all powders of the merchant?"

"It is the song of the Church," she went on, "as it searches for salvation as the bride of Christ."

"Behold his bed," Macbeatha quoted seductively, relentlessly, *"which is Solomon's; threescore valiant men are about it, of valiant Israel. They all hold swords—"* He spoke the word harshly, for emphasis. *"—being expert in war."* Again the pause. *"Every man hath his sword upon his thigh because of fear in the night."*

He stood now just before her, not a handsbreadth from her upturned face. But Gruoch neither flinched nor retreated. "You do not impress me, Macbeatha mac Findlaech," she said bluntly. "Just because a man can recite poetry, and Scripture, does not make him less a brute."

His laugh was soft and unkind. It would have chilled *me*, had I been in her shoes. "If you think I am a brute," he mocked, "wait until you meet Gillecomgain."

"All men are brutes," she said doggedly. "Except men of God. I expect nothing more from my husband. If you seek to frighten me, you fail."

"Is that what the sisters teach you?" he asked contemptuously. "That men are brutes? And which of them would know?"

"Not all my learning was done at the convent," she countered.

"Oh?" He backed off a bit, leaning negligently against the stall where the mare nickered uneasily and stomped one foot. "This sounds most intriguing. Pray tell, lady, where else and with whom you have studied the ways of men?"

That stymied her momentarily, for as he had guessed, she truly had been sheltered amongst women and clerics for most of her life. But she was not to be defeated so easily. "My brother comes to visit me," she maintained, "and his foster brother Alwin. They always come with several warriors as a guard, for my mother does not trust the High King. So I have met warriors before, sir, and I know their kind."

"And your brother," he baited. "Is he also a brute?"

"Of course not. He's only a boy, barely fourteen. Although," she added, "I'm sure those warriors will make a brute of him in due time."

Macbeatha leaned forward so his face was level with hers. "Pray they do, lady," he advised, "or his life will be short, indeed."

"Will you kill him?"

He barked a short laugh. "God forbid! I'm not so damnable a blackguard as to take advantage of a boy without the strength and skills to defend himself! Besides, regardless of what your mother may have told you, I am not Malcolm mac Kenneth's man." Again he leaned forward. "I am *my* man, and no other."

"That is what alarmed her."

Now it was his turn to pull back and consider. "What do you mean by that?"

"I know you came to her the winter before last," Gruoch said, having some control now and clearly enjoying it. "You asked for my hand, and promised to keep me safe in the bowels of Moray—yes, and my brother, too. That part of the offer was interesting to my mother, for she knows Malcolm's arm does not extend to Moray." She paused, relishing this next part. "But you—you worried her. She knew you would use me as a stepping stone to the high kingship—and that, Moray, is not your office. It belongs to my brother. Yet she did not despair, for there was another prince in Moray, one whose ambitions were to the northwest, not to the south."

I saw Macbeatha stiffen in the moonlight as he realized what had happened.

"So she sought Gillecomgain for me," Gruoch concluded with wicked satisfaction. "To have the safety you had offered, but without your price."

Chapter Twenty-Three

Rarely did I see Macbeatha so surprised that his emotions showed naked on his face, but this was one of those times. He had been the cause of his own downfall, and the truth of that choked him. He had given Boite the right reasons for a marriage alliance, and she had used them to outwit him. "Your mother is a crafty woman," he grated. "Cold as iron in January, but crafty."

"You are not one to speak of coldness," Gruoch replied. "You men, who barter for wives without a care for their natures or their feelings, so long as they bring you power."

"There you are mistaken," he snapped, his swagger returning. "And I see now I must thank God your mother bound you to Gillecomgain instead of me. I wish him luck trying to get an heir on a work of stone like you."

"Men will rut with anything."

He took a step forward and loomed over her. "What would you know of the ways of men and women? You, who were raised among nuns and churchmen?"

The air hung thick and static between them. I, who was only a step behind Gruoch's shoulder, had been totally excluded, as though I were no more than a pitchfork or a post. "And would you teach me?" she challenged, her eyes never wavering from his. "Think again, for I have powerful kin. If you lay a hand on me, they will not rest until they have hunted you down and staked your carcass for the ravens."

As she stood there, toe to toe with him, her face upturned, her eyes bright with challenge, I thought: Silly girl. She *wants* him to.

So strong was the temptation to rule her that for a moment I thought he would give in and force himself upon her, if only to still her mocking. But then common sense filtered back to him and he eased off slightly. "Teach you? Why, to teach you the ways of men and women, I would first have to find a woman." Reaching around her, he grabbed my wrist and drew me to him. "Now, here," he told Gruoch, "is a woman." And with great deliberation he gathered me in his arms and kissed me a long, intimate kiss. "You see?" he said, his honeyed voice growing rough now with passion as he pushed back the blanket I had thrown around my shoulders and began to fondle my breasts through the thin fabric of my shift. "Soft, and yielding, and responsive ..." I let my head fall back while he nuzzled my neck.

Gruoch stood frozen there, watching us, though with what expression I cannot say. Then, as Macbeatha caught hold of my shift and began to draw it off over my head, she turned on her heel and stalked out of the stable.

We finished our business in an empty stall, for her taunts and her challenges had stirred him beyond any possibility of stopping. I suppose I should have been upset that he used me as a substitute, that in his mind it was someone else he ravished; but there was something so primal about his full-blown lust that he swept me along with him. After all, why should it matter who or what put him in such a high state of excitement? I was the one who reaped the rewards.

Still, I couldn't resist goading him a bit as we brushed the straw and dust from ourselves and dressed to return to the house. "I thought you were going to woo her," I complained as I shook out the blanket I'd used as a shawl. "Strange wooing, to take your slave girl in front of her."

"Not strange at all," he said easily, untying his belt to shake out his tunic, then retying it. "Virgin girls are fascinated by wicked men. They're drawn to us like ants to honey."

I lifted an eyebrow. "Oh? And you still think you will have won her heart by the time we reach Inverness?"

"Easily," he boasted. "The hard part will be keeping her out of my bed. I don't dare deliver a sullied bride to Gillecomgain. Too many tribes would withdraw their support of me if I dishonored him in such a low manner."

"Now, wait!" I protested, combing straw from my hair with my fingers. "It's all right to lead troops against him in open revolt, but it's not all right to sleep with his wife?"

Macbeatha looked blankly at me. "They're two different things," he said, as though that were perfectly obvious. "I can take over his office if I believe I can do it better than he, and I have the support to do so. I can't take over his wife because I believe I can do *that* better." He bloused his tunic over his belt. "And believe me, I can."

"I have every reason to believe you," I assured him, "although no basis for comparison. But really—" He draped his arm around my shoulders and we started back for the house. "Even if the lady does have a morbid fascination with putting her finger in a flame, I believe she was serious about having your carcass staked out for ravens if you tried to plow her furrow."

He laughed softly, a warm, sincere laugh that said I had relieved all his tensions and eased the frustration of this day for him. "She was quite graphic about that, wasn't she?" Then he sighed. "No, I must admit, evoking any tender feelings from that one may be a labor beyond even *my* Herculean charm."

I snuggled up against him, resting one hand on his strong, broad chest. "Nothing is beyond you," I said confidently. Then I asked, "What is Herculean?"

The next day Macbeatha and the abbot rowed out to the abbey, which is on an island in the loch. My lord was curious what books they had there. They came back late in the afternoon, discussing the merits of celibacy for clergy, and whether there was any real point in adopting the top-of-the-head tonsure practiced by the Roman church further south, as opposed to the frontal tonsure the followers of St. Colm used. Macbeatha maintained it cost nothing to shave your head in such a way as to keep the Holy Father happy; the abbot claimed that good Scots would accuse him of embracing foreign ideas and treat him as suspect in all areas of life. "The Holy Father will never know which tonsure my monks and I use," he maintained, "but every tribesman around the loch will. If it was good enough for St. Colm, they think it should be good enough for us."

"I'm sure Christ doesn't care one way or the other," Macbeatha demurred.

I had spent a fairly strained morning helping Gruoch and the others pack her trunks, which were too numerous for the pack animals we had brought. She made no reference to the previous night nor my part in it, but that in itself made me uncomfortable. She made no reference to Macbeatha, either, nor to the several days we would all travel together. Gillecomgain's name was mentioned once or twice in passing, but that was all. Perhaps she was just tired.

The evening was better. After supper we told stories, mostly of saints lives, and then the abbot brought out his *clarsach*, that wonderful Scottish harp. Gruoch joined more readily in the music, though it seemed to me a sadness underlay her singing. I remembered how I felt, leaving everyone I knew and loved for a strange country and a strange person and an unknown future. That night when she had crawled into her own bed for the last time, I came and knelt beside it, lowering my voice so the others couldn't hear.

"I, too, came to Inverness from far away," I confided, "leaving everything I knew behind. It was hard for me. But someone there cared for me, and helped me to be strong, and comforted me when I cried. I would have died a thousand deaths if not for his kindness."

She looked at me with pity in her eyes. "Poor Kelda," she said softly. "Is that why you are so devoted to him?"

Somehow I hadn't expected her to know I meant Macbeatha. "My lord is a good man," I told her sincerely. "Gentle to the weak, cruel to the wicked, fair and honorable to his clients."

"Dear Kelda." She reached out to stroke my cheek, her tone tender in contrast to her words. "He is arrogant, and selfish, and ruthless in his pursuit of power. Those are not qualities that endear him to me."

Now I was more confused than ever. How could she speak so gently to me, and call me dear, yet say such things about Macbeatha? And say them with regret! This woman made less sense to me the longer I knew her. I tried to forge on. "It is only your harsh words that make him behave so. He would be your protector, and your friend, if you would not try so hard to make him angry."

But she snuggled down in her feather bed and said, "Gillecomgain must be those things for me. I know you wish the world would love your Macbeatha the way you do, but I can't.

Gillecomgain has been chosen for me, and to him only will I give my trust."

I went to bed with a heavy heart, wishing Gillecomgain were worthy of her innocent ideals.

The next morning Macbeatha gave orders to his men regarding the journey, then sat back to let me shave him. This practice had caused some raised eyebrows the previous day, and this morning it drew more direct attention. Ailean and Maisie, who were supposed to be helping Gruoch prepare to leave, sat fascinated as I sharpened the shaving knife on a goatskin strap, tested it across my own forearm, and then began to scrape away the bright red stubble of Macbeatha's beard. As I did, Gruoch came down from the loft, holding her skirts in one hand and an ornate flat box in the other. "My trunks are ready," she announced. "You can have the men take them out to the cart any time." The abbot's wife had hired an ox-cart from a neighbor to take Gruoch's luggage as far as the port.

Then she turned and saw Ailean and Maisie gaping as I stroked the knife across Macbeatha's throat. For a moment she, too, watched the activity; then she shook her head and moved on toward the door. "You are a trusting soul, mac Findlaech," she said as she passed. "Letting a woman put a knife to your throat."

I stopped and stared at her, both surprised and annoyed. "I would sooner cut my own throat," I protested.

She paused and looked back. "I did not intend it to reflect on you, Kelda," she said dryly.

"No, it was me she intended to wound," Macbeatha said, catching my wrist and holding the knife out of his way while he lifted his head to turn menacing green eyes on her. "She has an agile and spiteful tongue, but I doubt her hands can match it."

"Meaning?" she demanded.

"Kelda, give her the knife."

I balked. It had taken me weeks of practice before I dared set the blade against his skin. What if her hand slipped? "Lord, it is *my* task," I whimpered.

But he was paying me no attention. His eyes were on her, challenging her, drawing her in. Gruoch stood unmoving for a moment, then reached a decision and stepped briskly to his side. "If you are that big a fool," she said abruptly. Entrusting her parcel to Ailean, she took the knife from my hand and turned to him. I could only step back and watch, my heart in my throat.

But Macbeatha's lips curled slightly in grim satisfaction, as they had when he'd lured Ivarr into the swordfight. Then he tilted his head back and waited.

Now Gruoch hesitated. Her chest rose and fell sharply with her rapid and shallow breathing, and the knuckles of her hand clutching the knife were white. "You must hold the blade easily," I coached softly. "Let it glide over the skin ..." She stretched out her arm, relaxing her grip, then pulled it back in, trying her best to look business-like and efficient. Studying his chin as though it were a pig's hide or a plucked fowl, she reached out with her left hand and laid it on his cheek, as she had seen me do, to steady it. But when she brought the knife up and held it near to his face, her hand trembled.

She stared at the tremor in the blade, willing it to stop, but it would not. She took one deep breath, and then another, and then—

"This is a mistake," she said, dropping her hands. "It is not my office to shave you. I almost let you goad me into it, Moray, but no. I will not." With that she handed the knife back to me, retrieved her parcel, and strode out the door.

Macbeatha raised his head slowly to watch her go, then turned to the other two girls. "Go outside and make sure everything is to her liking," he told them. When they had left, he permit himself a small chuckle.

"That was a dangerous thing to do," I chided him.

But he shrugged. "The worst she could do was nick me. I, on the other hand—I could not lose. Whether she refused the task, or did that which only a wife or servant does-- But she is made of strong stuff, isn't she?" Admiration colored his voice. "To stand down from a challenge, but cast the blame back on her adversary— It is more than I expected from her."

"She never does what one expects," I agreed. "Rather like someone else I know."

He chuckled again. Then the chuckle became a laugh. Then he slumped down in the chair with his head tilted back for me to finish shaving him.

When the train was ready and tearful farewells done, Gruoch turned to mount the mare we had brought. But Macbeatha stopped her with an announcement. "There is one more thing before we depart."

Everyone stopped what they were doing to listen. He had that kind of voice, you know: it carried over almost any kind of commotion, and people automatically turned to hear. With everyone looking on, he approached Gruoch. "Lady, what is in that case you carry?" he asked, indicating the ornate box she had requested be strapped to her saddle, for she did not trust it to the van.

"It is something my father gave me," she replied. "I will not be parted from it."

"From the way you handle it, I would guess it is an artifact of a religious nature. Is that correct?"

She hesitated. "Yes. It is a cross, worked in gold. I keep it with me, that I may always have a place for meditation and worship."

"As befits your pious nature," he agreed. Then, "Lady, will you hold it out for me? I would swear an oath on it."

Her eyes widened, but after a moment's consideration, she unstrapped the box and held it before her in both hands.

"Reverend Abbot," my lord addressed our host, "when I first arrived, you were concerned I might be a scoundrel come to abduct this child—" Gruoch winced when he called her that. "—and do her harm."

"I have satisfied myself otherwise," the abbot assured him.

"Nevertheless, I would give you further comfort, and one I hope you will pass on to the Lady Boite, who doubtless is concerned for her daughter's welfare as she journeys to a distant country."

Dropping to his knees in the dust before Gruoch, Macbeatha placed his hand upon the case she held. "I swear before these witnesses," he said, "and by this holy cross, and by the blood of Christ, that I will deliver the Lady Gruoch safely into the hands of her betrothed, Gillecomgain mac Maelbrighde; and that I will protect her and defend her with my own life, placing her honor before mine, not only for this journey—" His voice dropped to a whisper. "—but always."

Good God, I was such a fool, I thought he only practiced his wiles on her, to win her heart out of spite for Gillecomgain. But I should have known it then.

Ah, Fionna, I should have known it then.

Chapter Twenty-Four

Upon returning to Inverness we learned to our sorrow that Thorfinn, as my lord had joked, *had* decided to return Gillecomgain's visit. However, he was not fool enough to sail up the Moray Firth and assault the fortress at Inverness. Instead he landed at Burghead on the northeastern shore of the firth, where he occupied a formidable old stronghold surrounded on three sides by water, with three redoubts and a great deal of marshland before its walls on the fourth. From this base, he ravished the countryside in both directions along the coast. The warband my lord had left behind in Forres rushed to give battle, led by Dufflach. It was a bloody conflict that ended in a stalemate, with Thorfinn still ensconced in Burghead but no longer able to sally forth and wreak havoc at will.

Dufflach took a grievous wound in the battle, and though Macbeatha galloped directly from Inverness to join his men, Dufflach expired before he arrived. So as Gillecomgain wed Gruoch in the cathedral at Inverness, my lord sent to his sister the painful news that she was a widow. She had been delivered of a child only the week before, and I could not help but weep for her.

Everyone waited to see what Macbeatha would do about Thorfinn. I thought it unfair they expected him to solve the problem, since it was Gillecomgain who had caused it by invading Sutherland. But the friendship between my lord and Thorfinn was no secret, and men wanted to know where his loyalty lay.

"Let Thorfinn show his face outside that fort," Macbeatha said grimly, "and you shall see the color of a Morayman's courage—and the color of a Norseman's blood. But I will not attack the fortress. That is a fool's errand, and I am no fool."

Gillecomgain was furious at his cousin's inaction. Although the wound on his leg was still painful, he mounted a horse and led a fresh contingent of warriors up the coast. There, they say, he argued bitterly with Macbeatha, who maintained that an assault on Burghead would cost the lives of many fine warriors, and budge Thorfinn not one fingerlength. But Gillecomgain would have none of it. Rallying a large number of men, he rushed the fortress like a madman—and the results were as my lord had predicted. A good many Scots lay dead and dying on the field, and Thorfinn was still in his place.

"Go back to your new wife," Macbeatha told his hot-headed cousin. "Leave the removal of Thorfinn to me. I have more patience than you and he put together—I will starve him out of his sanctuary. He will be gone by autumn."

And so he was. As the Scots waiting outside Burghead began to drift away, needing to harvest their fields and move their cattle, the Norsemen also grew restless. One evening, when the moon was new, Macbeatha called in all his watchmen and damped his fires, and the next morning the fortress was empty. Under cover of darkness, Thorfinn had retreated to his longboats, moored off the point out of reach of the Scots, and headed home.

Did they have it planned? Was it agreed between them? I do not know. Macbeatha sent for me after Gillecomgain left, that he might have pleasant company while he kept his vigil outside Burghead, but he never spoke of any arrangement, and I saw no traffic between them. I only know that, though he smiled and joked with his men, in private his heart was heavy and his sighs deep. Some nights he stood in the opening of his tent and stared into the darkness for hours, and others he cradled his head in my lap while I stroked his forehead and massaged his temples. It was no easy time for him.

When it was over, we all rode back to Inverness with great pomp and ceremony, as though we had won some valorous campaign rather than having out-waited the Norsemen. Macbeatha paraded his entire warband to the fortress to announce that the Viking prince had been forced from the shores of Moray and was unlikely to trouble us again soon. Gillecomgain stood at the entrance to his hall for this show, with the Lady Gruoch beside him. She wore much finer clothes than she'd worn in Fife, and was adorned with gold and silver. Such things suited her, cool and aloof as she was. I tried to read on her face what two months of marriage to Gillecomgain had done to her, but I could not detect so much as a shadow under her eye. If marriage disagreed with her, she gave no sign. If it pleased her, she gave no sign of that, either.

We all dined at the fortress that night, by invitation of Gillecomgain, and my lord—both as tanist and as hero of the day—sat next to his cousin and the new mistress of the hall. I was pleased to see he and Gruoch were polite to each other, for during the entire journey from Loch Leven to Inverness, they had continued to harry one another unmercifully. She had taken every opportunity to cast aspersions upon his character, his intelligence, and the fate of his immortal soul. But he, rather than defending himself or refuting her indictments, had smiled (or leered) and agreed with her, and if there was not sufficient evidence to condemn him, he invented it. Then he had praised her lavishly for those qualities she failed to demonstrate toward him, such as kindness, graciousness, and tolerance. Never had a harsh word or a cruel phrase passed his lips with regard to the Lady Gruoch—but never had a compliment rung true.

Here in the fortress, however, where she was queen and Macbeatha an honored guest, Gruoch seemed to have surrendered her querulous ways and was, instead, gracious and thoughtful. Perhaps it was only that she had been frightened on that journey to an unknown land and an unknown husband, and sought to vent her unhappiness on the target least likely to suffer damage. Or perhaps, having seen Gillecomgain's brutish nature, she thought better now of his charming, if roguish, cousin.

Or perhaps, I thought briefly, she found fulfillment in those pleasures she shared with her husband, and so became more tractable— But no. No, it could not be that *any* woman should find pleasure in Gillecomgain's touch.

Yet pride and satisfaction were evident on the mormaer's face any time he chanced to look at his wife; and the only smiles I saw on her lips that night were those bestowed upon her husband.

The harvest was a bountiful one for us, and Macbeatha gained many clients in the area Thorfinn had raided, for he leased stock to them and provided grain to be paid for in goods and services during the following year. These arrangements were made with the chieftains, of course, who in turn made contracts with the men of their tribes, so that both high and low were provided for—and all owed their loyalty, directly or indirectly, to Macbeatha. Then, when the last of the reaping was done and the cattle had been moved down from the hills into their winter pastures, Macbeatha mounted his favorite horse and rode up into the Highlands to fetch Brenna and her babe to Inverness for the winter.

Motherhood and widowhood had taken some of the fight out of Brenna. The child, called Hagenlaoch or "little hero," was a fussy and demanding baby, so Brenna was tired most of the time and slept whenever he would permit. Macbeatha offered to get a nurse for the boy, but she preferred to care for him herself, saying it gave her comfort and took her mind off the loss of her husband. I think it was a good thing, for it made her content to let Sosanna run the household.

Sosanna was the wife of Girc, grandson of old Donn, and had been overseeing Macbeatha's household for the past year. She also had a young son, and I was curious how Macbeatha would react to having two small babies in the house for the winter. Men who are unaccustomed to babes often have little patience with their fussing and squalling. But while I saw irritation on his face now and again, mostly he seemed awed by them. One might find him standing by Hagenlaoch's cradle, staring in wonder at the tiny person inside. Or he would put out a long, blunt finger and gently stroke the cheek of the sleeping child. "His skin is so soft," he might remark. "Hard to imagine he will grow to be a tough old warrior like his grandfather." Or, "See how his brow furrows while he sleeps. What do you suppose one so small can dream of, that would make him scowl so?" His fascination only made the ache inside me worsen. There was still no sign of a child in my womb.

Then, to make matters worse, Brenna had hardly been there a week when we had a visitor.

Gruoch came to the door, accompanied by her maid Maisie and one of Gillecomgain's warriors. "You must be Brenna!" she greeted my lord's sister, smiling warmly and holding out both hands to her. "I am Gruoch, your cousin's wife. When I heard you would be in Inverness for the winter, I was so pleased! My husband speaks well of you, and I have been anxious to meet you."

My jaw must have dropped to the floor, I was so surprised to hear this congenial talk from a woman normally so distant. Yet she and Brenna sat down together and chatted on as though they had known each other since birth. Sosanna joined them, and the three were a most lively trio, laughing and playing with the two babies. Gruoch adored the babies, cooing over them and cuddling them, just like any other young girl who wishes to have one of her own.

Maisie sat with them, but I knew better than to stay too near Brenna for very long, so I wandered out back to the kitchen to help Aithne until a shout went up, and I knew Macbeatha was coming home. I ran, as always, to draw a horn of ale for him and greet him in the hall. He came through the door panting and laughing and wiping the sweat from his brow, for he had been out with Girc, Donn's grandson, and they had raced each other back. "Ho, here is my Valkyrie!" he sang out when he saw me waiting. "She always knows what a man wants when he walks through the door and is ready to supply it, be it a draught of ale—" Here he took the horn and drained it. "—or a willing mouth." Then he cast aside the empty horn and caught me up in a lascivious kiss.

"Brother," Brenna called in chilly tones from her place by the fire, "we have a guest."

Macbeatha set me back on my feet and turned to see who it was.

All merriment vanished from his face in an instant. He looked almost as grim as he had when Thorfinn sat in the fortress at Burghead, and his own loyalty was in question.

Then a crafty smile twisted his lips and his eyes took on a malicious sparkle. "Why, Lady Gruoch," he greeted with a courtly gesture, "how nice to see you. Please forgive my boisterous entrance, but then, it is only to be expected from a beast such as I."

Sosanna giggled—she thought it was a joke. Brenna made an impatient little noise, then said, "Oh, don't be such a tease, Macbeatha."

But the Lady Gruoch smiled archly and replied, "Pray, do not chastise yourself, lord, for there is a touch of the beast in us all. Perhaps our strength lies in knowing what will rouse it in us."

Macbeatha hesitated, no doubt unable (like myself) to understand the gist of that remark. How could he respond to it when he wasn't sure what it meant? Then he straightened himself and tried his usual tack. "You grace my house, lady, with your presence. I trust my kinswomen have greeted you in a worthy manner, and made you at ease?" His smile was most beneficent, his manner most smug.

Gruoch laughed gaily, again throwing him off balance. I don't believe he had ever heard her laugh gaily before. The other ladies joined her, and she exclaimed, "Oh, we have had the most delightful afternoon! I cannot tell you how I cherish the company of such lively and gentle ladies. My husband has seen to my every comfort at the fortress, but as yet he has not enticed any of his noble kinswomen to come visit us—though I understand his sister-in-law will come for Christmas. So while I lack for nothing in goods and authority, I do long for the friendship of other women." Here she extended a hand each to Brenna and Sosanna. "But this afternoon I have discovered that, with these two so nearby, I now lack nothing." And she seemed genuinely happy.

It pierced my lord through like a slender spear. Through all his wrangling with Gruoch, and behind each insult, veiled or unveiled, that he loosed in her direction, was the gleeful conviction that as Gillecomgain's wife, this sharp-tongued, self-righteous churchmaid would know unparalleled misery. The ultimate vindication of his suffering her unjust invectives was the knowledge that in Gillecomgain, she had gained a husband who was every vile thing she accused him of being. How he relished the thought—for he told me many times—of her weeping in her bed, and cursing the day her mother had sold her, for her brother's future, to Gillecomgain.

So this profession of her complete happiness went hard on him.

"They have been remiss in one thing, though," Gruoch added, at which Brenna and Sosanna looked horrified and Macbeatha quite stunned. But she smiled warmly. "Why, they have not yet invited me to stay and dine, and I don't know how I shall forgive them if they make me go back home when we are having such fun!"

Then they laughed again, the three of them, and Macbeatha pulled a face. There were quick and repeated urgings by both women that she stay, to which Gruoch readily succumbed. Sosanna went off to the kitchen to see what special treats could be added to the menu in Gruoch's honor, Girc went off to find his grandfather, and I drew another horn of ale for Macbeatha. Then my lord spotted the warrior who had accompanied Gruoch hence. "Niall! What, does Gillecomgain send you to spy on his wife?"

"To see her safely here and back," Niall protested, blushing at the jest.

"My husband is ever concerned for my welfare," Gruoch interjected. "Although I'm sure you do not understand it, he treasures me and worries that some harm might befall me if I go out with only my maid for company."

"Ha!" Macbeatha laughed, eyes sparkling with merriment. "He's afraid I shall steal you away from him." Throwing himself onto one knee at her feet, he clasped her hand and made to bring it to his lips. Gruoch snatched it away and glared at him.

"The day my husband has to worry about me falling victim to your charms," she snapped, "is the day a mother starling lays her eggs out for the fox!"

This was the behavior he expected of her, and Macbeatha rose to his feet chuckling wickedly. "Niall," he called, "go tell my cousin his wife dines with us tonight—and don't bother to come back. One of us will see her and her maid safely home." Then he turned and caught me around the shoulders with one arm, ushering me toward the back of the house with him. "That ought to bring Gillecomgain running," he said softly.

Chapter Twenty-Five

He was right. The meal was scarcely ended when Gillecomgain halloed from outside and was bidden to enter. "Join us, cousin!" Macbeatha invited heartily. "Kelda, bring him some ale!"

Gillecomgain looked nervous and almost embarrassed. He approached his wife and kissed her hand. "I missed your presence at table, lady," he mumbled.

Gruoch beamed a smile as warm as summer sun. "Oh, indulge me, lord!" she entreated prettily. "I find I so enjoy the company of the women in this house. Do be good enough to let me visit them often, won't you?"

Blushing, Gillecomgain cleared his throat and answered, "Be sure, you may visit as often as it pleases you. Far be it from me to deny you the company of your own sex." But he could not keep from glancing out the corner of his eye at Macbeatha.

So it came to be that once each week, Gruoch would visit Brenna and Sosanna; and in the evening, as men returned from their tasks, Gillecomgain would show up to keep an eye on her. The women chattered away and worked at spinning or sewing or some other such handiwork, while the men played *brandub* or chess and told tales. It was quite a cozy little scene, except for the underlying tension between the two cousins. Macbeatha created this intentionally, for he disliked Gillecomgain's company in general, and he hated seeing domestic harmony between the mormaer and his wife. Nothing wounded his pride so grievously as to think this woman, this *girl*, actually preferred Gillecomgain to him. It galled him. It puzzled him. It puzzled me, frankly. But do you know, I think that was the reason she came to visit—just to flaunt her matrimonial contentment in his face.

At any rate, Macbeatha quickly grew tired of his cousin's regular visits, and so he set about making the mormaer uncomfortable—not overtly, of course, for Gillecomgain would have taken offense, and that was not in Macbeatha's plan. So he used the simple ploy of beating the man at chess.

Gillecomgain hated to lose. In prior years, when the two of them had played, Macbeatha had been tactful enough to let his cousin win occasionally, but such grace went by the wayside now. He beat Gillecomgain quickly, and he beat him consistently, until one night the mormaer sent his regrets and one of his warriors to escort his wife home. Macbeatha smiled with satisfaction and asked Girc if he wanted to play.

Now, Girc was a fine steward, gradually taking over for his grandfather as Donn found himself troubled by rheumatism and a mysterious shortness of breath. He was also a decent warrior, having as much common sense as courage and skill. But he was not much of a chess player. He was less of a challenge than Gillecomgain, and Macbeatha was disinclined to hurt the young man's feelings by repeated drubbings. Donn provided a better game, but he often nodded off by the fire, and my lord was loath to disturb him. So while the women chattered, and Girc worked at making a drum, and Donn dozed in his chair, Macbeatha paced the hall restlessly, seeking some occupation for his active mind.

Mind you, he had no trouble on the nights when Gruoch was not there—I see that now. But her presence put him on edge: like a challenge left unanswered, he could neither ignore it nor tear himself from it. So he paced, and fretted, until one evening he looked at the chessboard with its simply-carved figures and asked, without looking up, "Lady Gruoch, do you play chess?"

She looked up from her needlework, as did the other two women. But while their mouths gaped in amazement, Gruoch seemed to find nothing odd in the question. "My brother speaks enthusiastically of the game, but the Reverend Abbot did not indulge in it, and so I have not learned much about it."

Still he did not look at her. "Would you like to?"

She considered that a moment, but only a moment. "It could not be less entertaining than stitching this kerchief," she admitted.

Putting her needlework aside, she rose and crossed to where the board was set up.

Macbeatha seated her at the table, but he himself did not sit down. Instead, he stood several steps off, leaning negligently against a post that supported the loft, and described for her each of the pieces and their peculiar methods of movement on the board. Gruoch listened quite seriously, then proceeded to repeat the information back to him as she moved the players around on the board, reinforcing with eye and hand what her ears had taken in. They began a game, with him coaching her as they went, and she moving both her markers and his, for he would not sit down at the board with her.

This went on until nearly Christmas, when the arrival of visitors at the fortress kept the lady in her own hall for many weeks. It was near to the Festival of Bride, then, before she came once more to my lord's house. He was not there, having ridden out to Nairn to speak with one of his clients. It was nearly dark when at last he returned, but he had hardly given greetings and shed his cloak when something about her appearance caught his attention. Crossing to her immediately, he took her face in one hand and tilted it this way and that in the light from the hearth. Then he let go and took a step back. "And when does Gillecomgain expect his heir?"

Gruoch blushed to the roots of her dark brown hair—possibly the only time I have ever seen her do so—and replied, in the most even tone she could muster, "At midsummer, I think."

Exclamations of surprise and excitement erupted from the other women, but Macbeatha kept right on. "And does he know of it?"

"I have confided it to him."

"Good." He went to the peg where I had just hung his cloak and took it down again. "For I intend to invite myself to his table tonight, and I didn't want to congratulate him on his good fortune if you had not yet shared the news. I wish you much joy, Lady, and hope your time will go easy on you." Then with a swirl of the cloak, he went out the door and did not come back until morning.

Now, it was not unusual for Macbeatha to stay the night at the fortress. But it was unusual for Owen to bring him home the next day so blinded by headache and nausea that he couldn't stand on his own feet. It was also unusual for him to lie on his bed the rest of the day with the shutters fastened and the door closed, and to snarl at anyone who disturbed him. I was not foolish enough to venture near him. I knew why he was so distressed. Gillecomgain, his hated cousin and rival, was to have an heir, while Macbeatha had none. And it was my fault.

I wanted to crawl into a hole and die. When he had stalked out of the house the previous evening, I fled to the stable and flung myself weeping into a pile of cold and dusty straw. I was cursed, and no longer could he ignore it. Only after I had cried myself tearless did I realize how stupid I was being. I shouldn't wait for him to find another, I should do it for him. I should find him a comely and fertile wench to bear his babes, and then he would love me for bringing her to him. I would a thousand times rather give over half my nights to another and see him happy, with a child of his own, than keep him all to myself and know his heart was sore.

But in the morning when he returned with Owen and I saw what state he was in, my tears started afresh and I fled back to the stable to lament my fate. It was there Aithne found me. "What is it?" she asked anxiously. "Are you all right? Are you hurt?"

All I could force out between my sobs was, "My fault. It's all my fault."

It took her some time to calm me down enough to get the sense of my sorrow. Then she only clicked her tongue and shook her head. "Ach, don't take on so hard, lass. The Lord gives, and the Lord withholds—we mustn't fret ourselves over His decisions. Now, dry your eyes and think more cheerful thoughts, so when Macbeatha shows his face at the fire, you'll give him no more to fret about. He frets himself enough about things he can't control."

But I couldn't do it. I skimmed the milk with hands that shook, and churned butter with tears leaking down my cheeks; and when evening came and Sosanna bade me climb upstairs and tell Macbeatha the meal was ready, I ran away and hid. I simply could not face him, for shame at my inadequacy and fear of what he must think of me.

Donn limped out to the stable to find me. "Stop making such a fuss, girl," he said sharply, and I was mortified to realize Aithne must have told him why I wept. "Babies are not the be-all and end-all of the world."

"Then what is?" I demanded, and he had no answer for that.

I spent a cold night in the stable, burrowed into the straw with two cats for bedfellows—I was sure I deserved nothing more. In the morning I crept inside to find a crust of bread—why should anyone waste good food on me?--but when I heard my lord call for me, I could not bear to face him and see the reproach in his face. I fled once more to my retreat.

Before long, the door was flung open and in stomped Macbeatha, tall and stern in the gray dawn. He marched directly to where I cowered and stood over me, fists planted on his hips, his chin and cheeks rough with two days growth of beard. "Well," he grumbled. "This is an odd place for a *house* maid."

It was not like him to take that petulant tone with me so early in the day. It confirmed my fear that he had grown weary of my childlessness and would now condemn me for it. "Please don't send me away, lord," I whimpered, rising to my knees but unable to meet his eyes. I could bear any punishment but to be parted from him.

"Send you— By St. Drostan's tooth, who put that idea in your head?" he swore crossly. "I'll have a choice word or two with whomever it was. I don't need a sobbing slave girl first thing in the morning. It was Brenna, wasn't it?"

"No, lord," I answered hastily. "It was my own idea."

"Why on earth would you think I might send you away?" he demanded, both astonished and annoyed.

"B-b-because I—I—" The words would scarcely tear loose from my trembling lips. "I cannot—cannot give you—a—a child," I managed finally, and broke out in fresh sobs.

His silence was palpable, like a great cold that crystallized around him and then spread out through the stable, freezing everything it touched and stifling my sobs. I waited in agony for his rebuke. When he finally spoke, his tone was meant to be gentle, but he could not keep the hoarseness from his voice. "Silly goose," he rasped. "And I suppose no one in my house had the courage to point out that none of my wenches has ever borne me a child."

The breath vanished from my lungs as if the horse in the next stall had kicked me in the stomach. None of his wenches ... I grew dizzy and swayed on my knees. But—but he was so—so—

He snorted softly and spoke with what was meant to be wry humor, but failed miserably. "If you turned up with child, I should wonder whose bed you had been warming while I was gone."

No child? Ever? No red-haired bastard tucked away in the hills? No husband studying his wife's offspring with suspicion? No— no—

Suddenly all the anguish, all the self-recriminations, I had known for my own inadequacy, I felt aching in his heart. Oh, how could Fate be so cruel to him, to deny him a son, an heir? How could the Christian god be so heartless, to one so faithful and so valiant and so strong and so— Leaping to my feet, I launched myself at him and clung to him, wishing I could take back on myself all the pain and emptiness I now knew were his. "Oh, it's not fair!" I cried, pressing my face to his breast. "You should have a son—a dozen sons—all as handsome and as brave as you. You should have daughters to pet and spoil, and boys to make mischief and a house full of laughter and shouts and ..."

His arms came around me as I ran out of breath and thought both. "Filling the house doesn't seem to be a problem," he remarked dryly. "As for the other ..." His fingers twined themselves in my hair. "Do you want a child so badly?" he asked softly.

"Only if it's yours," I replied fiercely, and I felt his arms tighten around me.

After a moment he said, "Such things are in God's hands, and it may be He will change His mind some day. In the meantime, let us speak no more about it." Then he loosed himself from my grip and started back toward the house. "As soon as your hands are steady," he said flatly, "I need a shave."

The next time Gruoch came to visit, Macbeatha contrived to have business elsewhere; but before he left he set up the chess board, moved one of his players, and said to Brenna, "Tell Lady Gruoch it is her move."

Upon receiving that directive, Gruoch sat at the board and pondered it carefully for a long while At last she moved one of her pieces, then went back to her needlework and her gossip.

So it went from Bride to Easter. Each would ponder the chess board, alone, make one move, and go on with other things. Sometimes Macbeatha would laugh out loud when he saw how she countered him; other times Gruoch would mutter under her breath as she saw what fresh trap he had lured her into. Once Maisie bumped into the board and sent all the pieces tumbling, much to her dismay; but Gruoch was not the least bit flustered. "It's all right," she assured the frightened girl. "I know where they all were." Without hesitation she set all the players back right, and when Macbeatha came the next day to study the board, his sharp eye detected nothing amiss.

Then, just as the weather was warming and the ground was turning to mud underfoot, just as everyone began to feel the approach of Beltaine and the joy of spring, little Hagenlaoch began to wheeze. Macbeatha sent for an old woman who knew of healing herbs and potions, and Brenna sent money to the bishop to have a special service of healing spoken for her son, but it was to no avail. The baby wheezed, and coughed, and turned blue, and died.

Brenna, of course, took the loss of her son very badly. And not surprisingly, she found a target for all her anguish and her pain—me. The child had scarcely coughed his last cough and grown still in his cradle when the distraught mother turned on me. "You did it!" she screamed. "You put the Evil Eye on him!" And if Sosanna had not stepped between us, I believe she would have plunged her dagger into my heart on the spot.

It took Sosanna and one of the other servants to hold her back while I fled the room. I went first to find Macbeatha, and tell him the bad news. He was heartbroken. "I would have made him my heir," he whispered in my ear, his arms wrapped tight around me. "In the old days, in my grandmother's tribe, a man's heir was his sister's son—I wouldn't have minded that." Then, of course, I could not add to his sorrow by telling him about Brenna's accusation. Besides, I thought if I took myself out of the house for a time, her first reaction would pass and she would grow more rational.

Ha. Though I wandered about the town, and dawdled at the dairy with the milk maids before returning to the house, I found her anger had not cooled. But Macbeatha was there now, so when she charged at me with arms flailing, he caught her around the waist and flung her back into her chair. "That's enough!" he roared.

"She killed my baby!" Brenna sobbed.

"She did nothing of the kind," he snapped. "You wouldn't let her touch him, or even go near him." That was true—she had warned me from the first day she entered the house what would happen if I went near her son.

"She put the Evil Eye on him!"

"Nonsense! There were enough rowan sprigs on his cradle to protect him from any ill magic. He died of a cough, not a curse."

"I want her out of this house!"

Now he leaned over her chair and looked her straight in the eye. "She is my slave," he said, "and this is my house. If you do not like the situation, it is you who must leave."

That seemed a terrible, cruel thing to say when she had just lost her baby, so I tugged at his arm and said, "Please, lord, don't send her—"

"I'm not sending her anywhere," he said firmly. "But you are not leaving—not until I do. Is that clear, Brenna?"

Brenna turned from us both and began a loud keening over her child, who was laid out on a tiny bier with rush candles burning brightly at head and foot to keep the demons away.

I stayed out of the house as much as I could during the seven days of mourning. After that, any time I entered a room where she was, Brenna got up and left. Macbeatha had forbidden her to speak any more of the Evil Eye, and so she held her tongue, but the damage was done. I noticed her maids would make a sign to ward off evil whenever I approached, and even Sosanna—that sweet and gentle creature—grew nervous if I came too near her baby's cradle. I prayed fervently that Macbeatha would take me with him on campaign again that summer, and not leave me in the house while he was gone.

Then, like manna from heaven, came the messenger from High King Malcolm.

He bore a letter which my lord opened hastily, but he was already grinning before he broke the seal. Letter-writing was not much practiced in the north, except by clerics, so I had noted when Macbeatha sent a letter by courier to the High King just after Bride. Apparently he anticipated a favorable answer, and he got it. "Dhui!" he shouted, and his young servant came running. "Send my token around to all my guardsmen, and any others who would have glory and riches. Horsemen only—I take no foot on this campaign. Tell them to be ready on the second day after the Beltaine fire. We ride for Bernicia, to serve the High King there!" In his joy he lifted me up into the air and twirled me around, adding, "And no doubt some fat cattle across the border in Northumbria will decide to follow us home."

So we escaped for the summer, I from Brenna's vindictiveness, and he from Gillecomgain's obvious fertility and his war with Thorfinn. During the pleasant months that followed, I told myself by the time we returned to Inverness, things would have sorted themselves out. With any luck, Thorfinn would kill Gillecomgain and my lord could become mormaer—and marry the widow, if she would consent, and have his claim to the high kingship in future years. Oh, yes, they still did verbal combat, trying their best to savage one another with words, but there have been worse marriages made, and for poorer reasons. If she would not suffer him to her bed, at least it would not deprive him of an heir—and they could always play chess in the evenings.

Do you know, they kept that chess game going the entire time he was gone? He would send his move back in a message to Donn, and she would forward hers through that same intermediary. Wherever we went, Macbeatha's chess board went with him, and the only thing that pleased him more than a successful cattle raid was to have Gruoch's next move, so he could ponder his response.

My problem with Brenna did vanish over the summer, for while we were gone, Raghallach's second son, Farrell, arrived in Inverness for Midsummer. He now had his dead brother's inheritance, and wished to have his wife as well. Brenna consented and went back with him into the highlands. As a widow, she no longer needed her brother's consent, although I'm sure she would have had it. Macbeatha still needed his ties to Raghallach.

To Macbeatha, she left a message: "Come visit me and enjoy my hospitality as I have enjoyed yours; but do not bring that heathen girl with you. This is *my* house." It didn't bother me; I knew Macbeatha would never stay with her for very long at a time. So my problem was solved.

His, however, was a little more complicated.

Chapter Twenty-Six

Gillecomgain was unhappy to see his cousin go south that summer. He was especially unhappy to see him take so many fine horsemen with him. They came from the length and breadth of Moray, young men eager to see the land beyond the Mounth, and seasoned warriors who had grown distrustful of Gillecomgain's leadership. They all followed the ruddy young tanist, even if it was into Malcolm's service they went. After all, it was not Malcolm who would be telling them what to do, it was Macbeatha; and at Dunglas and Dunkeld and, yes, even at Burghead, he had shown that he knew, not only how to fight and to lead warriors, but how to plan and execute successful campaigns. They trusted him.

"You steal the heart of my warband!" Gillecomgain raged.

Macbeatha only laughed. We were in Gillecomgain's hall, where my lord was taking his leave. Five hundred men waited for him outside. "I steal nothing," he said. "They are clients of mine as well as yours, and they may choose freely with whom they ride. They choose me."

"You weaken my invasion of Caithness!" cried the mormaer.

A nasty snarl curled Macbeatha's lips. "Then stay home. Patrol the lands you have, and pray Thorfinn turns his attention elsewhere."

It was calculated to inflame Gillecomgain, and it did. "I do not fear that great Norse toad!" he roared. "I will drive him out of my lands and into the sea!"

Macbeatha gave a great sigh. "Very well, go play in Caithness. Try to take back your mother's lands, where your father failed. Me,

I'd rather play in Bernicia. I won't find the Northumbrians camped at my gate come autumn." Then he turned and approached the Lady Gruoch, to whom I was returning a scarf she had chanced to leave behind by the chess board. "If you have performed your errand, Kelda, it is time for us to go," he said.

But though Macbeatha addressed me, it was Gruoch's eyes he met. They were dark with silent fury. "You are a cold bastard," she accused, too softly for her husband to hear.

"Why?" my lord mocked in equally low tones. "Because I would steal Northumbrian cattle, but not have them steal mine?"

"Because you goad my husband so he must fight Thorfinn. What if he is killed?"

Macbeatha smiled wickedly. "Why, lady, then I should become mormaer, and marry his grieving widow."

Her mouth gaped in shock and her eyes blazed with outrage. "I would burn in hell before I'd marry you!" she hissed.

"You can do both," he suggested roguishly. "We could burn in company, you and I, together for eternity."

Now Gillecomgain began to wonder at this soft murmuring between his wife and his tanist, and he came nearer. "That is most gracious of you, lady," Macbeatha invented smoothly, "to pray for our safety. But I would rather you prayed for our success." Her mouth tightened at the lie, but she could hardly object with her husband standing by. "What shall I bring you from Northumbria?"

"Only victory," she replied tightly.

"I know what you should bring her," I told him when we were outside. "Bring her two or three heads to wash. That would take some of the vinegar out of her."

The High King was at Edinburgh that summer. If he harbored any anger against my lord for his part in the raid on Dunkeld two years before, he never spoke of it. But Crinan did not come to court that season, sending his son Maldred instead with a contingent of Athollmen. After my lord had paid his respects to the High King, he took his warband on to Bernicia, giving no opportunity for the two rival tribes to clash.

Many men of high rank arrived to wait upon Malcolm in Edinburgh, including Macbeatha's friend Bowen with his uncle Echmarcach, who was King of the Isles and a client of the High King. Echmarcach stayed at court, but Bowen said he could think of nothing more exciting than to spend the summer romping around

Bernicia with Macbeatha, checking under the skirts of Lothian women and sneaking into Northumbria to fight a few Danes. He joined us where we camped on the coast near Lindisfarne.

The district of Bernicia lies part in Lothian—which belonged then to the Scots—and part in Northumbria, which belonged in some manner to the Anglish king, who was not Anglish at all but Danish—as were all the overlords of Northumbria. For years the Scots and the Danes had battled over Bernicia, for it was a rich place, and the Angles who dwelt there acknowledged first one sovereign and then the other, depending on which served their purposes better. So while Bernicia was technically Malcolm's, the residents were not particularly hospitable to armies of Scots tramping about the countryside.

My lord, however, was most gracious to the Bernicians and did his best to keep his men from making too much mischief there. Instead, he led them on raids into Northumbria, where he had no compunction about mischief but looted and capered to his heart's content. He and Bowen would come back in high spirits, their horses laden with trinkets of brass and silver, usually with a cask or two of honey mead lashed to their saddles, and driving a herd of cattle or sheep which were promptly slaughtered for feasting. Then they would get roaring drunk and sit by the fire with their warriors, boasting about the men they had killed and the women they had ravished. If I believed one tenth of the stories they told, there would not have been a soul left living or undefiled between Lindisfarne and York.

Soon after the Festival of St. Mary we received word that the Lady Gruoch had been delivered of a boy child and had named him Lulach. All the Moray tribesmen rejoiced that their mormaer had an heir, and they drank to the health of mother and child (but pissed on Gillecomgain, whom they loathed to a man). Macbeatha was the heartiest well-wisher, proposing toast after toast, inventing wild accolades to the child, prophesying Lulach would be such a great warrior that wind and water would bend to his will, and the *tarve uisge* would rise out of Loch Ness to sing his lullaby. When he came to bed he was quite drunk, but as he lay beside me on the camp bed, his joy seemed to dribble away like water from an ill-made trough.

Knowing how his heart ached for a child of his own, I held him and stroked him and murmured comforting sounds. He lay limp and unresisting, content to be so solaced, until out of the blue he said, "My grandfather's going to be so-o-o-o-o-o angry."

"Why?" I asked, wondering if I had missed something or if he was just that drunk.

"Because there's another male in the line of Kenneth mac Dubh. The boy could grow up to challenge him—or more likely, to challenge Duncan. He's going to be furious."

"It doesn't matter, does it?" I soothed. *"You're* going to be High King, anyway—even if you have to marry the old aunt—so what difference does one small baby make?"

"You're right," he agreed. "It is Gillecomgain who is in the way just now, for I must hold Moray before I can take Alba. I'm afraid I shall have to kill him, if Thorfinn doesn't do it for me. And oh, God, won't she hate me then?"

I didn't have to ask him who.

Not long after, we received tidings that Gillecomgain, filled with bravado upon the birth of his son, had actually won an engagement against the Norsemen near Duncansby and now occupied that town. Thorfinn was up in the Orkneys at the time, collecting *skatt,* but everyone knew he would not let the matter rest. It was no surprise that, by the time men in Lindisfarne began to think of going home to help with the harvest, word came to us that Thorfinn and Thorkel had raised an army in the Orkneys and come swarming down the coastline toward Duncansby. Gillecomgain, with unaccustomed wisdom, chose to march gloriously back to Inverness before they arrived, so each side went home claiming the victory.

As autumn approached, Macbeatha brought his men back to Edinburgh where he loaded a ship with the booty he had acquired and sent it back to Inverness. But he himself seemed reluctant to go. Half his company departed, brimming with satisfaction at the summer's campaign, while the rest talked half-heartedly about one more raid before they settled down to the domestic chores of harvest, and a long winter rich with tales of their exploits. Bowen and his uncle stayed, too, the lot of them drinking the king's ale and eating at his board. They were there when a messenger burst into the hall shouting that Cnut, king of the Danes, was sailing up the coast of Lothian toward Alba.

Cnut was a fierce and ruthless man with powerful armies at his command. Not only was he king of the Danes, but of Norway, and more importantly, of Angleland. It was his nobles and retainers who ruled in Northumbria. He had been on a pilgrimage to Rome, one reason Macbeatha had chosen this particular summer to make mischief in his lands. The jarl of Northumbrian—Eadulf, I think it was—was a force to be reckoned with, make no mistake, but the Scots knew they could meet him on equal terms if he came into Lothian after them. Cnut was another matter.

Malcolm had no time to muster a large army, although he sent messengers immediately to Crinan, Duncan, and the mormaers of Fortriu and Ce. If Cnut came on the attack, Malcolm would have to meet him with the forces at hand: Fife, some Athollmen under Duncan's brother Maldred, Echmarcach's fifty, and Macbeatha and his two hundred and some Moray horsemen.

The air in the hall hung heavy as fog while we awaited further news. There were only five ships in Cnut's fleet, and no sign of a land army, yet no one rested easy. As soon as they turned to sail up the Firth of Forth, merchants began burying their silver, and women and children gathered inside the fortress and the cathedral for refuge. Herdsmen drove their beasts far up into the Pentland Hills to hide them in small glens and caves.

"He does not come to fight," my lord predicted to the king. "Even if there were fifty—even if there were a hundred—armed men on each ship, it is not enough for him to attack Edinburgh. He knows we are five times that, with more on the way."

"I agree," Malcolm said. "He comes to talk, or I would not have let him draw this close without testing him."

Macbeatha leaned and spoke low in the High King's ear. "Let me set the defenses. We'll line the roadway, but at a distance, and in hiding. We'll put spearmen on every hill between here and the firth, again in hiding. Let him approach without knowing our strength, or our mind."

"It is not your place to command the defense," Malcolm said firmly. "Fife will command for us." He called the mormaer of that Great Tribe to him. "Take charge of the defenses. Place your men along the Leith Walk and other likely routes from the firth, but well back, out of sight. Put your best spearmen upon the heights. Send Maldred to greet Cnut and escort him hither, with his men at Cnut's back. And Moray ..." He glanced back at his Macbeatha and Bowen, who had been his fosterlings. "Post Moray and the Isles on the walls of the fortress in plain view. Let Cnut know I am not unattended."

A smile spread over Macbeatha's face. Though Malcolm had denied him command, the king had heeded his advice and given his troops the premier assignment.

As men rushed to do the king's bidding, Malcolm called to my lord. "Well, Moray," he said with a twinkle in his aging eyes, "it would seem you are in control of this fortress. What an opportunity for you!"

Macbeatha answered with a sly grin that faded to gravity. "I may be an ambitious man, lord, but I am a Scot first. When Alba is threatened, I stand fast by her king. No man will find fault with me there."

"Really." The twinkle in Malcolm's eye changed to a cold glitter. "And if Moray were threatened?"

A shadow passed over my lord's face. "I have my quarrels with my cousin," he said, "but he is chieftain of my tribe and blood of my blood. Who stands against Moray, stands against us both."

I wondered then, crouched quiet as a mouse near the stairs, what was meant by this exchange between them. I did not learn for some months, but then it became abundantly clear.

Cnut put ashore at the port of Leith, which is on the Firth of Forth a short distance from Edinburgh. The king's grandson Maldred, younger brother to Duncan, met the Danish ruler with a conspicuous escort and brought him along a road watched by a thousand pairs of Scottish eyes. But when Cnut reached the outskirts of the city, he would not come in. There he pitched his tents and set up his camp and waited for Malcolm to come to him.

This Malcolm did, after a suitable length of time, and a good long argument with his advisors. Fife was against it. "You're no damned lackey, that you should go to his tent like a steward to his master."

But, "If I were in his place," said Macbeatha, "I certainly would not walk into the jaws of the wolf. To meet in an open place, before the city, is a good choice. He came many leagues to see you; you can go one or two to see him."

So Malcolm had his own tent pitched across the road from Cnut, along with those of Maldred, Macbeatha, and the Isles. Fife stayed in Edinburgh. I went with my lord, to wait upon him— but also, I was surprised to hear, at the High King's request. "The language of the Orkneys is only slightly different from the language of the Danish kings," Malcolm had said. "Let her wait upon us, and our guests, when we meet. Who knows what she may hear that does not reach our ears?"

For that same reason, he wanted Macbeatha and Echmarcach with him when he and Cnut met, for they both spoke Norn and could hear the Danish king's words from his own lips, rather than through an interpreter. Maldred he bade stand watch outside the tent where the meeting took place. His grandson did not look happy at being left out; on top of that, there was a slight drizzle that dripped off his leather helmet into his eyes and soaked through his fine woolen cloak.

By careful arrangement, we entered through one end of the tent at the exact moment Cnut and his entourage entered through the other. Both kings were dressed regally, in elaborately embroidered linen garments with rich woolen cloaks that pinned at the right shoulder and left their sword arms free. Gold twinkled from their necks, arms, and fingers, and their scabbards glittered with jewels.

"I greet you, Cnut, king of the Danes and of Norway and Angleland," said Malcolm.

"And I greet you, Malcolm, High King of Alba and ruler of the Scots," Cnut replied. He had the look of a true Norseman: tall, fair-haired, and handsome, except for a crooked nose most likely broken in some battle or brawl. He was perhaps thirty-five winters, whereas Malcolm had seen nearly twice that. Two or three noblemen attended him, one in particular who was rather young and glowered unaccountably at Macbeatha.

The two kings sat in chairs, and I served ale to them, but not to their men. Each had a translator at his elbow, and they spoke back and forth of many things: Cnut's recent pilgrimage to Rome, the harvest now underway, the Jarl of Northumbria, and the king of Dublin, who was also a Dane. Finally Cnut came to the point.

"Your warriors have been troubling my farmers in Northumbria."

At that, the glowering young nobleman stared directly Macbeatha. I glanced at my lord, but there was no twitch of recognition in his face.

"Have they?" Malcolm inquired in all innocence. "I myself have been here in Edinburgh all summer."

When that had been translated for the Danes, the glowerer growled something I couldn't hear to Cnut, who shushed him. "They speak of one whose hair is red like gold," the Danish king said, his eyes going pointedly to Macbeatha, who still showed no trace of emotion. In the dim interior of the tent, his hair looked only a dull yellow, but his mustaches were unmistakable.

"Many Scots have red hair," Malcolm replied easily. "And it is not unknown among your people. Does not the god Thor have red-gold hair?"

This Cnut acknowledged with a slight nod of his head. "As I told my nobles, where two great rivers meet, the waters are always turbulent. Whatever fish swim in such waters must expect to be battered about."

This did not please the glowerer; I could read on his lips the curse he dared not voice.

"However," Cnut went on, "it is another matter if one of those rivers should flood the land."

Malcolm gave him a quizzical look.

"We have spoken of Dublin," Cnut explained. "In past generations, the men of Dublin have sometimes cross the land of the Scots to lay siege to York."

This was true. The Norse rulers of Dublin had on more than one occasion sailed their ships up the Firth of Clyde, deep into the heart of Scottish territory, and marched from thence to Northumbria to make war on the Danes there. Using this tactic, they could arrive almost without warning, and without the risk of a sea voyage either north, through the treacherous Pentland Firth, or south, around Anglish territory for several days.

"The men of Alba have no quarrel with the men of Dublin," Malcolm said pointedly. His wife had been a woman of Leinster, and so he had some ties to Ireland.

"Neither have I any quarrel with the Scots of Alba," Cnut replied. "Unless they allow such a crossing while I am king." He leaned forward in his chair, eyes narrowing. "Then I would count them my enemies; and I am a very bad man to have as an enemy."

For a moment Malcolm only smiled back, and I thought: That is just what Macbeatha does. He smiles at his enemy, all the while he is thinking how to get the best of him.

Then Malcolm said, "The Irish are across the sea from Alba; you, neighbor, are near at hand. It is better to worry about the wolf in the kitchen than the fox in the hen house."

Now Cnut smiled, but it was a cold smile. "I was told you are a wise man. I have come here, neighbor, to make a pact with you.

Northumbria chafes to return the visits your warriors have made, with a force ten times that which bit him. If you were to declare yourself my friend and ally, I would bid him stay his hand."

The glowerer's jaw muscles bunched noticeably.

"And what is required of your friend and ally?" Malcolm wanted to know.

"That you will come to my aid, by land or by sea, if Dublin comes against me."

Malcolm chewed on his mustaches thoughtfully for a moment. Finally he said, "A good enemy is better than a false friend. Alba does not wish to see foreign troops, Anglish or Irish, set foot upon her land. Should Dublin come from the west, we would oppose him." A small smile curved his mouth. "Should Northumbria come from the south, we would oppose that, too."

"Then we are agreed." Cnut rose from his chair. "You will be my man by land or sea, if needed."

"If needed," Malcolm echoed. "I will let no Irishman cross my lands unopposed. Nor any Dane or Angle."

"I never doubted it."

Malcolm called for ale, and I filled the horns of the two high kings, as well as those of the nobles attending them, and they all drank to the alliance. The glowerer hesitated, but I whispered to him, "Drink, lord. He will not be king forever."

The man's eyes widened in surprise when I spoke to him in a language he understood; then they narrowed again, and a small smile touched his lips. He lifted his horn to Macbeatha across the way, and drank. It sent a chill through me.

"And who," Cnut asked cannily, "is this gold-haired warrior who stands with you, Malcolm? He almost looks like a Dane."

"A northern prince," the High King replied. "He is Macbeatha of Moray; and the other is Echmarcach, King of the Isles." He nodded toward the glowerer. "And who is that with you?"

"A kinsman of the jarl of Northumbria," Cnut replied. "His name is Siward." Siward nodded to the High King. but then turned his head and locked eyes with Macbeatha. It was clear from the look that passed between them that these two had met before in the fields of Northumbria; and that someday, on another field, they would meet again.

Chapter Twenty-Seven

"What can your girl tell us?" Malcolm asked my lord after our party had retired to his tent.

I spoke to Macbeatha in Norn, and he translated for the king. "She says Cnut was very crafty in his speech, but our interpreter replied with equal skill."

"Good, good," Malcolm murmured.

"She also says Cnut's interpreter was not entirely accurate. He told Cnut I was a king."

Malcolm waved that off. "A small point."

"And as they departed, Cnut told one of his aides to tell the troops you had submitted to him and promised to be his man."

"The bastard!" Malcolm exploded. "I said no such thing!"

But Macbeatha laughed. "Be at ease, Grandfather. Cnut knows what you did and did not promise; his interpreter was clear on that point, and Cnut is not a stupid man. If he chooses to tell his troops you 'submitted'—well, it doesn't really matter, as long as he doesn't bring them against you."

"Damned Norsemen," Malcolm grumbled. "By the time they finish a tale, a salmon is a whale and a sucking pig is a boar."

"Yes, we Scots are much more reliable," my lord said dryly. "We only turn a turtle into a sea monster."

That amused the High King. "Will you come back to Scone with us for the winter? I miss your wit."

"You are most gracious and hospitable. It will be an honor. But I wish to stop at the community of St. Serf at Loch Leven on my way, if you don't mind the delay in my coming. Having fed my warrior's heart all summer, I would nourish soul and mind for a time in the company of clerics and learned men."

The High King sighed, but he did not object. "It is good to keep a balance in life. By all means, go cleanse yourself of sin and open yourself to the teaching of scholars. But don't tarry too long." He reached out and pinched my bosom. "Or shall I keep this one as a hostage, to make sure you hasten along?"

Macbeatha shrugged indifferently. "Take her, if you want. There are plenty of girls near Loch Leven."

"Yes, but most of them are married to God."

"Married women are the best," my lord said with a wink. "You taught me that."

"Only if you outrank their husbands," Malcolm chided. "I know you are ambitious, Macbeatha, but surely the Almighty is safe from your grasping."

My lord laughed, conceding the victory in their verbal match. "Once Cnut has sailed away, I plan to host a feast for my troops, before they return to Moray. Will you honor us, my liege?"

"Not this time. But I shall provide a loaf for every man, to take on his journey home. Maldred—" He turned to his grandson, who had stood simmering to one side during this convivial exchange. "Send my steward in, will you?"

"Let the girl fetch him," Maldred snapped. "That's what servants are for."

Malcolm raised hard eyes to the young man, but Macbeatha intervened quickly, bidding me in Norn to fetch the king's steward. I ran off at once, so I do not know how that conversation ended. But Maldred came to Macbeatha's feast in his grandfather's place, so I suppose my lord smoothed things over somehow. He was very good at that. There Maldred laughed and was merry, and my lord persuaded one of the serving girls to sweeten his evening, so by dawn the two princes were great comrades. But Maldred was still Duncan's brother, and when it counted most, the good will my lord earned at that feast did not help him.

In later years I looked back on that winter as the end of my childhood. I was eighteen and spoiled by an indulgent master, with no duties heavier than shaving his ruddy face and cleaning and mending his clothes. I believed implicitly that he would rise first to mormaer and eventually to High King, and that I would be there to wait on him and admire the kingly way he conducted his affairs. It never occurred to me he might fail. It never occurred to me he might be slain by Gillecomgain, or Duncan, or a simple Northumbrian warrior. It never occurred to me that *my* life might be in danger. And yet I came as near to punishment and death that winter as when pride-stung Ivarr threatened me with his knife.

We traveled first to Scone, where jugglers, acrobats, mummers and clowns came to entertain the High King. Next we followed him to Loch Lomond on a hunting expedition, and finally to Aberfeldy to partake of Crinan's hospitality. That was awkward, for Crinan clearly still fumed over Macbeatha's part in burning his town of Dunkeld. (The abbey had not yet been rebuilt, which was why Crinan was at Aberfeldy.) I did hear him say once that he held Gillecomgain responsible for burning the abbey itself, believing Macbeatha tried to stop this action. But he harbored no love for my lord, as evidenced by his glares at table and his cutting remarks made in and out of my lord's hearing.

While we were with Crinan, the High King suffered an illness and lay for several weeks in bed, coughing and wheezing and burning with fever. The doctors hovered over him, and Duncan came up from Cumbria—hoping, no doubt, the time had come for him to take over the kingdom—but that sly old fox surprised them all by recovering. Still, he was weak and unfit for travel, requiring many more weeks to recuperate, and his retinue had to entertain itself at Crinan's expense for some time. My lord and his men did a lot of hunting because it got them out of the hall and away from the ugly tempers of Crinan's warband. That left me with little to occupy my time. Finally I asked my lord if I might wait upon the High King in his absence, for it gave me something to do and might prove useful to him.

Thereafter I spent several mornings a week as a nurse in the High King's bedchamber, happily making his other servants look dimwitted and inconsiderate by comparison. I was quicker to do his bidding, more solicitous of his needs, and I did not hesitate to lean across his bed to adjust his covers and dangle my finer attributes before his face. He would eat the soup or porridge I fed him whilst he refused it from others, and he allowed me to bathe his face and neck with cool cloths, whereas he sent others away with an irritated gesture. All in all, we got along splendidly.

As his health improved, various noble clients came to consult with him, and assuming I was ignorant of their language, they never bothered to shoo me from the room. Malcolm himself might do so, and I always went cheerfully and obediently so as not to arouse any suspicion. But Macbeatha was so discreet with the information I garnered, Malcolm relaxed his guard and often allowed me to stay while he discussed his business with these men. So it happened I was in his room on an early spring day when Duncan came to converse with his grandfather.

"By your leave, I will return to Cumbria tomorrow," he told the king. "I want to be there in time for the Beltaine games. Macbeatha said he might come with me."

I looked up at the sound of my lord's name and smiled in my innocent fashion, and Duncan smiled back, but the king was in a grumpy mood. "Macbeatha should be in Moray," he growled.

"Well, I wouldn't mind trading him," Duncan replied. "I'd like to go up into Moray and have a crack at Thorfinn, but I don't suppose Gillecomgain would take kindly to me showing him up in his own kingdom."

"It is not his kingdom!" Malcolm snarled. "It is *my* kingdom, and he is my mormaer. And you let Thorfinn be. He is my mormaer as well, and entitled to your respect."

"When he comes and swears loyalty, *then* I'll respect him."

"He will come," Malcolm said stubbornly. "He is my grandson, just as you are. When the time arrives, he will come and swear Caithness to you." Then the king started to cough. I hastily brought him some honey mead to sip, scolding Duncan in Norn. The latter looked cross, but the king smiled. "She doesn't want you upsetting me. Says she'll take a stick to you if you do it again." Actually, I had accused Duncan of having manners akin to a cow, and if he upset his grandfather again I would take a cow prod and chase him from the room. Then, "You're a good girl, Kelda," the High King told me in Norn, patting my hand and letting his eyes trail across my bosom.

I smiled smugly and returned to my spindle.

"I've been thinking about something," Malcolm continued, returning his attention to Duncan. "You very nearly became High King this winter, you know." Duncan tried to protest, but Malcolm waved off his objections. "Don't be an ass. I won't live much longer, and we both know it. So let us leave sentiment behind and look to the future. There won't be any problem having you confirmed as High King—there is no one else of age in either royal house, except

Thorfinn, and he's gone too Norse for the Great Tribes to accept him. Even if Macbeatha were to join him—"

"What! Macbeatha back Thorfinn for High King?" Duncan demanded incredulously.

I twirled my spindle and pretended not to hear them.

"It is not the least bit far-fetched!" Malcolm snapped. "If Macbeatha held Moray already, and Thorfinn all of the Orkneys, their combined might could well challenge you! But Macbeatha is reluctant to take Moray by force, and Thorfinn still struggles with his half-brother, so no alliance is possible as yet. That leaves you as the only logical choice. Today."

Duncan frowned. "But tomorrow?" he ventured.

"There is a prince of the house of Kenneth mac Dubh," Malcolm reminded him. "In two or three years he will come of age, and if he does not meet his death on a battlefield, in a very short time he could challenge you. So far I have not been able to find him; if you can, you know what to do."

"Aye." Duncan nodded with grim satisfaction. "That I do."

"And now there is another potential claimant in that line."

Again Duncan frowned, puzzled.

"Gillecomgain," Malcolm explained in exasperation at his grandson's lack of acumen. "Under Brehon law, by his marriage to Gruoch, Gillecomgain could challenge you for the kingship."

"Gillecomgain is no threat," Duncan scoffed.

"Most likely not. He is obsessed with conquering Caithness, which makes him little more than a nuisance. No, it is his wife who is the threat, and their son."

"*She* can't be king!" Duncan laughed. "And the brat's no problem for at least twenty years."

"Stop and think a moment," Malcolm advised with a feverish gleam in his eyes. "What will happen to Gillecomgain of Moray eventually?"

Duncan knew the answer to that. "Macbeatha will kill him."

"And before too long, I think. Then what happens to Gruoch?"

That took him a moment to reason out, but he did come to it. "She becomes a widow, and she can marry someone else. Someone more ambitious. Someone like ..." His voice trailed off and he glanced back at me.

I smiled and drew out the thread from my spindle. But Malcolm saw me there and frowned. "Kelda," he called in Norn, "I am hungry. Go fetch me something to eat."

"Apples with cinnamon?" I offered brightly.

"Yes, yes, that would be nice," he agreed. "And close the door as you go out."

I put down my spinning and hurried for the door, but I did not go far beyond it once it was closed. Instead I pressed my ear to the wood.

"So you see, it is Gruoch who is dangerous," Malcolm was telling his heir. "Very dangerous."

"What do you suggest we do about it?"

They had dropped their voices, and I had to strain to hear. "I've been thinking about that all morning," the king mused. "Did you know Gillecomgain has gone to Urquhart to visit his brother's widow?"

"I heard one of Macbeatha's men speak of it."

"Urquhart is not as well defended as Inverness. Nor as well fortified. In fact, the house where they stay is not even within the fortress walls. If a small force of men—say a hundred—were to arrive unexpectedly ..."

I could almost hear the slow smile spreading across Duncan's face. "You know, I think I will leave for Cumbria tomorrow," he told his grandfather. "But I won't ask Macbeatha to join me. I have only fifty men here, but my father will give me fifty more. Perhaps we'll do a little hunting along the way." He gave a mirthless chuckle. "It will be great sport."

"Don't be too noble," Malcolm advised him. "Get the brat, too—he'll only rise to haunt us later."

I didn't dare wait any longer, but fled to the kitchen to find the apples I'd promised the king. I managed to be on my way back up the stairs, only slightly out of breath, as Duncan was coming down.

For hours after Duncan's visit I sat with the High King, spinning and singing songs for him, and wishing desperately that Macbeatha would return from his hunt soon. Noon came, and another serving girl took my place, but I could do nothing other than go silently about my work, pretending nothing was wrong. Finally the light began to fade, and I walked out in the direction my lord had gone, hoping to catch him as he returned with his guard.

I was not disappointed. When I saw them trotting back toward Crinan's house, I waved frantically. Macbeatha thought I was playing and charged his horse at me, but I shouted at him with such urgency, he reined in and dropped to the ground beside me. "What is it?" he asked. "What's happened?" And I told him.

"Bastard!" exclaimed Dougal, for they had all clustered around to hear the news. "He would murder a woman and child?"

"I wouldn't mind leaving Gillecomgain to Duncan's tender mercies," Weylin began, "but the lady—"

Suddenly my lord seized Weylin by the front of his tunic and hauled him up nose to nose. Macbeatha was clearly furious, and his voice came through clenched teeth. "Gillecomgain is duly elected king of Moray," he gritted, "and no Athollman is going to take him in his own lands!"

Weylin, abashed, mumbled an apology.

"We can leave right now," Owen suggested. "From here. We'll get to Urquhart before Duncan and raise their men to arms."

But Macbeatha shook his head. "Our horses are tired, and we've no supplies. They'd guess where we had gone and overtake us. No, we must be crafty about this." I could see his mind spinning as he quickly made plans. "Tomorrow, we'll take leave of Duncan and pretend to go hunting. But we'll circle around and see which road he takes to Moray. If he goes by Drumochter Pass, we'll go by Loch Tay. If he goes by Loch Tay, we'll take Drumochter. Either way we'll outrun him, because he can't move a hundred warriors at our pace without attracting attention he doesn't want."

"And supplies?" Goll asked.

"We'll buy them along the way. I have a purse heavy enough yet to do that, and I can hide it on my person—though I'll have to leave a good many things behind that I hate to lose. So must you all—it can't be helped. There is the honor of Moray; and besides—" He looked grim. "I swore once I would protect that lady, and so I must do."

His men nodded and turned back toward their horses. But it seemed to me he had forgotten one little detail—one very important to a particular Norse serving girl. "And what of me, lord?" I asked plaintively.

Macbeatha glanced at me as though I had suddenly appeared from nowhere. "You'll have to stay behind this time," he said. "If I bring you along, Malcolm will suspect something and send men to stop us."

All the color drained from my face and my heart nearly exploded within my chest. "But, lord," I whispered hoarsely, "when you do not return in the evening, he will know what has happened—and who told you about it."

With his foot in the stirrup, Macbeatha paused and looked back at me again. I could see him struggle with the problem, needing to fly, not wanting to be burdened with a woman— "I can't take you along," he protested again. "You won't be able to keep up with us. Go to the priests, they'll give you sanctuary. Or—or—"

"To Crinan's monks?" I asked quietly. "And will any churchman be able to protect a heathen bedwench from Malcolm's men?" My blood ran colder than the River Ness. What Malcolm would do to me when he put two and two together ... "But nevermind, lord," I said in a voice that was steady, if hollow. "Perhaps the High King will take pity on me because I was kind to him, and give me a quick death. Go to the aid of your kinsman and his noble lady; they are of your house and need your protection." I forced a shrug and a poor smile. "What is one slave girl, more or less?"

Though my voice quavered and my mien was humble, my words were carefully and craftily chosen. I had lived with him long enough to know just which of his heartstrings to tug at. Many times he had disparaged the bond of blood binding him to Gillecomgain, and espoused the Christian precept that even a slave has value in the sight of the Lord Jesus. As once I had professed ignorance of the Christian faith to persuade Thorfinn to rescue me and my mother, so now I pretended to devalue myself in relation to his cousin, knowing he thought me worth ten Gillecomgains. I counted on him to act accordingly.

And it worked. Though he struggled a moment longer, finally he turned decisively to Dougal. "I need you to say your horse threw you today and you've wrenched your back. Tomorrow you will beg off hunting and go instead into the village seeking a liniment. Take Kelda with you, say she is to pick out some cloth for a new cloak for me for Beltaine. Then buy her a good horse—forget that stupid pony she rides—and one for yourself, and get us some supplies. We'll meet you by the road to Loch Tay."

He turned to me. "If you slow us down too much, I'll have to leave you somewhere along the way. But it will be somewhere safe,

I promise. It is because of you that we have this news, and it would be poor payment for your faithfulness to abandon you to Malcolm's mercy. Besides." He swung up into his saddle, then reached down and tugged me up in front of him. "I should have to find someone else to shave me, and there aren't many these days I'd trust to put a knife to my throat."

* * *

Fionna drew a blanket up over Kelda and took the cup from her limp hand. The force which kept the Norse woman going had ebbed and allowed sleep to overtake her. Out of habit, Fionna muttered a blessing of healing over her guest, as one would over a sick child or a wounded man, but she knew it would not help. The wound in Kelda's heart was too great for such magic to be of any use.

It irked Fionna that she had grown so fond of this stranger in so short a time. Kelda was not her concern—only curiosity had prompted her to take in the Norsewoman. It was the tale of Macbeatha that should concern her, not the woman. She had always been too tender-hearted—even her mother had said so. Her sisters had chided her as well, and her husband in that brief year before a temper that was quicker than his sword had cut his life short. Over the years Fionna had grown tougher, had learned the wisdom of staying distant from the world and its goings on, had found it was easier to help people if you did not care too much about them.

But it was always the wounded ones who sought her out. "Fionna, please, a healing potion for my baby." "Fionna, I beg you, a purge to cast out the child in my womb, for I cannot feed another mouth." "Fionna, Fionna, something to ease the pain, something for my mother ... my wife ... my grandsire ..." And Fionna steeled her heart and sold them her potions and tried not to think about what they would and wouldn't do.

Now here was Kelda, and Fionna knew what the Norsewoman wanted: a potion, one Fionna did not part with lightly, or to just anyone who asked. She would never have given it to the gay young thing Kelda had been in her youth. But now? With such sorrow in her heart?

Fionna didn't know. She just didn't know.

Chapter Twenty-Eight

In Fiona's hut

Kelda awoke and rubbed at her eyes. "I'm sorry," she apologized. "I must have nodded off. Did I sleep long?"

"No more than you needed," Fionna replied, pouring a cup of clear water for her guest.

"Where did I leave off?" Kelda took the cup from Fionna's hand. "I'm not sure what I spoke, and what I dreamed..."

"You were riding to Urquhart. To warn the Lady Gruoch that her life was in danger."

Kelda nodded. "Oh, yes..."

* * *

Duncan and his men chose to go to Urquhart by Loch Tay and the Glen Dochart, so Macbeatha and his men cut north through the Strath of Appin and over the hills to Glen Garry. It was a punishing ride, up through Drumochter Pass, and I was hard pressed to keep up with the men, for I was never a good rider. We suffered several delays along the way: a horse that broke its leg, a section of mountain track that had crumbled away, a flooded glen we had to go around. These gave me some relief, but cost us precious time. When we reached the road above Loch Ness, we could look back from a high place and see Duncan's band of warriors in the distance, coming on a leisurely trot.

We reached Urquhart at dusk, and my lord burst into the house where Gillecomgain was staying. The mormaer's men stood with their hands on their sword hilts, for they knew not why Macbeatha came so urgently demanding admittance. Among the ladies at the hearth I saw Gruoch nursing her baby, and I wondered if somehow she knew of the danger, for she sat pale and drawn, looking as if she had ridden as hard and as long as I. Then her eyes fixed on Macbeatha, and a light sprang back into her.

"Macbeatha!" exclaimed Vevina, Maelcolm's widow and mistress of the house. "Why have you come?"

"To bring warning," my lord panted. "Duncan mac Crinan is not four hours behind me with a hundred warriors, bent on the destruction of the mormaer and his family."

Now Gillecomgain staggered to his feet, and I saw why he had not come forward sooner: he was clearly drunk, though the sun was just down and the board not yet set for the evening meal. "My destruction, eh?" he bellowed. "Well, bring him on. We shall see whose destruction this night brings!"

Macbeatha turned on him with a look of sheer contempt. "If you are drunk at this hour, Duncan will need no help working your destruction. Where is Ellar?" My lord found the captain of Gillecomgain's guard among the faces confronting him. "How many warriors are here?"

"Just my ten," the man replied. "But there are four other captains in the village; we can have fifty men within a few hours."

"Get them," Macbeatha commanded. "With my guard, we are sixty. But Duncan has a hundred; we have to move into the fortress."

"What, tonight?" Ellar protested. "Surely Duncan won't attack in the middle of the night. Tomorrow morning—"

"Tomorrow morning we may find ourselves surrounded," Macbeatha snapped. "We have to move this entire household *tonight.* Lady." He turned to Vevina. "Are your children here?"

She bristled a little, for she still did not trust him; her children could one day challenge him for power. "They are in fosterage," she answered. "Quite safe, I assure you."

"Good, because Duncan is not likely to spare children, nor women. He has never seen the Lady Gruoch and is apt to kill every woman in the house, rather than risk her escape—"

"Gruoch!" Gillecomgain interrupted, as though called from a haze by the mention of his wife's name. "What has Gruoch to do with this?" His face was ugly with suspicion and hatred.

"You stupid ass!" Macbeatha hissed at him. "It's *her* Duncan wants, not you! Oh, he'll kill you, make no mistake, but she's the real threat to his sovereignty—she and the babe. Malcolm has smelled his own death this winter, and he is no longer willing to leave the succession in God's hands. The lady needs to get out of here, she and her son—"

"No one's going anywhere!" Gillecomgain roared. "I am perfectly capable of protecting my own wife and child! Let Duncan come on! I'll gut him myself!"

"He'll be sober by morning," Ellar said quietly. "If we can just wait till morning—"

"Damn it man, Duncan is in the heart of Moray!" Macbeatha barked. "He's not going to wait around till daylight and challenge you to a pitched battle! He's going to burst in here at midnight and murder you in your beds! Can't you understand that?"

"Then we'll be ready for him!" Gillecomgain insisted. "See? See?" He took his drinking horn and cast it into the fire. "No more ale. We'll lie here in wait—fifty of us. Sixty, with you. We'll pretend we're asleep, and when he rushes in, it'll be him who is surprised. Yes?" His twisted face looked to Macbeatha for approval. "You'll stand with us, cousin, and we'll send them all to hell. We've done it before, against worse odds, haven't we? Remember Dunglas?" He nudged Macbeatha clumsily. "Come, cousin. You and me, against the House of Malcolm. Moray against Atholl. What do you say?"

My lord hesitated as he considered this plan. Then, "On one condition," he said.

"Condition?" Gillecomgain snarled, his wheedling changing quickly to ire.

"Get the women and children out of here now. And the servants."

For a long moment Gillecomgain balked. Then Vevina slipped to his side. "We would only be in your way, brother," she soothed. "Let us get out from underfoot, and let warriors do what warriors were born to do. Guthrie," she called to her steward. "Tell all the servants to go out to their kin in the valley tonight, and hush about this. We don't want the Athollmen to know we are expecting them.

Gruoch, sister, gather your things and come with me to my father's house. It is not far, and—"

"No," Gruoch said flatly.

Macbeatha turned on her with a baleful glare.

"I will not be the cause of your deaths, Vevina," she said in the same flat tone. "Wherever I am found, it will not go well for the people of that house."

"She's right," Macbeatha agreed grudgingly. "If Duncan finds only warriors here, he may send men to search the village."

Weylin spoke up. "There are caves hereabout," he offered. "I was fostered not far from here, and I can think of several places that Duncan will never find."

"Good," my lord said decisively. "Lady, gather your things, and what you need for the child, and go with Weylin. You will be safe, for he will guard your life as he would mine."

But Gruoch was not through being obstinate. "No," she said again.

"You are not being given a choice!"

"I will go," she told him, "but only if you take me there yourself."

"What!?" roared Macbeatha and Gillecomgain together.

"You swore on the cross," she reminded Macbeatha. "When you took me away from Loch Leven. You swore on the cross that you would protect me and defend me with your own life, placing my honor before your own."

"And I have ridden here in defiance of the High King and at peril of both life and health to keep that vow!" he shouted. "What nonsense is this?"

"It is not nonsense!" she shouted back, her voice edged with hysteria. "My life and my son's life are in danger, and you swore to me that you—*you*—would protect me. Not one of your men, not ten of your men, but *you*. If there are assassins abroad, I will have *you* to protect me and my son."

She was trembling and Macbeatha started to reach out to her, but whether to comfort or strangle her, it was hard to say. He stopped, anyway. He could hardly lay hands on another man's wife with that man right in the room. But it was clear that Gruoch had Macbeatha tight by his most sensitive part—his honor. The vow he had gallantly sworn to impress a young girl was coming back to bite him now.

"It's not far," Weylin intervened, always the peacemaker. "We can be there and back before Duncan arrives."

"Will that satisfy you, lady?" Macbeatha asked through clenched teeth. "If I see you safely installed in some hiding place, and then return here to aid your husband?"

Gruoch stepped back from him and smoothed her hair, as calm as though they had only been discussing the melting of the snow on the nearby mountains. "I would have it no other way," she said with maddening aplomb. "Of course, you must be here to stand with your lord. I expect you to see him through this battle faithfully and victoriously."

With fresh horses from Vevina's stable, we made our way by narrow mountain tracks to a cave high above Loch Ness. We were eight: the Lady Gruoch, her son and her maid; Macbeatha and three of his guardsmen; and me. It took longer than Weylin remembered, and the first cave smelled strongly of animal occupants, so he found another. Macbeatha instructed Dougal to stay with us, much to the young man's chagrin; then he, Owen and Weylin made their way through the darkness back to Urquhart.

Owen told me later they were not halfway down the mountain when they saw flames in the town below. Alarmed, they urged their horses on at a reckless pace, with only the moonlight to illuminate their treacherous path, but it was not fast enough. Duncan had been craftier than any of them had given him credit for. Leading a small party of men forward from his main column, he had reached Urquhart about the time we reached our sanctuary. With no warning, and no intention of engaging in combat, he had set fire to the timber house.

By the time my lord and his men reached the small settlement, the rest of Duncan's warband was drawing near from the south. Stopping in the deep shadows of a larch grove, they dismounted and crept forward, but the situation was hopeless. They watched, appalled, as a dozen warriors burst out of the burning house, only to be cut down by Cumbrian bowmen. From inside came the screams of men who could not reach door or window, and Macbeatha lunged toward the inferno. It took both Owen and Weylin to hold him back. "It's no use, lord," Owen said. "They're not fighting like men. It serves nothing to throw your life away with the others."

"Oh, God!" Macbeatha moaned, sagging to his knees to watch in helpless agony as his countrymen perished. "Oh, God, I cursed him with this!"

"Cursed who?" Owen asked, puzzled.

"Gillecomgain." Tears streamed down Macbeatha's face, stained an eerie red by the livid light of the flames. "When he set fire to the little village church after we raided Dunglas. I called for all the fires of hell to consume him for that deed. And they have." With a groan, the roof timbers gave way and crashed in upon the poor souls still trapped inside the house. "But oh, God, he's taken fifty good men with him. Fifty, plus six. My six."

They stayed until the vanguard of Duncan's column came into view, and it was no longer safe. Then they melted back into the trees and made their way slowly up the mountain.

In the cave above Loch Ness, we knew nothing of this, though we could see flames in the village below and feared tragedy. It was a dreadful night, cold and miserable, and though I had kindled a small fire against the chill, it could not reach my heart. Gruoch sat on a stone near its meager warmth, or rose and paced to the mouth of the cave and back, or knelt in prayer. What she prayed for, I do not know; but before we had left Vevina's house, Maisie whispered to me that Gillecomgain's regard for his young queen had slipped after the child was born. Wounded again in battle, the mormaer had been soured by pain and drunk most of the time, and Maisie had seen him strike her more than once. Perhaps in the cave that night, Gruoch prayed for deliverance, and not only from Duncan.

The hours dragged by until dawn. I think Maisie slept a bit, but she was the only one. We were all awake when Macbeatha came back to us, dirty and sweaty and smelling of smoke. I rushed to him, overjoyed to see him alive and whole, but he brushed me aside and dropped to his knees before Gruoch. Head down and shoulders sagging, he croaked, "Lady, I have failed you."

Her face told nothing as she sat cradling Lulach in her arms. "How so?"

In a broken voice he told her of Duncan's treachery, and Gillecomgain's awful death in the fire with all his men. "Forgive me, lady," he finished.

I saw the agony in his soul and knew his grief was real, but it seemed unlikely to me that the querulous widow would believe him sincere. I waited for her wrath, for the scorn she would heap upon him; but after a moment's silence she said, "You did what you could, kinsman. You have saved me and my son, at least. God will not fault you, nor will I."

Only then did he raise his eyes with something like hope in them.

"Moray will be yours now," she went on. "My child and I must look to you for our defense from Duncan mac Crinan."

"Lady, I swear it to you again," he said urgently. "I shall protect and defend you at all cost—and your child, too." His eyes fell on the curly dark head of the babe sleeping in her arms with a wistfulness that twisted my heart.

Gruoch cast a look at Owen and Weylin, sagging in the firelight. "Maisie, find food for these gallant men," she commanded. "Brave hearts, rest yourselves here by the fire. I would have a word with your lord in private." Then she rose, still cradling Lulach, and stepped to the mouth of the cave. Macbeatha followed.

The others were polite enough to busy themselves at the fire, but I had not their scruples. I slipped into the shadows and waited breathlessly to hear what she would say to my lord. She took a deep breath, gazing out over the fog-filled valley. "You once asked my mother for my hand in marriage," she began. "Would you still be interested in such a match?"

He sucked in his breath. "Lady, you know I am."

"There are advantages to me, as well. But there are certain disadvantages, and so I must ask you for several conditions before I agree to—to be your wife." The phrase came hard to her.

"Lady, we need not speak of this now," he whispered. "There is time enough—"

"There is no time," she contradicted sharply. "I have a son, and he is in danger. I would have your promise this day, before I must go out from here and face—and face the duties of a widow and a queen. So these are my conditions: One, that you must not hinder nor harm my brother, whose place it is to rule as High King one day."

He hesitated, of course, for it was the office he himself sought. "I will not harm your brother," he agreed carefully, "nor stand in his way if he proves himself worthy to seek the high kingship. In fact, if I achieve that goal before him, I will name him as my tanist. Will that satisfy you, lady?"

"Yes," she decided. "It will not satisfy my mother, but it will satisfy me, for I have seen how you carry out your vows." Then she went on. "Two, in the matter of my son Lulach, that by your support and encouragement, you endeavor to place in his hand the scepter of Moray—in favor of any sons of your flesh."

"Done," he said quickly. "Lady, he shall be as my own son, and none shall take precedence over him."

Surprise showed on her face, and in the pale light I could see her trying to fathom why he had not balked, wondering what plan he had in mind. As if it were a game of chess, she considered the position of all the players, searching for the trap he might spring.

The sun was creeping above the eastern highlands, sending bright, clear rays down to melt away the mist. "Then it is agreed," she said finally "I shall lend you my support in your bid for the mormaership, although I don't know who would oppose you. And by my marriage to you, I give you claim to the high kingship, when the day comes. Only let me mourn my husband for a time, and then it shall be done."

And though I had hoped for just such an outcome for my master, I was suddenly seized with a great fear. This marriage would give him Moray, without contest, and open the way to the High Kingship someday. No one wanted that more than I. But my world was about to change, and in a way I was afraid would do me no good.

Chapter Twenty-Nine

When Duncan and his band of marauders had gone, we ventured down from our hiding place to seek warmth and sustenance in the house of Vevina's father. Soon we were joined by dozens of armed men, for in the hills around the loch, men had seen the flames and come swarming down, thinking Thorfinn had attacked. How surprised they were to learn it had been Duncan, come by stealth into Moray's lands! By noon, there were thirty mounted men ready to ride after him, and Macbeatha would suffer no other to lead them forth; so he left us there and galloped away, taking his three remaining guardsmen with him.

I wept and wept when I saw what was left of Vevina's house. Six of the dead were Macbeatha's men. I had served them ale and braided their hair and tended their wounds, and now they were only blackened lumps amid the ashes. We couldn't even tell who was who. I thought of the wives and children back in Ross and Inverness who would never see their men again, not even to bury, for we took only Gillecomgain's body back with us, to be mourned and buried with the kings of Moray. Him we knew by the gold chains melted into his chest.

At nightfall, Macbeatha and the other warriors returned, tired and bloody, but victorious. Duncan, aware he was deep in hostile territory, split his men at the south end of the loch, sending half southeast across the river and half southwest along Loch Oich. My lord chose the latter trail as more likely to be Duncan's, and when he caught up to the culprits, he fell upon them with such fury, his Moraymen slaughtered every man, despite being outnumbered. But

Duncan was not among them. He had ridden with his guard in yet another direction, slipping to safety among the lochs and glens of western Atholl. Furious, but unable to follow further without rest and supplies, my lord returned to Urquhart.

News of the tragedy traveled quickly, and by the next evening, three hundred men were ready to go after Duncan and further revenge their king, but Macbeatha sent them home again. There would be no catching up to Duncan at this point, and if Moray crossed into Atholl with three hundred warriors, they were sure to be met by the combined forces of Crinan and Duncan. They would have to be content, he said, with having slain fifty of the culprits.

This did not please the Lady Gruoch at all. She looked up at him from the shrouded body of her husband with eyes that could have burned holes through an oak tree. The cause of her anger was soon plain: she wanted him to raise the whole of Moray and launch a full-scale attack on Duncan in Cumbria. As long as Duncan lived, she told him, her son was in danger.

"And if I were so stupid as to throw my life away in such a futile war," he demanded, "who would protect you and the child? And your precious brother."

She argued a bit more, but he counseled patience. Duncan would fall soon enough.

"Not soon enough for me," she hissed.

"In God's good time, lady," he chided her. "And in mine. But that time is not now."

She hardly spoke to him the entire journey to Inverness. When we reached the fortress, she thanked him with great courtesy for his efforts on her behalf, and for the duty he had shown his cousin. But there was no warmth in her voice, and I wondered if she would renege on her promise of marriage. Only the two of them had been party to it—my testimony would hardly count for anything. Macbeatha, however, laughed at such fears. "She will honor her bargain. It was carefully made, with cunning and logic, and it will serve her well. She needs me."

"How so?" I asked.

"Malcolm seeks to destroy her to prevent her marrying an ambitious man. Like me. Once the deed is done, the danger to her is removed. Having made her my wife, I can make my claim with or without her."

It made sense, I had to admit—and Gruoch was a most sensible woman, even then. Still, the whole matter made me uneasy.

"And what of me?" I asked petulantly. "Will you send me away, as your friend Bowen sent Myrna away when he married?"

His arms fastened tight around me and he pressed his lips to my ear. "I shall never send you away. You are far too valuable to me."

"And if your new wife demands it?"

He stroked my hair in a comforting gesture. "The lady and I have done our bargaining; your name did not come up. If it does, I will make it clear enough to whom she owes her life, and that of her son. Have no fear, Kelda."

But somehow, I was not reassured. I knew how badly he wanted to be High King, and I had seen how near he came to abandoning me once before. If I stood between him and his chance at the Stone of Destiny, I knew just how long his promise would hold.

Once Gillecomgain was buried, the council of churchmen and nobles met to consider Macbeatha's claim and to elect him the new mormaer. There was only one dissenting vote, so my lord was duly installed within a fortnight. The morning after his investiture, Sosanna found old Donn cold in his bed, his spirit having fled during the night. No one was surprised; the old steward had not been well for some time, hardly rising from his bed, and we all knew this was what he had been waiting to see. But Macbeatha would miss his wise counsel in the years ahead—and so would I.

Nothing was said at that time of my lord's betrothal to Gruoch, for it would have been unseemly to announce it when Gillecomgain was hardly cold. Instead, the new mormaer announced that, in deference to her grief, the widow need not move out of her residence at the fortress until after the harvest. He would content himself with the hospitality of his clients and keep his house and household where they were until Hallowmas. Gruoch thanked him most graciously for this kindness, and I thought, what a pair! Liars both, and it was a toss-up which was better at it.

Next, Macbeatha set about cementing his authority as mormaer. It was customary for a new leader to put on a demonstration of his power and abilities as a military leader. Sometimes this is done with a raid, as Gillecomgain had done, but Macbeatha chose a royal circuit instead. He paraded the length and breadth of Moray collecting his *conveth* in person, taking a sizeable warband, for it is customary the mormaer should display his strength this way—men often need reminding of why they should pay hospitality rent. Sometimes a chieftain will refuse to pay unless the mormaer comes in person and shows himself powerful enough to take what is his, if need be.

Only one chieftain challenged my lord's right that summer. Griogar of the mac Fearchair had been the one dissenting vote in Macbeatha's election. He practically accused my lord of leading Duncan to Gillecomgain, and of intentionally abandoning his cousin to the flames with the goal of taking over Moray. When the Lady Gruoch heard this and protested, Griogar insinuated complicity between them in the matter.

Do I need to tell you what happened? Macbeatha called upon all the men of Moray to rally to his banner. Then they went in and wiped out the tribe of the mac Fearchair to a man. "Thus to all who impugn my honor, or that of the Lady Gruoch," he declared grimly. No one else in Moray ever challenged him again.

But he never boasted of that battle. In fact, he never spoke of it at all.

Though he spent most of the summer quartered with one chieftain or another, he returned to Inverness from time to time, in part to badger Lady Gruoch for when he might announce their betrothal, and in part to entertain warriors who came to pledge him their support. It was shortly after Midsummer, as he feasted in his own hall, that a stranger arrived and was ushered in.

How shall I describe him? He had dark hair braided like snakes, and a pointed beard as black as pitch. He swaggered into the hall with his sword clanking at his side, wearing dirty woolen trews and a stained, sleeveless pigskin tunic. The muscles in his upper arms rippled in the firelight, and his forearms—which were coated with dark curling hair—seemed larger around than those of any other man I'd met. His thighs were so thick with muscle, he appeared bowlegged when he stood still—

—and the top of his head came no higher than my nose.

Now, at the sight of this ferocious little man, a murmur of laughter ran through the crowded hall. Dwarfs are well known among the Norse, and honored as the best of swordsmiths; but I had always imagined those dwarfs to be grotesque and misshapen. That is how the stories of them are told. This man was as finely built as any warrior I had seen, only he was ... small.

"I seek Macbeatha mac Findlaech, grandson of Gia of the Kanteai-tuatha," the little man announced in a voice so deep it provoked another murmur of laughter for its incongruity.

My lord rose from his seat with a glint of amusement in his eye. "I am he."

"I hear you lost six good men of your guard to the coward Duncan mac Crinan," boomed the stranger, looking up at my lord in an appraising manner.

The amusement vanished from Macbeatha's face at the mention of his lost men. "That I did." There had been many candidates to fill those six vacant spots, but at that time, my lord had chosen only four. These were the men who would guard his life; he chose them very carefully.

"I heard of your plight in the east," the little man declared. "I have come to offer my service."

Laughter now surged through the hall, and although Macbeatha did not join in it, his lips did twitch with a longing to smile. "And who are you, man, that I should have need of your service?" he asked.

The stranger scowled at the warriors closest to him and, oddly enough, the laughter died on their lips. "I am Venko mac Nechtan," he announced, "of the Kanteai-tuatha. I am a cousin of the granddaughter of your grandmother's brother, and thus your kinsman. When I heard you had need of the finest warriors in the land to serve in your guard, I felt I must come."

"Warrior!" Weylin hooted. "And what do you ride into battle, a goat?" That brought another roar of laughter.

In the blink of an eye the little man had drawn his sword, and it was pointed squarely at Weylin's nose. "It is not what a man rides, but how he wields his weapon," Venko said evenly. "Will you cross your sword with mine?"

Weylin drew back, disconcerted, for the sword had been drawn before he even thought to reach for his own. "Macbeatha," he said, "I have no wish to harm your kinsman, if such he is. Yet if he leaves that sword in my face, I shall have to teach him to respect his betters."

"The only better I might have in this place," Venko said coldly, "would be my kinsman, and he will have to prove that to me."

Now Owen stepped between Venko and the new mormaer. "Lord, let me dispose of this nuisance for you," he offered.

But my lord was obviously intrigued by the little man. "The courage and battle prowess of the Kanteai are well known to me," he said courteously. "But only in legend. I did not think any lived who clung to that tradition."

"We are not what we once were," Venko admitted, never taking his eyes from Weylin for a minute. "We are few in number, and most have become clients of the mac Craine. But there are those of us left who uphold the honor of our ancestors."

Moving Owen aside with one hand, my lord came to stand beside the stranger, who reached only to his shoulder. "Do you bear the mark?"

Slowly Venko lowered his sword, then turned his left shoulder toward my lord. There, blazed across his upper arm, was a double-circle tattoo identical to Macbeatha's, except there was no zigzag across it. "Well, cousin," my lord acknowledged. "I am pleased that the Kanteai call me kin. But you will have to convince me of your skill as a warrior before I take you into my guard."

"Let one of these men fight me," Venko said, gesturing at those closest. "Then you will see."

"First blood," Macbeatha cautioned. "You do me no good to pledge your service if you kill one of my men."

"You would still be better off," Venko insisted, "but very well. First blood."

"Outside, then," my lord commanded. "Dougal—do Venko mac Nechtan the honor."

We all traipsed out into the late summer twilight. It is a treacherous time of day to fight, when the sun rests half below the hills, and the shadows conceal so much. But Dougal took up a shield, drew his sword, and faced the stranger.

Before anyone knew what happened, Venko darted in and sliced a wicked cut along Dougal's shoulder. "Wait!" Dougal shouted, staggering back. "I wasn't ready for him!"

"You mean you didn't take him seriously," Macbeatha snapped. "Owen, perhaps you can do better."

So Owen drew his sword and stepped up to the little man. They looked comical, for Owen was a full head taller than his opponent, and almost twice as big around. Yet he was light on his feet, and he did, indeed, do better than Dougal had. They exchanged a dozen strokes before Venko got under Owen's shield and put a gash in his calf just above his boot.

"Very impressive," Macbeatha admitted. "But if you are not too tired, I would give you one more opponent."

"I could fight an army," Venko declared.

"You don't need to fight an army tonight," Macbeatha said as he drew his own sword. "Only me."

Venko took his stance, then noticed that Macbeatha held sword his left-handed. Puzzled, the little man took a step back, considered the phenomenon, then shrugged and took up his stance again.

The two combatants circled carefully until Macbeatha feinted and Venko struck in response. But as the little man swung his sword, my lord reached out with his long arm and made an upward stroke that slashed the tunic over Venko's right breast. His own left arm was carried up out of the path of Venko's sword, which he caught deftly on his shield. Venko stopped with a bewildered look, then glanced down at his chest to see the trickle of blood welling through the rent in his tunic.

"Forgive me, kinsman," Macbeatha apologized, "but I could not let you draw blood of two of my men without spilling your own. Now come sit at my right hand in the hall, and Kelda shall tend your wound for you while we drink and make merry. When I next ride into battle, I want you with me, for only after a man has fought at my side will I take him into my guard. That is, if you will serve a lord who fights with the devil's hand."

Venko straightened up. "As long as that hand is turned on our enemies."

So we all trooped back inside, where Macbeatha made much of his new warrior, bidding Dhui bring a fine linen tunic to replace Venko's damaged garment, and sending me to fetch ointment and bandages for all three wounded men.

As I approached Venko to minister to him, his eyes grew wide, and he looked me up and down in the way that men do. "A Viking!" he exclaimed, noting my fair hair and tall stature.

"*My* Viking," Macbeatha corrected.

"Ah." Still he looked me up and down as I washed his cut—which was really quite shallow—and applied ointment to it. Then, as I laid a bandage upon it, he leaned over and sniffed my neck. "Mm. She smells wonderful."

I sat back on my heels and put my hands on my hips. "*She* has a name," I informed him.

Venko's eyebrows shot up. "She speaks a civilized tongue!" he exclaimed. "I didn't know you could train a Viking."

"This one is quite biddable," my lord assured him with a twinkle in his eye. "I've trained Kelda to do a great many things."

"Oh?" Venko's eyes lit with keen interest. "I have heard that Viking women are quite free with their favors."

"They do as their masters command," Macbeatha replied. "I command this one to serve *me.*"

Venko looked so crestfallen that Macbeatha laughed out loud. "Don't worry, my friend, there are plenty of maids who esteem the mormaer's warriors. I'm sure we can find you a pleasant companion somewhere."

Venko uttered a deep sigh as I finished wrapping the bandage around his chest. "Yes, but this one is so ... *big,*" he said plaintively.

That, too, made my lord laugh. "Well, then, when she has finished tending the others and returns to wait on us, you may hold her on your lap, if you like."

That brightened Venko's countenance considerably, and as I helped him into the fresh tunic Dhui had brought, and showed him how to blouse it properly over his belt, he sniffed me again. "Ahhhh! So much woman!"

In the following months, Venko's eyes followed me wistfully whenever I served in the hall. He never missed an opportunity to tug me into his lap, and he would hold me for as long as Macbeatha would let him. I can't say I objected—it's hard to dislike someone who has such open admiration for you. "If you were my wench," he would murmur into my bosom—for he loved to rest his head on my ample breasts—"I would wear myself out with pleasure."

Yet he never tried to force himself on me, for he honored Macbeatha's word as though it were law. Sometimes I found myself wishing he would try, for as the responsibilities of my lord's office began to weigh on him, he had less time and energy to be playful with me. When Venko whispered of keeping me awake all through the night with his attentions, it reminded me of the early years with Macbeatha when our pleasure would go on for hours. Now, the nights when he was not tired or preoccupied grew fewer and further apart; and soon, he would have a wife ...

They announced their betrothal not long afterward, and then my lord rode off again to collect his *conveth* from across Loch

Ness. While he was gone, Girc met with the Lady Gruoch to discuss moving Macbeatha's household into the fortress. When Girc returned and said the Lady wanted to speak to me, my stomach drew up in a knot and stayed that way all the long walk up the hill and into her presence.

Chapter Thirty

Gruoch sat at a table in her work chamber off the main hall. A brazier burned on the floor near her feet, for the small window high in the wall which admitted the light, also admitted the crisp fall air. Even with the brazier burning, she had a blanket draped across her knees and a heavy shawl wrapped around her shoulders. She was not one to wear much jewelry unless she was going out in public; only her ornate gold earrings and a thick necklace of braided gold ornamented her plain woolen shift. She was scratching marks on a sheet of vellum as I came in.

"Thank you for coming, Kelda," she said without looking up. "I know you are not my servant as yet, but I wanted to talk about what will be expected when you come here to live."

My heart lurched and I tried to swallow, but my throat was too dry and the muscles would not work. It didn't even occur to me to try speaking.

"How long have you served Macbeatha?" she asked.

My mind was so numb it took me several attempts to reason out the figure. "Fo—four winters, Lady," I stammered at last.

"Do you feel you know his habits quite well?"

Try as I might, I could not understand the significance of this. His habits? What habits? In bed? Was that what she meant? No, no, the lady would never ask such a question. What did she mean, his habits? When he rose and when he slept? What he ate? It made no sense to me.

Finally she glanced up at me and I realized I had been silent and stupefied for some time. "I—I suppose so, Lady," I managed.

For a long moment she stared at me with those cool gray-blue eyes of hers. Then, "I won't bite you," she said softly.

"Forgive me, Lady," I blurted out, "but I don't know what you want of me!"

"I only want to know," she said with a touch of impatience, "if I should put you in charge of the chamber servants, or those in the hall. You are familiar with his habits, and so you know how he likes his chamber kept, and you could direct the chamber servants to keep his room and those of his guests in proper order. But you also know what he expects from his servants in the hall, and so you could train them accordingly."

This was not something I had imagined the Lady Gruoch might wish to discuss. I blinked, and my mouth gaped open, and finally I said, "But Murdock manages—"

"Murdock is too old to manage anything," she interrupted with a dismissive wave of her hand. "Let him doze by the fire in his old age, and leave the running of a mormaer's household to those who have the energy for it. From what I have seen of you, I believe you quite capable of keeping a dozen other servants in line, and I will need that kind of assistance. Macbeatha will be quite a different sort of mormaer than Gillecomgain was, and we can expect a great deal more activity here than we have had in the past. Now." She began to scratch on the vellum with her quill again. "I think I shall ask you to serve in the hall. Hospitality in the hall is critical, and you seem to have a flair for it. Do you agree?"

I didn't think it was my place to disagree. "I love serving in the hall, Lady," I told her truthfully.

"Then I shall count on you."

That seemed to be a dismissal, so I bowed and turned to leave. I had almost gained the door when she spoke again.

"Do you have any children, Kelda?"

I was so startled I think I actually gasped. She had been in and out of Macbeatha's house dozens of times, and the doings of his servants were no secret in the town of Inverness, anyway. Surely she knew perfectly well that I had no children!

Then I realized it was not me she was inquiring about. Carefully I turned back to face her. "God has not blessed me, Lady," I said quite contritely, having heard that phrase often enough to know it was what a Christian like herself might expect.

"So that's it," she murmured.

"That's what, Lady?" I asked innocently.

"Just a puzzle I've been trying to work out. Thank you, Kelda. You may go."

The more I thought about her conversation, the more it confused me. Why would Lady Gruoch want to put me in charge of other servants? I would have asked Macbeatha what it meant, but he was gone. So was Donn, who might have explained it. To this day, Fionna, I do not understand why she offered to put me either on public display in the hall, or in private proximity to my lord's bedchamber. Had Macbeatha asked her to? Was it her way of saying she didn't care if he kept me? Did she think to distract me with additional responsibilities? or disguise my function in the household? I do not know. I shall never know.

By the time Macbeatha returned to finish up the harvest and make the final preparations for his wedding day, we had already begun to move many aspects of his household over to the fortress. The other servants in the hall there were none too willing to take orders from me, but I threatened them not only with Macbeatha's displeasure, but the Lady Gruoch's as well. One or two tried to get me into trouble by intentionally doing things wrong and then saying I had told them to. Were they surprised when the Lady Gruoch saw right through their ploy and took my part against them! To tell the truth, I was surprised, too. She was always fair to me, Gruoch was. I know I speak uncharitably of her, but it is for other reasons, and not for her behavior toward me.

The whole idea of moving into the fortress, of taking responsibility for the servants in the hall, of sharing my lord's bed while his Christian wife was just down the hall—Christian wives don't think highly of bedwenches and concubines, I had come to learn. In fact, Norse wives don't always think very highly of them, either, but they can't do much about it. I hated to think what Gruoch could do, if she wanted.

But what bothered me most of all was Macbeatha. He seemed so *happy* about this wedding. Well, of course, it put him within reach of his dream of becoming High King one day. But never did I hear him voice any uncertainty about the match, any regret for the baggage that came with his royal claim. All this change, the household turned upside down, and Macbeatha only grinned like an idiot and said, "Fine, fine," to everything. When I told him I was to have charge of the servants in the hall, he only grinned more wickedly and reminded me what he liked most was to have two or three plump maids who were willing to slip their skirts up if a warrior craved some pleasure. I replied rather tartly that his lady had picked the servants, and not me.

For a moment he frowned, but only a moment. "You'll just have to help me corrupt them, then," he decided, and off he went with Girc to select the pigs for the wedding feast.

The night before his wedding he was as amorous as I had ever seen him, while I was nervous and distracted. Long after he had fallen asleep, I tossed and turned and cried into the pillow. Finally dawn came, and I rose and set about preparing him to be bound legally to another woman. I tried to tell myself it would be no different than his various romantic intrigues, that in due time he would tire of Gruoch as he tired of all the others—especially since she was so cold and quarrelsome. But somehow I could not calm that last vestige of panic in my heart. And so, on this day that was so important to him, my hand on the shaving knife trembled, and I nicked him.

He flinched, more startled than anything, and I staggered back horrified. "I'm sorry, lord!" I sobbed, and tears streamed down my face.

Slowly he reached up to touch the tiny cut; then he gazed at the smear on his fingertip as though he had never seen his own blood before. Finally he turned to look at me with questioning eyes.

I knew he would never understand how I felt, and what I meant to say was, "It's all this commotion and the household being upset," or maybe just, "Everything's changing and I can't seem to keep up." But what came out of my mouth was, "Will you want her to shave you now?"

At that his eyes grew soft, and he reached out and drew me onto his lap. Laying his stubbly cheek next to mine, he whispered in my ear, "No one shall ever shave me but you, Kelda." Then I wept in his arms, even though I knew it wasn't true. It was sweet of him to say it, anyway. He kissed the tears from my cheeks and held me until I grew calm again. Finally he set me back on my feet and instructed me to continue my task.

"A wise choice, if you ask me," I sniffled, forcing my hand to be steady once more. "I wouldn't trust that lady with a knife at my throat."

I'm afraid I can't tell you much about the ceremony. It was in the big cathedral, and everyone who could cram into the building or crowd around the windows was there, so I couldn't see much. I suppose they exchanged vows—that's the way a Christian wedding goes—and the priest murmured some incantations and sprinkled them with water from a sacred well. Then the monks sang psalms and hymns and recited prayers, and finally the two of them turned to leave the church. But before they took a step, Maisie brought the child Lulach, who was just over a year old then, and gave him to his mother; and when Gruoch had kissed him, she turned and presented him to her new husband.

A look of wonder filled Macbeatha's face as he took Lulach in his arms. I don't believe he had been allowed to touch the child before that moment. But he nested Lulach there as though the crook of his arm were made for nothing other than holding a squirming little boy, and a radiant smile broke across his face like sunlight breaking through the fog. Then, with Gruoch on one arm and Lulach in the other, the happiest man in Alba proceeded out of the church.

Tears stung my eyes as they passed by without even noticing me. Damn her. She'd given him Moray by keeping him away from the fire that destroyed Gillecomgain; she'd given him Alba, or as good as, by becoming his wife; now she gave him the only thing I ever wanted to give him, and couldn't—a son.

The feast afterwards was the most sumptuous affair I had seen outside the High King's court, and I worked myself to exhaustion. Of course, I worked all the *other* servants to exhaustion, too, and Macbeatha finally bade me ease up a bit and let them enjoy the occasion, too. So once the boards were removed and the dancing began, as long as everyone's horn was filled, I said no more. And when I filled Venko's tankard and he pulled me down into his lap, I collapsed there gratefully.

Venko was not like the others, who might tease me or pinch me but would never try to hold me—at least not without a sideways glance at Macbeatha to see if it was all right. Macbeatha had given him permission once, and he assumed that was good until it was rescinded. In many ways he was like a child, earnest and trusting, and without any real sense of the politics that are rife in every royal household. It never occurred to Venko that his lord might take offense at the attention paid to his wench. If a man admires another's fine horse, or the cut of his clothes, is the owner jealous?

And there was nothing lurid, or even very playful, about Venko's attention. He was nothing if not sincere. In fact, that was true of Venko in every circumstance: he had no deep, hidden motives, no intentions other than those he told you. While Scots on the whole are given to exaggeration and boasting, Venko said only what he believed, and boasted only of what was true. If he claimed to be a better swordsman than Owen, it's because he was. If he called me the finest creature God had ever made, it was because he believed that.

Consequently, tales spread that Macbeatha had passed me off on his man. My lord no longer cuddled me openly in the hall, not with Gruoch around, and since Venko was always being familiar, rumors naturally arose. As long as Macbeatha did not believe them, I didn't care; they gave the Lady Gruoch an excuse to turn a blind eye, for though my lord no longer caressed me in public, he continued to do so in private. Not that he neglected his wife, mind you—most of his nights were spent in her bed that winter. But when her menses flowed, or if Lulach was cutting a tooth and fussing in the night, my lord preferred to sleep in his own bed, and he preferred not to do so alone.

Then the spring came and he went off to visit his clients, so Gruoch saw no more of him than I. Sometimes he would take me along in his entourage; sometimes he would take her and Lulach as well, for he loved showing off his stepson to anyone who would pay attention. But most often he rode prepared for battle. There was trouble stirring in the east—Crinan's Athollmen were making mischief along the Dee and the Don Rivers. These were not in Moray, exactly, being more in the territories of Cirech and Ce, but the mormaers of those Great Tribes allied traditionally with Moray. There were many marriage alliances between them, and should they find the Athollmen posing a serious threat, they might call upon Moray for aid.

There was nothing my lord wanted more.

He got his wish, of course, and whether that just happened or he did something to help it along, I will never know. But as he tarried near Essie, word came that Atholl warriors had crossed into Moray itself and raided fifty head of cattle from one of Macbeatha's clients. It was all the excuse he needed. He went thundering after them with his warband, and there was a great fracas somewhere around Craigearn. I'm not sure we got so many cattle back, and I'm not sure the poor farmers who pastured their own herds thereabouts were very pleased with the results. But my lord taught the Athollmen that Macbeatha mac Findlaech was not a man to be trifled with, and that was what mattered.

Then, as though the Lord Jesus himself wanted Macbeatha to have the opportunity to establish his skill as a general, three boatloads of Danish vikings landed on the coast below Aberdeen. That was the territory of Cirech, but the mormaer there was all too glad to have Macbeatha rush in with his hundred and fifty picked troops to repel the invasion.

Yes, he was quite a hero that summer. I wish you could have known him then! Still young and full of vinegar, in pursuit of a destiny that would not be denied. Each battle was a step on the road to Scone, and cost be damned. Fortune rode upon his shoulder, and he glowed with the radiance of—of—

* * *

"The sun," Fionna finished for Kelda. "He glowed with the radiance of the summer sun, which dazzles the eye and brings life to the land: warms it, thrills it ..."

"Yes!" Kelda's face held a look of wonder that Fionna should know just what she meant. The old one smiled wryly. In fact, she had met the High King at that time, and the description was most apt. It was the only time she had ever seen him, but the pulsing of life and power within the man was unmistakable.

But those of the Old Race knew the sun had two natures: in summer, it brought warmth and life; in winter, only cold reproach. Fionna had seen this the day she and her two sisters met Macbeatha upon the moors ...

Chapter Thirty-One

*I*t had been twenty-five years ago, and even then Fionna had felt like an old woman. She had outlived two husbands and five children; she had seen those who practiced the old ways die out, or be harassed into the new religion; and only she and her two sisters were left to practice their arts in this isolated place, far from the villages of Christians who both feared them and begged their services. Heartsore and bitter with her grief, by the time Macbeatha mac Findlaech wedded the land of Moray to become her guardian and king, Fionna only watched with detached curiosity the omens that told of his rise.

Her sisters saw them, too, and noted this northern prince bore the mark of a Pictish tribe. Neass, eldest of them, saw it in the stars and cried exultantly, "Our people shall rise again!"

Taeve, their middle sister, was more subdued as she gazed into a bowl of still water and saw images her sisters could not. "He is a Scot," she said quietly. "Though there is Picti blood in him, he is a Scot in nature. See him, tall and golden with a shaved chin, as no man of the Old Race was ever shaved."

Fionna snorted in contempt. "His is the House of the Sun, and the sun has two natures: one fair, one foul." She had no use for duplicity, nor for the princes of the Scots.

Yet she could hardly cast the stones that autumn without hearing them speak of this ruler, this Macbeatha about whom all the country of eastern Moray was a-buzz. Why was that? It irritated her that her stones should supply her with such useless information, but deny her any knowledge of the coming winter, whether it be *harsh or mild, short or long. It irritated her even more when the stones announced this prince was on his way to her. What business had she with the king of Moray?*

He came in early morning, when the fog had rolled in from the sea to bathe the land in eerie whiteness. Fionna waited with her sisters outside their stone huts, hearing the muffled footfalls of the horses before their dark shapes appeared. Then the beasts materialized before them, snorting nervously as they smelled Fionna's herbs and potions on the air.

Two men sat astride, and Fionna caught her breath. One was a warrior of the Old Race, small in stature but sturdy of build, the symbol of his House emblazoned upon his leather tunic in the deep brown of dried blood. His saddle and bridle were decked with gaudy ribbons, and two severed heads gaped and sneered from a rope draped across his horse's withers.

"What is your business here?" Neass called out in a strident voice. "What do you seek, men of blood and iron?"

Her words died without echo in the swirling fog.

"We were told in the village there are wise women here," came the bold reply from Macbeatha. "Are you those women?"

Fionna turned her eyes to him and saw Taeve's description had not been wrong. He sat like a giant upon his horse, tall as a Norseman, with golden hair caught up in braids and flowing mustaches of bright red. But what struck Fionna was his cat-green eyes. They were ablaze with confidence, sparkling with excitement.

"We are three sisters of the Old Race," Neass responded solemnly, "whose honor it is to preserve the knowledge and the arts of our ancestors, though we are the last to do so." Her eyes strayed to the smaller warrior and she, too, was intrigued. "And who are you?"

"If you are so wise," bantered Macbeatha, "you should know who we are."

Fionna lifted her jaded eyes to meet his and announced, "You are Macbeatha mac Findlaech, ruler of Moray, king of the House of Loarn—and soon to be High King of Alba."

That gave him pause. He gazed at the sisters with new respect.

"You see?" cried the small warrior excitedly. "You see, it is true, they are seers, they are! I know they can help us." He climbed down from his horse and approached, fishing inside his tunic.

"The old days have come back to us," Neass interrupted, gazing wistfully at Macbeatha, "when a king of the realm seeks advice from those of our House."

Now the great lord dismounted, too, tossing a leg over his horse's head and sliding deftly to the ground. His momentary surprise at being recognized had vanished, and he sauntered casually toward the three sisters, focusing on Neass. "I am not yet High King," he pointed out. "And it is my kinsman who has the question."

Arrogant man! "There is a question in your heart, too," Fionna said sharply. "It beats there like a pulse beneath your tunic, steady and insistent. Do you deny it?"

He swung his head over to her, and a slow smile turned up the corners of his mouth. "I deny neither the question, nor your ability to see it beating." The twinkle in his eyes and the gentle humor in his voice caught Fionna off guard. *Perhaps there was more to this warrior than to most.* "But it is Venko's question that brings us here. Mine has been with me a long time—it can wait a while. If you answer Venko's question, though, you will be well paid for your services."

Now the little warrior stepped forward, his expression earnest as he thrust out his palm, where lay a silver ring. "Look at this."

On the band, a Christian cross had been worked against a background of interlaced lines. Fionna eyed it critically. "I see it."

Then he thrust his other hand at her, and she saw he wore a duplicate of the first ring. "It is just like mine," he said, "which I had from my father's hand. But I took this ring from a Viking." He pointed to one of the heads hanging from his horse. "That one. Does it mean anything, do you think? That the enemy I slew wore the same ring as I?"

It means you, too, will die by the sword, you silly nit! Fionna thought. But she knew better than to voice such bitter speculation, so she only shook her head and said, "It means your enemy had an eye for fine workmanship."

The little man looked absolutely crestfallen. Then he scowled impatiently. "No, really," he insisted. "Is it a warning? A blessing?"

She sighed wearily. "If the gods meant anything by it, they have not bothered to tell me." With that she turned away from the visitors, intending to go back into her hut and do something useful.

But Taeve was still intrigued with the tall warrior. "And what is it you seek, Macbeatha mac Findlaech?" she asked.

"Wisdom," was his cryptic reply.

Fionna stopped with a harsh laugh. "Wisdom, is it?" She took a step toward him through the swirling fog. *"Wisdom is paid for in heartache and loss. Are you sure you have the price?"*

"Say rather," he modified, "that I would know what the future holds for me."

"Oh, the future," Fionna mocked. "Well, that is quite a different thing. To know the future is not necessarily to be wise."

"Some would say, in fact, that a wise man does not wish to know the future."

He was baiting her; there was a definite challenge in those green eyes. But baiting her to do what? And why? "What do you say?" she asked.

"I say a wise man prepares for the future, and he can do that better if he knows what it is."

"Sometimes," she conceded. "Sometimes he can do nothing about it, and he only grows angry and fearful waiting for what must come to pass. Will you take that chance, Macbeatha of Moray?"

A smile broke across his face that ought to have chased the fog away with its brilliance. "My destiny is upon me," he declared softly. "If I feared it, I should have wasted away long ago."

And finally Fionna realized it was for the danger itself that Macbeatha baited her. This was a contest: could she tell him of his future? Could he bear to know? "Come inside, then," she bade him, and led the way into her hut.

He entered without fear, though Venko shivered and crossed himself as he came behind. Neass and Taeve followed them, as eager to see the contest as any spectators. Fionna directed them all to seats near the fire, while she fetched her basket of stones. When they were all seated on the dirt floor, she laid out the Cycle of Life between them: Birth, Puberty, Marriage, Death, with the sun on one side and the moon on the other. Then she chose five other stones from her basket. Cupping them in her hands, she shook them once, twice, thrice, and cast them across the Cycle.

The pattern revealed no surprises. "Alba will not fall into your hands," *she told Macbeatha,* "but you must take her in battle."

"I never doubted it," *he replied.*

She peered at him carefully, then selected another set of stones and cast them across the pattern, too. "Hmph," *she muttered.* "Be not hasty—haste brings ruin. But patience brings a long reign and good harvests."

"Ah," *Macbeatha sighed in resignation. He was a man who knew the value of patience, though she suspected the lesson was hard-learned.*

She could have quit then, but she knew he would not be satisfied. Besides, there was a perverse streak in her that wanted to give him something to chew on. This time she selected stones of a more ominous nature and flung them into the pattern.

They clattered and thudded to their places on the hardpacked earth. She bent over them to see what they bespoke. "Blood," *she said after a moment.* "I see much blood."

"That is a warrior's life," *he said, unperturbed. Then,* "Is it my blood?"

It was a curious thing, the way these stones were grouped. Fionna forgot her desire to bring the cocky young ruler down a peg or two as she studied the symbols and tried to discern their meaning. "No, the blood is in Fife," *she told him, shaking her head slightly,* "but it will cling to you." *The mocking icon of Irony winked up at her, sending a chill along her shoulder blades.* "Beware Fife. There is danger in Fife you would do well to avoid."

He was silent for a long moment. Then, "Fife is not my province, not yet," *he said.* "It should be easy to avoid."

She lifted mocking eyes to his. "Easy, you say! Easy when you sit in my house, snug in the womb of the earth. When the battle frenzy is upon you, see how easy it is."

"Will it be a battle, then?" *he asked, wetting his lips in anticipation.*

She waved a hand over her stones. "Ask them. They do not tell me the nature of the danger." *They were whispering, the stones were, words that only she could hear and understand; but they were not telling her what she wished to know.*

Now she plunged her hand into her basket and drew stones out at random. A practiced flick of her wrist strewed them across the Cycle of Life, and she looked to see what the gods had chosen to reveal to Macbeatha of Moray. "Health," she pronounced, almost in disgust. "Wealth. Peace. And then—" The stone was overturned; Fionna righted it carefully. "Defeat."

The smile drained from Macbeatha's face as water drained through cheesecloth. "When?"

Fionna could only shrug. "Not for a long time."

"At whose hand?"

She raised her eyes to his again. "It would be better not to know."

"If your stones tell you, then you ought to tell me."

Suddenly Fionna didn't want to very badly. It was always this way with her: she was sure she wished to tell her suppliants things to horrify them; but when the stones gave bad news, her desire to hurt vanished like a shadow when a torch is extinguished. Almost mechanically, her hand turned the stone that would answer, and she saw a strange sign. "The rowan," she murmured, perplexed to find that stone here.

Macbeatha, too, was puzzled. "The rowan tree brings good fortune. What does this mean, the rowan shall defeat me?"

She could only shrug. "I do not know. It is very curious. Let me cast again."

Once more she plunged her hand into the basket, drawing out three or four random stones. Scattering them across the floor, she bent forward to see what they were.

Death stared at her from the winter quarter.

Macbeatha reached forward as if to touch the stone, then slowly he drew back his hand. "That is Death, is it not?" His voice was devoid of emotion.

"Death will find you, as it finds all men," she defended. "Did you think you would be spared?"

"And what stone is that?" He pointed toward a green and black pebble that lay in a line between Death and the Double Sun.

"Something unholy," she murmured.

"Unholy?" He searched her face cautiously. "What do you mean? A demon? A ban sidhe?"

But Fionna shook her head slowly. "Not unholy in that way, but ... Bent." She didn't know how else to put it. "Life requires a balance, and this man—if man he is—is all to one side. He is south and not north, he is odd and not even, he is night and not day, he is left and not right. Something has pushed him all to one side, *and there is no balance in him ..."* A prickling sensation crawled along Fionna's skin: one of the stones had fallen face down, and her heart pounded as she turned it over. When she saw it, her hand drew back convulsively. Immediately she scattered the stones from their pattern.

"What else?" Macbeatha demanded harshly, catching at her wrist.

"He is a dark warrior," she hissed at him. "Dark with old blood—and in all the world, only he can destroy you."

His eyes bored into her; she could feel them, but she would not meet them. Finally he let her go, and Fionna collected her stones back into her basket.

When she had done, Macbeatha reached inside his cloak and drew out a small pouch that looked and sounded heavy. "I will not insult your art, old one, by offering to pay you" he said. "But perhaps your sisters—" He tossed the pouch to Neass. "—will see your belly does not go empty this winter, nor your bones suffer from the cold."

"We take care of each other," Fionna agreed.

Still he seemed reluctant to go. "Are your prophecies always so gloomy?"

She snorted. "I promised you a long reign, health, and riches. If you find those gloomy, you do not have my pity."

"What about my kinsman?" He nodded toward Venko. "You could not answer his question about the ring, but can you tell him something of his future, something not too gloomy?"

She could not help smiling just a little. What an odd king, to turn from the tale of his own destruction to ask for happy news for his kinsman! She set the Cycle of Life again, then grabbed a random handful of stones and tossed them across it, vowing silently to tell only the good things she saw. It was not hard. "Kings," she said. "There are kings in his future."

"Kings!" Venko exclaimed in surprise. "More than one?"

"Many kings. Good and bad, great and small—but all with one thing in common."

"What is that?"

Slowly Fionna lifted her eyes to the little man, a man of her own kind, and she was glad to tell him what the stones revealed. "They shall call you their father," she pronounced. "All these kings shall call you their father."

Anger and disappointment flashed in Macbeatha's eyes, but he forced it away. "There, my friend, you see?" he said cajolingly to Venko. "In that you shall be greater than I. You shall have royal sons."

Venko's eyes had grown wide at this prophecy. "Truly? My sons shall be kings?"

Fionna scanned the stones again and saw a subtle warning, but she decided to ignore it. "You are a fortunate man," she said instead. "Both of you are fortunate in what this world gives you. Now go in peace, for truly the gods watch over you both."

Her sisters ushered the two warriors out then, while Fionna picked up her stones one by one and returned them to her basket. When finally she crawled out of her hut, the strangers were already vanishing into the mist on their horses. A chill seized her, and she called out, "Beware, Macbeatha! Beware Fife. Beware the rowan that rises against you. And beware the unnatural one." Her words fell like stones in the thick, gloomy air. The steady clop-clop of hooves sounded a moment longer; then that, too, was swallowed by the fog.

Neass came up behind her and put her mouth close to Fionna's ear. "What was it you did not tell the king about his death?" she asked suspiciously.

Fionna continued to stare at the place where the two men had disappeared. "The bent one," she replied softly. "The dark warrior who shall spill the king's blood. It is Macbeatha himself who shall warp him."

Chapter Thirty-Two

In Fionna's hut

The gods had an odd sense of humor, Fionna thought now: to raise up a powerful king like Macbeatha, and then dash him down by means of a creature he himself had made. But then, did not all great men carry within them the seeds of their own destruction? "Things changed for him that season, didn't they?" she asked Kelda.

"Changed?" The Norsewoman shook her head. "Not his good fortune, for he continued to climb like a hawk, circling ever higher, reaching for his destiny. But—yes, something did change that autumn. Something ..." She sighed deeply as the weight of hindsight dragged on her weary frame.

* * *

If there was a time when Macbeatha began to understand the cost of his desires, it was the second autumn of his mormaership. He had built a new fortress called Bradanmor in the east, near his friend Fergus, and we all went there for the summer. But word came of a Viking attack south of Aberdeen, and off he went with all of his men, all of Fergus's men, and a hasty message sent to Brenna's husband Farrell in the Highlands to bring all his as well. Weeks trickled by with no word. Harvest began, and we wondered if Girc needed us back in Ross, but he sent no messenger. More weeks passed, and harvest was done, but still Macbeatha did not come, though word of his success reached us. So there we sat, fretting over his safety and wondering how long we should wait before returning to Inverness without him.

The Lady Gruoch would have been happy not to return at all, for this country was more like her lowland home than Inverness, which was in the cleft of the Great Glen with the mountains rising up like stone armies on both sides. Aithne muttered that the mormaer and his kin ought to celebrate Hallowmas at home, not off in some foreign country, as she deemed anything outside of Ross or Inverness. Hadn't her Siusan died when she came east to this Godforsaken place?

"That was in the Highlands," Gruoch said patiently. "Here the winters are mild, the winds clean and fresh. It is a much better spot for Lulach to winter than Inverness, where it is often stormy and the waves on the Firth leap up as high as houses."

She measured everything by its advantages and disadvantages for Lulach. He was two by then, and what a rambunctious little boy he was! That, of course, was Macbeatha's doing, and none of his mother's. My lord would ride Lulach on his shoulders and gallop around the yard like a fool, or put him astride one of the hounds—"to teach him balance," he insisted. By Midsummer that year my lord had him sitting on a pony, and he and Gruoch had the greatest argument over when Macbeatha could give the boy his first wooden sword.

While we waited for Macbeatha's return from war that autumn, a messenger arrived with news of another rambunctious boy, one who had now reached *aimser togu,* the age of choice. This was Gruoch's mysterious brother whom I had never met. The message said he intended to accept Macbeatha's invitation and come north to join his warband. Gruoch was ecstatic and sent a reply off immediately for him to come as soon as possible.

Shortly thereafter Macbeatha returned with fresh Viking heads attached to his saddle and a clean chin. I asked neither who had shaved him, nor who had cleaned those ghastly heads. Gruoch took no notice of either, but could hardly wait for him to dismount before telling him her brother was coming. That made him smile, and he kissed her on both cheeks. I, of course, stood by with a horn of ale for him, and when Gruoch grew tired of his war stories and went to bed early, he kissed more than my cheeks.

Actually, it wasn't the war stories that disturbed her, though they were grisly enough. It was his tale of three sisters he encountered upon the moors, seers who prophesied greatness for him. Gruoch had no use for pagan mystics, and she crossed herself quickly at the mention of them. "It is dangerous to consort with demons, husband," I heard her say in a low voice.

Macbeatha laughed at her. "They were no more demons than you and I. They were just old women, flattering a new mormaer."

"The *Cailleach*," Gruoch murmured, and crossed herself again. The Hag.

"Peace, woman," he chided gently, laying a hand on her arm. "There was no evil in them. Wait till you hear what they said." The prophecies he related were so convenient as to make me suspect he had invented them himself, from his own wishes: to be High King of Alba, with a long reign of good harvests. For his new guardsman Venko, they had prophesied kings for sons, if you can imagine! Another case of wishful thinking. Venko was a fierce warrior, but a fairly simple soul with no deceit in him and, therefore, no head for politics. Plus, he was of the Old Race whom men did not respect. Could such a man father kings?

One would have thought Gruoch could at least smile at such predictions. Instead she murmured a charm against evil, then begged her lord's leave to go to her chamber for a time of prayer in thanksgiving for his return. Nor, apparently, was she the only one disturbed by the mystics and their prophecies. Lying with Macbeatha in his chamber that night, after our passions had been sated, I felt him drifting into distracted thoughts rather than sleep. "Lord?" I whispered in the darkness. "What troubles you?"

He sighed and tugged me closer in the soft feather bed. "Silly thoughts," he dismissed. "Don't worry."

"But you are worried," I replied, running my fingertips lightly across his furrowed brow. "What is it? What troubles you in the face of such happy prophecies?"

"The sisters gave me warnings as well as accolades," he confided. "I'm to avoid some danger in Fife, and to beware of rowan trees, if you can make any sense of that, for somehow the rowan shall defeat me."

"But the rowan is good luck!" I protested.

"Not for me, apparently. And my life shall end at the hands of one unholy born. Twisted, she said. Bent. A dark warrior."

It sent a chill through me, and I shivered there in his arms. He only wrapped himself tighter around me and went on, "Oh, don't worry, my little Valkyrie! If I am to have a long and happy reign before then, what more should a warrior desire?"

Still, he slept fitfully that night—and so did I.

It was only three days later that Sloane, one of my lord's couriers, rode in with a wounded and bedraggled priest. Sloane looked white as a ghost, and at first we thought he had been injured, too, but he brushed off concerned hands saying, "We must speak to Macbeatha. Bring the priest inside; he must tell Macbeatha his story."

My lord was playing chess with Gruoch in the hall, but he rose when Sloane entered with the priest draped on a servant's shoulder and a dozen other curious servants on their heels. "Sloane, cousin," he greeted worriedly. "What news? What has happened?"

"This man can tell you." Sloane nodded to the priest. "I found him in the Cairn o' Mount Pass."

The Cairn o' Mount Pass is one of several routes to reach eastern Moray from the south. It was at least two days' journey for a wounded man, and I wondered that Sloane had not sought care for the injured priest before bringing him on. But we learned it was the priest himself who had insisted. Raising his head, he addressed not my lord, but his wife. "Lady Gruoch," he croaked.

She started in her chair. "Father Tuthald!" she cried. "Oh, Father Tuthald, what's happened, where is my brother?"

"Malcolm's men," the priest panted, clutching at a wound in his side which, from the smell about him, had begun to fester. "Don't know how they knew ... but they lay in wait for us. The big one—I know him. Duff, his name is. Duff mac Moryn—" Tears streamed down the poor priest's cheeks. "Never let him draw his sword. Looked him in the face, called him by name, and then—" His voice choked off.

"NOOOOOOOO!!" shrieked Gruoch, falling to her knees on the straw-strew stones. *"NO NO NO NO NO—!"*

My lord rushed to her and tried to raise her up, but her back and her knees were like water and would not support her. Only her fists seemed to have any strength, and with these she beat upon his chest. "Assassins!" she wailed. "God curse Malcolm mac Kenneth and his hell-hounds! God curse him, God curse him, God—!" She broke off in incoherent weeping.

Macbeatha carried her off to her chamber, calling for a surgeon to attend the priest, and for two or three ladies to come help him with Gruoch. By the time he returned, the priest had been laid on a cot near the hearth, and I was applying an oatmeal poultice to the angry cut along his ribs. Sloane stood nearby, fidgeting with his dagger.

"Sloane," Macbeatha snapped. "What happened?"

"Uchtan was with them," Sloane said quietly. Uchtan was the messenger Lady Gruoch had sent to her brother. "Run through with a spear. I thought this one was dead, too, but ..." He glanced at the priest, then recounted the tale as he had been able to reconstruct it from the cleric's ravings. Tuthald had been the boy's *culdee,* teaching him Latin and Greek, poetry and law. At Lady Boite's urging, the priest had agreed to accompany his erstwhile pupil to Moray. Not only was Boite concerned for her son's spiritual welfare—for she considered the faith of all Northerners suspect—but Tuthald had spent time at Malcolm's court and knew many of his retainers on sight. Should any come looking for the boy, Tuthald would know who they were—and whom they served.

Reasoning that a large escort would draw Malcolm's attention, Uchtan, Tuthald and the boy had set out alone by little-known ways to cross Atholl into Moray. What gave them away, no one ever knew, but there was an ambush waiting in a narrow part of the pass. Six men rode out of the trees, felling Uchtan with the first spear. Then, having seen the boy's face and confirmed his identity, Duff mac Moryn simply ran him through with a lance. No challenge to combat, no pretense that this was anything other than an assassination. They hacked the priest for good measure and rode off.

"One other thing," Sloane said quietly as he finished his tale. "They took the boy's head. I imagine they've gone back to Malcolm with it, to claim a reward."

Macbeatha had listened to this whole story grim-faced. "He never let the boy touch his sword?"

Tuthald stirred on his cot. "Murderers," he whispered. "Honorless men."

"The sword was still in its sheath," Sloane confirmed. "They didn't even bother to thieve the corpses."

Macbeatha nodded and turned stonily away.

"I suppose you ought to send word to the Lady Boite that—"

"What I ought to do," thundered Macbeatha, rounding on his man, "is hunt down the piece of filth who killed the boy and slit him belly to chin! Not to allow the lad to draw his sword and defend himself—! God damn him to everlasting fire! What kind of a coward does that? And to assassinate a *boy*—seventeen years old, what threat was he to Malcolm? None, today. But he was on his way to me—"

Suddenly my lord stopped and looked down, for a round-faced cherub was tugging on the hem of his tunic and gazing up with frightened eyes. Lulach was now the only heir of old king Kenneth mac Dubh, and a new fear wrote itself across Macbeatha's face. Scooping up his tiny stepson, he clutched the child close to his breast. Then, when poor Lulach began to whimper at the strength of his stepfather's grip, Macbeatha kissed the boy and handed him over to me. "Owen! Call my guard. Two horses each and travel rations. We're going to track this cowardly dog back to his master, and both shall pay—*both!*" With that he spun on his heel and strode toward the stairs.

I took Lulach up to Gruoch, but one of the old servants had given her a potion to calm her, and it had put her to sleep. So I gave him to Maisie and went to help my lord with his preparations. Macbeatha was more angry than I had ever seen him, and it was a cold anger—the kind that freezes the blood of those who look upon it. I feared for him that day as I had never feared for him when he rode off to battle. How he would deal with the killer did not concern me—it would be vicious and cruel, and rightly so. But the High King? How would he deal with Malcolm mac Kenneth, who had hired the assassin?

It was long dark, and they had been gone for hours, when the Lady Gruoch finally awoke and called for her son. Hearing the whispers among the servants, I went up to her chamber to peer in and see how she fared. She sat on her bed, eyes glazed, clothing rumpled, watching Lulach stare at himself in her polished silver mirror. He squinted at his reflection, then touched a finger to his nose to see if the image would mimic his action. Normally such antics made her smile, but now she just stared at him in a dazed fashion, then let her eyes wander around the room.

As soon as they lit on me, I wished I had ducked back out of the chamber, but of course it was too late. "Kelda—where is my husband?"

"Gone out, lady," I replied, not knowing how sound her wits were at that moment. She certainly looked deranged.

Her eyes unfocussed again as her gaze bent inward. "He swore to protect him," she whimpered. "He swore he would protect my brother and keep him from harm."

"He wasn't here, lady," I reminded her. "He was off slaying Vikings when the message came."

"I know." Tears welled up in her eyes and I felt oddly uncomfortable. Lady Gruoch wasn't the kind to let servants see her tears. "He would have gone to fetch my brother, if I'd asked him. I should have asked him. I should have waited until he came home and …" Her voice trailed off.

Maisie threw herself half onto the bed and wrapped her arms around Gruoch's waist. "It wasn't your fault, lady!" she sobbed. "Don't ever think it was your fault. It was that heathen of a high king and his devil-spawned minions—not you."

Her outburst seemed to calm Gruoch. It threw her back into a familiar role, that of being strong and in control for the sake of the weaker ones around her. "Hush, Maisie," she soothed. "Take Lulach and put him back to bed, I shouldn't have wakened him. Find him a sweet to quiet him, there's a good girl."

When Maisie had gone, I helped Gruoch unfasten her shawl and slip off her shoes, then settled her under the blankets and firs. "We were so close in age, we were almost like twins," she said as I tucked her long, dark hair into a night cap. I gathered she was speaking of her brother, though her mind wandered from subject to subject without apparent provocation. "He said when he was king, he would have me always at court; and I said I would marry the king of Northumbria and give that land to him as a present." She giggled a little. "We were just children, we knew nothing of politics. I should have said—" With a sigh, she settled her head on her pillow as two tears trickled down her cheeks. "I should have said I would marry the King of the North … and given him that …" Mercifully, she drifted off to sleep then and I escaped to the hall, leaving others to watch over her during the night.

I awoke in the late autumn dawn with old Isobail shaking me. "It's the Lady Gruoch," she whispered. "She's calling out in her sleep for Lord Macbeatha, and for her brother. Over and over, I don't know if I should wake her …"

Groaning, I stumbled to my feet, wondering why Isobail picked me to solve this crisis. But I scrambled dutifully up the stairs to see what was going on.

By the time I got there, some brave soul had wakened the tormented sleeper, and I found her sitting up in bed, staring wide-eyed about the room. When her eyes fell on me they pulled back into focus and she asked, with a hint of her usual haughtiness, "Kelda! Where is my husband?"

"He's gone out, lady," I said again.

She tugged at her shift to make sure she was decently covered by it. "And why has he gone, at such a time? A lady has a right to expect her lord to stay close by in her time of grief."

"Can't you guess?" I groused. "He has sworn vengeance on your brother's killer, and on Malcolm, and ridden off with his guard to carry out his threat."

Gruoch's jaw dropped and her eyes grew wide. "What?"

"He's gone to revenge your brother," I repeated impatiently. "So don't chide him for not being here by your—"

"When?" she demanded, frantically clawing her way out of the bedding and seizing me by both arms. "When did they leave?"

"Yesterday," I told her, startled at this reaction. "Just after you took to your bed."

At the news, she grew unexpectedly pale, sagging so I had to catch her to keep her from sliding to the floor. "No," she breathed. "Oh, no. No, he mustn't. He can't take on Malcolm mac Kenneth, not with just his guard. It's madness! He—" Now her eyes searched mine in desperation. "You must stop him."

"Lady, I cannot," I said in exasperation. "He has already gone!"

"Then go after him! Tell him he must give up this madness. Tell him I said so. Tell him we will avenge my brother another way, another time, but Kelda—Kelda!" She shook me. "Kelda, he met the Hag on the moors, and now he rides to grave danger-- Stop him! I fear for his life!"

I feared for him, too, although I did not understand the Scots' anxiety over this "hag," this old woman whom they think is a harbinger of evil. But for *me* to stop *Macbeatha*-- "Lady, you must send warriors to stop him. Sloane can show them the way, but-- Send Fergus. Now, there's a good plan. Fergus is not half a day's ride from here—"

"No!" she shouted, her voice edged with hysteria. "No, I will not wait for Fergus! Macbeatha wouldn't listen to Fergus, anyway. No man can turn him from this deed, Kelda, for they all think he's right. Blood paid for in blood. He'll listen to you, though. He trusts you. Tell him I sent you. Tell him I prayed to the Virgin Mother, and she told me in a dream that he must not seek vengeance, but must forgive." That had the uncanny ring of truth to it, the way she said it. Who knows what dreams she had in that drug-clouded sleep? "You know how to talk to him to make him listen," she pleaded. "You're the only one who can. Please, please, you *must* go after him! Take as many men as you need, but find him and stop him!"

Now she had me frightened, but I could see only one obstacle after another. "Lady, the men will not take orders from me," I protested.

"They'll take orders from me!" she snapped. "And if I tell them to take you to Macbeatha, that is what they will do!" With that she snatched her shawl from a peg on the wall, scuffed her feet quickly into her slippers, and strode out the open door toward the stairs with maids trailing after her.

Well, when Gruoch sets her mind to a thing, no one can stop her except possibly Macbeatha, and he wasn't there. So within the hour she had assembled a cavalcade of ten warriors with arms and supplies, plus Sloane as scout, to accompany me on my journey. "I would go myself," she told me, handing me a letter she had prepared for Macbeatha, "but I can't leave Lulach. Tell my husband I will wait for him here."

I was touched momentarily by her concern for Macbeatha. It was a new thing in her, to put aside her own desire for revenge, in favor of her husband's safety. I thought perhaps she cared more for him than she let on.

"Now, go," she bade me urgently. "He is the only protection I have for my son—I cannot afford to lose him on such an ill-considered venture."

Lulach again! I might have known. To others, Macbeatha was leader, protector, steward, or political tool. I mounted my horse firm in the belief that in all the land, I alone cared about the man.

Chapter Thirty-Three

How can I express what madness it was, that pursuit of Macbeatha? For a slave girl to ride with ten warriors for protection! To even hope we might catch up to him, when he had such a head start. Perhaps the warriors by themselves could have gained on him, but with me slowing them down, it seemed impossible.

Yet we reached Cairn o' Mount well before nightfall on the second day and found signs of my lord's passage. His trail led straight down the pass, and we sheltered that night at an inn where the host reported having seen a company of ten men thunder past just before noon that day. This cheered everyone. They had only half a day on us, and they had to go more slowly now to track this man Duff. Didn't they?

They didn't. Arrogant Duff, thinking no one would find the bodies for weeks, hadn't bothered to conceal his tracks, or his passage. We followed Macbeatha's trail and his directly to Scone. When we reached the royal residence, though, it was cold and dark—Malcolm had gone to Glamis to spend Hallowmas, for that was where his ancestors were buried. But Macbeatha, said people in the town, had crossed the Tay and gone south.

"He's after Duff then," Sloane muttered to Lauman, who led our expedition.

A dairymaid agreed. "Duff was here, all right, antsy as a ewe smelling wolf on the wind. Saw the king just before he left, then lit out for home." As to where "home" was, she wasn't as sure. "Western Fife, I think. Or maybe into Fortriu."

Fife! My blood turned as cold as the waters of the Tay, which we must now ford. It meant nothing to the others, of course—Macbeatha had not told them of the warning he received from the three seers.

In Perth, a small boy told us he had seen a prince and his guard pass by earlier that day, heading south into the hills. We struck off in that direction, and Sloane soon picked up the trail.

My bones ached, I hurt in places I didn't know I had, and yet I pressed on. By nightfall, I could hardly keep the reins clutched in my frozen hands. When Lauman called a halt at a small cottage, I did not argue. I knew we ought to keep going, but I couldn't, I just couldn't. I had grown numb with cold and fatigue and the constant pounding of the ride.

"Sloane, take two men and go ahead," Lauman directed as I tugged one leg over my horse's rump and slid to the ground. There I collapsed in a heap, for my knees would not bear my weight. One of the warriors caught my elbow and hauled me to my feet. "Come to the fire," he said in a voice that was gruff but not unkind. Then he half-dragged me into that poor cottage and deposited me by the hearth, where I stretched out and went promptly to sleep.

When I awoke at dawn, it was to the clamor of voices and men stirring in the yard. One of the scouts had returned. "We've found him," he announced as he burst into the little hut, letting a draft of cold air in with him. "He would not turn back, so Sloane offered to scout the trail for him, planning to delay him till we can catch up."

"Up! Up!" shouted Lauman. "To your horses! And someone lash the girl to her mount, I'll not have her falling off halfway there."

I didn't resist nor even object, but they needn't have taken such pleasure in it. Unlike Macbeatha's guard, which had grown accustomed to my presence, these men resented having to drag me along. "The Lady Gruoch was right," I croaked at Lauman when he shoved an oatcake into my hands. "None of you can get him to turn back. Only me. Only me."

The trouble with having Sloane lead Macbeatha a merry chase was he led *us* a merry chase as well, and so it was near nightfall before we came upon the second of his companions, who had turned back to find us. But let me tell you what I have since learned from others about Macbeatha's journey, up until the point I finally reached him.

At Scone, when he found the king gone to Glamis, Macbeatha had cursed and considered briefly, then decided to follow Duff. Perhaps it was beginning to come to him what a problem it would be to confront the High King and accuse him of murder. But when Sloane caught up to him and reported the Lady Gruoch asked her husband to turn back, he laughed harshly and said, "Oh, I'll turn back, all right. I'll turn back when I have that brute's head in my hand to throw at my lady's feet."

Then Sloane tried to lead Macbeatha astray, but my lord was too good a tracker himself to be fooled for long. When he saw what his man was up to, he lashed poor Sloane across the face with his reins, cutting a gash that left a scar Sloane bore to the end of his days. Then on he pressed with renewed anger.

They reached the little steading of Duff mac Moryn just at dusk on All Hallow's Eve. Macbeatha's men were nervous; despite the priests' insistence that Hallowmas was a festival to honor the departed saints of the Christian faith, every Scot knew it was *Samhain,* the Feast of the Dead. On this night the door between our world and the Otherworld is open so spirits may pass back and forth. Perhaps the good Christian saints are indeed abroad that night, and a man might be visited by his grandfather or his favorite uncle or some great warrior ancestor, but there are other spirits abroad, as well. Spirits whose intent is evil. Spirits who will try to steal a man from his tribe and kin, dragging him back with them to the Otherworld.

That was the night on which Macbeatha tore down the house of Duff mac Moryn.

It was a mean hut of wattle and daub, so it did not take much tearing. When my lord called to those within and demanded that Duff come out, Duff refused. "Go away!" cried a frightened female voice. "Evil spirit, go away! We will not come out this night!" They imagined, you see, that he was a demon from the Otherworld. He might as well have been.

"I am Macbeatha mac Findlaech!" roared my lord. "Ruler of Moray, king of the House of Loarn, and brother-in-law to the son of Boite, whose life you took in Cairn o' Mount Pass! Come out and face justice!"

Of course, this did not increase Duff's willingness to unbar his door. So my lord took the hatchet from his saddle and hacked into the mud daubing of the house, hooked the weapon around a framing stick, and gave a mighty jerk. A chunk tore loose from the wall. "Come out and face me, Duff!" he bellowed, chopping another hole and making the whole house shiver. Then he ran a rope through the two holes and urged his horse back.

Voices shrieked from within as the wall pulled away completely. The remaining three walls listed, and the thatched roof tilted at a crazy angle. "Come out, mac Moryn!" my lord shouted, riding his horse into the hut and sending Duff's poor wife scurrying to get her children out from under its hooves.

"Mercy, lord!" cried Duff, falling on his knees. "I beg you mercy! Spare my house and my family!"

"Your family had best run for the hills, if they would be spared!" Macbeatha snarled, looping his rope around a roof pole.

So they ran, with pigs and goats and two cows getting tangled up in the rush to escape. My lord rode his horse out, pulling the roof down into the hearth fire. Soon the whole cottage was ablaze.

It was that light which guided us the last distance to him. Lauman and the others gaped in wonder at the sight before them, while I squirmed against the straps lashing me to my horse. "Cut me loose, you fools!" I shouted at them. And to Macbeatha, "Lord! Lord, stop! Lord, it is I, Kelda, come from your lady with an urgent message. Oh, stop! Please, stop!"

But he could not hear me, for a terrible rage was upon him.

Duff tried to run, but Macbeatha leaped from his horse and brought the man to earth, tumbling round and round with him in the dry grass. "Mercy, lord!" Duff croaked.

"Stand up!" my lord commanded, clambering to his own feet. "Stand up and draw your sword!"

"No, lord," Duff whined, coming only to his knees. "No, I will not draw against you."

"You only draw against boys, is that it?" Macbeatha demanded, launching a fierce kick which doubled the man up. "Boys who don't have a chance to draw their own swords in defense. Isn't that right?" Another kick sent Duff sprawling in the dirt. "Now, draw your sword, coward, and fight a real warrior!"

"Mercy!" Duff cried again, blood gushing from his nose in the eerie light of his burning house. "God forgive me, I have sinned, I know I have sinned. Only have mercy, and I will be your servant forever."

"My servant? My *servant!* I wouldn't have a servant like you!" Macbeatha seized Duff's tunic and jerked him to his knees. "You're not fit to lick the boots of my servants!" And his powerful left fist lashed out, striking Duff in the face.

"Mercy, lord!" the assassin sobbed, for he was a great coward at heart, as all who knew him would testify. "In the name of God and the Holy Mother, have mercy!" But Macbeatha struck him again. He wore a ring with a green jewel in it—a wedding gift from the Lady Gruoch. Now it caught the firelight as his left fist lashed out again and again, pounding into Duff's face and stomach.

By this time I was frantic. I carried my lord's shaving knife with me always, and when I realized the men were not paying any attention to my pleas, I struggled to loose that blade from its hiding place beneath my skirts. It was a small thing, but very sharp; I sawed urgently at my bonds with it.

Finally Lauman saw what I was about and remembered his mission. With a muttered curse he drew his dagger and slashed away the cords holding me in the saddle. I stumbled to the ground and lurched toward Macbeatha, crying. "Lord, stop this! Your lady beseeches you! *I* beseech you!" In my worried and wearied condition, I could not think what to say beyond that. "Lord, the Hag," I panted. "Lady Gruoch says she had a dream—lord, please—"

But Macbeatha had hold of Duff's hair and was hauling the battered man to his feet. "I said *fight me!*" he roared at his victim, landing a punch deep in his gut.

I would have thought Duff had no breath left to speak, but he managed to gasp, "Mercy," before he crumpled to his knees.

"Did you have mercy on the boy?" Macbeatha thundered, locking his fists together and swinging them like a club at Duff's face. We could hear the crack of breaking bones as his cheek caved in. "Did you have mercy on Uchtan?" Another blow, this from the other side. "Did you have mercy on the *priest? A priest,* for God's sake! You would have murdered a man of God!"

Now at last I reached him, lunging at him from behind, trying to seize one arm, "Lord, stop!" I begged. "Lord, you mustn't! You're a king, you must show mercy."

Annoyed at this interruption, Macbeatha swung around to see who inhibited him. There was madness in his green eyes, a hate so insatiable that for a moment I thought he would kill me, too. But then he seemed to know me. "The boy was under my protection," he grated. "I swore to her that I would protect his life."

"To Lady Gruoch?" I pounced on a slim hope. "And it is she who sent me to you, lord, counseling restraint."

But he tossed me aside, and his eyes went back to the bleeding lump before him. "I swore it to her!" he bellowed, seizing Duff by the hair again. "I swore it to her, and you have made a mockery of my vow—!"

Before he could land another blow, however, another arm, stronger than mine, stayed him. "Enough, lord," growled Owen; and when Macbeatha made to use his right hand to strike Duff again, he found that, too, seized. "It is done," said Venko gently. "The deed is done, lord. The man is dead."

And so he was. With animals bawling in terror and flames shooting up into the night, Macbeatha looked back on the awkwardly sprawled form of Duff mac Moryn and saw it was lifeless clay. Slowly the madness drained from his eyes and the tension from his limbs. I ran to him again and threw my arms around him, weeping. I had failed. I had failed his lady, and worse, I had failed him.

There was a squeal and a groan like a banshee's wail as the last walls of Duff's house fell in. Overhead in the winter sky the Pleiades glimmered, those stars that herald the supremacy of night over day, of the dark of winter over the warmth and light of summer. There was the sound of sobbing: Duff's wife cradled one child in her arms while another clutched tightly at her leg, and firelight lit the streams of her tears. She was a pitiful sight to behold, and my heart ached for her. How would she and her children survive this winter, with no house and no husband?

The little boy clinging to her leg was perhaps four or five winters. He was blond of hair and fair of face, though his countenance was stained red by the flames. He stared with horror at the fierce, towering warrior who had just beaten his father to death. Macbeatha's eyes met his across the trampled yard, and I felt my lord suck in his breath. Did he know, in that moment, what he had done?

Beware Fife, the Hag had told him. Beware the Dark Warrior. Duff means black, you see, and though Duff was dead, there stood his son: mac Duff.

Epilog

In Fionna's hut

With that final word, Kelda seemed to collapse in on herself. "Hush, now," Fionna soothed, laying aside her stones. "Rest a while. You can finish your tale in the morning." She crawled to the wall where hides and blankets were rolled and tied in neat bundles. "Here, I will make you a bed."

"I'm sorry to be so slow in telling my story," Kelda apologized. "It's just that when I get started, I seem to remember everything ..."

"Only the young are in a hurry," Fionna replied, spreading the bedding on the floor near the fire. The man seeking her hut had stopped for the night in the village nearby; he would not take up his quest again until morning. Likewise, the royal cortege bearing the High King to the Isle of Iona had stopped to rest for the night. "Old ones like me know there is plenty of time."

"Is there?" Kelda asked softly.

"Time is all we have, you and I. Once it was different: we had plans and ambitions and dreams like everyone else. But mine have fled, and yours have been stolen. What good is the time left us, if we cannot use it to savor that which is still ours: our memories, and our understanding."

Kelda shook her head slightly as she stretched out on the thick hides. "I don't think I have any understanding."

"You understand all you need." For Kelda, understanding was the ache in her heart: aching for the widow in the firelight of a burning hut, aching for the king enacting his own doom. But for Fionna ...

With a sigh, she turned back to the elaborate pattern of stones laid out on her floor. The sign of the Norse jarl still perched just outside the circle—he would come into play somehow. And the Fallen Foe—Gillecomgain? No, that one was never associated with Scone. Duncan? Fionna had tried so hard to ignore such kings, so she knew little about that one. And this Gruoch who wedded Macbeatha—the stones had not spoken of her yet. Was she more than just a path to the high kingship?

Disgusted, Fionna swept an arm across the floor, gathering the stones toward her. There were days when she cursed her gift of hearing them whisper. Tomorrow she would cast them again, for they would not be silent unless she did.

Tomorrow, and tomorrow, and tomorrow ...

BOOK TWO

Prolog

Larkin mac Duff knew that he was not like other people. Even without his brother telling him, or his mother weeping in despair, he knew it. He would lose bits of time. He would find objects under his pillow, and not know where they came from. He became so engrossed in the use of his sword or his knife that he forgot if this was a wooden post he was attacking, or really a man. That didn't happen to other people. It certainly didn't happen to Malcolm Canmore. Malcolm always knew where he was, and what he was doing, and why he was doing it.

Larkin didn't. He didn't know why he did certain things. He didn't always remember that he'd done them. But he didn't let it trouble him anymore. He hadn't let it trouble him for a long time. His mother had explained it to him once, long ago. "Oh, it's the Devil in ye, Larkin," she had sobbed when she found him stabbing his knife over and over into the side of Aunt Morven's goat. "The Devil came into you that night, and you've not been the same since."

Larkin knew exactly which night she meant, and it made sense to him because that was the night he'd discovered the power in his left hand.

Da had come home just a day or two before, laughing and throwing his boys up in the air and calling out to his wife for ale. "We'll celebrate!" he cried. "It's Hallowmas soon, and what a feast we'll have! I've pleased the High King, and he's been good to us—oh, yes, indeed! We'll have a roast pig for our feast this year, see if we don't!"

So on All Hallow's Eve, with the pig snoring by the hearth without a clue what was in store for it on the morrow, they'd bolted their door against evil spirits and said their prayers, and the two little boys had been tucked into their beds.

But the bolt had done no good against the Devil who arrived that night. He'd torn their house down—torn out the walls and let it all collapse into the fire! Then he'd hauled Da into the yard and begun to beat him.

Larkin had watched, clinging to his mother's skirt, unable to take his eyes away. Down came that mighty fist, smash! into Da's face. Then it raised up and down it came again. Smash! Blood spurted from Da's nose. Smash! Larkin was sure he saw teeth go flying into the night. They caught the light of the burning house and glimmered just a moment before disappearing like sparks into the darkness. Smash! The fist came down again and drove Da to his knees.

Da was crying, begging the Devil to have mercy. Da called on the Holy Mother, but she didn't do anything. The Devil was stronger than the Holy Mother. He pulled Da up by his tunic front and smash! Larkin could hear bones breaking. Mother was sobbing and clutching Ewan to her breast. Sometimes she would push Larkin back behind her, but he always struggled forward again to watch. Smash! Da doubled up over that fist. Da was the strongest man Larkin knew. It would take an awful lot to make Da double up like that.

Then something caught Larkin's eye: a flash of green in the firelight. There was something shiny and green on that hand, that powerful hand that was making a ruin of Da's face, knocking him down again and again and again. It was a ring, a great green ring, and it gave added force to that smashing fist. Up from the dirt the fist lifted Da, lifted him and then, thud! Da gave a great oof! as all the breath went out of him. Thud! It struck him again, but this time there was no breath left to rush out, only a cracking sound that could have been Da's voice, or his ribs. A flash of green, a mighty swing, and—

—and it was his left hand. The Devil was using his left hand to beat Da. And as he stood triumphant in the firelight, looming over Da's crumpled body, the Devil raised his head and looked directly into Larkin's eyes.

Larkin's jaw dropped, and he felt the hair on the back of his neck stand up. He wanted to back away, to hide behind Mother, but found that he couldn't. Helpless, he stood there staring at the Devil until the Devil turned away from him at last.

Suddenly, Larkin's face felt cold. He felt as though he'd been facing a raging fire which had abruptly gone out. His knees began to shake.

And then, Larkin felt his left hand twitch. Surprised, he shoved it behind him as though it were no part of him, but it twitched again. Slowly, he drew the hand out and looked at it. It didn't look any different. But it felt ... odd. Experimentally, he pounded it against his right palm. Smack. It felt strong. He pounded it again. Yes, he was sure it was stronger than it had been that morning. He pounded it again, and again—

Then the Devil's warriors were gathered around him and Mother and Ewan, putting them on a horse and leading it away toward Aunt Morven's house. Larkin turned around for one last look at the Devil standing in the light of the burning house. "I'll get you!" Larkin shouted, still smacking his left hand into his right. "I'll get you and I'll make you pay!" But no one heard Larkin because he shouted inside his head. He did not speak his anger aloud. He did not speak aloud at all for a very long time.

Chapter One

In Fionna's hut

A strange apprehension filled Fionna as she scattered her stones once more upon the hard earthen floor of her mound home. Though it was August, the air inside her stone-lined refuge held a chill. The man following Kelda had taken up his hunt again, and soon he would be here. What was his intent, this man who tracked the Norsewoman?

Nearby, Kelda stirred on her pallet and clutched at a small leather pouch she had kept close ever since she arrived. It smelled strongly of cedar oil, and Fionna had not asked what was in it. Slowly the Norsewoman opened her eyes and peered around the dim interior, lit only by a shaft of sunlight seeping through the hut's smoke hole, and a small cooking fire. Finally she dragged herself into a sitting position and pushed a stray lock of graying hair from her face as she looked at the pattern Fionna was creating. "What do your stones tell you today?"

Fionna scowled. "Only what they told me yesterday, as you began your tale." She strewed another handful of pebbles across the floor. "This Duff that Macbeatha slew—Did the king know what he had done?"

Kelda considered that. "I'm not sure. He knew-- He knew he had transgressed the prophecies," she said carefully. "'Beware Fife,' the Cailleach had told him. 'Beware the Dark Warrior, the Unholy One.' Yet in his great rage, he chased the assassin into Fife and beat him to death on Samhain Eve." She sighed. "In the light *of that burning hut, he knew he had done evil, yes. But when he looked into the eyes of the child—when he looked at mac Duff—"* Kelda shivered.

Fionna poured her guest a cup of the brew she had warming at her fire. "Go on," she encouraged.

* * *

Donn told me once that Macbeatha had a fierce temper, but he had learned to keep a tight rein on it. He lost the reins that night in Fife, and the monster that killed Duff mac Moryn was nothing like the warrior who led his men into battle, or the king who ruled long and well. Perhaps it was some Samhain spirit that possessed him, after all. But when Duff was dead and there was only the distraught widow and her two small children, that evil thing vanished like fog at midday.

Someone found a pouch with gold Anglish coins stuffed in Duff's boot—payment, no doubt, for having delivered the head of Gruoch's brother to the High King. Macbeatha handed it over to the widow without counting it, as the price of her husband's life. Then he had Weylin take her and the two boys to a kinsman's house nearby. We bedded down for the night in a small church, and in the darkness of that place, where no man could see, I felt him trembling in my arms.

Upon our return to Bradanmor, the Lady Gruoch met her husband at the gate, her face a pale question. His look held no answer for her, so her gaze passed from him to me. I only shook my head. She did not blink, but her eyes dulled a little and her chin sagged ever so slightly before she turned back to my lord. "Welcome home, husband," she greeted formally, as though he had just returned from a visit to some client.

Macbeatha swung a leg over his horse's head and slid wearily to the ground. "I fear your plea for restraint did not reach me in time," he said. "But I am not sorry your brother is avenged. May Duff mac Moryn rot in hell for his cowardly deed."

"Come inside, lord," she said, as if she hadn't heard at all. "It is cold, and you've had a long journey." Taking him by the arm, she led him into the house as though he were a child.

What did they say to each other when they were in private? I do not know. But I know he would not pass a whole night in her bed for months, fearing to wake her with his violent dreams. So he woke me instead, and I never minded. I would hold him and rock him and soothe him until he could sleep again.

It was a dismal winter. But spring came, as spring will do, and upon our return to Inverness for the Feast of St. Brigid—which we still called the Festival of Bride—a messenger arrived from Thorfinn. He wanted Macbeatha to meet with him.

I was delirious at the prospect. My lord's guardsmen were troubled—they mistrusted Thorfinn in general, and this would be the first meeting between him and Macbeatha since the latter had besieged the former in the ruined fortress at Burghead. But since my lord had somehow arranged for each side to withdraw from the field with honor intact, I feared no hostility. No, my thoughts were of seeing men I had known in childhood, men who could tell me how my mother fared, and my little brother Hakon. How old would Hakon be now? Nine? Ten?

Once, it passed through my mind that Ivarr could be among Thorfinn's warriors, and I shivered. I had no desire to see the man who had threatened me with mutilation and death. But I trusted in Macbeatha's protection, and I could not curb my excitement as I accompanied my lord and his guard up the coast to the Dornach Firth. We turned in there, traveling northwest and along the Oykel River, through territory Scots and Norsemen have battled over for generations, until we came to the meeting place.

Several Norsemen waited on the riverbank and guided us through a stand of trees to a meadow. There, several tents had been pitched, and a fire sputtered over a roasting pit. I searched the faces in the camp for Thorkel Fosterer, who owned my mother, but I did not find it. I was having a second look for Ivarr when a tent flap snapped back and out came Thorfinn Sigurdsson himself.

My former master had grown burlier with the passing years, so there was no trace of the rangy youth left in him. Instead, he had a chest like a bull's and legs like house pillars. For a moment his fierce, craggy face scowled at us; then he bellowed out a laugh. "By God, Macbeatha, you have kept her all this time!" he roared. "You used to change wenches like you change tunics—one for each new festival. Perhaps age slows you down?"

"Cast not your sins upon me," Macbeatha mocked, his eyes twinkling. "The wenches still come and go, but that's no reason to give up a servant who can speak two languages. Especially when Duncan thinks she can only speak one."

At that, they both howled with laughter and clapped each other on the back, then stomped toward the fire arm in arm.

I slipped away, for I had spotted a young warrior named Turolf who had been but a boy when I was in Thorfinn's hall. He remembered me, too, and when I pressed him eagerly for news about my mother, he was most obliging. She had at last bought her freedom, as well as that of Hakon and a younger son named Solmund, who was born after I left home. Thorkel, who had fathered both boys, showed no interest in formally acknowledging either, but he often brought them presents. Just last fall he had given Hakon a small bronze sword. Turolf assured me my brother showed great promise with it and would surely be invited to join Thorfinn's warband when he was old enough.

Just then I heard my name bellowed playfully from the fire. "Kelda! Do you still remember how to serve ale to thirsty warriors, or has this barbarian ruined you entirely?"

I dashed toward a nearby cask, snatched up two drinking horns that lay beside it, and drew ale for the two jarls. A light mist had begun to fall, and they were headed into Thorfinn's tent. "Kelda has made it her mission in life," Macbeatha boasted, "to keep my drinking horn filled—and my other horn emptied." Both men laughed raucously, and I waggled my fleshy parts to support his assertion before following them with the ale. While they drank, I fetched a pitcher, returning in time to refill both horns.

When I had refilled their horns, Macbeatha drew me onto his lap, somewhat to my surprise. Of late, he had not been very playful with me in the hall, even when Gruoch was not present, and I wondered if his interest waned. Perhaps Thorfinn's presence reminded him of how we had carried on in the early days; or perhaps it was a ploy, to flaunt in Thorfinn's face what he had given away. Whatever the reason, I was not inclined to object.

"I see taking a wife hasn't dulled your appetite," Thorfinn observed dryly, as Macbeatha slipped his free hand up under my shawl.

"Why should it? Although they do keep me panting sometimes," he fabricated blithely, "hopping from one bed to another, three, four times in a night."

Thorfinn made a rude noise.

"And you?" Macbeatha probed. "Are you going to give up bedding your slave girls once you marry—who is it? Inger--Inga—"

"Ingebjorg," Thorfinn supplied. "That depends on how unreasonable she is. I met her once—she's quite the Christian. I can see a fight or two coming over the subject." Then he stretched his long legs out in front of him and dropped his eyes to his drinking horn. "How is my grandfather these days?"

Macbeatha's green eyes began to whirl at the mention of the High King. "Death hailed him from the gates this winter, but was sent away. As for next winter ..." He shrugged. "Who knows?"

"Indeed," Thorfinn mumbled, still pointedly not looking at Macbeatha, who would look nowhere but at him.

"Will you go to see him?" my lord asked. "I can grant you safe harbor in Moray, and arrange it in Cirech, till you reach the Tay. Atholl I cannot speak for."

"No, no," Thorfinn growled. "I'll not go to Alba while my grandfather lives." His face darkened and his eyes grew distant. "Not as a client, anyway."

I thought he meant because he had sworn allegiance to the Norse king, and feared his Scottish grandfather's displeasure. But Macbeatha read something deeper. "Do you intend to challenge Duncan?" he asked bluntly.

Thorfinn threw him a sidelong look. "I've as much right to be High King as he does."

Now Macbeatha stared down at his own horn of ale. Here was a wrinkle he hadn't considered. It had always been in his mind to rise to the office of High King—but what if he had to challenge Thorfinn for it? After a moment he said, "They won't accept you."

Thorfinn sat back in surprise. "Who won't?"

"The churchmen and the nobles who elect the High King. They'll pick Duncan over you."

"Not if he's dead."

Macbeatha shunted me aside and rose to his feet, slowly shaking his head. "You don't understand. It's not just Duncan's army you'd have to fight. It's every Scot, every tribesman, north and south." Crossing to the tent's opening, he push the flap aside enough to see it was still misting outdoors.

"North?" Thorfinn echoed coldly.

Now my lord turned to face him again. "Try to understand, cousin. You're not a Scot. You're a Norse jarl, and the Scots will never accept you as High King of Alba. If I tried to back you, I'd be challenged by every male member of my tribe until one of them got lucky and killed me."

"You mean you'll swear allegiance to Duncan?" Thorfinn demanded incredulously.

Macbeatha gave a crooked smile. "Not by preference. If your grandfather will hang on for two or three more years ..."

Thorfinn stared at his guest, and stared, and stared; and finally, the light dawned in his eyes. *"You* would challenge Duncan for the high kingship?"

"In time."

This notion was clearly foreign to Thorfinn. "What, on the strength of that old yarn that your mother was Malcolm's daughter?"

Macbeatha sipped his ale carefully. "More on the strength of my wife's claim."

Now Thorfinn rose and paced the short distance to the tent's back wall, cursing under his breath. "Good God, Macbeatha. I'd always counted on ..." Wearily he grasped the tent frame with one hand, sagging from the effort of dealing with this new twist.

"You hold all of the Orkneys now, don't you?" my lord asked, for Thorfinn's half-brother Brusi had died and Thorfinn had assumed control of the remaining third of those islands. "And half the Hebrides—I know, for Bowen's been fighting you every inch of the way. Caithness and Sutherland are yours—I won't contest you. Nor will I ask you to swear allegiance to me, should I become High King. You are a Norse jarl, Thorfinn; you'll have as great a jarldom as your father did, and at an earlier age. Be strong in it! Hold it long and well. But Alba is mine." He tossed off the last of his ale. "Alba is mine."

I crouched on the stool Macbeatha had vacated, waiting for Thorfinn to respond. He stood slumped by the back wall for a long time; finally he straightened himself, shaking that shaggy dark hair of his. "My claim is better than yours."

"If only you were a Scot," my lord said sadly.

Their eyes met across the dim interior. Slowly Macbeatha smiled. "Of course, if I'm killed trying to take Duncan, you have my permission to step in and finish the matter."

Thorfinn snorted. "You have more gall than any man I've known, Macbeatha."

"Thank you," my lord mocked, with a gracious bow. "I suspect we may not come to terms on this issue today; but God willing, it is still a few years off. Let us agree on one thing: I will not challenge you for any part of what you now hold, and you will not try to make further inroads into Moray. Is that fair?"

"Fair enough," Thorfinn agreed. He held out his empty horn, and I filled it, along with Macbeatha's. "Moray for you, Caithness and Sutherland for me," Thorfinn toasted, and they both drank.

"Good neighbors always," Macbeatha proposed.

"Skoll!" They drank again.

"And in all other things ..." Macbeatha shrugged. "We will talk before we raise our swords. Agreed?"

Thorfinn agreed to that, too, and they drank one more toast. Then they clapped each other on the back and marched out into the drizzle, roaring for food and bickering over who would get the kidneys of the calf that had been roasting in a pit all day. In the end they split those, too.

But the Fates were not inclined to give them two or three years to settle the issue of who would challenge Duncan for their grandfather Malcolm's kingdom. Macbeatha said no more of confronting the High King over the assassination of Gruoch's brother, nor did his wife. The risk was too great. But Boite, the boy's mother, felt differently. She and her kin conspired with another family whom the High King had also cut off from royal succession, and together they launched an attack on Malcolm. He was at his fortress in Glamis, preparing to return to Scone for the winter, when the combined forces of the two Houses came against him.

Now, Malcolm had not survived as High King for thirty years without reason. He was well-liked by his warriors, and mightily respected by his mormaers. As soon as the hostile army approached, men flocked to Malcolm's banner. Though his health was not good, his iron will was not one bit rusty. Scorning armor in true Scottish fashion, but with shield brightly painted and standards flying in the crisp November air, Malcolm mounted his horse and led his warband out to meet the enemy. They say he wielded his sword with as much vigor and skill as a man of twenty winters, and Boite's vengeful army was forced to retreat, broken by the numbers and ferocity of Malcolm's followers.

But in that battle the High King took his death blow. His kinsmen carried him back to Glamis, where he lingered for three days until Duncan arrived, the latter cursing that he was too late to participate in the battle. As soon as Malcolm beheld his eldest grandson, he smiled faintly and breathed his last.

I know warriors, and you cannot tell me Malcolm did not choose this last battle as his end. There was no need for him to lead his own troops, except that he chose to meet his death, not lying in his bed like a cow in the straw, but on horseback with his blade in his hand. That is a noble death, one befitting such a great ruler. I did respect him, you know. He was wicked, but no more than most, and he took care of his kingdom: seizing Lothian for its riches, making marriage alliances with potential foes, protecting Alba from foreigners with his sword and his cunning. If he was blind in the matter of choosing Duncan as heir, it did not make him any less a great king.

I never thought of it before, but—how like him Macbeatha was …

Well. What was my lord doing during all this? Because of his close connection to Malcolm, Boite chose not to involve Macbeatha in her conspiracy. That was a mistake on her part. Moray's army, and Macbeatha's leadership, would have tilted the scales in the other direction: Boite would have had victory instead of defeat. But even after his vicious revenge on Duff, she did not trust her son-in-law. It's quite possible she didn't so much fear his siding with Malcolm as she feared his seizing power should they win. However it may be, she attacked without him.

Macbeatha was furious. He stormed about the fortress raging at Boite's lack of trust, and the waste of the good men of his wife's kin because he had not been there to aid them. Would he really have joined them against the man he called his grandfather? Oh, yes—but not for the murdered boy's sake, or because of his marriage alliance with the family of Kenneth mac Dubh. He would have done it for the very reason I just told you: leading those combined forces to the attack—for none was better qualified—he would certainly have won the day, and then he could have claimed the high kingship by virtue of his victory. Boite had denied him this, and that was the real reason he stormed about the fortress, barking out orders and cursing under his breath.

But there was nothing to be done about it, and he soon gave up his rage for a more practical course. With fifty warriors and a suitable retinue, he set out for Scone. As Mormaer of Moray, he must help elect the new High King. We traveled down the Great Glen this time, it being a shorter if more arduous route, and then crossed boldly through Atholl. From time to time one chieftain or another would approach to ask our business, but they always let us pass without incident. The election of a High King was not to be hindered.

In the end, there wasn't much of a contest. Duncan had royal ancestors, a decent record as a warrior, experience as king of Strathclyde and Cumbria, and Malcolm's blessing. Whose claim could be better? Not Macbeatha's, certainly. His claim was largely through his marriage to Gruoch, whose family had just been defeated in battle. He was not foolish enough to suggest himself as a candidate that year.

But his meeting with Thorfinn was fresh in his mind, and in our moments alone I could see the anxiety written on his brow, wondering what his friend would do now. Thorfinn was, as he had pointed out, as much a grandson as Duncan, and his reputation as a warrior was undeniable. To Thorfinn's stubborn mind, his claim was as good as his cousin's. Macbeatha was right, though: the Scots knew Duncan, whereas they did not know Thorfinn. To them, he was a marauder who tried to steal control of the Western Isles. Why would they choose an enemy as a king? The only way Thorfinn could have established his claim to Alba was, as Macbeatha had told him, with an army.

The question then was, would he try it?

Chapter Two

Whether it was the season—for winter was upon us—or Macbeatha's warning not to expect aid from Moray, I do not know, but Thorfinn did not appear at Scone to put forth his claim to the high kingship. Neither did he, as Mormaer of Caithness, pledge Duncan his support.

Macbeatha did. On the last day of November he stood with the other mormaers as each in turn hailed Duncan *ard righ,* high king. One laid the royal cloak on Duncan's shoulders; another handed him the white rod that was the symbol of office; and yet another raised him up from his place, seated on the *Lia Fáil,* the Stone of Destiny. My lord stood by smiling graciously, and he banged upon his shield as loudly as the rest during the acclamation, but I knew how it galled him to have to acknowledge Duncan as High King.

We stayed and feasted at the new king's table for several weeks, with Macbeatha up to his old trick of letting Duncan win at chess. They were most convivial to each other, and neither spoke of Gillecomgain. (I was surprised to learn that everyone at court assumed it was Thorfinn, not Duncan, who had burned Gillecomgain in his house. That is a Norse tactic, of course, to surround a house and burn it; and perhaps that had been Duncan's strategy, to cast the blame on his Norse cousin. More likely it was Malcolm's strategy, for I doubt Duncan could have been so artful.)

Duncan was in a high state, with all the adulation and flattery heaped upon him. He was drunk most of the time—but then, so were most of the mormaers and other chieftains—and bragged incessantly about his past triumphs in Cumbria, and how all Alba would now grow rich under his leadership. The nobles gathered around him were little concerned with past glory, however. They wanted to know where the new High King would lead his warband first. Each, of course, had his own suggestion. Jarrow was a great favorite, and someone even suggested York, although he must have been very drunk to suggest striking so deep into Northumbria. My lord surprised them all by proposing Durham. That is a walled city in Northumbria—very rich, and not so far over the border as York, but very well protected.

"If it were easy, it wouldn't be worthy of a high king," he said when Fife balked. "And with the proper planning and strategy, I believe it can be done."

But Duncan kept mostly silent during this discussion, munching on walnuts that a serving boy cracked for him and washing them down with ale. Finally Crinan turned to his son with a sly look I did not much like. "And what say you, Duncan of Alba? What says the High King?"

"I say no," Duncan replied flatly.

"What?" exclaimed the others, and "Why not?" and "Then where shall we strike?"

"I'm not planning any raid this summer," the new king announced smugly, brushing at the crumbs on his chest but succeeding only in chasing them deeper into the folds of his clothing.

"No raid!" the warriors objected, seeing the wealth of Durham vanish before their eyes. "Why not?" and "You're the High King!" and "But you must lead a campaign." Macbeatha kept quiet, watching Crinan and Duncan by turns.

"First we must bind Alba together," Duncan continued. "That's what my grandfather said." It did sound more like Malcolm's thought than Duncan's. "So this summer I'm going to make a royal circuit. Pay a call to each of my faithful mormaers."

At that, Macbeatha's eyes grew dark and dangerous. It was one thing to bite his tongue and abide Duncan's presence there in Scone; it was quite another to let him ride into Moray. I thought of the blackened ruins of Vevina's house in Urquhart, of all the Moraymen in that area eager to chase this weasel back into its hole, not three years past. And did Duncan expect to ride peacefully through Moray?

"What's to be gained by parading through your own kingdom?" complained Ce, who did not want a high king's company squatting at his fortress and eating up the meager supplies he had.

"Splendid idea for a new king!" exclaimed Fortriu, who could afford to feed Duncan and his men for months, and far preferred that to sleeping on the cold ground or a lumpy camp bed. After all, what was *conveth* but a "hospitality rent," a set amount of food and goods supplied for the king's upkeep? What did it matter if Duncan ate them in Fortriu, or carried them away with him?

Macbeatha had put on a careful look of indifference. "You will go to your brother, too?" he asked conversationally. Upon Duncan's election, Maldred had been named king of Strathclyde and Cumbria in his brother's place.

"Of course."

"Perhaps there first," Macbeatha jested, for upon his appointment, Maldred had gone charging off to claim his prize, declining Duncan's invitation to stay and celebrate with him. The new high king had been quite irked.

"No, not first," Duncan drawled, trying unsuccessfully to keep a smirk from his features. "Not to Strathclyde first—nor to you, Ce," he assured the surly mormaer. "I know you have had hard times, as have Cirech and the Isles. No, no, it is not you I shall visit first."

I saw Macbeatha's jaw clench.

"We ride first to Moray."

The moment we left the hall, Macbeatha's brow furrowed and he stomped heavily to his guest chamber. "We leave for Inverness day after tomorrow," he said brusquely. "See that all my things are packed, and that we get what supplies we need for the journey."

"Aren't we staying for Twelfthnight?" I asked innocently.

"I won't suffer another day with that obnoxious turd!"

I know I shouldn't have baited him, but I couldn't help it. "The longer we stay here," I pointed out, "the longer you have to figure out how you're going to tell the Lady Gruoch that the man who murdered her first husband is to be a guest in her house."

"It is my house!" he roared, not at all amused. "And as my wife, it is her duty to honor my guests, and I will hear no more about it!"

I arched an eyebrow. "Well, perhaps if you put it to her in just such tones, that will help."

My jest brought him up short and he sank wearily onto his bed. "If only he would go to the south first," Macbeatha groaned. "To Fife, and across Fortriu to Strathclyde, and back to his father in Dunkeld. That would take him the whole summer. Then by next year—" He wiped an arm across his furrowed brow. "By next year I would be ready for him."

"Ready for him?" I asked quizzically, climbing onto the bed behind him and starting to massage his great shoulders.

"Malcolm was greatly feared and much respected," he said, "and Duncan was his choice. The tide of feeling won't turn against him for at least a year. Damn Malcolm, for putting this idea in Duncan's head!"

Abruptly he rose and began to pace the room. "It was probably Malcolm's idea for him to come to me first, as well. Crafty old devil! He knew I'm the most dangerous of the lot, especially since I married Gruoch. He knew the only time Duncan would have a hope of facing me down is in this first year. The others will watch, cautiously, to see how Duncan does. If I dig in my heels and refuse to let him enter Moray, they'll be happy enough to join the fray on his side for a share of the riches."

"Not Cirech, surely!" I cried, for Cirech is Moray's neighbor in the north, with little love for Southerners; not to mention they owed my lord a great debt after he chased the pirates from their shores. "And Bowen won't let his uncle join with Duncan!"

"Bowen and his uncle will have their hands full with Thorfinn," Macbeatha predicted. "The Isles won't be able to come in on either side. And though Cirech and Ce might come to me, they're more likely to call me a fool and stay in their own lands. The others will all join Duncan. Damn him! If only he would come to me last."

He flung himself back down on the bed and my fingers took up where they had left off, rubbing the bunched muscles of his shoulders and neck. "A year from now," he went on, "people will begin to question why he has done nothing but ride around the countryside, living off the hospitality of his clients and getting fat on their labor. By then he will have made an ass of himself in front of every mormaer and his lady—especially his lady. Then, let him come. I could feign some insult—even claim a threat to my wife— and challenge him to combat as he approaches Inverness. I need

Duncan deep in my territory, without the resources of his damned Atholl kinsmen to draw on. I need to challenge him to honorable combat. But not this year." He let his head loll forward under my ministrations. "It won't work if he comes to Moray this year."

"So you'll lure him back again. When you're ready, you'll lure him up there on some pretext."

"But I cannot suffer him to come into Moray!" he gritted through clenched teeth. "I do not grieve that Gillecomgain is dead, but I cannot forgive Duncan the treachery by which he accomplished it."

For several moments my lord just sat there, slowly relaxing under the prodding of my practiced fingers. "And you're right about Gruoch," he finally said. "It's bad enough I have to go back and tell her we elected the murdering craven as high king. If I tell her he's marching into Moray ..."

I wanted to remind him there was plenty of room in my bed, but that was a poor and petty thing to say, so I didn't say it. "You won't have to tell her at all," I soothed instead. "Because by the time we leave, you'll have thought of a way to talk Duncan out of this foolishness."

He smiled then, and chuckled. "You think so, eh?"

"You're the thinker, lord," I demurred. "I'm not a thinker, so it must be plain truth."

Then he laughed and reached around to pull me to him, flopping back on the bed with his arms around me. "You are a saucy wench!" he declared happily. "Every man should have a wench like you."

"Oh, no," I protested. "Because then every man could become high king, as you shall be."

That made him roar with laughter; and though you may not believe it, of all the pleasures we shared that night, none gave me greater joy than to fill him with such laughter.

We did not leave so soon after all, but lingered while Macbeatha tried to cajole the High King gently to some other plan of action. Duncan, however, was nothing if not stubborn. He had announced before all his nobles that he would visit Moray first, and so he would.

My lord then pursued another course. Pleading a promise to be home with his lady by Christmas, he made a significant show of packing, bade the High King a regretful good-bye, and left with great fanfare. His last words to Duncan—who was going out to hunt—were, "We'll see you at Beltaine. You'll find we Northerners put on the best Beltaine games." Grinning broadly, he poked the High King's burgeoning belly. "And the best feasts." Then we were off up the Strathmore with our cavalcade and our carts full of luggage while Duncan and his party headed into the hills above Scone.

Scarcely were we out of sight of the watchtower when Macbeatha and his guard turned back. Few know what he did then, for Macbeatha never boasted of it, and Duncan certainly wasn't telling. But I had the whole of it from Venko, who was a fierce warrior and as loyal a man as Macbeatha ever had, but whose mouth ran on more than it should.

They slipped into the hills and tracked down the king's hunting party as it chased a red deer the hounds had scared up. Five of Duncan's men rode ahead to trap it and keep the hounds from killing it—that was to be Duncan's privilege. The other four hung back with their lord, but even they were caught up in the chase and gave little thought to what other dangers might come out of the woods. One stopped to answer a call of nature and was shocked when his well-trained horse bolted abruptly, leaving him afoot. Another was unhorsed by a tree branch that appeared from nowhere.

Duncan and his two remaining warriors followed the shouts and hurrahs of the lead men, only to find themselves suddenly alone, with no sight or sound of the hunt. Weylin and several others, you see, had emulated noises of the chase to lead the High King away from his own men. Venko giggled like a crazed person as he told me how puzzled Duncan and his two guards were at the sudden disappearance of companions who had been so loud and vocal only moments before. Suddenly cautious, they peered through the trees but saw nothing untoward—only a little hut with a curl of smoke coming from the smokehole in its thatched roof.

"The curs!" Duncan exclaimed. "They have given up and are resting by a fire!"

One of Duncan's men ventured to disagree, but the king cursed and urged his horse toward the hut. Indeed, there were tracks round about it, and it never occurred to Duncan they might be those of any but his own men.

It is possible he did not notice one guard disappear as they dismounted and approached the hut. But I don't care what Venko says, I am *sure* he realized the man who followed so closely behind him as he opened the door, never made it inside.

Imagine the look of shock on Duncan's broad and florid face as he swung the door open and found Macbeatha waiting for him! "Come in, cousin," my lord greeted with that glint in his eye that could make men tremble. "Warm yourself at the hearth."

What passed through Duncan's mind as he found himself in Moray's power? He had to know it was possible he would never leave the hut alive. Perhaps he reasoned Macbeatha would not have gone to such lengths to get him alone if he intended to kill him—but I like to think the pit of his royal stomach grew cold with fear.

"What do you want?" Duncan demanded, even as the door closed with a thump behind him. The two mac Erc brothers stood on either side of the door, while Venko and Owen stood before him, flanking my lord.

"Only to talk, cousin," Macbeatha assured him. "We need to come to an understanding, you and I."

At that Duncan scowled menacingly and retorted, "We are not cousins. You are no blood of mine."

"If that is true," my lord told him with a cold smile, "it is a great relief to me. But be that as it may, there is something we need to get straight between us."

Still Duncan did not perceive his danger. "If there is any straightening to do, it is I, the High King, who will do it!"

At a nod from Macbeatha, the two mac Ercs seized the king's arms and held him fast. All color drained from Duncan's face.

Macbeatha came then to the king and looked him squarely in the eye. "I will make this simple, so you can get back to your hunt and I can get back to the lands where I am king. Yes, *king!*" he snapped as he saw Duncan begin to object. "In Moray, I am a *king!* I have hailed you High King and feasted at your table, and offered to ride into battle with you, and I will continue to do all of those things—here, where you reign. Before your mormaers and in your hall, I will continue to acknowledge your suzerainty and pay you all respect. But know this, Duncan mac Crinan." His voice grated low and threateningly: "Do not come into Moray."

I can well imagine the fury in Macbeatha's green eyes, and how he held Duncan breathless with the ferocity of his gaze as he continued in the same harsh tones. "There is a house in Urquhart where six of my men died—friends and kinsmen both. With them died fifty good men of Moray and the chief of the House of Loarn. The head of my family, in his own lands! Do not think for one instant that I have forgotten—or that Moray will ever forgive."

For a long moment more he held Duncan in that withering glare; then he turned away toward the crackling fire. "So when spring comes," he went on in a lighter tone, "I suggest you find something else to do. Raid a Northumbrian city, or find a menace of some sort that needs your attention. Because if you come near Moray, you will find an army waiting to oppose you. A very large army of very angry men. And cousin or no, I will have your head, Duncan. I will have your head for Gillecomgain's widow."

Now, I don't know if Venko was inventing this part, but he insists when the mac Ercs escorted Duncan back outside and gave him the reins to his horse, there was a wet stain creeping down the High King's leg.

Chapter Three

Duncan decided to accept my lord's advice. This was made easier by Thorfinn choosing that next spring to ravage the western mainland of Atholl: Duncan was far too busy leading his warband to the rescue to be bothered making any royal circuit through Moray. The following year he responded to incursions by a band of Northumbrians in Lothian. Macbeatha even went to help him with that, although Duncan didn't really do much except make a few reprisals across the border, taking as much toll of his Lothian hosts as he did of his Northumbrian enemies.

Whether it was Duncan's company or the weight of thirty-one winters, I do not know, but my lord seemed different than the last time we had campaigned in Lothian. His mien lacked reckless abandon; it smacked instead of calculated cunning. He bore himself with more dignity, spoke with more authority, and seduced his women with less single-minded vigor. It struck me that he was no longer a young prince, but a *righ,* a king.

We never again wintered at the High King's court: for one thing, Macbeatha could not bear to be parted from Lulach for so long. The boy grew and changed from one week to the next, and my lord was loath to miss a day of it. But that year, we did stop at Scone on our way back to Moray from Lothian. Duncan had not yet arrived, having gone first to Strathclyde, where he still had a mistress he doted on. His wife was in the residence, though, along with his two sons, Malcolm and Donall.

Malcolm mac Duncan, or Colmbeag "Little Colm"—as we called him, was then five, and his brother, three. They loved

Macbeatha, for he played rough and tumble with them just as he did with Lulach, who was of an age with Colmbeag. My lord would get on his knees for a mock sword fight with the elder, and he would blow on Donall's stomach with a loud *bbllattt!* and make him laugh. You would think their mother would be delighted that a warrior of Macbeatha's stature took time to tease them and wrestle with them and tell them stories of great heroes and famous battles.

But Aelflaed had, from the very beginning, a great disdain for my lord. She was a Northumbrian noblewoman, tall and large-boned, with pale blond hair and a rather stern face. Whenever my lord appeared, she scowled at him, and if she spoke to him at all it was to scold him for wreaking havoc with her relatives in Northumbria. Macbeatha sloughed this off good-naturedly, telling her if she didn't like his campaigning practices, she should speak to her husband—it was by Duncan's order they crossed the border to return Northumbria's spears point first.

One day Aelflaed walked into the cheery room where her boys played on cold days to find them both in Macbeatha's lap, one on each knee, while he told them a story. Whether it was the obvious worship in those little blue eyes, or something else I cannot fathom, Aelflaed snapped. Snatching up Donall and pushing Colmbeag behind her, she launched into a bitter diatribe against my lord and told him he was never to lay hands on her boys again.

He looked so shocked. While mother shouted and sons bawled, he sat there gape-mouthed like a stunned salmon until finally Aelflaed ran out of breath. Then he rose and said sadly, "Lady, I have nothing but love for your sons. I am sorry to have you place such a ban on me; but I must respect your wishes, as they are your sons. I will leave tomorrow for my home and my own son. Please give your husband my apologies that I could not await his return."

That night he was very quiet and melancholy in bed. Pressing myself up against his back, an arm wrapped around his chest, I could almost feel the hurting of his heart through his flesh. But all I could do was nestle my face against him and hold him until he slept.

The next few years were quiet, with the exception of the great battle between my lord and his lady over Lulach's fosterage. Gruoch wanted to keep Lulach there at Inverness and bring the sons of several of their clients to be fostered with him; she thought the warriors of Macbeatha's guard could instruct them in weapons, and Father Tuthald, who had stayed on with us, could teach them Latin and poetry and such. This, Macbeatha refused to consider. "You coddle the boy, lady," he told her bluntly, "and will continue to do so. *I* coddle him, for that matter, and it is time he went where he will be treated as a warrior in training, not the pulse of his mother's heart and the apple of his father's eye. Besides," he added. "It is safer to have him elsewhere."

At first Gruoch put her back up and objected that Lulach was *her* son, but Macbeatha shot back that the boy was *his* heir, destined to rule Moray one day, or even Alba, and they had an obligation beyond that of a parent toward a son. She said no more in front of us servants, but I knew by the hardness in her eyes, she did not intend to let the matter drop. What words or what wiles she tried on him behind closed doors, I do not know, but she did so in vain. When Lulach's seventh summer arrived, off he went into the western highlands to a prince called Indulf.

Nor was this the only conflict over Lulach's fosterage. Duncan once sent for Macbeatha to join him in Dunkeld, where he had gone for Hallowmas. As they sat at table on the day of the feast, the High King turned to my lord and suggested Lulach come to him at Scone, to be fostered with Colmbeag.

Macbeatha laughed. Loudly. "Oh, no, my dear cousin, I am not so big a fool as that."

Duncan bristled at this dismissal. "Do you imply that some harm would come to him in my care?"

"Your grandfather had Lulach's uncle beheaded to assure your kingship," Macbeatha said frankly, but without a trace of rancor. In fact, he sounded quite merry. "Should I then trust the last heir of Kenneth mac Dubh to your care?"

"I only seek to do you honor," Duncan grumbled, "offering to foster the boy."

"You seek a hostage," my lord said. "I give you none."

Duncan voiced another protest, claiming disrespect and distrust were unworthy of a mormaer, or "great steward," toward his king. What my lord replied I could not hear, for he spoke so softly, the man at his other elbow did not know what was said. When I asked him afterward, though, he smiled at me. "Why, I told Duncan if he kept on, there would be a war between us; and since Thorfinn is already in open rebellion, it would look bad for another of his mormaers to rise against him."

Before we left, however, Macbeatha proposed a marriage alliance between his house and Duncan's, as a sort of sop to the High King's pride. Duncan had a nephew named Maelduin, his sister's son, who was a handsome young man and well versed in the noble arts of war and poetry. Macbeatha was much impressed with him and proposed to recommend him to Vevina, his cousin's widow, for her daughter Bainen.

The idea of a blood claim on the tribes of western Moray appealed to Duncan, and he lent his approval to the match. Maelduin's father Eoganan was reluctant, for the enmity between the tribes of western Atholl and the Moraymen of the Great Glen is old and bitter. When my lord pointed out, however, that the couple would live in Atholl, where Bainen would serve as a sort of hostage for her kinsmen's good behavior, Eoganan was mollified and said he would be open to negotiations on such a marriage.

It remained, then, for Macbeatha to convince Vevina this was a good match. She had no love of Duncan, after he burned her house with the men of her family still in it; and although my lord had shown himself to be her friend and protector, she was still anxious about his motives.

"I don't want Duncan in Moray," he told her flatly. "With Maelduin tied to us by blood, he becomes the logical emissary between Atholl and Moray, and Duncan can stay well away. I've met the lad, Vevina; he has none of Duncan's stink about him. He's practical, forthright, and not too ambitious. Let him come to visit and see if you don't agree." Vevina consented, and upon meeting the young man, she concurred with my lord's estimation, so a match was arranged.

The wedding was to take place at Midsummer, and my lord himself promised to deliver the bride. But before the day arrived, the Northumbrian jarl Ealdred invaded Strathclyde and punished the inhabitants severely. Marching up and down the countryside, burning and looting, his army was more than Maldred could handle, and so the young king of Strathclyde and Cumbria appealed to his brother Duncan for help.

My lord waited anxiously for a summons to join in a great army to stop the Northumbrians, but it did not come. The time arrived to take Bainen to her wedding, and he delayed his departure for Urquhart by a day, hoping for a messenger, but none came. He delayed it yet again, and finally had to set out on a quick march to make up for lost time.

We arrived late in the day to find Bainen frantic with worry over the match. Maelduin was an *Athollman,* after all, and what if he murdered her in her bed? What if he kept her a prisoner in his fortress, and never let her come back to see her beloved mother again? What if he kept her in chains, or killed her children as they were born, or—

Upon hearing these frightful imaginings from the sobbing girl, my lord gently scooped her up in his arms, carried her to the hearth, and sat there holding her in his lap like a child. He rocked her and soothed her, assuring her Maelduin was no monster, that he was too honorable a man to murder a woman, let alone harm his own sons, and of course, she could come to visit her mother. Macbeatha would see to it personally. He would ride down to Loch Rannoch and fetch her home for a visit any time she wanted. Gradually Bainen's sobbing subsided and she actually fell asleep with her head on my lord's shoulder. It is a comfortable spot, I can tell you.

The next morning, a servant pounded on our door to announce that Bainen had locked herself in her chamber and would not come out.

With a groan, Macbeatha forced himself from our cozy bed, threw on his tunic and cinched it with a belt, pulled on his boots, and clomped out to where a knot of people had gathered around Bainen's door. Wrapping a shawl over my shift, I padded after him.

Vevina gave him a pleading look. "I'm sorry to disturb you, lord," she apologized, "but last night you did so much to calm her fears. I thought perhaps she would listen to you again this morning."

Macbeatha mumbled something, rubbed at his face, and then turned to the door. "Bainen?" he called gently. "It is Macbeatha. Will you not come out?"

"No!" shrieked the hysterical bride. "I don't want to get married. I want to be a nun and live in a convent. Go away!"

Macbeatha closed his eyes with a pained sigh. Then his muscles bunched, and with one powerful kick he shattered the puny latch holding the door. "Get her ready," he growled at the startled maidservants. "I intend to leave here in one hour, and Bainen will be in that horsecart if I have to carry her out and lash her to the seat myself!" Then down the stairway he went, and out the front door of the hall.

I scurried after him, tying up my belt as I went. It was a cool, sweet summer morn, and the mist clung to the loch like a comforter. I could hear fishermen preparing their boats to go out, though I could not see them in the whiteness, and the quiet lapping of the waves on the shore reminded me of my childhood by the sea. Beneath her blanket of fog, Loch Ness seemed to stretch endlessly to north and south, while the highlands on both sides rose like giants out of legend.

"Lord, wait," I called as Macbeatha turned toward the water and its peaceful sounds.

He waited, and when I caught up to him, he put an arm around my shoulders. "Why can't more women be like you, Kelda?" he grumbled as we walked into the swirling mist. "Agreeable and compliant and—"

"Saucy?" I reminded him. A smile tugged at his lips. "Then how would you know what a treasure I am, if there were so many more like me?"

That elicited a chuckle. "I suppose that's true," he admitted. Reaching the lake shore, we turned and walked south along the wet strand.

"But I see my lord forgets the day he found me sobbing my heart out in the stable," I reminded him. "You must forgive Bainen her little tantrum, lord. Think how frightening it is to be abandoned amongst one's traditional enemies, with nothing to protect you but a smile and a pretty face."

"Then Bainen is well armed," he commented dryly. Then he turned to study my face. "Do you still long for a child, Kelda?" he asked soberly.

"I long for your child, lord," I told him honestly, "and always will. I pray to the Holy Mother Mary every day." I did not tell him I also prayed to Freya, for I knew how he felt about that. But Freya seemed more likely to grant such a prayer than the Virgin Mother.

He stopped walking then and locked his strong hands behind my back. "Would not the child of another man do?" he asked softly.

His eyes bored straight into mine, and it was the hardest answer I ever made. "No, lord," I said stoutly.

With a great sigh he closed his eyes and leaned his forehead against mine. "You always know just when to lie," he said wearily. "Thank you." Then he kissed me long and gratefully.

It was a lie, Fionna, I must tell you. When I looked around at the other serving girls with their babes—when I saw Gruoch, or even Maisie, fussing over Lulach—how my heart ached for a child of my own! To hold a little one in my arms, to nurse it at my breast, to teach it and watch over it and see it grow day by day ... But I could never deceive my lord. If I went to another to sire my child, he would know it, and I would not risk his anger or his scorn. If he wanted to offer me to another man, that was his choice: I was his slave. In truth, I didn't understand why he chose not to do so. But it was not for me to offer myself.

"I cannot let another have you," he whispered as if he had read my thoughts. "Not only because I delight so much in you myself, but also because you are mine. You are mine, and if I let another trifle with you, it will be said that I cannot hold what is my own. If a seed grew in your womb which I had not planted, it would be a mockery of my strength, and I will not be mocked. Forgive me, Kelda, that I am so selfish, but a king cannot be mocked. Not if he hopes to stay king."

I promised him that I understood, that I desired no other man, and that if he could find me a sturdy tree to lean up against, I would lift my skirt and prove it. That turned his mood, and he led me up the bank to just such a tree where he would have accepted my invitation, but that we heard an eerie noise on the mist.

His head jerked around and he searched in the direction of the loch. "What is it?" I asked, for I had never heard such a sound in my life.

"Sh," he cautioned, and the noise came again, like the trumpeting of an angry cow, or the roaring of a bull seal, but not at all like either one. Then upon the loch there was a surging of water, the mist rolled to one side as though fleeing from that sound, and a great dark shape appeared skimming just on the surface.

"Look, a whale!" I cried, for that was what it looked like. But there are no whales in Loch Ness.

Just then a head reared up out of the water and emitted that piercing, mournful wail again—and believe me, no whale has a head like that, nor any seal or walrus, either. I stood frozen, clinging to my lord as the creature sank from sight and the water closed over the place where it had been.

"What was it?" I asked when I could find my voice.

"The *tarve uisge,*" Macbeatha breathed. "The water bull. I have heard him before, but never have I seen him, until now." His face was pale beneath its ruddy stubble of beard. "What omen is this, that I should see him now?"

Looking back, I cannot say yet if the omen was good or evil; for what came of the marriage between Bainen and Maelduin was both. Most of all, it was inevitable. Given Duncan and Macbeatha and the conflict between them, it was inevitable.

Chapter Four

We arrived for the wedding with Macbeatha and his men ready to continue on to Strathclyde and redden their blades with Northumbrian blood. But, "Oh, we've plenty of time," Duncan assured them. "Things are not so desperate as Maldred says. We can feast our kinsmen here, give Maelduin a week or two with his new bride, and then take him with us to Strathclyde to settle accounts with Northumbria."

So Duncan feasted, and Macbeatha fretted, until at last they set out for the south. By the time they got there, the Jarl of Northumbria had devastated the land and cantered back into his own country, crowing like a cock on a dung heap.

Macbeatha was furious. "The marriage could have waited!" he roared at Duncan. "We should have been here weeks ago! Now he's back inside his walled city, gloating, and bragging to his king how he slaughtered the Scots in their own land!"

"He won't gloat for long," Duncan promised. "We'll get him."

"When?" Macbeatha demanded.

Duncan hemmed and hawed and finally promised to strike in September. But later he decided he needed a council of war first. It was after harvest before that was done, and then it was too late to assemble an army before winter. "In the spring," Duncan promised. "We'll get him in the spring."

Next Macbeatha badgered him for a plan. Where would they strike? Would they challenge the Northumbrians to a pitched battle? Would they arrive by stealth? What did Duncan think?

Clearly, Duncan did not know what to think. But Macbeatha did. He wanted Durham. After York, it was the most important city in Northumbria. It was a busy and prosperous trading center, and it had an abbey where lay the remains of St. Cuthbert. The many pilgrims who visited were so generous to their saint, the abbey was rich beyond what Scots think is decent for churchmen to be—especially Northumbrian churchmen.

"It's got walls," Duncan protested.

"So had Carham," Macbeatha pointed out, and that about tied the package. Duncan bragged incessantly about his participation in his grandfather's famous battle for Carham, so he could hardly afford to admit he'd had little to do with the victory there. Nor did he want to look a poorer king than old Malcolm. "Durham, then," he agreed. "In the spring."

How regal my lord looked that spring, riding out at the head of two thousand Moray tribesmen! I wish I could have gone along, but he expected a fearsome battle and took no camp followers. And a fearsome battle it was, but not the kind of which he could boast in years to come.

After elaborate preparations, and dragging a baggage train twice as large as necessary across the River Tyne and into Northumbria, Duncan and his army reached the woods north of the Durham. Surrounded by his mormaers, the High King looked out from the trees toward the formidable city surrounded on three sides by water, and he saw the gates wide open.

"It can't be," Macbeatha muttered, sitting upon his horse at Duncan's side.

"They must know we are coming," Crinan agreed, himself out of patience with his son's unwieldy march.

"It is a gift from God," Duncan declared. "We must attack immediately, and take what God has willed us to take!"

"No!" Macbeatha objected. "We send a few men in, to capture the gates," for that was the battle plan he had coerced from Duncan: to approach the city by stealth, sending a handful of picked men inside to capture the gates and prevent them being closed

"I've changed my mind," Duncan insisted. "We strike, now!"

"They'll only close the gates when they see us coming," whined Ce.

"That is why we send our cavalry first," Duncan replied. "They will be swiftly through the gates before the lazy gatekeepers can act. Do we not have the Reliquary of St. Colm with us?"

Macbeatha turned to Crinan, as though he would stop his son from such madness. Crinan, dressed in his abbot's robes in order to carry the Reliquary and ensure the assistance of God and the saint, rubbed his chin and stared down at the city. "Perhaps no word has reached them ..."

"Impossible!" Macbeatha exclaimed.

"An angel has stopped up their ears!" Duncan declared. "It is a sign from God! He has given us the victory!"

Macbeatha tried to stay the king from his course, citing a story about Joshua in the Bible having sent spies into Jericho before he attacked it, but Duncan only heard what he wanted to hear. "Jericho, yes!" he shouted. "The walls of Durham shall be like the walls of Jericho, tumbling down before our onslaught. Take the word to your warbands, all of you! Spread out through the woods here, and at my signal, you will all send your horsemen rushing down upon them. Victory is ours!"

He was always one for brave speeches, was Duncan. Stupid, but brave. The mormaers went back to their warbands, including Macbeatha, and the word was passed down to the chieftains who followed them, and to their individual companies. Everyone waited for the signal.

But before it came, Gillivray dashed up on his horse. Several days earlier, my lord had sent him and a handful of others on ahead, when he'd left his own baggage train north of Tweed. "Ealdred's inside!" Gillivray shouted. "He got here two days ago with his housecarls, and they've mustered every able-bodied man in the city!"

Macbeatha jerked his head toward the mockingly open gates, like a deer that has scented the hounds. "It's a trap, then. They're waiting for us. Dhui! Ride over to Fergus, tell him not to charge. Moray does not charge! Dougal, the same message to Aod and Gabran; Venko, to the rest of the horse. I will tell the High King."

Tell him he did, but Duncan only called him a liar and a coward and sent his cavalry off anyway. Macbeatha raced back to his troops to see his contrary orders enforced and found that Aod and Gabran had held, but Fergus had not. Poor Dhui's horse had stumbled and broken its leg, and though the brave serving boy had unhorsed an armed warrior to take the message onward, the delay had been too much. Fergus mac Mhuire and five hundred Moray horsemen had rushed to their deaths against the walls of Durham.

For as soon as the cavalry charged out from cover, the gates of Durham slammed shut, and the horsemen ran headlong into a hail of Anglish arrows. From the heights, wave after wave of the deadly shafts came down at them, tumbling horse and rider indiscriminately. When Duncan saw the slaughter, he panicked and sent in his foot soldiers, as though they could tilt the balance; but at that point the gates reopened and squads of Northumbrian horsemen rode out to cut down these warriors, as well.

Only then did Macbeatha lead his warband forth, harrying the Northumbrians with the five hundred cavalry left to him; but there were easily fifteen hundred Danish and Anglish horsemen, and it was futile. Macbeatha bought his own warriors a bit of time to retreat, which all the Scots were doing with great haste, and so they brought home to Moray three hundred of their thousand horse, and maybe five hundred foot. Others fared worse: Ce lay dead on the field, and valiant Fife. Crinan lost his nephew who led the charge for Atholl. Fortriu was devastated by the loss of his entire warband, and his grandson who led them. Cirech, who saw Macbeatha hold and so broke off early, was outraged by the stupidity of Duncan's conduct under fire. But none was as angry as Macbeatha.

"I told you it was a trap!" he raged at the High King as their troops sloshed across the River Tyne.

"I told you to send in your horse!" Duncan shouted back.

"Only a fool throws his horse against walls crowned by archers! If I hadn't held back, we would all be dead, and who would cover your retreat?"

"Maybe if you had done what you were told, we wouldn't have to retreat!"

Macbeatha's answer was to slash at the High King with his reins.

Duncan roared in outrage. "You're a dead man, Macbeatha!"

"No. *Those* are dead men," my lord said, pointing back through the trees toward Durham. "Thousands of them—*thousands!*--and I shall live to see you pay for it."

The Northumbrians chased the Scots all the way to the River Tweed, where at last they fell off. There they camped upon the south bank and plundered the surrounding countryside while the remnants of Duncan's army slunk back into Bernicia like wounded curs. From that day forward, Northumbria held the southern portion of Lothian that Malcolm had earlier won, up to the River Tweed.

News of the debacle spread like wildfire. Brenna rode down from the Highlands to meet her brother at the Cairn o' Mount Pass, frantic after the welfare of her second husband. Farrell's leg had been badly broken when his horse fell on him, but he still lived, and Macbeatha was relieved he did not have to tell his sister she was widowed a second time. Still, it was clear Farrell might never go a-horse again, and Brenna cursed Duncan as blue as any good warrior, which shocked my lord's guardsmen but surprises me not at all. She can hate with more venom than anyone else I know.

Macbeatha came home to us bitter with sorrow and out of patience with the High King. Word had come that the Northumbrians took the heads of all the fallen Scots to hang upon their walls as trophies. The heads of his kin, his clients—Fergus mac Mhuire's head, hanging upon the walls of Durham! It was the last straw, Macbeatha said. No more would he acknowledge Duncan as High King, nor have Moray support him. When Duncan's men came to collect his *conveth,* Macbeatha would refuse to pay. Let Duncan try to take it, if he thought he could. If Durham was any example of how well Duncan could fight, they had nothing to fear.

Lady Gruoch soothed him in ways I could not. She spoke to him calmly and sensibly of testing the waters before launching a ship of rebellion. How did the other mormaers feel about the defeat at Durham? They must send messengers to find out. And they must be careful not to place young Maelduin in the middle of this conflict, for it would be well to keep him on their side. His father was a powerful chieftain and could be very useful to them when they ruled Alba.

Odd, isn't it? She who had been furious when Macbeatha wouldn't take an army into Cumbria to revenge Gillecomgain—she now counseled patience and caution. But eight years had passed, and how we can change in eight years! The sharpness of her tongue had abated, and if she had not grown any warmer that I could see, at least the corners of her granite character had softened a bit, rounded by experience and responsibility. One thinks less upon one's own grievances when one has the care of an entire household—or in her case, an entire Great Tribe—to consider.

So it was Gruoch who brought Macbeatha back from the depth of his pain, from the flaming anger over the loss of so many of his own; brought him back to reasoning, to thinking, to laying plans for how he could use the crushing loss at Durham to his own advantage. I could knead the knots from his shoulders and stroke the furrows from his brow, but it was Gruoch who drew the tension from his mind. They spoke together of how the defeat at Durham could drive a wedge between Duncan and his supporters. They observed to one another that what remained now was to step back and wait until Duncan did something else stupid.

They hadn't long to wait. The ashes of the Beltaine fire were scarcely cold when a messenger rode in with news of Duncan's next stupidity.

Chapter Five

In Fionna's hut

"It had to do with the Northman, didn't it?" Fionna asked, eyeing the stone with its twin wolf heads that represented the northern prince.

"Yes," Kelda agreed. "Thorfinn, who was a cousin to Duncan, though he never swore allegiance to him. I don't know if Duncan didn't know Thorfinn was bound to Olaf of Norway, or if he just stubbornly refused to admit it. At any rate —" She sighed and took the cup of brew Fionna handed her.

* * *

As any bully will do, who seeks to avoid the fact that he has been trounced, Duncan looked around for someone else on whom to focus his ire. In this case, Jarl Thorfinn had just made another of his spring raids on Ireland, stopping to plunder a number of Scottish islands on his way home. When Duncan heard of it, he bellowed like a bull in rut. Thorfinn was supposed to be his mormaer, and not only did he refuse to pay *conveth*, he attacked Scottish lands and looted them! He had been doing it for years, of course, but now Duncan raged and roared and declared Thorfinn had forfeited his position as Mormaer of Caithness, which their grandfather Malcolm had granted him so long ago. Duncan would replace him.

Of course, the very idea that Duncan could replace Thorfinn was laughable in itself. But wait till you hear who Duncan named as the new Mormaer of Caithness: his nephew Maelduin. Yes, Maelduin who had just married Vevina's daughter. Duncan told the young man to raise an army and go take his province away from Thorfinn.

Now, Maelduin had a good heart and a level head, but like all Scottish warriors, he lusted for battle, believing it his destiny to live bravely and die gloriously. So when his uncle the High King of Scots told him to raise an army and go to war, that is exactly what Maelduin did. And the most direct route from his home in western Atholl to Thorfinn's stronghold in the north was up the Great Glen, right through Moray.

Macbeatha met him where he crossed the river north of Loch Lochy. Picture Maelduin and his army of five or six hundred men marching down to the river and looking across at Macbeatha and a thousand Moray warriors. A thousand *visible* Moray warriors. At first Maelduin was overjoyed, thinking Macbeatha and his army had come to join the Athollmen in routing the rebellious Thorfinn from his lands. Were not the Scots of Moray and the Norse of Caithness old enemies? He and his guard splashed their horses out into the ford to greet his fellow mormaer.

Imagine his surprise, then, when Macbeatha's response to his friendly invitation to join ranks was that Thorfinn was as much his kinsman as Duncan—and a better warrior, to boot—and that Moray would not join in any war to give an ass like Duncan control of Caithness.

I was not there, but I can well credit how stunned that young man looked. His smile drained away like the water at his feet, they say, and his jaw went slack as he tried to comprehend this turn of events. There he was at a restricted river crossing in the narrow confines of the Great Glen with a thousand Moraymen between him and his objective. "Will you oppose me?" he asked hoarsely.

It was a question to which no one knew the answer until Macbeatha spoke. Perhaps he himself did not know until he got there and looked Maelduin in the eye. But after a long pause my lord chuckled and said, "I do not need to oppose you. You will find Thorfinn opposition enough, and I would not have your blood on my hands." Then he warned Maelduin to harm nothing of Moray in his path, neither man nor beast nor crop nor house. Having made that clear, he signaled to his men and they all dispersed into the woods like spirits vanishing into mist.

They say it was comical how Maelduin picked his way through the countryside, as a house cat might pick its way across a muddy yard. He stopped with his wife's kin in Urquhart, then moved northward in close ranks along well-used paths so he did not trespass any fields. He made his men march on the rations they carried, taking nothing from the land, and their horses were grazed only where a local chieftain gave permission. Maelduin did not fear to face the Viking lord of Caithness, whom he had never met, but he had no desire to cross blades with the lord of Moray. The rumors had started even then, you see. He was not only two-handed, but charmed, was Moray. The *sidhe* protected him, and he conferred with witches upon the moors. Maelduin might not have believed such when he first heard it of his new kinsman, but when he sat upon his horse in the middle of that river ford and looked into Macbeatha's whirling green eyes, Maelduin believed. I know he believed.

Did Macbeatha send warning to his friend Thorfinn? He may have, but no doubt Thorfinn already knew. A warband of that size marching up the Great Glen could hardly go unnoticed. As you can well imagine, Thorfinn was ready for them. He and Thorkel Fosterer had put together an army the size of which caused Maelduin to attempt a hasty retreat.

Thorfinn was not about to let him escape unscathed, however. He followed Maelduin well beyond the Oykel River and halfway to Cromarty Firth, with Maelduin engaging in defensive rear actions while the main part of his army fled. It is said that Moraymen jeered him all the way to his own lands. After all, they had been unable to defeat Thorfinn under Gillecomgain; it would have looked very bad if Maelduin and his Athollmen had walked in and done it.

It was an unhappy report young Maelduin had to give his uncle the High King. The next thing we knew, a messenger came from Duncan demanding to know why Macbeatha had not gone to his kinsman's aid.

"Tell Duncan," my lord instructed the messenger, "he is lucky I allowed an army of Athollmen to pass through my lands. I have no quarrel with our cousin Thorfinn, and the *King* of Moray—" I saw the messenger blanch as Macbeatha emphasized that title. "—was not consulted in this action, and did not think it advisable to participate."

What a flurry of messengers my lord sent abroad after that! They went to Thorfinn, they went to all the mormaers, they traveled the length and breadth of Alba. Duncan had ensconced himself in some seaport in Lothian, licking his wounds after Durham, and his nobles were grumbling that the High King stayed like a hound in his kennel.

Thorfinn did not linger in Moray lands, but seeing Maelduin well on his way south, he withdrew into Sutherland once more. Macbeatha met with him not long afterward. Thorfinn had acquired a scar on his chin somewhere along the way, but not from Maelduin. "Who was that young man?" he inquired contemptuously as I served ale to them both.

"Duncan's nephew," my lord replied. "And Gillecomgain's by marriage, so he considers himself a kinsman of mine. You should have seen his face when I told him you were my cousin and I would not oppose you."

Thorfinn snorted and took a long drink of his ale, which left white foam on his black mustaches. "I can't believe he thought he could walk into my territory and just take it away from me. Truly an action worthy of the nephew of Karl Hundison."

"Of whom?" Macbeatha asked.

Thorfinn laughed roundly. "Karl Hundison," he repeated. "It's what Arnor the *skald* calls Gillecomgain in his tales."

"Because his father was known as Jarl Hundi," I guessed.

Macbeatha put on that mock wounded face of his. "The dog jarl? I'm not sure I like that." But I assured him it was a compliment to Maelbrighde's tenacity and fierceness as a warrior. The skalds always spoke highly of Macbeatha's uncle, and of his father Findlaech. "But Karl?" my lord pressed. "I don't know that word. What does it mean?"

Thorfinn shrugged. "It's a joke. Because it sounds like jarl. Its meaning is ... I don't know. Common, I guess. Unremarkable. Almost ... unsavory."

"Well, it's an apt description of Gillecomgain, I'll grant you that."

We were meeting in that meadow again, where we had come the summer before old Malcolm died. By agreement, each man had brought only nine warriors and two servants to this meeting.

"It wasn't me that killed him, you know," Thorfinn said abruptly. "Gillecomgain."

Macbeatha's face went blank. "It wasn't me, either." That rumor floated around, too.

"Not that I would have minded burning the scoundrel," Thorfinn added gruffly. "I just wanted you to know I didn't go stealing through your lands to do it."

"I'd have fought you if you had," Macbeatha told him simply, and drank deeply from his tankard.

They talked of other things, then. Thorfinn told me my brother Hakon was now part of his warband and had acquitted himself well against Maelduin. Eventually they worked their conversation around to Duncan and the butchery at Durham. Macbeatha's visage darkened as he spoke. "Duncan will fall," he vowed. "And soon."

"He will if he tries to drive me out of Caithness."

Then they raised their eyes to each other and knew they had still not resolved the matter of who should rule Alba. Thorfinn had just lost a large piece of his territory to his nephew Ragnvald, and although he would not admit it, he was angry and vengeful. Taking Duncan's kingdom from him would have been sweet salve on his wounded pride.

But Macbeatha had worked long and carefully toward this end, and he would not let anyone—even Thorfinn—walk in and claim his prize. Alba was his. The Scots would accept him as their leader, whereas they wouldn't accept Thorfinn.

Thorfinn didn't much care if the Scots accepted him or not. He would rule as he ruled in the Western Isles he had wrested from Echmarcach: by brute force. The Scots would pay him respect, and pay him *skatt,* or they would lose everything.

All of this they managed to say without speaking a word of it. It was in their eyes, in the meaning behind their careful conversation. When they parted the next morning, it was without the joy and high spirits that usually punctuated their clandestine meetings. Macbeatha had hoped to persuade his boyhood friend not to pursue a course in conflict with his own; but as they faced each other in the morning mist, no assurance had been gained.

That was the day I knew I was no longer Norse. If these two great rulers—both of whom I had served and loved—ever met in battle, I knew whom I wanted the victor to be. I knew I would betray Thorfinn in an instant, to aid Macbeatha. I knew if my lord were vanquished, I could never go back to my mother and my countrymen. My life was in Alba. I was a Scot.

Only they would never let me be one of them, Fionna. They would never let me be.

Macbeatha had one last thing to say to Thorfinn before we left that morning. "Duncan is in Berwick-upon-Tweed," he told his friend. "On the eastern coast."

"Berwick!" Thorfinn's shaggy black eyebrows shot up, and he sneered. He had developed a very ugly sneer. "What does he do there, make faces at the Northumbrians across the water?"

"I don't think so." Macbeatha wiped the mist from his face, for it was so heavy it felt almost like a light rain. "They say he's buying ships."

Thorfinn's sneer changed to a frown. "How many?"

Macbeatha only shrugged. "I don't know. I'm not even sure if it's true about the ships. But I thought I'd tell you what I heard."

Thorfinn nodded, and then they embraced. "You have been more kinsman to me than Duncan ever was," he acknowledged, and his voice held a note of gratitude.

"Pray we can keep it that way," Macbeatha answered, and we departed.

Duncan was indeed buying ships, as we learned at Midsummer. Eleven warships were reported sailing up the coast, past Aberdeen and then Banff. Macbeatha was in the highlands along the River Spey when word reached him, and he came thundering back to Inverness with a warband five hundred strong. "Eleven ships!" Gruoch exclaimed when she heard.

"They're Danish ships, too," my lord growled. "Sleek, fast— and he's recruited Danish steersmen. They know how to maneuver those longboats like a weaver his shuttle."

"Oh, dear." Gruoch turned a bit pale. Then she told him the news we had received just that morning from his steward in Ross. Maelduin had raised another army; but wary of his wife's kin, he had led only a small company up the Great Glen on pretext of visiting Vevina. While the tribes of that region watched him parading by, the bulk of his army had slipped through the highlands west of the Glen and into Ross. There he met up with them, and even now they were marching deep into Sutherland, their goal unknown.

Macbeatha was unsurprised. "I feared as much," he told Gruoch. "Duncan has sent for Irish levies, and those will most likely be foot warriors, for a land battle." Duncan's grandmother was Irish, you see, and from time to time his family called upon their distant kin for aid in warfare, and vice versa. "But with his usual discretion, he hasn't waited for them to arrive, but must have after Thorfinn with all haste."

"If he defeats Thorfinn," Gruoch asked in a small voice, "will he come for us?"

Now Macbeatha looked at his slender wife, all stony-faced and stiff. She had been out in the fishhouse, supervising the salting and packing of a large catch, and so she was dressed for working. With her dark hair pulled back from her pale face and her brown woolen shawl unadorned by gold or lace, she looked so cold and unappealing to me. But my lord laughed aloud and hugged her affectionately, as though she did not smell of salmon and mackerel. "Pray he does, my love!" he exclaimed. "For I am ready to take him. I will march over Duncan and his eleven warship and his Irish levies, right into Scone!"

their distant kin for aid in warfare, and vice versa. "But with his usual discretion, he hasn't waited for them to arrive, but must have after Thorfinn with all haste."

"If he defeats Thorfinn," Gruoch asked in a small voice, "will he come for us?"

Now Macbeatha looked at his slender wife, all stony-faced and stiff. She had been out in the fishhouse, supervising the salting and packing of a large catch, and so she was dressed for working. With her dark hair pulled back from her pale face and her brown woolen shawl unadorned by gold or lace, she looked so cold and unappealing to me. But my lord laughed aloud and hugged her affectionately, as though she did not smell of salmon and mackerel. "Pray he does, my love!" he exclaimed. "For I am ready to take him. I will march over Duncan and his eleven warship and his Irish levies, right into Scone!"

Chapter Six

There was a great sea battle between Thorfinn and Duncan, and though Thorfinn was badly outnumbered, he managed to win. Macbeatha hardly blinked when he heard of it, for he said Duncan had no grace upon the water, being unaccustomed to it, whereas Thorfinn was like a *selkie,* that creature which is a seal in the water and a human on land.

Afterward, Duncan came sailing back into the Moray Firth with half his fleet, all that was left him. He stuck to the Southerland shore, no doubt looking for his nephew or his Irish levies to reinforce him. Maelduin, it turned out, had been killed in a clash with Thorkel Fosterer. South of the Oykel River, though, Duncan finally found the Irishmen near Tarbatness, which is an old battleground.

Thorfinn, having followed Duncan down the coast, caught up with him there and challenged him. This land battle also went badly for the Scots, and before long Duncan broke and fled in his ships, leaving the Irish mercenaries to find their own way home. He sailed east across the Firth and beached his ships on the Moray side near Burghead, retreating inland toward Elgin. There he threw up a camp on the banks of the River Lossie near the town of Bothgowan and sent an imperious message to Macbeatha, demanding my lord raise reinforcements and come help him go back after Thorfinn.

Macbeatha raised an army, all right. As soon as he got word Duncan had landed, my lord sent out his token across the breadth of Moray calling all the fighting men to his banner. How many thousands were there? I don't know. It was high summer and the weather was fine, and every man who could bear arms came down from the Highlands, or traveled across the moors, to join King Macbeatha's warband.

They poured into Inverness from both sides of the Great Glen, with nearly every tribe represented. They camped around the fortress and in the hills above the town, and on the shores of the River Ness and the loch. As the chieftains came to pledge their loyalty, Macbeatha called each by name, knowing his House and the lands belonging to his tribe. The storehouses were thrown open and gifts of food distributed. Cooks baked bread from before dawn until after dusk, fires in the yard crackled with the fat of roasting animals, and every night there was feasting in the hall. Then after the guests retired, and the household servants fell exhausted into their beds, Macbeatha stood at the window of his fortress and looked down on the sea of men who had come to fight for him, who had come to make him High King of Alba; and his eyes glittered like jewels in his ruddy face.

When the flow of men into Inverness finally dwindled to a trickle, he called out to the crowd in his hall that they would depart on the morrow. Out came the war drums—great *bodhran* that rumbled through Inverness like thunder, echoing back from the surrounding hills. Around a huge bonfire in the yard, men danced in a frenzy as the drums throbbed. In the lingering dusk we saw dozens of fires in the outlying camps and knew men were dancing there as well, filled with the music of the war drums.

What do they stir in our souls, those drums? I do not know, but every one of us felt it. There was not a maid in the town that night who did not fall down before some warrior, and I'm sure it was the same in the outlying camps. I myself waited in Macbeatha's room, though he had gone to his wife's chamber that night. I was afraid if I stayed in the hall, I would surrender to Venko. Let him find one of the chambermaids, or that plump cook's helper he loved to corner in the pantry. This night, of all nights, I must be Macbeatha's wench—even if that meant spending the night alone.

Darkness was long in coming, for Midsummer was just past. Yet there were stars plainly visible in the sky when at last the door opened and my lord entered his chamber. He came to me smelling of Gruoch, a smell I had come to hate; but as he stood at the window with me locked in his arms, staring down at the warriors drifting away from the fire with this maid or that, I knew there was still hunger enough in him for me. Oh, how he loved power, Fionna!

Gazing down at those men, at the power that was his to command, kindled hunger enough to ravish a dozen women. Nor was I disappointed. And when at last the drums ceased, and he slept, it was in my arms—not hers.

The next morning we watched them go, banners flying, drums rumbling across the land once more. My lord wore a cloak of scarlet draped over one shoulder, a tunic with blue and red embroidery, and on his head a bonnet of deep green. His golden torc and armbands glittered in the August sunlight, and his hair—ah, it fairly blazed red! With his shield slung over his back and throwing spears bristling from his saddle, he looked every bit of what he was: the most dangerous and powerful man in Alba.

Lady Gruoch and I watched from the steps of the hall as they pranced out of the yard, Macbeatha's strong hand on the reins keeping his jittery mount under control. Owen rode out in front with my lord's standard, and the remainder of his guard fell in behind. The rest of the cavalcade followed, raising their voices in a lusty battle hymn, and my heart nearly burst with excitement at the splendor of it all.

"Oh, how I wish I could be there to see Duncan fall under his sword!" I exclaimed, for he took only Dhui to attend him.

A strange look came over Gruoch's face, and she turned to regard me with eyes half glazed. At first I thought I had offended her with my spontaneous outburst. But then a gleam came into her eye. "We *shall* go," she announced.

My mouth fell open.

"And why not?" she demanded. "We deserve to be there, you and I. We have nursed his wounds, and flattered his guests, and catered to his humors— *We deserve to be there.*" With a swish of her skirts, she turned and began snapping out orders to the servants. "Maisie! Lay out my riding clothes and pack my comb and mirror. Leish! Have someone saddle my horse, and one for Kelda; then send two or three boys to watch the roads for any latecomers who wish to join my husband—we will need warriors for an escort. As soon as there are six or seven, we will depart."

"Nine, lady," I prompted her. "If a king must have nine in his bodyguard, so must a queen, don't you think?"

"Very well, nine warriors," she amended. "Yes, everything must be done properly, and with all ceremony. This is the Queen of Moray who goes to watch her enemy fall. And, oh, Kelda!" she finished, her lips twisted in a smile almost as wicked as Macbeatha's had been. "How I shall relish the fall of him!" But I couldn't help wondering, Fionna, was her hatred of Duncan on behalf of her husband? or her brother?

Or was it still for the burning of Gillecomgain?

How many people tried to talk her out of it? Everyone with a pennyweight of sense, I'm sure. And Maisie, who had less than a pennyweight but knew ladies of quality did not ride to war. Gruoch would hear none of them. "I am the Queen of Moray and granddaughter of a High King," she said doggedly, "and I shall see my enemy vanquished and my husband victorious." Still the servants dragged their feet in packing our baggage, for they did not know whether to obey the lady who bade them do it, or the lord's steward who bade them stop. I took care of that. A few good pinches and a well-placed kick got them all moving, and I packed the lady's comb and mirror myself.

At noon we rode out of the yard, attended by nine warriors, two horseboys, a porter, old Father Finbar, and only two pack animals. Gruoch wanted all speed, so we carried a minimum of baggage. She spoke hardly at all on that trip. Her face was set in its customary unsmiling manner, but something glowed within her like a torch through an oiled skin. She was dressed in deep blue, which always flattered her fair complexion, and her copious gold jewelry sparkled in the sunlight. She sat her mount with grace and confidence, both legs to one side, her knee hooked around a knob on the saddle. In every aspect of her bearing, she was a queen.

We traveled late that first night, since the day is so long at that time of year, and reached the village of Forres where the startled wife of its chieftain gave us hospitality for the night. We slept little and were off without breakfast, knowing my lord would have reached Elgin in a single day's march. There he had arranged to meet with additional forces from the eastern lands of Moray, and he might even now be issuing his challenge to Duncan.

But luck was with us. Having arrived at Bothgowan quite late the previous day, Macbeatha was in no hurry to seek out his adversary. Although the first of the eastern warbands had arrived, many others would not reach the site until noon, and Macbeatha wanted to wait for every one. So he stayed in his camp in the hills just above Duncan, who had foolishly pitched his tents in an exposed position near the river.

Gruoch searched the landscape anxiously as we approached the two camps, trying to determine the state of affairs. She was relieved to see no battle was in progress, and her husband's standard flew in his camp along with those of twenty or thirty other notable Houses. Her face brightened at the sight. Then she brought our train to a halt and, of all things, broke out her own standard. "My mother sent it to me," she explained, "after her forces fought Malcolm. It is the standard of the royal house of Kenneth mac Dubh, and in my brother's place, I bring it to my husband today. Let Duncan tremble to behold it in Macbeatha's van!"

I don't know if it got Duncan's attention, but it certainly got Macbeatha's. We were not yet within shouting distance of his camp when a group of horsemen thundered out to meet us, Macbeatha at their head. His eyes blazed as he reined in scarcely an arm's length in front of us. "What are you doing here?" he demanded, glaring first at Gruoch and then at me.

"The Queen of Moray comes to see her enemy vanquished," Gruoch declared, meeting his look with an eye as fierce as his own.

"The Queen of Moray would have done well to stay out of harm's way!" he snapped. "I have enough things on my mind without worrying about your safety!"

At that she bridled even more, lifting her chin in the haughty way she had. "No harm will come to me," she replied archly. "Do you see any rowan trees marching up the slopes? We shall not be defeated until they do, was that not what the *Cailleach* foretold?"

Macbeatha's jaw tightened, and I wondered if he would point out that the wise women had not prophesied *how* the rowan would defeat him. Or that his success in battle did not necessarily equate to the queen's safety. But he said neither of these things. Instead he swung around on me. "I expected you to have more sense than this. Why didn't you stop her?"

I gave him my stupid cow look. "I am only a slave girl," I answered innocently. "Who am I to tell the Queen of Moray what she may and may not do?"

Now he turned back to his wife and opened his mouth to speak again, but she was quicker, cutting him off. "Before you say more, husband," she warned, "I do not intend to leave this field. And unless you wish to suffer the disgrace of a disobedient wife before all your men, I suggest you do not order me hence."

What rage burned in his eyes!

And what lust.

I tell you, Fionna, it was as if they were back in that stable at Loch Leven, when he tried to bend her to his will and she would not soften. For all he praised my compliant nature, it was her obstinacy that kindled his strongest passion. They sat there upon their horses, eyes locked in fearsome combat, and the desire between them was so tangible I could have sharpened his shaving knife on it.

Finally he tore his eyes away and gestured back at the ridge where his standard flew. "Set your tent next to mine," he commanded. "And stay in it! You'll see all you need from the doorway. You—" He pointed at the captain of our guard. "Take my lady's standard and set it beside mine, at the same height. And *you!*" He jabbed a finger at me, his eyes like green fire. "You keep her out of trouble, if you have to throw her down and sit on her—and I know you can do it! And don't give me any more nonsense—" Actually, he didn't say nonsense, and the Lady Gruoch flushed at his language. "—about being only a slave girl. You are *my* slave girl, and you will do as I say!" Then he wheeled his horse around and galloped back into camp.

When we reached the ridge, Macbeatha met us with a smile and helped Gruoch down from her horse in the most charming and courteous manner. "Good Lady of Moray, welcome!" he greeted, and taking both her hands, he kissed them. "How can we fail, when a lady of such grace and beauty brings us her standard with the Holy Cross upon it?"

"It is the banner of the royal house of Kenneth mac Dubh," she announced in a clear voice that carried nearly as well as his. "And with it comes the strength and support of all my kin."

Gods above, did you ever know such a pair of liars?

It was now mid-afternoon, and a messenger came from Duncan, wanting to know why Macbeatha delayed in waiting upon the High King. What my lord answered, I don't know, but it must have been clever and deceptive rather than curt, for a meeting was set between them. As Gruoch's tent went up, he departed with only his nine guardsmen in attendance.

Duncan and his guard rode out to meet them, and the two parties converged in a meadow at the foot of the hills. There they dismounted, and we could see the two leaders as they strode toward each other, their men trailing behind. Neither was dressed for battle, though of course they wore their swords. There are different accounts as to what happened, but it went something like this.

"Cousin!" Duncan sang out with a broad grin. It was the only time Duncan had ever called Macbeatha cousin, but now he was all too ready to claim kinship to the commander of five thousand warriors. "Now we shall go back across the Firth and drive that Viking dog into the sea!"

Macbeatha, however, displayed a most cold and cruel countenance, making Duncan hesitate and look with curiosity upon him. For a long moment my lord did not speak, holding the king transfixed with his green eyes. Finally, "I told you never to come into Moray," he rasped.

Duncan stared at his mormaer in shock; then all the color drained from his florid face. "What are you saying?"

"I'm saying these men at my back have not come to fight Vikings."

Fear wrote itself across Duncan's visage. "Surely you do not takes arms against your king!"

"You are not my king," Macbeatha said flatly. "You are no longer worthy of the office."

"What do you mean?" Duncan shouted, enraged. "I *am* the king! I am the High King! My grandfather named me! The nobles of the land confirmed it! The Bishop of Scone sanctified it! You yourself swore allegiance to me upon the Stone of Destiny, and *who are you to say I am not worthy!*"

"I am Macbeatha mac Findlaech!" my lord shouted back. "King of Moray and of the House of Loarn, descended from high kings of both Dalriada and Pictland! And I say that you are a *coward* and a *fool.*"

"I, a coward!" Duncan howled. "It was you who refused to join my nephew against Thorfinn last spring! Because of your cowardice, I had to sail up here myself to make war on the miscreant."

"And what a glorious venture that has been!" Macbeatha mocked. "Eleven ships to five, and who won, Duncan? Tell me, *who won?*"

Duncan didn't know what to say to that, so my lord continued. "A high king cannot order Moray or any other Great Tribe to war. Each tribe decides for itself whether or not to follow. The strike against Thorfinn was a fool's errand, and I am no fool. But you, obviously, are, for only a fool takes a land army and tries to make them fight on ships. Yet what else could I expect of the man who bungled the battle before Durham? I told you then and I tell you now, it was sheer stupidity to throw cavalry against the walls of a city without having secured the gates! Three thousand brave warriors suffered the consequences, and had I not held back my horsemen, your head might even now be decorating a pole in the marketplace of Durham.

"You know how to feast, and talk, and beat upon your chest," my lord concluded, "but you do not know how to do the one thing that makes a king: you do not know how to fight."

With a roar, Duncan stepped back from Macbeatha and drew his sword.

Chapter Seven

This was not what my lord had planned. He had intended to challenge Duncan formally and meet him on the field with a set number of men. Confident of the prophecy that he would be High King, and of Duncan's ineptitude in war, Macbeatha had planned to arrange an even match so no one could say Duncan had been beaten unfairly. But when Duncan drew his blade, Macbeatha was quick to respond in kind. He had to, for Duncan charged at him like a raging bull, and soon the air rang with the song of iron striking iron. Duncan lashed out in rage and Macbeatha countered coolly, deflecting each blow, until Duncan's initial fury had spent itself. Then Macbeatha went on the offensive.

Neither man bore a shield, for they had not come prepared to fight; nor did they wear leather helms or any other kind of armor. It was a duel in the finest tradition of the Scots: two warriors facing each other with naked blades and naked courage. Word flashed throughout both camps, and soon men lined the meadow on all sides, amazed by this unexpected event.

Duncan was as tall as Macbeatha, and once he had been of the same muscular build; but the High King had eaten and drunk too well for the past several years. His belly sagged over his sword belt, and he soon became winded. Behind him, his guard of Atholl tribesmen grew worried, watching Duncan fade while Macbeatha seemed to grow stronger with every lightning slash of his blade. They shifted uneasily, fingered their own weapons, and looked from one to another in despair.

"You've ... no ... *right!*" Duncan panted as he lunged forward with a mighty swing and missed. Immediately Macbeatha's sword lashed back and its broad blade bit deeply into the High King's thigh. With a roar, Duncan went down upon his knees.

For a moment Macbeatha stood over him, his blade stained with the High King's blood. "I have made it my right," he snarled. "Let him who thinks he can stop me, try." Then he raised his sword in his right hand for the killing stroke.

Suddenly a knife flew and buried itself in Macbeatha's biceps. Stunned, he staggered back half a step and looked up to see the captain of Duncan's guard, who had shamefully interfered in the battle between the two kings. But there was no need for my lord to respond; even as his eye went to the Athollman, Owen's dagger sprouted in the man's gullet, bone haft gleaming in the afternoon sunlight.

Macbeatha spared one sweeping, contemptuous glance for the rest of the High King's bodyguard; then he tossed the hilt of his sword deftly to his left hand. With a feral cry, he raised his blade once more and delivered a last, slashing stroke to the wounded High King, a stroke so powerful it severed Duncan's arm and chewed into his ribs.

Howling in rage, Duncan's guard rushed at Macbeatha, and Macbeatha's guard leaped to defend their lord. More warriors from both sides sprang forward, and soon there was a general battle going on. In the camp above, Moraymen discovered they were missing out on the action and rushed to join the melee. It was like watching the sea rush toward the shore: wave after wave of men swept down the slopes, screaming their warcries and crashing upon the field in a foam. They flooded over the Athollmen and into the High King's camp, taking everything they could find as plunder.

Seeing they were overwhelmed, the Athollmen retreated, scattering in all directions. Somehow Duncan clung to life, and his guardsmen bore him away to Elgin where a priest gave him the last rites before he died. The battle done, my lord left the field and returned to his camp. He had no need of plunder. What he desired lay far to the south, in the royal city of Scone, and now it would be his.

As soon as he dismounted before his tent, I rushed to bind his arm while he and Gruoch gazed at each other. "I would have brought you Duncan's head, lady," he told her, "but his guard prevented me."

"Give me his kingdom instead."

A slow smile curved his lips. "It shall be yours, as it is mine. And it shall go to Lulach after me."

Only then did she seem to notice his hurt, and the blood that had dripped all down his arm. "Is it bad?" she asked of me anxiously.

"It is deep," I told her, "but the bleeding was almost stopped before he reached us. I have bound it tightly, which should take care of it. If he will *sit still* now, and keep his arm raised so it does not start bleeding again, it should be all right. Wounds that bleed freely seldom grow poisonous."

She studied the binding on his arm for a moment, then observed, "You know so much about tending wounds, Kelda."

"I've tended enough of them," I sighed.

"Will you show me how?"

Can you imagine? The slave girl, teaching the queen how to bind wounds! It was too tempting to leave alone. "If you've a good length of cloth for bandages," I said impishly, "you can come with me now. Heaven knows there will be plenty to practice on today."

So she took her shawl—her own shawl of fine spun wool—and followed me into the camp.

I'll give you one thing about Gruoch: she never shied from any task before her. Through the blood and the stink, though she looked a bit green from time to time, she never once faltered. She tore up her shawl, and then began to tear strips from the hem of her shift, until I ran back to the tent for my spare one, which was older and not so fine, and made better bandages. She washed wounds and made oatmeal poultices until the last of the summer sun faded from the sky. Then Dhui came to say Macbeatha wanted us—wanted *me*, actually, and oh, what a face Gruoch made at that! But we both hurried back to where his tent stood next to hers.

Macbeatha ducked out from under his tent flap as he heard us approach. "Kelda!" he snapped. "Be prepared to ride at daybreak. I've just received word: Thorfinn has landed at Burghead."

Ah, Thorfinn. Macbeatha had killed Duncan, and gladly, to clear his road to the high kingship, but would he fight Thorfinn as well? I hardly slept for worrying what might transpire the next day—and for thinking of Gruoch and Macbeatha together in his tent. I doubt they passed the night discussing political strategy and the ramifications of a war with Thorfinn. Not from the way he looked at her over the fire.

All too soon the early summer dawn was upon us, and I dragged my weary bones up from my spot on the ground in Gruoch's tent—not even a camp bed for me there! I truly was spoiled. Macbeatha looked pale and tired—the loss of blood, I thought. I rushed to check the dressing on his wound and see if it had bled any more during the night. The dressing was fresh. "At least let me shave you this morning, lord," I begged. "You must look fine when you meet with Thorfinn."

He gave me a crooked smile. "If he lifts his sword against me, it won't matter that I have some stubble on my chin." Then he sighed heavily and the smile slipped away to be replaced by a furrowed brow. "Let us hope he will at least speak to me first. Yes, yes, Kelda, find me something to sit on and you shall shave me before we leave."

From the camp it was only a short space west and north to Burghead. We were there by mid-morning. Eight longboats had anchored off the point, and men camped outside the crumbling fortress walls as well as within. We approached slowly, Macbeatha's banner standing out in the sea breeze, and waited on the landward side of the salt marshes.

"We should have brought more warriors," grumbled Owen, for there was only my lord and his guard and me.

"Thorfinn is my friend," Macbeatha insisted, "and like a kinsman to me. We are not in danger unless we draw our weapons."

Before long a small group of men came out from the Norse encampment, headed by Thorfinn himself. Thorkel Fosterer walked at his elbow as they climbed the triple row of crumbled bulwarks and crossed the salt marshes to meet us. We dismounted as the Norsemen drew near and all stood facing each other.

"Cousin," Macbeatha greeted.

Thorfinn hesitated only a moment, then threw his arms wide and the two men embraced each other.

After that they stood back from one another, an awkward silence between them. "What news of Duncan?" Thorfinn asked finally.

"Duncan is dead."

"By your hand, I assume?" Thorfinn's face was a mask, betraying no emotion.

"In single combat," Macbeatha affirmed, likewise keeping his face blank.

Thorfinn nodded, not the least bit surprised. "I had hoped to have that honor myself, but if it couldn't be me, I'm glad it was you."

Finally some warmth showed in Macbeatha's countenance. "It's good to hear you say that."

"I had him in my grasp twice," Thorfinn grumbled, relaxing into a grimace himself, "but he slipped away both times, running like a cowardly dog with his tail between his legs."

"Perhaps," Macbeatha suggested, "the Fates are trying to tell you something." Thorfinn scowled at the idea, but my lord continued. "Think of it, cousin: twice within your reach, but it was not to be. It was to my sword he fell."

Thorfinn said nothing, but his eyes glittered dangerously. Sorrow settled upon Macbeatha's features, as it does upon those of a parent who must refused the request of a beloved child. "You may as well know, I met a *petta*-woman upon the moors some years ago, and she prophesied that I would become High King."

Now Thorkel spoke up. "Prophets have been wrong before," he growled. His weathered face was sun-reddened, and his flowing mustaches stood out more white than blond.

Macbeatha turned sad eyes upon Thorkel for a moment, knowing the weight this man's opinion carried with Thorfinn; then he returned his gaze to his childhood friend. "I will march for Scone tomorrow," he said simply. "We have been good neighbors for eight years, and friends much longer. I don't want that to change."

Thorfinn ran a hand through his unruly black hair and made a noise of frustration. "Only what am I to tell my men?" he demanded irritably. "It's gone all through camp that I am to be the next King of Scots. I think Arnor started it, but it doesn't matter. They all say it now. How can I back down without losing my honor?"

"March with me," Macbeatha suggested impulsively. "We'll show our solidarity. Then you go back to Caithness and the Orkneys, and it will be between us as it has been."

Still Thorfinn shook his head, knowing his men would not be satisfied.

Some memory tickled at me, something about an old Norse custom … "You should walk under the sod together," I blurted, and both men turned to me in surprise. "No, think of it," I rushed on, "if you walk under the sod together, then you are as foster brothers. What one has belongs to the other, and vice versa. Therefore, all the lands belonging to Macbeatha belong to Thorfinn as well, and what is Thorfinn's is also Macbeatha's."

Hope gleamed in my lord's eyes and he turned to his friend with a questioning look. Thorfinn rubbed at the scar on his face as he considered. "It might be enough," he admitted. "Certainly, once we walked under the sod together, it would be unthinkable to take up arms against one another."

"Then let's do it!" my lord exclaimed. "We'll be brothers under the sod, and our kinship will be beyond question."

Thorfinn looked back at Thorkel Fosterer, and the older man nodded his grudging concurrence, though I could see it went hard on him. He always wanted Thorfinn's greatness as much as Thorfinn did. "It is the wisest choice, I think. You have Ragnvald to deal with, Thorfinn, and soon, I'm afraid. No point in having enemies on two sides."

So Thorfinn gave his ascent, and we had the ceremony that very afternoon. A large arch was cut from the sod, and the two princes walked beneath it, side by side. Such a great shout went up, you could hardly hear the oath they swore to one another. Then they embraced; but suffused with the joy in their faces were very different emotions. For Macbeatha, there was victory and relief: the high kingship was as good as his, and without the cost of fighting his childhood friend for it. For Thorfinn, there was resignation and regret. He had wanted the high kingship of the Scots for himself, but now it was not to be. It was not ever to be. He must look to the Orkneys, to the Western Isles and to Ireland for his kingdom.

That night we feasted on roasted beef (which my lord pretended not to know was stolen Scottish cattle). With a bubbling heart, I waited upon both Thorfinn and Macbeatha, smiling wide enough to split my face. I was glowing like a candle at Christmas when I turned from refilling my pitcher at a barrel and nearly ran into a tall, sturdy young warrior. I knew his face in an instant, and terror gripped me. It was my old nemesis, the man who had forced me from Thorfinn's hall, and I stepped back with a gasp. "Ivarr!"

But the blond warrior looked startled and said quickly, "No, no, I'm not Ivarr, I'm Hakon!"

It was my own brother Hakon! Relief surged through me, and joy. Ivarr, I realized, would be much older now, whereas Hakon was just of the age Ivarr had been when I left Thorfinn's hall. Looking closer, I could see it was not Ivarr's face, although they bore a striking resemblance when they reached manhood, having both the same father.

I dragged Hakon before Macbeatha, wild with excitement, and my lord bade me leave off serving for a time so I could get all the news of my family. Mother was quite well, Hakon said, especially now that she had two grown sons to work her land. Of course, Solmund—who had been born after I left—wasn't exactly grown, nor was he a warrior like Hakon. But he was a strong, cheerful lad who took good care of Mother when Hakon was away.

"She must be proud of you," I said, with no little pride myself. "And Thorkel, too. Did you fight beside him in this campaign?"

"No, he wasn't there either time." Disappointment showed on my brother's face as he explained that Thorkel had arrived too late for the sea battle. Then, while Hakon went with Thorfinn to Tarbatness, Thorkel went to Thurso where he found Maelduin's forces in possession of the town.

"But you're sure Mother is all right?" I asked anxiously, for her plot of land lay between the town and Thorfinn's *huseby*.

Hakon waved a dismissive hand. "They were warned and everyone got away before the Scots arrived. And when Thorkel got there, he gathered all the *bønders* and freemen and thralls in the area, any man who could hold a stick or a torch, and they marched on the town." Soon, he said, the Scots were all pushed back into a couple of houses on the waterfront. "And do you know what Thorkel did?" My brother grinned in delight. "He set fire to the houses. Men came pouring out, and they died on the blades of Thorkel's warband. And Maelduin—" His grin became a chortle. "Maelduin tried to get away by jumping out a second-story window, and guess what Thorkel did!" Hakon made a whistling sound as he swung an imaginary blade. "Cut his head off, just like that, as Maelduin sailed through the air. I hear it landed in a dungheap!"

Poor Maelduin! What a brave, foolish young man. But I had no time to ponder his fate, for Venko came and said Macbeatha wanted me. As I arrived bright-eyed and breathless at my lord's feet, he smiled indulgently and pulled me into his lap. "Oh, you're going to make me regret this before I've even done it, aren't you?" he sighed. "You're not to come back to Elgin with me tomorrow. I need you to go to Inverness and pack up my things instead, everything I'll need to make my entry into Scone in style and splendor. Venko will go with you. Then come by boat to Aberdeen—I'll meet you there and we'll go on by horse."

I pouted just a little, never liking to be separated from him, but the ship sounded better than an overland journey. And what a grand entrance we would make into Scone! There, the leaders of all the Great Tribes would come and swear their support of my master, Macbeatha mac Findlaech, for I never doubted his election. Who could oppose him? Besides, the three sisters had foretold it for him.

They had foretold other things as well, Fionna, and it's not that I didn't think about them—they just seemed so far away. I saw nothing ahead but long, happy years for my lord and myself. The Fates had a nasty surprise in store for me, though, before another summer came to the land. And I didn't even see it coming.

Chapter Eight

Thorfinn traveled with Macbeatha only as far as Aberdeen. He had sworn to march all the way to Fife and beyond, for he was curious to see Edinburgh, but he couldn't keep his men under control. There were only a hundred with him, the others having returned home in their longboats, but they couldn't resist harassing the local Scots, which put Macbeatha all out of sorts. So at Aberdeen Thorfinn splashed into the tide, declared in Norn that this was Fife and that he had traversed Alba from end to end, and none of his men was the wiser. His honor redeemed, he promptly secured two ships and sailed home.

So he was not there to distract from Macbeatha's entrance into Scone. How grand my lord looked, and how fierce, mounted on a dapple-gray stallion with his shield upon his back, sword hilt gleaming, and his warband stretching out behind him like a river of menace. It had rained off and on that morning, but as we entered the town, the clouds broke and the sunlight streamed down on his hair, touching it with flame. He had seen thirty-five winters, eight of those as leader of his Great Tribe, and now he came to make his claim upon the highest office in the land.

The Bishop of Scone met him as he entered the town. "Why have you come here with this army, Macbeatha of Moray?" he asked formally, to which my lord replied, "I have come to make my claim to the office of High King; and I make that claim in my own name, and in the name of my wife."

Gruoch was not there: she would not set foot in the place until she came as its queen, she said. It was in Atholl, after all, and her kin had not been treated kindly there. She and Lulach waited at St. Andrews for Macbeatha to send word of his election.

The council of nobles had to wait for Crinan, who had taken his son Duncan's body to the Isle of Iona for burial. When he returned, he objected strenuously to Macbeatha's claim. His other son, Maldred, was Duncan's tanist, a grandson of Malcolm mac Kenneth like his brother. How could they let an upstart like mac Findlaech be High King over Maldred? There were no high kings in his family for at least ten generations!

But there was Gruoch's claim, and the old rumor that Macbeatha's mother was really Malcolm's daughter. Above all, there was the immutable fact that Macbeatha had defeated Duncan in single combat, and that he commanded thousands of warriors. He was without doubt the most powerful warlord in the land.

Common sense won out, and Macbeatha's claim carried the day. While he waited for Gruoch to arrive, my lord rode into the yard of the royal residence where Aelflaed, Duncan's widow, still stayed with her three sons, guarded by a hundred Atholl tribesmen. Not wanting to frighten her, my lord brought only his ten guardsmen, and me. He wished to speak to the lady in her own language, and if he did not know a particular word, he hoped I could help.

We were surprised to find a horsecart packed, and two ponies, and a mounted guard ready to escort them. Aelflaed had already heard of Macbeatha's election, and she was on her way out with all haste.

As we stood wondering in the yard, Maldred came out with Aelflaed on his arm, a nurse carrying the baby Morggan, and young Malcolm and Donall trailing behind. The widow hauled up short when she saw my lord and turned a look of pure hatred on him.

"Lady Aelflaed," he began, but she cut him off.

"Do not speak to me, you butcher," she said in perfectly good Scots.

His eyes widened, but then he composed his features and tried again. "Do not go in such haste, lady," he pleaded. "I would not have it said that I chased you from the town."

"As though I would stay in the same place where you dwell!" she snapped. "If I were a man, I would kill you on the spot!"

Macbeatha managed a roguish smile, the kind that normally charms women right into his bed. "Then I have double reason to thank God such a lovely creature as yourself was born female."

Do you know what she did? *She drew her dagger on him!* Thus his reward for trying to charm that Northumbrian shrew. The smile dropped from his face as she waved the knife menacingly.

Maldred caught her arm. "Put that away, lady," he said uncomfortably. "The man is king."

"My son is king!" Aelflaed shouted, for it is the custom of the Danes and Angles, as it is of the Norse, that a son inherits his father's position.

Not so among the Scots, of course. But Macbeatha tried to mollify her. "Some day he may be king," my lord agreed. "His father was High King, and his great-grandfather. When he comes of age, if he proves himself a strong leader of men, then he may well come to lead Alba, as I lead it now."

"Murderer!" she snarled. "You have slain your king and stolen his crown!"

How silly. The Scots don't have a crown. Macbeatha tried to reason with her once more. "Lady, I have fought your husband in single combat, and won. That is not murder. And now I have made my claim to the office of High King, and it has been confirmed by the nobles. I have stolen nothing."

"Only my son's birthright!"

"There is no right of birth, only of power!" he retorted, then quickly relented. "Lady, I bear you and your sons no ill will. They are princes and should be raised as such. Do not send them into hiding, as my wife and her brother were forced to hide. Let Colmbeag become my fosterling—he is the same age as my own son. I will have them raised together, here in the royal court. They shall be as brothers."

But Aelflaed was not swayed from her determination. "You shall not see or know of my son until he puts a sword to your neck!" she vowed.

After that my lord did not try to persuade her, but stood aside and let her pass with her three boys. I thought it curious that she spoke of Malcolm as though he were her only son, and we heard later that when she and Malcolm went to the Anglish king, young Donall was left behind with his uncle in Cumbria. The babe, I think, wound up with his Northumbrian kin. But that day in Scone, I didn't understand how a woman could care for one child more than another. Of course, at that time, I myself would have given every possession I had, and years of my own life, just to have *any* child of my own.

I suppose that's why I asked Macbeatha for the lamb. Oh, I made some excuse to him and to myself about my mother having been given a sheep of her own by Thorkel. But it was just that I saw this little lamb, and its mother was dead, and I felt so sorry for it. It was half-grown already, but it had been wounded by the same wolves that killed its dam, so it needed nursing. Macbeatha laughed at me for being so tender-hearted and said it was mine if I wanted it.

So I fixed up a sling for the little creature—Galvan, I called it—for it could not walk on its injured leg; and I carried it with me everywhere. I even slept in the stable with it, since my lord kept himself to Gruoch's chamber at night. There were plenty of servants to wait on him, so he didn't mind that I shirked some of my duties to carry Galvan about.

I was happy, too—foolishly, clownishly happy. Aelflaed's servants had gone off with her, and Duncan's had gone to Duncan's kin, but many others were bound to the office of the High King. Since Lady Gruoch left me in charge of all the servers in the hall, they had to follow my directions. Some had been rude to me in the past, when they thought I was a stupid Northerner who didn't speak their language, so their grudging submission to my authority made me grin.

Why they thought so ill of me carrying my lamb around, I don't know. Looking back, I suppose they had to find fault with something, and this business of a serving girl carting a lamb around in a sling was odd enough to draw their contempt. But the more they grumbled about it, the more I smiled, for there wasn't a thing any of them could do. Macbeatha had given me the lamb, and until he told me otherwise, I could care for it as I pleased. I put a green ribbon around its neck and declared, "Now you are *my* slave," though I must say, his green ribbon was much prettier than my worn leather slave collar.

On the day of my lord's investiture, I boldly took Galvan with me to watch the great ceremony. "Now all the other sheep will envy you," I told him, "because you saw the High King made upon the *Lia Fail.*" I don't think little Galvan was much impressed, but I was. This inauguration was worlds different from the ceremony

I had attended for Duncan. This was *my* lord being installed, and I didn't hesitate to let everyone know it, even a lamb.

It started in the church, of course, with Mass and Holy Communion, and the Bishop of St. Andrews poured oil upon Macbeatha's head, as the prophets of old did to kings chosen by God. Then we processed to the Hill of Law with four stout warriors carrying the *Lia Fail,* the Stone of Destiny, on two poles, each slid through an iron ring on either end. My lord looked so solemn and so spiritual, dressed in white with his torc and armbands gleaming, and two or three rings on each hand. When the warriors set the *Lia Fail* down upon the Hill, Macbeatha knelt before it and, placing his hands on its surface, swore by his honor to serve the commonweal of Alba, and to defend her people.

There were more prayers and exhortations, after which the churchmen retired and more ancient customs were observed: The new High King was sprinkled with the blood of a young bull, and he ate of its liver to ensure the fertility of the land under his care. The heads of the Great Tribes handed him the white rod, the symbol of his office, and one by one they hailed him as their *ard righ,* High King. When they had done, the crowd broke into a shout of acclamation, and warriors banged their spears upon their shield bosses.

There was more, but when it was done, Gruoch came forward with Lulach, and Macbeatha rose to greet them. Lulach was nine then, a dark-haired rascal with more mischief on his mind than there are fish in the sea, but he stood straight and somber in his best clothes, wearing the boots he so hated and looking just as princely as any grown man. Macbeatha hailed Gruoch as Queen of Alba, daughter of Boite, daughter of Kenneth mac Dubh; and the people cheered again, though I don't know why. When you think of it, I suppose it did unite both South and North of Alba as never before. More likely the story of how Gruoch had dressed the wounds of the warriors after the battle with Duncan—which, you will recall, I had suggested—traveled like a ship under full sail, and that was why they cheered her.

At the end of the ceremony, everyone was invited to a great feast, and off they went to gorge and drink themselves senseless. Knowing my lord would not have need of me for some time, I stayed behind. I should have gone to help serve, but it was much more fun to play with Galvan in the sunshine. We sat there in the sweet grass watching as the crowd drifted away until only two people remained: Crinan of Atholl and his son Maldred, king of Strathclyde and Cumbria.

They did not see me, for they were staring in the direction the crowds had gone, and Crinan's face was as black and bitter as a winter storm. "It's done, Da," I heard Maldred say. "He won't be such a bad king, I think."

"Do you understand *nothing?*" Crinan demanded of his son. "He is *Moray*. He is the House of Loarn He swore loyalty to your brother upon this very hill, then took up arms against him! Is that the kind of man you can trust?"

At first Maldred was silent. He had some courage, but it always took him a moment or two to find it. Finally he shrugged. "And now you have hailed him High King upon the same hill. Will you show more faith than he?"

Crinan's hand flinched toward his sword—he was in warrior's dress this day, not his abbot's robes—and for a heartbeat I thought I would witness murder upon the Hill of Law. But then he let his arm drop, and the rage quieted in his mien. "I am a man of God," he said proudly. "I will lead no rebellion."

But the countenance he turned after my lord was dark with hate. "The king needs to be taught, though, that he cannot flaunt the laws of men nor the laws of God. And I shall see him humbled by both before I am through. I shall see him humbled."

Chapter Nine

At Edinburgh

Malcolm mac Duncan paced an upstairs corridor in his cousin's house in Edinburgh. The young man looked more like a Dane than a Scot: tall and broad shouldered, with fair hair and blue eyes. His hair grew wild and curly about his head, earning him the nickname Canmore, or "Big Head," among the Scots. But aside from his unbraided hair, he looked no more foreign than any number of Scottish princes whose mothers or grandmothers had been Norse. It was in his thinking that Malcolm Canmore was a foreigner, and that was more difficult for the Scots to accept.

But by Christ, he would make them.

Turning abruptly into an empty chamber, Malcolm strode to the open window and looked down upon the Leith road, eyeing the traffic that came and went. He liked the hustle and bustle of Edinburgh, its cathedral and its mighty fortress, but he knew he should not be here. He should be in the royal residence at Scone, and God damn the soul of the man who had denied him!

Malcolm had been nine years old when he had last departed Scone. Sometimes it was hard to remember what his life had been like before then. He remembered the house in detail, every rough stone and frayed tapestry of it. He remembered the yard with its many stables and storehouses, and of course, the watchtower. He remembered the priest who had drilled him in Latin, and he vaguely remembered a bard who taught him songs—but he could *not remember how it all felt. He could not remember the emotions which ran through him, or what games he had played with his brother Donall, or what he was doing the night his brother Morggan was born. It was as though some other boy had lived all that and only told Malcolm about it.*

It seemed his own life began the day their steward called him aside from the other boys in the yard and said, "Go to your mother. She has something to tell you." From the steward's tone, Malcolm knew it was nothing good.

Mother sat in the sun house with her ladies gathered around her, and several of them were weeping. Mother was not. Mother's face was as dark and angry as a winter storm, her mouth set in a grim line. Donall stood at her knee, but as soon as Malcolm appeared in the doorway, Mother turned to him and muttered, "Oh, my son! What they have stolen from you!"

Curious, and a bit fearful, Malcolm edged closer. "What's wrong, Mother?"

She rose and took him by the shoulders. "Your father is dead," she said simply. "The traitor Macbeatha has slain him by deceit and treachery, and now he comes to Scone to kill us as well."

Malcolm still remembered the cold sensation that had swept through him, knowing he would die. He pictured his mother run through with a sword, and Donall with his throat cut like a pig, and the baby-- What would they do to the baby? Cut him in half? Throw him in the river?

But days passed, and the traitor did not come. Instead, Malcolm's father was brought home. He remembered looking at the dead king wrapped in a shroud, lying on a table in the hall, and wanting to pull the cloth aside to see who it really was under there, for he suspected it was not his father. Duncan had been a huge man, an enormous man, and this-- This man was just a man, no bigger than any other. Where was his father? And what had his father looked like? He could not remember the slightest detail, either the color of his hair or the size of his nose.

Ladies had gathered around that shrouded corpse and wept and wailed, and monks had come to chant over it night and day. Mother had wailed, too, although she didn't weep. Malcolm couldn't recall his mother ever weeping. Finally men came to take the king's body away for burial, and Malcolm was sure his mother was relieved to see it go. "Now, my son," she said as the bier rolled out of the yard in a horsecart. "Now we will see whether your father's kinsmen are brave men or cowards. Now we will see if they rise up and smite this usurper, or if they lie timidly like hares in their warrens while the traitor marches in here to seize this place and murder us all."

But the demon jarl—that's what Mother took to calling him later—had not assaulted Scone. Malcolm didn't know why, exactly, but he remembered his uncle Maldred scoffing at the notion, while Mother paced in the hall and declared the traitor would cut off all their heads and mount them on pikes. Donall, who was only seven, started to cry, and Maldred back-handed him, telling him to be a man, now, and that no such thing was going to happen to him. "Macbeatha loves children," he insisted.

"Yes, roasted to a turn!" Mother snarled. "He wants my son's crown, do you think he will hesitate to chop off the head where that crown belongs?"

The men of Atholl had not risen to defend them, though, and Macbeatha approached the city unopposed. When Mother finally saw that no one was going to take up arms against the conqueror, she started packing. Mother was a terror when she was packing; Malcolm and Donall both ran and hid in the stable, trying to stay out of her way. She snapped at the servants and railed at the grooms for daydreaming while the wolf licked his chops and circled their house.

They were on their way out of the hall when The Monster rode into the yard.

To this day, Malcolm could remember how he looked, his bare arms swollen with muscle and gleaming with sweat and gold armbands. His hair was a dark gold, glinting red in the sunlight, and his face was shaven, except for his flowing red mustaches. There was something about those mustaches ... Malcolm was sure he had seen those mustaches before ... How kingly the man looked, though, seated upon his dapple gray horse! Malcolm remembered thinking, I wonder if Satan himself looks so fine?

It was a strange thing, to remember that face, when he could not remember his own father ...

Malcolm shook himself now and turned from the window. It no longer mattered which face he remembered—both men were dead. It seemed strange to think they would soon lie side by side upon the Hill of the Dead there at Iona, the Traitor and the Betrayed. It wasn't right. When he was High King—but no, the Isle of Iona was *sacred, and he couldn't go digging up holy ground. Some things were better left alone.*

But by God, suffering the Usurper's step-son to sit upon his throne was not one of them! Surely the Scottish nobles gathering in Scone could see that! They would not, could not, ratify Lulach's claim to the High Kingship!

Could they?

Chapter Ten

In Fionna's hut

*K*elda watched Fionna casting her stones. *"Is he here?"* she asked quietly.

"The man who follows you? No, but he is close by," Fionna replied, seeing how the stones fell in the dirt. *"He will not find us unless I want him to. And I am not ready for him. Not just yet."* She picked up the stone of the Twin Wolves. *"You were speaking of Crinan, of his threat against the king."*

Kelda nodded and pushed a lock of graying hair back from her face.

* * *

I worried a little about Crinan's threat, but not for long. I was sure Macbeatha was more than equal to any machinations of the Mormaer of Atholl. Besides, there was far too much going on to be concerned about Crinan's disaffection.

People came from everywhere to visit the new High King. There was a constant parade of guests in and out of the hall, and a variety of entertainers to amuse the guests. Among the musicians was a monk who played pipes of a kind I had never seen before. They were attached to a pig's bladder, which was filled with air by blowing down a tube into it. When the monk squeezed the bladder under his arm, air rushed out through the pipes, making the most awful noise. Macbeatha said this instrument was much fancied among the Irish, and he rather liked its mournful quality. It reminded him of the wind rushing through the trees and crags of the Highlands, or the creak of timbers on a boat under sail. To me, it sounded like the screeching of birds when a predator approaches their nests.

Then there were the relatives who showed up. Brenna was the first, sweeping into town in all her finery in time to see her brother inaugurated, then announcing her intention to stay through the winter. My lord had promised her a winter at Scone, you remember, all those years before, and she was going to have it now, in style. But she was not the worst of the relatives who showed up to share in my lord's victory. Oh, no. When the inauguration was over and those who had to help with the harvest hurried home, another of his kin made her appearance: Boite.

Gruoch was, at first, delighted to see her mother, and distressed that they had just sent Lulach back to Moray with his fosterer. Macbeatha, too, greeted his mother-in-law with great courtesy, offering her his hospitality and protection. But the old hostility was still in Boite's eyes. Since her failed uprising six years before, she had been in hiding; now, with Duncan dead and her daughter the reigning queen, she could return to the places and the people she had known when her father was High King, and to whom did she owe it? That cursed Morayman whose father had taken arms against her father. Malcolm's upstart fosterling, whom she had once denied Gruoch's hand. It went hard with her.

Macbeatha seemed not to mind. She sniped at him then as Gruoch had done when they first met, and he handled it the same way: he smiled smugly at her and offered all manner of praise and flattery, taking special delight in giving her gifts of things she could no longer afford to buy for herself. Her wretched estate pleased him to no end.

Before too many days, though, it became clear there was going to be a problem between Boite and her daughter. Gruoch had seen almost nothing of her mother since being placed in fosterage at the age of seven. Now suddenly, here was Boite—with, I might add, the same penchant to command and direct as her daughter—invading the one province Gruoch had dreamed of holding since the death of her brother: the household of the High King.

Many of the servants found themselves in a quandary, knowing they ought to take orders from Gruoch but finding Boite's edicts difficult to evade. The mother was far more critical than her daughter, who actually had a great deal of patience and compassion for her servants. That might even have been what caused Boite to pick at them so relentlessly, thinking they were taking advantage of her daughter's good nature.

She tried picking at me, of course, but I have always been ornery of temperament. The first day she was there, she scolded me for bringing my lamb into a king's house, then stopped and studied my face. "You were with him, weren't you?" she remembered. "When he came to see me at Abernethy."

"With who, lady?" I asked innocently.

"With my daughter's husband!" she snapped, for she never called him by name. It was always "him," or "the king," or even yet, "Moray."

"I was his excuse for making the journey," I said. "So Malcolm would not suspect."

Now her eyes narrowed shrewdly as she looked me up and down. "Are you his mistress, then?" she asked bluntly.

I decided my stupid cow look would not serve with this one—she was far too clever. "I am his servant, lady," I said, indicating the slave collar at my neck.

"And where do you serve him? In his bed?"

"I serve him wherever he desires."

"He takes advantage of his station, then," she pronounced, and turned to go.

I could not let that slide. "He takes nothing I do not freely give," I called after her.

Boite turned and glared at me. "I do not know why my daughter tolerates your presence here. I would have sold you to an Irishman, and long ago."

"That is not her choice to make. I am not her slave."

Boite harumphed and put her noble nose in the air.

"And I don't only serve my lord in his bed," I informed her. "Sometimes I serve him in the straw of the stable ... or upon a bench in the hall ... Once I served him upon the table in his map room ..."

Boite gathered what dignity she could and left the room.

But it was in the matter of Lulach that Gruoch and her mother quarreled most often. Until her son's death, Boite had paid her grandson no attention, never coming to visit or even sending gifts.

Now Lulach represented her family's hope of regaining the High Kingship, and she wanted the boy raised in close proximity to the nobles of the land who would one day elect him. "You must bring Lulach back from fosterage," she told her daughter.

"He is safer with Indulf," Gruoch replied, although she herself had asked Macbeatha if they couldn't bring him back. "Duncan still has many supporters here in the south."

"Is your husband so weak a king, he cannot protect his stepson in his own hall?"

"He's not weak, he's wise," Gruoch corrected. "He knows better than to expose Lulach to danger unnecessarily."

"How can the boy learn anything in the wild Highlands of Moray?"

"He will learn strength and perseverance; and he will return to us when he reaches the Age of Choice. Then he will ride in Macbeatha's warband with the finest warriors in the land. He shall learn what it means to be king."

I could see it was a good thing Boite hadn't come to Macbeatha for sanctuary after her House was defeated by Malcolm. If mother and daughter argued like this now, what would they have done while Lulach was still at home? Boite seemed determined to shape her grandson's life, even in his absence.

"You will write to Lulach's foster mother," she directed one day. The sun was bright, and several of us sat sewing in the women's house by the south wall. Galvan wandered in and out of the open door, his green ribbon setting him apart him from the king's sheep. "There are certain foods Lulach should eat to make him healthy and strong, which no doubt such a backwards woman will not know about. Pig's liver, for instance, and fried blood. And be sure to instruct her to tie a rowan sprig to his bed, one with berries upon it, to keep the fairies away."

"The rowan is not good luck for Macbeatha," Gruoch said. "He would be singularly unhappy if I requested it for Lulach."

"Well, he's not the child's father! When he has children of his own, he can make decisions about them."

At that, Gruoch put down her sewing and left the room without a word. In all the years I knew her, she would never respond to any remark about Macbeatha's childlessness.

Irritated by her daughter's intransigence, Boite turned on me. "Why do you insist on tying a ribbon around that creature's neck?"

she demanded, for Galvan was trying to reach the ends of his ribbon to nibble on them.

I favored her with my stupid cow look. "Macbeatha said I may do with him as I please. He belongs to me."

This reference to my lord's indulgence only irritated her the more—and she *hated* my stupid cow look—but there was little she could do except grumble, which she did. "Dressing an animal like a child. Against nature. Just what you'd expect from a pagan."

Knowing how serious it could be if people thought I was not a Christian, I rose to the defense. "The Lady Gruoch told me she once had a pet lamb. Its mother had died and the Reverend Abbot gave it to her to care for. She fitted a leather teat over a jug of milk and nursed it that way, and raised it up till it was strong enough to eat grass. And she kept a ribbon around its neck, too. A red one." That was true. Of all the people in the household, only the Lady Gruoch really understood what Galvan meant to me—but then, one couldn't ask for better protection than that.

Of course, the story would have had a better effect if Galvan hadn't chosen that moment to drop his business in the middle of the floor.

Soon the harvest started, and even I went out to the fields to help gather it in. Galvan no longer rode in a sling, but he followed me around, still limping from his wounds, as I picked apples or tied up sheaves of barley. One afternoon one of the harvesters—a short, stocky brute of a man with only three teeth showing—scolded me for letting Galvan nibble some grain in a field that had not yet been reaped, so I pouted and took my lamb off away from the people toiling in the fields. Feeling they could do very well without me, I wandered over the hills to a pleasant little spot by a creek where I sat down in the sun to watch Galvan crop the sweet grass.

I was singing a little tune, something I had learned as a child, when a band of horsemen came through the trees: my lord and his guard, come to check on the harvest and do a little hunting. They had heard my voice and followed it to the creek. Stopping at the edge of the glade, Macbeatha leaned on his horse's neck and smiled down at me. "Now, there's a lass looks like her skirt needs lifting," he remarked, eyes radiating a familiar hunger.

My response was to twitch the hem of my shift slowly up over my knees.

"If you are busy, lord, I can see to it," Venko offered.

But my lord grinned and said, "No, no, busy as I am, there are one or two things I really must do for myself." Then he bade them go on without him and slid off his horse to join me in the grass.

He had had but little time for me since we arrived in Scone, and little time for himself, as well. The press of people around a new ruler is always great; and the more important the ruler, the greater the press. Entertainers wanted licenses; clients wanted to lease additional cattle; churchmen wanted surcease of the *conveth* required of them; and warlords wanted to know when he would strike into Northumbria. So I was glad for his sake, as well as mine, that he chose to enjoy an afternoon away from all that. We took our time and drew out our pleasure in an indulgent fashion.

At first little Galvan was unhappy about my lord's attention to me, nudging my shoulder or butting his little head into Macbeatha's back. It was quite comical, and we laughed and laughed over it. Finally the little sheep grew bored with our antics and wandered off to investigate the flowers beneath the larch trees, and we were able to continue uninterrupted.

It was some time after the culmination of our pleasure that I noticed Galvan was gone. I called out to him, but he did not come. Then Macbeatha and I both hunted amongst the trees, but there was no trace of him. Just over the hill a flock of sheep grazed and I ran to it, hoping my lamb had joined his kindred, but I could not spot his green ribbon anywhere and he did not answer to my voice.

As my distress grew, Macbeatha's patience decreased. Oh, he did not scoff at me or deride my unhappiness, but I could see in his eyes that he did not understand why I made such a fuss over a sheep. "He's probably gone home to his stable, Kelda," my lord suggested. "Come on, you can ride behind me on my horse, and we'll get there quickly." I thanked him, but told him to go on alone—I would search a little longer. He hesitated, but not for long. What is one sheep, after all, when one owns hundreds?

I searched and searched until the day began to fade, but to no avail. Then I searched all my long, slow way home, but my lamb was not to be found. Tears stung in my eyes, and a tight knot squeezed my heart as I stumbled at last, weary and defeated, into the yard.

And oh, what I came home to! Tearlach mac Erc, one of my lord's guardsmen, had been torn open by a boar while hunting. The others had brought him back, but the surgeon said there was no hope for him. Tearlach rose to consciousness only to scream in agony until he fainted again; and so when last rites had been said, Macbeatha himself cut Tearlach's throat to release him from his suffering.

Everyone retired early that night, except the mourners who keened over Tearlach's body, led by Lady Gruoch herself. I would have stayed, too, but Macbeatha whispered to me to come to his chamber. There I massaged my lord's neck and shoulders, stroked him with loving hands, and held him close through the night. I knew what grief was in his heart, having had to hasten the death of his own man. It was a long time before he slept.

He was still sleeping the next morning when I slipped out of the room to see if perhaps my Galvan had returned during the night. The days were growing shorter now, and the daylight was still pale as I pushed open the stable door and peered inside.

At first, what I saw did not register. But then I stepped back with both hands clamped over my mouth to muffle the scream I could not contain. No one else was near, so I screamed and screamed into my hands until I got some little control of myself. Then I was sick. Coughing and gagging, I sank to my knees and pounded my fist helplessly against the dirt floor.

Someone had cut my little Galvan's throat, you see, and hung him by his hind feet there in the stable. The green ribbon, soaked now with blood, was still around his neck.

When I was able, I clambered to my feet and rushed out, fleeing across the yard and into the hall. Someone called out to me—one of the mourners, I suppose—but I ignored it and pounded up the stairs and into my lord's chamber.

He was still sleeping, so I just sank down in a corner, wadding up my shawl and sobbing into it so I wouldn't disturb him. Soon enough he woke, and seeing me there, he called softly, "Kelda? What is it? What's wrong?"

"I will miss Tearlach," I said, thinking it was better not to burden him with my grief when he had enough of his own.

He sat up on the edge of his bed and rubbed his face. The window was open and golden sunlight poured in, kindling the fire in his hair. There was, I noticed, some gray mixed with it now. "You didn't weep so last night," he remarked, for by the time we came to bed, I had done my crying for Tearlach. "Is there something else?"

I should have known better than to try to deceive him. "It's just—" I broke off and swallowed hard, trying to find the shortest way to get it out. "My lamb is dead."

He came to me then, full of sympathy. "That's all right," he soothed, his arms around me. "I'll give you another one."

But I shook my head. "I don't want another one. They'd only kill it, too."

At that he stopped and drew back to look at me sharply. "What do you mean, kill it? Someone *killed* your lamb?" I nodded. "Perhaps they mistook it for one of mine," he ventured, "and meant it for the table."

Again I shook my head. "He was still wearing his green ribbon."

That was the end of sympathy. Now he was angry. "What a vicious, spiteful thing to do! Do you know who it was?" I only shrugged. "Cowards! They're jealous," he declared. "I'll give you two sheep. No, six." He rose to his feet, as though he would go straight to the pastures to choose the sheep himself.

He didn't understand. Whoever killed Galvan hadn't done it to deprive me of property. They'd done it to hurt me. I loved Galvan, and they had deliberately killed the thing I loved and hung it up where they knew I would find it. And I was never, never going to let that happen to me again. "I don't want sheep," I told him boldly. "If you want to give me something, give me something they can't destroy." A memory surfaced from my youth. My mother had not only a sheep of her own, but-- "Land," I told him. "Give me a little piece of land for my own."

He sagged as he looked back at me. "Kelda, I can't do that. Among the Scots, *tribes* hold land—not people."

"But you're the High King!" I protested. "There are lands that belong to you."

"There are lands given into my care, yes," he admitted. "And I can give them into the care of another: one of my clients, one of my kinsmen. I suppose I could even give a parcel into your care— would that do?" he asked sincerely, lifting my stubborn chin in his hand. "A plot of land that you can work by yourself? You wouldn't really own it, but I can tell people it's your spot to work and no one else must touch it. Then—" He warmed to the idea. "Then we'll calculate what you grow on it, and I'll give you something of equal value for it when it is put in my storehouses. Would that be all right?"

He wanted it to be all right. He wanted to do something to take my pain away and fix the problem, and so I said it was fine, just to make him happy. But it was not what I wanted. What I wanted, really, was for people to respect me. The Norse respect people who own land. But I know now it wouldn't have made any difference.

That night in the hall he told a story which he claimed was from Holy Scripture. In it, a prophet came to the king and told him about two men: one very rich man who had lots of sheep, and one very poor man who had only one. The poor man loved his sheep like a child, and fed it from his table and slept with it in his bosom, or so Macbeatha said. That sounded a little too familiar to me, and I think he might have invented that part, for who there in the hall knew enough of Holy Scripture to contradict him? Anyway, my lord said that when the rich man had a guest, instead of killing one of his own sheep for the feast, he took the poor man's only sheep and killed it to serve to his guest.

Then Macbeatha called his steward over and gave him instructions: In the spring, when the flocks were taken up to higher pastures, he was to tie green ribbons around the necks of three fat ewes. And when they were brought down again in the fall, there had by God better be three healthy ewes with three healthy lambs wearing those ribbons; and all six were to be mine.

I doubt the Scots present learned any lesson from all this, but I did. I learned to cease my boasting in the hall, and to walk very carefully and humbly among my fellow servants. Never again did I show any partiality to one animal or another, to any whelp of Macbeatha's hounds or any foal of his horses. I fussed over no favorite shawl, nor any special hair ribbon or brooch. With my lord's warriors I was at ease, but with the guests who flowed in and out like water, and with the many servants who kept his beasts and tended his fields, I was cautious and discreet. Caring too much for any thing meant it could be used to hurt me, so I could not be seen to care.

If that is the price a slave girl pays, do you know what price is demanded of a king?

Chapter Eleven

They exacted their price at Christmas.

The Festival of Christmas is the longest one the Christians celebrate, going on for twelve days. Nearly everyone of importance came to Scone that first year: bishops and princes and many of Macbeatha's close kin. Even Crinan came, his eye bright as a hawk's, and I should have known he meant no good to my lord. I was in the alehouse counting up the casks when a white-faced servant dashed in to say Macbeatha wanted me in the hall, immediately.

The air crackled with his rage as I hurried into the room. Glancing around, I was surprised he had called for me with such august company present: a number of princes, ladies, and several churchmen. He usually kept me in the background when there were churchmen about. Boite was there, and Brenna—never a good sign for me. And Crinan was there, with a look of wicked delight poorly concealed on his square face.

"My lord sent for me?" I asked politely, bobbing my head in a respectful manner. There were no other servants in the hall, I noticed, and the musicians and jugglers and other entertainers had all been dismissed.

Macbeatha's rage was contained, as was his custom, but it blazed from his eyes and sounded in his voice like the growl of a bear who stands off a pack of wolves. They looked like wolves, those plotters gathered in the hall. Rising from his chair on the dais, my lord grated, "These good people are concerned for the immortal soul of their high king, and they have come to bid me change my ways."

The blood chilled in my veins, and my breathing stopped. If he had called me into the hall, there was only one change they wanted of him.

Now he turned his burning gaze on those who confronted him, one by one, until each flushed with the heat of it. "They have come to tell me it is improper for a high king to keep a slave," he said slowly, and each word was like the fall of a hammer meant to pummel this wolf pack; but it was my heart they pummeled. "They say that one Christian should not own another." He moved around the hall as he spoke, stopping in front of each man and looking him in the eye. "They say a king should be an example to his people." He stopped before the Bishop of Abernethy, whose eyes were riveted to the floor. "Isn't that right, Lord Bishop?"

Abernethy drew a great breath. "You keep the woman in a sinful relationship," he said doggedly, though he could not raise his eyes.

"A sinful relationship." Macbeatha moved to the next man, the Bishop of Perth. "A *sinful* relationship. And *you,* Lord Bishop. You have a wife, do you not?"

Surprise lit the Bishop of Perth's face. "We are married by law!"

"By law! But not by the Church, are you?" my lord demanded. "Because the Holy Father has forbidden clergy to marry. You are married before men, but not before God. Is that not a *sinful relationship?"*

The Bishop flushed from his shaven cheeks to the roots of his Columban tonsure. "It is too hard a thing to ask of a man," he protested. "The Holy Father has given us something to strive for, but not every man can be expected to attain it. We are not perfect."

"Ah, I see," Macbeatha mocked, going on to Crinan, who also had a wife. "So a Bishop—or an abbot—can have a wife because he is not expected to be perfect; but a king is, is that it?"

Crinan did not budge one mote before my lord's glare. "A king must be an example for his people," he said doggedly. "You must put the woman away from you and cleave to your wife."

"And did your son Duncan put away his mistress," Macbeatha demanded, "when he became High King?" Everyone knew there was a miller's daughter in Cumbria who had born Duncan two or three children.

"We are not speaking of my son," Crinan deflected.

"I see." Macbeatha moved on to Boite. "We are not speaking of past high kings, but of the present one. Is that it?" His eyes blazed down into her set features. "I would not think to find you in league with the son-in-law of Malcolm, lady."

She looked up at him through her eyelashes. "I am here for the sake of my daughter, and for no other reason."

"Did she bid you come?" he asked harshly.

"If she knew, she would—"

"Did she bid you come!" he roared.

The silence echoed a long moment. "No," Boite said finally. "She is too gentle and tractable for her own good."

A chuckle sounded low in Macbeatha's throat. "Tractable, eh? Then we speak of two different women, lady, for the one I married is made of sterner stuff than even you." Next he rounded on Father Tuthald, the priest who had been with Gruoch's brother when he died. "And you! These others do not surprise me, Father Tuthald, but you—"

Tuthald shifted his feet uncomfortably. "It is your immortal soul I am concerned for," he said, but his voice cracked as he spoke.

Macbeatha chuckled again, a dry, mirthless sound. "Well, I shall do you the service of believing that, Father. Of all the people in this room, you may actually mean it."

Brenna was next. "And you, dear sister? Here with my detractors?" There was a note of genuine sorrow in his voice when he addressed her.

"I fear that heathen wench will drag you down to Hell," she answered in a rush, but she could not meet her brother's eyes.

"Heathen! *Heathen?*" Macbeatha stormed across the floor to where I stood trembling and snatched the amulet from my bosom. "She wears the cross of Christ upon her breast! She goes to mass more often than you! She was baptized in Thorfinn's household— *what more do you want?* God forgives, Brenna—why can't you?"

Dropping the amulet, he turned and faced them all. "In all your concern for the welfare of others, have you thought of Kelda's welfare at all? 'Send her away,' you tell me, but what of her? What happens to her, to this Christian whose soul, the priests tell us, is as valuable as my own? Hm?" He went straight to the Abbot of Brechin. "What do you propose I do with her, Reverend Abbot? Sell her to a heathen? For according to you, no Christian should own another Christian, so are you therefore asking me to sell her into bondage to a heathen master who will seek to corrupt her?"

"Of course not," the Abbot muttered, flushing red.

"What then?" he badgered. "Send her back to Thorfinn?" He turned to a powerful chieftain whose lands were close by Scone. "Insult my cousin and start a war between us? Oh, you'd like that, wouldn't you? A war that drained Moray's resources and kept the High King in the north, leaving you here to do as you please. Yes, you'd like that very much, I think." Moving on to the King of the Isles, he said, "You'd like it, too, I suppose—keep Thorfinn tied up and out of your hair for a while. You might even pursue your ambition to retake Dublin, if Thorfinn were busy elsewhere."

"No one said you should send her back to Thorfinn," Echmarcach grumbled.

"No, no one said where I should send her," my lord agreed, turning his back on them for a moment. His voice carried throughout the hall, however. "No one has given any thought at all as to where I should send her—just 'away,' you said. Tell me, where is this 'away?' And who will she serve there?" He spun around. "You, Crinan? Perhaps you imagine you can learn my secrets from her, eh? Something you can use against me?"

The abbot's mouth fell open at the accusation.

"No, no, I can see you are too noble to stoop to such tactics," Macbeatha jibed. "Do you suppose the new Anglish king is that noble, as well? Not, of course," he scoffed, "that there are any rough fellows in Alba who would take advantage of a slave girl and give her into the hands of the Danes or the Anglish. In fact, there is probably a very poor market for a slave who has served a High King."

An uncomfortable silence reigned; no one had thought that to take me away from Macbeatha, was to place me at someone else's disposal.

Now his eyes narrowed and his tone grew savage. "You say that you come here out of concern for me, out of concern for Alba—but I say that you lie. It is out of concern for yourselves that you come, because you fear me. 'Macbeatha is too strong,' you say to yourselves. 'We cannot manipulate him, as we did Duncan. We cannot control him. So we must find some way to humble him, to strike at him and make him weaker.' And so you seek to hurt me. You seek to take away something I value. You presume to hold me to a higher standard than you have set for any other king."

With a sweep of his hand, he took them all in. "Well, *you are right!* You cannot control me. You cannot humble me with your transparent attempt to deprive me of the most loyal servant any man has ever had. You cannot, because *I accept your challenge.* I will *be* a better king than you have ever had before!"

Striding through the hall, he came back to where I stood, laid a hand on my head and forced me to my knees. It was not hard to do: my knees had no strength left to support me. My world was ending. My lord was sending me away.

"But do not think," he threatened the assemblage, "that you will benefit from this. Do not think for one moment than *any one of you* will gain by the loss I incur today." I heard his knife whistle from its sheath, heard someone gasp and cry him to stop. I could not see who it was, for the world had gone gray all around me, and there was nothing but the sound of his voice.

"Kelda," he said softly, gently. "Do you trust me?"

Did I trust him? After all these years! "Yes, lord," I croaked.

And then, as he had once before in Thorfinn's hall, he commanded me, "Bare your neck."

With shaking hands, I did as he bade: I pulled the shawl away from my neck and lifted my chin, though I could not meet his eyes. It was over, it was all over ... The world held nothing for me anymore. Macbeatha reached out with his knife; its blade caressed my cheek as mine had caressed his each morning for so many years; then it glided down to my throat and I closed my eyes, waiting.

Quickly, so quickly I hardly felt it, his blade slipped beneath my worn leather collar and sliced cleanly through it.

"From this day forth you are a free woman," he declared softly. "And for your years of service, one hundred and five cattle shall be yours, that you may be dependent on no man for your welfare."

Tears streamed down my face like a brook in spring flood. "And six sheep," I reminded him in a voice that cracked with sorrow. "You promised me six sheep."

* * *

In Fionna's hut

"I never wanted to be free of him," Kelda told her host. "Oh, there were times when I chafed at my bondage, at the fact that as a slave, I was looked down upon by people like Brenna and Boite, and even some of the other servants. But I never, for one moment, wanted to be free of him. It was the end of my world."

"At least he provided for you," Fionna pointed out. "One hundred and five
beasts—that is a great many."

"I was rich," Kelda said simply. "Rich enough to make many other people angry. That, of course, was his intent. They sought to hurt him, and wronged me in the process; that wrong he would redress, and he would rub their noses in it."

"So you gained many enemies."

"I gained no friends, surely. But then, I never had any in that room—except Macbeatha's guard, of course. Now that I was out of his care and keeping, though—and out of his hall—they could not protect me. Nor could he."

"So you had to find somewhere safe. Somewhere ... far away."

Kelda sighed, and her fingers stroked the leather pouch in her lap, her eyes still fixed on some distant place in her memory.

* * *

I don't think Macbeatha realized that, when he made me a rich woman. I think he truly believed I would settle nearby, perhaps build a house in the village and lease my cattle to clients. After all, I belonged to no tribe and therefore had no lands in which to graze my cattle, so what choice did I have?

One which never occurred to him, apparently, for a look of shock took his face when I told him what I planned to do. It was late that same night, after a cheerless supper in the hall where he presided with all the grace and good humor it was his custom to exhibit, while everyone else looked pale and strained—even his captain, Owen, can you imagine? I didn't think anything could affect Owen's appetite. I myself could not eat, and I wanted badly to be far, far away from these treacherous people. But I ventured to the hall in search of Venko, for my plan hinged on him.

Venko's tribe lives deep in the heart of eastern Moray, far from those who wished me and my lord harm. His kinsmen did not know I had been a slave, and probably would not have cared if they did. They were so proud of him: a member of the High King's guard, riding at the High King's elbow! He brought honor and glory back to his House. So I drew him from the hall that night and told him I would give him all my cattle and whatever children God would allow us, if he would take me back to Moray in time for the drawing of lots at Bride, when each man of the tribe is given a piece of ground to tend.

You should have seen Macbeatha's face when I told him. I stood with my meager bundle of things in my hand, Venko at my side. "I've come to return your shaving knife to you, lord," I said bluntly, "and to bid you farewell."

He stopped dead, his eyes frozen on my face.

I forced coldness into my voice; I dared not weep, he himself had taught me that. "Venko and I will be leaving in the morning."

"With your permission, lord," Venko added quickly, for he would not agree to my proposal without Macbeatha's permission. "I will be back after Bride, in plenty of time for campaigning."

Macbeatha stood speechless, his eyes wide with disbelief.

"But he will need to leave again," I pressed on, "to bring our cattle north, after the passes have opened. It will only take a few weeks."

Venko looked distinctly unhappy. "With your permission," he repeated. "The cattle should be there for the blessing at Beltaine. But I have many kinsmen who will see to it—I need not stay myself."

Never have I known Macbeatha to be so slow in piecing information together. "You—you'll marry her?" he managed at last.

I fixed him with a bold eye. "It is the only way I can get land," I told him. "I have to marry a Scot."

Denial filled his eyes and he opened his mouth to speak, but then he shut it again. After a moment he nodded. "Yes, of course, that is a good plan," he said. "Take as much time as you need, Venko. If you wish to spend some weeks with your kin, do so. Your place in my guard will always be here, whenever you choose to return."

And so we left, riding up Strathmore and skirting the line of hills called the Mounth, all the way to the coast. By the time we reached Aberdeen I was pregnant, but there was none of the joy I had always believed I would feel to discover I was with child. There was no joy in having my own house, no joy in tilling my own soil—that is, the plot we drew in the lottery that year—no joy in seeing my herd of cattle driven through the Beltaine fire. There was a great deal of satisfaction in all those things: I drew from them a sense of purpose and a course along which to steer my life. But there was no joy.

There was no joy in my life for a very long time.

Chapter Twelve

On the Isle of Iona

The wind blew fresh off the Western Sea, sweeping up over the little island and ruffling Brother Reardon's tunic as he followed quietly behind the High King's bier. Nine guardsmen bore it reverently toward the abbey's small chapel where it would lie until a grave had been dug with the other Scottish kings. Then Macbeatha would rest at last with his honored predecessors, there where the wind swept over them, fresh and clean, and the tangy scent of brine washed away any hint of corruption. It was a fitting place for the man, Reardon thought. He had always been one with the wind and the air, the sun and the sea ...

It was here in the west that Reardon had first met the Moray prince some thirty years ago, here within sight and smell of the sea. As a young monk, Reardon had come to Alba from Ireland, sure there had to be more heathens here to convert than could be found in Ulster. Weren't they all Gall Gaedhil, *foreign Gaels, bred of Viking conquerors who infested the land?* How surprised he had been to find the folk of Mull and other nearby islands bearing crosses around their necks and singing hymns at their hearths. There must be someplace else, Reardon had reasoned, where there were true heathens in need of his witness. "Send me into the highlands," he begged the abbot. "I know God has a mission for me there." And so, to silence the boy, the abbot had blessed his going and prayed God would protect the naive young monk. With only the roughest *directions from a fisherman on Mull, Reardon set forth in his little coracle to paddle up the rivers and lochs of the Great Glen.*

The wildness of the country had fascinated Reardon. Mountains soared up to a height he had never imagined, their bold, rocky faces catching the rays of the setting sun, and the cries of gulls echoed off the cliffs. He felt himself transported as he left his coracle on the bank of Loch Linhe and climbed up the slope to the west. The wind howled down from the heights; he heard its song in the trees and crags of the highlands above him and wanted to join in. Finding a sheltered spot under a rocky overhang, he sat himself down and opened his pack.

There was no food left in it—God will provide, he told himself. There was no book of Scripture in it, either—all the Scripture he needed was in his head. The only thing left in Reardon's pack was the only worldly thing he valued, and he valued it only because of the gift God had given him to draw music from it. It was na Pýoba, the pipes. He settled the bag under his arm with the drone pipes to one side, blew into the mouth tube to fill the bag, and took the chanter in his hands.

For a moment he just let the drones wail on their discordant notes, blending with the cry of the birds and the whine of the wind and the sighing of the trees around him. Then he let his fingers pick out a lilting melody, a hymn, that rose and fell like the hawk circling out over the glen on an updraft. Another song came to mind, one his mother used to sing to him as a child, so he played that, too. Then, from out of the rugged landscape of this place came another tune that was not anything he knew, but a rare gift from the Creator to his humble servant. Reardon played it again and again, lost in the rapture of the gift, unmindful of the sun setting behind the mountain at his back and the numbing chill which settled in the shadows.

Unmindful, that is, until his reverie was broken by the sharp sound of laughter, and a man's voice hooting, "It's a monk, Owen!" Then peals and peals of laughter followed, and Reardon jumped up in surprise to see three or four young warriors standing in the trees nearby. Actually, one was not standing at all, but rolling on the ground, overcome by mirth.

It was not derisive laughter, however. It was joyous, unrestrained laughter that tumbled like a brook over mountain stones, careening and splashing its way to the glen. Such was the force of that laughter, Reardon had to smile, even though he didn't understand the joke. One of the warriors, a dark, burly fellow who looked like he could stop a bull in full charge, did not find it pleasing, though. He scowled darkly at Reardon, and the monk was startled to see a drawn sword in the man's hand. Were these murderers, then? Men turned out by their tribes and forced to wander, kinless, throughout the land?

But no—the burly one wore a gold torc around his neck, as did the laugher, who had recovered himself somewhat and held out a hand to his friend to be helped to his feet. Then he sauntered over to Reardon in a casual but self-assured manner, with the others following behind him. "Forgive us, Brother, for interrupting you," *the laugher greeted,* "but Owen here was sure that sound was the banshee's wail, and that death awaited one of us on this trip. Indeed, I myself wasn't sure what it was, until we came through the trees there and saw you." *The laugher held out his hand to Reardon.* "I'm Macbeatha."

Reardon took the proffered hand cautiously, almost overwhelmed by the buoyant good humor of Macbeatha. "Brother Reardon," *he identified himself.* "Have you never heard the pipes, then?"

"Actually, I have, once," *Macbeatha told him, examining the instrument with unveiled curiosity.* "In my grandfather's hall. But I doubt any of my lads have ever heard it before. We're men of Moray, you see."

"Where is that?" *Reardon asked blankly.*

Macbeatha threw him a curious look, then grinned once more. "Up north, at the other end of this Great Glen. You're Irish, aren't you?" *he guessed.* "I can tell by your speech." *Reardon admitted that he was, and Macbeatha asked him,* "Where are your companions?"

"Companions?" *Reardon shrugged.* "I haven't any."

Macbeatha's eyebrows flew up. "You wander through such rugged country alone?"

"God will protect me."

Macbeatha's eyes seemed to whirl in the setting sun—they were green, those eyes—and then he laughed again. "And so He has done," *the Morayman agreed,* "for He sent us to take care of you! Come down the hill, we have a campfire started and we're roasting some fish."

So Reardon joined the band of warriors for the night. They had been in Cumbria for the winter and were now on their way back home. Reardon had never really spent any time among warriors since, at age seven, he had gone to the monastery at Kells. He found these young men quite different from the monks he had grown up among. They were so full of life: wild and untamed, like this land he passed through. It lifted his heart to be among them, even if they were a bit crude.

In truth, they were quite crude. One named Weylin teased Macbeatha about the bedwench he'd left behind in Cumbria. Reardon didn't understand most of the jests. Finally, "Behave yourselves," Macbeatha scolded the others through his laughter. "You're embarrassing poor Brother Reardon."

"Us? You started it," one reminded him.

"So I did," he admitted without a shred of repentance. "Well, we'll go visit Thorfinn next and have our fill of wenching up there, so let's be pious for a time. What do you say, Brother Reardon?" he asked. "Can you play us a hymn upon those pipes?"

Reardon was glad to oblige, but the looks on the faces of the Moraymen proved them to be as mystified at his music as he was at their jests. "That's a song of the Trinity, isn't it?" Macbeatha asked when he had finished.

"Yes, exactly." Reardon was surprised it had been hard to recognize. He knew he had played the melody flawlessly. "Shall I play you another?"

"No, that's all right," Macbeatha answered quickly. "We should get some sleep now—we want to press on early tomorrow. Will you travel with us for a way, Brother Reardon?"

Reardon couldn't think of any reason not to, and so he accompanied the warriors up the loch for a day. That night they camped again on the western shore. "Why don't you camp over there?" Reardon asked, pointing across to the eastern side where some huts clustered on the hillside, offering the possibility of hospitality for travelers.

Macbeatha's countenance darkened at the suggestion. "That's Atholl."

"Atholl?" Reardon echoed.

So Macbeatha explained about the feud between Atholl and Moray. Reardon well understood such hostilities between Great Tribes, for it was the same in Ireland. "It is a pity," he said sadly, "that we cannot all live in Christian brotherhood, as God intended us to do."

"Yes, it is a pity," Macbeatha agreed. "Think how great Alba could be if the tribes could forget their differences and live as one people."

"Think how dull it would be," Owen grumbled.

For a moment Macbeatha's eyes danced in merriment; then they softened with visions of far-off things. "There's never any lack of enemies," he said with certainty. "The trick is to look for them outside Alba."

"Only Satan is our enemy," Reardon contradicted. "The rest are brothers and sisters in Christ, who may or may not know Him yet."

They got distracted then in the business of making their camp, raising a simple tent against the light drizzle that had begun to fall. Once the shower had passed, the monk brought out his pipes and, seeing the unhappy looks on the faces of several of the warriors, he hiked away from the camp to a serene spot looking out over the water.

It was a clear night, now the rain was gone, and the stars were a dazzling canopy in the slice of sky framed by mountains and trees. Reardon played his new song again, and then another, older tune, before a voice came to him out of the darkness. "What is your destiny, Reardon? Do you know?"

It was Macbeatha's voice, of course, but Reardon could not see the man. He was cloaked in a pool of shadow somewhere to the monk's right, a bodiless voice asking a timeless question. "My destiny is in God's hands," Reardon said instinctively.

"And has He said nothing to you of what it is?"

For a while Reardon was silent, pondering the query. "Sometimes," he began slowly, "I think my destiny is martyrdom, at the hands of the heathen. But then I think, why would God glorify someone as mundane as me?"

There was a rustling sound, ferns brushing against one another, but still Reardon's eyes would not penetrate the darkness. "Well, don't count it a loss," came the voice of Macbeatha, tinged with mirth, "if you're not to die in agony, being jeered by barbarous fellows." Then the mirth vanished, and the voice said softly, "It's in the pipes."

"What is?" Reardon asked, finding this disembodied voice quite eerie.

"The voice of God," Macbeatha replied. "I know, because I've heard the pipes before, and they were just so much noise to me. But when you play..."

The notion settled over Reardon like a warmth. *The voice of God in na Pýoba*— Perhaps that was his destiny, then, to play the pipes among the heathen so they might hear the voice of God...

After several moments he asked, "What is your destiny, Macbeatha?"

But the voice was gone, and if a man had walked away from Reardon, the young monk never heard him.

In the morning Reardon took leave of his companions. "Are you sure you won't come with us?" Macbeatha asked. "We're going up into Caithness, among the Norsemen. No doubt you could find a few heathens there!"

But Reardon shook his head. "No, I believe God spoke to me last night," he said humbly. "I'm going to wander here for a while, in the highlands—on both sides of the loch."

Macbeatha nodded in understanding. "God go with you and your pipes, Brother Reardon," he said sincerely. Then his smile flashed and his eyes sparkled. "When I'm High King, you must come and play for me," he jested. And Reardon laughed. They all laughed.

But in the years that followed, Reardon often wondered about the red-haired prince. As he drifted from hut to hut, from settlement to settlement, he heard news now and again of Macbeatha mac Findlaech. When he did, he wondered about that conversation in the darkness, and about the jesting remark at parting. When, after years of ministry, he saw that people were, indeed, drawn by his piping and touched by his music, he began to think perhaps the northern prince was in fact a prophet. Had not King David been both a warrior and a prophet?

So it came as no surprise when, fourteen years after that encounter, he learned Macbeatha mac Findlaech was now High King of Alba. Upon hearing the news, Reardon set out immediately, inquiring his road as he went, until he reached Scone, where the High King was in residence..

The guards in the great hall frowned as they looked the ragged monk up and down, eyeing his pack suspiciously. "The king is with his counselors," they told him sourly. "Wait over there with the others." And it didn't matter how many times Reardon told them the king had invited him, they would not listen.

So he went out to an open place away from the hall and took up his pipes. At the sound, some sheep grazing nearby scattered bleating, only to return in a few minutes and continue cropping the grass. A flock of pigeons rose up, startled, and then settled in a grove of beech trees not far away. Men at work repairing the thatched roof of a stable stopped and stared at the piper. And before he had finished his second song, out came the High King himself.

The face was older, the shoulders and chest a little thicker, and the clothing much richer; but the smile on his face and the sparkling green eyes were the same. At the end of his song, Reardon leaned the mouth tube against his chest and observed the new monarch, resplendent now in gold and scarlet. "I see you found your destiny," he remarked.

"And you yours?" Macbeatha asked.

"I believe so."

Then the High King reached out a brotherly hand to the monk. "Come inside," he invited. "I asked you to come play in my hall, did I not?"

So Reardon passed the whole winter in the High King's court, sometimes playing in the hall, more often wandering out away from the village with Macbeatha and teaching him to play na Pýoba. *The king was a quick student, but he would never play where anyone else could hear him.* "This is something I do for myself alone, for the edification of my soul," *he said once.* "That is a luxury a king rarely enjoys. I will not let anyone find a way to use it against me."

In the spring there was a flurry of activity, and men came from across the land to form the largest warband anyone had ever seen. Reardon grew troubled by it and thought he would return to his highlands and his ministry there. He sought the king to take his leave, and found him sitting alone in his reading room, an open book upon the table before him, but with his chair and his eyes turned toward the window. A fresh breeze wafted in, ruffling the pages of the book.

"Lord?" Reardon called softly, hesitant to disturb him when he looked so deep in thought.

Macbeatha hardly stirred; but, "Come in, Brother Reardon," he bade, and so Reardon went in.

Reardon could see the creases now etched around the king's eyes and upon his brow, and in his hair winked strands of white. After a long moment of silence, Macbeatha said, "It bothers you, doesn't it? All these trappings of war, men bent on killing and looting-- Not the way God would have us live, I'm afraid."

Reardon shifted uncomfortably. "Joshua took Canaan by force of arms," he allowed, "and David conquered the Philistines in like manner." But he could not force any enthusiasm into his voice.

"Those were heathen enemies," Macbeatha replied, his gaze still fixed somewhere out the window. "It was in my mind to attack Northumbria and take back the portion of Lothian which Duncan lost. They have a new jarl who boasts he will capture even more of my territory, and I would strike at him before he strikes at me. I have called upon my ally Thorfinn of Orkney to join me. Even now he sails for the south of Strathclyde, where he will march across my lands and strike at Northumbria from the west. I will lead the main invasion force down from the north. I know this Jarl Siward; he is a fierce warrior, and a cunning leader, but he cannot hope to withstand us both."

Reardon swallowed hard, feeling a knot form in his stomach. He had seen what was left of a village after a marauding army went through. Whether this Siward attacked Macbeatha, or Macbeatha attacked Siward, the results would be much the same for the lowly residents of the land.

"It would be a great victory for the Scots," Macbeatha went on in an oddly detached voice. "Not to mention personal glory for me. It would wipe away the sting of Durham, and my name would be written in the chronicles that you monks keep—not to mention being sung in halls and hovels across the land."

"But?" Reardon prompted, sensing the codicil in Macbeatha's tone.

"But the Northumbrians are not heathens," Macbeatha responded. Turning at last from the window, he caught Reardon in his potent gaze. "And what right does one Christian king have to rise up against another?"

Reardon's heart flipped over in his chest.

Now Macbeatha rose from his chair and began to pace the room slowly. "I have been a man of war," he said. "I have used war to further my ends, even provoking it when need be. I have taken up my sword with glee, and sacrificed countless lives to my ambition. But now I have reached my goal and sworn to be guardian and protector of Alba and her people. I have sworn—" *His voice broke, the only time Reardon ever heard it do that.* "I have sworn to be a better king than has ever reigned in this land. Now how do I do that? By taking more territory, by claiming the goods and the lives of other Christians? Or by quelling the sword which would take Alban lives? Keeping my borders secure and protecting the lives and the property of my people?"

"I have seen families of Atholl devastated by the raids of your kinsmen," Reardon offered. "And I have watched children in Moray perish of hunger because all the cattle of their tribe had been stolen by men of Atholl. Plunder makes only a few warriors and their families rich; a good harvest makes everyone rich."

This was clearly not a new thought to the High King. "Yet Siward will surely strike at me," Macbeatha mused. "And Thorfinn has already set sail for Strathclyde. There are seven thousand men on their way to me—I can't send them home or next time I call, they will not come. I must do something with them."

Reardon shook his head. "These are things I know nothing about," he said. "All I know are the teachings of Holy Scripture, the Offices of the Church, and the pipes."

Returning to his chair, Macbeatha sat down and gazed out the window once more. "Then play the pipes for me, Brother Reardon," he sighed heavily. "Play the pipes, and perhaps the voice of God will speak to me."

So Reardon played for the king in the confines of his reading room. He played song after song while Macbeatha gazed out the window with a troubled countenance.

Then suddenly the king sat up in his chair, and his green eyes began to whirl with thought. Turning back to the table, he pushed the open book away and rested his elbows there, hands clasped, chewing absently on one thumb. Finally a smile spread over his features. When Reardon had finished his song, he put the pipes down.

"I'll be leaving for Edinburgh soon," the king said, "to gather my forces. From there we'll move south toward Northumbria."

His eyes twinkled with an unspoken secret. "Come with me, Brother Reardon. Come play your pipes when I meet the Jarl of Northumbria. Perhaps we shall all hear the voice of God."

Intrigued, Reardon agreed.

There were a thousand men from each of six Great Tribes, with an extra thousand from Strathclyde. As they traveled south they were joined by Scots who had settled in Lothian, and together with the porters, horseboys, servants, and camp followers, they were a great host. But as they stole through the hills of Lauderdale, and before they passed the monastery at Stow, Macbeatha left his baggage train in a high and defensible place. Then he divided his army into seven units and established a set of signals by which they would communicate with each other as they approached the River Tweed.

When they were within sight of the Tweed, they scattered their camp amongst the trees and waited.

The Tweed was no longer in flood, and its banks grew drier every day; soon large groups of men and horses would be able to cross at the fords. Messengers came to the king several times a day, and it wasn't long before one brought news that a small party of Northumbrians had crossed the Tweed further upriver, running smack into a contingent of Scots. In accordance with Macbeatha's orders, not one had been allowed to escape. Two days later another scouting party approached the Tweed at a different place, came across in small boats, and swiftly met a similar fate.

"That should flush the fox," Macbeatha said, and he continued to wait.

Now the king's spies told of messages flying back and forth between Siward and his brother-in-law Harald. Apparently the two had been riding north at the head of a large army when word came that Thorfinn of Orkney was raiding in the Uplands from a base camp in southern Strathclyde. Furious, Siward had taken half the army and ridden west to deal with this incursion, bidding his brother-in-law continue north and make some raids into Lothian.

When two small parties of warriors had vanished north of the Tweed, though, Harald found himself in a quandary. The Scots must be present there in large numbers—what else could explain the fact that not one warrior had returned? But where were they? And how many? More than Harald had? Would they attack? Should he attack?

Siward, who was finding Thorfinn more difficult to deal with than he had imagined, had no sympathy for his brother-in-law. If Harald was <u>afraid</u> to cross the river and engage the Scots, he could wait for Siward to arrive in a couple of weeks.

Harald had taken the insult as Siward had intended, a strike at his manhood. At the head of two hundred picked warriors, he crossed the Tweed.

Macbeatha gave orders to let these Northumbrians pass through the Scottish lines. Then, when they were surrounded, the Scots fell upon them. "I want two things," Macbeatha had told the captain of those Scottish forces. "Any man of God who is with them, alive; and Harald's head."

Reardon had been with the king when both articles were delivered, the latter wrapped in a cloth treated with cedar oil to preserve it, and the former in the person of a skinny priest. Macbeatha spoke to the hostage in Latin, the only language both shared. After assuring the priest no harm would come to him, the king gave the cleric a message to deliver to Jarl Siward. "Tell him that I have heard the voice of God, bidding the two of us to meet with all haste. Tell him, therefore, to meet me at the river crossing to speak." As a sign of good faith, Macbeatha would have his kinsman Thorfinn of Orkney withdraw. "And as a sign of my determination—" Macbeatha picked up the wrapped head of Siward's brother-in-law and slipped it into a leather sack. "Give him this."

That night Macbeatha asked Reardon to accompany him to the shore of the river in the darkness. There the king sat upon a tree trunk that had washed up in this year's flood, and he gazed across the water at the campfires of the Northumbrians while Reardon played upon the pipes. "For I imagine," Macbeatha told the monk, "the warriors camped yonder have never heard the sound of na Pýoba *before.*" So Reardon let his pipes wail on the still evening air while he drew out a tune of his own devising on the chanter.

Thorfinn withdrew, and it took only three days for Siward and the rest of his army to reach the river crossing. There he found the whole of Macbeatha's army, no longer hidden amongst the trees, but camped in their thousands upon the broad meadow above the northern shore. All the heads of the slain Northumbrian warriors were mounted on posts at the water's edge, so a bristling forest of gruesome trophies lined the bank.

Macbeatha and his guard rode down to the water's edge to await the Northumbrian jarl, bidding Reardon bring his pipes and accompany them. Before long a dozen Northumbrian warriors approached the other side with Siward at their head.

Jarl Siward was a big man, both tall and broad of chest. His fair hair was cut just above his neck, and it stuck out from under his leather helmet on every side. Macbeatha called across the water in Norn for him to come over. Siward, being no fool, called back for Macbeatha to come to his side. Smiling, Macbeatha replied that if they were to speak Scots, he would come to Siward; but if they were to speak in Siward's language, the jarl must come to him. Grudgingly—and cautiously—Siward urged his mount into the water.

As the Northumbrians reached the northern bank, Macbeatha left his guard behind and rode forward to meet them. How different he looked from the Northumbrian jarl, one hand resting arrogantly on his hip, red hair catching the sun, no armor to be seen—not even a helmet. Not as big through the chest as Siward, he was nonetheless unmistakably muscular, and he sat his dapple gray stallion with the grace of one used to long hours in the saddle. Rigdomnae, *Reardon thought to himself. The stuff of kings.*

Later on, Reardon asked the king what they said, those two warriors at the river crossing. "I told him his men had come into my lands without permission, and with the obvious intent of making mischief among the peaceful inhabitants—that is why they were killed." Macbeatha laughed. "He spat on the ground when I called the inhabitants peaceful. It seems that stories still circulate hereabouts of a certain red-haired warrior who caused much commotion among the Northumbrians ten or fifteen years ago."

"And what did you say to that?" Reardon asked.

Macbeatha's smile grew wistful at the monk's question. "I told him that was a young man, bent on making a name for himself, and he would no longer be found in these parts. Instead, I said, there was a king whose name was already well known." Then Siward had asked about Thorfinn, and his mysterious withdrawal from the Uplands of Northumbria. "I told him Jarl Thorfinn and I grew up as cousins, and although Thorfinn is his own man, we often see things the same way."

That in itself had given Siward pause. The Scots were always a force to be reckoned with; if they were joined by the powerful and ambitious Jarl of Orkney, it could be a very uncomfortable situation for their enemies.

A blunt man, Siward had asked next about Macbeatha's claim to have heard the voice of God. "Are you a saint?" he had asked with a derisive sneer.

Macbeatha only laughed. He was, he proclaimed, a warrior; he lusted for battle as other men lusted for women. It was food and drink to him, and nothing was so sweet as to split an enemy's skull with his mighty sword. But he was also a Christian, and God had bidden him save his wrath for those whose hearts were evil, who crossed into his lands to steal his cattle and to do harm among the folk there.

"I asked him if perhaps he had heard the voice, too," Macbeatha told Reardon. "I said it was an eerie sound, like the wail of women both north and south of the river, keening for their children. I said if he listened at nightfall, he would undoubtedly hear it again. It would say to him that if he did not raise his hand against the Christian king of Alba, neither would that king lift his hand against Northumbria."

Reardon had played his pipes again that night, praying Siward would indeed hear the voice of God, be it in the pipes or in Macbeatha's words. Something worked—the next morning the Northumbrians broke camp and marched away to the south. It would be six long years before they crossed the River Tweed in any numbers, then to be quickly and decisively beaten back and held there for eight years more.

This long span of peace was welcomed by the farmers and herdsmen in troubled Lothian, and no doubt those on the south side of the Tweed as well. That it was God's doing, Reardon had no doubt; but God had used a king called Macbeatha mac Findlaech to achieve His end. The peace Macbeatha established and maintained had been felt all the way into the highlands, where Reardon returned to do his ministry.

Only with the battle of Gowrie had it been shattered, and Reardon had felt that pain in his own heart, clutching at his chest and falling to the ground on the Feast of the Seven Sleepers—the very day on which the forces of Siward and the forces of Macbeatha met in fierce combat. For weeks Reardon had lain, pale and sweating, on a pallet in a shepherd's hut. Herbal brews and bed rest finally restored him, but never to his old vigor. Climbing the smallest hillock robbed him of breath, and he knew his ministry in the rugged, wild lands had come to an end. He returned at the end of his days to the abbey on Iona.

And now the king had come to the end of his days, as well. The monk put a hand to his aching heart. When would God send another such to rule in Alba? Reardon had met Lulach and knew him to be a decent young man, but-- There was just nothing extraordinary about him. He would probably be a fine king for a peaceful time, but Alba had not been at peace for three years now, and next summer promised to be worse. Canmore was determined to rule the Scots as his father Duncan had done, and he would not rest until he was victorious or dead.

And who knew if a brutish man like Canmore could hear the voice of God?

Chapter Thirteen

In Fionna's hut

"Did you find peace, at least, so far from your enemies?" Fionna asked.

A small laugh slipped from Kelda's lips. *"Peace? As much peace as a woman ever gets, raising a family and running a farm."* Then she thought about it. *"As much peace as my mother ever knew, surely. Even after she purchased her freedom, there was little change in her daily life. She still worked Thorkel's fields, and her own, and saved her earnings to buy Hakon a mail shirt, for her sons were everything to her. For her, peace was being treated fairly, and having no one take her children from her."* Kelda frowned. *"I mean, having no one cast them into the sea at their birth. I thought of her when I labored to deliver my first child, how she had been robbed of two babes by a cruel master. I thought, 'At least I don't have to worry someone will cast my daughter into the sea just to hurt me. At least I don't have to worry if her father will ever own her as his child ...'"*

* * *

She arrived early, while Venko was off campaigning with Macbeatha in Lothian—Siward had just become jarl of Northumbria and was eager to redress old grievances. The midwife said she came early because I would not stay out of the fields and let my clients do the harvesting, but I couldn't help it. They were *my* fields, and I toiled alongside the men and women who now looked to me for their support. I never much cared for field work—planting and cultivating and harvesting—but this was *my household* now, and I was determined to take care of it.

The baby was small but feisty, and she not only lived, she thrived. By the time Venko returned in October, she could look at him with bright eyes, and he could see the blood of his Pictish ancestors in her. But I wanted her to be a Scot, so I gave her the strongest Scottish name I knew—Siusan. I think she would have approved, my long-ago nemesis, for though my Siusan never grew to be so tall, she is every bit as tough and as willful.

Venko stayed with us that winter, trying his best to do what a lord of property should do, but he was restless. Meting out fodder, seeing that the tools were mended for spring, checking on the stock after a storm—these were not skills he had practiced. He loved little Siusan, and he was delighted finally to have me as his own, but his heart was in the south, with Macbeatha. His soul yearned for the companionship of his fellows, for the drinking and singing and storytelling of the hall.

When spring came, there was the plowing to oversee, the calving and the lambing, testing the ground to see when the frost had gone, the shearing-- Venko grew irritable as our steward asked him questions he did not know how to answer, sought opinions he could not formulate. Then a rider came in search of us, with a message from the High King. Oh, please, would we come and visit him at Aberdeen, where he tarried on the coast—he so wanted to see our new child and congratulate us on this blessing!

I tried everything I could to dissuade Venko, but he was determined. If the High King requested, we would oblige. My suggestion that Venko go alone was rebuffed—it was me Macbeatha wanted to see, Venko insisted, and the child, so we would all three go. Nothing I said would make him see how awkward it was going to be for me to face Macbeatha again, and with a child in my arms.

It was chilly in the hall when we arrived. My lord stood at the fire with his cloak draped around those powerful shoulders, his hair glinting red in the firelight. When he heard us come in, he looked up and I gasped. In place of his shaven chin was a full beard, as bright a red as his mustaches, although it was well salted with gray. Then a smile split his face that was like the sun rising over the sea, and he came to meet us with outstretched arms, embracing Venko first.

When he turned to me, my heart stopped. Even with the unaccustomed whiskers, he was so beautiful—as beautiful as he had ever been!--and I wanted to cast aside everything and throw myself into his arms. But of course, that was out of the question. I was no longer a slave girl, but the wife of his kinsman, and there were boundaries that could not be crossed. He reached out and touched my cheek, then my shoulder. "Lady," he greeted softly.

Lady! No one had ever called me "lady" before. Everything I had known in my head about my change in status, suddenly overwhelmed my heart, and I felt dizzy. Raising a hand, I touched the new whiskers on his face with a question in my eyes that my lips could not form. But he understood. "I promised you," he whispered. "No hand but yours shall ever shave me."

It was the pledge he had made me on his wedding day, a pledge he had not always kept in the past—but he was keeping it now. Tears sprang to my eyes.

He pretended not to notice. "You look well, Kelda," he observed in that ringing voice which was meant for other ears than mine. "Motherhood becomes you." I did not even try to stammer a response, and he went on. "May I assume that in this bundle of blankets somewhere, there is a child?"

"This—this is Siusan," I managed. Venko only stood to one side, grinning proudly.

Macbeatha's eyes sparkled as he recognized the name. "Siusan, eh? Well. We must send word back to old Aithne—she'll be so pleased!" Then he poked a calloused finger at the blankets, peering for a face underneath. "May I hold her?" he asked with the touch of awe that always crept into his voice when he beheld small children.

Carefully I transferred my precious bundle into his arms. His face went soft as he pushed back a flap here and a corner there until he could at last look upon the tiny, dark face of my child. Then, even as I watched him gaze at her, I saw the disappointment come over his features. Thank all gods that Venko did not notice—he would have been crushed. But I knew what it was.

Because she had been born early, you see, Macbeatha wondered if, perhaps, the child was his.

But she was not, and no stretch of the imagination would make it so. Macbeatha beamed at me then, and told Venko what a beautiful daughter he had, and clapped the happy father upon the back, and called for refreshments. Most likely no one else had seen the light dim in his eyes. But my heart ached for the pain I knew he felt, that this one little flame of hope he nurtured after so many years had been snuffed out.

You'd think he'd have wanted nothing to do with her after that, but no. I could hardly get her back from him. He carried her around the hall, showing her to everyone and saying, "Look at Venko's child! Isn't she a marvel? So exquisitely tiny and dark." It was as though, having seen for himself that the child was not his, he had to make sure everyone else knew it, too. No doubt he was right to do this, for if he had wondered, you can be sure every gossip in the land had speculated as well.

Then Gruoch entered the hall, followed by her women, and came straight to me with her hands held out. "Welcome, Kelda," she said politely, and kissed me on the cheek. Can you imagine? Gruoch, kissing me on the cheek as though I were the wife of any great warrior come to her husband's court. Well, I *was* a great warrior's wife—I just didn't feel like one. I had been a slave too many years.

Unfortunately for me, others felt the same. The queen may have greeted me with sisterly—if reserved—aplomb, but she was the only woman in the hall who did. They all knew I was the bedwench the king had been forced to put away, and they treated me with all the contempt that righteous Christian women have for bedwenches. When I sat at table in the hall—a very odd experience for me—no one wanted to sit next to me, and those forced to do so turned pointedly in the other direction to talk to their neighbor.

I was miserable. If I brought Siusan into the sun house where the women sat sewing and spinning, several would get up and leave. They would all have left, but Gruoch would not allow it. Carefully, deliberately, she called them by name and spoke of this or that, so they couldn't walk out while speaking to her; or sometimes she pointedly told them to sit down, that she desired their company, and would they be so good as to stay a while longer? It was sweet of her, but it was useless. You can't make people like someone they think is beneath them.

Walking down the corridor, I could hear the ill-concealed whispers: Viking slut. Heathen. Slave girl. King's wench. The men never said anything, although I could see them look askance when I entered a room, but the women were merciless. Finally I refused to go out from the guest chamber Venko and I had been given, pleading illness. There I sat crying all day, and I begged Venko at every opportunity to take me home.

After two days of my weeping, he was ready to comply. This bitter treatment of me had not escaped even his undiscerning eye, so you can well imagine it had not escaped Macbeatha's. When Venko announced to his lord that we would leave in the morning, Macbeatha had had enough. He sent for me.

The boards had been cleared from the hall, but everyone sat around the hearth with Macbeatha in a raised seat at their head. His eyes were cold and angry as I approached, so I felt like a slave girl again—one about to be reprimanded.

"Your husband tells me you wish to leave in the morning," he began. "But how can you think of traveling? I thought you were ill."

I said nothing.

"I think it is homesickness," Venko dissemble—badly. It goes hard on him to lie, and he doesn't do it well, so I bless his heart for trying. "I think she will be well once she is back home."

"No doubt," Macbeatha agreed, rising from his place to stroll around behind the benches and chairs. "There seems to be quite a *sickness* in this place. A general *malaise,* as it were." His hard eyes raked across those at the hearth, and the hall fell quiet. "I wonder if it has a name, this sickness? What do you think, Lady Mona?" he demanded of the mistress of the hall. "What should we call this foul spirit that seems to have infected everyone here? Shall we call it *pride,* I wonder?" He stopped just behind a pair of sisters and placed a hand on the shoulder of each, leaning over them. "Shall we call it a lack of Christian charity?"

The women sat with eyes downcast and cheeks flushed. "Perhaps we should just call it smallness of mind," he continued, moving on down the line. "Or meanness of spirit. Or perhaps we should call it *self-righteous hypocrisy."*

"Please, lord," I managed in a choked voice. "Let us just call it a mistake."

"A mistake!" he thundered. "There has been a mistake, all right, but it is not you who made it!"

"No, lord," I said quickly, finding my voice at last. "It is you who have made it."

He stopped dead, thunderstruck.

"Dogs bite, lord," I told him, "and bulls bellow, and eagles prey upon doves. We should not be surprised when they continue to do these things, even though we have bade them stop."

For a moment he did not know what to say. Then, "Men of reason are not beasts of the field," he argued.

"We all have our natures," I replied. "Mine is to serve, and I am no more comfortable sitting at table with these people than they are to have me. Please, lord. Let me take my child and go home. There I am mistress of my own household, and I am content in it." Before he could say more, I crossed to Gruoch and bobbed my head. "I thank you, lady, for your kindness," I told her sincerely, for I owed her that little word, at the very least; then turning to Mona, "and you, lady, for ... for shelter and for bread." Then, turning one last time to Macbeatha, I said, "Mercy becomes you, lord. Pray you, be not contemptuous of those who are weak, but teach them forgiveness by your example."

With that, I left the hall.

Oh, it was no great charity on my part, Fionna. If he had taken vengeance on them all, as they tell me he took vengeance on those who forced him to send me away, I couldn't have been happier. But he was the High King—he couldn't go about alienating his people because they snubbed a former slave girl. I should be flattered, I suppose, at his political blindness in this matter, but that is just what it was: blindness. I didn't want to be the cause of lost loyalties.

Besides, it was not only the attitude of the people in that hall that hurt me. To see him there, telling stories and dancing in the evening, mounting his horse to go hunting in the day—to have him call for ale, and me not fetch it! How I longed to cast aside my child and throw myself into his strong arms, to leave the bed I shared with Venko and crawl into his-- But all that was gone forever.

The next morning he came into the yard as we mounted our horses to leave. The red beard still looked odd to me, but a full beard is more common among Scots than a shaved chin, so I suppose it looked more natural to others. "Hurry back to us, Venko," he bade my husband. "I miss your strong arm at my side." Venko promised to come as soon as the planting was done. Then he came to stand beside my horse, and his eyes were soft.

"Forgive me, lord," I said with the steadiest voice I could manage, "for not being as strong as you would have me be."

"Forgive *me*," he said in return, "for not tearing you from that saddle and kissing you one last time."

"Done," I told him.

"And done," he replied.

We rode off into the chill morning, fog swirling around so that we could barely see the road, and before I was ever tempted to look back, he was lost from my sight. I did not see him again for many years.

Chapter Fourteen

In Fionna's hut

"What of Venko?" Fionna asked. "Did he stay on among his people, learning to raise cattle and sheep?"

Kelda shrugged. "He tried. But his interest in lambing and calving was short, and his patience with questions of when to plant and how much to slaughter for winter was even shorter. When spring came, I was glad enough to send him off to Macbeatha for the summer, and he was glad enough to go."

* * *

In the beginning, he came back every winter, but he came later and later each year, and some years he did not come at all. In truth, he was so little help when he was home, it was almost better not to have him around. He only told stories of battles and other events now far removed from my life, part of a world that was no longer mine.

Instead, I relied on our faithful steward, a kinsman of Venko's who was just as incapable of deceit or guile. And then there was Lonn. He was a man of property whose house was not far from ours, just over a hill and across a small stream. I often left my girls with Lonn's wife while I went out to work in the fields, for they liked the company of Lonn's children; and Ena, his wife, liked the ewe's milk and goose eggs and other such things I always brought her. Lonn was a great help to me as I learned the business of letting my cattle to clients, of calculating how many to send to market and how many to slaughter. He was a good friend and a source of strength, as well; and I do not know if my third child was his or Venko's, but it doesn't matter. The poor thing died within two weeks. My fourth child lived longer, but not much, and I began to despair that, like my mother, I should constantly labor and never know the fruits of my pain.

When my fifth child, a son, was born on a cold March eve and grew to be healthy and robust, I decided I had had enough. I named him Reagan, which means "little king," because the Hag said Venko would be the father of kings. When Venko returned that fall, I told him he should find whichever of the servants would accommodate him, but he was to come no more to my bed. I knew he kept a woman in Macbeatha's hall, and had at least two children by her—that I never begrudged him. But he would get no more children by me. My womb was closed.

I get ahead of myself, though. You want to know of Macbeatha, and I saw him once more during that time. It was before his pilgrimage to Rome—did you know he spoke with the Holy Father himself? And it was after the fever took my fourth child, so that sorrow and melancholy were my frequent companions, in spite of the fine June weather and how nicely the crops were coming in. There had been much raiding of cattle back and forth between Venko's people and another tribe, and on this day our younger men had gone off after the raiders.

With the men away, it was up to us women to tend the fields where the young plants were sprouting up. In no mood for company, I was by myself, hoeing in a stand of oats, my skirts tucked up around my waist, my bare feet and legs liberally coated with reddish dirt. Sweat trickled down my face as I hacked away at the offending weeds, my thoughts lost in some distant time. Suddenly I was seized from behind and a cold blade pressed to my throat. "Don't make a sound," a rough voice growled at me.

The hoe fell from my hand and I froze, casting my eyes frantically around to see just how far from the house I had gotten in my single-minded hoeing. Too far. Then there was a familiar chuckle in my ear, and the sweetest voice I knew said, "I suppose you're going to tell me you only wanted to see what was inside the chest."

The chest—? Oh, his sea chest! When Macbeatha had come to Thorfinn's hall and found me in his chamber, going through his things— "Damn you, Macbeatha, you scared the life out of me!" I exclaimed, my heart still hammering. "You're lucky I didn't die of fright right on the spot!" I remember thinking if I had been pregnant at the time, I might have miscarried—but of course, I didn't dare say that to him.

He loosened his grip on me then, and I turned in his arms to behold his eyes sparkling with delight. "Not you, you're too contentious to fall dead of a fright," he bantered. "But you're lucky I *wasn't* an outlaw, and it was not the sharp side of my blade at your throat. What are you doing, working this field by yourself?"

"Pretending I'm the lady of the hall," I grumbled. "Don't I look like one?" I stood back to indicate my filthy hands and legs, and the great smears of dirt on my skirts.

He threw back his head and laughed. "Ah, you are still my Kelda! I'm glad to see wealth and freedom have not changed you."

"Oh, they've changed me, all right," I assured him. "I never worked this hard when I was a slave." That made him laugh, too, and his joy was so infectious, I finally smiled grudgingly. "But what are you doing here?" I asked. "Is Venko with you?"

"My sister has spawned yet another son," he explained. "This one makes seven, and I have promised to receive him from the font at his baptism. We were on our way to her and ran into some of your folk chasing after cattle raiders. Since we were so close, I suggested to Venko that we come surprise you—but he was more interested in chasing the raiders. I told him if he hadn't the good sense to visit his wife when he had the opportunity, I would do it for him." Macbeatha's green eyes sparkled with that old wickedness. "So here I am."

There he was, indeed, as tall and handsome as ever he had been. His hair glittered with silver as well as gold now, but that only added dignity; and the lines that creased his forehead and framed his eyes and mouth simply carved more character into his regal countenance. "It's not fair," I said bluntly. "You show up after all these years looking like the god Thor himself, and I look like a—a—" I waved my dirty hands in frustration, unable to think of an apt comparison.

"Well, we can fix that!" he declared cheerfully; and without ceremony he scooped me up and carried me off across the field in the direction of a stream. I protested most of the way, but he only laughed and shifted me up and over his shoulder like a sack of oats, chiding me to hold still and not make a mess of his fine linen tunic. You can imagine how I responded to that: by the time we reached the stream, there were as many dirty finger prints on the back of his tunic as I could manage. It perturbed him not in the least. He waded out into the shallow, icy water and plopped me into it anyway. I shrieked and splashed at him, but he only laughed and grabbed one of my feet, rubbing at the dirt on it—which kept me from getting up, of course. In a matter of moments we were both soaked.

Then, as he raised me up and rubbed a streak of mud from my cheek with his calloused thumb, his eyes softened and the merry smile faded into wistfulness. Deep within me I felt an old familiar ache, so fierce it stopped my breath. Gently, oh, so gently, he took my face in both his hands and brushed his lips across mine. "How I have missed you," he whispered. Tears sprang to my eyes, and the only response I could make was to find his mouth with mine. The shock of that touch leapt to my breast like a flame.

Suddenly the flame swept through us both, igniting passions long dormant and tinder dry. We were consumed with our desire for each other, becoming a mindless inferno that must blaze like the Beltaine fire until there is nothing left to fuel it. We struggled out of our wet clothes and rutted on the bank of the stream like two wild things that come into season but once a year. The intensity of our joining left me gasping, as I had not had cause to gasp in a very long time.

For long, long moments afterwards we lay in each other's arms, our contented bodies warmed by the summer sunshine. I felt a kind of peace and security I had not felt since that day long ago when my little lamb did his best to interfere in our play. Oh, how desperately I wished for those days to come back! But they never would. Finally Macbeatha rolled off to one side of me, and I felt the breeze cool against my bare skin where he had lain.

"I wasn't going to do that," he said softly.

Finding that a curious notion, I turned onto my side and looked at him. "Why not?" I asked. Surely he didn't imagine Venko would mind! And my consent was rather obvious.

His mouth twisted in a wry smile. "Believe it or not," he told me, "I have been a faithful husband since the day you left."

Now I stared at him as though he had sprouted a third green eye in the center of his forehead. He laughed at my expression. "Upon the cross, it's true," he insisted ruefully. "Difficult, mind you, but true."

"Why?" I asked, mystified. "That is not in your nature."

He shrugged. "Perhaps *because* it is not in my nature. To prove to myself that I can." He plucked a blade of new green grass and put its stem between his lips. "To show my accusers that I could do without you or any other, save my wife." For a moment he chewed thoughtfully on the grass; then he cast it aside and admitted, "Because I would never again allow them to use anyone to strike at me that way."

With a sigh I rolled again onto my back and stared up at the puffy white clouds scudding across the sky, pushed by the southwesterly winds. "I can't believe I was ever that stupid," I told him. "Had I the good sense to be discreet ... I am sorry if I have been the source of any pain for you."

But he reached over and stroked my cheek. "You have never caused me any pain," he replied. "Some aggravation from time to time, but not pain. No one in this world has been less trouble to me than you."

"To leave off women entirely, though!" I exclaimed. "At the festival fires, too? And on campaign?" I knew how hot his blood flowed at such times. "I would never have left, if I thought you would be denied such comforts because of it."

He gave a regretful chuckle. "Your staying would have made no difference. It was my choice, not yours." Then he prodded me with an accusing finger. "And don't make it sound as though I had no woman to my bed at all. I have a wife, remember, and a very satisfactory one. She has never turned me from her chamber door."

That was not exactly what I wanted to hear about at that moment. But of the dozen things that sprang to my mind to say, I fortunately chose to voice none. Instead I turned onto my stomach and plucked at the grass growing so rich and lush around us. "And how is the Lady Gruoch?" I asked politely. At least, I meant it to be polite.

He hesitated a moment before he answered. "She is well," he replied simply. Then, sitting up, he said with more animation, "Lulach comes back from fosterage next spring. We will celebrate his coming of age at the Festival of St. Mary, and then he will ride with me in my warband. Can you believe it?" He rambled on for a time about the boy's exploits, his intelligence, his courage, and I wondered briefly how a question about Gruoch had become a discussion of Lulach's virtues.

At one point, he dutifully asked, "And how are your daughters?" I smiled and told him they were both well enough, growing like the weeds I'd been hoeing in the field. "No, not weeds!" he protested. "Like flowers. They must be comely children, with such a beautiful mother. Would that I could see them, but ..." He sighed contentedly and pulled me back into his arms. "I have only a few hours to spend with you, and I am too selfish to share you with your children for even one moment of that time." It was a lovely lie. I knew he had no great desire to look upon the children some other man had given me.

We talked for long hours then, and he told me of many events that had transpired since I'd last seen him. Moray and Atholl had gone on campaign together against marauding Irish, but a fracas had broken out and Crinan had been killed. Macbeatha was plainly disturbed by this; it had been his intent to heal the breach between the two Great Tribes, and instead, the rift had worsened. His old nemesis Siward, Jarl of Northumbria, had crossed the Tweed the previous summer and gotten all the way to the River Forth before Macbeatha arrived with five thousand men and pushed him back. Macbeatha said Siward would never have been so bold if Thorfinn hadn't been engaged in a civil war with his nephew Ragnvald.

My heart twinged, for I'd had a visit from my brother Hakon not long before and learned from him that my mother was dead. It was sad to think she never knew that I, too, had gained my freedom—that would have pleased her so. But I tried not to think of it, asking instead how my lord Thorfinn fared these days. Macbeatha's face brightened as he told me he would go visit him after he had seen Brenna. "Please give him my greetings," I said. "If that is not impertinent."

"You have always been impertinent—that is what I love about you." Then he gave me a wistful smile. "But you are a free woman now, Kelda, and a rich one. You may give greetings to whomever you please."

"May I truly?" I asked slyly. "Then give your sister my greetings when you see her."

He grimaced. "Perhaps it's best not to do that," he conceded. "Unless you want *her* men down here raiding your cattle, too."

"*Her* men?"

At that he laughed. "Oh, yes, I'm afraid so. Her husband Farrell hardly strays from his hearth anymore because of his bad leg—and because my sister bullies him, most likely. And although he has a cousin who leads his warband, I suspect it is Brenna who tells them when and where to fight. They joined me against Siward last year, and Brenna came along. She stayed in camp, of course, during the actual battle, but believe me, her presence was felt."

"Why, I'm shocked," said I, "knowing her gentle manner, and the peaceful nature of all her kin." Macbeatha laughed even more and cuddled me in his arms.

The sun now drifted toward the tops of the western mountains. Macbeatha noted its position regretfully. Somewhere during the course of our meeting I'd had the presence of mind to spread our clothes out to dry—but then, it seemed I was forever drying clothes, or mending them, or stitching new ones. I think my hands do these things on their own with no direction at all from my mind. Anyway, as he reached for his tunic, I put out a hand to stop him. "Take me once more," I whispered.

But he shook his head. "No," he said regretfully. "I should not have done it even one time. It is a vow I made to myself, and that is the worst kind to break. A man must be in charge of his nature, not his nature in charge of him." Still his eyes ran wistfully over my form, and he said with a smile, "But you have always been irresistible to me."

"And you have always been a liar. But lie to me anyway—I prefer it to the truth."

He reached out then and touched the soft creases that had begun to form at the corners of my mouth, as they also clustered around my eyes and across my forehead. And as I saw him study those marks of time, I knew he was comparing me, not to the girl he had once known, but to the wife whose face had begun to show the same marks. "Did she ever learn to smile?" I asked.

His eyes betrayed his startlement. "Gruoch?"

"Since there is no other."

A mask of indifference appeared on his face, and he shrugged. "She smiles. You know that."

"For others," I agreed. "But does she smile for you?"

He was a moment in answering. "She is everything a man could want in a wife."

"Is that a yes or a no?"

"It's a yes!" he snapped, then immediately repented his loss of temper. I could see it in his eyes. But I was not finished.

"She smiles for Lulach," I guessed.

His mouth twisted in a wry smile. "Everyone smiles for Lulach. He is a joy and a delight." Then he forced a laugh. "What, do you imagine I am jealous of my own son?" His smile faded only a little as he corrected himself. "Stepson."

Now it was me who reached for the clothing that lay drying on the grass. I dressed slowly while he watched; then I helped him into his tunic and trousers, and arranged the folds of his cloak carefully, as though I had never left his service. When I fastened the clasp on his chest, he put his arms around me once more. "Come back to court," he pleaded softly. "I miss you. I miss your smile and your laughter, your wit and your audacity. Don't come as my lover, but as my friend. A king has so few friends, Kelda."

But I shook my head. "Don't you remember what happened at Aberdeen? I will not live that way, Macbeatha, scorned by the people around me. Here I have dignity. Here I am respected. My daughters will grow up with pride, and no one will whisper behind their backs that their mother is a heathen Viking slut. No, my lord, I will come no more to your court, as lover or friend or anything else. My life is here now. Yours is there."

"I will come to you again," he whispered.

"No, you won't," I insisted. "Lord, do us both a favor and take a mistress somewhere. Keep her secret if you like, although flaunting her would be better, but give up this silly vow of faithfulness. It gives the Lady Gruoch too much power over you."

He pulled back, offended. "Gruoch has no power over me save that I choose to give her."

I sighed and disengaged his arms from around me, keeping his sword-hardened hands in mine. "She plays you like one of those chess pieces," I said wearily. "After all these years, she remains the one thing you have never quite conquered, and that is how she binds you to her. So put her back in her place: take a mistress. Let her wonder again who it is you really love. You will both be happier for it."

I could see the denial on his face, and the stubborn set of his features, so I gave up. "Good-bye, my lord," I said, brushing my lips against his one last time. Then I walked away from him, picked up my hoe, and went back to work.

Chapter Fifteen

At Edinburgh

"*L*ord?"

Malcolm Canmore looked up from his reverie to see a serving boy standing in the doorway. "Pardon, lord," the lad squeaked in his unchanged voice. "It's the Dark One. He's at one of the serving girls again, got her shoved up against a wall, threatening to cut her ear off."

Scowling, Malcolm strode from the chamber, muttering under his breath as he went. If it wasn't one trial, it was another. He hadn't really understood that when he fled Scone as a child, for when Mother had packed them up and bundled them out of the royal residence, they'd gone straight to his uncle Maldred in Strathclyde, and Malcolm had liked it there. It was a happy place, and there was his cousin Gospadruig who knew all manner of places to go snaring rabbits, and who loved to play at battles with Malcolm and Donall.

But Mother was unhappy, restless. She whined at Maldred to raise an army and go depose the usurper, until Maldred finally hit her and told her to shut up. When spring came and Maldred still gave no sign of taking up arms against Macbeatha, Mother packed again. She bade Malcolm mount his pony, and took Morggan in her arms, but Donall she left behind. "Foster him for me," she said to Maldred. "Three boys are too many for me to care for when I have no husband." And off they went to Mother's cousin Siward, who had recently become Jarl of Northumbria.

Siward welcomed them warmly, calling Malcolm a little king and listening sympathetically as Mother poured out her story about the demon jarl who murdered his sworn king and stole the kingdom away from the rightful heir. "Fear not, cousin," Siward had pronounced nobly, "I shall right this wrong for you. I will attack the Scots this very season and put the wretched usurper to flight."

But something had gone wrong. In later years, Malcolm learned that Macbeatha had turned out to be a more formidable enemy than Siward anticipated. That, he decided, was an error on Siward's part. Hadn't the usurper killed Duncan? One had to be a shrewd and powerful warrior to defeat a great king like Duncan. And Siward paid the price for underestimating Macbeatha: he came back to York without a victory, and had to listen to Mother haranguing him for the next year.

Actually, it took less than a year for Siward to tire of his cousin's tirade, and he sent her off to some other kinsman for a time. Then the prince Edward Aetheling, called Edward the Confessor, came back from exile in Normandy to be consecrated king of the Anglish, and there was a new power in the land. Mother packed again.

This time it was Morggan who was left behind.

Mother presented herself at Edward's court in the guise of a beleaguered widow, hounded by the usurper who had banished her and her son, and begged asylum. Edward graciously took her in. Thus Malcolm, who was then twelve, came to live among the pages and princes of King Edward's court.

He showed great promise as a warrior, and the royal armsmaster undertook his training with relish. King Edward himself took notice, praising Malcolm's quick mind and his beautiful singing voice, as well as his aptitude with sword and spear. This might have inspired the young prince to greater effort, except that Malcolm needed no further inspiration. He was already driven to excel by two things: his determination to win back his kingdom, and his hatred of the usurper who had stolen it.

Malcolm met all manner of powerful men at court, learning first-hand the intricacies and machinations of political intrigue. And whenever someone asked Edward who that intense young man was, the one with the curling hair and the strong face, King Edward would say, "Oh, that is the King of Scots. His father was murdered, you see, and he has come to me for sanctuary. Someday we shall see him back upon his throne."

See him back upon his throne! That must mean Edward intended to help. It had to mean Edward would help. Malcolm clung to the promise as tightly as he clung to his sword. But remembering Siward's experience, Malcolm knew he would have to be very strong to defeat Macbeatha in battle. So he trained hard, and he cultivated the friendship of the most promising young warriors. When he was old enough to engage in battles, he and his friends fought in skirmishes across the country; but always he returned to court, so that Edward might never forget about him. If he was to regain his kingdom, Malcolm needed an army, and who but Edward could give him one?

By this point Mother had become an embarrassment. Malcolm lived in dread that she would press Edward too hard about restoring her son's crown, and the offended monarch would send them away as Siward had done. But luck was with him: Mother had attached herself to Queen Edith, and when that lady's family fell from grace during political in-fighting, Mother was sent with Edith to an abbey in Hampshire, there to be imprisoned. Malcolm was so happy, he was tempted to help her pack.

Once she was gone, he began his careful campaign. While Edward's mind was occupied with internal strife, Malcolm spoke casually of the time when he would sit upon the throne of Alba and protect Edward's northern border for him. He spoke of the thousands of men he would command as a monarch, and how they would be available to aid Edward. When his kinsman, Siward of Northumbria, readied an army to defend the king against an exiled enemy's return, Malcolm—who was by then twenty-one—rushed to join the troops and prove his courage and worth to the Anglish king. "For I am rightwise king of Alba," he told Edward when he came again to court, "and I would not see another monarch thrust from his throne, as I was thrust from mine."

Edward had almost forgotten that this woolly young warrior was not one of his own subjects. He eyed the young man from head to toe and finally said, "Perhaps it is time to consider how we shall redress your grievance."

Time! It was past time, as far as Malcolm was concerned. His father had ruled Strathclyde and Cumbria from the age of eighteen; if Edward would only give him an army, he knew he could rule Alba.

But Edward had his own problems. A native faction of nobles had gained power, and to placate them, Edward must dispose of his Norman friends, who were viewed as odious foreigners. Two of the ousted Norman knights fled with their retinues to Alba, where they were received by the usurper. Malcolm did not hesitate to impart this knowledge to Edward, who grew uncomfortable at the thought of his disgruntled former retainers in league with the powerful king on his northern border.

But as carefully as he fanned this flame, Malcolm found his benefactor reluctant to take action upon it. No, no, he couldn't send an army north from London, he needed his army here. Yes, yes, he would put Malcolm back on his throne, but it had to be done carefully. Malcolm, he claimed, didn't understand the intricacies of politics. Malcolm, he said, was young and headstrong. Older, wiser heads were needed here.

Finally Malcolm seized upon a plan, which he set before Edward. Let his cousin Siward of Northumbria collect an army and lead it against Alba on Edward's behalf. Edward risked nothing, and Siward was a seasoned warrior who had fought the Scots before. Surely he was just the man to reinstate Malcolm.

This notion intrigued King Edward. Yes, Siward was a good man, and loyal. But asking him to attack a foreign power—would he undertake such a mission for his king?

Siward was more than ready to attack Macbeatha. He had been forced to retreat twice from the Scottish king, thwarting his designs to retake the rest of Lothian. If Edward would send money and supplies, Siward would lead an invasion. This one would be carefully planned. This one would involve a two-pronged attack: a land army going by horse up through Lothian, and a fleet sailing directly into the Firth of Tay. The ships would carry supplies as well as warriors. That had been the problem in the past: in order to carry the war up to Fife and even Atholl, one had to traverse the occupied portion of Lothian. A war leader was likely to find his supply lines cut off behind him.

After some wavering, Edward decided he would pronounce his blessing upon the adventure, providing a small purse and a few dozen men as a sign of his royal approval. Siward growled at the meager offering, but he took it. Malcolm rushed to his cousin's capital in York. The time was at hand. His destiny was upon him. They were about to invade Alba.

At least, that was what the young prince thought. Arriving in York, he was much surprised to find no assembled troops, no baggage train being loaded, no visible signs of preparation to march. Leaving Edward's men in the yard, Malcolm dismounted and clattered up the stairs into his kinsman's hall, demanding to see Siward. After being passed from one lackey to another, he was finally directed to Siward's map chamber where he found his mother's cousin, not pouring over charts of the eastern seaboard, but leaning back idly in a chair with his boots propped on a table, conversing with his steward about how much land had been seeded to oats this year.

Siward glanced up at the young man in the doorway. "Ah, Malcolm!" *he greeted cheerily.* "Come in, come in! How are things in the south?"

Stunned, Malcolm stepped into the room. "Where's your army?" *he asked, more stupefied than angry.* "Why are you not ready to march?"

Siward gave a short barking laugh. "March!" *He pulled his boots off the table one at a time, letting them clomp as they hit the floor.* "March! We don't march till we've done our planning, boy. Now that you're here, we can begin." *He dismissed his steward with a nod.*

"Begin!" *Malcolm squeaked, his voice breaking in an embarrassing fashion.* "Begin! I thought it was done! An army of horse by land, and a fleet by sea."

Now Siward's eyes glittered coldly. "You call that planning?" *he asked, with just the hint of a sneer.* "Oh, yes, you were tutored by Edward, weren't you. Well, here. Bring me that map." *He jabbed a thick finger at a rolled parchment lying on a small table by the window. Obligingly, Malcolm fetched the sheepskin and handed it to the older warrior. Siward spread it out on the table before them.* "All right. Here we are in York," *Siward said, stabbing a spot on the map where a delicate drawing of a tower inside a circle indicated the fortified city.* "Here's your country of Alba." *He gave a wave of his hand over a large expanse of crooked lines and inverted chevrons and circles with letters printed beside them.* "Show me how you will attack."

Malcolm studied the map carefully. He could read its symbols well enough, its wavy rivers and humped hills and sharp coastline. The letters meant nothing to him, for any attempt to teach him writing had ceased when he fled Alba, but he could identify the major settlements by their relationship to geographical features. "We strike for his heart," the prince said decisively. "We seek him out in his capital at Scone. Even if we don't kill him—which I intend to do—if we can take Scone, we take control of the valley called Strathmore, which is a veritable highway into Alba."

Locating that town on the map, he mused, "But to get to Scone by land, we should go up the coast here, by Jarrow." He traced the line with his finger. "We cross the Tyne here, the Tweed there, and go along the south bank of the River Forth till we reach a suitable crossing. Then it's across these hills and meet our fleet here, on the Firth of Tay. Rest, resupply, and up the Tay to Scone." Looking up at his kinsman, Malcolm beamed at his own grasp of strategy.

Siward did not look as impressed as the young man had expected. True, he nodded his head as he considered this, but then he said, "If we leave from York, it will take us three days to reach the Tweed. It's at least two days' march from the there to the Tay. Rest for a day, that makes six. What do you suppose the High King of Alba will be doing all this time?"

Malcolm looked blank. He hadn't thought about that. He thought about it now. "Will he know we're coming?" the young man asked uncertainly.

Siward snorted. "He has couriers and relays and signal fires and such all through northern Lothian," the jarl replied. "A fly doesn't break wind north of the Tyne but what Macbeatha hears of it by nightfall."

Malcolm stared at the map again. Six days ...

"You might like to find him in Scone," Siward continued, "but more likely he'll fall on you from the hills outside Edinburgh. If he can't get his warriors together fast enough to do that, he'll be waiting when you cross the Forth. And then what?"

Cheeks burning, Malcolm turned back to the map. He didn't want to fight the usurper at Edinburgh, or at the Forth, he wanted to fight him at Scone. He'd always dreamed of it: storming that fortress, chopping off the usurper's head with his sword and then hanging it from the battlements ... There must be a way. Men on horseback, in full armor, a baggage train—no. No baggage train. The baggage must go by ship. "A forced march," he said decisively. "No baggage. We gather in the uplands south of the Tweed, rather than here in York. Our movements are less likely to be noticed

in the hills, away from the main roads. Then we leave at night—preferably a cloudy night, hoping for fog in the morning to screen us even longer. We can be past Edinburgh and crossing the Forth before anyone knows we're on the march."

Now Siward raised an eyebrow. "That's a possibility," he admitted. "That's a good possibility. But between the Forth and the Tay lies Fife. The Jarl of Fife isn't going to let you trot through his province uncontested." He gave Malcolm a measuring look. "And your troops will be exhausted."

Malcolm frowned and shook his head. "Fife won't be able to raise more than five hundred, seven hundred men at short notice."

"So?"

"Surely he won't attack a much larger force with only seven hundred men!"

Siward gave a low chuckle. "You don't know your own people very well, do you?"

"Well, if he does attack with that number, we can handle it," Malcolm dismissed. "Then it's a short space through these hills to where we meet our fleet."

"And the High King's fleet? Where is it going to be?"

"Patrolling the seas, I assume," Malcolm answered airily. In fact, he hadn't known the usurper had a fleet.

Again Siward chuckled. "Oh, is that right? Very well, let's for the moment say that the Scottish fleet is off somewhere, completely unaware of our arrival, and that our army reaches the Tay without huge losses. Now you've got Macbeatha in his fortress at Scone—what do you do next? Lay siege?"

"He'll come out," Malcolm said confidently. "We could lay siege, with our fleet right there to supply us, but he'll come out. I know he will."

"Oh, he'll come out, all right," Siward agreed. "He'll come out when his Moraymen have come down your Strathmore valley from the north. He'll come out when Thorfinn of Orkney, his friend and ally, has sailed down to join the Scottish fleet in challenging ours. He'll come out on his terms, my young cousin, and not on yours."

"Then we'll fight him!" Malcolm cried impatiently. "That's why we're going!"

"You'll fight ten thousand men and two fleets?"

Malcolm paused, blood pounding, nostrils flaring. He had to fight the usurper, he had to get his throne back, he—he—

"What do you suggest?" he asked tightly.

A slow smile spread across Siward's face. "I'm glad you asked that," he said dryly. "You may make a king after all, if you can keep that temper in check. By the grace of God and the support of King Edward, I might be able to put you on the throne of Alba; but unless you can keep a level head and see things rationally, you'll never be able to hold it. So pull up a chair, boy, and pay attention, because I'm about to explain to you some very important facts—not only about waging war, but about your country and its people—most especially its present king. And if you don't take every word to heart, you'll be dead in six months, and I'll have to bide my time until I can put your little brother Morggan on the throne. Understand?"

Malcolm understood. Forcing away his pride, he drew up a chair while Siward began his instruction.

The first fact Siward impressed upon the young prince was just how dangerous a man Macbeatha, King of Scots, really was. Not only was he a fearless warrior, but he was a cunning strategist. He had never lost a battle. Never. Malcolm learned for the first time how his father Duncan had blundered at Durham against Siward's father-in-law Ealdred, and how the army of the Scots would not have escaped at all, had it not been for Macbeatha. This went down hard. Mother had never represented Duncan as anything other than a courageous warrior and a masterful king.

What made Macbeatha even more dangerous, Siward continued, was the broad-based support he had in Alba. Siward had seen him raise ten, fifteen thousand troops for a battle. It was easy to get men to fight for a king who'd never lost. Among the folk of Alba, it was widely believed that Macbeatha enjoyed magical protection, that his victory had been insured by charms, and that he himself could not be killed by an ordinary mortal.

But what gave his strength of numbers even more potency was the network of information that funneled in to the high king. He seemed always to know what was going on in every part of his kingdom. Couriers rode the length and breadth of the land, adding what they saw with their own eyes to the reports they carried back from the chieftains and the priests in hill and dale. There were signal fires set upon heights and in towers, and horns that blew at appointed times. He probably had informants in Edward's court, and it was quite likely he knew Malcolm was coming.

Malcolm considered that. "We could let out false information," he suggested.

Siward nodded. "The night march is a good idea. If we can find a quiet, out-of-the-way harbor to assemble our fleet, that will help, too. If we can attack him before all his forces are raised, we have a chance. But we can't spend weeks in a siege. We've got to draw him out somehow. And there's one other thing we can do." He grinned wolfishly at his kinsman. "Do you still have friends in Atholl?"

Malcolm brightened, seeing immediately where this was going. "I have kinsmen there, yes. My mother has kept in touch with them. And I have a brother in Cumbria—"

But Siward waved that off. "Your cousin Gospadruig may claim to be king in Cumbria, but Macbeatha's put one of his own kinsmen just north in Strathclyde. Your brother and your cousin will never get past him. These other kin of yours, though, where are they?"

"Dunkeld, I think, up the Tay from Scone."

"You think!" Siward growled. "Find out! Get in touch with them immediately—but discreetly. Find out their numbers. Find out how willing they are to support you for the high kingship. If they will rise up and join us ..." Siward's grin was malicious. "I have a strategy in mind that just might work."

Chapter Sixteen

In Fionna's hut

Time was short; Fionna could feel it. The man tracking Kelda was close now, following her trail through the heather, hunting her single-mindedly. The old woman knew her hut was well-hidden, but this man, the way he tracked-- She had cast her stones across the floor once more, but they said nothing of him, who he was or why he pursued the Norsewoman. Dipping up another draught of her brew, she pressed the cup into her guest's hand. Kelda trembled as she took it; but then she drew from some inner well and her face grew calm, her hands steady. She sipped carefully at the hot liquid, closing her eyes as it slid down her throat.

"That day by the stream—that was not the last you saw of the king," Fionna prodded.

"No," Kelda admitted. "But it was the last until after Dundee. Until after Dunsinnan."

* * *

We had heard, over the years, how Duncan's widow had carted her three sons around to their various kin after leaving Scone, urging anyone who would listen—and those who would not—to raise up an army and depose Macbeatha. She finally found welcome at the court of the new Anglish king, Edward the Confessor, and there she raised Colmbeag. Quite naturally, as he attained manhood, he took up his mother's plea for aid to set him upon the throne of Alba, which he considered his by right of birth.

Edward could hardly hold his own kingdom, let alone give a Scottish prince armies to march on Alba. Nevertheless, when the young man turned 21, Edward gave him a handful of warriors, promised him the aid of Siward of Northumbria, and sent him forth to conquer.

When Macbeatha learned that Canmore and Siward were amassing troops in Northumbria, he called for the largest warband in many seasons and spent most of the summer in Edinburgh, patrolling frequently in the area near the Tweed. The season wore on, though, and there was no sign of northward movement. Men grew weary of patrolling with no enemy to fight. Macbeatha took them over into Strathclyde for a change of scenery, and to acquaint Lulach with that country. Macbeatha had split it off from Cumbria and installed one of his clients to rule there, while Maldred's son Gospadruig held Cumbria. But it is traditional for the High King's tanist to hone his skills as king of Strathclyde and Cumbria, so everyone expected Lulach would soon claim them both.

Just before Midsummer, messengers brought word of an interesting development. Siward and Malcolm Canmore had quarreled, and Canmore had ridden back to Lincoln, taking Edward's men with him. Siward had disbanded his army and sent them home, saying he would not venture north for the glory of such a spoiled brat, and that King Edward had better teach the boy some manners if he expected Siward to do anything for him. Macbeatha breathed a sigh of relief; he had not wanted to fight against the boy he once bounced on his knee and coached in the use of his toy sword.

So Macbeatha returned to Scone, dismissing those warriors who wished to celebrate Midsummer at home. But a week before the festival, Siward attacked. Canmore's departure had been a ruse; they had reassembled their army in the Uplands and moved out in the blackness of a new moon, riding quickly through Lothian and past Edinburgh before they were sighted. The Mormaer of Fife caught them at the river crossing near Sterling on the Forth and took some toll of their numbers, but he hadn't a large enough force to do anything more than delay them. Still, he had done that, and the army that struggled out of the Ochil Hills to the south bank of the Tay was tired, hungry, and thinned out by Scottish spears.

In Scone, Macbeatha prepared for their assault. There were full two thousand men still with him, but Siward had twice that. Hurried messages were sent out to all the Great Tribes to recall those brave men who would fight the Northumbrians. In the meantime, the High King left only a small band to hold Scone while he and the bulk of his troops retreated into the Sidlaw Hills northeast of town to await their reinforcements. If Siward tried to cross the river and attack Scone, he would be outflanked by the warriors in the hills; and if he passed it by and came after Macbeatha, the Moraymen coming down from the north would take him from the rear.

But Siward did neither of these things. Instead, his army forded the Tay just before dawn—a time when no Scot would cross such a boundary for fear of crossing into the Otherworld—and took an abrupt right turn. Down the north shore toward the east they went, carefully skirting the hills where Macbeatha lay. As Venko tells it, the High King watched them pass, his forehead creased in a puzzled frown. "What is he doing?" Macbeatha murmured. "Does he think to outflank me? Surely he knows I can see everything he does ..."

Suddenly a fire kindled in his green eyes. "By God, he's got a fleet coming! The only way he could get this far this fast is to travel without baggage, with virtually no supplies. That means he expects supplies here, and that means a fleet. But it would be dangerous to bring a fleet this far up the Tay, where they could be trapped by our own ships, so it will meet him ..."

"At Dundee," Owen supplied.

"Exactly," Macbeatha agreed emphatically. "The firth is wide and the shore hospitable there. And once resupplied, he will challenge me here."

It was too late to hurry and take the fortress of Dundee, on the north bank of the Firth of Tay, but Macbeatha was not inclined to be cooped up inside fortress walls anyway. "We can ask no better position than these hills," he declared. "We'll fall on them from here—as soon as more warriors arrive." That meant they would have to give Siward's men a chance to rest and recuperate from their forced march. It was not what anyone wanted, but it was the best they could do under the circumstances.

That day seven hundred men arrived from Cirech, and five hundred more from Ce turned up the day after. Fortriu also sent five hundred, and Fife had now gathered additional men and joined the High King with near a thousand. Moray was on its way, but would not arrive for another day at least—longer for those coming from the western areas.

"Where is Atholl?" Macbeatha fretted. "Two hundred are still here, but I had five hundred earlier this season. The others haven't that far to return to me—where are they?"

"That's Malcolm mac Duncan with Siward," Owen reminded him. "Perhaps we don't want Atholl."

Macbeatha growled, counted his troops, and made a decision. "I won't wait any longer," he announced. "We attack tomorrow."

There were no surprises now; Siward knew where Macbeatha was, and Macbeatha knew where Siward was. The High King issued a formal challenge, and Siward accepted. Day came; priests on both sides gave absolution to their warriors; the morning fog rolled away; and the Scots howled down out of the hills toward the Northumbrians, their voices raised in their battle cry: *"Albanaich!"*—Men of Alba.

Before the hills lay the lowland of the Carse of Gowrie. Soon the sandy soil just west of Dundee drank the blood of the slain on both sides of the field. With their backs to the water, the Northumbrians had no place to retreat; with the soil of their homeland beneath their feet, the Scots had no intention of retiring. It was four days before Midsummer, and across the water in the cathedral at Abernethy, monks chanted the liturgy for the Feast of the Seven Sleepers; but in Gowrie, only the dead slept. Living men drove their horses at their enemies, swinging swords and casting spears and throwing axes.

Macbeatha sent horsemen around to the northeast in a flanking maneuver, but Siward had anticipated this. The night before, young Canmore had taken a force into position at the base of the hills there, lying in ambush. As the horses charged down the slope, they bypassed the hidden Northumbrians, then found themselves caught between two bodies of enemy warriors. They were cut down swiftly.

The loss of those horsemen was a terrible blow to Macbeatha. The Bishop of Scone sat high up on a hill overlooking the battlefield, bearing a reliquary of St. Colm and praying mightily for victory for the Scots, but things did not look good. Siward's fleet had delivered fresh infantry troops to augment his four thousand horse, and all wore armor. More than half Macbeatha's forces were afoot, men of great courage but poor means who lacked horse and armor both. The Northumbrian cavalry made a slaughter of them. The odds turned against the Scots, and they fought desperately to hold the field.

Macbeatha had just ridden to the top of a small rise to assess the situation when a messenger reached him. "What is that banner?" the messenger demanded, pointing across the field.

Macbeatha followed his finger. In the east, where his horsemen had been ambushed from the rear, a red banner flew with a gold design stitched upon it. "It must be Colmbeag," he guessed. "Those were his father's colors." Then when the breeze snapped the red cloth out full, he saw the emblem Canmore had chosen, and the color drained from his face. It was a slender twig with a cluster of tiny leaves: a sprig of rowan. The messenger addressed him grimly. "Lord, men of Atholl are coming down the Strathmore. A thousand, at least. But it is Canmore's name on their lips, and they all have sprigs of rowan fastened to their cloaks."

The rowan. We learned later that as they passed through Birnam Wood, the warriors of Atholl had cut sprigs from the trees there and pinned them to their cloaks as emblems of their support for Malcolm Canmore. At last Macbeatha knew what the Hag had meant when she prophesied the rowan would defeat him.

But she didn't say when, and my lord was determined it would not be that day. He called an immediate retreat, falling back into the hills. Siward's men rushed after them and paid the price for such foolishness. It is one thing to fight a man on level ground where there is room to swing a sword or cast a weapon; it is quite another to root him out of the forested hills. Siward called them back and retired to Dundee. Fifteen hundred Northumbrians died in the battle of Gowrie, or so they say, including Siward's nephew and his oldest son. But the Scots suffered worse: three thousand brave warriors did not return to their homes and their families except by the "low road," as the Scots say, the one that traverses the Otherworld with Death as its portal.

Macbeatha brought his remaining troops all the way through the hills to a place on the western edge called Dunsinnan, where an ancient hill fort crowned a steep bluff. In that crumbling but defensible place, they gathered and regrouped while Macbeatha paced the hilltop and thought, and thought, and thought. "We cannot let Atholl join with Siward," he said decisively. "They are too many in numbers, they will assail this hill and take it."

"Moray comes," Owen reminded him.

"Aye, but Atholl is between us and them. Even if Moray could reach us, together we would not be enough. Siward has numbers, and armor, and supplies. We are cut off."

"More will come, lord," Venko insisted.

"Not in time." Macbeatha shook his head, pacing still upon the brow of the hill. "And our men have lost heart after today's battle. They will lose even more once they learn Atholl has turned against me. No, we cannot fight under these conditions. I must go to Siward."

"You will surrender?" Venko asked in horror.

"I will never surrender!" Macbeatha snarled. "They'll have to separate my head from my body first. But I can bargain with Siward." He smiled coldly. "I know what he wants."

* * *

In Fionna's hut

Suddenly the hide covering on Fionna's door snapped back and a grizzled warrior thrust his head through the opening. "There you are!" he cried when he saw Kelda seated inside. "Now you will—" But his words were cut short as he gritted his teeth in agony and pitched forward onto the dirt floor.

Chapter Seventeen

At Edinburgh

As he clattered down the stairs ahead of the serving boy, Malcolm Canmore wondered at how naïve he had been when he first fought the usurper. So many things he hadn't understood about his enemy, about his allies-- Was it only three years ago? He felt he had aged a decade since then.

The invasion started out well enough. He and Siward had staged a quarrel that ended with Siward declaring he wouldn't waste men and money putting such a self-centered brat on the Scottish throne, and Malcolm leaving York as if returning to London. Then he'd turned back under cover of night and met up with the Northumbrian forces to begin their march north through Lothian. They had been crossing the River Forth before anyone tried to stop them.

In Fife they met resistance, and Malcolm learned firsthand the cursed tactics of the Scots of Alba: all the way from the Forth to the Tay, spears shot out from behind trees, small bands of warriors burst forth to cut down stragglers, and trip wires sprang traps that maimed their horses or unleashed tree branches to knock fully armed men from their mounts. They were pelted with stones and pierced with knives that seemed to spring like magic from the bushes themselves. But Siward, who had fought the Scots before, snapped and snarled at his troops like a sheepdog, rounding them up and keeping them in formation until they rested upon the shores of the Firth of Tay, where their fleet was scheduled to meet them.

There things began to go wrong. Troops aboard the fleet should have taken the town of Abernethy before the horsemen arrived, to provide a safe base for the march up the River Tay and the attack on Scone. But the fleet was not waiting, and the town was still in the hands of the Scots. Later they learned the Northumbrian admiral, seeing how well-defended it was, had not even tried to land, but instead left word for Siward to meet him at Dundee. It was, the admiral had said, a much better landing site.

No doubt it was better for the fleet, but it put the cavalry in a damned awkward position. In order to get there, they had to go practically across Macbeatha's doorstep. Even at this time of year, there was no suitable river crossing any nearer than the one at Scone. They might ferry across at Perth, but that would take time with so many men, and they would be vulnerable to attack during the maneuver. No, there was only one alternative: weary and worn as they were, the Northumbrians marched past Abernethy, past Perth, and on to the ford at Scone. There they crossed in the dim light of dawn, in full view of the watchtower, and turned quickly to the east. Siward watched nervously over his left shoulder as they hurried toward Dundee, expecting the Scots to charge down out of the hills on their flank at any moment, forcing his flagging troops to wheel and fight.

Fortunately, the usurper had chosen not to strike at them just yet. When they reached Dundee, its inhabitants had retreated into a fortress near the settlement, leaving the town itself to Siward and his army. They plundered everything they could, which made the men happy, but Malcolm chafed. He had no patience, waiting for the usurper to decide to do battle. He would have brought the attack, but the demon jarl stayed hidden up in the hills, and there was no getting him out of there till he was good and ready.

To compound the situation, Malcolm hadn't seen hide nor hair of his kin from Atholl. At Siward's urging, he had contacted them months earlier. His messenger had been well received, but the reply he brought back was enigmatic. "We know the son of Duncan, and he is our own," said the chieftains of several powerful Atholl tribes. "When the time has come, he will know us, and we will be his." Didn't that mean they were coming to fight for him? Then where were they? Damned Scots. Why couldn't they just say a thing plainly?

Finally a warrior from Macbeatha's camp arrived with a formal challenge, and the time of battle was set. Under cover of darkness, Malcolm took a small force of men and laid an ambush just northeast of the proposed battleground. It was a successful trap, and they caught a large contingent of horsemen in it. But Malcolm wanted the usurper. He wanted to sink his axe into that proud chest. He wanted that golden head with its red mustaches spiked on the point of his spear. The fighting was so intense, though, he couldn't get anywhere near the demon jarl.

Then, just when Malcolm thought he would have to slay every Scot on the field to get at the usurper, they all withdrew. His first thought was that his troops had beaten them, and the Scots were going home. But they had only fallen back to an ancient and crumbling fortress to await reinforcements. "You mean they'll come at us again?" *Malcolm cried in surprise when Siward told him.*

"They'll come at us tomorrow, and the day after, and as long as we stay on this shore!" *Siward snarled.* "Where are your damned kinsmen? We need to catch Macbeatha between us and squeeze him out of those hills. If we don't, he'll just keep falling back to the north, drawing us deeper and deeper with him. And God help us if he ever gets to Moray—he'll have so many men, you'll think the forest itself has taken up arms! If your kin don't show themselves tomorrow, we'll have to retreat."

"Retreat!" *Malcolm howled.* "But we're winning!"
"There is no winning or losing against the Scots," *Siward said bluntly.* "There's Macbeatha alive, and Macbeatha dead. Until he's dead, he'll come back at you from somewhere like a rabid terrier." *Malcolm would have debated that, but a messenger arrived just then. The King of Scots wanted a meeting.*

The usurper looked much as he had the day Malcolm and his mother had fled Scone. His hair had grayed considerably, and he sported a beard shot through with white, but he was just as tall, just as regal, his powerful arms folded across his chest. As Siward and Malcolm drew near, his eyes sparkled with challenge. "Jarl Siward," *he acknowledged, nodding his head at the jarl. Then he turned to Malcolm, and his voice softened unaccountably.* "Malcolm mac Duncan." *Malcolm felt an appraising eye run over his body with an almost physical touch.* "Yes, you've the look of your father about you. And that same curly hair that would not stay braided when you were a boy." A slight smile played over his lips.

Malcolm felt an uncanny tingling at the back of his neck. He didn't remember a thing about his hair not staying in braids, and he didn't understand how this man would know, anyway. Was he a witch?

Now the usurper turned his attention back to Siward. "I understand you lost both son and nephew today," he said. "It is a bitter thing to outlive one's heirs. Please accept my condolences."

"They died bravely," Siward replied stonily. "As did many others."

"Scots and Northumbrians both," Macbeatha agreed gravely.

Malcolm wanted to shout at the regicide. It's not supposed to be like this! You're not supposed to stand there and make civilized small talk, offering condolences. You're a monster! You're supposed to gloat over his pain!

But Siward took the conversation forward. "Half your men are dead upon the field," he said bluntly. "Do you come to sue for peace?"

The usurper's face grew grim. "We had a peace—you broke it. But more men are on their way to me. We can spill even more blood before I throw you off this shore—that is your choice."

Now, there was the monster Malcolm expected to see!

Siward gave a barking laugh. "My choice!" he marveled. "I can keep you throttled in your makeshift fortress with one hand while I rape Scone and the Tayside with the other. Your men will fade away into the hills like water leaking into the sand. If you want no more blood spilled, surrender to me today and acknowledge Malcolm mac Duncan as rightful king of Scotland!"

But the usurper curled his lip in a nasty smile. "Moray will be here tomorrow," he said, "with three thousand troops. They are even now at Glamis, where they have joined with two thousand of Atholl, all on their way to me. That makes us twice your number. Stay and perish. Leave, and young Malcolm here need not live with the ignominy of having lost his first campaign."

"I will win!" Malcolm snarled, unable to keep silent. "I will win this campaign, and take back from you that which you stole from my father!"

The eyes the usurper turned on him were surprisingly mild. "I took what your father could not keep," he said gently. "A nation must have the strongest leader she can, or her enemies will devour her. Kings are forged by the fires of war and politics, young Malcolm—not the accident of their birth."

Suddenly Malcolm felt Siward's restraining arm across his chest, and realized only then that he had lunged at the usurper. "Easy, easy," Siward cautioned. "This is a place for speech, not swords." Then he addressed Macbeatha. "Why do you come, if you are so confident of your victory?"

"Because there are widows enough in the land," the usurper replied. "I can push you back to your ships, but the price will be high for us both. There is a fat season upon the land, and a fine harvest to bring home. I would not trample the grain under the feet of warhorses, or stain good pastures with blood. Go back to your own country, Siward. See to your own harvest."

"My king has bade me put young Malcolm upon your throne. I cannot go back and tell him I slew half your men and walked away with nothing."

There was a pregnant pause. Then, "Take Lothian," the usurper said quietly.

Ah! They had him scared! His brave talk of reinforcements was so much wind, or he would never have surrendered territory. Malcolm could see his kinsman's mouth twisted in a small smile.

"My king did not bid me add to my territories," Siward replied with a trace of mirth in his voice. "He told me to put Malcolm on the throne of his fathers."

"It is for the Scots to say who shall rule Alba—not King Edward. Take what you can and go."

"Give Malcolm his father's inheritance," Siward badgered. "Then I will go."

Rage flashed in the usurper's eyes. "Duncan held Alba out of turn! Even then, by right his tanist should have been from the House of Kenneth mac Dubh. But its only heir was most foully murdered—and at whose bidding, do you suppose? Do not speak to me of rightful inheritance!"

Malcolm had never heard such nonsense before. Who was Kenneth mac Dubh, and why in God's name should he have any claim to the throne of Alba? The demon jarl was speaking gibberish.

"Yet it is true," the usurper continued, having calmed himself, "that Duncan served as king of the Cumbrians, and proved himself worthy in that." He hesitated slightly. "I will name young Malcolm *here as King of the Cumbrians in his cousin's place. That is my right to do."*

Malcolm's jaw dropped. King of what? Did this regicide truly think he would settle for Cumbria? Cumbria?!

"Duncan was king of Cumbria and Strathclyde," Siward came back. "Will you unite them again under one king?"

Malcolm turned to his kinsman in disbelief. "Surely you're not suggesting that we seriously consider—"

"Shut up," Siward growled.

"But we have him on the run!" Malcolm protested. "He wouldn't be making these concessions if—"

Siward seized him by the shirt front with a powerful fist and hauled him up short. "I said shut up!" the old warrior hissed in his face, "or I'll slit your throat myself!"

Malcolm could only stare at his kinsman in horror and pray that it was all part of some elaborate plot Siward had for outsmarting the usurper. That must be it. That had to be it. Siward would never cave in to such blatant—

"Very well," the regicide said softly. "King of Strathclyde and Cumbria." Then his voice raised. "But he's to go first to Cumbria, until I can send word for my kinsmen in Strathclyde to withdraw. And he's to pay conveth to me like any other subject king, or I will take Cumbria from him and give it to Lulach, do you understand? And then I will take Lothian back from you." The threat was harsh and ringing.

Siward chuckled. "If you can."

"Oh, I can," Macbeatha assured him with a cold more frightening than his anger had been. "Once, you saw me raise ten thousand men and stir them with the voice of God. Fourteen years of peace and plenty have brought another generation of warriors to manhood, and I can raise fifteen thousand today. And there is yet my cousin Thorfinn and his bloodthirsty Vikings. So do not try my patience, Siward of Northumbria, for it is brittle as old leather just now. Malcolm mac Duncan is a prince of Scots, and as such I give him the opportunity to rule as a client king. If he proves his worth, perhaps he will be elected steward of his Great Tribe of Atholl, for its current ruler has no satisfactory successor. He will rise in Alba as far as his own abilities will take him; but if he falters in his duties, he will pay the price his father paid."

In the silence that followed, Malcolm realized with a shock that Siward was going to accept this settlement. There was no protest, no railing, nothing but that damned smirk on Siward's face, and Malcolm knew he had been betrayed. It was Lothian that Siward had wanted all along. Malcolm had been an excuse to get King Edward's support, a way to add further import to this invasion, but Siward didn't really care if Malcolm took the Scottish crown this year, or ten years from now, or not at all. He was a goad, nothing more.

The shock of betrayal finally gave way in Malcolm to a murderous fury. Sold out, by his own kinsman! Cheated of his birthright by a greedy jarl who acted in league with this—this— "I will kill you!" *Malcolm swore to the regicide.* "And I will take for myself the kingdom of my father!"

Once more the usurper fixed him with those eyes which should have been hard, should have been hateful, but were not. "It may be that someday you will rule in Alba," *he said,* "for you are a prince of royal blood. But it will not be today, and it will not be because I or King Edward make you High King. It will be because the nobles of this nation accept you as their king under the law, and you have a great deal to prove to them before that can happen."

"Come," *Siward said softly, tugging Malcolm gently back from the confrontation. Macbeatha, too, drew back a step, and so Malcolm turned to leave in disgust. But a voice called after him.*

"Colmbeag."

Malcolm froze in his tracks. It had been a very long time since he'd heard that name, and the voice that called it was oddly familiar.

"Do you not remember at all," *it asked wistfully,* "when I rode you upon my shoulders, and got down upon my knees to play at wooden swords with you?"

Old memories swam to the surface, along with feelings long forgotten: a cozy room filled with laughter and love; a happiness that existed nowhere else in his childhood memories; and a warm, merry presence that hugged him close, and flattered him, and made him feel safe and strong— An image flashed in his brain: a smiling face, and a pair of bright red mustaches ...

No. NO! That could not have been this man, this usurper, this murderer. It wasn't his father, that much he knew, for he remembered wishing it were; but it couldn't—it couldn't— He and Donall, each

perched on a knee, listening to stories spun by a golden voice, and the smiling face and twinkling eyes of the storyteller were—
NNNOOOOOO!

He turned savagely to confront the demon, the monster, who conjured up feelings he had not owned since leaving Alba; who threw such images back at him now to dazzle him, to unman him at this most crucial time. "You killed my father!" he rasped, "and stole my kingdom, and I will see you in hell for it!" Then he turned and strode away, leaving Siward behind in his eagerness to put as much distance as possible between himself and this devil who tore at the fundamental principle upon which he had built his life. God damn Macbeatha mac Findlaech to everlasting hell!

Chapter Eighteen

In Fionna's hut

Kelda cradled the intruder's head in her lap, peering anxiously into his face. "What did you do to him?" she asked hoarsely.

"I have done nothing," Fionna replied, taking in the pallor of the man's skin beneath his pointed, graying beard, the blood seeping through his tunic. "Your husband was wounded defending the king, was he not?"

Kelda nodded, stroking Venko's shaggy hair.

"The wound has opened again, I think. And he has been tracking you for some days. He fainted, that is all." She retrieved a small pouch of dried herbs, opened it, and took out a pinch. "When he wakes, you must check the dressing to see how badly he bleeds." Then Fionna crushed the herbs between her fingers and waved them under Venko's nose.

He flinched away from the pungent odor, struggling back to consciousness. Slowly his eyes opened and he stared around him, befuddled. When he saw Fionna's stones scattered on the floor, his mouth gaped and he stared at the old woman. "You!"

"You know her?" Kelda asked in puzzlement.

"The three sisters," Venko said. "The Cailleach. The prophecy."

Kelda gazed at her host a moment, then closed her eyes and sighed as she understood. "Ah. I might have known."

Fionna was surprised Venko had found her hut, hidden as it was among the natural hills of this region, overgrown with grass and shrubs and wildflowers. But he had been here before, though it was long ago. She poured a cup of water and pressed it into his hand. "Drink this, and I will fill it again. Water is the source of life, and if you wish to recover from your wound, you must drink of it. Drink and drink and drink." Then she busied herself at a pot simmering over the fire, adding meal and dried berries and pine nuts.

Venko drained the cup of water, and Kelda refilled it for him from the skin that Fionna handed her. He drank the second cup more slowly, while she checked the dressing on his wound. "Why did you run away?" he demanded. "I would be with Owen and the others now, if not for you!"

"You could have gone," she said mildly, taking the ointment Fionna handed her to dab on the oozing cut. "You can still go, I won't stop you."

"You know I can't!" he snapped petulantly. "Macbeatha made me promise."

"Macbeatha is dead." The phrase echoed up from the emptiness of her soul.

Fionna watched them, knowing their sparring was that of old comrades so familiar they cannot wound one another. His grief was not as terrible as hers, but it was mortal, nonetheless. He would fight like a demon in the coming war between Lulach and Malcolm Canmore, with no wish to survive it. Such wishes were usually granted.

"What are you doing here with this wise woman?" Venko demanded of Kelda.

Fionna intervened quickly, afraid the Norsewoman, numb as she was, would reveal her true purpose in coming. "She is telling me a story. I asked her to tell me of the king, and so she is doing. We were just speaking of the retreat to Dunsinnan Hill."

"She was not there!"

"I have heard the tale often enough," Kelda said.

"Go on, then," Fionna bade her. "The man can correct you if you are wrong. You said the king went to meet Siward."

* * *

They met in a grove near the battlefield, Siward arriving with Canmore at his side, Macbeatha with Owen. They dickered as men will, each claiming superior strength, until my lord offered a compromise: if Siward would withdraw, Macbeatha would cede his holdings in Lothian to Siward, and he would make young Canmore a client king.

Canmore was not happy with the proposition, for he wanted Alba, not Strathclyde and Cumbria. But Siward found it to his liking. He told Canmore he was going home, and the lad could take what he was given or forge on alone. Having little choice, Canmore left with his kinsman and took ship back to York.

Lulach was not any happier than Canmore with the settlement. "Strathclyde was to be mine!" he shouted at his step-father, and those who had known Gillecomgain swore it was his shade upon Lulach's countenance, for his face seemed to twist all to the left.

"And it will be yours!" Macbeatha snapped back. "You'll have to take it, that's all. It will do you good, to fight for it rather than receive it from my hand. But for now, let Canmore have it. We can deal with him another day. It's the Athollmen coming down the Strathmore that concern us now."

"You have made a fool of me!" Lulach hissed.

"I have made a bargain to save your kingdom!" Macbeatha gritted back. "This kingdom, Alba! If Atholl and Siward united, your head and mine would be dangling from a pole in the marketplace of Scone before the week is out. Now, shut up and think about how we are to bring Atholl back into line!"

Of the fifteen hundred or more men left to Macbeatha, hundreds were wounded. They huddled behind their makeshift fortifications at Dunsinnan, waiting for daylight. Macbeatha himself had taken a shallow cut across his left breast, and though it was not serious, everyone knew that the enemy had drawn blood of their king. They wondered if the charm on his life had faded.

To insure that Atholl did not join forces with Siward and Canmore, Macbeatha sent riders to taunt the Athollmen and draw them up out of broad river valley called Strathmore, eastward to Dunsinnan Hill. Led by a man named Annon, they made their camp at its foot, and their fires glowed in the mid-summer twilight like the eyes of wolves waiting in the darkness for an injured man to fall asleep. The two hundred Athollmen who had fought with Macbeatha at Gowrie slipped away into the night, and little wonder.

Inside the crumbling fortress, the spirits of the High King's troops faltered, and their hearts were low.

"Do we strike at daylight?" his guardsmen asked.

But Macbeatha shook his head. "We will not strike first."

Weylin was appalled. "Lord, we cannot allow them to carry the battle to us!"

"They are *Albanaich!* They are my people!" Macbeatha snarled. "I will not strike the first blow!"

"These are your people, too," Owen told him, indicating the camp with a sweep of his hand. "They expect you to strike at the traitors."

Macbeatha mulled this over, then he said tightly, "I would buy more time for Moray to reach us. I will ask to speak to Annan tomorrow—that should delay things. I will tell him Canmore has gone home. Perhaps they will turn back without a fight."

"Perhaps we should slaughter them anyway," Owen murmured so softly that Macbeatha could not hear him.

The meeting was arranged, but it went badly. Annan had led Atholl since Crinan's death, and he came with a sprig of rowan pinned boldly to his cloak. From the very fact that Macbeatha had taken refuge in Dunsinnan, he knew Siward had got the best of the king, and he was like a wolf that had scented blood. Nor would he believe Canmore had gone. "Your face is filled with lies!" he accused Macbeatha. "I will have none of them. Come forth at dawn and meet me as an honorable man, or surrender your kingdom to Malcolm mac Duncan."

It was a clear challenge, and it could not be refused. The day had taken its toll of Macbeatha; his voice was hoarse as he replied, "Your head is mine. The surrender of your men will be accepted, but your own life is forfeit. Find a priest before morning, for at daylight I will claim what is mine."

And so he did. Rallying his troops, my lord led the charge out from Dunsinnan to meet the Athollmen. Annan went down in the first clash, and Macbeatha struck off his head, raising it aloft with a howl of triumph for all to see. But as he held that grisly trophy by its hair, a spear caught him in the right shoulder, changing his cry of triumph to one of pain. The weapon had not much force behind it, and Venko bound up the wound so the king could stay on the field. But his dispirited warband began to give ground, and Macbeatha soon had to call an orderly retreat before it became a rout. Back to Dunsinnan they went, step by backward step, ducking behind the crumbling stone walls of centuries past, and rough wooden barricades erected the day before.

Two or three women with healing arts had been brought to the camp after Gowrie, and one of them tended the king. She packed his wound with mud and uttered a charm of protection over him, then went on to others who were worse off. The king's physician was in Scone and, his guardsmen reasoned, would see to him soon enough. Tomorrow Moray would arrive, and they would catch Atholl between the two forces and smash it.

In the morning, however, the king burned with fever, his arm was swollen, and he had to grit his teeth against the pain. Lulach led a sortie down the hill against Atholl, while several messengers slipped out to reach the Moray troops and call them up into the hills—though it seemed the whole countryside must know where the High King lay, and what trouble had befallen him. The contingent he'd left behind to hold Scone, having assured themselves first of Siward's departure, rode now to the High King's relief, and joining their fellow Moraymen, they attacked the rebels from the west while Macbeatha's troops again struck down from the heights of Dunsinnan Hill.

Already nervous because Annan was dead and Malcolm Canmore was nowhere in sight, Atholl quickly fled the field, scattering where they could for safety and scurrying back to their various homes. Macbeatha sent word after them that once they had elected a new mormaer, he was to report to the High King at Scone to swear loyalty, or he could expect a visit from the royal warband to ensure his cooperation.

But Macbeatha did not lead his own troops that day, for his wound had grown poisonous, and the pain in his shoulder and arm was so great, it was all he could do to sit his horse without fainting. He watched while Lulach led the charge, and when the battle was won, his eye glistened with fever more than pride. He would not dismount where others could see him but called Owen and Venko behind a stretch of stockade where they had to lift him from his horse, and he came near to crying out when that right arm fell under its own weight against his side. They had no tents, no cot, to shield him from the rain or the stony ground. They made a shelter of tree limbs and found blankets to cushion his head and prop up his arm. Owen would hardly let another touch him. Weylin left immediately to fetch the surgeon from Scone. And Venko—Venko rode for the one person he believed could bring Macbeatha through any sickness. He came for me.

Chapter Nineteen

At Edinburgh

*M*alcolm Canmore pushed his way through the cluster of servants in the hall to find a wild-eyed warrior had a maid pinned bodily, face against the wall. She was whimpering in fear, while the young man clutched her hair roughly in one hand and held his knife poised against her exposed ear with the other. Malcolm folded his arms over his chest. "Larkin!" he barked.

The warrior turned a crazed eye toward Malcolm. He had the palest blue eyes Malcolm had ever seen, so pale they almost looked white. His hair was pale, as well: a bright, shining head of milk-white hair, cut short in the Danish style with bangs falling over his forehead. It was not for his appearance that everyone called him the Dark One.

Now he recognized Malcolm, and a wolfish grin split his face as a spark of sanity glimmered in his eye. "Oh, good day to you, my king!" His voice, as always, had a distant quality to it.

"What are you doing with the girl?" Malcolm asked sternly.

"What girl?" It was no facetious question—Larkin had forgotten all about his victim. Malcolm could read that in the man's face as awareness filtered in and Larkin eased his grip on the girl's hair. Then Larkin gave a small laugh, as though someone had played a good joke on him, sheathed his knife, and stepped away from her. "Oh, this girl." He looked a trifle embarrassed.

"Did she offend you?"

Larkin only shrugged, smiling amiably. "*Can't remember. Probably.*"

"*Probably not,*" *Malcolm growled. The girl slipped out from behind Larkin and fled the room sobbing.*

Larkin was actually older than Malcolm by a couple of years, but he looked younger, for he was of a more slender build and had delicate facial features. A careless man might assume Larkin was weak; but that careless man could wind up dead for his error. Beneath his coarse woolen shirt, the warrior's arms and shoulders were thick with muscle, and both his reflexes and his temper were razor-edged. Malcolm had seen him drive a man's jaw through his skull with a single blow from his fist.

His left fist.

It was for that reason, and that reason alone, that Malcolm tolerated the man's madness. The servants and others who knew Larkin swore he was possessed by a devil, and Malcolm thought they were probably right. But it took one devil to defeat another, and after the battle at Dundee, Malcolm had known that's what he was up against. That was when he had scoured the countryside for a man with a powerful left hand, and a powerful hatred to match. That was when he had first made the acquaintance of Larkin mac Duff.

Following Dundee, Malcolm and Siward had returned to Northumbria by ship, Siward because he wanted to accompany the bodies of his son and his nephew, and Malcolm because Siward insisted. The old jarl meant to ensure the hotheaded prince did not lead the remaining cavalry in an attack on the Scots in violation of the treaty they had just made. Once at sea, Malcolm confronted his kinsmen where he sat drinking in the tiny cabin below the poop. "You have betrayed me!" he raged, banging both fists on a small plank table bolted to the floor.

Siward was unimpressed. "*I have saved you,*" *he replied disgustedly.* "*Did you really think you could walk into a country and claim its throne when you haven't set foot there for fourteen years?*"

"*Edward did!*" *Edward had been in exile in Normandy longer than that before returning to claim the Anglish crown.*

"*But only when Edward had the support of the Anglish nobles,*" *Siward said harshly.* "*Which Scottish nobles support you, Malcolm? Your own kin did not turn out. Even if they had, Atholl alone isn't enough. These people don't know you, and a good many of them weren't fond of your father. In Alba, boy, you've got to make your own reputation. I've given you that chance; I've gotten Cumbria for you."*

Malcolm grumbled something about the inferior quality of Cumbria and its Brython natives, but Siward was in no mood for such thanklessness. The bright promise of his eldest son's life had been snuffed out, and for all his brave words, Siward's heart was bursting with grief. Malcolm could tell by the size of the wineskin Siward was pulling at and by his obvious intention to finish it without help from anyone.

So Malcolm went out on deck and stood looking over the rail at the coastline of Alba—of his country—slipping by, just as his hopes for ruling there slipped by. It was the end of July, and by the time he got to Edward, even if he could talk the king into giving him an army, there was no way to plan another invasion and return to Alba that year. No, he would have to do as Siward had suggested and take up the reins of Cumbria, doing what he could with that country.

As he thought about it, Malcolm began to see the advantages. Why, he would have an army there in Cumbria—a small one, probably, and not as well trained or well equipped as he would like, but he could fix that. He would fix that. And his brother was there. Siward had often accused Malcolm of not understanding his countrymen, and the prince had to admit that was true. But Donall could help him. Donall had grown up in Alba, or near to, and could help him understand the Scots. And the Cumbrians—surely the Cumbrians would support him in attacking Macbeatha! They had been ruled by Alba for years; now here was their chance to turn the tables, to put a Cumbrian king upon Alba's throne! Yes, yes, being king of Cumbria had definite possibilities ...

So Malcolm had gone to Cumbria, tossed aside his weak cousin Gospadruig and begun training his army. He was surprised, and greatly pleased, when a group of young warriors arrived from Atholl to pledge their loyalty and support. It was only then that he learned his kinsmen had, indeed, risen to support him, but the usurper had cut off the lines of communication between them, preventing word of their coming from reaching him. If only he had known— But that was water down the creek, and Malcolm set his sights on the future. Here, now, was the heart of a great warband, and with them he would build up the power he needed to throw the regicide off his stolen throne.

As soon as he had made himself and his band of warriors familiar with the land below the River Clyde, Malcolm marched northward and established his authority in Strathclyde, as well. When he reached the capital of Dumbarton, he found the usurper's kin well gone, as had been promised, but he took great delight in ferreting out any leftover loyalty to the former steward and squashing it. The people learned quickly that those who supported Malcolm knew his favor, and those who did not felt the heavy heel of his boot.

Malcolm's brother Donall was eager to assist the new king in taking control of both parts of his kingdom. At twenty-one, Donall had the same fair hair as his brother, and so he was called Donall Ban, meaning Donall the Pale. Malcolm found his brother's ways a bit odd at first, from his braided hair to his checked clothing, but the new king reminded himself that these were the ways of the Scots, and he'd better learn them.

Donall was an easy-going young man who found his brother's naiveté in the matter of Scottish customs amusing. But he did not find Malcolm's plan to overthrow Macbeatha amusing. "You can't kill him," he said bluntly. "I've seen the man fight—I've gone into battle with him—and he is unbeatable in single combat. He's switch-handed, you know—wields a sword with left as well as right. Most warriors don't know how to defend against a man who cuts from the left."

Malcolm thought about that. He didn't just want the usurper off his throne, he wanted him dead. "Then I need to find another man who fights left-handed."

Donall nodded thoughtfully. "The Beltaine games," he said. "We could hold a special competition for those who can use a sword in either hand."

But as it turned out, he didn't have to wait till Beltaine. Shortly after word went out about the special competition, a lord from eastern Strathclyde sidled up to the king. "If you want the fiercest two-handed fighter in the land," he said in a knowing undertone, "there's a lad in Dunblane you ought to see."

He and Donall had gone to Dunblane in secret, for it was not within his lands but across the border through Fortriu and into Fife. They had barely settled by the hearth at an inn there when the door burst open and a ragged boy with a wild look in his eye fairly leapt into the room. His pale hair was badly braided, with wisps jutting out in all directions. Barefoot, clad in a patched tunic smudged with dirt, the slender youth looked like a stick doll put together by clumsy hands.

"Larkin!" barked the man who kept the inn. "Go away! Don't be bothering our guests."

But Larkin's eyes had zeroed in on Malcolm and Donall by the fire and he swaggered closer, looking them up and down with ill-concealed rage. "Are you king's men?" he demanded.

Startled by the question, it took Malcolm a moment to realize that Larkin didn't mean King Edward's men, or even his own. He meant the usurper's men. "I serve only myself," growled Malcolm.

"Don't make trouble, Larkin," the innkeeper warned again. "I've given these people hospitality in the name of our tribe, and you'd best behave yourself or your brother will have to pay for any injury you cause."

That seemed to give Larkin pause; he straightened up, looked around as though embarrassed and gave a short, self-conscious laugh. "I only want to know who they are," he pleaded with the innkeeper.

"Guests," the man replied. "That's all you need to know."

But Larkin wiped at his mouth with the back of his hand, then began to circle slowly around the two brothers, eyeing them from all sides with pale eyes that shone brighter with madness at every step. Malcolm got slowly to his feet, turning carefully so he was always facing the madman. He could see now that this was no boy, but a grown man with childlike features. He could also see there was tension and strength in every muscle and sinew of the man's body.

"You are a warrior,," Malcolm guessed, never taking his eyes from the madman.

"I am," Larkin replied, his breathing shallow, his nostrils flaring like those of a warhorse scenting blood.

"You wear no sword."

Larkin stopped and thrust out his chin in an obvious pout. The beard upon it was thin and scraggly. "My brother took it away," he said petulantly. Then a giggle slipped out and he smiled wickedly. "I killed a king's man once, a messenger, and he had to pay the honor price. Now he won't let me play with swords anymore."

The innkeeper was edging closer to Larkin, obviously determined to intervene if the young man caused trouble. But Malcolm was not worried. It seemed Larkin had a grudge against king's men, and that intrigued him. "I'm a warrior myself," *he told Larkin.* "So we have something in common."

At that the madman sneered, hooking a finger inside the collar of his shirt and showing his bare neck. Malcolm became conscious of the gold torc around his own throat. "Not much," *Larkin snarled.*

Malcolm was not discouraged. Larkin had used his right index finger to tug at his collar, leaving his left hand free and poised above a knife, which hung in a sheath from the madman's belt. He wondered ... "You have a knife, there," *he said, nodding to the weapon.* "What do you say to a contest? We can choose a target and—"

With a move so swift it defied anticipation, Larkin sent the knife whizzing through the air just at Malcolm's ear. The young king had to lift a hand to his face to make sure the blade had not shaved the whiskers from his cheek in passing. Then, "You missed me," *he said dryly.*

"I wasn't aiming for you. I was aiming for that."

Malcolm turned to look where Larkin gestured and saw the knife protruding from the center of an iron harness ring hanging on the wall. The ring could not have been more than two inches in diameter. And the blade had flown from the man's left hand.

Slowly Malcolm crossed to the wall and inspected the knife. It was buried a full inch in the soft wood. "Very impressive," *he admitted, tugging it out.* "I will try to match it, though I doubt I can." *He brought the weapon back and offered it to its owner.* "You don't mind if I use my right hand, do you?"

Larkin's mouth twitched up into a lopsided smile that did not involve his eyes. Those still glistened with unnatural brightness. "You're no devil, then," *he said with a giggle. Taking the knife, he rotated his left wrist tauntingly.* "This is the devil's hand," *he announced in a hollow, detached voice.* "I discovered that long ago. It's stronger than God's hand." *Here he shook his right hand in limp-wristed fashion. But the left kept moving in circles.* "It kills without mercy, this left hand. It has no heart, and no soul." *Suddenly his hand snapped out and Malcolm found the tip of Larkin's knife pressed against his throat.* "And no reason."

Malcolm could hear Donall's chair scrape as he leapt to his feet behind them, but he himself did not flinch. He only held the madman's gaze as a smile tugged at his lips. "If I served the High King, though," he asked softly, "that would be a reason, wouldn't it?"

"Larkin, put it away!" the innkeeper hissed. "Think of your brother! You know how angry he'll be. You'll make a beggar of him if you injure a lord."

"Do you serve the Devil, then?" Larkin grated.

"I told you," Malcolm replied calmly. "I serve myself."

The giggled slipped in again. "Are you a great lord?" Larkin asked in a whisper.

A broad smile spread across Malcolm's face. "Better than that," he whispered back. "I'm a king."

But Larkin's eyes grew hard and dark, and his mouth drew into a grim line. "What manner of lie is this?"

"It is God's truth," Malcolm swore, but softly yet, for the innkeeper stood nearby. "I am the King of Cumbria: Malcolm mac Duncan."

It took a moment, but a moment only, for that to register in the madman's brain. Then his mouth fell slack with amazement and his hand drew back, letting the knife clatter uselessly to the floor. "Canmore," he breathed.

"Come back to Cumbria with me," Malcolm invited, "and you can kill the High King's men to your heart's delight. And, if chance favors you, the High King himself."

Slowly Larkin sank to his knees, lifting his arms to encircle Malcolm's waist. Burying his face in the king's shirt, he wept.

"Take a walk with me, Larkin," Malcolm invited now, laying a comradely arm across the Dark One's shoulders as he started for the door.

Outside in the yard, warriors practiced with their arms, or mended their tack, or flirted with the serving girls. Larkin accompanied Malcolm docilely through this commotion, which made Malcolm smile a little with an almost brotherly affection. How different was this Larkin from the one he'd met three years ago! That Larkin had been suspicious and obstinate, a wild thing without direction or control. Malcolm had changed all that. He'd won the man's obedience and trust by channeling his rage and *giving him the only thing he desired in life: an opportunity to kill Macbeatha mac Findlaech.*

But Malcolm was the only one who could control him. This incident with the serving girl was not the first, and not all had ended so well. What was he to do with the madman now? Set him after Lulach, of course. Larkin would like that. Yes, he was sure Larkin would like that.

Chapter Twenty

In Fionna's hut

With Venko settled on a pile of furs to rest, Kelda took another cup of the warm brew from Fionna's hand. "I had sworn I would not go to the king again," she said. "But when I heard what had happened... Siusan was then thirteen, or near to, and knew as much about running the household as I, so I left her in charge of it. Reagan, I gave into the keeping of my younger daughter, Netta. At eleven, she did more mothering of him than I, who was always in the fields or the dairy or the stables. And I ran to my lord. Ran with a cold terror in my heart, for I knew what the rowan meant to Macbeatha." She sipped at the cup, frowned slightly, then went on. "It was the prophecy—your prophecy—that the rowan would come against him, and so it had. We all knew what that meant.

"It was the beginning of the end."

* * *

There was a poor, rude hut tucked into a narrow glen near Dunsinnan, belonging to a humble man and his three children, and to this simple abode they had carried my lord at the surgeon's command. A small stream trickled through the glen, which the surgeon felt was key to drawing out an infection. The hut itself was light and airy, for it was summer and whole sections of the wattle and daub walls had been removed to let in the sun. When I rode up with Venko, I thought how pleased my lord must be to have all that fresh air. He always loved fresh air, did Macbeatha.

But when I ducked inside, my heart lurched in my breast, for there he lay on a pallet, eyes closed, face pale, with a priest hovering over him murmuring prayers. I bit my fist to keep from crying out, sure I was too late. Weylin, who kept watch beside him, jumped to his feet and hurried to us. "He's sleeping," Weylin assured me in hushed tones. He embraced Venko quickly, then turned and embraced me, too, and the tears spilled down his cheeks. "Now I know he'll get well," he said in a choked voice.

I was moved by his belief in me—or rather, his belief that when I was there, things were back in balance. I felt it myself. To be back among these men, and all of us waiting on my lord—it felt as though the ground under my feet had suddenly settled back into place after being slightly askew for many years. I had missed them all, not just Macbeatha. For fourteen years I had missed them all, and I knew it when Weylin put his arms around me.

But he let me go then, and I moved to the pallet as a flower turns its head toward the sun. Crouching beside my lord, I touched my hand to his fevered brow and rested my fingers lightly on the pulse in his neck to assure myself it beat strongly and rhythmically as always. His eyes fluttered open at my touch and wavered across my face, then fell shut as though he hadn't the strength to keep the lids up. "Is this Valhalla, then?" he asked in a dry, raspy voice. "For here is my Valkyrie waiting, as I always knew she would be."

Tears sprang to my eyes, but I forced them away. "No, no Valkyrie for you quite yet, lord," I replied with all the sauce I could muster. "Just some dried up old farm wife they've brought to tend you."

From his throat there came an odd, choking sound, and I feared it was the death rattle—but no. His lips twitched at the corners and I realized he was laughing. "Same sweet Kelda," he whispered. His hand drifted up, fumbling around until it found mine and clasped it. I could have cried at the weakness of that grip—a babe could have pulled away from him. I did not pull away, though. He said no more, but went back to sleep; and when he woke hours later, I was still there with his hand in mine.

That night my lord's fever finally broke. Venko likes to say it was my coming that did it, but that's not true. It was the surgeon's potions, and his poultices, that did it; or perhaps it was the charms that the little girl of the house liked to say over the royal stranger who lay on her father's bed. Whatever the cause, I bless it, for he woke in the morning wanting to sit up and eat something, the first time since the battle he had done so.

Just taking some broth and a few bites of bread seemed to exhaust him, and afterwards he lay back upon the pallet and closed his eyes. With a sigh he reached for my hand again, which I gave him gladly. "Will you stay now?" he asked.

"Lord, I will stay as long as you need me."

"Good." He shifted a little on his bed, as though he might find some way to settle himself so his shoulder pained him less. "And will you do something for me?" The thickness of his voice told me he would soon be asleep again.

"Anything," I whispered.

Rubbing my fingers across his bewhiskered cheek, he said, "Shave this damned beard off me, will you? There's so much gray in it, I look a hundred and ten."

I waited until he was awake again, and then I did as he asked, finding that my hands remembered well this familiar task. But oh, how funny he looked when I was through! His face was all pale where the beard had been, and I hoped no one gave him a mirror until he'd been out in the sun for a few weeks and browned his chin to match his forehead.

He slept much in the days that followed, for he was still very weak. I had to shoo away the men who came constantly to see for themselves how he improved—they had to tell him stories, you see, and ask him questions, and that tired him more than was good for him. In doing so, I saw how different my tactics had become. Once I would have pouted prettily and stamped my foot and waggled my large breasts at these men, and they would have grinned and gone off thinking what a lucky man Macbeatha was. But I no longer had the arsenal of my youth, so I found I must rebuke them as I did my children, with a motherly scolding and a firm insistence that they not overtax their lord. They heeded me just the same, however, for they knew I was right. Had they balked, I would simply have had Owen throw them out. I was determined to see Macbeatha well and strong, and quickly, for Alba needed him.

And I needed him. I needed to know he was in his place, doing what he had always done: guiding the nation as he guided his horse, coaxing and contriving to make things happen. After all those long years of being so far away, you would think I'd have learned how to live in a world without Macbeatha mac Findlaech in it, but I never had. I always knew he was there—not with me, but somewhere. He lived. He laughed. He was.

The surgeon smiled now when he came to check his illustrious patient, for it was clear my lord would recover. It was also clear who was going to oversee his treatment, so the surgeon gave me the potions, herbs and such that were needed, and I administered them faithfully. In a week he pronounced Macbeatha strong enough to ride the short distance back to Scone.

My lord had been up and walking around for a couple of days, and of course he insisted on visiting the makeshift hospital which had been set up nearby. I went with him to make sure he did not overtax himself, and I saw how the men's faces glowed when they saw their king recovering from his wounds. It gave them hope, for they believed with the hearts of simple men that as the king went, so went the land; and their king was alive, and vital, and had driven the enemy from their shore. Those who crossed to the Otherworld did so with hearts at peace for a battle they considered won.

Macbeatha did not consider it won. Although he wore a smile and laughed heartily during these visits, he came away from them with his face almost as gray as his beard had been. I would make him sit down under a tree to rest, and send away all the men who trailed after him, and there I would hold him with his head against my breast. "I have lost," he would whisper to me. "I have lost Lothian, and I have lost Atholl. They rose up for Canmore once; they will rise for him again. They wore sprigs of rowan, and the *Caillaech* said I would be defeated by the rowan.'"

"Oh, yes, you are quite defeated," I would chide him. "That's why Atholl tucked their tails between their legs and ran for home. That's why your lady waits safely in Scone for your return. You may as well die here on this spot," I would goad, "and let this boy Canmore have his way."

"He is not undeserving," my lord defended once.

"He is a spoiled brat," I told him. "Nearly as bad as your own son. Who spoils these boys, telling them they will grow up to be kings?" I have certainly said no such thing to my own son, despite the prophecy that Venko would father kings. I do not want my son to even imagine such a future. The price is too high.

Lulach came back from chasing the Athollmen and was bent on taking his small band down to Cumbria forthwith to take on Malcolm. But, "No," Macbeatha growled.

Lulach looked stunned. "No?"

"Not this season," Macbeatha told him, glowering in a manner Lulach was unaccustomed to see.

"Why not?" the young warrior demanded, defiance sparking in his blue eyes.

"Because the Mormaer of Moray is dead," my lord snapped. "He spent his life on the battlefield against Atholl. Go there, take control—no one will oppose you. Learn to rule. Learn to lead. Then you can raise an army and take Strathclyde away from Canmore."

For a moment Lulach looked as though he would still protest, but then he saw the wisdom of what his stepfather told him. "Yes. Yes, of course!" he said decisively. "I will lead Moray, as you did, as my father did. That is the best training ground for a high king. And next spring I will take my warband against Canmore." Then off rushed that precocious young man to take upon his shoulders the leadership of the Great Tribe of Moray. As if he could learn it all in the span of one winter!

It was a familiar cavalcade, then, that descended from the hills to enter the village of Scone: Macbeatha, his guard, and me. But we were a tired band this time, each feeling the weight of years upon him. Macbeatha had seen forty-nine winters, and Owen more than that. Dougal, who had been the youngest when I came to Macbeatha, was himself a grandfather.

And Dhui! Oh, I forgot about Dhui. He had ridden up from Scone earlier, to tell us the Lady Gruoch had returned safely from Fife where she had been visiting her kin when Canmore attacked. The little boy who had cared for the horses was now the father of seven children. He had grown broad-chested and powerful, and I thought, *If only someone put a sword in this man's hands, he could slay warriors as a reaper cuts barley!* Like his parents Aithne and Engus, though, Dhui was a *doer chele,* a base client, not entitled to bear arms.

The people of Scone turned out to shout huzzah and welcome home their king, who sat tall in his saddle, smiling and waving at them—with his left hand, of course. The surgeon had warned him the muscles in his right shoulder were damaged, and though he must exercise them when he had healed better, his right arm would never have the strength it had once had.

"It is fortunate, then," Macbeatha had responded, "that I have two arms."

He did work at getting the strength back in his right arm that winter, but he never afterward made pretense of preferring it. Sometimes I think he was secretly relieved that he now had license to use his left whenever he pleased.

All the High King's household waited in the yard outside his hall. On the steps stood the Lady Gruoch, as queenly and as proper as ever, surrounded by her ladies and a handful of servants. I wondered what she would say to see me with her husband; but before I could guess, I spotted another familiar face there on the stairs.

Brenna.

My lord's sister was as dainty as ever, with a tiny waist that showed not a trace of having born so many sons. Her face glowed when she beheld her brother sitting regally astride his horse. Knowing what would happen to that shining face if she saw me, I edged my pony around behind Dougal and slid to the ground.

"Welcome home, lord," said the Lady Gruoch, her mellow voice rich with emotion. I noted with surprise that moisture glistened in her eyes. If she attached any significance to his clean-shaven face, it did not show. Perhaps someone had warned her.

"Lady, I have much to tell you," her husband replied, leaning over his horse's neck with the casual air of the rogue he was. "Let me say first that your son is well; he fought most courageously in every battle we undertook, and I could not be more proud if he were the son of my flesh as well as of my heart."

The tears brimming in Gruoch's eyes began to trickle down her cheeks.

"We are saddened by the loss of many good men, however," Macbeatha continued, "not least among them our kinsman the Mormaer of Moray, who rides now in the vanguard of the King of Heaven—which is, I must admit," he added with a sparkle in his green eyes, "something of a promotion."

Gruoch must have known all this, of course, for messengers had been back and forth between them several times.

"And I have sent our brave Lulach back to Inverness," my lord went on "commending him to the nobles there who will choose the new mormaer. Let us pray God that soon we receive the happy news of Lulach's election."

I had reached the foot of the stairs now and began to climb them slowly, wondering how I could slip past Brenna and get to Macbeatha's chamber unnoticed, there to prepare the salve and bandages with which to dress his shoulder. Perhaps if I tugged my shawl up around my face ...

"But my lord, we can speak of all these things later," Gruoch said, brushing at a strand of hair that had not fallen out of place, and using that movement to cover the brushing of tears from her face. "You must be weary after your journey. Come into the hall where you can rest and refresh yourself, and we will speak at length of the battle, and the great heroes who fought in it."

Still Macbeatha made no move to get down from his horse, only continued to smile at his lady. "Aye, heroes indeed," he agreed. "There are names that should be honored in song, and we must ask the royal bard to compose ballads to our brave men who fell at Gowrie, and at Dunsinnan."

"So we shall," she concurred. "Come, lord, and when you are seated by the hearth in your own hall, we will bid the bard listen to your tales and make them into song."

Still Macbeatha sat upon his horse, leaning on his good arm. "Lady, how glad I am to be home again, and to find you waiting at my door."

Gruoch flushed, flattered by the compliment but obviously puzzled by his delay in coming inside. I was not puzzled, however. I knew exactly what the problem was, and I hurried up the last few steps to pause at her elbow. "He will not dismount while you watch, lady," I whispered, "and have you see that he needs assistance."

Her reaction was immediate and smooth as butter. Turning away from me as though it had been only a breeze that brushed at her ear, she took Brenna by the arm, saying, "Come inside, sister, and let us make a comfortable place for our lord by an open window. You know how he loves fresh air!" Then she whisked Brenna into the hall, bidding the rest of her retinue follow quickly.

I lingered in the doorway to block any view of him as he climbed slowly and painfully down from his horse, suffering Owen's firm grip in aid. Once balanced on his feet, he straightened himself, wiped all trace of pain from his features, and came toward the hall at a slow but steady pace. I slipped inside then, not wanting to see if he would need help halfway up the stairs.

The hall was familiar to me, even after fourteen years: the tall, narrow windows, the heavy wooden chairs for the nobles, the alcoves and doors leading off the main chamber. I made my way quickly toward the stairs, almost expecting old Shayla to waddle out of the shadows and scold me for dawdling when there was work to be done. A phantom collar chafed my throat, and I had to reach up and brush at it to make the sensation go away. In doing so, my shawl fell off my hair and away from my face.

Brenna's voice rang out from below. "You!"

I froze in my tracks, back rigid, waiting for the next outburst. But instead, it was Gruoch's voice that sounded clear and warm, like a shaft of sunlight illuminating the hall: "Yes, sister, was it not good of Venko to bring his wife to tend our lord's wound? She has the gentlest hands, you know. She always bound up Macbeatha's wounds for him, in the old days. I am so pleased she could come."

Turning to face her, I bobbed in courtesy. "You are most gracious, my lady," I replied. "Forgive me if I do not tarry here to greet you better, but I must prepare my lord's medicines as the surgeon instructed."

"Go, by all means," Gruoch bade me. "If there is anything you need, just tell one of the servants."

I nodded a second time and scurried up the stairs, repenting once again of every evil thing I'd ever said or thought about the queen. Whatever else she may be, she is the most gracious royal lady I have ever known. Of course, it is all for show and for politics, saying in public that which it is most discreet to say, but it is a role she plays to perfection, and bless her for it!

But I could feel Brenna's hateful eyes on me as I mounted the stairs, and I knew I had not heard the last from her.

Chapter Twenty-One

I was in Macbeatha's chamber, mixing a salve with water boiled on a brazier there, when a little serving girl found me. "If you please, lady," she chirped, "the queen asks would you come downstairs to dress my lord's shoulder. She doesn't want him to stir from his chair."

Like as not he couldn't have made it up the steps without aid, and so here was Gruoch saving face for him again. Gathering the things I needed, I followed the little mite out into the corridor. We chanced to pass by a room where two servant women were strewing fresh straw upon the floor, getting it ready for a guest, and I heard them gossiping. "... I don't know why we bother with it," one was saying. "She'll be down the way in the king's chamber, and Venko will be in the kitchen going at Sorcha."

"And did you hear the queen?" the other giggled. "'She has the gentlest hands ...' Yes, but what she does with them is another matter!"

They assumed, of course, that now I was back in Scone, I would also be back in Macbeatha's bed. Well, let them, I thought wearily. It was doubtful I could convince anyone otherwise. But my children were tucked away in Moray, far from the idle gossip of the court and any harm it might engender; and as for myself, I found that the older I got, the less I cared what other people thought of me.

In the hall, people had gathered around the king, everyone wanting to assure themselves that he was all right, that he would recover and rule as he had before. I pushed my way through to him, unhappy at how closely they pressed in upon him. The wound still looked vicious, and I did not want them gaping and gasping as I changed the dressing. "My lords," I addressed the warriors there, "be so good as to escort these ladies to another part of the hall while I tend the king's wound. Though he has no modesty himself, I am sure the ladies would find their hearts racing to see him half naked, so let us observe some decorum and provide him a bit of privacy."

There were some indrawn breaths at such suggestive speech, but it achieved its objective: they moved away, men and women both, encouraged by Weylin and Dougal. Owen and Venko stood staunchly at their lord's side, providing a screen.

Gruoch stayed, too. "May I see how it is done?" she asked. "Not that I would presume to take over what you obviously do so well, but if it should happen some time that ... you are indisposed, or ..."

I beckoned her to come closer and watch, precluding any need for her to continue her justification. The wound still seeped, crusting the bandage and sticking it to his skin, so I had to soak the dressing with warm water before I could remove it. Even so I could hear his involuntary intake of breath when I carefully peeled away the soiled cloth. Gruoch heard it, too, and gently slipped her slender fingers into his good left hand. He clasped them for a moment, then lifted them to his lips to kiss, and pointedly put her hand away from him. "It is not that I do not crave your hand in mine, heart," he said with a wry smile, "but when Kelda applies that salve, I am apt to crush your lovely fingers in my grip."

So Gruoch sat with no hand to clasp but her own, watching as I cleansed the angry wound and then applied the salve. He flinched, and sweat stood out on his brow, but he made no sound other than puffing his breath out with great force for a moment or two. Finally I settled the fresh bandage into place and bound it gently, and he gave a great sigh of relief.

"It looks simple enough," Gruoch said evenly, though her face seemed a bit pale. "But no doubt Kelda's practiced hands make a smooth job of what would be difficult and painful for one less skilled."

I said nothing but used a damp cloth to sponge away the perspiration on his brow. "She is a treasure," Macbeatha said fondly, for which I blotted his face as well.

Next I made him stretch out his right arm and bring it back several times, so it didn't grow too stiff. He grimaced a bit, but we had both seen men who coddled their healing wounds and found their tendons and muscles would never again stretch as they ought, so he bore through it. Soon I had him settled back in his chair, and he called to a serving girl for some ale.

"There is a potion which he must drink now," I told Gruoch, "and you would do well to give it to him before all his friends, so he will not balk and make faces, but swallow it down like a man." Macbeatha glared at me, but I paid no attention and kept right on. "There is another he should take upon retiring—I will give you that as well. It is sweeter and he takes it without a fuss, but he goes right to sleep with it. So make sure his boots are off and he is properly vented before you give it to him."

Gruoch looked startled. "But—I thought that—" she stammered, and then she actually blushed, if you can imagine. "That is to say, you are his nurse and—"

"I am also tired, lady," I told her frankly. "I would be most grateful if you could give him his medicines tonight, for I want nothing more than to find some bread and butter in the kitchen, and then steal away to a sleeping chamber, if there is one available for Venko and me. At the moment I crave nothing so much as a decent bed and a good night's rest."

The queen recovered her wits quickly and bade the little serving girl take me to a guest chamber and bring food for my supper. Venko wore a troubled look—no doubt he was expecting to have his mistress warm his bed that night. I told him frankly that he might join me or find his own place to sleep, only not to wake me if he came in.

Then I turned back to Macbeatha and prodded his chest with an accusing finger. "When you grow tired," I instructed, "you are to pretend you've had too much to drink and let Owen help you up those stairs. And that's to be early, do you understand?"

"What, am I a child?" he sulked.

"I shall see that he does," Gruoch promised.

"See how they conspire against me!" he complained to Owen, but Owen only gave him a look which said plainly that if my lord gave his wife any trouble about it, Owen would take the matter upon himself.

People began to drift back toward the king now, so I gave Gruoch the two potions and went back upstairs. In short order I had dined simply but well and was stretched out comfortably on a good straw tick with the shutters closed against the lingering twilight.

But I did not sleep right away. For the first time since I had come running to tend Macbeatha, I asked myself how long I was going to stay. Surely there were others at court who could take care of him now. But I had to admit, I did not want to surrender that duty. It felt so right to be with him again, to share his company, to hear him laugh. And to serve him-- I felt as though I had been only half a person for years upon years, and now suddenly I was made whole because I served him again. To fetch him his medicines, or simply a cup of water, made me feel *alive*. To give him my stout shoulders to lean upon when he walked, to stroke his brow while he worried and pined-- I didn't want to go back to being half a person. I wanted to stay with him for the rest of my life.

But I had children at home, and a harvest to bring in—that was what I had wanted when I married Venko, wasn't it? Land and children of my own, a place in my community, a sense of value and worth apart from Macbeatha. So here was the price of that comfort: I could not run out on my responsibilities. My oldest girl was now nearing *aimser togu,* the Age of Choice, and as she had no desire to marry God, I had better find her a suitable husband. Her sister would not be far behind, and since she always wanted whatever the elder had, the challenge would be to keep her from finding a boy at the festival fires before she was of a proper age for such escapades.

And little Reagan—I did not want very badly for him to be a warrior, but as the son of a great warrior, and such was his destiny. There was no one at home to teach him the skills he needed, so we must foster him out when he turned seven. That would be within a year, and we had not yet considered who might serve as his fosterer.

So I had to go home. I had to. But not yet. I would be home for Hallowmas, but surely they could get by without me until then. It would wait. It would all wait just a little while.

And with that thought I finally drifted off into exhausted slumber.

Although I had decided not to bother trying to convince any gossips that I was not sharing the king's bed, I found I *did* have to convince Macbeatha. In light of his self proclaimed vow of fidelity, I was surprised the first time his hand slipped under my shawl to fondle my breasts, which were as large as ever, if no longer so firm. "I see you're feeling better," I commented dryly.

"Better every day," he said cheerfully. "Come sit on my lap and I'll show you just how much better I feel."

It was mid-morning and we were alone in his reading room, for I had persuaded him not to go down to the hall quite yet. "Now, there's an offer to warm a maiden's heart," I responded to his invitation. "Let me find you a maiden who will warm yours in return." In fact, I had been looking around the hall for a suitable wench but hadn't found one who looked to be the right type. They were either too young, too thin, or married to someone who might object.

"I have the only maid I want," he insisted, letting his hand slide down to my waist and drawing me closer.

He used his injured arm as well as his good one, and so I let him continue tugging me nearer, thinking the exercise was good for it. But I snorted contemptuously. "Your eyes fail you, lord," I said, "for I'm no maid, but a dried up old woman with children of an age to be married, or nearly."

"And I'm a grandfather," he countered, "or as near as I'll ever come to it. What has that to do with anything?" With a quick, unexpected tug he threw me off balance and I landed with a soft thud in his lap, where I had not for a moment intended to be.

"What about your vow to yourself?" I demanded, struggling to get back up. "I thought you were a faithful husband these days."

"Ah, gently!" he warned as my struggles brought a hand too near his injured shoulder. Then he took advantage of my resultant leniency to explore further beneath my shawl. "And I have been a faithful husband. But all good things must come to an end, and I've a mind to end that particular condition."

"Well, I've made a vow of my own," I informed him. "I've made a vow to let no man—husband, king, or other lover—plant his seed in my furrow any more. I love my children, but three are more than enough for me."

He paused only for a moment before resuming his gentle questing. "You've nothing to fear from me, then," he said, keeping all trace of rancor out of his voice. "I've never planted a seed that grew." Leaning forward, he began to nuzzle my neck.

Oh, what a sizzling sensation shot through me at his touch! My blood warmed and I longed to press myself closer to him, instead of drawing away. But something in my head warned against such foolishness. "Ohhhh, no," I insisted, pushing his face firmly away from my neck. "With my luck, God would think it very funny to give me a child now, after all these years, when I really don't want one. He has an odd sense of humor, your Christian god." I struggled again to gain my feet.

This time he let me go with a sigh. He caught at my hand, though, after I had risen, and he lifted questioning eyes to mine. "Do you still worship Thor and Odin, Kelda?" he asked, and I could see the idea troubled him.

"No," I lied. "But I think of them as the gods of my people, and the Christian god as your god—whom I now worship," I added quickly. I did, after all. I went to mass and made my confession and said the Christian prayers and blessings—and I never spoke to my children of the old gods. I have raised them to be Scots, and that means being Christians. None shall ever have cause to call them heathen.

I'm not sure Macbeatha believed me. But he let the subject, and my hand, go.

Crossing behind him, I began to massage his neck and shoulders. After a moment, I whispered in his ear, "I can find you a wench, lord."

"Don't bother," he replied heavily. "Faithfulness is better for me."

I let my hand slide through the neck of his tunic to rub his chest, staying carefully away from his bandage. "A fine, big girl," I tempted. "Tall and buxom ... soft skin and firm flesh ..."

But he drew my hand out of his tunic, kissed it and put it aside. "There is no one else I trust," he said simply, and turned his attention back to his book.

That was not, however, the end of the matter. As he grew stronger, so did his desire—and he loved nothing so much as a challenge. He must conquer that which resisted. Within a week or so, he suggested I might speed his recovery by elevating his pulse in a pleasurable manner.

"Remember your vow," I reminded him patiently. We were in his chamber and I had just shaved him and changed his bandage, which now served only to keep his tunic from irritating the healing flesh.

"I've broken more vows than I can count," he sighed. "What's one more?"

I didn't like the tone of his voice: he sounded so discouraged. There is nothing so deadly to a warrior as melancholy. Melancholy kills their fighting spirit, and for warriors, to live is to do battle: if they lose the desire for one, they lose the desire for the other. I was not about to let my lord succumb to melancholy. So I knelt down in front of him and made him look into my eyes. "Name one," I challenged.

I thought he would speak of the duty he swore to Duncan, or the marriage vows he made to Gruoch; but instead, after a moment's thoughtful pause, he said, "I vowed to protect Alba. I have failed in that."

"Oh?" I arched an eyebrow. "I don't see any enemy of Alba wandering through the land unopposed, do you?" I was thinking, of course, of Siward, who had gone back to Northumbria and not, as yet, even come to Lothian to collect his *skatt*. Not that he wouldn't get there after the harvest, but he hadn't yet.

But Macbeatha answered soberly, "Canmore. Canmore is in Cumbria." Then he rose from his chair and began to pace. It pleased me to see him pace, for not long ago he hadn't the energy to do so; yet I was sorry to see him so agitated.

"I don't know what's happened to him, Kelda," he said of Canmore. "He has become his mother's son—she always hated me, even before I slew her husband. He is filled with that same hate, only fueled by his father's defeat. And he sits in Cumbria now, where I put him, and gathers his forces and binds that country to himself, so that he can march across its borders and attack me. The sons of Alba will die, because of his personal grudge against me."

"They will die because they are warriors. If they didn't fight Canmore, they'd find someone else to fight. That is what warriors do."

This simple truth did not comfort him. He sat on the edge of his bed, hands clasped as he rested his forearms on his knees. "But why does it have to be Colmbeag?" he asked sadly.

"Perhaps your father felt the same way," I suggested softly, "about Maelcolm and Gillecomgain."

That elicited a wry smile from him. "And I, like Colmbeag, hated them both because they slew my father." He shook his head. "You're right, Kelda. There is nothing new in Canmore's hatred, nor his desire to rule. Only it feels so different to be on the other side of the stream."

He looked so sad, and I longed to take him in my arms, to kiss and comfort him as I had in the old days, but I knew where that would lead and I was not ready to go there. So instead I chided him. "Oh, come, you sound like an old grandfather sitting by the fire mourning the loss of his teeth," I reproved. "You're not dead quite yet, I think."

"Come lie in this bed with me, and I'll show you how dead I am."

"And with twice the skill of Canmore, I'm sure," I agreed, rising to my feet and crossing to where he sat. "But I'm still not tempting the Fates." Then I leaned over, licked his ear and whispered, "Only you." He made a grab for me, but I scooted out of reach and left the room laughing. He could not be all that melancholy if I could still raise his blood, and his sense of humor.

Even as Macbeatha tried to coax me into his bed, Brenna tried to buy me out of it. I was in my bedchamber mending one of Venko's tunics—I told him he should have taken a mistress who could sew instead of cook, for his clothes were in a terrible state of disrepair—when Brenna stalked into the room and closed the door.

My hand went instinctively to the little shaving knife I once again kept hidden in the folds of my skirt; but Brenna kept her distance, posing in front of the door like a hawk on a crag. There were steaks of silver now in the brown hair that cascaded over her shoulders like a reckless stream, but she wore them like jewelry. From her waist there dangled a wicked looking knife in a gilded sheath. Too long for table use, it looked more like a warrior's blade—in fact, Brenna herself looked like some battlemaid: stern and hard and predatory. They say she rode at the head of Farrell's warband as they came to Dunsinnan, her sons flanking her. I do not doubt it.

"What will it take for you to leave?" she asked bluntly.

I studied her a moment and discovered I had grown tired of her senseless hostility. I held those dark eyes and replied with equal candor, "For Macbeatha to send me away."

She made a motion much like a hawk ruffling its feathers. "You have bewitched my brother," she declared. "I will not see him go down to Hell because of the spell you have placed upon him."

I arched an eyebrow at her. "Why? Don't you want his company there?"

Now her eyes blazed with anger. "I'm giving you fair warning, slut!" she hissed. "Leave now, or know my wrath!"

"I've known your wrath for twenty and more years," I said dryly. "I'm still here."

At that, her dainty little face turned harsh and ugly. "Remember that I know where your children live."

That was it. I was through trading words with this vindictive little she-wolf. Rising to my feet, I crossed to loom over her. "Remember that their father is your kinsman, and a warrior," I told her, "with a very long sword. And remember that you have children of your own who ride into battle with him." Then I brushed the princess aside like a serving girl and tugged the heavy door open. Pausing there, I said plainly, "I will stay as long as my lord has need of me."

Leaving the chamber, I went straight to Macbeatha and relayed her threat against my children. He was less patient than I. I'm told that later that day he invited her to accompany him to the church, where rested the Stone of Destiny. There he forced her head down upon that most awesome and holy block and, holding his knife to her cheek, threatened to scar her face if she did not swear upon the stone that she would do nothing to harm me or mine. It was not the first time he had taken my part against her in cruel measure, and yet she never ceased to love him. Can you explain to me, Fionna, why her love for him never faltered, and her hatred of me never dimmed?

Within two months of his injury, Macbeatha was riding to the hunt again, though it clearly exhausted him. His guard was careful that he not stay at it too long, and he grumbled about them coddling him, but he did not resist. Gruoch surprised him with a book she had commissioned for him, the writings of some dead Roman which they took turns reading aloud to each other. It gave him great delight and provided a more sedate pass-time. By the beginning of October, he had resigned himself to the tedious task of a slow but steady recovery. He had learned to pace himself so he used his injured shoulder enough to strengthen it without doing further damage. Under the watchful eyes of Owen and Gruoch and others strong enough to stand up to him, I knew he would be all right. I told Venko it was time to go home.

Macbeatha was surprised when I told him we would go back to Moray for the winter. "What need?" he asked, and his eyes pleaded for me to stay. "I shall be bored to tears if you go. Who will make me laugh as you do?"

"Lord, I have children," I reminded him patiently.

"Bring them to court."

We were in the hall, and the warriors and their ladies were beginning to assemble for the evening meal. I cast a glance over my shoulder at them. "Within reach of these predators?" I scoffed. "No thank you. I won't have my little ones called names to their faces, or gossiped about behind their backs." He started to object, but I hushed him with a finger to his lips. "And will you hold a knife to everyone's throat and make them swear? Be reasonable, lord. Let me see to my children this winter, and I will be back again in the spring."

His green eyes searched my face. "Promise?" he asked in a rough whisper.

I stamped my foot in mock petulance, putting my hands on my hips like the girl I used to be. "By the crozier of St. Colm," I swore like a good Scot, "it is not a life and death matter!" I disliked this tone of desperation that sometimes crept into his speech.

Taking my face in his calloused hands, he rubbed his thumbs gently across my cheeks. "Only I want my friends with me," he said quietly, "during these difficult times."

"That is your wound talking," I chided, pulling his hands firmly away before too many people saw. "And your wounded pride. You give too much weight to the prophecy of those old women." He never spoke of it in the hall, but I knew he fretted over Canmore's choice of the rowan as his emblem, and he searched the shadows for the Dark Warrior he'd been told would take his life.

"They said the rowan tree would come against me, and so it has—a great forest of rowan sprigs on the breast of those Athollmen. It looked like half of Birnam Wood."

"They also said you would have a long and prosperous reign," I reminded him. "And it is *not over*. Now, spend your winter at playing chess, and telling tales, and studying your books and maps. In the spring you'll see how many men come to you, and you'll feel better. Beltaine will make a new man of you."

"Will you spend it with me?" he teased. He never let me forget that Beltaine is a time to celebrate fertility in man and beasts, and it ought to be celebrated with sports, not only upon the field, but under the covers, as well.

"Why do you pursue an old cow when there are so many heifers about?" I asked.

"Because the milk is so rich," he purred.

I giggled. I couldn't help it. One could never get the better of Macbeatha in word games. "I surrender," I told him. Then I added craftily, "I promise I shall see to your Beltaine pleasure."

The sparkle in his eyes said he knew I was up to something, and I hoped the wicked anticipation would keep him amused that winter. It certainly warmed my lonely heart from time to time.

Chapter Twenty-Two

I managed to drag Venko back to Moray with me, though he was loath to leave Macbeatha at such a time. But there were family matters to take care of, and it was only right that he be involved in the decisions. We had very different views on some: he wanted to wed Siusan to a man of his tribe, but I argued a mac Craine was a much better choice, since his kin were mostly clients of the mac Craine. I finally got my way when I produced Fingon mac Craine, whose grandmother had been of Venko's tribe. Fingon was twenty-two, tall, fair-haired, and very bashful. He took one look at my dark, wild-eyed Siusan and went completely tongue-tied.

Siusan, unfortunately, was not equally impressed. Mostly, she had her heart set on one of Lonn's boys, with whom she had grown up. But the boy was unreliable, whereas Fingon was steady as a rock, the third of five sons and more concerned with cattle than with trophy heads. I was just puzzling how to make Siusan a bit more receptive to Fingon's suit when Netta solved the problem for me. One day, after her sister had criticized Fingon's lack of clever speech, Netta announced, "If you don't want him, Siusan, I will be glad to have him. I don't care if he can speak, as long as he can kiss."

There is nothing quite like sisterly jealousy to drive a romance forward. The next time Fingon came to call, Siusan lured him into the byre to discover for herself if kissing might, indeed, be the young man's redeeming quality. Apparently she liked what she discovered, for over the next several weeks we heard a slow but steady concession of Fingon's virtues. "Well, he does know an awful lot about tending beasts." "It's true, he is well-respected hereabouts." "At least he doesn't go off campaigning every summer, like his brother." And finally, "I do rather like that he's tall."

They could not be wed, of course, until she reached the Age of Choice late in the summer, but the arrangements were made, and Fingon came to take charge of our cattle while Venko and I were away. Siusan knew all that needed to be done, but the servants didn't always listen to her, whereas they would give Fingon no trouble. That was two matters laid to rest.

On the matter of Reagan's fosterage, though, Venko and I were agreed. Deep in the Highlands near the headwaters of the Findhorn is a tribe noted for the stern, fierce character of its warriors. Several had fought beside Macbeatha over the years, and one in particular was known to Venko. He was a brother to the chieftain and, Venko said, the third best swordsman in the kingdom—he and Macbeatha being first and second, of course. That was fine with me. All I cared was that he lived far from the turmoil brewing in the south. I kissed my son, and wept over him, and watched him out of sight, knowing I might never see him again. But he is safe there in the Highlands, my Reagan, for a little while. There is no safety for a warrior when he comes of age and the lust for battle seizes him, but while he is yet a boy without the means to defend himself, he is safe from his father's enemies, and from mine.

It was near to Beltaine before all these arrangements could be made. But finally we could leave with quiet hearts, knowing Reagan was in good hands and Fingon would see to Siusan and her sister. Then I shocked Venko by choosing a maid from among the servant girls and bringing her along to Scone. Until then I had scorned having a personal maid to brush my hair and tidy my chamber. But, "Most of the ladies at court have maids," I informed Venko with a sniff. "Perhaps they will stop thinking of me as a servant if I have one of my own." I didn't think that very likely, but I did think it was apt to give Brenna fits to see me waited upon. The very thought made me smile.

So it was that Flanna came to court with me. Flanna was nineteen or twenty—she wasn't quite sure—and had a little boy named Guarie, who came with us, too. Flanna had met Guarie's father at the Midsummer fire and gone to live with him for a year and a day, as is the custom before marriage. But he beat her, so when the year was up and she met him again across the Midsummer fire, she turned and walked away. Wise girl! Back to her father and mother she went, but there were five other children at home, and lots of hard work. When I told her what I wanted of a maid, she jumped at the chance.

As her name suggests, Flanna has reddish hair. She is not exactly beautiful, but neither is she ugly. She has a sort of plain face, with a generous sprinkling of freckles and clear blue eyes. She also has large breasts and a merry laugh, and she was no stranger to a man's bed, even then. I had promised to provide Macbeatha with his Beltaine pleasure—I hadn't said it would be in my own person.

Macbeatha looked his old self again when we arrived that spring, right down to his chin, which had magically stayed shaven while I was gone. Well recovered from his wound, his spirits had been lifted by a visit from the new Mormaer of Moray, Lulach mac Gillecomgain, and Lulach's son Maelsnechta. Both had gone back now to Moray, for Lulach intended to invade Strathclyde that summer and, if not dislodge Canmore, at least rattle his teeth a bit. It would have been inappropriate for Macbeatha to do so, since he had given Canmore the kingdom, but Lulach could hardly wait to challenge his rival. Macbeatha's face glowed as he talked of his stepson's ambitions, of the high caliber of his guardsmen, of the many men who flocked to his banner. It was as though Macbeatha himself climbed to the top of Alba's hierarchy once again.

How it warmed my heart to see the old sparkle in his smile, to feel his eyes rake me up and down like a hungry man beholding a roasted pig, and to see him walk with all the confidence and power that were ever his. He arched an eyebrow when he saw I had a girl to wait on me, for Flanna rearranged my cloak when we entered the hall, and brushed at my skirt to make it lie smoothly, all the while carrying Guarie tucked under one arm like a satchel. "I see you have come in style this time," my lord commented, watching her bustle about her work. "Is that your son she carries like a parcel?"

I laughed. "No, my son is much older. That's Flanna's boy."

"Flanna." He savored the name on his tongue as he ran an appreciative eye over her. She had found one of the household servants and was asking for my chamber, that she might see my trunks safely to it. Suddenly the smile dropped from Macbeatha's face and he turned to me with accusing eyes. "You haven't, by any chance, brought her along with me in mind, have you?"

I gave him an indignant look. "I brought her to serve me," I said, pretending to be offended at such a suggestion.

"Good." He took a step closer and leaned over to speak into my ear. "Because I don't accept substitutes."

"Yes, I know, faithful husband and all that," I agreed. "As though a man your age could catch a fresh young thing like Flanna, anyway."

Now he glared at me, then wagged a warning finger under my nose. "Don't give me your sauce, woman."

"Oh, but I must. It's why you keep me around, remember? And a good thing, because Lord knows I won't give you anything else."

He just grinned a smugly wicked grin and went off to join his men at the hearth.

For the next several days, his eyes followed Flanna quite a bit, as though he were trying to decide if she was tempting enough to risk indiscretion. Sometimes he would look from her to me with reproach in his eyes, as if I did him some disservice by flaunting a comely wench before him.

When Beltaine came, with games and feasting and much merrymaking, he joined in the festivities whole-heartedly—although he was not so foolish as to try beating the younger men at their sports. But he wagered recklessly, awarded prizes, and flirted with every woman in attendance, base or free. Then in the evening, when the bonfire was lit, he prowled the circle of its light like a predator, his gold jewelry winking an invitation.

Flanna stood at my elbow holding Guarie, and when Macbeatha came to her, he paused. He reached out to touch young Guarie first, for he loved babies still, but then his hand caressed Flanna's cheek. Slipping his fingers into her thick, red hair, he leaned to whisper something in her ear. Then he moved on around the circle.

"What did he say?" I asked her eagerly.

She looked puzzled. "He said if he were not the High King, he would ravish me on the spot." Flanna raised worried eyes to my face. "I thought I was supposed to— I mean, I understood you to say— Do you suppose it's because I—"

"It has nothing to do with you," I assured her. "He is being stubborn. He wants what he cannot have, therefore he will not take what is available. Only let me speak to him a moment."

Slipping through the crowd, I hurried to catch up to him. Finally I was able to reach out and catch his wrist as he stopped to take a bite of the cake in Lady Nuala's hand. He turned from her to me with glittering eyes and I pulled his head down toward mine so I could whisper in his ear. "Lord, they expect you to do more than flirt," I said. "If you go to your bed alone, people will say you are no longer able to take your pleasure of a wench."

Suddenly he wrenched me up tight against him, and I could feel that part of him which proclaimed he could and would have his pleasure that night. "Come to my chamber," he whispered hoarsely, "and we will prove them all wrong."

"I am your loyal man's wife," I reminded him. "It cannot be."

His eyes narrowed and his smile was cold. "Even so," he said, as though that had been his point. Then he let me go and moved on around the circle until he came to Gruoch. She was surrounded by her ladies, her graying hair plaited with flowers. Her figure had thickened a bit with age, though not to excess, and she reminded me of the way her mother had looked when I first met the Lady Boite: very dignified, and very regal. She smiled warmly at her husband, and then the smile faded as she noted the odd look in his eye.

Suddenly he pulled her to him as abruptly as he had me and locked her in a passionate kiss. It raised a heat in me just to watch them. When finally he let her go, Gruoch looked stunned, and a little weak in the knees. That was all right, for she didn't need her knees—Macbeatha scooped her up and tossed her across his shoulder like a sack of meal. You should have seen the look on her face! When she protested, he smacked her smartly upon the backside so that she jumped. Then he sauntered off toward the hall with the queen of Alba over his shoulder like a common serving wench.

Oh, he had style, had Macbeatha. I don't know that Gruoch appreciated it, but he had style. And do you know, Fionna? I think he was trying to make me jealous!

Chapter Twenty-Three

Not long after Beltaine, news reached us that Siward of Northumbria had died of an illness, and I was much relieved. I don't think Macbeatha really was. He had known Siward, known his methods and his ambitions. Now King Edward appointed his brother-in-law Tostig as the new Jarl of Northumbria, and that was cause for dismay because he was a friend of Canmore's from their youth in Edward's court. He took up Canmore's cause with relish, announcing boldly that he would lend whatever ships and men the Cumbrian king needed to seize the throne of Alba.

Who do they think they are, these Anglishmen, deciding who should rule over the Scots? It is not their nation! What do they know of our land, of our people, of our customs? I call them mine, Fionna, for I have lived twice as long among the Scots as I did among the Norse. I know how their law works, whereas these Angles speak of the "throne" of Alba and can't even get it straight in their heads that Alba has no throne, and no crown, to symbolize power, but a white rod. And it is *not* the right of the son to succeed his father—not here. These Anglishmen seek to impose their law, their customs upon the Scots, and why should that be?

Even now, the leaders of Alba meet in Scone to decide who will be the next High King, and it must be Lulach—there is no other prince in the land who is known to them all for his courage in battle and his constancy in friendship. He is the only one who can carry on the war against Canmore—for it will go on, this war. Canmore will not cease his quest for power until he succeeds or dies. And

Lulach is the best man to lead the fight against him, for Lulach has fought him before.

It was a merry young man who left Inverness that summer to lead his troops south to wrest Strathclyde from Canmore. But he was rudely surprised to find an army of Atholl lying between him and Dumbarton. He had to fight them first, before he could get to Canmore. So fight them he did, and win, too; but it is a prickly thing to leave a defeated enemy at your back while you march forward to meet another opponent.

Macbeatha decided this would be a good time to call upon the Mormaer of Fortriu, whose lands lie between Atholl and Strathclyde. With the High King and his sizeable warband sitting so close by, the Athollmen dared not harry Lulach's flank. On marched the Mormaer of Moray to challenge the Cumbrian king.

Yet many of the Athollmen slipped ahead to join Canmore's army. It gave him greater numbers than Lulach brought down from Moray. They met in a fierce battle near Loch Lomond, and I understand Lulach did considerable damage, but eventually he had to leave the field. That he acquitted himself well I do not doubt, for Canmore did not attempt to pursue him; but it was not the victory he had hoped for.

I accompanied my lord to Fortriu, so I was there when Lulach and his warband joined the High King to rest and recover from their wounds before returning to Moray. It tickled me that Macbeatha asked me to see to his stepson's hurts—minor things, a cut here, a scrape there.

We were in the mormaer's hall, and Lulach sat in a chair near an open window where the light was good. "I remember you, Kelda," he said as I dressed a scratch on his arm. "From when I was a little boy. I remember you racing through the hall when my father came home, your skirts bunched in one hand and a horn of ale sloshing in the other. I remember you sitting at his feet and laughing. I remember you shaving his cheek ..." His voice trailed off and he threw a glance at Macbeatha, who stood by watching us. "Why have you shaved your beard again, anyway?"

My lord replied without hesitation. "To find the man underneath." It was such a ready answer, I suspect he had been asked this question many times before.

Lulach didn't know what to make of this response, any more than I did, but after one puzzled look, his face lit up in a smile. "The man underneath? Why, I didn't know he was missing!" It was just the sort of thing Macbeatha himself might have said, and they both laughed at his wit. But as Macbeatha did not elaborate, the young prince asked, "But why did you stop shaving your beard in the first place?"

Tears stung in my eyes, even after so many years, and I was glad I was busy tying up the bandage so neither of them could see. "How many people would you trust with a knife to your throat?" Macbeatha asked.

That made Lulach frown; then he shook his head sadly. "I cannot understand how anyone can resort to treachery to slay a man. There is no honor in it; and what is there for a Scot except honor? That is what distinguishes us from barbarians."

Macbeatha's countenance grew dark, and I knew he was remembering Duff mac Moryn, who slew Gruoch's brother without letting him draw his sword. "You do not have to understand it," he growled at Lulach, "but believe it. Believe it, and beware of it, or your life will be brief and the bards will christen you Lulach the Foolish."

Lulach looked over at Flanna, who held the basin of water I had used to clean his cuts. "You would never cut my throat, would you?" he teased her. "If I asked you to shave me?"

"Not on purpose, lord," she replied innocently, which made the rest of us laugh.

Lulach's eyes lingered on her healthy bosom, and I was not surprised later on when Flanna brought Guarie to the sun house where I was spinning with the other women and tugged at my sleeve. Whispering in my ear, she asked if there was any harm in serving the son, since the father did not seem interested in her charms. With a sigh, I told her she might serve whomever she pleased, so long as she was discreet. Smiling, she handed little Guarie over to me and, like the child she was, she skipped lightly off to find her handsome warrior.

It made my heart ache with nostalgia to watch her go. I had been that girl once. I had been, and never would be again. But then, Macbeatha would never again be that brash young prince on his way to power, and I think it was worse for him than for me. We stole a moment alone that night, out in the yard, slipping away among the shadows like two naughty children. The night was cool, and my shawl was thin, but when he wrapped his great arms around me, I needed no other warmth.

For a long time we simply stood there, holding each other contentedly as only old, familiar lovers can, with no need for speech between us. Then he put his lips near my ear and spoke softly. "I do appreciate your present, you know, even though I haven't taken advantage of her."

"You mean Flanna?" I asked. "Oh, did you think she was for you?"

He chuckled quietly. "You always were a shameless wench. You knew just the kind of girl who would catch my eye. And believe me, Kelda, I thought about this one."

"Well, thinking is probably all an old man like you can do."

"Lift that skirt of yours, and I'll show you just what an old man like me can do." For a moment we struggled playfully, but he gave up rather quickly and went back to holding me close. A breeze played through the leaves overhead, and I could hear the skittering of night creatures through the grass and ferns nearby. Then, "It's not that a girl like Flanna doesn't rouse me anymore," he went on. "It's just that— There is always a price for such pleasure, and frankly, I'm no longer inclined to pay."

I knew what he meant. As a young woman, I could not have imagined it, but by then I had paid heavily for all my flirtations, and my naive refusal to be discreet. There is a cost to the heart for all such antics. Yes, I knew very well what he meant. "Whatever you wish, lord," I told him sincerely. "My only thought was for your comfort, and your pleasure."

He stroked my hair and kissed my brow. "Dearest Kelda," he sighed. "That is the only thought you have ever had."

Macbeatha honored us by coming to the wedding of our daughter Siusan at the end of summer. It was the first time he had seen her since she was a babe. He was his sly, wicked self, flirting outrageously with both our girls and teasing Fingon that if Siusan's father were anyone other than his own trusted man, he would steal her away from her groom. Netta begged to come back to court with us, but I was adamant. She knew I had once been the High King's servant, and being a very wise child for a twelve-year-old, I believe she suspected in what capacity I had served—but she didn't need to hear it from the likes of Brenna.

The number of nobles who came to court that winter was smaller than usual. It had been small the year before, Weylin told us, but everyone thought it was because Macbeatha was recovering from his wound. Now we had to admit there might be another reason, the one Macbeatha feared most: they had begun to doubt. A new chessman was on the board in Malcolm Canmore, and strengthened by Tostig of Northumbria, he set people to wondering. How long would it be before he struck at the High King once again? And in that strike, who would win?

It was interesting to see who did and did not come to call. Fortriu was conspicuously absent, though he may have been watching Canmore just to his west. Atholl came, but only briefly, with only half his *conveth*, pleading poverty. Macbeatha told him bluntly that the rest would be paid in the spring, or the High King would take it himself from the mormaer's herds and flocks, even if it left him nothing. The King of the Isles did not come, and several prominent nobles of Cirech and Fife also begged the king's pardon for not visiting.

But you'll never guess who *did* come: Donall mac Duncan, known as Donallban, brother to Malcolm Canmore.

The hall at Scone was decked for the Christmas feasting when we heard a commotion outside, and up the steps clattered a band of ten warriors, all with jaunty bonnets and smug smiles. At their head strode a young man in his early twenties, his hair as pale as mine and his blue eyes sparkling as though he had just tricked a churchman out of his habit and cross. "Greetings, lord!" he sang out to Macbeatha, who was seated at a chess board across from the Mormaer of Ce. "I am Donall mac Duncan, and I come seeking hospitality at your Christmas table."

Macbeatha rose slowly and regarded this upstart prince with the cocky smile and the brazen manner. "I had rather hoped to see your brother here," he told Donall. "Do you come on his behalf?"

"No, lord, I come as my own man," Donall replied cheerfully. "Am I welcome as such?"

Macbeatha inclined his head in regal ascent. "You are welcome, Donall mac Duncan. Perhaps more welcome than if you came in your brother's name, for he has not paid me his *conveth*; and if you do not bring it with you, then it is well you don't greet me as his representative."

Donall grinned, showing a row of white, even teeth. "I'm afraid my brother doesn't intend to pay you, lord," he said without apology. "But for my own self, I have brought gifts of bread and ale and wheat flour for the feasting."

What could Macbeatha do? Donall made all show of courtesy as a guest, offering no offense, breaching no protocol. Macbeatha gave him hospitality, having no choice. But we all knew very well why the young prince was there. He came to spy on us—and to tweak the High King's nose.

It was the funniest thing to watch Macbeatha watching Donall. It was like a lead hound watching an insolent pup parade across his territory. "Damned cock-sure whelp!" the king muttered one day when the prince had gone out of the hall to show off his new clothes in the marketplace. "I ought to send his head back to Canmore in a sack!"

"But you won't," I said serenely.

"No," he admitted. "But how does he know I won't?"

"Because, lord," I told him, looking him square in the eye, "he's just like you."

Oh, he didn't like that. He cursed and fumed and declared that all women were simpletons, taken in by a handsome face and a brazen air. It seems Gruoch had made much the same comment earlier.

Finally, after Twelfthnight, Donall came to take his leave of the king.

"Tell your brother I missed him," Macbeatha said gruffly. "And tell him I'll be around in a month or so to collect my *conveth*."

"I'm sure he's expecting you," Donall replied. "In fact, I believe he and mac Duff can hardly wait for your arrival."

Suddenly an unreadable expression settled over my lord's features. "Mac Duff?" he said with feigned nonchalance. "Which mac Duff would that be?"

Though he controlled himself carefully, there was no mistaking the pleasure with which Donall savored his response: "Larkin mac Duff mac Moryn."

"The only Duff mac Moryn I knew," Macbeatha said evenly, "was a coward and a murderer, and he deserved no better death than he got."

"That would be the man."

"And his son wants my head, I suppose,"

Donall laughed. "He's obsessed with it. Practices with his weapons day and night. Hardly sleeps, he's so busy inventing various ways to kill you."

"Obsessed, you say?" Still Macbeatha's face and voice revealed no trace of anxiety. "Well, tell him he'll get his chance. I'm due my *conveth,* and I'll take it from Malcolm's storehouses and pastures myself if he doesn't hand it over. Oh, and Donall— If I see you at your brother's side resisting me, I'll hold you as guilty as him."

"Oh, I'll be there," Donall assured him with a smile. "It's all to my advantage, and I wouldn't want to miss the fun."

Macbeatha arched an eyebrow. "How so?"

"If Malcolm is killed, I am in line to become king of Cumbria, since I am his tanist. And if *you're* killed and Malcolm becomes High King, I'll still become king of Cumbria. And I'll gladly pay *conveth* to whomever rules, by the way. I'm not so greedy as my brother, nor so idealistic."

"Then stay out of the way of my spears," Macbeatha advised him. "For I do not hesitated to cut down those who oppose me, whether they have dined at my table or not."

"I don't doubt it. But between your spears and me will be not only my own shield and courage, but mac Duff— and he is the fiercest madman I have ever seen." Then the Cumbrian prince turned on his heel and left.

Slowly Macbeatha rose to his feet, trembling with controlled rage. "Fetch Sloane to me now," he hissed. "I need a man to go into Cumbria and find this mac Duff. I need to know just how mad a madman he is."

Chapter Twenty-Four

In Fionna's hut

"And he was the dark warrior, this mac Duff?" Fionna guessed.

Kelda nodded, and in her lap, Venko stirred. "Bent out of nature," Venko said softly. "All to one side: south and not north, odd and not even, night and not day—" He sighed deeply. "Left, and not right. A man with no balance in him."

Fionna knew those had been her very words, twenty-five years before. Venko had carried them as a nagging weight all this time, so when the hour came, he did not have far to reach for that prophecy. "And did you know it then?" she asked.

"Not then," he told her. "Only later, when I saw him fight."

"Macbeatha knew, though," Kelda said. "When Sloane returned, my lord received his report in private and would not divulge its contents; but those of us who knew him well, knew he was disturbed. Only I could guess why, for I had been with him when Donall taunted him with news of mac Duff."

* * *

There were, as you can well imagine, many outrageous tales which circulated about the king: that he could catch a spear in midair and hurl it back; that when he danced a war dance upon his shield, you could hear the drums of the *sidhe,* the fair folk, coming from the forest. Some said he had the Second Sight and knew where an enemy lurked before that enemy showed himself. Others claimed he had tricked an angel out of his heavenly speech, and that was how he could strike such shrewd bargains with people like Thorfinn. But the most interesting and persistent tale to crop up in halls and hovels across the land was that his life was enchanted.

Some said it was his Pictish grandmother who cast a spell of protection over him, so that no man born of woman could harm him. Others said he had bedded a queen of the *sidhe* who was so impressed with his prowess that she granted him this boon. Still others whispered he'd made a pact with the Devil. But they all agreed: no ordinary man could kill Macbeatha mac Findlaech. And fortified by the prophecy of the *Cailleach*, he himself had sauntered through life confident that only one man could destroy him, and that was the Dark Warrior foretold.

But when the rowan came against him at Dunsinnan, and a wound that seemed minor grew unexpectedly foul and fearsome, Macbeatha became like a bull that has scented the wolf. For years he had ignored his own mortality, believing in the long reign promised to him; but fifteen years is a long time for a man to be King of Scots, and we all knew it.

Late that night after Sloane brought his news, after the hall had quieted down, Macbeatha stole down the empty passageway to my chamber and let himself in. I had not been asleep—how could I sleep, knowing what Sloane must have said?—and so I stirred in my bed when he opened the door. "Don't be frightened," he whispered, "it's only me."

I told him I hardly imagined it was Venko, who had discarded his old mistress in favor of a plump widow he found in the village. Then I made room for Macbeatha on the edge of my bed, and he sat down facing me.

"Sloane has seen mac Duff," he said quietly, reaching out in the darkness and finding my cheek with his fingers.

I could not speak. Instead I ran my hand gently along his outstretched arm in a comforting gesture.

"He is everything that Donall claimed," he continued. "Fierce—deadly—mad." His fingers slipped now from my cheek into my hair and twined themselves there. After a moment he added, "He fights left-handed."

"That doesn't make him the Dark Warrior," I said, though I did not believe that, and I knew he wouldn't, either.

"Dark with old blood." He sighed. "The old woman said he would be dark with old blood. None is any older or any darker than that of Duff mac Moryn."

I wanted to deny it, to say, *Oh, pooh! You've killed a hundred men or more in your time, and a good share of them before you ever met Duff. Why not one of their sons?* But I knew it was all wind through a tattered sail. So I kept quiet.

In the darkness he bent over and laid his head upon my breast. I rubbed his neck and stroked him, as I had done so many times in years gone by. There was such an ache in him—not a longing for pleasures of the flesh, but the need to be held and comforted. So I pulled back the blankets and furs and let him come into the bed with me, which he did with a grateful and ragged sigh. Troubled as he was, he did not attempt to take advantage, but was content to hold me tightly to him. There, twined in each others arms as of old, we finally slept and did not wake until morning.

The winter dawn was slow in coming, so noises in the yard and the hall woke us before any daylight filtered into the room. For some time we lay there in silence, touching each other and remembering a thousand similar mornings; and I was tempted to discard my resolve and encourage him to indiscretion. It had been eight years since he had visited me in Moray and we had coupled there on the stream bank. But as I contemplated the wisdom—or the foolishness—of it, he sat up and put his feet on the floor. "I suppose your maid will be coming up soon," he said, for Flanna and Guarie usually slept in the hall with the other servants and retainers. "I shouldn't be seen here."

I snorted contemptuously. "As though it won't be all over the village by midday that you spent the night in my chamber."

"I know," he sighed, rubbing at his face sleepily. "But I couldn't worry Gruoch with my fears, and I couldn't bear to sleep alone." I heard the weariness in his voice and reached up to rub his back.

"I have to fight Canmore, you know," he said defeatedly. "I can't let him get away with not paying his *conveth*. So I have to go down there, as soon as I can assemble a large enough warband, and make him pay up. I have to go face mac Duff."

It wounded me to hear him sound so dispirited. "And did they say, those old women, that you would fall the first time you met this Dark Warrior?" I challenged.

No, he had to admit that wasn't what they'd said. "They said there was a dark warrior, and in all the world, only he could destroy me."

"So there," I pronounced triumphantly. "You might fight him ten, fifteen times before he gets the best of you."

Macbeatha gave me a wry smile. "You do have a way of looking at things that sets the world back on its feet."

"Nonsense. You just have a way of looking at it slantwise. Now, I forbid you to be melancholy." I gave him a gentle shove to encourage him off the bed. "Go be the kind of king I know you are. Call up your warband. Go thrash recalcitrant Atholl to whet your appetite, and then descend upon Malcolm Canmore like the Seven Hounds of Hell."

In the dim light I could see his grin. "Like the Hounds of Hell, eh?" he asked, reaching back to rub my neck, and then letting his hand slide down to take liberties elsewhere. "And will you come with me?"

"Where you go, I follow," I promised.

His hand began to tug at my shift. "Just like the old days?" he asked slyly.

I balked, but it was so good to see the light come back into his eyes. "What do you mean, 'old days'?" I asked. "Wasn't it just yesterday I fetched your ale, and cleaned your boots, and sat in your lap by the campfire while you reached under my skirt to play?"

"What a salacious wench you were," he remembered, letting his hand find my thighs. "By St. Brigit, I never knew a woman so eager for pleasure as you. And I knew quite a few." Then his hand stopped and his smile dimmed. "But no more, eh?"

With heart pounding, I took a deep breath and decided to risk the caprice of the gods. Surely they had better things to notice than what I was doing. "So I said," I told him coyly. "And where is the warrior man enough to change my mind?"

How his eye sparked at the challenge! And how I did enjoy my surrender. But it was for him I did it, and not myself. He needed to be a conqueror again, so I hoped to fuel his appetite for the conquest of his enemies with his conquest of me. And who can say I was not right to do so? For he went forth from my chamber, ready to take charge of his destiny again, eager once more for the battle. Perhaps it would have been so anyway, but I like to think I contributed in my small way.

We rode out against Atholl before Beltaine, before they could assemble too great a warband. The mormaer and his guard met us outside Dunkeld and challenged Macbeatha to a battle of fifty. To this my lord agreed, and the time was set for the following day. But Macbeatha shocked everyone by not choosing his personal guard to engage in the battle. Instead, he chose thirty seasoned warriors from his standing warband, and twenty fresh young men of Moray who had marched to join him for the first time that spring.

Venko and the others were not happy to be left out of the fighting, but no one was more unhappy, I think, than the Mormaer of Atholl. He had chosen fifty of his youngest, fiercest men, thinking their quickness and vigor would carry the day in a battle of equal numbers. But the same thing had occurred to Macbeatha, which was why he had chosen his own younger, yet experienced, men to fight. And while the battle sounded in the glen, his wily, war-wise guardsmen were driving off two hundred and more of the Mormaer's cattle that had been gathered for the upcoming Beltaine blessing. When the Athollmen were finally forced from the field, my lord already had his overdue *conveth* in possession. He bade farewell to a chastened Atholl and went to celebrate Beltaine with Fortriu.

As we camped about Aberfoyle, news reached us that the Mormaer of Fife had crossed into Northumbria and intercepted two hundred of Jarl Tostig's men who rode to aid Canmore. This was just what we had feared, the Anglish lending Canmore support. "Lord, you must send for Thorfinn," I urged him.

But he balked at the suggestion. "I met with Thorfinn as he returned from a pilgrimage to Rome," he told me. "He has put up his sword to keep the peace in his own country, and to serve God in the building of a church. I don't know if he will heed a call to war."

I made an exasperated noise. "He is a warrior," I said disparagingly. "And he is your brother under the sod. If you call him, he cannot refuse to come."

"Yet I hate to ask it of him," Macbeatha said softly, "for it is a noble work he does. Fife has served me well in stopping the Northumbrians. Let us hope that, for this season at least, my Scots are enough to teach young Canmore a lesson."

So on the eve of Beltaine, with the show of revelry being provided by the folk of Aberfoyle, Macbeatha and his warband stole south and surprised Canmore at Dumbarton. Caught inside the fortress there, with all his cattle, sheep and horses gathered outside for the Beltaine blessing, Canmore mustered those warriors who were camped around him and marched out to defend his property. They had little success and were soon beaten back inside the fortress walls. At least, that is the way it was told to me—I was left behind at Aberfoyle.

I do know that Macbeatha and his warband returned to us victorious with a great many beasts, and that they continued to battle back and forth throughout the summer: the Scots raided into Cumbria in small parties as they wished, and the Cumbrians raided back into Fortriu to recoup their losses. In his younger days, Macbeatha would have found this sort of activity quite entertaining and been content to amuse himself with it until well after Midsummer—but no longer. After that first battle, he led hardly any raids himself, only presiding over the sporadic strikes that followed. He looked weary in the evenings, and as the summer rains poured down, he would rub at the ache in his right shoulder and talk of returning to Scone to oversee the harvest there.

And around the campfires, when the laughter had died and the singing wound to a close, men would speak in hushed tones of Malcolm Canmore, who was brave as a bull and canny as a wolf. "And who is that madman who rides with him?" they would ask one another. "The one with the pale hair cut in the Danish fashion. I saw him run through two men with one spear, and every stroke of his sword takes a man's head ..." The Dark One, they called him, and The Lunatic. And sometimes, The Changeling.

Macbeatha had set up court for himself at Aberfoyle, even letting Gruoch come to show how safe he felt. Many important nobles came to see how he fared against the young challenger, and he entertained them in grand style. Then, when Midsummer had passed, he packed up his entourage and left Fortriu for Loch Tay and some deer hunting. This sort of kingly aplomb was supposed to tweak the beard of young Canmore, and it probably did. But it made no friends in Fortriu. When the king and his men had gone, they were left to suffer the Cumbrians' reprisals with only those warriors of Fife and Cirech who lingered on to aid them.

"Let there be empty bellies in Strathclyde this winter," Macbeatha had grated as he drove off all the beasts he had collected earlier in the summer, sending them back to his own lands near Scone. But the Cumbrians were not about to suffer alone, not when there were cattle and sheep in Fortriu. So there were empty bellies in both places that winter.

When we returned to Scone for Hallowmas, Venko and I learned our Siusan had given birth to a daughter, and after witnessing the ordeal, Netta had vowed to marry the Church. That didn't last, of course, for she took such delight in the new babe, Fingon had to practically lock her in the house to keep her from rushing out to make one of her own.

Lulach also had a daughter that winter, and Gruoch could hardly wait for spring so she could rush to gaze upon this angelic creature. That is the only good news we had that winter. Word came that Jarl Tostig had assembled two thousand horsemen and was sending them to his friend Malcolm Canmore. Canmore could easily raise that many again in Cumbria, plus there were tribes in Atholl spoiling for the opportunity to rise up against Macbeatha and drive the hated House of Loarn from power. And after what we had done to Fortriu, it would surprise no one if that Great Tribe struck a bargain with its powerful neighbor.

Macbeatha called for a thousand men from each of his mormaers. And at last, upon the insistence of both myself and the Lady Gruoch, he wrote to his friend Jarl Thorfinn and requested his aid in taking young Canmore out of power. "The time has come to challenge the Fates," he told me. "Perhaps when the old woman said to beware the rowan, it meant I should not underestimate Canmore—which I have done by giving Cumbria to him. Now it is time to rectify that mistake."

Of the Dark Warrior, he did not speak.

The requested warbands came from Cirech and Ce, from Moray and Fife, and even some from the Western Isles, although not so many as my lord would have liked. But none came from Atholl, and none from Fortriu. Macbeatha had hired five hundred Irish mercenaries, as well, and with his standing warband and a number of warriors who showed up just for the glory of it all, his troops numbered nigh six thousand. Patrols went all through the hills north of Strathclyde, and along the River Forth, with others sent to watch the western coastal lands of Atholl where my lord feared Canmore might invade by sea and be joined by his kinsmen. My lord planned to lead the bulk of his forces to Doune in Fortriu, from whence he could strike in any direction.

But before we could depart, there came the worst news of all. I saw the messenger from the Orkneys arrive, a young-looking priest with the crown of his head shaved in a Roman tonsure. As soon as Macbeatha had sent him off to the kitchen to find a meal, I rushed into my lord's reading room, where he stood gazing out the window with a sheet of velum in his hand. "Is he coming?" I asked eagerly. "Will Hakon be with him, do you suppose?"

My lord did not turn from the window. In a flat voice, he said, "Thorfinn is dead."

Chapter Twenty-Five

All the breath left my body in a rush. It was a moment before I could speak. Thorfinn, dead? "How?" I demanded. "He died of an illness just after Christmas."

I could scarcely take it in. Thorfinn, who had survived the treachery of half-brothers and nephew, dead? Thorfinn, the warrior by whom all other Norsemen set their standards, dead? And of an illness? I burst into tears.

Bless Macbeatha for trying to comfort me when his own heart must have been so sore. Putting his arms around me, he murmured, "He was your first love, wasn't he?"

"You don't understand," I sobbed. "To die of an illness—in his bed— That is no way for such a great warrior to die! A warrior should die in battle, with his sword in his hand, not in the straw like a cow!" It is a great shame for a Norse warlord to die so.

For a long moment Macbeatha said nothing, and I could almost feel the ache inside him for the man who was close kin of his soul, if not of his flesh. Finally, in a voice thick with grief, he said, "Perhaps he did as they say my old enemy Sigurd did: dressed in his armor and had his men stand him upon his feet so he could meet death with a spear in one hand and an axe in the other."

It was a hopeful thought, and it gave me a moment's comfort— enough, at least, to realize what this meant for the coming campaign. I drew back to look at my lord "Surely his sons will come to your aid, won't they?" I asked tentatively. "Will they not honor the love their father bore you and sail with their *hird* to fight against Canmore?"

But he shook his head and waved the piece of vellum listlessly as he returned to the window. "I have been told politely but firmly that the Orkneys will not interfere in the affairs of Alba and her neighbors. Both Paul and Erlend have made their marks on it." He gave a wry smile. "It seems they are waiting to see who wins, before they make an alliance with one or the other of us."

"There can be no doubt who will win!" I exclaimed indignantly. "And even less so if they were to come in on your side!"

"Well..." Macbeatha rolled up the vellum slowly and held it in both hands. "I met Thorfinn's sons once. I found them to be spoiled, self-serving, sanctimonious little monsters, and I didn't like them a bit. Apparently," he added dryly, "the feeling was mutual."

"Now what will you do?"

"Do?" he echoed with a lift of one eyebrow. "The same as I would do *with* Thorfinn's aid: attack Canmore. I still have more warriors than he. I will take them west and see where he assembles his men. Once I know his whereabouts, I will draw him onto a field of my choosing and teach him a lesson he'll take to his grave." There was hard iron in his voice as he spoke, and that look which made brave men tremble had come again into his eye.

Canmore was not particularly easy to find, however. We knew where he was mostly by which of our scouts did not return. That is a sad thing, but it is true. And even that we could not trust, for when scouts returned to us alive and unharmed, did that mean Canmore's men were truly not in that region? or that they were hiding there, and chose to let the scouts return so as to throw Macbeatha off the track?

"He cannot hide that many men," Weylin insisted.

"Not his Northumbrians," Macbeatha agreed. "They are at Dumfries, that we know. But Cumbrians? Uplanders? They could be anywhere—fifty here, two hundred there, and you'd never know it."

There was no air of pageantry or kingly leisure about our departure that spring. This was deadly serious business, and everyone knew it. It was the seventeenth year of Macbeatha's reign, and the first real challenge to his kingdom since the battle at Gowrie three years earlier. He tried to leave me behind, but I was no longer his slave—I simply waved him good-bye, waited until the head of the column was out of sight, then snatched up my bundle of belongings and joined the tail end of the baggage train.

It was three days before he even knew I was there. He tried sending me back, but I pointed out that I would only return to him as soon as my escort had gone. Growling and snarling, he finally gave up the idea. It was all the harder on him because he had tried to pack Gruoch off to Inverness to visit her new grandchild, but for once she would not be enticed. "I shall wait here in Scone for you, lord," she said patiently, obstinately.

"A month ago you couldn't *wait* to go see your granddaughter!" he cried in frustration. "What happened?"

"I changed my mind."

"And when do you think you might change it back?"

"When you bring me victory," she said, and went on with her embroidery.

When we had been in camp two weeks, Macbeatha decided he could wait no longer for proper information and must lead a raid somewhere into Strathclyde. Rumors had Canmore encamped with a small army on the shores of Loch Lomond in the west, and since that was as likely a place as any, my lord struck against it. They did meet resistance there, but it was not led by Canmore, and there were no more than two or three hundred of them. They faded back into the hills rather quickly and only harried the High King's warband as they returned to Doune.

Next it was the Campsie Fells from which his scouts did not return, and so he marched there. Again he found a pocket of Cumbrians, this time with fifty Northumbrian horsemen to support them, and they fought a brief but bloody battle from which the outnumbered Cumbrians retreated rapidly. Canmore's banner was captured, and some said they had seen the Cumbrian king directing his troops from a hilltop, but he showed none of the tenacity and fury for which he was known.

"Damn him!" Macbeatha exclaimed when he returned to Doune once more. "He's playing me like a *fhidheall*. He draws me to one place for a skirmish, then to another, and for what? Not for the glory of retreating each time, certainly. What's he about? Where is the main body of his warband?"

And where, I wondered, was mac Duff? No one had seen the Dark One that season.

"Perhaps he's dead," Weylin, ever the optimist, suggested with a shrug. "A man like that is as dangerous to his friends as he is to his enemies. Maybe he ran afoul of the wrong person and was killed for it."

But Macbeatha fretted and pondered and tried to think what Canmore's strategy might be. He stopped leading assaults himself and instead let his captains take their men into Cumbria as they had the previous season, to rattle the bushes and try to shake Canmore out of hiding. But the Feast of Saints Peter and Paul went by, and that of the Seven Sleepers approached, and all we knew was that the Northumbrians who had arrived at Dumbarton earlier in the year were no longer there, and that Canmore did not seem to be in any of his fortresses along the River Clyde.

Finally Macbeatha decided to turn the tables on his young rival. "I'm tired of searching for him," he announced. "I'm going home for Midsummer. Let him come find me." So back to Scone we went with half his warband. The other half he left in Fortriu under Lulach's care, that he might not be surprised from that quarter.

"Perhaps he has gone to Ireland to hire mercenaries," I suggested as we splashed across the Tay and turned our weary horses toward the village of Scone.

Macbeatha grunted. "Or back to King Edward, looking for ships." He gnawed at his lower lip. "Damn the boy! He's got those warriors from Tostig, what does he intend to do with them?"

Like a hound with a greasy rag, he was still worrying it when we rode into the yard. Gruoch was there to meet him, her face beaming, but he was not in much of a mood to appreciate it. "I fear I cannot bring you the word you wish to hear," he told her bluntly. "Canmore hides like a duck in a bog, and I cannot flush him. I've left Lulach there to poke about some more, but there is no point in my remaining."

Gruoch seemed not to care. "Husband, look who's come to join us!" she exclaimed, pushing a young warrior forward. "Maccrea!"

Maccrea was one of Brenna's many sons. He had been fostered at Scone, and Gruoch had mothered him in a way she had not done with any other fosterling. Perhaps it was because Maccrea was close kin; or perhaps it was because he looked and acted like a younger version of Lulach.

"Where's your mother?" Macbeatha snapped at the boy, dismounting.

"She won't come to court while I'm here," I reminded him as I climbed off my own horse. Not since he had threatened to cut her face if she misbehaved

"Is that any reason not to send your father's warband down here to help me?" he demanded, advancing toward the hall with his brow still furrowed, but without really looking at Maccrea. It was not the boy he was angry with.

But Maccrea, who couldn't have been more than twenty, didn't know that. "I—I'm sorry, Uncle," he stammered. "Mother said Lulach had his thousand without us, and—but I wanted to come myself, so after we killed the wolf pack that was taking our sheep, I—"

Shaking his head sadly, Macbeatha waved the boy to silence. "Pay me no mind, Maccrea," he apologized. "I have been wrestling with a problem on my journey, and it has me all out of sorts. I am glad to see you, lad, and in truth, I wouldn't know what to do with another hundred warriors just now." He sighed deeply, draping an arm around his nephew's shoulders. "I can't fight an enemy I can't find."

But like Lulach, Maccrea would have done almost anything to please Macbeatha, and no matter how many times his uncle told him otherwise, he persisted in the notion that the High King wanted Farrell's warband to come fight for him. He offered several times to go and fetch them, but Macbeatha always refused. "Until I know where Canmore is," he insisted, "I have no need of them."

You know how young men are. When the Midsummer feasting was done, Maccrea and his three companions set off up the Strathmore without a word to anyone.

"I suppose you'll tell me I was that headstrong when I was his age," Macbeatha grumbled to Gruoch when he learned of Maccrea's departure.

"Headstrong, yes," she agreed. "But you would have assessed the situation better." It was early August, and men were thinking of returning home soon, rather than riding out to war. If Canmore did not show himself in the next month, Macbeatha would be hard pressed to keep any warriors in camp. In fact, Macbeatha wondered aloud once if that wasn't Canmore's intention: to wait until the Scots began to drift home and the High King's forces were depleted.

In fact, Canmore had another strategy, one so brazen it had never occurred to my lord or his lady or any of their advisors. Only four days after he had left, Maccrea staggered back into the yard, having ridden his horse to death and covered the last bit on foot.

We had seen signal fires the night before and knew there was some kind of trouble in the northeast, but we had no idea of its nature until Maccrea arrived. "We stopped—at Inverbervie," he gasped. "Maelwyn's horse—lame." Inverbervie is on the coast going north. "We saw—ships—go past. Five, maybe six."

"Vikings?" Macbeatha asked anxiously. That was all we needed now, a Viking attack! In fact, my lord had sent his fleet up north, to patrol the waters above Aberdeen, because he feared just such a strike while he was busy with Canmore in the south.

But Maccrea shook his head. "Headed north. Anglish ships." Macbeatha's eyes widened as he began to understand what the boy was trying to tell him. "We took—a small boat—to get closer. See who they were." He swallowed, reaching for the dipperful of water some servant had the wits to bring him. "Archers—shot at us. Killed Maelwyn. Wounded Egann. The priest there said—arrows were—Cumbrian."

Macbeatha seized his nephew in a crushing embrace, kissed his forehead, then released him and left him to the care of Gruoch and her women. "Owen!" he snapped. "Get us ready to ride. It would seem Canmore thinks he can outflank me and strike into Moray!"

"If he was at Inverbervie—what, two days ago?" Weylin objected, "he'll be at Aberdeen or beyond by now. And it will take us four days to move this warband up the coast—"

"Leave the warband here to defend Scone," Macbeatha directed. "This is the town he hungers for, from all reports. The ten of us will go. In two days we can reach Moray through the hills—there we'll find all the willing warriors we need. If Canmore means to come south down the Strathmore, he'll find this warband waiting, and we can come at him from behind. Or if he continues north into Moray, we'll deal with him there." Next he turned to his wife, who was on her way into the hall. "Send word to Lulach," he instructed. "This may or may not be a diversionary measure. Either way, he must know of it and know to expect the unexpected."

When he had finished giving orders, I tugged at his sleeve. Looking down at me, he saw my face pale and drawn. "Lord, my children are in Moray," I whispered.

He started to say something harsh but thought better of it. Instead he touched my cheek and assured me, "Venko and I will see that no harm comes to them."

"Let me come with you," I pleaded. "I can ride hard, you know I can. I rode to Urquhart with you once, and followed you to Fife with Sloane. I can go for two days, and if not, you can leave me along the way. Please, lord." Tears welled in my eyes. "I must go with you to Moray."

For a moment he struggled with it, but he hadn't time to waste talking me out of the notion, so he nodded curtly. "See to our food," he commanded crisply. "Pack nothing else. We leave as soon as the horses are ready."

I hastened to do his bidding; but I must tell you, it wasn't my children I was really worried about. They were far from the coast, in an area unlikely to be caught in the fighting. No, it was for my lord I feared. Canmore had surprised him once again, striking where unexpected. And at Canmore's side would be the man who had not been seen in any of the skirmishes in Cumbria: mac Duff. The Dark Warrior.

Chapter Twenty-Six

In Fionna's hut

"You went because you feared for him?" Venko asked, shaking his head. "He let you come because he feared for you. In Moray was safety—or so he thought. And for whatever reason you were willing to go, he would take you, so long as you stayed there."

Kelda's lips twisted into a wry smile. "So we deceived each other," she said. "Not the first time. But I had decided when I bade my little Reagan good-bye and went back to Macbeatha, I would not be left behind again. No, I would never be left behind again."

* * *

Beside his guard, there were only Dhui and I who left Scone with Macbeatha that day. We rode well into the night, and at first light we were on our way again. Cutting through the hills, we came eventually to the River Dee, heading for the ford near Creag Faire. There, by chance, we encountered a man who was bringing his cattle down to market, and he offered to send his three sons as messengers to raise the fighting men of the Highlands. "You need only wait here for them," he promised

Macbeatha, however, could not bear to wait anywhere. "My sister is not far," he said. "Let us at least cross the River Dee and be that much closer to Moray." So off we went into the twilight. We forded the Dee and skirted Creag Faire, The Rock of Watching. I shuddered as we passed that towering height, feeling its stare upon us.

The sun had long since disappeared behind the Hill of Mortlich as we crossed over one of its forested feet. The summer twilight lingered, but the shadows were long and deep around us, and the men were uneasy in their saddles. Twilight, they tell me, is a time when demons and faeries cross back and forth between their world and ours.

They were no faeries, though, that rushed out of the trees at us, but six warriors on horseback, swords raised and harsh cries sounding on their lips. Poor Dougal was cut down even as he loosed his spear, and the others barely had time to draw their swords before the enemy was upon us. Yet there were more of us than of them, and although they fought fiercely for a time with swords ringing and horses snorting, they soon withdrew and retreated along the road toward the ford.

Owen and Venko set out in pursuit of them, but Macbeatha called them back. "They were Canmore's men," he said gruffly. "I recognized the one with the bad eye. Mostly likely they are only a scouting party, so there could be more nearby. Or it may be they're trying to draw us into a trap." It was a well-used tactic, to bait an armed party with a rider or two, then draw them into the clutches of a larger warband.

"What do we do?" Owen asked. "We're indefensible on this road. The Abbey at Aboyne is the closest haven, but we'd have to cross the ford again to reach it. That's the way those bastards were headed."

"We go on," Macbeatha said decisively. "There's a little village with a church on the road between Alford and Banchory. Lumphanan. Remember it, Owen?"

"Aye," the burly warrior growled. "All swampy and full of mist."

"Exactly," my lord replied. "We can make it by nightfall and sleep in the church. Then in the morning, under cover of the mist, we can slip away. We'll not follow the road, but climb up into the hills and go directly to my sister. She has the largest warband near to us."

So we put Dougal's body upon his horse and pressed on toward Lumphanan. I wept the whole way, but silently. How long had I known Dougal? He had been with Macbeatha when I first met him at Thorfinn's *huseby*, thirty years before. Now he was gone, and I couldn't even keen aloud because I was afraid—I was so afraid!--of what might lie between us and Lumphanan.

Yet Macbeatha's incredible luck held, and we managed to reach the little settlement safely. It was hardly more than five or six huts on the bank of a loch, with a small church dedicated to St. Finian. Macbeatha gave the priest one of the rings he wore—not the green one he'd gotten from Gruoch, for he would never part with that—and asked him to see to Dougal's funeral mass and burial. Then we laid out the fallen warrior properly with a candle at his head and another at his feet. Macbeatha put pebbles upon his eyes and one in his mouth, so his spirit would not become confused and go back into his body, but would find its way to Heaven.

It was full dark now. Low clouds had rolled in from the east, and a light drizzle fell. Neither moon nor stars could pierce that damp, gloomy darkness.

The church had no hearth, so we huddled together for warmth and tried to sleep a little. The warriors took turns standing guard, and Macbeatha took me in his arms for a time to comfort me. Or was it I who comforted him? A warrior loses so many friends in his lifetime. But somehow I could not shake the feeling that Macbeatha knew in his heart that Dougal was only the first, and they would all join him soon. I sobbed against his shoulder, and finally toward dawn I fell asleep.

I awoke in the gloom of the fog-shrouded village to discover they had gone. Dhui sat in the doorway of the church looking unhappy and a little guilty. "I'm to stay with you," he said when he saw me sit up. "Since I'm not allowed to bear arms, I wouldn't be any good to them anyway." I wondered if Macbeatha knew how bitter that was for Dhui, not to be able to carry a sword like his lord.

"How long ago did they leave?" I asked, struggling to rise. My bones ached and my head throbbed, but I was determined to continue somehow.

From his slowness to respond, I guessed that they had only just gone. But when I bolted for the door, Dhui rose to stop me, throwing both arms around me to keep me from clawing past him. "No!" he said firmly. "I may not be allowed to fight, but I can do what I'm told, and that I will!"

Just then from outside, muted by the fog, there came to us the shrill whinnies of horses and the howl of savage warcries. "Let me go, let me go!" I shrieked, struggling mightily against Dhui as the sound of iron striking iron drifted back to us through the mists. But he held me fast, and we both stood there weeping in the doorway of the church as the man we loved above all others led his guard in one final charge against the enemy.

* * *

Kelda's voice trailed off, and it was clear she could not go on. Fionna turned to Venko, her eyes asking him to take up the story. The little warrior cleared his throat once, twice. Fionna handed him a cup of her hot brew; he sipped at it for a moment, and then took up where his wife had left off.

They had, indeed, tried to slip away from the church while Kelda was sleeping, he said, for Macbeatha knew she would raise a fuss about being left behind. But the king was determined to keep her out of harm's way, whether she liked it or not. "When all this is over," he instructed Venko severely, "you are to take her home, do you understand? Take her home and tie her to the doorpost if you must, but make sure she stays there. She ought to be with her children now, not following an old warrior like me around the land." And so Venko had promised he would do whatever was necessary to take Kelda back to Moray and make her stay there.

"The fog was so thick I could hardly see my horse's nose," he told Fionna now. "Then, as we started out of the village, a breeze stirred and began to lift the fog away. It had just cleared enough for us to see our way around loch and bog when we heard riders approaching."

It was a larger band than before, coming up the road from the south behind them. Breaking to the north and west, the king and his guard tried to escape, weaving between the swampy patches—but such was not to be. The enemy followed doggedly, led by sound when sight would not suffice them. The fox was scented, and the hounds were in pursuit. Reaching the solid, if steep, footing of a small hill, Macbeatha urged his horse up its slope into a stand of trees, then reined in sharply. His guard followed suit. Wheeling their mounts, they faced the advancing pack of horsemen. To continue running was only to postpone the inevitable. It was time to stand and fight.

They could see the Cumbrians then, advancing through shreds of mist that lingered over the wet ground. There were probably twenty-one of them: two bands of ten with one of Canmore's lieutenants at their head. Canmore himself was not there. Later on they learned he was camped nearer to the coast, somewhere south of Aberdeen. Being unfamiliar with the territory, he had sent scouting parties in several directions to determine if the local chieftains had raised any warbands that might cause him trouble. Venko did not know why Canmore had chosen to make landfall so far north of Scone, except someone suggested he was trying to cut Macbeatha off from his men in the north, who had come to save him three years before at Dunsinnan.

Whatever the reason, Canmore's men were there, at Lumphanan, and they were closing in on the High King and his guard.

"Two to one," Macbeatha said with his old cheerfulness. "Well, we've faced worse odds and lived to tell of it, haven't we, lads?" Smiling, he drew his sword from its sheath and unslung his shield. "Say a prayer, then, and let's have at them!" Venko barely had time to cross himself before Macbeatha raised his sword high and gave the warcry of his House. "Up the Loarn!" he roared, and charged down the hill at their pursuers.

Venko was hard after him on his left, Owen on his right. They set upon the Cumbrians like demons, and Venko saw Macbeatha's first opponent go down in a spray of blood. It had been his intention to stay close to his lord, but a horse went down between them, and then an attack from the left drew Venko away. By the time he could afford to look up and see where Macbeatha was, the mist had blown up from the loch and once more impeded their vision.

"I could hear him," Venko told Fionna urgently. "I could hear him snarl as he swung his sword, hear his enemies howl in pain. I heard his horse squeal and go down, heard him curse as he jumped free of it. All around me were the sounds and the smells of battle: blood, iron, the snorting of horses, the grunting of men. There was the rattle of spears drawn from their places on the Cumbrian saddles, and I thought, What fools! You can hardly see a man at arm's length, much lest at a distance to cast spears! And then one grazed my ribs ..."

His hand went to the wound, healing cleanly now, but still painful. "Yet I fought on," he told Fionna. "I tried to find Macbeatha in the fog, but I could no longer hear his voice—only *the bold ringing of iron on iron which told me he still battled the enemy. I cannot say how I knew that sword was his, but I did. It was his father's sword, and its song seemed different from that of other swords."*

Clearly the king faced a vicious opponent. He struck quickly, savagely, with a force that sang through his blade and threatened to snap the rigid iron that met it. Venko tried to work his way nearer, but the fog fooled his ear. Were they to his right, or his left? He leapt off his horse, hoping that away from the snorting beast, he could hear better—but still he could not tell. And when he thought he'd found them, the figure that materialized out of the mist was a Cumbrian swordsman who attacked him with fury. Venko could not seem to cast him off.

"It was an enchantment," the small warrior insisted. *"I am the best swordsman in Alba! No Cumbrian could stand to my blade except by enchantment."*

And when at last he had dispatched his relentless enemy, Venko could no longer hear the sword of the king.

"There were shouts in the fog," he told Fionna. *"Weylin. Gallwen. But not the king."* He covered his face with a hand, overcome.

Kelda laid a hand on her husband's arm. *"I will tell it,"* she said, her voice calm and empty. Then she shivered, although it was not cold in the hut, and pulled her shawl closer around her.

Chapter Twenty-Seven

At first we could only hear them. From the door of the church where Dhui held me fast, we could hear their battle cries, hear the horses squealing and the crack of sword on shield. Then the fog lifted a little and we could see them. They were outnumbered. Blessed Virgin, they were so badly outnumbered! But what could either one of us do?

I ceased struggling, for I knew Dhui would never let me go while I fought him. So I forced myself to be still, and we leaned on each other to support our grief, but I had to get away. I knew I had to get away. Looking around, I saw Dougal's body stretched out nearby, the candles at head and feet burning low. "Look," I said to Dhui, nodding toward it. "He still bears his sword."

Dhui gave me a suspicious look. "And why not?"

I waited an artful moment, chewed on my lower lip for effect, then said, "They could use another sword up there, Dhui."

Now he saw what I meant and stood back, aghast. "I cannot take up arms!" he said. "You know that!"

I forced a scornful laugh. "Do you think they care just now whose hand wields the sword that aids them? Nevermind." I pulled away from him, back into the church where he did not stop me from going. "I will bear it up the hill myself."

"You can't!"

"Why not?" I demanded. "I am a warrior's wife now, not a slave. I can take up a sword if I wish."

"You'll only get hurt," he objected. "Macbeatha wanted you safe, and I can't let you take up a sword like a fool and go charging after him."

"Then you take it," I challenged A wooden cross hung on the wall near Dougal; I took it down from its place. "If you take Dougal's sword, I'll stay behind and pray." The cross was heavy, being perhaps half the height of a man.

Dhui regarded me with suspicion as I held the cross reverently before me. But his eyes trailed to that sword, lying useless in its scabbard at a dead man's side. He stepped toward the body, glancing around nervously, but there was no one else to see what he did. How easy, just to slide it out of its sheath, to feel the weight of it in his hands ...

And while he debated, I slipped behind him and swung the cross with all my might, smacking it against the backs of his knees. He yelped in surprise as his legs buckled beneath him. I bunched up my skirts and bolted for the door.

I could hear him calling my name as I fled between the huts of the village toward the battlefield. I thought, somehow, if I were there, if I were only there near Macbeatha, he would not be killed. Whether through magic or prayer or sheer force of will, my being there would somehow prevent his dying. Hadn't I brought him back from death's door at Dunsinnan? Hadn't he known nothing but victory while I was with him? Strange, the things you can make yourself believe when you want to.

Fog shifted and snaked around me like a living thing, hiding me from Dhui, hiding the battle from me. Often I had to follow the sounds of the fighting rather than its sight, but follow it I did. More than once I stepped into mud and water that reached to mid-calf, but always I managed to pull myself free and struggle on.

Finally I was on that hillside, panting as I climbed upward, every breath a stabbing pain in my chest. The sounds were nearby now. Carefully, carefully, I worked my way forward, from one tree to the next, willing the mist to clear. It would do the king no good for me to become a casualty. The fog fooled my ear, and I could not tell from which direction the grunts and cries and clanging swords came. And then, like the breath of Freya, a breeze swirled around me, lifting my skirts. It lifted the mist, as well, and I saw them.

Macbeatha stood with dripping sword, hunched over the body of a Cumbrian. Before him stood another warrior, a younger man,

not large but with powerful arms. No helmet covered his bright
blond hair, and he carried no shield. My lord looked up at him with
battle lust written on his face. "Are you next?" he snarled.

The warrior smiled, a cold and disquieting smile. Nothing of
fear showed on his face, but a hatred so pure it glittered. Then
slowly he raised his sword in his hand.

His left hand.

The snarl faded from Macbeatha's lips. "You are mac Duff,
then," he said.

"Mac Duff, the Dark One," his opponent sang gleefully. "Mac
Duff, the Changeling. Mac Duff, born not of a woman, but of a
devil. Aye, I am he. What do you say to that, Devil? Eh?" A laugh
escaped him, a tittering, child-like laugh.

For a moment longer Macbeatha stared at him. Then, "So this
is where it ends," he said with a calm that put ice in my breast.
"Here, in a piss-ant fight on a God-forsaken hillside in the back of
nowhere—" Slowly a smile spread across his lips. "Well, then, so
be it," he sneered, bringing his sword and shield to the ready. "But
I'll not go to hell alone!"

Then they were at each other, striking and parrying, lunging
and weaving, while I stood paralyzed, clinging to a tree for support.
A blow shattered the king's shield; he flung the remnants in mac
Duff's face and attacked furiously. Clang, clang, clang, scrrraape!
went their swords. Their weapons locked hilt to hilt, and then the
king's fist rammed against his opponent's midsection, forcing mac
Duff back. Clang, clang, clang, clang--! The Dark One's back was
up against a tree now, not three paces from where I stood. Macbeatha
pressed his advantage: clang, clang, clang, scrrraaaa— They came
together again, swords crossed, eyes locked, neither moving—

And then Macbeatha staggered back, clutching at his belly. I
did not know then what had happened, did not know that instead of
a shield, mac Duff carried a long knife in his right hand, and he had
plunged it into my lord's gut. I only knew Macbeatha dropped to
his knees on soggy ground, hunched in agony. I screamed.

The Dark One pushed himself away from the tree trunk and
loomed over the king, shreds of mist swirling around his knees.
Macbeatha lifted his head and his mouth worked as though he
would say something to his nemesis, but no sound came forth. Then
slowly his face steeled, his shoulders lifted, and he raised his sword
once more.

With one swift stroke, mac Duff severed the king's hand at the wrist. I screamed again as Macbeatha howled and collapsed over the spurting stump. For a moment mac Duff watched him warily; then he stepped to where the dismembered hand had fallen, still clutching the sword. "You can't have this anymore," he said, kicking both hand and sword out of reach. "I have the Devil's hand, you know, so you can't have it, too." The fog crept in closer.

"God damn you to hell with your father!" hissed the king.

"You first," whispered mac Duff, and raising his arm, he aimed one last stroke at Macbeatha's neck.

"NNNOOOOO!"

Out of the mist to my right, a body hurtled through the air. Brave Dhui had followed me, and having no shield and no sword, he did the only thing he could: he launched himself between them and took the fatal blow on his own broad chest, falling back upon the king. Macbeatha cried out as Dhui's weight crushed him, and then they both lay still.

From somewhere nearby a horn sounded, and mac Duff's head came up, testing the air like a hound. Voices sounded flat upon the fog, men calling to each other, and something else: hoofbeats. Riders were coming, and not just a few. Mac Duff gave a short, sharp laugh and melted into the mist.

Horsemen thudded past us in the cloaking fog, and I ran to Macbeatha, fearful lest he be trampled. When the riders were gone, I clawed Dhui's bulk aside, I know not how, to reach the king. Blood stained his fine tunic, and his face was pale and lifeless. But I thought maybe—maybe— Bending my ear to his lips, I felt the barest tickle upon my cheek.

He was alive! Just barely, but he breathed. He breathed! He was not dead. And now that I was with him— "To the king!" I shouted with all my might, for I could hear his warriors up the slope from us. "He breathes, he breathes! Oh, help me, please!"

And then they were all around us: Owen first, and then Venko, and after them Weylin and all the others. "He breathes!" I shouted again, and Owen bent to check his lord's wounds. The stump of Macbeatha's hand he bound quickly, using his belt to pinch off the bleeding. There was a piece of my shift staunching the flow of blood from the king's abdomen, though I do not remember putting it there; but when Owen peeled it away gently, that great hulk of a warrior groaned in despair and put the cloth back, tears streaming down his cheeks. He knew then what I would, could not, admit: Macbeatha would die. He might linger for a time, but he would not recover. Dhui had prolonged his lord's life by giving up his own, but he could not save it. None of us could save it.

We made a litter and carried him down from the hillside to a little well that served the village. There I washed his wounds as best I could, and cleaned the blood of other men from his face and arms, hoping it might revive him, but he lay still as death. Venko fetched the priest out from the village, and there by the well that good man gave him last rites while I wept bitterly, protesting that he would live—he must live!—although the faces of all around me denied it. The priest had hardly finished when Brenna appeared.

She rode her horse astride, a leather helmet capping her head and a shield upon her arm, carrying a tall thrusting spear like a battlemaid. The horsemen who passed me in the fog had been hers, responding to the messenger sent out the day before. Leading her husband's warband forth, she had come to Lumphanan just as my lord and his guard clashed with the Cumbrian scouting party.

And oh, what a scene she made! I think she would have killed me—for everything was my fault, with her—but Owen caught her up in a bear hug until she dissolved in a fit of hysterical weeping. I could not hate her at that moment. How could I hate anyone who loved Macbeatha so much? Finally she calmed down enough to beg Owen to let her go to the king. Venko made me give up my place at my lord's side, so there would be no trouble between us. Then she knelt beside Macbeatha, her brown and silver hair a tangle beneath her helm, and called his name softly.

Macbeatha stirred.

It was the first time he had fluttered so much as an eyelid since I found him. Now that I was not there, he stirred, and Venko had to hold me back so I did not rush within Brenna's reach to be near him. His voice was so faint I could not hear it, but Brenna could. He told her to find Canmore. If mac Duff was here, then Canmore had to be somewhere between Lumphanan and the coast. She was to gather all the warbands of Moray and lead them against Canmore. They would follow her, he said. They wouldn't dare do otherwise.

And do you know, they did? Owen and Venko went with her, which no doubt helped. Gallwen, too, and they rallied all the tribes of Moray to drive Canmore out of his encampment and back to his ships. There were only five hundred of the enemy, but it wouldn't have mattered if there were five thousand. Every warrior within a day's travel came, and even those men who were not allowed to bear arms, took up pitchforks and farm axes and sharpened sticks to attack the invaders.

As for those of us left behind, we might have stayed there in Lumphanan, afraid to move the king lest we hasten his death, but he would not have it. The next time he roused to consciousness, he gave his instructions to Weylin, senior among those guardsmen left with him. "Take me home," he whispered.

"To Inverness, lord?" Weylin asked in bewilderment.

"Scone," he breathed. "Take me back to Scone."

I argued with Weylin, but he shook his head at me. "We can stay here and watch him die," he said. "Or we can carry him forward and watch him die. Either way, the result is the same. If he wants to go to Scone, then by Christ and the Virgin Mary, I will find some way to get him there."

Even if an oxcart had been available in that remote place, the ride would have killed him before we reached the river. So four of his guards picked up the litter and carried it, while the rest of us followed on foot. When we reached the River Dee, we resorted to coracles whenever possible, to smooth his ride and speed us on our way. How I prayed on that voyage! I prayed to the Christian god, for he is the only one I know who ever brought a man back from the dead. If anyone could save my lord, it was he. But I never had any luck getting the Christian god to hear my prayers.

By nightfall of the second day, we had reached Aberdeen, and there we received news of Brenna's victory. Canmore had fled south in his ships, they said. The threat was ended. Macbeatha smiled at the news. "Tell her—Scone," he whispered in the raspy voice that was left him. "Ride to Scone. Celebrate ... victory."

At Aberdeen we hired a ship. Macbeatha clung to life, his breathing shallow, his pulse slow. I stayed by his side every moment, clutching his remaining hand in mine. Whether the voyage was two days or three, I could not tell you; I lived, not by the rising and setting of the sun, but by the times my lord roused to consciousness. So great was his pain while awake that I almost wished he would sleep the whole time; and yet I craved his presence, the feeble squeeze of his hand, the breathy word he spoke.

"Take Venko back," he whispered once.

"Back where?" I asked petulantly, not wanting to think about Venko just then.

"Your bed," he replied with a wry twist of his mouth. "Have one more baby. A boy. For me."

"As if there aren't a hundred little boys named Macbeatha in your honor," I scoffed, tears leaking down my cheeks. "I've called my son Reagan, 'little king'—isn't that enough for you?"

"The sisters said ... Venko would father kings," he reminded me.

"And I have given him the means," I replied. Then I added, with some bitterness, "Let the Fates take care of the rest, since they seem to defy my every attempt to thwart them. They can expect no further assistance from me." *I want no offspring of mine to be a king, Fionna. Kings pay too dear a price.*

Eventually we docked at Perth, and there we shifted my lord to a raft that was pulled upstream by horses on the bank. Owen, Gallwen and Venko joined us there; they had ridden ahead, first to Scone to bear the news to Gruoch, and now to meet us. They intended to carry my lord on his last entry into the town. But although he suffered the litter up from the ford, when we drew near the village, Macbeatha squeezed my hand and asked for Owen.

Setting him gently on the ground, his guardsmen gathered around to hear his instructions. Owen bent close to hear his breathy voice. "Put me ... on my horse," the king directed.

Owen drew back. "Lord, I can't! It will kill you if we move you from this litter!"

Macbeatha gave a weak, wheezing laugh, a sound that chilled me. "Damned fool," he whispered. "I'm dead anyway. Now, put me on my horse and let me ride into Scone like a king."

I knelt closest of them all, for I would never let go his hand, so he turned to me. "Tell them," he commanded feebly.

"No, lord," I sobbed. "I won't tell them to do that. You're bleeding inside, and every move costs you. Let them carry you into—"

"On my horse!" he roared—only it was no roar at all, but only the breathiest of whispers that sprayed droplets of blood from his lips. The wound in his belly continued to ooze, and the stump of his left wrist had begun to smell fetid. Even I knew he would not survive the day. Owen looked at me, and I begged him with my eyes not to do it, but I could see he would.

"Weylin, help me with him," Owen growled. "Venko! Hold that mare still. If it's one last procession he wants ..."

Through my fresh spate of tears, I saw Macbeatha smile.

Gently, oh, so gently, they lifted him from his litter—and still his face twisted in agony as his wounds tore. But they set him in the saddle and held him there, Owen on one side and Weylin on the other. Then slowly, slowly, my lord raised himself up from his slumped position and sat straight.

"Cloak," he commanded, though the August sun shone fiercely that day. I found a decent cloak among our baggage, and when Gallwen threw it across Macbeatha's shoulder, my lord pulled it over his bandages. Vain man! Then he squared his jaw and nodded at Venko to lead the mare forward.

The whole village awaited us, for the watchmen had seen our barge from the tower and raised the cry. Now a shout went up as people saw their High King riding once more into Scone, wounded but alive, bent but not broken. From the royal residence, a cavalcade came to meet us, Gruoch at its head.

I walked behind Weylin, watching my lord fearfully lest he lose his balance and slip in the saddle; but his guardsmen held him firmly, hands discreetly hidden by the cloak, and he lifted his head high. What that cost him, I will never know. But he was a king, and he would not appear to his people in any other guise. As the crowd pressed in, he stopped and looked around at those adoring faces, at the awe-struck children and the gleeful old men, at the queen hurrying toward us. Keeping the stump of his left wrist hidden beneath the cloak, he lifted his right fist in the air. "Victory!" he cried with every ounce of breath that was left him.

Then he pitched forward and tumbled into the street.

Shrieking in anguish, I clawed my way past Weylin to reach him, to cradle his head once more in my lap, but it was too late. Blood trickled from the corner of his mouth and his beautiful green eyes stared unseeing at the sky. All the world I ever knew had come to an end.

My lord was dead.

Chapter Twenty-Eight

At Scone

A breeze slithered in from the open window and touched Gruoch's neck, making her shiver where she sat at her writing desk. Without wanting to, she remembered that this was the day. Yes, unless there had been trouble in crossing Atholl—and there had better not have been!—this was the day they should reach Iona and lay him to rest in the sacred ground ...

Tears sprang unbidden to her eyes, and Gruoch rose in disgust. Weeping would not bring him back. He had lived a warrior's life and died a warrior's death, and she had been powerless to change that. So what was the point in weeping?

Crossing to the window, she breathed deeply of the fresh air. What was there about a man that craved battle? What was there about risking his life that satisfied some urgent need in a man, and made him do it again and again and again? The pitting of one's wits against another, of testing one's reasoning skills against an adversary, that Gruoch could understand. But brute strength? Animal cunning? Why?

Still, whispered a secret voice inside her head, would you have had any other kind of man?

With a sigh, Gruoch looked down at the village below and tried to imagine herself as a miller's wife, or a merchant's, or even a churchman's. She tried to imagine herself with a man who stayed home every summer, who sat by the fire and discussed the wheat harvest or the snow depth or the price of wool, instead of a man who *talked of manipulating princes and bringing Great Tribes under his sway. Love a man who wanted nothing more from life than a full belly and a comfortable bed? Never!*

Ambitious men like Macbeatha were dangerous, as her mother had warned her, but it was the very danger of him that had seduced her. When she met him in her fosterer's house, the sight of him had stolen her breath. This is he, *her heart had sung.* This is the man I was meant to marry—not the one my mother so carefully chose, but this one: this radiant, powerful, beautiful man ... *Then he'd spoken to her, and his arrogance cut through her like a knife. He knew. He knew just how mesmerizing he was, and he expected her to fall madly in love with him. In that terrible instant Gruoch had realized she could never let him see the depth of her feelings; for the moment he felt he had conquered her, she would be just another victim of his charm, and she would lose him.*

So she had scorned him to protect herself, and to keep him in his place. But the power and the passion burning up from the depths of his soul had laid waste to hers. She had chided him for his warlike nature, all the while she lusted for his savage spirit. Who but a warrior could give her what she desired? Even before her brother was killed and the honor of her House fell to her and her son, what had she wished for him but conquest? The very first time she saw him off to war, and she still wedded to his cousin, what had she asked him to bring her? "Only victory."

Victory!

It had become her habit, after that. Each time he left on campaign, he would ask the same question in various ways, and she would respond in kind. "What riches shall I bring you, lady?" "Only victory." "What do you desire upon my return?" "The news of victory." "What shall I send you while I'm gone?" "Word of your victory." *And so powerful was he, so single-minded in his ambition, he had never failed to give her what she asked, even after Dunsinnan. The crushing blow at Dundee he had turned away, and then wreaked his vengeance on the attackers from Atholl. So when he set out on that mad flight up to their farm to find Canmore—was it only a fortnight ago?--how could she have imagined it would be different?*

He had come to her chamber, where she knelt in prayer for his safety, and tried once more to get her out of Scone. "Take your ladies and go," *he pleaded frankly, since all his subterfuge had failed. "Ride to Perth and take a ship to Inverness. I would know you are safe in the stronghold of Moray, far from these treacherous Southerners."*

"I shall be quite safe here," she demurred.

"What can I say to make you go?" he begged, his eyes so full of the love she would never let him admit, unable to respond in kind.

Putting out a hand to soothe his brow, so aged and fraught with worry, she wondered if he could read in her face the feeling she would never speak. "Only send word of your victory over Canmore," she told him, "and then I will go." So he had ridden off with his guard, and with no word of love from her.

But that is the way we were, *she reminded herself now. They had shared their passions in private, and spoken their tender sentiments with their eyes, but they had never given them voice. It was her way of holding him; it was his way of denying he was bound. It was a safety each of them needed.*

And for her, the price of that safety was watching Kelda ride away with him, knowing when he lay down to rest, she would be there to comfort him and keep him warm.

After all the years, Gruoch had never grown numb to that hurt. When she wedded Macbeatha, she had promised herself never to mention his intimacy with his Norse slave. She would never acknowledge the girl as a competitor, and in due time, Kelda would cease to matter. In public and in private, in court and in closet, Gruoch would be everything he needed and desired, and Kelda's services would become unnecessary. There would be no fuss, no confrontation. Kelda would simply grow less and less important, fading into the background, until Macbeatha thought no more of her than of any other woman.

But that had never happened. When Macbeatha suffered in spirit—after the killing of Duff, for instance—it was always to Kelda he went for solace. Gruoch opened her arms to him, pleaded with her eyes for him to share the torments of his soul, but he never did. His anger he might share with her, his frustrations and his dilemmas, but never his sorrow. It was as though with her, he could never be anything but a king, and the one thing a king could not show was weakness. When it was comforting he wanted, when it was sanctuary from the world he craved, he went to Kelda.

Those who forced the Norsewoman from him had done Gruoch no favors. She had wailed aloud when she learned of it. The woman was gone, but not because he did not want her. Not because he preferred Gruoch. They had driven her away, and in her absence, he had never allowed the queen nor any other to fill that place. Gruoch had watched her husband endure the trials of kingship with no comforter at all, watched him grow gray and weary because he would share with no one his doubts, his fears, his regrets.

So when he'd been wounded at Dunsinnan, Gruoch had been glad enough to see Kelda return. At least he had someone, then. Kelda became the queen's surrogate, tending his weakness which he would not let Gruoch see. Even at the end, he would not let her see ...

Signal fires had announced a victory, and watchers on the coast sent word that Canmore's ships had sailed back toward Angleland. What relief Gruoch had known! Canmore, beaten off yet again, and her Macbeatha victorious!

It was not until three of his guardsmen rode into the yard that she learned the cost of that victory.

They faced her with looks of such abject misery, her heart rose in her throat. "What is it?" she demanded, seeing Owen and Gallwen unable to meet her eyes, and Venko looking like a hound whose master was dead. "What news of my husband? Is he well? Is he wounded?" The words tumbled over each other like water over rapids.

At first they could not speak. Finally Gallwen tried. "Canmore is defeated," he began.

"Yes, yes, I know. But what of the king?" Why could she not say his name, even then?

"He is wounded, lady," Venko managed. "Badly wounded."

Her throat tightened so she could not speak, and the blood pounded in her ears so she was afraid she would shame Macbeatha and herself by fainting. She could do naught but wait for the three warriors to continue.

"He comes to you, lady," Gallwen managed. "But—he—" Gallwen could not finish.

"He is dying," Owen said finally in his rough voice. "I do not know that he will survive the journey."

The strength went out of Gruoch's knees and she groped feebly for a chair. One came under her hand—had someone moved it there?—and she eased herself into it carefully. But she did not faint. She did not faint, and she did not weep. "Then I shall wait for him here," she whispered hoarsely, hating the sound of weakness in her own voice. That was unworthy of him. "I shall wait here, and implore our Lord Jesus Christ for a miracle."

And so she had, night and day, until the watchmen called from the tower that the king's raft was at the ford, that the king was coming into the village. All they could see, though, was a body on a litter. They could not tell if he were alive or dead.

Carefully Gruoch rose from her knees, knowing her eyes must be puffy and dark from lack of sleep, and she smoothed her clothing. Sure that Maisie was in no state to help her, she brushed her own hair and tied it smoothly with a blue and red ribbon. But then her patience failed her, and she called for a horse. "Let us go forward to meet our lord," she told her retainers, brushing past them and out of the hall as though it were a prison.

Before the others were ready, Gruoch had climbed up to her side-saddle and urged her mount to a trot. A bend in the street this way, around a house that way, and she could see—

Dear God be praised, he was astride his horse! They had been wrong after all! Cunning Macbeatha had fooled them all again: he had cheated death and returned to her once more. There he was, coming like a king, coming in triumph as he had always come! God had heard her prayers and spared his life. Joyfully, Gruoch urged her horse to greater speed, cantering toward him.

But before she reached him, he stopped in the center of the street. His eyes seemed to find her in the crowd—oh, yes, he looked right at her!—and he rose up in his saddle to give her the word she had asked him to bring: "Victory!"

Then he fell, pitching forward off his horse in a manner that dashed her hopes like spray upon the rocks. It was only a show. Vain man, arrogant man! He tried to fool the people, tried to fool her, into thinking he was all right — Gruoch whipped her horse into a run, heedless of those in her path. When the crowd became too thick, she reined in and slid to the ground, pushing her way through. She could hear voices around her: "Make way! Make way, it is the queen! Stand back, here, let the queen through!" They were distant and vague, like voices in a dream, as a way opened before her and she burst through at last—

Too late! Gruoch saw in an instant that she was too late. Kelda knelt in the dirt with his head in her lap, sobbing her grief, and his eyes—his beautiful, green eyes that could sparkle with mirth or snap with cold anger—were blank and lifeless. Someone pulled Kelda away—the Norsewoman shrieked and wailed and fought— but although Gruoch saw it, she could not feel one way or the other about it. Only there was Macbeatha, soaked in his own blood, lying in the street, dead—dead—

Slowly she dropped to her knees and touched his lifeless cheek, felt the mortal clay already grown cool to her touch, and knew she could never tell him now. She might shout it at the top of her lungs here in the streets of Scone, but where he had gone, he could not hear her. I love you! *Lifting him in her arms, she cradled his graying head against her bosom.* I love you, and I selfishly wanted to bind you to me, only me—!

Perhaps in Heaven he already knew. Perhaps in Heaven he understood why she could never say it to him. Perhaps in Heaven he would forgive her reticence.

But here on earth, where he had lived and breathed and felt and needed ... he had died in Kelda's arms.

Chapter Twenty-Nine

In Fionna's hut

Fionna took the empty cup from Kelda's slack hands and set it aside, then blotted the tears from the Norsewoman's cheeks.

Venko sighed a sigh that was more of a groan. "I would be with them now," he said in a voice thick with grief. "I would be with them now on Iona, but Macbeatha made me promise. He made me promise I would take Kelda home to Moray."

"I would have waited," Kelda said softly.

"I could not leave you there in Scone. I could not leave you there, with Macbeatha dead and us gone. There are people who—who thought it was—" He did not finish.

"Inappropriate," Fionna supplied.

"She wept as though it were her husband!" Venko accused. "When he fell from his horse, it took two of us to pull her back so the Lady Gruoch could kneel beside him!"

Kelda offered no defense, only sat staring at nothing. The cloak had slipped from her shoulders, but her hands still clasped the small pouch that smelled of cedar oil.

"So I brought her here to Moray. When we stopped Lumphanan, though, to see about Dougal and Dhui—to see they had been buried properly, and a mass said for each—she ran away."

"I walked out to the well while he talked to the priest." Kelda's tongue was thick in her mouth, and she formed her words carefully. "There was a boy there. Three boys. But one had this." She cradled the pouch, stroking it gently. "He'd found it near the battlefield and *wrapped it in a cloth with cedar oil. It still bears the green ring Gruoch gave him at their wedding."*

Venko blinked. "Macbeatha's hand?" He reached for the pouch, but Kelda skittered away from him like a wild creature, huddling against the far wall with her prize. "What will you do with it?" he asked in bewilderment.

"I will take it to him. In Odin's hall. He will need it there." A secretive smile touched her lips. "In Valhalla, the Hall of the Slain, warriors contend in battle every day; then they are restored to wholeness at night and feast together. He loved the battle, did Macbeatha. I know there will be a place for him in Odin's hall."

"That is blasphemy!" Venko cried, more surprised than offended.

"Not to a Norseman," she replied. Then she raised hopeful eyes to the old mystic. "The potion I asked for?"

"It was in the last cup."

"Potion? What potion?" Venko demanded.

"Among the Norse," Kelda explained, "when a great man dies, he is accompanied to the Otherworld by his wife, or a concubine or slave girl. So there will be a woman to give him pleasure there, along with the other delights of Odin's hall."

Venko's eyes grew wide in horror as he realized what Kelda intended. "You cannot do this!" he gasped. "I forbid you to do this thing!"

"It is done," Fionna told him. "The potion itself is deadly."

"Not quite done," Kelda said. "There is more to it, but I am a coward—I do not want such suffering. And I have to do it all myself, for there is no Valkyrie, no Angel of Death, to assist me. That's why I wanted the potion, to ease my way." She drew a ragged breath. "I saw an oak grove by the river. An oak grove is a sacred place, and it is there I shall fix my rope to a branch."

"No!" Venko cried in anguish. "No, do not do this thing!" Frantically he clutched her hand, covering it with kisses.

"And will you do any differently?" Fionna asked harshly. "Going to war for Lulach, throwing yourself upon the swords of Malcolm Canmore? I have seen the sign of Lulach mac Gillecomgain: it lies in the season of Death, with Macbeatha! And it is in your heart to join them, is it not?"

At first Venko could say nothing to her accusation. Finally, "That is the fate of a warrior," he defended.

"And this is the fate of the king's woman. Do not deny her what you grant yourself—the privilege to serve him one last time."

Now Kelda reached out and patted her husband's bowed head. "He always called me his little Valkyrie," she reminded him. "They bury him today, and I must be there when he arrives, waiting with a horn of ale to refresh him after his journey."

"But our children!" he protested.

Kelda shook her head. "I have given all that I can to our daughters."

"And Reagan?"

"His foster father will ... will care for him." Her speech was badly slurred now. "If things go badly for Lulach ... it will be better if people didn't know whose son ..." With an effort, she drew a deep breath. "I wish she hadn't promised you kings."

Then she struggled to her knees. "I can fix the rope myself," she said, "only I don't know how I ... A sacrifice to Odin is both strangled and stabbed," she rambled, "and I ... how will I ... Help me, Venko," she pleaded, resting a hand on his shoulder. "Help me get to the oak grove, and—and—"

Venko sobbed aloud once; but then he quieted himself, drew a great, shuddering breath, and wiped at his face with his arm. "I promised him I would keep you safe," he protested.

"There is no place safer than Odin's hall," Kelda assured him. "At least I will never meet Brenna there."

The oak grove was a peaceful place, cool and green and sweet, with the soft sound of a stream chuckling not far away. Kelda felt a great calmness wrapped like a cloak around her. "This is good," she said, unwrapping the rope she had wound about her waist.

Venko dropped his horse's reins and let the beast graze. "Don't do this," he pleaded one last time.

Her head buzzed as if she had drunk too much ale. "The potion has done it," she replied, weaving a little. "Only now I must fulfill the requirements ..." The sun glared between the leafy tree tops, and she squinted as she peered upward. "I need a branch—there, that one." With clumsy fingers she coiled the bulk of her rope and tossed it up toward the branch. It peaked hopelessly short of its goal and tumbled back to earth.

Patiently she recoiled it, but as she made to toss it again, Venko stopped her with a hand on her arm. "Here, you are too weak," he *grumbled. With a strong arm and a keen eye, he lofted the coil so it snaked up and over the branch.*

The loose end now dangled just within her reach. Forcing her sluggish fingers to make a knot, she fed the other end through, then drew it up tight against the branch. "Now, how shall I get myself up off the ground—" *She looked around the glade.* "Ah. I will sit on your horse," *she announced. Reluctantly Venko fetched the beast to her, then helped her up to sit sideways in the saddle. She giggled.* "Just like a lady."

"You are a lady," *he growled.* "If you would only act like one."

"Never. Ladies have no fun." *With slow but practiced hands she made the dangling end of the rope into a noose.* "Now you must take your knife, and while the rope squeezes my breath, you must pierce me between my ribs. Three or four times is plenty." *Then, thinking about the sharp jabs, she amended,* "Three is plenty."

"I cannot draw your blood!" *Venko protested, tears flowing freely down his cheeks.*

"Of course, you can. You are a warrior." *Not much of a husband, but yes, a fine warrior.*

Forcing her mind to focus, Kelda reviewed her arrangements and saw that everything was ready. Yet as she tried to lift the noose over her head, she found her arms curiously reluctant to move. The choking of the rope, the jab of the knife— Perhaps she should wait. Let the potion take care of it. But then, would she reach Odin's hall? She must get there, and quickly; she must be waiting when Macbeatha arrived. Still her hands balked at this simple task—

Then she heard his voice over the murmur of the stream, over the twittering of birds in the trees. Kelda, do you trust me?

Yes, lord.

Bare your neck.

Slowly, slowly, she maneuvered the loop around her head, gently tugging her long hair free of it. Carefully she adjusted it to fit snuggly, like the leather slave collar she had worn during the happiest years of her life. Then she took one last breath and slid off the horse.

Venko cried out as Kelda lurched to the end of the rope, swinging slightly and struggling against the rough hemp. Though her mind was at ease with her decision, her body still reacted instinctively, legs twitching, hands straining toward her neck. Venko covered his face for a moment; then he drew his dagger quickly. With a sure hand, he pierced her ribs once, twice, thrice—then he thrust the blade deep into Kelda's heart, and her struggling ceased.

Miles away on the Isle of Iona, the Bishop of St. Andrews scattered the first handful of dirt across the shrouded body of the king.

Epilogue

Alone now in her hut, Fionna frowned and reached into her basket of mystic stones. She had been moved by Kelda's story, a story of devotion so deep it made that of the king's warriors pale. It was a legacy Fionna hoped would survive the Norsewoman, but she feared it would not. She understood the stones now: it was not just Macbeatha mac Findlaech who passed from this world, but the way of the Scots as he had lived it. Cunmore's sign lay in the spring quarter along with the Turning Demon, who upset the ways of men and threw everything topsy-turvy. That was what Canmore, raised in a foreign court, would do for Alba. A new culture was coming into the land, and the old ways of Macbeatha and his predecessors would be swept away. They would be seen by the new rulers, not as the ways of another time, but as evil; and the king whose long reign was marked by good harvests would be remembered by future generations as a Traitor, a Usurper.

But she was curious now about the prophecy she had given Venko long ago. Kings, many kings, would call him father. Sons of his daughters? she wondered. That would be the old way, the way of Fionna's people. But that was not the way of Malcolm Canmore and those who came after him. So the boy, Reagan-- In her basket of stones, Fionna found the one she sought, a flat disk with a hole bored through it. Gazing intently through the opening, she called up an image of the boy, Kelda's son, the one who called Venko father.

He stood on a high and barren hilltop, a nine-year-old boy laughing at the companions he had raced to the top. Bracing his

legs against the whistling wind, he was a rugged, healthy boy: fair of face and bright of eye ...
   ... with a shining head of golden-red hair.

AUTHOR'S NOTE

If the historical sources covering the time of Macbeth have one thing in common, it's that they hardly have one thing in common. Dates, places, events, and people differ from one source to the next, and the views of modern scholars are equally divergent. You'll find several who state categorically that Duncan and Macbeth were cousins, while others say that evidence of this is late and rather questionable.

Most of what we "know" about Scotland and its environs during the eleventh century was not written down until two or three hundred years after the fact. Sources dating to that time come from outside Scotland, so they were not written by eye witnesses, and they reflect a foreign perspective. See my web site at http://www.sff.net/people/catherine-wells/machome.htm to find the bare historical facts as I understand them.

For Scottish culture of that time period, I relied heavily on what is known of contemporary Irish culture. But the Scots had co-mingled with the Norse for several centuries, and absorbed the Picts before that. I did a good bit of looking at Scottish culture of later centuries, then peering backward through the mists, imagining how it came to be.

As for the Picts, whose residual culture figures in my story— *nothing* is known for certain of these elusive people, except that they carved a series of symbols on marker stones and left them for us to puzzle over. Everything else is speculation.

This dearth of concrete knowledge creates considerable difficulty for the historian.

But it's *great* for a novelist.

I've done my research as carefully as I can, but the truth is, a lot of what passes for historical fact is, in reality, extrapolation, interpretation, or downright speculation. Like Shakespeare, I have reviewed the historical sources available (although my sources are more extensive than those Will had) and gone from there. I believe what lies within the covers of this book is as likely a story as any the historians can give us.

Catherine Wells
October 30, 2006

P.S. — Oh, all right, I've used a date for Thorfinn's death that is earlier than the accepted one, which scholars have inferred from the Norse *Sagas*. The *Sagas* were not written down until 200 years after the fact. They could have made a mistake.